Praise for #1 N... ...or

"Miller tugs at the h... ...authors can."
—*Publishers Weekly*

"Miller's name is synonymous with the finest in Western romance."
—*RT Book Reviews*

"Linda Lael Miller creates vibrant characters and stories I defy you to forget."
—#1 *New York Times* bestselling author Debbie Macomber

"Miller is one of the finest American writers in the genre."
—*RT Book Reviews*

Praise for *USA TODAY* bestselling author Maisey Yates

"Fans of Robyn Carr and RaeAnne Thayne will enjoy [Yates's] small-town romance."
—*Booklist* on *Part Time Cowboy*

"Passionate, energetic and jam-packed with personality."
—*USA TODAY* on *Part Time Cowboy*

"Wraps up nicely, leaving readers with a desire to read more about the feisty duo."
—*Publishers Weekly* on *Bad News Cowboy*

LINDA LAEL MILLER

MAISEY YATES

The
Cowboy
Way

HQN™

ISBN-13: 978-0-373-78988-7

Recycling programs for this product may not exist in your area.

The Cowboy Way

Copyright © 2016 by Harlequin Books S.A.

The publisher acknowledges the copyright holders of the individual works as follows:

A Creed in Stone Creek
Copyright © 2011 by Linda Lael Miller

Part Time Cowboy
Copyright © 2015 by Maisey Yates

Printed in U.S.A.

CONTENTS

A CREED IN STONE CREEK

Linda Lael Miller

For Sheri and Kat
You're brave and you're funny and I love you both.

CHAPTER ONE

Some instinct—or maybe just a stir of a breeze—awakened Steven Creed; he sat up in bed, took a fraction of a moment to orient himself to unfamiliar surroundings. One by one, the mental tumblers clicked into place:

Room 6. Happy Wanderer Motel and Campground. Stone Creek, Arizona.

The door stood open to the fresh high-country air, which was crisply cool on this early June night, but not cold, and the little boy—Steven's newly adopted son—sat on the cement step outside. A bundle—probably his favorite toy, a plush skunk named Fred, rolled up in his blanket—rested beside him, and the boy's tiny frame was rimmed in an aura of silvery-gold moonlight.

Something tightened in Steven's throat at the poignancy of the sight.

Poor kid. It wasn't hard to guess who he was waiting for. Matt was small, with his dad's dark hair and his mother's violet eyes, and he was exceptionally intelligent—maybe even gifted—but he was still only five years old.

How could he be expected to comprehend that his folks, Zack and Jillie St. John, were gone for good? That they wouldn't be coming to pick him up, no matter how hard he hoped or how many stars he wished on, that night or any other.

Steven's eyes burned, and he had to swallow the hard ache that rose in his throat.

Jillie had succumbed to a particularly virulent form of breast cancer a year and a half ago, and Zack had only lasted a few months before the grief dragged him under, too—however indirectly.

"Hey, Tex," Steven said, trying to sound casual as he sat up on the thin, lumpy mattress of the foldout sofa—he'd given the bed to the child when they checked in that evening. Steven shoved a hand through his own dark blond hair. "What's the trouble?" His voice was hoarse. "Can't sleep?"

Matt looked back at him, shook his head instead of answering aloud.

He looked even smaller than usual, sitting there in the expanse of that wide-open doorway.

Steven rolled out of bed, shirtless and barefoot, wearing a pair of black sweatpants that had seen better days.

He crossed the scuffed linoleum floor, stepped over the threshold and sat down beside Matt on the step, interlacing his fingers, letting his elbows rest on his knees. There was enough of a chill in the air to raise goose bumps wherever his skin was bare, so he figured Matt had to be cold, too, sitting there in his cotton pajamas. With a sigh, Steven squinted to make out the winding sparkle of the nearby creek, sprinkled in starlight, edged by oak trees, with night-purple mountains for a backdrop.

Matt leaned into him a little, a gesture that further melted Steven's already-bruised heart.

Carefully, Steven put an arm around the boy, to lend not only reassurance, but warmth, too. "Having second thoughts about turning rancher this late in your life?" he teased, thinking he couldn't have loved Matt any more if he'd been his own child, instead of his best friend's.

In the morning, Steven would attend the closing over at the Cattleman's Bank, and sign the papers making him the legal owner of a fifty-acre spread with a sturdy though run-down two-story house and a good well but not much else going for it. The rickety fences had toppled over years ago, defeated by decades of heavy snow in winter and pounding rain come springtime, and the barn was unsalvageable. Yet something about the place had reached out to him and grabbed hold, just the same.

The small ranch had been a home once, and it could be one again, with a lot of elbow grease—and a serious chunk of change. Fortunately, money wasn't a problem for Steven, which wasn't to say there weren't plenty of other things to chap his figurative hide.

Sometimes, he felt just as lost as Matt did.

Matt's mouth quirked up at one side in a flimsy attempt at a smile, all the more touching because of the obvious effort involved. "I'm *only* five years and three months old," he said, in belated reply to Steven's question, in that oddly mature way of his. "It's not late in my life, because my life just got started." The little guy had skipped the baby-talk stage entirely; he hadn't even tried to talk until he was past two, but he'd spoken in full sentences from then on.

"Five, huh?" Steven teased, raising one eyebrow. "If you weren't so short, I'd say you were lying about your age. Come on, admit it—you're really somebody's grandfather, posing as a kid."

The joke, a well-worn favorite, fell flat. Matt's small shoulders moved with the force of his sigh, and he leaned a little more heavily into Steven's side.

"Feeling lonesome?" Steven asked, after clearing his throat.

Matt nodded, looking up at Steven. His eyes were huge and luminous in the predawn darkness. "I need a dog," the boy announced solemnly.

Steven chuckled, ruffled Matt's hair, gleaming dark as a raven's wing in the night. Relief swelled inside him, flailed behind his chest wall like a living thing doing its best to escape. A dog was something he could manage.

"Soon as we're settled," he promised, "we'll visit the animal shelter and pick out a mutt."

"Do they have ponies at the shelter, too?" The question cheered Steven; Matt was pushing the envelope, so to speak, and that had to be a good sign.

They'd already had the pony discussion—repeatedly.

"You know the deal, Tex," he reminded the little boy quietly. "The fences need to be replaced before we can keep horses, and the barn, too."

Matt sighed again, deeply. "That might take a long time," he lamented, "since you'll be working in town every day."

Steven fully intended to settle down in Stone Creek, build a normal life for his young charge and for himself. And to him, *normal* meant showing up somewhere on weekday mornings and putting in eight hours—whether he needed the paycheck or not.

He'd had to fight just to get through high school, let alone prelaw in college, and then earn the graduate degree that had qualified him to take the bar exam—a frustrating variety of learning disorders had all but crippled him early in his life. Although they'd been corrected, thanks to several perceptive teachers, he'd had a lot of catching up to do.

Still felt as if he was scrambling, some of the time.

Steven ruffled Matt's hair. "Yep," he agreed. "I'll be working."

"What about me? Where will I be when you're gone?"

They'd already covered that ground, numerous times, but after everything—and everybody—the little guy had lost over the past couple of years, it wasn't surprising that he needed almost constant reassurance. "You'll be in day camp," Steven said. "Until you start first grade in the fall, anyhow."

Matt's chin jutted out a little way, the angle obstinate and so reminiscent of Zack that the backs of Steven's eyes stung again. Zack St. John had been his best friend since middle school, a popular athlete, excellent student and all-around good guy. Losing Jillie had been a terrible blow, knocking Zack for the proverbial loop—he'd gone wild and finally died when, driving too fast down a narrow mountain road, he'd lost control somehow and laid his motorcycle down.

"Couldn't I just go to the office with you?" the boy asked, his voice even smaller than he was. "I might not like day camp. Anyhow, it's summer. Who goes to day camp in *summer*?"

Steven sighed and got to his feet. "Lots of kids do," he said. "And you might just wind up thinking day camp is the greatest thing since 3D TV." He extended a hand. "Come on, Tex. Let's get you back to bed. Tomorrow might be a long day, and you'll need your rest."

Matt reached for the stuffed skunk, and wound up in the now-tattered blanket he always kept close at hand. Jillie had knitted that herself, especially to bring her and Zack's infant son home from the hospital in, but the thing had been through some serious wear-and-tear since then.

Steven supposed that Matt was too old to be so attached to a baby blanket, but he didn't have the heart to take it away.

So he watched as the little boy got to his feet, trundled back inside, took a brief detour to the bathroom and then stood in the middle of the small room, looking forlorn.

"Can I sleep with you?" he asked. "Just for tonight?"

Steven tossed back the covers on the sofa bed and stretched out, resigned to the knowledge that he probably wouldn't close his eyes again before the morning was right on top of him. "Yeah," he said. "Hop in."

Matt scrambled onto the bad mattress and squirmed a little before settling down.

Steven stretched to switch off the lamp on the bedside table.

"Thanks," Matt said, in the darkness.

"You're welcome," Steven replied.

"I dreamed about Mom and Dad," Matt confided, after a silence so long that Steven thought he'd gone to sleep. "They were coming to get me, in a big red truck. That's why I was sitting on the step when you woke up. It took me a little while to figure out that it was just a dream."

"I thought it was something like that," Steven said, when he could trust himself to speak.

"I really miss them," Matt admitted.

"Me, too," Steven agreed, his voice hoarse.

"But we're gonna make it, right? You and me? Because we're pardners till the end?"

Steven swallowed, blinked a couple of times, glad of the darkness. "Pardners till the end," he promised. "And we are definitely gonna make it."

"Okay," Matt yawned, apparently satisfied. For the moment, anyhow. He'd ask again soon. "'Night."

"'Night," Steven replied.

Soon, the child was asleep.

Eventually, though he would have bet it wouldn't happen, Steven slept, too.

MELISSA O'BALLIVAN WHIPPED her prized convertible roadster, cherry-red with plenty of gleaming chrome, up to the curb in front of the Sunflower Bakery and Café in downtown Stone Creek, shifted into Neutral and shoved open the door to jump out.

It was a nice day, one of those blue-sky wonders, so she had the top down.

Setting the emergency brake and then leaving the engine running, she dashed into the small restaurant, owned and operated by her brother-in-law Tanner Quinn's sister, Tessa, and made her way between jam-packed tables to the counter.

Six days a week, Melissa breakfasted on fruit smoothies with a scoop of protein powder blended in, but most Fridays, she permitted herself to stop by the popular eatery for her favorite takeout—Tessa made a mean turkey-sausage biscuit with cheese and egg whites.

"The usual?" Tessa grinned at her from behind the counter, but she was already holding up the fragrant brown paper bag.

Melissa returned the cheerful greetings of several other customers and nodded, fishing in her wallet for money as she reached the register. Out of the corner of her eye, she spotted a face she didn't recognize—a good-looking guy with dark blond hair, a little on the shaggy side, perched on one of the stools in front of the counter. He wore black slacks and an expensive sports shirt that accented the periwinkle-blue of his eyes.

For some reason Melissa couldn't have explained, she was suddenly picturing him in old jeans, beat-up boots and the kind of Western-cut shirt most of the men around Stone Creek wore for every day.

She looked away quickly—but not quickly enough, going by the slight grin that tugged at a corner of the stranger's mouth as he studied her. Who *was* this? Melissa wondered, while she waited impatiently for Tessa to hand back change for a ten-dollar bill.

Just somebody passing through, she decided, completing the transaction and noticing, somewhat after the fact, that the mystery man wasn't alone. A small boy sat beside him, busily tucking into a short stack of Tessa's incomparable blueberry-walnut pancakes.

Melissa accepted her change and her breakfast and turned on one high-heeled shoe, consulting her watch in the same motion. Her meeting with Judge J. P. Carpenter was due to start in just fifteen minutes, which meant she'd have to gobble down the sandwich instead of savoring it at her desk while she listened to her voice mail, as she usually did on Fridays.

Even without looking, she knew the stranger was watching her leave the café; she could feel his gaze like a heartbeat between her shoulder blades, feel it right through her lightweight green corduroy blazer and the white cotton blouse and lacy bra beneath.

Outside, Alice McCoy, the oldest meter maid in America, by Melissa's reckoning, had pulled up beside the roadster in her special vehicle, a rig resembling a three-wheeled golf cart. A yellow light whirled slowly on the roof as, ticket book in hand, mouth pursed with disapproval, Alice scribbled away.

"Not another traffic citation, Alice," Melissa protested. "I was only gone for two seconds—just long enough to pick up my breakfast!" She held up her sandwich bag as evidence. *"Two seconds,"* she repeated.

Alice bristled. "This is a no parking zone," she pointed out firmly. "Two seconds or two hours, it makes no never-mind to me. A violation is a violation." She made a little huffing sound and tore off the ticket, leaning to snap it in under one of the windshield wipers, even though Melissa was standing close enough to reach out and take the bit of paper directly from the woman's hand. "You're the county prosecutor," Alice finished, still affronted. "You should know better." She shook her head. "Leaving your car running like that, too. One of these days, it's bound to get stolen and *then* you'll be piping a different tune, young lady."

Melissa sighed, retrieved the ticket from her windshield, and stuffed it unceremoniously into the pocket of her blazer. "This is Stone Creek, Arizona," she said, knowing this was an argument she couldn't possibly win but unable to avoid trying. She was, after all, a lawyer—and a card-carrying O'Ballivan. "Not the inner city."

"Crime is everywhere," Alice remarked, with a sniff. "If you ask me, the whole world's going to hell in a handbasket. I shouldn't have to tell *you* that, of all people."

Melissa gave up, climbed into the sports car and set her bagged breakfast on the other seat, on top of her briefcase. She drove to the single-story courthouse, a brick building that also served as the local DMV, town jail and sheriff's office, parked in her customary spot in the shade of a venerable old oak tree and hurried inside, juggling her purse, the briefcase, and her rapidly cooling sandwich.

Melissa's official headquarters, barely larger than her assistant Andrea's cubicle, opened off the same corridor as the single courtroom and the two small cells reserved for the rare prisoner.

Andrea, at nineteen, wore too much eye makeup and constantly chewed gum, but she could take messages and field phone calls well enough. Because those things comprised her entire job description, Melissa kept her opinions to herself.

Dashing past Andrea's desk, Melissa elbowed open her office door, since both hands were full and her assistant showed no sign of coming to her aid, set the bag from the café-bakery on her desk and dropped her purse and briefcase onto the seat of the short couch under her framed diplomas and a whole slew of family photos. She ducked into her tiny private restroom to wash her hands and quickly returned, stomach grumbling, to consume the sandwich.

Andrea, popping her gum, slouched in the office doorway, a sheaf of pink message forms in one hand. Her fingernails were long and decorated with what looked, from a distance, like tiny skulls and crossbones. A sparkle indicated that the design might include itty-bitty rhinestones.

The girl wore her abundant reddish-brown hair short, with little spikes sticking straight up from her crown, and her outfit consisted of black jeans and a T-shirt with a motorcycle logo on the front.

Melissa sighed. "We really should talk about the way you dress, Andrea," she said, plunking into her chair and rummaging in the paper bag for her wrapped sandwich and the accompanying wad of paper napkins.

"It's Casual Friday," Andrea reminded her, with a faintly petulant note in her voice, fanning herself with the messages and frowning. Her gaze moved over Melissa's expensive slacks, blouse and blazer, and she shook her head once. "Remember?"

The sandwich, though nearly cold, still tasted like the best thing ever. "Is there coffee?" Melissa chanced to inquire, once she'd chewed and swallowed the first mouthful.

Andrea arched one pierced eyebrow, still fluttering the messages. "How should I know?" she asked. "When you hired me, you said it wasn't my job to make coffee—just to file and answer the phone and make sure you got all your messages."

Melissa rolled her eyes. "Speaking of messages?" she prompted.

Andrea sashayed across the span of floor between the door and the desk and laid the little pink sheets on Melissa's blotter. "Just the usual boring stuff," she said.

Melissa glanced at the messages, chewing.

There was one from her twin sister, Ashley. Ashley and her husband, Jack, were in Chicago, showing off their adorable two-year-old daughter at a family reunion.

Olivia, Ashley and Melissa's older sister, was looking after Ashley's cat, Mrs. Wiggins, but there were long-term guests—a group of elderly pals—staying at the B&B, and Ashley, who owned the establishment, was counting on her twin to stop by once a day to make sure the wild bunch were still kicking. Since one of them was a retired chef, they cooked for themselves.

The second message was from her dentist's receptionist. She was due for a six-month checkup and a cleaning.

The third: the biography she'd ordered last week was waiting at the bookstore over in Indian Rock.

"Sometimes," she joked dryly, losing her appetite halfway through the sandwich and dropping it back into the paper bag, which she promptly crumpled and tossed into the trash, "I wonder how I stand all the pressures of this job."

Andrea looked blank. "Pressures?"

"Never mind," Melissa said, resigned.

Just then, Judge Carpenter appeared behind Andrea, wearing a nifty summer suit some thirty years out of style and a wide grin. His hair was a wild gray nimbus around his face, and his blue eyes danced.

He'd always reminded Melissa of Hal Holbrook, doing his Mark Twain impersonation.

Andrea moseyed on out, and Melissa saw that J.P. was holding a steaming cup of coffee in each hand.

"God bless you," Melissa said.

J.P. chuckled and advanced into the room, pushing the door shut with a jaunty thrust of one heel. He set a cup before Melissa and sipped from his own after pulling up a chair facing her desk.

"He's here," J.P. announced. He wasn't much for preambles.

Melissa frowned, confused. "Who?" she asked, watching the judge over the rim of her cup.

J.P. leaned forward a little way, and dropped his voice to a confidential tone. "Steven Creed," he said.

Melissa's mind flashed on the drop-dead gorgeous man she'd encountered at the Sunflower that morning. He and the little boy were probably the only people in town she didn't know, since she'd grown up on a ranch just outside of Stone Creek.

Except for college and law school, and then a stint

in Phoenix, working for the Maricopa County prosecutor, she'd lived in the community all her life. So, by process of elimination...

"Oh," she said. "Right. Steven Creed."

Word had it that Creed was a distant cousin of the McKettrick clan, over at Indian Rock, and he was in the process of buying the old Emerson place, bordered by Stone Creek Ranch, the sprawling cattle operation that had been in Melissa's own family for better than a century. Her brother, Brad, lived there now, with his wife, Meg, herself a McKettrick, and their rapidly growing family.

"He rented that space next door to the dry cleaners," J.P. went on. "He's a lawyer, you know. He'll be hanging out a shingle any day now, I'm told."

"Stone Creek could use a good attorney," Melissa said, largely uninterested. Was this the reason J.P. had asked for a Friday morning meeting—because he wanted to shoot the breeze about Steven Creed? "Since Lou Spencer retired, folks have had to have their legal work done in Flagstaff or Indian Rock."

J.P. took a loud sip from his coffee cup. "I hear Mr. Creed plans on working pro bono," he added. "Championing the downtrodden, and all that."

That caught Melissa's full attention. Stone Creek wasn't exactly a hotbed of litigation, but it had its share of potential plaintiffs as well as defendants, that was for sure. There were disputes over property lines and water rights, Sheriff Parker hauled in the occasional drunk driver, and some of the kids in town seemed to gravitate toward trouble.

"That's interesting," Melissa said, vaguely unsettled as some pertinent recollection niggled at the back of her brain, just out of reach. As for Mr. Creed, well, she tended to be suspicious of do-gooders—they usually had hidden agendas, in her experience—but she was also intrigued. Even a little pleased to learn that Steven Creed wasn't just passing through town on his way to somewhere more fashionable, like Scottsdale or Sedona.

She remembered the child, his ebony hair a gleaming contrast to Creed's light-caramel locks. "The boy must take after his mother," she mused.

"Boy?" J.P. echoed, sounding puzzled. Then a light seemed to go on inside his head. "Oh, yes, the boy," he said, shifting around on his chair. "His name's Matthew. He's five years old, and he's adopted."

Melissa blinked, a little taken aback by the extent of his knowledge until she recalled that J.P.'s youngest daughter, Elaine, had moved back to Stone Creek after a divorce two years before, and opened a private, year-round preschool called Creekside Academy.

Of course. Creed must have enrolled the child in advance—and Elaine had passed the juicy details on to her father.

J.P. finished up with a flourish. "And there's no *Mrs.* Creed, either," he said.

According to Elaine—she and Melissa had gone through school together—from the day she'd jettisoned the loser husband and returned to the old hometown to make a fresh start, her dad had been after her to "get out more, meet people, kick up your heels a little... As if Stone Creek were *overrun* with single men," Elaine had grumbled, the last time Melissa had run into her, a few days before, over at the drugstore.

Melissa, who hadn't had a date in over a year herself, had sympathized. Between her sisters, Ashley and Olivia, and her big brother, Brad, somebody was always after her to go on out there and find True Love. Easy for *them* to say. Brad had Meg. Olivia had Tanner. And Ashley had Jack. The unspoken question seemed to be, So what's your problem, Melissa? When are you going to get with the program and corral yourself a husband?

Melissa frowned.

J.P. either missed the expression or ignored it. Rising to his feet, he lobbed his empty coffee cup into the circular file with the grace of a much younger man. Back in the day, during high school and college, Judge Carpenter had been a basketball star, but in the end, he'd chosen to pursue a career in the law. "Well," he said cheerfully, "I hereby declare this meeting over."

"That was a meeting?" Melissa asked, arching one eyebrow. The subtext was: *I wolfed down the one turkey-sausage biscuit I allow myself per week just so you could tell me Steven Creed is single?*

"Yes," J.P. said. "Now, I think I'll go fishing."

Melissa laughed and shook her head.

J.P. had just left when Sheriff Tom Parker peeked in from the doorway. Tom was a hometown boy, a tall, lean man with dark hair and, usually, a serious look on his face.

"Hey," he said.

"Hey." Melissa smiled. She and Tom were old friends. Nothing more than that, though—he was attractive, in a rustic sort of way, if shy, and he'd been divorced from his high school sweetheart, Shirleen, for years. Everybody in Stone Creek knew he'd fallen head over heels for Tessa Quinn the day she opened the Sunflower Bakery and Café—everybody, that is, except Tessa.

"Just wanted to remind you that Byron Cahill gets

out of jail today," Tom said, looking spiffy in his summer uniform of brown khaki.

Melissa felt a mild shiver trip down her spine. Two years ago, when Cahill was still a teenager, he'd gotten high one Saturday afternoon, compounded the problem with copious amounts of alcohol, swiped his mother's car keys and gone on a joyride. The joy was short-lived, as it turned out, and so was fifteen-year-old Chavonne Rowan, who was riding shotgun.

When the "borrowed" car blew a tire on a sharp curve outside of town, it shot through a guardrail, plunged down a steep cliff into Stone Creek, teetered on its nose, according to witnesses, and went under. Two fishermen had rescued Byron; he came out of the wreck with a few cuts and bruises and a really bad attitude. Chavonne, it turned out, had died on impact.

Byron was arrested as he left the hospital in Flagstaff, where he'd been taken by ambulance, as a precaution. Although uninjured, he'd been admitted for a week of detox.

Melissa had successfully petitioned the Court to have young Cahill tried as an adult, over his mother's frantic protests that he was a good boy, just a little highspirited, that was all, and then Melissa had thrown the proverbial book at him.

It was a slam dunk. Byron was convicted of seconddegree manslaughter and dispatched to a correctional facility near Phoenix to serve his sentence—just over eighteen months, as it turned out.

Velda Cahill, his mother, who cleaned motel rooms and served cocktails to make ends meet, rarely missed a chance to corner Melissa and tell her about all the things poor Byron was missing out on, all because she,

Melissa, "a high-and-mighty O'Ballivan," had wanted to show off. Let everybody know that the new county prosecutor was nobody to mess with.

Melissa felt sorry for Velda. Never reminded her that Chavonne Rowan was missing out on plenty—*the rest of her life*—and so were her devastated parents.

Tom Parker knotted one hand into a loose fist and tapped his knuckles against the framework of the door to get Melissa's attention, bring her back to the present moment.

"You be careful now," he said. "If Cahill so much as looks cross-eyed at you, call me. Right away."

Melissa blinked a couple of times, dredged up a smile. "You don't think he'd come back to Stone Creek, do you?" she asked. "It's not as if the town would throw a parade to welcome him home, you know."

Tom tried to smile back, but the light didn't spark in his eyes. "I think Cahill's the type to move back in with his mother and mooch for as long as she'll let him. And you know Velda—she won't turn her baby boy out into the cold, cruel world." He paused, rapped at the doorframe again, for emphasis. "Be careful," he repeated.

"I will," Melissa said. She wasn't afraid of Byron Cahill or anybody else.

Tom hesitated. "And speaking of parades—"

Melissa, who had turned her attention to a file by then, looked up. She was getting a headache.

"That was a figure of speech, Tom," she said patiently.

"We've got Stone Creek Rodeo Days coming up next month," Tom persisted. "And Aunt Ona had to resign from the Parade Committee because of gallbladder problems. She's been heading it up for thirty years, you know. Since you and I were just babies."

Melissa saw it coming then. Yes, sir, the light at the end of the tunnel was actually a train. And it was bearing down on her, fast.

"Listen, Tom," she said earnestly, leaning forward and folding her hands on her desktop. "I'm a good citizen, an elected official. I vote in every election. I pay my taxes. On top of all that, I fulfill my civic duty by keeping the town—and the county—safe for democracy. Believe me when I tell you, I feel as much sympathy for Ona and her gallbladder as anyone else does." She paused, sucked in a deep breath. "But that doesn't mean I'm going to join the Parade Committee."

Tom blushed a little. "Actually," he said, after clearing his throat, "we were hoping you'd take over, sort of spearhead the thing."

Again, Melissa thought of her siblings.

Olivia, a veterinarian and a regular Dr. Doolittle to boot, apparently able to converse with critters of all species, through some weird form of telepathy, oversaw the operation of the local state-of-the-art animal shelter, and directed the corresponding foundation.

Ashley, too, was almost continually involved in one fundraising event or another—and their brother, Brad? He was a country-music superstar, even though he'd technically retired around the time he and Meg McKettrick got married. *His* specialty was writing whopping checks for pretty much any worthy cause—and doing the occasional benefit performance.

"You have the wrong O'Ballivan," she told Tom, feeling like a slacker. They were overachievers, her sibs,

with a tendency to make her look bad. "Talk to Olivia—
or Ashley. Better yet, have Brad *buy* you a parade."

Tom grinned faintly and then gave his head a sad
little shake. "Olivia's too busy," he said. "Ashley is out
of town. And Brad has his hands full running Stone
Creek Ranch—"

"No," Melissa broke in, to stop the flow. "Really.
I wouldn't be any good at organizing a parade. I've
watched a lot of them, on TV and right here in Stone
Creek. I've seen *Miracle on 34th Street* four million
times. But that's the whole scope of my experience—I
wouldn't know the first thing about putting something
like that together."

The sheriff colored up a little, under the jaw and
around his ears. "You think Aunt Ona was an expert
on parades, back when she took over? No, ma'am. She
just pushed up her sleeves and plunged right in. Learned
on the job."

"There must be someone else who could do this,"
Melissa said weakly.

But Tom shook his head again, harder this time. "We
got the Food Concession Committee, and the Arts and
Crafts Show Committee, and the committee to deal with
the carnival folks. Everybody's either already volunteer-
ing, doing something else or out of town."

Melissa set her jaw. By then, she was starting to feel
downright guilty, but that didn't mean she was going
to give in.

Out front, Andrea chirped a sunny greeting to someone. Melissa felt an odd little zip in the air, like the
charge before a summer thunderstorm.

"Then I guess you'll have to cancel the parade this
year," Melissa said.

And that was when the little boy she'd seen at the café that morning, eating pancakes at the counter, popped into her office.

He looked up at Tom, then over at Melissa, his dark violet eyes troubled. His lower lip began to wobble.

"There isn't going to be a parade?" he asked.

CHAPTER TWO

QUICKLY—BUT NOT quite quickly enough, as it turned out—Steven pursued Matt through the open doorway, scooped him up from behind and immediately locked eyeballs with the certifiably hot woman he'd checked out while he and the boy were having breakfast earlier that morning, over at the café.

When their glances connected, his-meets-hers, there was an actual *impact,* it seemed to Steven. He half expected things to explode all over the place, walls to tumble, ceilings to collapse, founts of fire to shoot up out of the floor, as in some apocalyptic action movie.

Damn, he thought, dazed by the strength of his reaction. He'd known plenty of beautiful women in his time, none of whom had ever affected him in just this way. Was it the amazing body, the face, the crazy mane of thick brown hair, falling past her shoulders in spiral curls, the jarringly blue eyes that seemed to see past all his defenses?

Who knew? He glanced down at the nameplate on her desk.

Melissa O'Ballivan. Prosecutor.

Uh-oh, he thought. Been there, done that.

After what Cindy Ryan had done to him, he'd sworn off dating other lawyers—especially DAs and their assistants.

"Sorry," Steven said, finally finding his voice and

dredging up the patented, lopsided grin that had been serving Creed men well for generations. "We stopped by to pay a parking ticket, and Matt here got away from me."

It was only then that he noticed the uniformed lawman standing just inside the small room, arms folded, assessing him with a certain noncommittal detachment, as if he might be running through a mental database of wanted criminals, in case he could match up Steven's face to one of them. Here was a man who took his job seriously.

Maybe he'd been the one to write that ticket and place it neatly under the windshield wiper of Steven's old truck.

Either way, Steven liked him right off, and figured that liking would stick. His first impressions of people were usually, though not always, accurate ones.

"County Clerk's office is just down the hall," the cop said, relaxing visibly. "You can settle up on the ticket there." That said, he put out his hand in that quintessentially small-town way Steven knew so well. "Tom Parker," he said.

"Steven Creed," Steven replied, setting a squirmy Matt on his own two feet.

"How come there isn't going to be a parade?" Matt piped up. He wheeled to look up at Steven. "*You said there would be a parade.* And a rodeo, too. That's the main reason I didn't run away from home when you told me we were moving here!"

By that time, the spectacularly sexy Ms. O'Ballivan had pushed back her chair and stood, soon rounding the desk to face the boy. There was no telling what she thought of Steven, if he'd even registered on her radar, but the lady had obviously fallen for Matt, hook, line and sinker.

"Hi," she said, with a smile that tugged at Steven's gut like a fishhook, even though she was looking down at the child, not at him. "My name is Melissa O'Ballivan. What's yours?"

"Matt Creed," the boy responded, somewhat warily because he'd been taught to be careful of strangers, and Steven felt another tug, this time at his emotions. He'd given Matt the choice, when the adoption became final, of keeping his folks' last name—St. John—or taking on his new father's. And it still touched him that Matt, who remembered Zack and Jillie with a clarity Steven did everything he could to maintain, had decided to go by *Creed*.

"Matt," Steven managed, clearing his throat. He still had that weird feeling going on inside and he wanted to get away, so he could mull it over, come to terms, make some sort of sense of it.

Whatever "it" was.

"Let's go take care of that parking ticket," he prompted, after an entirely rhetorical glance at his watch, failing completely to note the time. "We're due to sign the papers for the ranch in a few minutes."

"You said there would be a parade," Matt repeated, turning away from the dazzle of Melissa O'Ballivan to frown up at Steven. The kid could be bone-stubborn when he'd made up his mind about something, which meant the Creed name would suit him just fine.

The lawman, Parker, cleared his throat. Slanted a glance at Ms. O'Ballivan. "Aunt Ona already did most of the work," he told her. "Laid the groundwork, signed off on the different floats and even arranged for all the permits. Only thing you'd have to do is oversee a couple of meetings, check stuff off on a clipboard. Make sure folks live up to their commitments."

Melissa laid a hand on top of Matt's head and ruffled his dark hair slightly. Her shoulders rose and fell as she drew in a big breath and sighed it out, looking cheerfully doomed. "Welcome to Stone Creek, Matt Creed," she said. "And here's hoping you'll enjoy the parade."

Mollified, Matt punched the air with one small fist and turned to Steven. *"Yes!"* he said, with a grin.

By then, Steven had pieced the scenario together in his mind, or part of it, at least. Ms. O'Ballivan hadn't wanted to oversee the upcoming event, but she'd been roped in anyhow—by the sheriff, from the sound of it.

Steven allowed himself a long look at Melissa—an indulgence, considering the way she shook him up. The Realtor who'd sold him the Emerson ranch had touted both the parade and the rodeo as "longstanding community traditions," in addition to other selling points, and Steven had made a big deal about the festivities so Matt would have something to look forward to, besides the relatively immediate dog and the eventual pony.

"Thanks," Steven told Melissa, and the word came out sounding gruff.

She made a comical face. "Don't mention it," she replied, rueful.

"Maybe I could help out somehow," Steven heard himself say, as he took Matt's hand and started to turn away. "Not that I know much about parades."

"Join the club," Melissa said, with another of those lethal smiles of hers.

Steven grinned, nodded and managed to peel himself away.

He forgot all about paying the parking ticket, though,

because his mind was full of Melissa O'Ballivan, and it was bound to stay that way.

All through the closing, held in a meeting room over at the Cattleman's Bank, Matt fidgeted. Steven signed papers, handed over a cashier's check covering the cost of the property in full, probably came across as a man who knew what he was doing.

Adopting a little boy. Quitting the prestigious Denver firm where he'd worked since he'd left the family business. Winding up so far from the Creed ranch outside Lonesome Bend, Colorado, which had been in the family for well over a hundred years, only to buy a rundown spread in another state.

Was he a man who knew what he was doing? Before he'd encountered Ms. O'Ballivan, Steven would have answered with an unqualified "yes." Now, he wasn't so sure.

"WHAT JUST HAPPENED HERE?" Melissa asked, widening her eyes at Tom Parker and laying the splayed fingers of one hand to her chest. Steven Creed and his little boy, Matt, had probably been gone for all of thirty seconds, but it seemed as if they'd taken all the oxygen in the room away with them, leaving a vacuum.

Tom chuckled. "Stone Creek has itself a new chairman for the Parade Committee," he said, looking pleased and maybe a little smug on top of that. Then, about to leave, he paused in the doorway to wink at her. "And unless I miss my guess, the earth just moved." With that, he was gone.

Melissa stood in the middle of the office floor for a few moments, flustered. Then, because she was nothing if not professional, she walked over, gave her door a firm shove with one palm to shut it and marched back to her desk.

She didn't have many cases to prosecute; things had been pretty quiet around Stone Creek since Byron Cahill got himself sent up, but there were a few, and she always had reports to make, files to review, emails to read and respond to. If she'd been smart, she thought to herself, she'd have gone fishing with J.P.

At midmorning, Andrea rapped on the office door and stuck her head in to say that she needed to go home because she had cramps and there was nothing to do around that place anyway.

Peering at the girl over the tops of her reading glasses, Melissa mouthed the word *go* and logged on to her computer. Andrea might or might not have been suffering from cramps, but there was no arguing with the fact that both of them were, for today at least, underworked.

Melissa, grateful to be putting in eight-hour days, like normal people, didn't miss the high stress levels and double workweeks of her previous jobs. She liked having the time to paint the rooms of her little house evenings and weekends, read stacks of books, enjoy her growing gaggle of nieces and nephews and even garden a little.

Okay, so she'd been through a romantic—not to mention sexual—dry spell since her breakup with Dan Guthrie, several long and eventful years before. Nobody had everything, did they?

Something sagged inside Melissa when she asked herself that question. Her *sisters* had everything a person could reasonably want, it seemed to her—babies, hunky husbands who adored them, work they loved— and it went without saying that Brad had caught the brass ring. During his amazing career, he'd collected more than a dozen awards from the Country Music Association, along with a few Grammys for good measure, his marriage to Meg McKettrick was beyond happy, and they were building a beautiful family together.

Melissa sighed. Time to put away the tiny violin, stop comparing herself to her brother and sisters. Sure, she was a little lonely from time to time, but so what? She was healthy. She had kin, people who loved her. Stone Creek Ranch, with its long and colorful history, was still home. She had a fine education, no mortgage, a jazzy car custom-built to look just like a 1954 MG Roadster, and enough money socked away to retire at forty if she wanted to.

Which she probably wouldn't, but that wasn't the point, was it?

For Melissa, success meant having options. It meant freedom.

If she had a notion to pull up stakes and throw herself body and soul into a job in a more exciting place—say, L.A. or New York—she could do that. There was nothing to tie her down: she could simply resign from her present position, rent out her house or even sell it, say another goodbye to Stone Creek and boogie.

She loved her sisters and her brother. She had lots of friends, people she'd known all her life. But it was the idea of leaving her nieces and nephews, not being there, in person, to see them grow up but instead settling for digital photos, phone calls, rare visits and emails that made a hard knot form in her throat.

And why was she even thinking these thoughts, anyway? Because Tom had been right, that was why.

Steven Creed and his little boy had appeared in her office and, at some point, the earth *had* moved. Shifted right off its axis. Gravity was suspended. Up was down and down was up, and the proof of that could be stated in one short, simple sentence: She'd agreed to head the Parade Committee.

Melissa drew in a breath, huffed it out hard enough to make her bangs flutter, and scanned the list of new messages on her computer screen.

Tom Parker, sitting three doors down at his own keyboard, IMed her to say that time was wasting and she really ought to schedule a meeting so she could get on the same page with everybody on the Parade Committee.

The response she sent was not something one would normally say to a police officer, face-to-face *or* via email. But this was Tom, the guy she'd grown up with, the man who'd named his dog Elvis, for Pete's sake.

Tom replied with a smiley-face icon wearing big sunglasses and displaying a raised middle finger.

Melissa laughed at that—she couldn't help it—and went back to the official stuff.

Eustace Blake, who was ninety if he was a day and nonetheless managed to navigate the public computer over at the library just fine, thank you very much, had hunted-and-pecked his way through a complaint he'd made many times before, with subtle variations. Visitors from some faraway planet had landed in his cornfield—*again*—and scared his chickens so badly that the hens wouldn't lay eggs anymore, and for all he knew, they'd contaminated his stretch of the creek, too, and by God he wanted something done about it.

Smiling to herself, wishing mightily for a fresh cup of coffee, Melissa wrote back, politely inquiring as to whether or not Eustace had reported the most recent incident to Sheriff Parker. Because, she assured the old man, he was absolutely right. Something had to be done. She even included Tom's cell number.

The next half-dozen messages were advertisements—find love, get rich quick, clear up her skin, enlarge her penis. She deleted those.

Then there was the one from Velda Cahill—Melissa would have known that email address anywhere, since she'd practically been barraged with communiqués since Byron's arrest. This time, the subject line was in caps. FROM A TAX PAYING CITIZEN, it read.

Melissa sighed. For a moment, her finger hovered over the delete key, but in the end, she couldn't make herself do that. Velda might be a crank—make that a royal pain in the posterior—but she *was* a citizen and a taxpayer. As such, she had the inalienable right to harangue public officials, up to a point. She'd written:

My boy will be coming home today, on the afternoon bus. Not that I'd expect you to be happy about it, like I am. Byron and me, we're just ordinary people—we don't have anybody famous in our family, like you do, or rich, neither. What little we've got, we've had to *work* for. Nobody ever gave us nothing and we never asked. But I'm asking now. Don't be sending Sheriff Parker or one of his deputies by our place every five minutes to see if Byron's behaving himself. And don't come knocking at our door whenever somebody runs a red light or smashes a row of mailboxes with a baseball bat. It won't be Byron that done it, I can promise you that. Just please leave us alone and let my son and me get on with things.
Sincerely, Velda.

Sincerely, Velda. Melissa sighed again, then clicked on Reply. She wrote:

Hello, Velda. Thank you for getting in touch. I can assure you that as long as Byron doesn't break the law, neither Sheriff Parker nor I will bother him. Best wishes, Melissa O'Ballivan.

After that, she plunked her elbows on the edge of her desk and rubbed her temples with the fingertips of both hands.

She really should have gone fishing with J.P.

"IT'S ALL OURS," Steven told Matt, as they made the turn off the road and onto their dirt driveway. "Downed fences, rusty nails, weeds and all."

Matt, firmly fastened into his safety seat, looked over at him and grinned. "Can we go to the shelter and get a dog now?" he asked.

Steven laughed and downshifted. The tires of the old truck thumped across the cattle guard. *Now to buy cattle,* he thought, trying to remember when he'd last felt so hopeful about the future. Since Zack and Jillie's death—hell, long before that, if he was honest with himself—he'd concentrated on putting one foot in front of the other. Doing the next logical thing, large or small.

What was different about today?

It wasn't just the ranch; he could admit that in the privacy of his own mind, if not out loud. Today, he'd met Melissa O'Ballivan. And he knew that making her acquaintance would turn out to be either one of the best—or one of the worst—things that had ever happened to him. Thanks to Cindy, he figured, the odds favored the latter.

"I liked her a lot," Matt said, as they jostled up the driveway, flinging out a cloud of red Arizona dust behind them.

"Who?" Steven asked, though he knew.

"The parade lady," Matt told him, using a tone of exaggerated forbearance. "Miss O—Miss O—"

"O'Ballivan," Steven said. It wasn't that she was anything special to him, or anything like that. He'd always had a knack for remembering names, that was all.

"Is she anybody's mommy?" Matt wanted to know.

Steven swallowed. Just when he thought he had a handle on the single-dad thing, the kid would throw him a curve. "I don't know, Tex," he answered. "Why do you ask?"

"I like her," Matt said. Simple as that. *I like her.* "I like the way she smiles, and the way she smells."

Me, too, Steven thought. "She seems nice enough."

But, then, so had his live-in girlfriend/fiancée. With the face and body of an angel, Cindy had been sweetness itself—until Zack died and Steven told her that Matt would be moving in for good so he thought they ought to go ahead and get married. They'd planned to anyhow—someday.

He'd never forgotten the scornful look she'd given him, or the way her lip had curled, let alone what she'd actually said.

"The kid is a deal breaker," she'd told Steven coolly. "It's him or me."

Stunned—it wasn't as if they'd never talked about the provision in his best friends' wills, after all—and coldly furious, Steven had made his choice without hesitation.

"Then I guess it has to be Matt," he'd replied.

Cindy had left right away, storming out of the condo, slamming the door behind her, the tires of her expensive car laying rubber as she screeched out of the driveway. She'd removed her stuff in stages, however, and even said she'd thought things over and she regretted flying off the handle the way she had. Was there a chance they could try again?

Steven wished there had been, but it was too late. Some kind of line had been crossed, and it wasn't that he *wouldn't* go back. It was that he couldn't.

"So if she's not already somebody's mommy, she might want to be mine," Matt speculated.

Steven's eyes burned. How was he supposed to answer that one?

"*And* she's going to make a parade," Matt enthused.

As they reached the ruin of a barn, Steven put the truck in park and shut off the motor. Off to the left, the house loomed like a benevolent ghost hoping for simple grace.

They had camping gear, and the electricity had been turned on. The plumber Steven had sent ahead said the well pump was working fine, and there was water. *Cold* water, but, hey, the stuff was wet. They could drink it. Steven could make coffee. And if the stove worked, they could take baths the old-fashioned way, in a metal washtub in the kitchen, using water heated in big kettles.

Shades of the old days.

"Yeah," Steven said in belated answer, getting out and rounding the truck to open the door and help Matt out of his safety gear. The pickup was too old to have a backseat, but Steven had a new rig on order, one with an extended cab and all the extras. "Ms. O'Ballivan is going to make a parade."

"And you offered to help her," Matt said. That kind of confidence was hard to shoot down. In fact, it was impossible.

The reminder made Steven sigh. "Right," he said. Then he lifted Matt down out of the truck, and they started for the house.

"This place is *awesome,*" Matt exclaimed, taking in the sagging screened porch, the peeling paint, the falling gutter spouts and the loose shingles sliding off the edges of the roof. "Maybe it's even haunted!"

Steven laughed and put out a hand, gratified when Matt took it. "Maybe," he said. The boy would be too big for hand-holding pretty soon. "But I doubt it."

"Ghosts like old houses," Matt said, as they mounted the back steps. Steven had paused to test them with his own weight before he allowed the child to follow. "Especially when there's renovation going on. That stirs them up."

"Have you been watching those spooky reality shows on TV again?" Steven asked, pushing open the back door. There was no need for a key; the lock had rusted away years ago.

"I wouldn't do that," Matt said sweetly. "It's against the rules and everything."

Steven chuckled. "Far be it from you to break any rules," he said, remembering Zack. Matt's father had *lived* to break rules. In the end, it seemed to have been that trait that got him killed.

The kitchen was worse than Steven remembered. Cupboards sagged. The linoleum was scuffed in the best places, where it wasn't peeling to the layer of black subflooring underneath. The faucets and spigot in the sink were bent. The refrigerator door was not only dented but peeling at the corners, and the handle dangled by a single loose screw.

"Are we going to live here?" Matt asked, sounding

a little worried now. So much for his interest in ghost hunting.

"Not right away," Steven said, suppressing a sigh. This place wasn't even fit to *camp* in, let alone call home. The thought of returning to the Happy Wanderer Motel depressed him thoroughly, but there weren't a lot of choices in Stone Creek, and the next town, Indian Rock, where there was a fairly good hotel, was forty miles away.

"Good," Matt said, sounding—and looking—relieved. "The people at the shelter probably wouldn't *let* us adopt a dog if they knew we were going to bring it here to live."

Steven laughed. It seemed better than crying. He crouched, so he could look straight into Matt's face, and took him gently by the shoulders. "We'll make this work," he said. "I promise."

"I believe you," Matt said, breaking Steven's heart, as he often did with a few trusting words. "Can we look at my room before we go back to town?"

"Sure," Steven said, standing up straight.

Matt, always resilient, was already having second thoughts about leaving. "Maybe we ought to stay here," he said. "It's better than the motel."

Steven grinned. "I won't argue with you on that one," he said, "but the Happy Wanderer has hot water, which is a plus."

"We could skip taking showers for a couple of days," Matt suggested. Unless he was going swimming, the kid hated to get wet. "Where's my room?"

Steven led the way through the dining room. Although there was a second floor, there was no way anybody would be sleeping up there before the renovations were finished and the fire alarm system had been wired and tested.

"Here you go," he said, opening a door and stepping back so Matt could go inside. It was, as Steven remembered from his visit with the Realtor a few months before, a spacious room, with lots of light pouring in through the tall, narrow windows.

"Where's your room from here?" Matt wanted to know. He stood in the middle of that dusty chamber, his head tilted back, staring up in wonder like they were visiting a European cathedral instead of an old ranch house in Arizona.

Steven smiled. Cocked a thumb to his right. "Just next door," he said.

"Can I see?" Matt asked.

Steven ruffled the boy's hair. "Sure," he said.

His room was smaller. There was a slight slant to the floor, and the wallpaper hung down in big, untidy loops.

Steven thought of his expensive condominium in Denver and wanted to laugh. There, he'd had a fine view of the city, skylights and a retractable TV screen that disappeared into the ceiling at the push of a button.

What a contrast.

"It's not so bad," Matt decided, taking in the results of years of dedicated neglect.

Steven rubbed his chin, considering options. "I guess we could go back to town and buy ourselves a tent," he said. "The weather's good, so we could take baths in the creek. Carry our own water, cook over a campfire, sleep under the stars. Back to the land and all that."

Matt grinned. "Awesome," he said. "Let's go buy a tent."

"Better unload the camping gear and the grub first,"

Steven answered. "If we don't, there won't be room in the truck for a tent."

"They don't come all set up, silly," Matt informed him as the two of them headed back through the house, toward the kitchen door. "They're sold in *boxes*."

"Thanks for bringing me up to speed on that one," Steven said, mussing Matt's hair once again.

Matt supervised while Steven carried in suitcases, supplies of dried and canned food, sleeping bags and the camp stove, piling everything in the kitchen.

He returned to find Matt standing in the bed of the truck, one hand shading his eyes from the sun, following a trail of dust down on the road.

"Look," the boy cried, sounding delighted. "Somebody's coming!"

Steven was relieved when the rig, a big, fancy red truck, turned in at their driveway. Matt would have been pretty disappointed if they'd gone on by, whoever they were.

He recognized his cousin Meg right away. She leaned out the window on the passenger side and waved, beaming, her bright blond hair catching the dusty light. Her husband, Brad, was at the wheel.

As soon as the truck came to a stop, Meg was out, sprinting across the yard to throw her arms around Steven's neck. "You're here!" she cried.

Steven laughed. It had been a while since he'd felt this welcome anyplace.

Matt scrambled down out of the truck bed, eager for company.

Brad unfolded his long, lanky frame from the interior of the pickup and approached, and the two men shook hands while Meg bent to look into Matt's eyes and smile.

"You must be Matt," she said.

Matt nodded. "And you must be Steven's cousin," he replied. "I forget your name, though."

"Meg," she said gently.

Brad, looking like a rancher in his old jeans, long-sleeved chambray work shirt and ancient boots, jabbed a thumb in the direction of the house and said, "Looks like this place is in even worse shape than I thought."

Meg surveyed it with her hands resting on her trim, blue-jeaned hips. Her white cotton top was fitted and sleeveless, and it didn't seem possible that she was old enough to be married, let alone the mother of a couple of kids.

She could have passed for seventeen.

"Brad O'Ballivan," she scolded, sounding wholly good-natured, "I've told you a thousand times that it's a train wreck over here."

Brad grinned. "It's better than the barn, though," he drawled.

Matt had recognized him by then. "Are you that famous guy who's on TV sometimes?" he asked. Before Brad could answer, he went on. "We know somebody *else* with the same last name as yours. Melissa."

"Melissa is my sister," Brad said, obviously enjoying the exchange.

"You have a sister?" Matt made it sound like the eighth wonder. He was an only child, of course, and so was Steven. Did the child long for a sister, the way Steven himself had, growing up?

Brad crouched, so he could look directly into Matt's face. "Actually," he said, "I have *three* sisters. There's Olivia—she's a veterinarian and she can talk to animals. And Ashley—she and Melissa are twins."

Steven felt a pang at the mention of twins, the way

he always did when the subject came up. It made him think of his cousins Conner and Brody and their complex family history. They were a matched set, those two.

"Do they look alike?" Matt asked. "Ashley and Melissa?"

"Nope," Brad answered. "They're not those kind of twins."

"Oh," Matt said, absorbing the information. Then he brightened, looking from Brad, who straightened to his full height and must have looked pretty tall to the child against that sunlit Arizona sky, to Meg, then back again. "You're famous, though, huh?"

"Yeah," Brad admitted, sounding almost shy. "Sort of."

Matt nodded and moved on, over the celebrity aspect of the encounter, evidently. "We're going to get a tent and camp out!" he announced. "And we're adopting a *dog,* too!"

Meg beamed. "That's great," she said.

Matt absorbed her approval like it was sunlight.

"You could use Brad's old tour bus," she told Steven, a few moments later. The two of them had only known each other for about six months; turned out Meg was something of an amateur genealogist, and she'd tracked him down on the internet and sent him an email. Steven didn't have a lot of kin, and he wasn't taking any chances on alienating his cousin by imposing on her generosity.

Brad nodded, though, and rested a light hand against the small of Meg's back. "That's a good idea," he said, before Steven could get a word out. "It's pretty well-equipped, and nobody's used it in a while."

Steven opened his mouth to say something along the lines of "It's okay, I appreciate the offer, but the tent will be fine for now," but Meg already had her cell phone out. She dialed, stuck a finger in her free ear, smiling fit to blow every transformer within a fifty-mile radius and asked whoever was on the other end to please bring the bus next door.

Brad, meanwhile, had wandered over to look at the barn. Or what was left of it, anyway. "Good for firewood and not much else," he said, scanning the ruins.

Steven nodded in agreement, shoved a hand through his hair. "Listen, about the bus, I wouldn't want you and Meg going to a lot trouble. We'll be okay with a tent…."

Brad listened, grinning. But he was shaking his head the whole time.

Steven's protest fell away when he heard Matt give a peal of happy laughter. He glanced in the boy's direction and saw that Meg was leaning down again, her hands braced on her thighs, so she could look into Matt's eyes. Her own were dancing with delight.

Matt must have told her one of his infamous knock-knock jokes, Steven thought. The kid did tend to laugh at his own jokes.

"Never look a gift bus in the grillwork," Brad said.

Steven looked back at him, blinked. "Huh?"

Brad laughed. "Never mind," he said, and started off toward Meg again.

It was almost as though the two of them were magnetized to each other, Steven observed, feeling just a little envious.

Ten minutes later, the gleaming bus was rolling up the driveway, and it was a thing of beauty.

CHAPTER THREE

IT WAS 5:30 P.M., by Melissa's watch. The bus from Tucson and Phoenix would have disgorged any passengers it might be carrying—Byron Cahill, for instance—at 5:00 sharp, before heading on to Indian Rock and then making a swing back to stop in Flagstaff and heading south again. She was familiar with the bus route because she'd ridden it so often, as a college student, when she couldn't afford a car.

Although she usually looked forward to going home after work, today was different. Home sounded like a lonely place, since there wouldn't be anybody there waiting for her.

Maybe, she thought, she should give in to Olivia's constant nagging—well, okay, Olivia didn't exactly *nag;* she just suggested things in a big-sister kind of way—and adopt a cat or a dog. Or both.

Just the thought of all that fur and pet dander made her sneeze, loudly and with vigor. Since she'd been tested for allergies more than once, and the results were consistently negative, Melissa secretly thought Olivia and Ashley might be right—her sensitivities were psychosomatic. Deep down, her sisters agreed, Melissa was afraid to open her heart, lest it be broken. It was a wonder, they further maintained, that she didn't sneeze whenever she encountered a man, given her wariness in the arena of love and romance.

There might be some truth to that theory, too, she thought now. She adored the children in the family, and that felt risky enough, considering the shape the world was in.

How could she afford to love a man? Or compound her fretful concerns by letting herself care for an animal? Especially considering that critters had very short life spans, compared to humans.

Feeling a little demoralized, Melissa logged off her computer, pulled her purse from the large bottom drawer of her desk, and sighed with relief because the workday was over. Not that she'd really done much work.

It troubled her conscience, accepting a paycheck mostly for warming a desk chair all day; in the O'Ballivan family, going clear back to old Sam, the founding father of today's ever-expanding clan, character was measured by the kind of *contribution* a person made. Slackers were not admired.

Telling herself she didn't need to be admired anyway, dammit, Melissa left her office, locking up behind her. She paused, passing Andrea's deserted desk, frowned at the ivy plant slowly drying up in one corner.

It wasn't her plant, she reminded herself.

It is a living thing, and it is thirsty, that self retorted silently.

With a sigh, Melissa put down her purse, searched until she found the empty coffee tin Andrea used as a watering can—when she remembered to water the indoor foliage, which was a crapshoot—filled the humble vessel at the sink in the women's restroom, returned to the cubicle and carefully doused the ivy.

It seemed to rally, right before her eyes, that bedraggled snippet of greenery, standing up a little straighter, stretching its fragile limbs a bit wider instead of shriveling. Melissa made a mental note to speak to Andrea about the subtleties of responsibility—she wasn't a bad kid. Just sort of—*distracted* all the time. And little wonder, given all she'd been through.

Andrea had arrived in Stone Creek as a runaway, when she was just fourteen, riding the same bus that had probably brought Byron Cahill back to town that very afternoon. Out of money and out of options, she'd spent her first night sleeping behind the potted rosebushes in the garden center at the local discount store.

Upon discovering her there, first thing the next morning, the clerk had called Tom Parker, a natural thing to do. Especially since Andrea sat cross-legged against the wall, stubbornly refusing to come out.

Tom had soon arrived, accompanied by his portly mixed-breed retriever, Elvis, who pushed his way right through those spiky-spined rosebushes to lick Andrea's face in friendly consolation. After a while, Tom—or had it been Elvis?—managed to persuade Andrea to take a chance on the kindness of strangers and leave her erstwhile hiding place.

Over breakfast at the Lucky Horseshoe Café, since closed, the girl had confided in Tom, told him about her less-than-wholesome home life, down in Phoenix. Her mother was on drugs, she claimed, and her stepfather, who had done time for a variety of crimes, was about to get out of jail. Rather than be at his mercy, Andrea said, she'd decided to take off, try to make it on her own.

Of course, Tom checked the story out, and it held up to scrutiny, so agencies were consulted and legal steps were taken, and Andrea moved in with the elderly Crockett sisters, Mamie and Marge, who lived directly across the street from Tom's aunt Ona, she of Parade-

Committee fame, as a foster child. Andrea still lived in the small apartment above the Crocketts' detached garage, proudly paying rent and looking after the old ladies *and* their many cats.

Melissa was thinking all these thoughts as she left the courthouse, head bent, rummaging through her purse for her car keys as she crossed the gravel lot.

"Did you get my email?"

The question jolted Melissa and she came to an abrupt halt, her heart scrabbling in her throat.

"Velda," Melissa said, when she had regained enough breath to speak. "You scared me."

Byron's mother, probably in her early fifties and emaciated almost to the point of anorexia, stood near the roadster, dappled in the leaf shadows of the oak tree. Velda wore an old cotton blouse without sleeves, plastic flip-flops and jeans so well-worn that the fabric couldn't have been described as blue, but only as a hint of that color.

"Sorry," Velda said, her voice scratchy from several decades of smoking unfiltered cigarettes and half again that much regret, probably, her expression insincere. Lines spiked out around her mouth, giving her lips a pursed look. "I wouldn't want to do that. Scare anybody, I mean."

"Good," Melissa said, steady enough by then to be annoyed instead of frightened.

Velda stood between Melissa and the driver's-side door of the car, her skinny arms folded. Her hair was iron-gray, with faint streaks of yellow, and fell well past her shoulders. Pink plastic barrettes, shaped like little hearts, held the locks back at the sides of her head, creating an unfortunate effect of attempted girlishness.

"Did you get my email?" Velda asked again.

"Yes," Melissa replied, holding her keys in her right hand. "And I answered it. The situation is really pretty simple, Velda. As long as Byron stays out of trouble, he won't have to worry about my office or the police."

Velda smiled wanly, shrugged her bony shoulders. She sidled out of Melissa's way, rather than stepping, as if it would be too much trouble to lift her feet. Clearly, there was more she wanted to say.

Melissa got behind the wheel of her car and turned the key in the ignition, but she didn't drive away. She waited.

"It's hard enough for him," Velda went on, at last, as if Melissa hadn't said anything at all, "knowing that poor young girl died because of what he did. Byron's got to live with that for the rest of his life. But he's not some hardened criminal, that's all I'm saying. He's not some monster everybody ought to be afraid of."

As she'd spoken, Velda had curled her fingers along the edge of the car window, so the knuckles whitened.

Melissa sighed, something softening inside her, and patted Velda's hand. "Byron is your son," she said quietly, looking straight up into the faded-denim blue of the other woman's eyes, "and you love him. I understand that. But, Velda, the best thing you can probably do to help Byron right now is to lighten up a little. Give him some time—and some space—to adjust to being back on the outside."

Tears welled up in Velda's eyes; she sniffled once and stared off into some invisible distance for a long moment before looking back at Melissa. Her voice was very small when she spoke.

"Byron wasn't on the bus," she said slowly. "He was supposed to be on that bus, and he wasn't."

Melissa felt a mild charge of something that might

have been alarm. "Maybe there was some kind of delay on the other end—didn't he call you?"

Velda's expression was rueful. The bitterness was back. "Call me? Not everybody can afford a cell phone, you know."

Melissa looked around. Except for Tom's cruiser, the roadster was the only vehicle in the lot. "Where's your car?"

"It's broken down," Velda said, still with that tinge of resentful irony. "That's why I was late getting over to the station to meet the bus. It was gone when I got there, and there was no sign of Byron. I asked inside the station, and Al told me he didn't see my boy get off."

"Get in," Melissa said, nodding to indicate the passenger seat, leaning to move her purse to the floorboards so Velda would have room to sit down.

Velda hesitated, then rounded the hood of the car and opened the door. Once she'd settled in and snapped on her seat belt, she met Melissa's gaze.

"What are we going to do now?" she asked.

Melissa leaned to dig her cell out of her purse and handed it to Velda. "Call Byron's parole officer," she said, by way of an answer, certain that Velda would know the number, even if she couldn't afford a mobile phone of her own. "He—or she—will know if there was some sort of hitch with his release."

Velda hesitated, then took the phone from Melissa. She studied the keypad for a few moments, while Melissa shifted into First and gave the roadster some gas, but soon, Byron's mom was punching in a sequence of numbers, biting her lower lip as she waited to ring through.

BRAD O'BALLIVAN'S TOUR BUS, it turned out, was equipped with solar panels, satellite TV, and high-speed internet service. It boasted two large bedrooms, a full bath and a kitchen with full-size appliances.

"Must have been tough," Steven joked as Brad showed him and Matt through the place, "having to rough it like this while you were on the road."

Outside, a couple of workers from Brad and Meg's ranch were already hooking up the water supply and installing the secondary generator. That would serve as backup to the solar gear.

Brad grinned modestly, shrugged, slid his hands into the front pockets of his jeans in a way that was characteristic of him. "The band used it, mostly," he admitted. "I traveled by plane."

"Right," Steven said, amused. "More like a private jet, I think."

Brad shrugged again and looked away for a moment, the grin still tugging at the corner of his mouth.

Steven had never met a famous person before—not one from the entertainment world, anyway—and he was pleasantly surprised by this one. O'Ballivan was not only a down-to-earth guy, he was generous. He clearly loved his wife and kids more than he'd ever loved bright lights and ticket sales.

"I appreciate this," Steven said.

"Just being neighborly," Brad answered, his tone easy. *No big deal,* was the unspoken part of the message. He turned, paused beside the door to scrawl a couple of numbers onto the small blackboard above the desk. "Let us know if you need anything," he said.

Steven nodded. "Thanks," he replied.

He stood in the doorway and watched as Meg and Brad drove away in their truck. Matt was so excited, he was practically bouncing off the walls.

"This is *amazing*," he marveled. "Can I have the room with the bunk beds?"

With a chuckle, Steven turned to look down at Matt. The kid's face was joy-polished; his eyes glowed with excitement.

"Sure," Steven replied.

"Can we go back to town and get a dog now that we don't have to live in a tent while our house gets fixed up?" The question itself was luminous, like the boy.

Steven felt like a heartless bastard, but he had to refuse. "Probably not a good idea, Tex," he said gently. "This bus is borrowed, remember? And it's pretty darn fancy, too. A dog might do some damage, and that would not be cool."

Matt's face worked as he processed Steven's response. "Even if we were really, *really* careful to pick a really, really good dog?"

"*Good* has nothing to do with it, Bud," Steven said, sitting down on the leather-upholstered bench that doubled as a couch so he'd be at eye level with the child. "Dogs are dogs. They do what they do, at least until they've been trained."

Matt blinked. Behind that little forehead, with its faint sprinkling of freckles, the cogs were turning, big-time. He finally turned slightly and inclined his head toward the blackboard over the desk. "Maybe you could call Brad and Meg," he ventured reasonably. "You could ask them if they'd mind. If we had a dog, I mean."

"Tex—"

"I'd clean up any messes," Matt hastened to promise. He seemed to be holding his breath.

Steven sighed. Got out his cell phone. "You're the one who wants to get the dog now instead of later," he said. "So you can do the asking."

Matt beamed, nodded. "Okay," he said, practically crowing the word.

Steven keyed in one of the numbers Brad had written on the board, the one with a *C* beside it in parenthesis. When it started to ring, he handed the device to Matt.

"Hello?" he said, after a couple of moments. "It's Matt Creed calling. Is this Mr. O'Ballivan?"

The timbre of the responding voice was male, though Steven couldn't make out the words.

"My new dad says we can go to the animal shelter in town and adopt a dog if it's all right with you," Matt chimed in next. Inwardly, Steven groaned. *My new dad says...*

The boy listened for a few more seconds, nodding rapidly. "If my dog makes any messes," he finished manfully, throwing his small shoulders back and raising his chin as he spoke, "I promise to clean them up."

Brad said something in response, after which Matt said thank you and then goodbye and finally snapped the phone shut, held it out to Steven with an air of *there-you-go*.

Steven accepted the phone, dropped it into his shirt pocket, and ran a hand through his hair. "Well?" he asked, though it was pretty obvious what Brad's answer must have been.

"It's okay to get a dog," Matt announced, all but jumping up and down with excitement by then. "Let's go." He grabbed for Steven's hand, tried to pull him to his feet. "Right now!"

Laughing, Steven stood up. Mussed up Matt's hair again.

Someone rapped at the door just then, and Steven answered. The ranch hands Brad had sent over were standing outside, thumbs hooked into the waistbands of their jeans, sun-browned faces upturned beneath the brims of their hats.

"Electricity ought to be working," one of them said, without preamble. "Water, too."

"Mind flipping a switch and turning on a faucet to make sure?" the other one asked.

"No problem," Steven said. "Come on in."

He'd spent a lot of time on a ranch, so he wasn't surprised to glance back and see they hadn't moved.

Matt was already switching the light on and off.

The faucet in the kitchen sink snorted a blast of air, chortled out some brown water, then ran clear.

"All set," Steven said. "Thanks."

The ranch hands grinned and nodded, and then they got into their beat-up work truck and drove away, dust pluming behind them.

Steven locked up the bus. Matt scrambled into their old pickup and expertly fastened himself into his safety seat, but Steven still checked to make sure every snap was engaged, just the same.

A minute or so later, they were on the road, making a dust plume of their own.

Stone Creek's animal shelter was a sight to behold, a two-story brick structure with Dr. Olivia O'Ballivan Quinn's veterinary clinic occupying part of the first floor. The entrance to the shelter itself was at the other end of the building, so Steven and Matt headed that way.

The walls of the reception area were decorated with original paintings of dogs, cats and birds, of the whimsical, brightly colored variety, and there were plenty of comfortable chairs. A display of pet supplies occupied a corner, fronted with a handwritten sign saying all proceeds went toward the care of the four-legged residents.

There was no one behind the long, counter-type desk,

but a young man in jeans and a lightweight sweatshirt crouched on the floor, a scruffy duffel bag beside him, ruffling the lopsided ears of a black-and-white sheep-dog.

The girl Steven had seen at Melissa's office that morning stood by, watching, and for some reason she blushed when her gaze connected with his.

"You could adopt him," the girl said, addressing her companion.

But the young man shook his head, straightened with a sigh. "Not without a job, Andrea," he said quietly. His hair was brown, a little long, his eyes a pale shade of amber, and full of sadness. "How would I pay for his food? And what if he gets sick and needs to go to the vet?"

"*I've* got a job," Andrea said. "I can help out with expenses for a while."

"You work for Melissa," Matt piped up happily, smiling at Andrea.

Her smile faltered slightly, but it was friendly. She nodded, then turned back to her friend. "Byron—" she began.

But Byron silenced her with a shake of his head.

Just then, a chubby woman with frizzy brown hair came out of the back, greeting Steven and Matt with a cheerful hello and an I'll-be-right-with-you before turning her attention to Byron and Andrea and the sheep-dog.

"Well?" she asked hopefully. "Have we made a decision?"

Steven thought he detected a note of compassion in her tone.

Once again, Byron shook his head. "It just won't work," he said. "Not right now."

The woman sighed. Her nametag read *Becky,* and she wore print scrubs in bright shades of pink and green and blue. "Your mom must be happy to have you back home," she said gently.

By then, Matt was down on one knee, petting the sheepdog, and Byron watched with a sad smile.

"She doesn't know I'm here yet," Byron answered, his gaze bouncing off Andrea once before landing on Becky. "I got off the bus to hitchhike the rest of the way, but then Andrea came along and picked me up just this side of Flagstaff. I needed to be around a dog to get myself centered, so we came here first."

Andrea winced slightly, as though Byron had inadvertently revealed some vital secret.

Byron looked at Steven briefly, then at Matt. "He's a nice dog, isn't he?" he asked, indicating the hopeful critter.

Matt nodded. "We're here to get ourselves a dog," he told Byron. "We have a ranch. Right now, we live in a bus, but we're going to have a house and a yard pretty soon."

Byron smiled, but there was still something forlorn about him. "Sounds like you'd be a good match for this fella, then."

"Don't you want him?" Matt asked. He might have been only five years old, but he was perceptive. He'd picked up on the reluctance in Byron's decision not to adopt this particular dog.

"He needs a home," Byron said. "Just now, I can't give him one—not the right kind, anyway. So if you think he's the dog for you, and your dad says it's okay, you probably ought to take him home with you."

Andrea started to cry, silently. She turned away when she realized Steven was looking at her.

Becky, on the other hand, was still on the other subject. "You'd better let your mom know you're home, Byron," she said in motherly tones. "Velda's been looking forward to having you back in Stone Creek. She probably met the bus. And when there was no sign of you—"

Byron's shoulders drooped slightly, and he sighed. Nodded. Turned to Andrea, who had stopped crying, though her eyes were red-rimmed and her lashes were spiky with moisture. "Give me a ride home?" he asked her.

"Sure," she said.

"We can always use volunteers around here, Byron," Becky added. "Folks to feed the animals, and play with them, and clean out kennels."

Byron smiled at her. "That would be good," he said. Then after pausing to pat the sheepdog on the head once, in regretful farewell, he followed Andrea out of the building without looking back.

"That poor kid," Becky said, and her eyes welled up as she stared after Byron and Andrea. Then she seemed to give herself an inward shake. Turning her smile on Steven and Matt, she said, "May I help you?"

"We're here to adopt a dog," Steven answered, still vaguely unsettled by the sense of sorrow Byron and Andrea had left in their wake.

"Well," Becky said, with enthusiasm, gesturing toward the sheepdog, "as you can see, we have a prime candidate right here."

The dog's name was Zeke, Steven and Matt soon learned, and he was about two years old, housebroken and, for the most part, well-behaved. His former owner, an older gentleman, had gone into a nursing home a few weeks ago, suffering from an advanced case of

Alzheimer's, and his daughter had brought Zeke to the shelter in hopes that he'd find a new home.

"Can we have him?" Matt asked, looking up at Steven. "Please?"

Steven was pretty taken with Zeke himself, but then, he'd never met a dog he didn't like. He'd have adopted every critter in the shelter, if he had his way. "Wouldn't you like to check out a few others before you decide?" he asked.

Matt wrapped both arms around Zeke's neck and held on, shaking his head. "He's the one," he said, with certainty. "Zeke's the one."

Zeke obligingly licked the boy's cheek.

Steven glanced at Becky, who was beaming with approval. Clearly, she agreed.

"Okay," Steven said, smiling.

He filled out the forms, paid the fees and bought a big sack of the recommended brand of kibble. Zeke came with a leash and a collar, left over from his former life.

He rode back to the ranch in the bed of the truck, since there was no room inside, but he seemed at home there, in the way of country dogs.

Matt sat half-turned in his car seat the whole way, keeping an eye on Zeke, who'd stuck his head through the sliding window at the back of the cab.

"I bet Zeke misses his person," the boy said.

Steven felt a pang at that, figuring there might be some transference going on. It was no trick to connect the dots: Matt missed *his* people, too.

"Might be," Steven agreed carefully.

Matt had referred to him as "my new dad" that day, as he sometimes did. It was probably the only way he could think of to differentiate Steven from Zack. And the boy wanted desperately to remember his birth father.

He had slightly more difficulty recalling Jillie, since he'd been younger when his mother died.

"Do you miss anybody?" Matt asked. His voice was slight, like his frame, and a little breathless.

"Yeah," Steven said. "I miss your mom and dad. I miss my own mom, and my granddad, too."

"Do you miss Davis and Kim? And your cousins?"

Davis was Steven's father, Kim his stepmother. They were alive and well, living on the Creed ranch in Colorado, though they'd turned the main house and much of the day-to-day responsibility over to Conner.

Brody, not being the responsible type, had left home years ago, and stayed gone.

"Yes," Steven answered. They went through this litany of the missing whenever the boy needed to do it. "I miss them a lot."

"But we can go visit Davis and Kim and Conner. And they can visit us," Matt said, as the sheepdog panted happily and drooled all over the gearshift. "My mommy and daddy are *dead*."

Steven reached across to squeeze Matt's shoulder lightly. As much as he might have wanted to—the kid wasn't even old enough to go to school yet, after all, let alone understand death—he never dodged the subject just because it was difficult. If Matt brought up the topic, they talked it over. It was an unwritten rule: tell the truth and things will work out. Steven believed that.

Matt lapsed into his own thoughts, idly patting Zeke's head as they traveled along that curvy country road, toward the ranch. Toward the borrowed tour bus they'd be calling home for a while.

Steven wondered, certainly not for the first time, what Jillie and Zack would think about the way he was raising their son, their only child. Also not for the first time, he reflected that they must have trusted him. Within a month of Matt's birth, they'd drafted a will declaring Steven to be their son's legal guardian, should both of them die or become incapacitated.

It hadn't seemed likely, to say the least, that the two of them wouldn't live well into old age, but neither Jillie nor Zack had any other living relatives, besides their infant son, and Jillie had insisted it was better to be safe than sorry.

He'd do his damnedest to keep Matt safe, Steven thought, but he'd always be sorry, too. Much as he loved this little boy, Steven never forgot that the child rightly belonged to his lost parents first.

He slowed for the turn, signaled.

"Will you show me my daddy and mommy's picture again?" Matt asked, when they reached the top of the driveway and Steven stopped the truck and shut off the engine.

"Sure," he said. The word came out sounding hoarse.

"I don't want to forget what they look like," Matt said. Then, sadly, "I do, sometimes. Forget, I mean. Almost."

"That's okay, Tex. It happens to the best of us." Steven got out of the truck, walked around behind it, dropped the tailgate and hoisted an eager Zeke to the ground before going on to open Matt's door and unbuckle him from all his gear. "Now that we're going to stay put, we'll unpack that picture you like so much, and you can keep it in your room."

Matt nodded, mercifully distracted by the dog, and the two of them—kid and critter—ran wildly around in the tall grass for a while, letting off steam.

Steven carried the kibble into the tour bus and stowed it in the little room where the stacking washer and dryer kept a hot-water tank company. He spent the next twenty minutes carrying suitcases and dry goods and a few boxes containing pots and pans from the house to the bus, keeping an eye on Matt and Zeke as they explored.

"Stay away from the barn," Steven ordered. "There are bound to be some rusty nails, and if you step on one, it means a tetanus shot."

Matt made a face. "No shots!" he decreed, setting his hands on his hips.

Zeke barked happily, as if to back up the assertion.

Without answering, Steven went inside, filled a bowl with water and brought it outside.

Zeke rushed over, drank noisily until he'd had his fill.

That done, he proceeded to lift his leg against one of the bus tires.

"That's good, isn't it?" Matt asked, observing. "He's going *outside*."

Steven chuckled. "It's good," he confirmed. "How about some supper?"

Matt liked the idea, and he and Zeke followed Steven back into the bus. Steven opened the kibble sack, and Matt filled a saucepan and set it down on the floor for the dog.

While Zeke crunched and munched, Steven scrubbed his hands and forearms at the sink, plucked a tin of beef ravioli from the stash of groceries he and Matt had brought along on the road trip, used a can opener and scooped two portions out onto plates, shoved the first one into the microwave oven.

"Time to wash up," he told Matt.

"What about the picture of Mommy and Daddy?"

"We'll find it after supper, Tex. A man's got to eat, if he's going to run a ranch."

Matt rushed off to the bathroom; Steven heard water running. Grinned.

By the time Matt returned and took his place at the booth-type table next to the partition that separated the cab of the bus from the living quarters, Steven was taking the second plate of ravioli out of the oven.

"Ravioli again? Yum!" Matt said, picking up his plastic fork and digging in with obvious relish.

"Yeah," Steven admitted, joining the boy at the table. "It's good."

I might have to expand my culinary repertoire, though, he thought. Couldn't expect the kid to grow up on processed food, even if it was quick and tasty.

Maybe they'd plant a garden.

Chewing, Steven recalled all the weeding, watering, hoeing and shoveling he'd done every summer when he came home to the ranch in Colorado. Kim, his dad's wife, always grew a lot of vegetables—tomatoes and corn, lettuce and green beans, onions and spuds and a whole slew of other things—freezing and canning the excess.

The work had been never-ending.

Maybe they *wouldn't* plant a garden, he decided.

Zeke, meanwhile, having finished his kibble, curled up on the rug in front of the door with a big canine sigh, rested his muzzle on his forelegs and closed his eyes for a snooze.

Matt eyed the animal fondly. "Thanks," he said, when he was facing Steven again. "I really wanted a dog."

"I think I knew that," Steven teased. "And you're welcome."

Matt finished his ravioli and pushed his plate away. Steven added *milk* to a mental grocery list.

"Can Zeke go to day camp with me?" Matt asked, a few minutes later, when Steven was washing off their plates at the sink.

"No," Steven answered. "Probably not."

Matt looked worried. "What will he *do* all day?"

"He can come to the office with me," Steven heard himself say.

Fatherhood. Maybe, in spite of the ravioli supper, he was getting the hang of it.

CHAPTER FOUR

VELDA RELAYED THE parole officer's remarks to Melissa, after saying goodbye and shutting the phone.

"Byron got out this morning," she said, the cell resting on her lap now, her gaze fixed on something well beyond the windshield of Melissa's quirky little car. "Just like he was supposed to. He had a ticket back to Stone Creek, and somebody dropped him off at the bus station, right on schedule."

Parked at a stop sign, Melissa didn't move until the driver behind her honked impatiently. Then she made a right, pulled up to the curb and stopped the car. "Maybe he decided to get off in Flagstaff or somewhere," she said. With permission from the authorities, Byron could settle anyplace in the state, after all—except that he would have needed his parole officer's permission to do that.

Color flared in Velda's otherwise pale cheeks. "You'd like that, wouldn't you?" she snapped, glaring over at Melissa. "If Byron didn't come back to Stone Creek, I mean? That way, you wouldn't have to think about him, now would you? You or anybody else in this crappy town!"

Melissa sighed. "Velda, calm down. I'm only trying to help you figure out what's going on here and find Byron."

But Velda shoved her door open and practically

leaped out of the car. "If you *really* wanted to help," she accused, "you wouldn't have pushed so hard for my boy to do time!"

"A girl died," Melissa said quietly.

The reminder fell on deaf ears, apparently. Maybe it was just too much for Velda to face, the reality that her only child had caused someone's death.

"Do you know what he did while he was in jail, Melissa?" Velda ranted on, standing on the shady sidewalk and trembling even though it was warm out. "Do you know what Byron Cahill, the horrible criminal, *did* every day, while he was locked up?"

Melissa swallowed, shook her head, braced for some dreadful prison story.

"He helped train dogs from the shelters to be service animals. Search-and-rescue, seeing-eye dogs, dogs to help deaf people, too. He's a *good boy,* dammit!"

"Velda," Melissa said, after nodding to acknowledge that Byron Cahill might actually have an admirable side, like just about everybody else on the planet, "let me take you home. Maybe Byron's there. Maybe he caught a ride with somebody instead of getting on the bus, or something like that."

But Velda shook her head. A tear slipped down her right cheek. Then she pivoted on the worn heel of one flip-flop and marched off down the sidewalk, probably headed toward the trailer park where she rented a single-wide, but maybe not.

Melissa, feeling as though she'd aged a decade in the last half hour, watched as Velda's thin frame disappeared into a copse of trees. She hoped Byron would be at home when his mother arrived but, at that point, nothing would have surprised her.

After checking to make sure the way was clear, Melissa pulled back out onto the road, executed a U-turn, and headed for Ashley's B&B.

Mentally, she reviewed her original impressions of young Mr. Cahill. He'd been sixteen when he was convicted and sentenced. Against the advice of his duly appointed public defender, but apparently with his mother's encouragement, Byron had waived a jury trial.

Melissa, in her capacity as prosecutor, and the public defender, a newly minted attorney imported from Flagstaff, had tried to negotiate some kind of deal, but in the end, they couldn't come to an agreement.

The defense wanted probation, with no jail time, and comprehensive substance-abuse treatment in return for a guilty plea. After all, the argument ran, Byron was very young, and he'd never been in any real trouble before.

Melissa had been in favor of the treatment program, but probation wasn't enough. Chavonne Rowan had been young, too. And thanks to Byron Cahill's reckless actions, she wasn't going to get any older. She would never go to college, have a career, fall in love, get married, have children. Naturally, the girl's family was devastated.

Not that Byron's going to jail would bring Chavonne back.

Secretly, Melissa had agonized over the case, but she'd presented a strong, confident face to the public, and even to her own family and close friends. She'd examined her conscience repeatedly, taken her responsibilities to heart, and she had the reputation as a ruthless legal commando to prove it.

Except for those few who knew her through and through—Brad, Olivia, Ashley and one or two close girlfriends—most people probably thought she was a real hard-ass. Even a ballbuster.

And when Melissa allowed herself to think about that, it grieved her.

Sure, she'd wanted an education and a career. She loved the law, complicated as it was, and she loved justice even more. Justice, of course, was an elusive thing, very subjective in some ways, too often more of a concept than a reality, but without the *pursuit* of that ideal, where would humanity be?

She thrust out a sigh. Shifted the car *and* her mood. She'd done the best she could with the Cahill case. And that had to be good enough.

With no reason to hurry home, Melissa decided she might as well stop by the B&B—the octogenarian guests were due in the night before—thereby fulfilling her promise to Ashley. She'd look in on the old folks, make sure they were having a good time. And still breathing, of course.

Five minutes later, she bumped up the driveway next to the spacious two-story Victorian house Ashley had turned into the Mountain View Bed and Breakfast several years before.

Ashley.

Melissa felt a stab, missing her twin sister sorely. Although they were different in many ways, Ashley domestic, Melissa anything but; Ashley blond, with a love of cotton print dresses and gossamer skirts, Melissa dark-haired, fond of tailored suits and slacks—they had always been close.

Hurry home, Ash, Melissa thought, as she parked and got out of the car.

A shrill wolf whistle from the front yard of the B&B stopped her in her tracks.

She shaded her eyes with one hand, since the sun was still bright, and spotted an elderly gentleman standing just inside the fence, in the shadow of Ashley's prized lilac bush, wearing white Bermuda shorts, a white polo shirt, white shoes and white knee socks.

"Now that," the old man said, gazing past Melissa to the roadster, "is *some* car." He shook his leonine head of snowy hair. "Beautiful. Simply beautiful."

Melissa smiled. At least he wasn't a masher. "Thank you," she said, pausing to look back at the car with undiminished admiration. "I like it, too."

"You must be Mrs. McKenzie's sister," the man said, shifting his focus from the car to Melissa.

Mrs. McKenzie, of course, was Ashley.

Melissa was still getting used to that—Ashley married, and a mother. Sometimes, it seemed incredible.

"You must be one of the current guests," she replied, smiling, extending a hand across the picket fence. "Melissa O'Ballivan," she said.

"I'm John P. Winthrop IV," the man replied, with a nod and a very wide—and very white—smile. "But you can call me John."

"How's it going, John?" Melissa asked, thinking she might be able to wrap up this interview quickly and dash off an honest email to Ashley when she got home, assuring her that the B&B was still standing. "Is there anything you or any of the other guests need?"

He beamed. "Well, we can always use another croquet player," he said, making a grand gesture toward the nearby side gate, which led into Ashley's beautifully kept garden of specially cultivated wildflowers.

A teenage boy from the neighborhood did the watering and mowed the lawn, so the flowers, a profusion of reds and blues and pinks and oranges, looked good, if a little weedy here and there.

"I wouldn't be an asset to any self-respecting croquet team." Melissa smiled. She ran two miles every morning, but that was the extent of her athletic efforts. "But I would like to meet your friends."

John P. Winthrop IV rushed to work the latch and swing the gate open. "You look like you could use an ice-cold glass of lemonade," he said.

Try a shot of whiskey, Melissa thought wryly, recalling the Velda debacle. She hoped Byron Cahill had been waiting when his mother got home. If he'd taken off for parts unknown, he was in all sorts of trouble.

"Thanks," she said aloud, bringing herself back to the moment. "Lemonade sounds good."

Mr. Winthrop closed the gate and sprinted to catch up to Melissa on the flagstone walk. He seemed pretty agile for a man of advancing years.

Maybe it was the croquet playing.

"There is one thing," he said hastily.

Something in his tone, a sort of mild urgency, made Melissa stop and look up into his kindly and somewhat abashed face.

"We're a little—different, my friends and I," Mr. Winthrop said.

"Different?" Melissa asked, while inside her head, a voice warned, *Here we go.*

Mr. Winthrop cleared his throat. "Mabel should have told your sister in advance, when we booked the rooms," he said. "But we were all counting so on this little getaway and when it turned out we were going to have the whole place to ourselves, well, it all just seemed meant to be—"

Melissa squinted, still several beats behind. "Mabel?"

"Mabel Elliott," Mr. Winthrop said helpfully. "We're all retired, living in the same community, and relatively comfortable financially, and we take a lot of these little jaunts. Mabel knows how to use the internet, so she's in charge of arranging accommodations."

"I see," Melissa said, still mystified, and beginning to wish she hadn't agreed to that glass of lemonade. She could be home in a couple of minutes, taking a cool shower, donning shorts and a tank top and sandals, puttering around in her struggling vegetable garden and generally minding her own business.

Mr. Winthrop took her elbow, in a courtly way. "And with all the foliage surrounding the backyard," he added, dropping his voice, "there's really no harm done anyway, now is there?"

He still sounded nervous, though. And Melissa could relate, because she was feeling downright jittery by now. What could possibly be going on?

They rounded the back corner of the house, and Melissa froze, her mouth open.

Five people, three women and two men, all having a grand old time, were playing croquet in the green, well-shaded grass.

And every last one of them was stark naked.

THE PICTURE OF JILLIE and Zack, taken on their honeymoon, showed them parachuting in tandem, somewhere in Mexico, their faces alight with celebration as they mugged for the skydiving photographer jumping with them.

There were lots of photos of the St. Johns, but this one was Matt's favorite.

"Tell me again about when this picture was taken," Matt said, snuggling down into his sleeping bag, while

Steven perched on the edge of the lower bunk and Zeke made himself comfortable on an improvised dog bed nearby.

Holding the framed photograph in his hands, Steven smiled, taking in those familiar faces. Even now, it seemed impossible that two people with so much life in them could be gone.

"Well," Steven began, as he had a hundred times before, since he'd become Matt's legal guardian and then his adoptive father, "we all went to school together, your mom, your dad and me, and right from the first, they were a real pair—"

"Tell me about the wedding," Matt prompted, with a yawn. It was all part of the pattern—he would fight sleep for a while, then lose the battle. "You were the best man, right?"

"I was the best man," Steven confirmed huskily.

"And you and my daddy had to wear *penguin suits.*"

Steven chuckled, wondering if the kid was picturing him and Zack dressed up like short, squat birds from the Frozen North.

But, no—he knew what a tuxedo looked like. Matt had seen the wedding pictures a million times—usually, he asked why he wasn't in them.

The answer—*you weren't born yet*—never seemed to sink in.

"Yeah," Steven said belatedly. "We had to wear penguin suits."

"Mommy had on a pretty white dress, though," Matt chimed in.

"Yep."

"And out of all three of you, she was the best-looking."

"A rose between two thorns," Steven said, playing the game.

"A petunia in an onion patch," Matt responded, on cue.

They laughed, the man and the boy. There was a ragged quality to the sound.

"Tell me more about my mommy and daddy," Matt said.

Steven talked, his heart in his throat much of the time, until the boy finally nodded off. When he was sure Matt was asleep, he left the room, stepping carefully around the dog.

Out in the living room/kitchen area, Steven opened his laptop, booted it up and logged on. He hadn't checked his email in a few days.

Once he'd weeded out the junk, and the stuff he didn't feel like dealing with at the moment, he opened a recent message from his stepmother, Kim. It was dated that afternoon.

"Are you there yet?" she'd written. "Let us know when you get settled in Stone Creek, and your dad and I will come for a visit."

Smiling, Steven tapped out a brief reply. Kim had always treated him with warmth and good humor during those growing-up summers, never trying to take his mother's place. "We're here," he wrote, "and living the high life in a country-music star's tour bus. There are bunk beds in Matt's room, so you and Dad could sleep there."

The thought of that made his grin widen.

He added a description of Zeke, the sheepdog, recounting the pet-adoption saga, assured Kim that he and Matt were both fine, and signed off with love.

A second message came from Conner. "I'll be in

Stone Creek for the rodeo next month," it read. "Save me a bed."

And that was the whole thing.

Steven chuckled. His cousin was definitely a man of few words.

He hit Reply and told Conner he was always welcome and there would be a bed waiting when the time came. Compared to his cousin's email, Steven's was downright verbose.

A low whimper distracted him from the computer; he looked up and saw Zeke standing with his nose to the door crack, wanting to go outside.

Steven left the laptop on the table and accompanied Zeke out into the yard.

It wasn't quite dark, but a few stars had begun to pop out here and there, and the ghost of a three-quarter moon peeked over the horizon, like a performer waiting in the wings.

Zeke sniffed around for a while, did his business and went back to the door, ready to go in.

Steven opened the door and the dog mounted the steps, then went directly back to Matt's room.

Wide-awake, already bored with the internet and in no mood to watch TV, Steven sat on the fold-down metal steps in front of the threshold and looked out over what he could see of his ranch.

Some ranch, he thought. Most of the fences are down, the barn probably collapsed ten years ago and the house is a disaster.

He sighed and combed the fingers of his right hand through his hair, something he always did when he was questioning his own decisions.

His dad and Conner had both tried to persuade

him to stay in Colorado and raise Matt on the family's spread. Set up a law practice in Lonesome Bend.

He wasn't sure they understood, his father and his cousin, why he'd needed to strike out on his own, create something new for himself and Matt and any generations that might follow.

He wasn't sure *he* understood, either.

The Creed ranch was rightfully Conner's, Steven figured, Conner's and Brody's. Their dad, dead since the brothers were hardly more than babies, had been Davis's older brother and, therefore, the heir to the kingdom.

Not that anybody knew exactly where Conner's identical twin brother was keeping himself these days. He'd had some kind of knock-down-drag-out with Conner, Brody had, and except for a Christmas card every few years, with a terse message scrawled somewhere inside, the family hadn't heard from him in a decade.

Conner, like the good elder brother in the parable of the Prodigal Son, had worked shoulder to shoulder with Davis to make the ranch prosper, and it had. Even with the ups and downs of the economy and the ever-changing beef prices, it was a profitable operation.

When he was younger, shuttling back and forth between his mother's place back East, where he lived fall, winter and spring, and the ranch, which he'd thought of as home, Steven had been more than a little jealous of his cousins. Two years younger than he was, the twins got to live on the land year-round, and Davis was a substitute father to them, the kind he couldn't be to Steven, for the better part of every year, because of the distance between Lonesome Bend and Boston.

So, Steven had essentially lived a double life. Summers, he'd been a ranch kid, a cowboy. He'd herded cattle on horseback, mended fences, skinny-dipped in the lake, brawled with his cousins like a wolf cub in a litter, competed in rodeos.

All too soon, though, fall would roll around, and he'd find himself on an airplane, wearing preppy clothes instead of jeans and a T-shirt and old boots, with his hair cut short and brushed shiny.

In Boston, Steven played tennis and held a spot on the rowing team. He dated girls with trust funds. Even as a relatively little kid, he had his own suite of rooms in his grandfather's sprawling mansion, and it was generally agreed—make that, *assumed*—that he would one day join the prestigious law firm, founded well before the Civil War broke out, where his mother, two uncles and, of course, Granddad, carried on the family business.

School was difficult for Steven, at least in the beginning, a fact that troubled his mother to no end, but he'd worked hard, gotten the grades, made it through college and law school, and joined the company as a junior clerk, just like any other newbie.

Within a year, both Steven's mother and his grandfather were gone, his mother having died of pneumonia, which had started out as an ordinary case of the flu, Granddad of a heart attack.

Steven had soon realized he couldn't work for his uncles.

They resented the fact that he'd inherited his mother's share of the family fortune, as well as a chunk that had been set aside for him at birth and gathering interest ever since. His uncles had never understood what had possessed their sister to hook up with a cowboy in some shithole town out West during a summer road trip with her college roommates, get herself pregnant and compound the everlasting disgrace by keeping the baby.

But there were other reasons for the break, too; Michael and Edward Fletcher had never shared their father's commitment to excellence, not to mention integrity, and his death hadn't changed that. Nor could they match their sister's keen intelligence.

A few months after the second funeral, his grandfather's, Steven had called his best friend from school, Zack St. John, and Zack had recommended him for a position at the Denver firm where he worked.

The rest, as they say, was history.

In Boston, in the operation his mother had referred to as the "store," Steven had practiced corporate law. As soon as he'd made the move to Denver, however, he'd switched to criminal defense.

And he'd loved it.

He and Zack had worked together a lot, and they made a crack team. Steven was proud of their record, not just the wins, but the losses, too.

In every case, they'd done their absolute best.

Just then, Steven's cell phone rang in his pocket, and the sound jolted him. For the briefest fraction of a moment, he'd forgotten that Zack was dead and gone, expected to hear his voice.

"Hello?" he said, still sitting in the doorway of the tour bus, realizing that the night was turning chilly.

"Why didn't you call?" Kim asked, with a smile in her voice.

Steven went inside, shut the door, kept his reply low because he didn't want Matt waking up. The boy needed his rest, especially since he'd be starting day camp on Monday morning.

"Because I sent an email instead," he answered. His dad and stepmother had never had any children of their own, which was a pity, because they both had a real way with kids. They were good people, decent and responsible, and he loved them.

"So tell me all about Stone Creek," Kim said.

MELISSA PLUCKED HER formerly frozen diet dinner out of the microwave and plunked it on the kitchen counter to cool, getting a mild steam-burn in the process. With her other hand, she held the cordless phone to her ear.

"I tell you that there are eighty-plus-year-old *nudists* cavorting on your property, Ashley O'Ballivan, and all you can do is laugh?"

"The name is McKenzie," Ashley replied cheerfully. "What did you *expect* me to do, Melissa? Call out the National Guard to restore order?"

"I didn't think you'd *laugh,* that's all," Melissa said, miffed and not entirely sure why.

"Why wouldn't I laugh?" Ashley asked reasonably. "It's *funny.*"

"Not to mention illegal." A belated giggle escaped Melissa. "I guess you're right," she admitted, eyeing her food warily. The microwaved dish looked more like a plastic replica of lasagna than the real thing, the kind that might be sold in a joke shop—assuming there was even a market for stuff like that. "But trust me, it was also a shock. You haven't lived, my dear, until you've seen a pack of bare-ass naked senior citizens engaged in a lively game of croquet."

"And you without a fire hose," Ashley quipped.

"Ha-ha," Melissa said, carefully peeling the cellophane cover from her lasagna. Ashley was the one with the cooking talent; Julia Child was her patron saint. Melissa had never really caught the culinary bug; in fact, she'd all but had herself vaccinated against it. "When are you coming home? I miss the pity suppers."

Ashley laughed again, but the underlying tone was gentle, and betrayed a slight degree of worry. "'Pity' suppers, is it?" she countered. "You *know* when we're coming home. I've told you nineteen times, it'll be early next week." She paused, drew in a breath. "Melissa, what's going on? Besides the nudist uprising, I mean?"

"Interesting choice of words," Melissa commented dryly, giving up on the lasagna and shoving it toward the back of the counter. "And it's already Friday, so 'early next week' might be—"

"Okay, Tuesday," Ashley said with a chuckle, then waited stubbornly for an answer to *Melissa, what's going on?*

"Byron Cahill got out of jail this morning," Melissa told her.

"Yes," Ashley prompted, sounding only mildly concerned.

"He didn't show up on schedule," Melissa said. "Velda was upset."

"What else is happening?" Ashley pressed. "Velda's *been* upset for years, and you knew Byron's release date all along."

I met a man, Melissa imagined herself saying. *His name is Steven Creed. He's all wrong for me, and I think he's beyond hot.*

While she might well have confided in Ashley in person, she wasn't ready to talk about Steven over the telephone. And, anyway, what was there to say? It wasn't as if anything had happened.

Still, Ashley was an O'Ballivan and, among other things, that meant she wouldn't give up until she got a story she could buy.

So Melissa threw something out there. "I was roped into heading up the Parade Committee," she said.

"Oh, my," Ashley replied, sounding taken aback. "How did *that* happen?"

"I'm not sure, beyond the fact that Ona Frame can't serve on the committee this year because her gallbladder exploded."

"It—*exploded?*"

"Not literally, Ash. And thank heaven for that, because you can just imagine the fallout—"

"Melissa," Ashley groaned.

"Sorry," Melissa lied brightly. She had always loved grossing Ashley out.

Another chuckle came from Ashley's end. "Not that you deserve this," she began, "but as soon as Jack and Katie and I get back from Chicago, I'll see what I can do to help you get the parade—well—rolling."

It was Melissa's turn to groan. "Bad pun," she complained, but she was grateful—wildly and instantly so—and she wanted Ashley to know it. "You're merely saving my life," she said next.

"How hard can it be?" Ashley asked. "One small-town parade with—what?—fifteen floats, a high-school marching band, Veterans of Foreign Wars and the sheriff's posse riding their horses?"

How hard can it be?

"Don't tempt fate," Melissa said. "Just because poor Ona has made it *look* easy all these years, that doesn't mean it is."

Ashley sighed. "Try to stay calm," she said, but she still sounded buoyantly optimistic, and why wouldn't she? Ashley was happy. Completely in love with her husband, Jack, and thoroughly loved in return. The mother of beautiful Katie and expecting a second child in six months or so. "And since when are you superstitious enough to worry about tempting fate?"

Maybe since always, Melissa thought.

In many ways, their childhoods hadn't been easy—their mother had left home for good when she and Ashley were small, and their father had been killed in a freak accident while herding cattle on Stone Creek Ranch, struck by lightning.

After that, the four young O'Ballivans had been raised by their grandfather, Big John. While Big John had really stepped up, loving them with all his strong, kindly heart, of course there were issues. Weren't there always issues?

Did *anybody* make it to adulthood unscathed? Melissa didn't think so.

"Melissa?" Ashley said, when she'd been quiet too long.

"I'm perfectly fine," Melissa insisted. She bit her lower lip, peering into her fridge now, finding nothing that appealed to her. "But what do you want me to do if the vice squad raids your house on grounds of lewd conduct?"

Ashley laughed.

It was a sound Melissa knew well, and loved.

As much a part of her as it was of her sister since, at some level, it sometimes seemed they were one and the same person.

"What do I want you to do?" Ashley teased. "Well, you could maybe loosen up a little. Sign up for the croquet team or something."

"You are just too hilarious."

"Melissa?"

"What?"

"Thanks for calling. I love you, I'll see you in a few days and goodbye."

Melissa made a face at the receiver and hung up.

Hunger finally drove her to get back to her car, drive to the supermarket, and invest in a salad from the deli department, a carton of low-fat yogurt for breakfast and the new issue of *Vanity Fair*.

She was on her way back to her car, shopping bag in hand, when she saw Andrea drive up. Spotting Melissa at the last moment, it seemed, the girl didn't have time to hide her guilty expression.

Melissa smiled cordially and waited until her assistant got out of her old car, slung her purse strap over one shoulder, and nodded a shy "Hello."

"Feeling better?" Melissa asked, keeping her voice sunny. "Cramps can be pretty terrible."

Andrea's taste in clothing was questionable, and so was her memory for watering plants and things like that, but she was basically honest, and Melissa knew she was intelligent, too. If Andrea ever learned to believe in herself, there would be no stopping her.

"I was faking," the girl said miserably, her confession coming in a breathy little rush. "I didn't really have cramps."

"No kidding?" Melissa chimed.

Andrea didn't catch the faint sarcasm in her boss's tone. "I went to pick Byron up," she said, looking down at the asphalt of the parking lot instead of directly at Melissa. "Byron Cahill, I mean."

"I see," Melissa said, though she was genuinely surprised. She'd had no clue that Andrea and Byron were friends.

With obvious effort, Andrea made herself meet Melissa's eyes. Now, there was an obstinate set to the girl's jaw as she waited for—what? Recriminations? A lecture? The verbal equivalent of a pink slip?

"Byron's mother was pretty worried when he didn't

get off the bus this afternoon," Melissa said, feeling weary again. "She thought something bad must have happened."

Andrea nodded, and her shoulders dropped a little. "I know," she said, small-voiced. "But everything's all right now. I took Byron home, and his mom was there, and she's making pizza. I just came up here to get some sodas and rent a couple of movies." She had the good grace to blush. "Since it's Friday night and everything."

"And everything," Melissa said lightly.

Andrea straightened her spine. "Are you going to fire me?"

"Probably not," Melissa answered, thinking how ironic it was that Andrea, Velda and Byron would spend a chummy evening eating pizza and watching DVDs together, while she dined alone on a deli salad. "For future reference, though, if you have personal plans that will take you away from work, just say so. Unless there's something pressing I need you to do, Andrea, I'll be happy to give you time off."

Andrea took that in, looking ashamed again. "It's just that I thought you'd disapprove. Of Byron and me going together, I mean."

Melissa looked around to make sure none of the local gossips were hovering nearby, with an ear cocked in their direction. "'Going together'?" she repeated. "How could you and Byron be—'going together'—when he's been in jail for the better part of two years?"

"We were pen pals," Andrea said. "I'd see Velda around town sometimes, and she'd tell me how lonesome Byron was, locked away like some kind of criminal—"

Melissa put up a hand. In a courtroom, she would have snapped out, "Objection!" In the supermarket parking lot, facing a young woman who'd had a drug-addicted mother and the very elderly Crockett sisters for her main female role models, she took a different tack.

"Hold it," she said, very quietly. "Byron *did* get high, consume alcohol, then climb behind the wheel of a car and get into a terrible accident. And someone died in that accident, Andrea."

Andrea's eyes widened. She swallowed visibly and then nodded. "I was just telling you what Velda told me," she said reasonably, softly. "I started writing to Byron, because I know what it's like to feel all alone, and he wrote back. We got to be friends." She paused, drew in a breath. "Byron understands how wrong it was, what he did, and so do I."

Melissa closed her eyes for a moment, surprised to find that they were scalding with tears. "Yes," she said. She was remembering Chavonne's funeral, and the graveside service, and how the dead girl's mother had let out a cry of such raw grief when the coffin was lowered into the ground that Melissa could still hear it, sometimes, in her nightmares.

Andrea stooped a little, peered at Melissa. Moved to touch her arm and then drew back. "Are—are you all right? You look sort of—I don't know—pale or something."

Melissa shook her head, not in answer but to indicate that she didn't want to talk any more that night, and stepped around Andrea to get into the roadster.

It wasn't until she'd set the grocery bag on the passenger seat, fumbled for her keys, started the engine and driven to the edge of the lot that she looked into her rearview mirror and saw that Andrea hadn't moved.

She was still standing in exactly the same spot, staring down at the ground.

CHAPTER FIVE

MATT, STEVEN AND Zeke the Wonder Dog were up early the next morning, even though it was a Saturday, normally a sleep-in day.

Steven showered, then Matt, and both of them dressed "cowboy," in jeans and boots. Matt wore a T-shirt, while Steven pulled on an old cotton chambray shirt, a favorite from years ago when he was still riding and roping on the ranch.

"Here's the plan," Steven said, sipping from a mug of instant coffee while Matt fed Zeke his morning ration of kibble and put fresh water in his bowl. "We'll go into town, have some breakfast at the Sunflower Café, or whatever it is, then take a spin by the day camp so you can get a look."

"Can Zeke come, too?" Matt asked, stroking the animal's back as he spoke.

Zeke didn't slow down on the kibble.

"Sure," Steven replied. "Today, anyway."

Matt nodded, but it was obvious that he had reservations.

"What?" Steven asked, setting his coffee mug in the sink.

Matt looked up at him, eyes wide with concerns that probably wouldn't even have occurred to most five-year-olds. "Zeke can go to work with you when I'm in day camp, right? And this fall, after school starts?"

"Right," Steven said, reaching for the truck keys and his cell phone. "But there will be days when that won't be possible, Tex."

"Like if you have to be in court or something?"

Steven smiled, gave the boy's shoulder a light squeeze. "Like if I have to be in court or something."

"But sometimes he'll be out here all alone? Shut up in the bus?"

Steven dropped to his haunches. Some conversations had to be held eye to eye, and this was one of them. "I plan on having the contractors put in a yard and fence it off as soon as the renovations are under way," he said. "We'll outfit Zeke with a nice, big doghouse and he'll be fine while I'm working and you're at school."

By then, Zeke had wiped out the kibble and moved on to lap loudly from his water bowl.

"What if the coyotes get him?" Matt asked.

Back home in Colorado, it hadn't been uncommon for people to lose the occasional pet to coyotes, even in the middle of town; as their habitats shrank, the animals were getting ever bolder. Because they traveled in packs, even large dogs were often at a disadvantage in a confrontation.

"We'll make sure the fence is real high, so they can't get over it," Steven said, straightening up because his knees were beginning to ache a little in the crouch.

"How high?" Matt persisted.

"Really, *really* high," Steven promised.

Matt brightened. "Okay," he said, making for the door, with Zeke right behind him. "Let's roll."

Steven laughed and, fifteen minutes later, they were nosing the truck into a parking spot in the lot beside the Sunflower Bakery and Café. Recalling yesterday's parking ticket, he made sure there were no fire hydrants within fifty feet.

They brought Zeke as far as the front of the restaurant and secured one end of his leash to a pole with a sign on it that read, "Park pets here." An oversize pie pan full of fresh water waited within reach.

Steven was just straightening his back, about to follow Matt inside the café, when Melissa O'Ballivan came jogging around a corner and up the sidewalk, straight toward him.

She wore pink shorts, a skimpy white T-shirt, and one of those visor caps with no crown. Her abundance of spirally chestnut-brown hair bobbed on top of her head in a ponytail.

Her smile nearly knocked Steven over—even if it *was* focused on Matt and the dog with such intensity that he might as well have been invisible.

Holy crap, Steven thought, because the ground shook under his feet and the sky tilted at such a strange angle that his equilibrium was skewed. He gave his head a shake, in an effort to clear away some cobwebs.

"Morning," Melissa said, jogging in place.

All the right things bounced, Steven noticed, grinning down at her like a damn fool. "Morning," he responded, after clearing his throat.

She looked up at him with a surprised expression in her blue eyes, as though she'd momentarily forgotten that he was standing there. Or never noticed him at all.

She apparently wanted to give that impression, anyway, and he was intrigued.

"Would you mind opening the door?" she asked, unplugging the white earbuds attached to an armband MP3 player from her head.

It took Steven a moment to register what that simple phrase actually meant.

She wanted to go inside the café.

Feeling his neck warm, Steven pushed the door open and held it, so she could jog over the threshold and across to the take-out counter.

Morning greetings and the scents of fresh coffee, baked goods and frying bacon washed over Steven, but starved though he was, he barely noticed. He couldn't seem to take his eyes off Melissa O'Ballivan's springy, perfect little backside.

"Over here!" Matt whooped, mercifully distracting Steven. If he was lucky, maybe nobody had seen him staring like a pervert while the county prosecutor ran in place in front of the counter, placing a breathy order for a bottle of *very cold* water to go.

The boy had found a table by one of the front windows.

Zeke, just on the other side, put his big paws up on the sill and pressed his nose to the glass.

Steven laughed, and that broke the tension—until Melissa jogged past again, water bottle in hand. A truck driver got up from his booth and opened the door for her, and Steven felt a stab of irritation—or was it plain old ordinary jealousy?

Outside, Melissa trotted by the window, favoring Zeke with a smile Steven wanted for himself.

"What'll it be this morning, fellas?" a pleasant female voice asked, and Steven turned to see Tessa Quinn, the lovely owner of the establishment, wearing a floral print cobbler's apron over jeans and a tank top and looking gorgeous.

He'd recognized her on sight the day before—she'd had a major role in a long-running TV series when she was younger—but evidently she'd exchanged her SAG card for a small-town café and an apron.

Matt asked politely for a short stack of blueberry pancakes and a big glass of milk, and Steven went for coffee and the ham-and-egg special.

Tessa smiled and said, "Coming right up," and the smile lingered on in her eyes when she glanced up briefly at the window Melissa had just passed.

MELISSA'S NORMAL JOGGING route took her by the B&B most mornings, but not that one.

What was she afraid of? she asked herself, giving a wry chortle as she picked up her pace, going two streets out of her way just to avoid passing Ashley and Jack's place. That the nude croquet game might have been moved to the front yard?

You're getting to be a real party pooper, Melissa O'Ballivan, she told herself.

At home, she went through her front gate and did a few cool-down moves and some stretches on the lawn. She finished off her water, started for the porch and nearly choked, she was so startled.

There, in the shadows of the grand old lady peony bushes on either side of the walk, their huge white blossoms already fading as June wore on toward July, sat Byron Cahill.

Andrea was beside him, and seeing Melissa's expression, the two kids touched shoulders, maybe trying to give each other courage.

"Well," Melissa said, not sure what to think. "Good morning."

Byron got to his feet. He was probably just being polite, and there was nothing threatening in his stance, but he was a big kid, and Melissa automatically took a step back.

"Andrea tells me you might need somebody to mow the lawn and trim the shrubbery and stuff," Byron said gravely. He'd filled out in jail, and he was neatly dressed in inexpensive jeans, high-top sneakers and a clean T-shirt. While he was away, his acne had cleared up, too.

He was actually quite good-looking, though still a kid.

Melissa *had* made a few noises around the office about hiring somebody to whip her yard into shape, but it had never occurred to her that Andrea was listening, let alone planning to bring her recently released boyfriend by to apply for the job.

"Well—" she said, looking at the overgrown peony bushes.

The grass was so deep that small animals could get lost in it, and the branches of the venerable old maple tree were practically scraping the sidewalk in front of her picket fence. Which could use sanding down and painting.

"I can borrow a mower," Byron said, and there was a catch in his voice. One that gave Melissa a twinge of sympathy.

Times were tough. There weren't a lot of jobs in Stone Creek, especially for kids with a police record.

Andrea watched Melissa hopefully, chewing on her lower lip before blurting, "Miss Mamie and Miss Marge hired Byron to reline the koi pond in the backyard over at their place. You know, empty it out and put down new plastic and then fill it and put all the fish back in—"

Evidently, this was Andrea's idea of a sales pitch, but it fell away in midstream when Byron gave the girl's hand a squeeze.

"I thought I'd ask," he said to Melissa. There was resignation in his tone, but his gaze was direct. If she'd stepped aside, he would have walked past her, toward the gate.

But Melissa didn't step aside.

"It's a big job," she said, sizing him up again. "And probably temporary." Mike Smith, the teenager who took care of Ashley and Jack's grass and flowerbeds, usually did yardwork for Melissa, too. This year, though, Mike was attending summer school, and he was running short on spare time.

Byron's eyes widened slightly, and a smile tugged at a corner of his mouth. "I'm not afraid of big jobs," he said. "As for the temporary part, I can deal with that."

Melissa wondered if Andrea had nagged him into asking her for work, or if he'd thought of it on his own. Either way, it took guts to come over here and make the request, considering past history.

"When could you start?" Melissa asked. She named an hourly wage that seemed to please him.

He shoved a hand through his sandy-brown hair. Considered his answer. "Well," he said, "Miss Mamie and Miss Marge need to come first, since all their fish are swimming around in buckets waiting for me to clean out the pond."

Melissa smiled at the colorful image that popped into her mind. "Tomorrow, then?" she asked.

"Sure," Byron answered.

Melissa finally moved, so he could descend the steps. He paused, facing her, Andrea still clinging to his left hand.

He put his right out to Melissa. "Thanks," he said.

She hesitated only a moment before taking the offered hand. "If you screw up," she told him, frankly but in a friendly tone, "you are so out of here."

He laughed. "Yes, ma'am," he said.

He started toward the gate, and Andrea double-stepped behind him, looking back at Melissa and mouthing, "Thank you!" as she went.

Hoping she'd done the right thing, Melissa went on into the house and walked straight through to the kitchen. There she popped her empty water bottle into the recycling bin and hesitated in front of her old-fashioned wall phone.

It was Saturday morning—*early* Saturday morning.

Surely no emergencies had taken place while she was out for her run—she hadn't been gone more than an hour.

Even prosecutors had weekends off, didn't they?

Melissa's mind flashed on Steven Creed, standing in front of the Sunflower Café a little while before, when she stopped by for water, not that she expected *him* to call or anything.

But *hot damn,* the way he looked in those rancher's clothes she'd fantasized about seeing him in the day before. It ought to require some kind of legal permit, being that handsome.

Melissa sighed—not being able to ignore voice mail was the curse of the competent, she reminded herself—and reached out for the receiver. If she didn't check for messages, she wouldn't relax and enjoy her time off.

There had been one caller.

Ona Frame's recorded voice rang over the wire. "Melissa? I hope it isn't too early to be calling you, dear, but I was just so excited when Tommy stopped by this morning and told me you were willing to fill in for me on the Parade Committee this year—" Here, the older woman paused, turned tearful. "You see, I'm going to have to have this darn ol' gallbladder of mine removed, and there's nothing for it, but we've kicked off the annual rodeo with a parade every single year for nigh on half a century now and I don't mind telling you, it almost broke my heart to think of canceling—"

While she was out for her run, Melissa had come up with seven or eight really good excuses for turning down parade duty, but they all flew away as she listened to Ona rant on. And on. The message lasted so long, in fact, that Ona had to call back because she'd timed out on the first run.

The essence of it was that the committee meeting had been scheduled for three o'clock that very afternoon, all along. It was to be held in the community room over at the Creekside Academy, and since the whole crew had been planning on attending anyway, she thought it was the perfect opportunity to present Melissa as their new leader.

"Call me and let me know if you can make it!" Ona finished off merrily. "And I do hope you weren't sleeping in or something, and I spoiled it by calling—"

Melissa hung up, let her sweaty forehead rest against a cupboard door while she drew slow, deep breaths.

There was no getting out of it. She was stuck. Might as well accept the fact and move on, she thought.

She did allow herself one indulgence before returning Ona's call and committing herself to the job, though. Melissa took her shower first.

DURING BREAKFAST, STEVEN got a call on his cell phone from the Flagstaff auto dealership he'd contacted several weeks before; the extended cab truck he'd custom-ordered was in, and they could deliver it that day if he wanted.

Steven agreed, relieved that he'd have a backseat for Matt and Zeke to ride in now. Plus, his old rig looked like it had been driven West in the '30s by some family fleeing the Dust Bowl, though, of course, it wasn't quite old enough for that scenario.

He smiled, remembering his dad's apt description of the vehicle.

Steven's got himself one of those two-toned rigs, Davis Creed had told a friend, tongue firmly planted in his cheek. *And one of those tones is rust.*

"Do I have to clean up my plate?" Matt asked, anxious to get outside and keep Zeke company.

Steven was still thinking about rigs. In Denver, he'd driven a candy-apple-red Corvette—also unsuitable for carting around a little boy and a dog.

But Melissa O'Ballivan would look mighty fine riding shotgun in the sports car, he thought. He pictured her wearing a blue-and-white polka-dot sundress, strapless, with her hair tumbling down around her bare shoulders and her lips all glossy.

"Steven?" Matt said, waving one hand in his face.

"Go see to Zeke," Steven replied, with a chuckle, as he pushed away his plate. "While I take care of the bill."

Matt scooted away from the table and zipped to the door, and Steven waited until he saw the boy with Zeke before he turned from the window.

A few minutes later, he joined them outside.

"We might as well go over and see if the office is fit for human habitation," he told Matt, shoving his wallet into his hip pocket as he spoke.

"Okay," Matt said, conscientiously, "but Zeke drank

all the dog water." He held up the empty pan as proof. "See?"

Steven mussed the boy's hair and nodded. "Good call," he said. "You figure you're tall enough to reach the faucet on the men's room sink and fill it up again, then get all the way back out here without spilling?"

Matt nodded and headed for the door, pausing only to say, "Keep an eye on Zeke while I'm gone."

Steven grinned and executed an affirmative half salute.

Matt proved to be a competent water bearer, and they headed for the office on foot, since it was just down the street.

As it turned out, the place was in fairly good shape. The property management people had had the walls painted a subtle off-white, as requested, and the utilitarian gray carpet looked clean.

Two desks, some file cabinets and a half-dozen bookshelves had been delivered, and when Steven picked up the handset on the three-line phone his assistant would use—once he'd hired an assistant, anyway—there was a dial tone.

"Looks like we're in business, Tex," he told Matt, who was busy exploring the small place with Zeke.

There wasn't much *to* explore, actually—just an inner office, a storage closet and a unisex restroom that was hardly big enough to turn around in.

And all that was fine with Steven.

He probably wouldn't have all that many cases anyway, even though his services would be free. Stone Creek wasn't what you'd call crime-ridden, after all, and that, too, was fine with him.

It was one of the main reasons he'd chosen to come

here. He'd wanted to raise Matt in a small town—a small town that *wasn't* Lonesome Bend, Colorado.

"Are we going to look at the day-camp place now?" Matt asked, once he'd peeked into every corner of the office. He didn't sound overly enthusiastic about the prospect.

Steven checked his watch. "The dealer said we'd have our new truck within an hour and a half," he replied. "Why don't we go back out to the ranch and wait for it to be delivered, then swing into town again and visit Creekside Academy?"

Matt liked that idea, and it was settled.

They headed back home, and when they got there and piled out of the ancient pickup, Zeke ran around and around in happy circles in the grass, glorying in his freedom or maybe just glad to be alive, and obviously a country kind of dog.

Two and a half hours later, the new vehicle was delivered, sky-blue and shiny, with the chrome gleaming fit to dazzle the eye. A second man followed in a small car, to give the driver a ride back.

Steven signed for his purchase, accepted the keys and waved the deliverymen off in the second car.

Matt, meanwhile, had climbed onto the running board, probably hoping to stick his face against the driver's-side window and peer inside. Too bad he was so short.

Chuckling, Steven walked over, hooked the boy around the waist with one arm, and opened the truck door with the other. He hoisted Matt inside, and watched, grinning, as he plunked himself on the seat, gripped the wheel and made that time-honored, spit-flinging *varoom-varoom* sound kids use to mimic the roar of an engine.

"It won't be long," Matt crowed, steering speedily, "until I'm old enough to drive!"

The words saddened Steven a little, because he knew they were true. Like all kids, Matt would grow up way too soon.

"Yeah," Steven agreed, with a laugh, "but as of today, you're still too vertically challenged to see over the dashboard."

"Varoom!" Matt yelled, undaunted.

Steven went to the other truck for Matt's car seat, brought it over and installed it carefully in back of the new rig while the boy continued to "drive" up front. Zeke, evidently feeling left out of the action, put his front paws up on the running board and whined to get inside.

With a shake of his head, Steven finished rigging up the car seat, shut the door and went around to the other side, whistling for Zeke to follow.

He opened the door behind the driver's seat and Zeke leaped right up, nimble as a pup, and sat panting happily on the heretofore spotless leather upholstery, waiting for the next adventure to begin.

"Come on, buddy," Steven said to Matt, when the kid didn't move from behind the wheel. "Time to switch seats."

"Can't I ride in front, like I did in the old truck?" Matt asked. He sounded a touch on the whiny side—probably needed a nap—but since Steven knew the boy wouldn't take one, he couldn't see any sense in allowing himself to dream of an hour or two of peace and quiet when there was no hope of it happening. ·

"No," Steven said firmly, "you can't. Anyhow, Zeke will get lonely if he has to sit back here all by himself."

Matt couldn't argue with that logic. The dog's well-being was at stake, after all.

So the boy scrambled between the front seats to the back and only sighed a couple of times while Steven was buckling him in.

"Let's see how this thing runs," Steven said, when Matt was secure.

Zeke had moved over next to Matt, probably lending moral support, and when Steven got into the truck and started it up, the dog's big hairy head was blocking the rearview mirror. So Steven had to reach back and maneuver Zeke out of his way, a tricky proposition at best.

By the time they finally hit the road, Steven was starting to think they ought to save the visit to the day camp for another day, but he decided against the idea because their wheels were already turning and, besides, Matt was supposed to start on Monday morning.

The place would probably be locked up tomorrow, since it was Sunday, and that would mean no advance reconnaissance mission for Matt. He was five, a new kid in a new community. Steven wanted to give him every chance to get his bearings.

On the way back into Stone Creek, Matt nodded off. Zeke, ever the sport, sank down on the seat and went to sleep, too. The peace and quiet was a wash, though, because that dog snored like a buzz saw gnawing into hardwood.

As soon as they pulled up in front of Creekside Academy, a long, low redbrick structure with green shutters on the windows, a large fenced playground and a tall flagpole, with Old Glory up there flapping in the breeze, Matt and Zeke woke up.

Zeke barked jubilantly. Maybe he was patriotic.

Considering that it was Saturday afternoon, it

seemed to Steven that there were a lot of cars in the paved parking lot, which looked out over the creek mentioned in the school's name. He knew Creekside was open six days a week, though, and figured the camp must be doing a brisk business.

He parked the truck beside a spiffy replica of a 1954 MG Roadster, looking over one shoulder to admire it while he stood beside the rear passenger door of his new truck, helping Matt with all his fastenings.

They walked Zeke, cleaned up after him and put him back in the truck, where he promptly curled up on the seat, with a big dog sigh, and resumed the nap he'd started earlier.

Elaine Carpenter, owner and founder of Creekside Academy, greeted Steven and Matt at the front desk. She was an interesting character, Elaine was, her buzz cut at considerable variance with her ruffled cotton sundress and ankle-strap sandals.

Steven introduced himself and Matt, since he'd never met Elaine in person, and she made serious business of leaning down, looking straight into the little boy's eyes, and solemnly shaking his hand.

"Welcome to Creekside Academy, Matt," she said. "I know you'll like it here."

Matt returned the handshake—and the solemn gaze. "I don't suppose you allow dogs to come to school," he ventured.

Elaine smiled at Steven as she straightened, but her expression was regretful when she looked at Matt again. "Only on show-and-tell days, I'm afraid," she said. She held out her hand to Matt, and he took it. "Let's have a look around."

"Where is everybody?" Matt asked, not pulling

away. "There are lots of cars in the lot, but I don't see any kids around."

Elaine tilted her head toward a closed door, opposite her desk. Through the glass window, Steven saw several heads moving around, most of them female, but it was the sign taped beneath that caught his attention:

PARADE COMMITTEE MEETING 3:00 P.M.
HELP US WELCOME MELISSA O'BALLIVAN
TO OUR GROUP!

Steven smiled.

Guided by Elaine, he and Matt toured the day camp, checked out the mini-gym, the art room, the music room and the colorfully decorated classrooms.

The place was kid-heaven, and Steven was impressed, though part of his mind didn't make the journey but stayed right there in front of that door with the sign on it, coming up with all kinds of ways to welcome Melissa O'Ballivan—to all kinds of places.

Like his bed, for instance.

It was an inappropriate train of thought, for sure, but there you go.

He was an adoptive father, settling his young son into a new community, introducing him to a new school.

He was also a man, one who'd been alone too long.

And Melissa was definitely a woman.

By the time they'd gone full circle, Elaine wanted to meet Zeke in person, so to speak, since he must be a pretty magnificent dog, given the way Matt sang his praises.

Elaine raised an eyebrow at Steven, who was lingering outside the community-room door. "Would that be all right?"

Steven nodded, handed her the keys to his truck, so she could open the door and meet Zeke face-to-face.

Matt, holding Elaine's hand as he led the way outside, didn't even look back at Steven. He was busy chattering on about life as he knew it. As they disappeared through the front doors, Matt was explaining how their barn had fallen down and there were rusty nails in it, and that it would mean a "titanic" shot if he stepped on one. As soon as the barn was fixed, he was saying, when the doors started to close behind him and Elaine, he was going to have his very own pony to ride.

Steven waited until the woman and the boy had vanished. Then he drew a deep breath, pushed open the door with the sign taped to it and walked into the community room.

Melissa was up front, clad in linen slacks and a matching top, her hair twisted and then clamped into a knot on top of her head with one of those plastic squeeze combs. She wore almost no makeup, but her toenails, peeking out of her simple sandals, were painted hot pink.

It was harder to think of her as the county prosecutor when she looked like that, so he silently reminded himself that there was surely another side to the lady. She might *appear* soft and sexy, but in court, pushing for a guilty verdict, she'd be ruthless and barracuda-tough.

Like Cindy.

Noticing Steven, Melissa widened her eyes for a moment, then turned her attention back to the people filling the rows of folding chairs, studiously ignoring him.

Steven took a seat in the back, watching her, struggling against a strange and not entirely unpleasant sensation that he was being reeled in, like a fish at the end of a line.

Mentally, he dug in his heels. But the truth was that even from that distance, he could see the pulse pounding at the hollow of her throat. He wanted—hell, *needed*—to kiss her there.

And a few other places.

This is crazy, he told himself, and shifted in the chair, but that didn't help much.

He folded his hands loosely in his lap, as a camouflage maneuver, and listened to Ms. O'Ballivan as earnestly as if she'd been conducting a White House press conference.

"I'm counting on all of you to follow through with your original plans," Melissa said, in the process of bringing the gathering to a close, it would seem. "We have less than a month until Rodeo Days start, but after reviewing all your presentations, I think we have a handle on the situation. Questions?"

A plump woman near the front raised a hand.

"Yes, Bea?" Melissa responded pleasantly.

"I'd just like to remind everyone about the rule we instituted last year, concerning the use of toilet tissue in place of crepe-paper streamers on some of the more—creative floats." Bea stood and made a slow half turn, sweeping the spectators up in one ominous glance. "Toilet tissue is in very bad taste and it has been banned in favor of good old-fashioned crepe paper."

No one argued the point, but when Bea faced front and sat down, there were a few subtle raspberries from the crowd.

Seeing the expression on Melissa's face, Steven wanted to laugh out loud.

Talk about somebody who didn't want to be where she was.

He raised his hand.

"Mr. Creed?" Melissa acknowledged, blushing slightly.

"Steven," he corrected. "Are you still looking for volunteers?"

CHAPTER SIX

ARE YOU STILL looking for volunteers?

Melissa narrowed her eyes at Steven Creed for a moment, wondering what the heck he was up to. Wondering what he was even *doing* at the Parade Committee meeting in the first place.

Okay, sure, he was new in town, and he'd said something in her office the day before about helping out. Joining groups was a good way of getting acquainted with the locals, and all that, but, *still.* Could he really be all that concerned about whether or not toilet paper could be used to bedeck floats in the Fourth of July parade?

"I guess," she said, well aware that her tone was lackluster.

A low, speculative murmur moved through the crowd.

Stone Creek liked to think of itself as a friendly place, extending a ready welcome to newcomers, and it was.

Mostly.

Steven Creed merely grinned, probably enjoying Melissa's discomfort, though only in the kindest possible way, of course.

And he waited for the proverbial ball to bounce back into his court.

Melissa worked up a smile. "Sure," she said. "We can always use another volunteer—can't we, people?"

Everybody clapped.

"Okay," Melissa went on, wobbly-smiled, ready to bring this thing in for a landing so she could go home, weed her tomato plants, dine on canned soup or something equally easy to prepare and curl up in the corner of her couch to read. "Remember—we're doing a walk-through next Saturday afternoon, in the parking lot behind the high school. Nobody bring an actual float, though. We'll be tweaking the marching order, that's all."

There were nods and comments, but the meeting was finally over.

Melissa collected her purse and her clipboard, hanging back while the dozen or so parade participants and general committee members meandered out.

Steven Creed didn't leave with them.

He stood near the door now, watching her, his arms folded, a twinkle in those summer-blue eyes.

Hoping he'd just go because, frankly, she didn't have the first idea how to deal with him, Melissa nodded, coolly cordial, and got busy folding up the chairs and stacking them against the far wall.

Steven remained. In fact, he helped her put away the chairs.

"I didn't expect to run into you here," she said, when the work was done and there was no avoiding looking at him.

"Matt starts day camp here on Monday, so I brought him out for a tour," he explained, just as the boy appeared behind him, half dragged by the sheepdog she'd seen them with that morning, at the Sunflower.

Elaine Carpenter, J.P.'s daughter and a friend of Melissa's, brought up the rear, smiling.

"Ms. Carpenter said I could show Zeke the inside of the school building," Matt told his father. "So far, he likes it."

He was such a cute kid, and so bright. Just looking at the little guy made Melissa's biological clock tick audibly. And here she'd thought the battery was dead.

Seeing Melissa, Matt beamed at her and said hello.

Melissa relaxed a little, though she was still conscious of the man standing so nearby that she could actually *feel* the hard warmth of his body.

Okay, maybe she'd just assumed the "hard" part. It wasn't difficult to make the leap, since he looked so lean and yet so muscular...

What was it about him that set off all her internal alarm bells?

"Hello, again," she told the child.

"We're staying in your brother's tour bus," Matt told her exuberantly. "He says you've got a twin sister, but the two of you don't look anything alike."

Melissa smiled, nodded. "Ashley and I are fraternal twins," she said.

The boy frowned, holding Zeke's leash in both hands to restrain the animal. "What's *fraternal?*" he asked.

Steven Creed's eyes twinkled at that, and his mouth had a "you're-on-your-own" kind of hitch at one corner.

Not about to explain the fertilization process to a child, Melissa brightened her smile and replied, "I think you should ask your dad about that."

"My real dad died," Matt said, wiping that smile right off her face. "But I could ask Steven."

Melissa saw pain mute the twinkle in Steven's eyes,

and she felt a twinge of regret. J.P. had mentioned that the child was adopted, but she'd forgotten. "Oh," she said.

"We haven't exactly worked out what I should be called," Steven told her.

Elaine had already left the room by that time, so it was just the three of them and, of course, the dog.

Melissa felt a strange, hollow ache in her throat. This time, she couldn't even manage an "Oh."

For the next few moments, the room seemed to pulse, like a quiet heartbeat.

Then Steven smiled at her and said, "I've never helped out with a parade before, but I'm pretty good with a hammer and nails."

"It's kind of you to offer," Melissa said, finding her voice at last.

"Do you want to come out to our place and have supper?" Matt asked her, out of the blue.

Steven looked a little taken aback, though he had the good grace not to come right out and say it wasn't a good idea.

Melissa was oddly reluctant to see Steven Creed go, even though she hadn't wanted him there in the first place.

He was just too—*much*. Too good-looking. Too sexy. Too lots of things.

All of which worked together to make her say the crazy thing she said next.

"What if you and your—you and Mr. Creed—came to *my* house for supper, instead?" I'm not the greatest cook in the world, Melissa thought to herself, but my sister is, and I'm willing to raid her freezer for an entrée even though it means risking another encounter with a naked croquet team.

Matt giggled, probably at the reference to "Mr. Creed,"

and then swung around to look up at the man standing behind him.

"Can we?" he asked eagerly. "Please?"

Steven's smile seemed a touch wistful to Melissa; he probably thought she'd suggested supper at her place to be polite, as a way of letting him off the hook for the impulsive invitation Matt had issued.

He'd be right, if he thought that, Melissa concluded, but she still hoped he'd say yes. And it surprised her how *much* she hoped that.

"Six o'clock?" Melissa added, when Steven still hesitated.

He sighed, looked down at Matt, shook his head. "We didn't leave the lady with much choice now, did we?" he said to the boy.

"It would be nice to have company," Melissa heard herself say. Her voice was softer than usual, and a little tentative. It came to her that she was going to be very disappointed if Steven refused, which was just one more indication that she was losing her ever-loving mind, since she should have been relieved. "And it's no trouble. Really."

That last part was certainly no lie. She'd snitch one of the culinary triumphs Ashley always kept on hand, in case of God knew what kind of food emergency, slip some foil-covered casserole dish into the oven at her place, and gladly accept all the accolades.

Without actually claiming the cooking credit, of course. If anybody asked, she wouldn't lie. If they *didn't* ask, on the other hand, why say anything at all?

Steven still looked troubled, but Melissa could tell that he wanted to take her up on the offer, too, and that knowledge did funny things to her heart.

"How else are you going to get to know people in

Stone Creek," Melissa urged, starting toward the door as though supper were a done deal, "if you don't let them feed you? It's the way we country folks do things, you know. Your best bull dies? We feed you. Your house burns down? We feed you. Not that being new in town falls into that kind of category—"

Why was she rattling on like this, making an idiot of herself?

At last, Steven made a decision. "Okay, six o'clock," he said. "Can we bring anything?"

Matt let out a whoop of delight, and the dog joined the celebration with a happy bark.

"Just bring yourselves," Melissa said.

Steven, Matt and the dog followed her out into the brightness of afternoon. Splotches of silver and gold sunlight danced and flickered on the waters of the creek as they burbled by.

A smile flashed in Steven's eyes when Melissa tossed her purse and clipboard into the passenger seat of her roadster.

"That's some ride," he said. "I was admiring it earlier."

The remark seemed oddly personal, as though he'd commented on the shape of her backside or the curve of her breasts or the scent of her hair.

And Melissa was immensely pleased.

"Thanks," she replied, her tone modest, her cheeks warm.

"One question, though," Steven went on, opening the door of the ginormous blue truck parked next to the roadster. The dog went in first, then the little boy, who submitted fretfully to being fastened into a safety seat. Melissa waited for the question to come.

Steven didn't ask it until he'd shut the truck door

again and turned to face her. "Where exactly do you live?"

Their toes were practically touching; Melissa breathed in the green-grass, sun-dried laundry smell of him, felt dizzy.

"I've never been very good at giving directions," she said, when she thought she could talk without sounding weird. "Why don't you follow me over right now? That way, when you come back later, you'll know the way."

"Okay," Steven said, with a little nod. His expression, though, had turned serious again. "I still think you've been painted into a corner here, Melissa, because you didn't want to hurt Matt's feelings about all of us having supper together, and while I certainly appreciate that, I'm not real comfortable with the idea of imposing on you, especially on short notice."

"It's only one meal," she pointed out.

If it was "only one meal," another part of her mind wanted to know, why was her heart beating so hard and so fast? Why was her breath shallow and why, pray tell, did she feel all warm and melty in places where she had no damn *business* feeling all warm and melty?

Steven was quiet, absorbing her answer.

It was disturbing for Melissa to realize that she even liked watching this man *think*.

"You're right," he said at last, with a sigh that was all the more wicked for its boyish innocence. "It's only supper. We'll be there at six."

"Good," Melissa said, wondering exactly when—and how—she'd lost her reason. Hadn't she been down this same road with Dan Guthrie a few years ago?

Dan, the sexy rancher, widowed father of two charming little boys.

Dan, the patient, fiery lover who'd turned her inside

out in his bed on the nights when they managed to have the house to themselves.

Dan, who'd finally dumped her, in no uncertain terms, claiming she couldn't commit to a serious relationship, and had taken up with a waitress named Holly, from over in Indian Rock?

Dan and Holly were married now. Expecting a baby.

And the little boys Melissa had come to love like her own children called Holly *Mom.*

Inwardly, she took a step back from Steven Creed, and he seemed to know it, because a shadow fell across his eyes and, for just a millisecond, a muscle bunched in his jaw. He wanted to lodge a protest, she guessed, having sensed her sudden reticence, but he didn't know what *about.*

"Follow me," Melissa said, in the voice of a sleepwalker.

Steven sighed, like a man who thought better of the idea but couldn't think of an alternative, and nodded.

Melissa drove slowly from the parking lot of Creekside Academy, out onto the main road, and straight into Stone Creek.

Every few moments, she checked her rearview, and the big blue truck was back there each time, Steven an indiscernible shadow at the wheel.

You just want to sleep with him, Melissa accused herself silently. *And what does that say about your character?*

Melissa squared her shoulders and answered the accusation out loud, since there was no one else in the roadster to overhear. "It says that I'm a natural woman, with red blood flowing through my veins," she replied.

You'll start caring for Steven Creed. Worse, you'll

*start caring for Matt. It's a case of burn me once, shame
on you, burn me twice, shame on me.*

*Have you forgotten how much it hurt, losing Dan
and the boys? It was like losing your mom and dad all
over again, wasn't it?*

"Oh, shut up," Melissa said. "I'm serving the man
supper, not a night of steamy sex." She sighed. She
could really have used a night of steamy sex. "And the
joke's on you. I already care for Matt."

You need a child of your own. Not a substitute.

"Didn't I ask you to shut up?" Melissa countered,
almost forgetting to stop at a sign.

Sure enough, Tom Parker's cruiser slipped in between her car and Steven's truck, lights whirling. The
siren gave an irritating little whine, for good measure.

As if she wouldn't have noticed him back there.

Swearing, Melissa kept driving the half block to her
own house, and parked.

"Did you see that stop sign?" Tom asked cordially,
climbing out of the squad car. His dog, Elvis, rode in
the passenger seat. In Stone Creek, Elvis counted as
backup.

"Yes," Melissa said tersely, "and I *stopped* for it."

"Just barely," Tom pointed out, glancing back at Steven's rig.

Melissa watched as the flashy blue truck, which
probably sucked up enough gas for four or five cars to
run on, drew up alongside her roadster, and the front
passenger-side window buzzed down.

"Is everything all right?" Steven leaned across to
ask. His eyes were doing that mischievous little dance
again, generating blue heat.

Tom waved at him, smiled cordially. "Everything's
fine."

Steven studied Melissa for a long moment, and when she didn't refute Tom's statement, he seemed satisfied. "See you at six," he said.

And then he just drove away.

Just like that.

Not that that annoyed her or anything.

Melissa folded her arms. "What's this all about?" she demanded. "You know damn well you had no business pulling me over. *I stopped for that sign.*"

Tom was still gazing after Steven's truck. "I just wanted to say hello," he lied.

"What a load," Melissa replied. "The truth is, you're just as nosy as your aunt Ona. You saw Steven following me and you wanted to know what was going on."

"He said, 'See you at six,'" Tom went on, as if she hadn't spoken. "You two have a date or something?"

"Or something," Melissa said. "Not that it's any of your business." She flexed her fingers, then regripped the steering wheel, hard. "This is harassment," she pointed out.

Tom chuckled, shook his head. But there was something watchful in his eyes. "At least let me run a check on Creed's background before you get involved," he said. "A person can't be too careful these days."

"Oh, for Pete's sake," Melissa retorted, exasperated. "A person *can* be too careful. Like you, for instance. When are you going to ask Tessa Quinn out for dinner and a movie, you big coward?"

Tom blinked. Straightened his spine. "When I get around to it," he said, in a mildly affronted tone.

"Have you run a background check on her yet?"

"Of course I haven't."

"A person can't be too careful," Melissa threw out. Then she sighed and changed the subject. "I was just coming from the Parade Committee meeting," she said pointedly. "You know, that little thing I'm doing because your aunt, Ms. Ona Frame, has to have her gall-bladder out? You *owe* me, Sheriff Parker. And if you think I'm going to put up with being pulled over for no reason—"

Tom did a parody of righteous horror. Laid a hand to his chest. Back in the squad car, Elvis let out a yip, as though putting in his two cents' worth. Then Tom laughed, held up both hands, palms out. Elvis yipped again.

Melissa leaned to retrieve her purse and that stupid clipboard.

He laughed again. "He's got you pretty flustered, that Creed yahoo," he said, looking pleased at the re-alization. "I haven't seen you this worked up since you were dating Dan Guthrie—"

Too late, Tom seemed to realize he'd struck a raw nerve. He stopped, reddened, and flung his hands out from his sides. "I'm sorry."

"You should be," Melissa huffed, turning on one heel.

Tom followed her as far as her front gate. "It's not as if you're the only person who's ever loved and lost, Melissa O'Ballivan," he blurted out, in a furious under tone. "Imagine how it feels to be crazy about a woman who looks right through you like you were transparent!"

"I can't *begin* to imagine that, for obvious reasons," Melissa replied, heading up the walk.

Elvis howled.

Tom stuck with Melissa until she'd mounted the first two porch steps and rounded to look down into his up-turned face. "You deliberately misunderstood that," he accused, but he'd lost most of his steam by then.

Melissa sighed. "You were referring to Tessa Quinn,

I presume?" she asked, though everybody in town and for miles around knew that Tom loved the woman with a passion of truly epic proportions. Everybody, with the probable exception of Tessa herself, that is.

Tessa was either clueless, playing it cool or just not interested in Tom Parker.

Tom thrust out a miserable breath. "You know damn well it's Tessa," he said.

Melissa cocked a thumb toward the squad car and said, "Get Elvis and come inside. I made a pitcher of iced tea before I went out."

But Tom shook his head. "I'm supposed to be on patrol," he said.

"Well, that's noble," Melissa replied, as the dog gave another long, plaintive howl, "but I'm not sure Elvis is onboard with the plan."

"I was just taking him over to the Groom-and-Bloom for his weekly bath," Tom said. He took very good care of Elvis; everybody knew that as well as they knew his feelings for Tessa. "He's just worried about missing his appointment, that's all. He's particular about his appearance, Elvis is."

Melissa smiled. Nodded. "Tom?"

He was turning away. "What?"

"Why don't you ask Tessa for a date?"

He looked all of fourteen as he considered that idea. His neck went a dull red, and his earlobes glowed like they were lit up from the inside. "She might say no."

"Here's a thought, Tom. She might say yes. Then what would you do?"

"Probably have a coronary on the spot." Tom sounded pretty serious, but there was a tentative smile playing around his lips. "Same as if she said no."

"So you're damned if you do and damned if you don't."

"That's about the size of it," Tom said.

"I dare you," Melissa said. When they were kids, that was the way to get Tom Parker to do just about anything. Of course, she hadn't tried it since playground days.

He flushed again, and his eyes narrowed. "What?"

"You heard me, Parker," Melissa said, jutting her chin out a little ways. "I double-dog *dare* you to ask Tessa Quinn out to dinner. Or to a movie. Or to a dance—there's one next weekend, at the Grange Hall. And if you don't ask her out, well, you're just plain—chicken."

Instantly, they were both nine years old again.

Tom stepped closer and glared up at her. "Oh, yeah?" he said.

"Yeah," Melissa replied stoutly.

"You're on," Tom told her.

"Good," Melissa answered, without smiling.

"What do I get if you lose?" Tom wanted to know.

Melissa thought quickly. "I'll buy you dinner."

"As long as you're not cooking," Tom specified, looking and sounding dead serious.

This was a bet Melissa *wanted* to lose. "I'll recruit Ashley," she said. "She can do those specially marinated spare ribs you like so much."

"Deal," Tom said, without cracking a smile. Even as a little kid, he'd been a sucker for a bet.

"Wait just a second," Melissa said. "What if *I* win? What happens then?"

"I'll take over as chairman of the Parade Committee," Tom told her, after some thought.

"Deal," Melissa agreed, putting out her free hand.

They shook on it, then Tom turned and stalked back

to the gate, through it and down the sidewalk to his car.
"Just remember one thing!" he called back to her.

"What?" Melissa retorted, about to turn around and
open her front door.

"Two can play this game," Tom said.

Then he got into the cruiser, slammed his door and
ground the engine to life with a twist of the key in the
ignition, leaving Melissa to wonder what the hell he'd
meant by *that*.

He made the siren give one eloquent moan as he
drove on past her house and vanished around the corner.

"Damn," Melissa said, as the answer dawned on her.

Now she'd gone and done it.

Tom would lie awake nights until he came up with
a dare for her. And it would be a doozy, knowing him.

But she didn't dwell on the problem too long, because
she had things to do. Like go over to Ashley's, thereby
braving the wild bunch, who might well be swinging
from the chandeliers in their birthday suits, to steal a
main course and a dessert from one of the freezers.

"Next time," Steven told the rearview reflection of a
chagrined Matt, as they drove out of town, "it would
be a *really* good idea to talk it over with me before you
go inviting people to our place for supper."

Matt was no pouter, but his lower lip poked out a-
ways, and he was blinking real fast, both of which were
signs that he might cry.

It killed Steven when he cried.

"I was just trying to be a good neighbor," Matt explained, sounding as wounded as he looked. "Anyhow,
I *like* Ms. O'Ballivan, don't you?"

"Yes," he said, tightening his fingers on the steering wheel, then relaxing them again. "I understand that

your intentions were good," he went on quietly. "But sometimes, if that person happens to have other plans, or some other reason why they need to say no, it puts them on the spot. There's no graceful way for them to turn you down."

Matt listened in silence, sniffling a couple of times.

"Do you know what I'm saying, here?" Steven asked, keeping his voice gentle.

Matt nodded. "Yeah," he said. "I get it. I'm gifted, remember?"

Steven laughed. "There's no forgetting that," he said.

"Are you mad at me?"

An ache went through Steven, like a sharp pole jabbed down through the top of his heart to lodge at the bottom. "No," he said. "If I straighten you out about something, it doesn't mean I'm angry. It just means I want you to think things through a little better the next time."

Matt let out a long sigh, back there in the peanut gallery, one of his arms wrapped around Zeke, who was panting and, incredibly, managing to keep his canine head from blocking the rearview mirror.

"It's kind of weird, calling you Steven," Matt said, after a long time. He was looking out the window by then, but even with just a glance at the boy's reflection to go on, Steven could see the tension he was trying to hide.

"Who says so?" Steven asked carefully. Conversations like this one always made his stomach clench.

"I do," Matt told him. His voice was small.

The turn onto their road was just ahead; Steven flipped the signal lever and slowed to make a dusty left. "What would you like to call me?" he asked.

"Dad," Matt said simply.

Steven's eyes scalded, and his vision blurred.

"But that doesn't seem right, because I used to have another dad," Matt went on. "Do you think it would hurt my first daddy's feelings if I went around calling somebody else 'Dad'?"

"I think your dad would want you to be happy," Steven said. It was almost a croak, that statement, but, fortunately, Matt didn't seem to notice. They'd reached the top of the driveway, so Steven pulled up beside the old two-tone truck and shifted out of gear. Shut the motor off. And just sat there, not knowing what to say. Or do.

"If he was *Daddy*," Matt reasoned, "then I guess it would be all right if you were Dad."

Steven's throat constricted. He literally couldn't speak just then, so he shoved open the truck door and got out. Stood staring off toward the foothills and the mountains beyond for a few moments, until he'd recovered some measure of control.

When he turned around again, both Matt and Zeke had their faces pressed to the window, gumming it up big-time with their breaths.

He laughed and carefully opened the door, so Zeke wouldn't plunge right over Matt and his safety seat and take a header onto the ground.

"I think that's a great idea," Steven said.

"So I can call you *Dad?*" Matt asked.

"Yeah," Steven replied, ducking his head slightly while he undid the snaps and buckles. "You can call me *Dad*."

"That's good," Matt said. A pause. "Dad?" He said the word softly, like he was trying it on for size.

"What?" Steven ground out, hoisting the little boy to the ground, and then the dog.

"How come your eyes are all red?"

Steven sniffled, ran a forearm across his face. "I guess it's the dust," he said. He pretended to assess the sky, sprawling blue from horizon to horizon. "A good rain would help."

"HELLO?" MELISSA RAPPED lightly at her sister's kitchen door, though she'd already opened it and stuck her head inside. "Anybody home?"

There was no answer, but she could hear voices coming from the dining room.

Melissa hadn't seen a car parked outside, so she'd hoped the lively group had gone out, maybe to play miniature golf or take in a movie. She would have loved to raid the freezer and duck out again, unnoticed, but she was afraid one of the oldsters would wander in, be startled and collapse from a massive coronary.

So she moved to the middle of the floor and tried again. "Hello?"

This time, they heard her. "Melissa, is that you?" a woman's voice called cheerfully.

"Yes," she answered. Then she drew a deep breath, proceeded to the inside door and drew another deep breath before pushing it open.

The guests were gathered at one end of the formal dining table, playing cards. And they were all wearing clothes.

Melissa was so profoundly relieved that she gave a nervous, high-pitched giggle and put one hand to her heart.

How amused Ashley and Olivia and Brad would be if they could see her now. In her family, she did *not* have a reputation for shyness, and her sibs would have gotten a major kick out of her newfound fear of naked croquet players.

"Come and join us," Mr. Winthrop said, rising from his seat. "We're playing gin rummy, and I'm afraid we've all known each other so well, for so long, that there just aren't any new tricks."

I'll just bet there aren't, Melissa thought, but not with rancor. Initial embarrassment aside, she liked these people. They had spirit. Imagination. Wrinkles. Lots and lots of wrinkles.

"I can't stay," she said, and the regret in her tone was only partly feigned. She enjoyed gin rummy and, heck, everybody was *dressed,* weren't they? "I'm having company tonight, so I came by to borrow a few things." She waggled her fingers at them, backing toward the swinging door. "Enjoy your game."

"Don't take the roast duck," one of the women sang out, shuffling the deck for another hand of cards. "Your sister promised that to us. It's Herbert's favorite, and he's turning ninety tomorrow."

"Hands off the duck," Melissa promised, palms up and facing the group at the table, and then she slipped out. She was smiling to herself as she headed for the large storage room, off the kitchen, where Ashley had two huge freezers, invariably well-stocked.

One was reserved for desserts, one for main courses. She selected a container marked *Game Hens with Cranberries and Wild Rice, Serves 6,* Ashley's graceful handwriting looping across the label. Melissa hoped that Matt liked chicken, as most kids did, and would therefore accept a reasonable facsimile.

For dessert, she purloined a lovely blueberry cobbler. *Best with Vanilla Ice Cream,* Ashley had written on the sticker. It was almost as if she'd known, somehow, that her twin would be breaking into her frozen-food supply soon and would need guidance.

Melissa set the food on the counter, went back to the inside door to poke her head in and say goodbye.

The card players were still clothed and so normal-looking that she could almost believe she'd *imagined* the notorious backyard croquet game. Maybe she really was going nuts.

"See you," Melissa said stupidly, her face strangely hot as she backed away from the door.

She turned, grabbed the food containers and boogied out the back door, glad she'd parked her car in the alley, so she wouldn't have to walk around front, where she might have to stop and chat with one of her sister's neighbors. She wasn't feeling very sociable at the moment.

She made a quick stop at the supermarket for ice cream and a premade spinach salad, then hurried home.

When she got there, Byron was working, shirtless, in the front yard, pruning shears in hand, snipping errant branches off the maple tree and stemming its invasion of the sidewalk.

Nathan Carter, a local dropout with a history of misdemeanors to his credit and not much else, sat cross-legged in the as-yet-unmowed grass, watching him.

"I thought you couldn't come until tomorrow," Melissa said, addressing Byron but shooting a curious glance at Nathan as she spoke, then grappling with Ashley's plastic containers and the stuff she'd bought at the store. "Something about relining the Crocketts' koi pond?"

Nathan returned her look, smirking. She'd never liked the kid; a sort of latter-day James Dean type, he seemed to fancy himself a rebel without a cause.

He was also without a job, a house or a car, as far as she knew. He came and went, turning up every so often to bunk on his cousin Lulu's screened-in side porch and stir up whatever trouble he could.

Byron, sweating, paused and pulled an arm across his forehead. His eyes were wary, and oddly hopeful, as he watched Melissa and nodded once. "Got that done," he said. "Those fish are back in the pond, swimming around like they had good sense. I'll be back in the morning to finish up around here, but I thought I'd whack off some of these branches tonight."

Melissa looked from Byron to Nathan and back to Byron, tempted to take her temporary yard man aside and remind him that he ought to be careful who he hung around with, given that he was on parole.

"Byron, here," Nathan put in helpfully, "is a little short on cash."

"I could advance you a few dollars," Melissa said.

Nathan and Byron responded simultaneously.

"Awesome," Nathan drawled, his tone oily, like his mouse-brown hair and his filthy T-shirt and jeans.

"I wouldn't feel right taking money," said Byron, with a decisive shake of his head. "Not when I haven't finished the job."

Had this kid changed in jail, Melissa wondered, or had she misjudged him, way back when? There had never been any question of his guilt, that was true, but maybe Velda had been right.

Maybe she should have tried for mandatory treatment in a drug and alcohol facility instead of time behind bars.... No. She had considered every angle, consulted experts, lain awake nights. She'd done what she thought was right and there was no use second-guessing the decision now.

She turned her thoughts to her supper guests—Steven and Matt Creed. Nathan dropped off her radar, a nonentity.

And she immediately felt better.

The containers of frozen food, now beginning to thaw, stung like dry ice through the front of Melissa's top and she still wanted to tidy up the house a little, choose an outfit—nothing too come-hither—do something with her hair, and put on some makeup. A touch of mascara, some lip gloss, that was all.

Maybe a little perfume.

The message she wanted to send was, *Welcome to Stone Creek,* not, *Hey, big guy, what do you say we hire a sitter, slip out of here, and go find ourselves a place to get it on?*

She blushed, because the second version wasn't without a certain appeal, then realized she hadn't responded to Byron's last statement. "Okay, then," she told him, ignoring Nathan, tugging open the screen door with a quick motion of one hand and holding it open with her hip. "See you tomorrow."

Byron nodded and went back to snipping branches off the maple tree.

CHAPTER SEVEN

By 5:59 P.M., MELISSA was ready to serve supper—the game hens, warming in the seldom-used oven, filled her small, bright kitchen with their savory aroma. The cobbler, already thawed and heated through, sat cooling on the counter nearest the stove, covered by a clean dishtowel. The antique table, which too often served as a catchall for newspapers and junk mail, looked like something straight off the cover of *Country Living* magazine.

Melissa took a moment to admire the crisp white tablecloth, the green-tinted glass jar in the center, spilling over with perfect white peonies from the bushes on either side of the front steps. The plates, purchased on impulse in, of all places, an airport gift shop, were decorated with checks and flowers and polka dots.

She tilted her head to one side, considering the look. Fussy, yes. Feminine, definitely. Cheerful, to the max.

But was it *too* fussy, feminine and cheerful?

After all, this wasn't a reunion of her high school cheerleading squad; she was entertaining a little boy and a grown man.

And *what* a man. There should have been a law.

Melissa chewed briefly on one fingernail, fretting. With the exception of the flowers in the jar, none of this was at all like her—the fancy dishes had been gathering dust in the cupboard above the refrigerator for a couple of years, she hadn't cooked the food and she had exactly one tablecloth to her name—*this* one. It didn't even have any sentimental value, that tablecloth—it hadn't been passed down through generations of O'Ballivans, like the various linens Ashley and Olivia so prized. No, Melissa had bought it on clearance at a discount store, just in case she might need it someday—her share of the heirlooms were stored in a chest, out on the ranch. Did she have time to drive out there and grab some?

Deep breath, she instructed herself silently.

Just as she drew in air, a rap sounded at the front door. *They're here.*

No time to tone down—or tone *up*—the decorations now, obviously.

Melissa, feeling especially womanly in her summery dress, a multicolored Southwestern print with touches of turquoise and magenta, gold and black, went to greet her company.

Matt stood on the porch with his nose pressed into the screen door, his damp hair already beginning to rebel against a recent combing, springing up into a rooster tail at the back of his head and swirling into little cowlick eddies here and there.

Melissa's heart melted at the sight of him; a smile rose up within her and spilled across her face, warm on her mouth. Of course she was aware of Steven, standing behind the boy—how could she *not* have been aware?—but she didn't make eye contact right away.

No, she needed a few more deep breaths before she could risk that.

So she concentrated on Matt—unlocking and opening the screen door, stepping back so he could spill into her house, all energy and eagerness and *boy*.

"You look very handsome," she told the child, re-

sisting a motherly urge to smooth down the rooster tail
with a light pass of her hand.

Matt's smile seemed to encompass her, like an actual embrace. "And *you* look beautiful!" he responded.

"Amen," Steven said huskily. That single word
coursed right over Matt's head to lodge itself in Melissa like a velvet arrow.

Her throat caught, and her gaze betrayed her, going
straight to him long before she was ready.

Steven wore jeans, a little newer than the ones he'd
had on earlier, along with polished black boots and a
white, collarless shirt of the sort men favored back in
the Old West days. His hair was damp from a recent
shower, like Matt's, but there were no cowlicks and
no rooster tails, and he smelled like a field of newly
sprouted clover after a soft rain.

A free-fall sensation seized Melissa, buffeted the
breath from her lungs, as though she were skydiving
without a parachute, or riding a runaway roller coaster.

The feeling was stunning. Terrifying, in fact.

And categorically *wonderful.*

"I hope you're both hungry," she heard herself say,
and the normality of her tone amazed her, because on
the inside, she was still being swept along, helter-skel-
ter, like a swimmer caught in a fast current.

"We're *starved,*" Matt answered, looking around the
living room, as alert as a detective scanning for clues.

Steven smiled and cleared his throat slightly, raising one eyebrow when Matt turned to look up at him.

"Well, we *are,*" the boy insisted, folding his small
arms.

Steven grinned, unwittingly—or *wittingly*—sending a charge of electricity through Melissa. His eyes,
so very blue and with a touch of lavender to them that

reminded her of summer twilights and late-blooming lilacs, ranged idly over her, pausing here and there, lingering to light small fires under her skin. It seemed lazy-slow, that look, but she knew it couldn't have lasted more than a fraction of a moment.

"Then let's get you some supper," Melissa told Matt, extra glad he was there, and not just because she was already so fond of him. If she'd been alone with Steven Creed, considering her strange state of mind, she might have jumped the man's bones right there in the living room.

Okay, so maybe that was an exaggeration. But she was definitely attracted to him, and she couldn't shake the feeling that she was on dangerous ground.

Remembering her duties as a hostess, she led the way into the kitchen.

Matt started toward the table the moment they entered the room, but Steven caught the child lightly by one shoulder and stopped him.

"Where do we wash up?" Steven asked, looking at Melissa.

She pointed toward the hallway just to the left of the stove. "The bathroom is that way," she said.

The Creed men disappeared in the direction she'd indicated, then returned a couple of minutes later.

Melissa was just setting out the main course. Since she didn't own a platter, she'd left the food in Ashley's freezer-to-oven casserole dish.

"Are those chickens?" Matt asked, eyeing the halved game hens dubiously.

Steven chuckled. "Yes," he said mildly. "They're chickens." And then he caught Melissa's eye, waiting for something.

After an awkward moment, Melissa pointed to one

of the chairs. Steven pulled it back, let Matt scramble up onto the seat.

"Can I eat with my fingers?" Matt wanted to know.

Steven answered without taking his eyes off Melissa. "Thanks for asking," he said, in an easy drawl. "But no, Tex, you can't eat with your fingers."

It finally came home to Melissa that Steven wasn't going to sit down until she was seated. She moved toward the middle chair, oddly embarrassed, waited for Steven to pull it out for her and sat.

She noticed a sparkle in the man's eyes as he joined her and Matt.

"I don't think those are really chickens," Matt said, in a tone of good-natured skepticism, peering into the casserole dish in the center of the table.

Melissa began to wish she'd served something little-boy friendly, like pizza or hamburgers or hot dogs.

Steven, perhaps hoping to put her at ease, speared one of the game hens with the serving fork, dropped it onto his plate, and began cutting it into bite-size pieces. His movements were quick and deft, with a subtle elegance about them.

Don't think about his hands.

Melissa blinked, snapping out of yet another mini-daze.

Steven switched plates with Matt, who nibbled at a bite, then began to eat in earnest.

"Slow down," Steven said, helping himself when Melissa didn't move to dish up a portion of her own.

Matt nodded, chewing and swallowing. "You're a good cook," he told Melissa.

Melissa felt heat pulse under her cheeks, longing to fib and take all the credit—and completely unable to do so. She was terminally honest; it was her personal cross to bear.

"My sister Ashley is," she clarified. "I—well—sort of *borrowed* supper from her."

Steven's eyes danced with blue mischief, but he didn't offer a comment. He did seem to be enjoying Ashley's culinary expertise, though.

Everybody did.

"Oh," Matt said. Having taken the edge off his appetite, he paused, looking across the table at Steven. "Do you think Zeke is okay?" he asked.

Zeke? Then Melissa remembered the dog.

"Zeke," Steven said easily, "is just fine."

"I wanted to bring him with us," Matt confided to Melissa, who, by then, had begun to eat, however tentatively. "But Dad wouldn't let me. He said it wouldn't be polite to do that."

Melissa smiled, willing herself to relax. Steven Creed, with his broad shoulders and his quiet confidence and his mere *presence,* seemed to fill that small kitchen, breathing all the air, absorbing the light.

Absorbing *her.* The experience, though disquieting, had a certain zip to it, too.

"Zeke," Steven repeated, his eyes smiling as he looked at Matt, *"is just fine."*

"You could bring him next time," Melissa said.

Next time? Who said there was going to be a "next time"?

Matt cheered at the news.

"Bring it down a few decibels," Steven instructed.

Matt grinned. "I'm too loud sometimes," he said to Melissa, in a stage whisper.

She laughed and stopped just short of ruffling his hair. "That's okay," she whispered back.

After that, a companionable silence fell.

It wasn't until the meal was over, and they were contemplating dessert, that Matt got down to brass tacks.

"Are you married?" he asked Melissa bluntly. "Do you have any kids?"

Steven, so far unflappable, it seemed to Melissa, reddened slightly. Narrowed his eyes at Matt and started to speak.

Melissa cut him off before he could say a word. "No," she told Matt. "I'm not married, and I don't have any kids."

Matt's smile was glorious, like dawn breaking after a cold and moonless night. "Good!" he said. "Then you could marry my dad and be my mom. We'd help with the cooking, so you wouldn't have to keep borrowing supper from your sister, and even do the laundry."

"Matt," Steven said, fighting a smile.

Without thinking about it first—if she had, she would surely have stopped herself—Melissa rested a hand on Steven's forearm. Felt the muscles tighten and then ease again under her fingertips.

"It's okay," she said, very softly.

Matt looked from Steven to Melissa, and his small shoulders stooped a little. "I guess I shouldn't have said that stuff about marrying Dad and me," he admitted.

"Ya think?" Steven asked.

Melissa smiled, anxious to reassure the child. "Know what?" she said, addressing Matt, finally removing her hand from Steven's arm.

"What?" Matt asked.

"If I'm ever lucky enough to have a little boy of my own, I hope he'll be just like you."

It came again, then. That beaming smile.

When this kid grew up, he was going to be a heart-breaker, no doubt about it.

"Really?" Matt asked.

Steven shifted in his chair, but said nothing.

"Really," Melissa confirmed. "Now, who wants ice cream and cobbler?"

MATT RESTED OVER Steven's right shoulder, like a sack of potatoes. Once the kid hit the proverbial wall and gave himself over to sleep, that was it. His surroundings didn't matter—he was down for the count.

Melissa, looking better than any dessert ever could have, walked out to the truck alongside Steven, hugging herself against the chill of a high country night.

There was hardly anything to that sundress of hers, which was fine with Steven, except that he didn't want her catching pneumonia or anything.

"Thank you," he said gruffly, pausing on the sidewalk, turning toward her.

He wanted to kiss Melissa, but holding Matt the way he was, the logistics were just plain off.

Melissa smiled, reached past him to open the rear door of the rig.

Matt mumbled something as Steven set him in the car seat and began buckling him in but, true to form, he didn't wake up.

"He's terrific," she said softly.

"I agree," Steven told her, after Matt was secured. They stood facing each other now, on that darkened sidewalk. "Of course it *would* be a real plus if he'd stop proposing to women."

There was something flirty in Melissa's smile, but something vulnerable, too. "Does he do that a lot? Ask people to marry you, I mean?"

Steven chuckled, even though he felt inexplicably nervous, and shook his head. "No," he replied. "Actually, Matt is pretty discerning when it comes to women." A grin tugged at one corner of his mouth. "He doesn't suggest marriage and instant motherhood to just *anybody,* you know."

Melissa laughed at that; it was soft and musical, that sound, and it found a place inside Steven and stowed away there, perhaps for keeps. "He's sweet," she said.

Again—*still*—Steven wanted to kiss Melissa O'Ballivan. Full on the mouth, with tongue.

Since the direct approach might scare her away, he settled for leaning in and giving her a light peck on the forehead.

"Tonight was great," he said, resting his hands on her shoulders.

Given that the sundress left that part of her bare, the gesture might have been misguided. Melissa's skin felt warm and smooth under his palms, taut with vitality. Steven tightened his fingers, briefly and almost imperceptibly, then withdrew, letting his hands fall to his sides.

"Thanks," he said again, grinding out the word.

He saw the heat flash in her eyes, the knowing, a desire that might even match his own, and everything inside him soared.

It was inevitable, he realized. Written in the stars.

Right or wrong, for better or for worse, at some point, he and Melissa O'Ballivan *would* make love.

Whoa, you big dumb cowboy, said the voice of reason, causing Steven to sigh. *You just met the woman yesterday.*

Once, before Matt became a part of his day-to-day life, Steven would have countered the voice with a resounding *So what?* living, as he had, by the philosophy that he-who-hesitates-is-lost, especially when it came to beautiful women and the opportunity to bed them.

Melissa certainly qualified as beautiful, and that was the least of it. He sensed a vastness within her, a fascinating inner landscape he yearned to explore.

In time.

"Go inside," he told her, smiling down into her eyes, "you're shivering."

"Yes, I really should," she agreed, shivering harder.

But she didn't move and neither did he.

They just stood there, looking at each other.

Finally, Melissa rolled up onto the balls of her feet and touched her mouth to his, the contact light and brief, over almost before it began.

The kiss electrified Steven, left him confounded.

In the next moment, a wistful little smile playing on her lips, Melissa turned and hurried back through the gate, up the walk, across the porch, finally disappearing into the house.

Steven, wondering what the hell had just hit him, *still* didn't move.

Then he heard one of the truck windows open, with a whirring sound, turned to see Matt looking out at him, rubbing his eyes once with the heels of his palms and then grinning sleepily. "Melissa *kissed* you," he said.

Steven chuckled and rounded the truck, climbed behind the wheel.

"She did," Matt insisted, as they pulled away from the curb. "I *saw* Melissa kiss you."

"Okay," Steven said, adjusting the mirrors. "She kissed me. It was no big deal, Tex. Just 'good-night.'"

"Melissa *likes* you."

"I like her, too."

"I bet she doesn't go around kissing *everybody* she likes," Matt went on.

"Go back to sleep," Steven responded, with a smile in his voice.

Matt giggled. He was wide-awake—so much for his usual tendency to sleep through anything. "Are you going to ask Melissa out for a date?"

Steven suppressed a broad grin. They were on the main street of Stone Creek now, headed in the direction of home.

Such as home was.

"You're five," he pointed out. "What would make you ask a question like that?"

Matt gave a huge sigh. "I know what dating is," he said, very patiently. "I watch TV. Guys on TV give lots of women roses and take them on dates, in limos. At the end of the season, the guy has to decide which one of them is a keeper and gets down on one knee and gives her a ring."

"And you watched all this stuff *when?*" Steven asked. In their household, television was strictly monitored, especially the "reality" kind.

"Mrs. Hooper has this big set of DVDs. We watched all of them."

Mrs. Hooper had been Matt's babysitter back in Denver. Steven had worked a lot of nights, tying up loose ends at his old law firm before making the move to Stone Creek.

"You didn't mention that at the time," Steven said dryly. Once they were past the city limits, he shifted gears and sped up a little.

"You never once asked me if Mrs. Hooper and I were watching smoochy dating shows on TV," Matt informed him.

"You'd make a great lawyer, you know that?"

"I don't want to be a lawyer," Matt said. "I want to be a cowboy." A pause. "I just need a *horse,* that's all. You can't be a cowboy without a horse. So, when are we going to build the new barn?"

Steven laughed and shoved his left hand through his hair, keeping his right on the steering wheel. "When I've had a chance to get some estimates and hire a contractor," he answered. "Until then, you'll just have to be patient."

Another sigh.

"What?" Steven asked.

"I was just wondering something."

"And that would be—?"

"Are you going to ask Melissa out on a date?"

Now it was Steven who sighed. "Guess what?" he said. "That just happens to be none of your darned business, buddy."

"How am I *ever* supposed to get a mom if you won't go out with women?"

"I *do* go out with women, Matt."

"Okay," Matt conceded. "You went out sometimes when we lived in *Denver.* But this is Stone Creek."

"And we haven't even been here two full days," Steven said reasonably. "Give me a chance, will you?"

"So you'll do it?"

"So I'll do what?"

Matt sounded exasperated. "Ask. Melissa. Out. On. A. Date."

Steven laughed again, harder this time. They were bumping their way over a country road now. Their turn-off was just ahead and he switched on the signal, even though there was no one behind them. "Do you ever give up?"

"No," Matt replied, without hesitation. "Do you?"

Steven sighed. "No," he admitted.

"Because a Creed never gives up, right?"

Steven didn't answer.

"Right?" Matt persisted, through a yawn.

"Okay," Steven said. "Yes. That's right."

"And you're going to ask Melissa to go out with you, right?"

Steven stopped the rig near the tour bus, shut off the engine and turned in his seat to look back at Matt. "If I say yes, will you shut up about it?" he asked, not unkindly.

Inside the bus, Zeke began to bark.

"Yes," Matt said, and Steven thought his expression might have been a little smug, though that could have been a trick of the light.

"Promise?"

"Promise," Matt confirmed. "But you have to promise, too."

Steven got out of the truck, went to open Matt's door and began unhitching the kid from his safety gear. "All right, I promise. But if she says no, that's it, understand?" He lifted Matt into his arms. "You don't get to pester me about it until the crack of doom."

Matt squeezed his neck. "Melissa *won't say no,* Dad," he said. "She likes you, remember? She kissed you."

Steven sighed. It sure felt good to be called "Dad," though.

Reaching the bus, he opened the door and stepped aside just before Zeke shot out of the interior like a hairy bullet.

"One other thing," Steven said.

Matt yawned again, watching fondly as Zeke ran in

widening circles, barking his brains out. "What?" the boy asked, sounding only mildly interested.

Steven set him down, and they both waited for the dog to do his thing.

"When it comes to dating," Steven said, "three's a crowd, old buddy. You'll have to stay home with a baby-sitter."

Zeke raised a hind leg and christened the left rear tire of Steven's new truck.

"Okay," Matt agreed solemnly. "It's a deal."

When the dog was finished, Steven reached to switch on a light. Then the three of them went into the flashy tour bus with a silhouette of Brad O'Ballivan's head painted on the side.

Within a few minutes, Matt was washed up and in his pajamas, his breath smelling of mint from a vigorous tooth-brushing session at the bathroom sink. Steven tucked the boy in and pretended not to notice when Zeke immediately jumped up onto the mattress and settled himself in for the night.

Smiling slightly, Steven stepped out of Matt's room, remembering his own childhood. In Boston, he wasn't allowed to have a dog—his mother said the antique Persian rugs in Granddad's house were far too valuable to put at risk and besides, animals were generally noisy—but on the ranch outside Lonesome Bend, the plank floors were hardwood, worn smooth by a century of use, and the rugs were all washable. Nobody seemed to mind the occasional mess and the near-constant clamor of kids and dogs banging in and out of the doors.

There had been a succession of pets over the years; Brody and Conner each had their own mutt, and so did Steven. His had been a lop-eared Yellow Lab named Lucky, and when he arrived in the spring, right after school let out, that dog would be waiting at the ranch gate when they pulled in.

The reunions were always joyous.

The goodbyes, when the end of August came around, and it was time for Steven to return to Boston, were an ache he could still feel, even after all those years.

Of course, Brody and Conner had looked out for Lucky while he was gone, but it couldn't have been the same as when Steven was there. Brody had Fletch and Conner had Hannibal, and that made Lucky odd dog out, any way you looked at it.

Summer after summer, though, Lucky had been there to offer a lively welcome when Steven came back, and the two of them had been inseparable, together 24/7.

His throat tight and his eyes hot, Steven tried to shake off the recollection of that dog, because he still missed him, no matter how much time had gone by. Lucky had been one of the truest friends he'd ever had, or expected to have.

Steven cleared his throat, then set about locating the drawings he'd been working on intermittently since he decided to buy fifty acres, a two-story house and a wreck of a barn outside Stone Creek, Arizona. Over the last several weeks, he'd redesigned the house a couple of times, and come up with what he considered a workable plan for the outbuildings, too.

Looking at the sketches, all of them scrawled on the now-scruffy yellow pages of a legal pad, Steven figured he was ready to hire an architect and start getting estimates from local contractors. Not that there were likely to be all that many in a community the size of Stone Creek.

He flipped through the pages, checking and rechecking. Somewhere along the line, he'd learned to multitask—a part of his mind was still back there on that sidewalk in town, face-to-face with Melissa O'Ballivan, who might as well have zapped him with a cattle prod as kiss him, even quickly and lightly, the way she had.

The effect had been about the same, as far as he could tell. On the other hand, he figured a *real* kiss probably would have struck him dead on the spot, like a bolt of lightning.

And then there was Matt, campaigning to marry him off ASAP, preferably to Melissa, but if that didn't fly, the kid was bound to zero in on another candidate without much delay.

Roses and limos and engagement rings offered on bended knee indeed, he thought, smiling.

A ringing noise jolted Steven out of his musings. He checked the caller ID panel on his cell phone—he didn't recognize the number—and answered with his name.

"This is Brody," replied his long-lost cousin. Brody's voice was so much like his twin brother's that Steven might have thought the call was from Conner, if it hadn't been for the opening announcement.

Relief and temper surged up in Steven, all tangled up. "Where the *hell* are you?" he demanded, in a ragged whisper. If it hadn't been for Matt, he probably would have yelled that question.

"It's good to talk to you again, too," Brody said, employing the exaggerated drawl he used when he didn't give a rat's ass whether he pissed off whoever he happened to be talking to. Which was all the time.

Steven let out a long breath, and he had to press it between his teeth, since his jaw was clamped down hard.

"You still there, Boston?" Brody asked.

The old nickname, once a taunt, enabled Steven to relax a little. And relaxing made it possible to work the hinges on his jawbones so he could open his mouth to answer.

"I'm here," he said. The second time he asked Brody where he was, he managed a civil tone.

Brody chuckled before he replied, "Now, cousin, if you followed the rodeo the way you used to, you'd know I've been out there on the circuit. In plain sight, you might say."

Steven's anger revved up again, like an engine locked in Neutral and pumped full of gas. "*Dammit,* Brody," he growled, braced on one elbow, with his fingers spread out wide through his hair. "I did follow the rodeo, online and sometimes in person, and I didn't hear your name or see your face even one time."

"I might have been in Canada for a while there," Brody allowed.

"Or doing time somewhere," Steven said, voicing his second worst fear. His first, of course, had been the distinct possibility that Brody was dead.

Brody laughed, and there was something broken in the sound. "I've been tossed into the hoosegow once or twice in my illustrious career," he replied. "But I've never served a stretch, Boston, and I don't mind admitting that I'm a little indignant over your lack of faith in the quality of my character."

Steven tried again. "Where are you, Brody?"

"Denver," Brody answered readily. "But I won't be here for long. Just passin' through, as they say."

"Have you been to the ranch?" Lonesome Bend wasn't that far from Denver; maybe Brody had paid a visit to the home folks. Mended fences with Conner, spent some time with Steven's dad and with Kim, both of whom loved both the twins like their own.

Even as the thought crossed his mind, he knew it was too much to hope for.

A Creed never gave up. Especially not on a grudge.

Brody gave another laugh, as raw as the last one. Maybe a little more so. "No," he said. "I'm not ready for that."

"It's been a lot of years," Steven said, straightening his spine, letting his hand drop to the tabletop. He glanced toward the hall, half expecting to see Matt standing there, watching him. "You planning on being 'ready' anytime soon?"

"Probably not."

"But you called me."

"Yeah," Brody agreed, with a sigh that said he didn't quite believe it himself. "I hooked up with a pretty girl in a cowboy bar last night, and it turned out that she used to work for you and Zack St. John, as a secretary or an assistant or something like that. Jessica, I think her name was."

Steven smiled sadly. Some things never changed. "You 'hooked up' with her, and you're not sure what her name was?"

"Hey," Brody said, "not everybody is detail-oriented the way you are, Boston. She was definitely a Jessica."

"Or maybe a Jennifer," Steven said. He'd never worked with anybody named Jessica, but there had been a Jennifer Adams at the law firm in Denver when he was there. She'd been a highly skilled paralegal.

"Maybe that was it," Brody admitted, with a chuckle. "Anyhow, she said you'd moved to Stone Creek, Arizona. When I heard that, I decided to get in touch, and damned if she didn't have your cell number handy."

"Whatever the reason was, Brody, I'm really glad to hear from you."

"There's a rodeo coming up," Brody went on, gliding right over any hint of sentiment, the way he always had. "There in Stone Creek, I mean."

"So I hear," Steven said mildly. "You mean to enter, Brody? Compared to what you're used to, it's small potatoes."

"It isn't so little," Brody said. "I've been there before. Nice buckle and a good paycheck, if I draw the right bronc and the competition isn't too bad."

"It would be mighty good to see you again, cousin," Steven said, knowing full well that Conner would be in town then, too. It didn't seem right to keep that fact from Brody, but Steven didn't want to risk losing contact again, and he figured Brody was bound to hang up at the mention of his brother's name.

"I was hoping you'd say that," Brody answered.

CHAPTER EIGHT

MONDAY MORNING ROLLED around way too soon, as it is inclined to do. Grumbling under her breath, Melissa practically *crawled* out of bed, went to the window and peered out between the slats of the wooden blinds.

Great.

The gray sky looked heavy-bellied with rain and, somewhere in the distance, thunder rolled, like a sound effect from the old Garth Brooks song.

The night before, feeling optimistic about the weather, she'd set out shorts and a tank top with a built-in sports bra, along with socks, running shoes and cotton underpants. Now, disheartened, Melissa opted for sweats, instead of the shorts and top, pulled her hair back and up in a ponytail, and went out into the front yard to stretch.

The fresh air, with its misty chill, did a lot to revive her, made her glad she'd overcome her first waking instinct of the day—to go straight back to sleep.

The lawn certainly looked a lot better, she thought, as she opened the gate in her picket fence and stepped out onto the sidewalk. Byron had spent the whole afternoon mowing and clipping and weeding, and the results were impressive.

Melissa breathed in the moist green scent of newly cut grass.

The branches of the maple tree no longer hung low

over the sidewalk, and millions of tiny raindrops dotted the leaves, shimmering like bits of crystal, finely ground and then sprinkled on.

She started off at a slow trot, warming up. A light drizzle began before she got as far as the corner, and another clap of thunder sounded, way outside of town but ominous.

Melissa raised the hood of her sweatshirt and picked up her pace. She liked to vary her route and that day she circled the town's small, well-kept park three times before turning onto Main Street.

Most of the businesses were still closed, of course, since it was only about 7:30 a.m., but the Sunflower was open, along with the feed store and the auto repair shop.

Tessa Quinn stood outside her café, her long, dark brown hair tumbling down her back, pouring fresh water into the community dog dish. She smiled and waved as Melissa trotted past on the opposite side of the street.

Melissa waved back, pondering an idea that had been rattling around in the back of her brain for a while now: playing matchmaker by inviting both Tessa and Tom over for supper on the same night. Of course it would mean borrowing more food from Ashley's freezer stash—or even convincing her twin to whip up some culinary wonder befitting the occasion. Sure, it would be a risk—Tom and Tessa might wind up disliking not only each other, but *her* as well—but suppose luck was with them? Suppose it was the start of something big?

She smiled at the thought. Maybe, so she wouldn't feel like a third wheel, and *Tom* wouldn't feel outnumbered, she would ask Steven to come back, too. This time, of course, she wouldn't practically tackle the man on the sidewalk at the end of the evening and kiss his face.

Remembering, Melissa blushed. She'd had the remainder of Saturday night and all of Sunday to get over giving in to that one foolhardy impulse, but here she was, still obsessing about it. What *was* her problem? She decided to hold off on the matchmaking, at least until Ashley got back from Chicago and could serve as a sort of advisor.

Lord, she missed her sister.

Melissa jogged on, passing by the library, and the log post office, with its large green lawn, flag and flagpole, and the row of bright blue mailboxes facing the street. It was time to head for home, she decided, leaving Main for the oak-shaded residential street that lay parallel to it.

Every house was familiar; Melissa knew who lived there now and who had lived there before that, and before *that*. She knew the people and their histories and their hopes and the names of their pets, living and gone.

That was life in a small town for you.

Eventually, she reached Ashley's B&B, and was pleased to note a conspicuous absence of naked croquet players, at least in the front yard. Maybe it was the inclement weather, she thought, with a smile.

Or they could be around back, cavorting away.

Melissa was so distracted by those thoughts, and so used to running along that street in the early morning, that she wasn't paying attention, and nearly got run over as she crossed the dirt-and-gravel alley between the B&B and the Crockett sisters' place.

Brakes screeched, shrill as fingernails on some celestial blackboard, and tiny rocks peppered Melissa's skin. Even though the rain was still coming down, dust boiled up around her in a cloud. Trying to fling herself out of the path of doom, she leaped for the nearest patch of grass, stumbled and tore open the knees of her sweatpants when she fell just short of her aim.

Moments passed, taking their sweet time.

Everything seemed to vibrate around Melissa, like some void. Sounds dragged, as though someone had put a finger on an old vinyl record as it went around on the turntable.

And then Andrea was crouching in front of her, taking her firmly by the shoulders. "Are you all right?" the girl croaked out. "Oh, my God, Melissa, are you hurt?"

Melissa stood up, with some help from Andrea, trembling and coughing wet dust out of her lungs and shaking her head, all at once. It was then that she saw Byron standing nearby, looking worried, his hair sleep-rumpled. His clothes had that hastily put-on look.

Andrea followed Melissa's glance then focused on her face again and rushed on. "I'm sorry—I'm *so* sorry—"

"Maybe she ought to see a doctor," Byron said.

Again, Melissa shook her head. She'd gotten a scare, and she'd scraped her knees, but she wasn't seriously injured. At home, she'd shower and, if it turned out she'd broken any skin, she could apply antibacterial ointment and bandages.

None of which meant she was going to let the incident pass without comment, however. Yes, she should have watched where she was going, should have looked before sprinting across the alley. Yet that old car *had* been going way too fast.

"Who was driving?" she asked, looking from Byron to Andrea.

A flush of color moved up Byron's neck, and he shoved a hand through his hair.

"*I* was," Andrea said, a mite too quickly. "It's my car."

Melissa wasn't convinced that Andrea had been behind the wheel, but she'd made her point, and no laws had been broken, after all. She bent to pull the torn fabric of her sweatpants away from her knees, and the burning sensation made her wince.

Byron started to move, hesitated, and then took a resolute step toward her. "You might be hurt," he said.

A swift and wholly unexpected rage swelled within Melissa in that moment, stealing her breath away, no doubt triggered by the near miss she'd just had. Her mind flashed on the photos of Chavonne Rowan's small, broken body, taken at the medical examiner's office in Flagstaff. And those images were still vivid in her recollection; as if she'd seen them only moments before.

You might be hurt.

Hurt, indeed. The way Chavonne had been hurt?

"At least let us give you a ride home," Andrea pleaded, her expressive eyes brimming. "Please?"

Melissa paused, then nodded. Her house wasn't far away, but the rain was coming down harder now, and the flesh on her knees burned and she felt mildly sick to her stomach.

Byron didn't actually take her arm, though that had probably been his original intention. Instead, he just sort of herded her toward Andrea's car, opening the heavy door on the passenger side and waiting for her to get in. Andrea scrambled behind the wheel.

Melissa noticed that Andrea had to scoot the seat forward to reach the gas and brake pedals, but she didn't remark on it. She noticed a *lot* of things—being detail-oriented was part of her nature as well as her job—but even so, she tended to take most observations with a grain of salt. It was too easy to jump to conclusions.

Andrea's car was practically a relic, she reminded

herself, and it was possible that the seat had to be adjusted every time she sat in it. Big John had owned an old rattletrap of a work truck like that once, back in the day. The seat had had a mind of its own and needed constant adjustment.

Andrea tightened her grip on the steering wheel and glanced at the rearview as Byron got into the back.

Melissa, understandably distracted, finally got it then. Byron had spent the night with Andrea, in her little apartment over the Crockett sisters' garage, and *whoever* had been driving had been in a hurry because neither of them wanted the elderly ladies to know about the rendezvous. Chances were, Velda wouldn't be thrilled that her son had pulled an all-nighter, either, especially so soon after getting out of jail.

It was no wonder the kids were rattled. They'd nearly flattened the county prosecutor under the front wheels.

"I'll be at work on time," Andrea told her boss a couple of minutes later, as she pulled the car to a stop at Melissa's front gate.

"Fine," Melissa said, shoving open her door to climb out. Since she was in good shape, it surprised her to discover that she was stiff all over, sore and achy.

Byron got out, too, and stood waiting on the sidewalk, the rain making his hair curl, watching her intently.

Melissa felt a sudden need to reassure him. Maybe it was that he looked so young, standing there, and so vulnerable, a regular Lost Boy.

"You did a great job with the yard," she said.

"Thanks," he said, and she realized he was waiting to walk her to her front door.

Melissa waved to Andrea and turned to go through the gate, only to find Byron one step ahead, holding it open for her. Her skeptical side—after all, she was a prosecuting attorney—warned her not to be too trusting. Being softhearted too often translated to being soft-*headed,* in her experience.

It might well be true that Byron was basically a good kid who'd made a serious mistake and paid the price for it. On the other hand, he could be putting on an act. The next drug fix, the next tragedy, might be right around the corner.

Rain slid off the roof over Melissa's porch, and she and Byron ducked through, like people passing beneath a waterfall.

Melissa wore her door key on a chain around her neck when she ran, and she pulled it out through the neck of her sweatshirt then, her hand still slightly unsteady. She'd gotten a powerful jolt of adrenaline a little while before, and it hadn't completely subsided.

Gently, Byron took the key from her hand, inserted it into the lock and opened the door for her, handed the key back when she turned on the threshold to meet his gaze.

"I'm sorry," he said hoarsely.

Melissa nodded. "Be more careful next time," she said.

He nodded. "You're sure you'll be okay?"

"I'm sure," Melissa replied, because she was. Growing up on a working ranch, she'd been thrown by horses and stepped on by cows. She'd fallen out of hay mows and off the backs of trucks and tractors, all with relatively little damage.

By comparison, this was nothing.

"Byron?" she ventured.

He still looked miserable. "Yeah."

"Choose your friends carefully. Nathan Carter is bad news, in case you've forgotten."

Byron absorbed that, his face pale and taut. "Right now," he answered, quietly and at some length, "I can't afford to be that picky. A guy needs friends, and right now, Andrea and Nathan are the only ones I have."

Sadness pinched the back of Melissa's throat. She said nothing more, but simply nodded in response to Byron's words.

Fifteen minutes later, having showered and gingerly dried herself off with little dabbing motions of her towel, she'd forgotten the brief conversation entirely. There were small cuts on both her knees, but they weren't deep, and the bleeding had stopped. The rest of her body felt bruised, though, as if she'd actually been struck by Andrea's car.

After bundling herself into a robe, she padded along the hallway to the kitchen, whipped up her protein smoothie, and gulped down a couple of over-the-counter pain pills with the first sip. In another few minutes, she told herself, watching dully as water sheeted down outside of the window over the sink, she'd be right as— well—rain.

Dressing took twice as long as usual, since every motion made some joint or muscle ache, but Melissa remained undaunted. She got herself into a pink-floral print skirt and a long white sweater, summer-light, and flicked on a few swipes of mascara and lip gloss.

Between the rain and her recent shower, her hair had frizzed out, and she was in no mood to spend half an hour taming it with a blow-dryer and a brush, so she clamped the stuff into a loose roll at the back of her head with an enormous plastic clip and called it good.

Tendrils drifted down around her cheeks and her

neck—the look was softer than her usual tailored approach, more Ashley's style than her own, but it pleased her, nonetheless.

While she was inside, the rain had stopped, and the sun was out, bright as polished brass.

When Melissa limped into her office, just before nine, Andrea was already there, standing in the middle of the floor like a sentinel and grasping a plain glass vase containing a huge bouquet of purple and white irises, most likely appropriated from the Crockett sisters' garden, in both hands.

"These are for you," Andrea said anxiously.

Melissa smiled, took the flowers and started to go around the nervous young woman, toward her own office. "Thanks, Andrea," she said. "But you shouldn't have. It really wasn't necessary."

"You could have been badly hurt," Andrea burst out, "or even—"

Melissa paused, frowning. "I'm *all right,* Andrea."

Andrea's eyes clouded over with tears. "I know you think—you think Byron was driving this morning, and that I'm covering for him, because of what happened before, to that girl, Chavonne. But *I* was behind the wheel, not Byron."

Melissa sighed, continued into her office and set the vase of flowers carefully on a corner of her desk.

They really were beautiful, dewy and vibrantly colored.

"What you do in your personal life is none of my business," she said, looking at the irises instead of Andrea. They'd both learned a lesson; now, it was time to move on.

"But—?" Andrea prompted, without inflection. Clearly, she wasn't ready to let the subject drop. Melissa, on the other hand, would have preferred to pretend that it hadn't happened.

"You've come a long way since your foster-home days, Andrea," Melissa replied, after drawing in and expelling a deep breath. "I hope you won't throw all that away by doing anything foolish."

Andrea blushed miserably. "Like going out with Byron Cahill?"

"I didn't say that," Melissa pointed out.

"You didn't have to," Andrea said. Still, there was no anger in her tone or her expression.

Melissa rested a hand on the young woman's forearm. "Okay, for what it's worth, here's my opinion. Byron has to be going through some major adjustments right now. He has a lot to deal with, and so do you. Maybe it would be better to let the dust settle a little before you get too—involved."

Andrea tensed slightly. "Because he was in prison."

"Partly, yes," Melissa answered. "And partly because both of you are young."

"Right," Andrea said, her tone turning crisp as she turned on one heel to leave Melissa's office. "I'll get your messages."

Bemused, and still aching all over from the tumble she'd taken into the gravel that morning, Melissa put her purse away, sat down in her chair and booted up her computer.

A tap at the framework of her open door alerted her to Tom's presence. Melissa smiled, and even *that* hurt a little.

Tom glanced in Andrea's direction and then came inside Melissa's office and closed the door.

"We've got trouble," he said. His tone was solemn.

Melissa looked up at him, her smile a thing of the past. "Sit down, Tom," she said.

But he shook his head. "I've had a complaint from Ashley and Jack's neighbors," he told her. "About the guests. Since it's sort of a—delicate matter, I wanted to run the report by you before I go over there."

Melissa closed her eyes for a moment. Dammit, that bunch of geriatric outlaws were running around naked again, and this time, someone had seen them.

She did *not* need this.

The B&B should have been Ashley's problem, not hers.

Tom cleared his throat, and his expression was diplomatic. His eyes twinkled, though, and he wasn't in any rush to state his business, it seemed to Melissa. "They're disturbing the peace," he said.

Melissa rolled her eyes. *"Disturbing the peace?"*

"Apparently, they're playing the stereo at top volume. Practicing the tango on the back patio." Tom drew in a breath, his eyes still dancing with amusement. "The Crockett sisters are worried that the noise will scare their fish."

"Their *fish?*"

"You know. Those fancy goldfish they have."

"And this is *my* problem because—?"

"Well," Tom said, "because Ashley and Jack left you in charge of the B&B, for all intents and purposes. I thought you'd want to know what was going on."

"Good heavens," Melissa said.

Tom chuckled. "I'm fixing to go on over there and have a word with those good folks, of course," he went on. "I'm sure they don't mean any harm. You can come along or stay here—your choice."

Melissa groaned as the weight of twin responsibility settled on her shoulders. "I'd better go with you."

Tom nodded. "That would probably be a good idea," he allowed, his mouth twitching at one corner, "but maybe I should go in first, just in case."

"Just in case what?" Melissa asked, feeling testy. The over-the-counter pain pills she'd taken with her morning smoothie, before leaving home, were taking the edge off, but that was about it. "Last I heard, the tango wasn't dangerous. Not for spectators, at least."

Tom gave her a wry look as he opened the office door and waited for her to step through before following.

Andrea was just rising from her chair, the usual handful of pink phone messages clutched in one hand. She looked pale, and there were faint shadows under her eyes.

"Anything important?" Melissa asked, with a glance at the messages.

"I'm not sure," Andrea admitted. "There was a call from a woman complaining that one of her neighbors is buying too much toilet paper—way more than anybody needs, especially when they live alone."

Melissa frowned, puzzled.

But Tom gave a chuckle and a low whistle that brought the faithful Elvis click-click-clicking down the hallway from his master's office on canine toenails and said, "Sounds like the same old controversy Aunt Ona has to deal with every year when rodeo time rolls around."

"Mr. Creed called, too," Andrea added, while Melissa was still pondering Tom's cryptic remark. "I guess he didn't have your home number. Anyway, he said he and Matt really enjoyed supper last night and they'd like to reciprocate as soon as possible."

Melissa blushed slightly. "Okay," she said, avoiding Andrea's gaze. She could actually *feel* Tom's grin, though she didn't look at him, either.

"We'll be back in a while," Tom explained to Andrea.

Out of the corner of her eye, Melissa saw Andrea nod before turning and going back to her own desk.

Moments later, Tom, Melissa and Elvis were in the squad car.

Melissa flipped through the messages to make sure there was nothing urgent, then shoved them into her purse. All except for the toilet paper concern, of course.

The caller, not surprisingly, had been Bea Brady, one of the more vocal members of the Parade Committee. She'd spoken up during the meeting out at Creekside Academy, Melissa remembered.

"Some people," she said, with a long sigh, "have *way* too much free time."

Tom's mouth quirked at one corner. Elvis, meanwhile, sat in the middle of the backseat, behind the metal grill. "I suppose you realize," he said dryly, "that there are a few people around Stone Creek who'd say that about us. The big joke down at the barbershop is that I don't even need to load my service revolver—I can just carry a single bullet around in my shirt pocket, like Barney Fife."

A giggle escaped Melissa, in spite of everything, but when she spoke, she was utterly serious. "Sometimes I think I'm in the wrong line of work," she admitted, surprising herself as well as Tom.

Tom, already signaling to turn onto Ashley's street, cast a quizzical glance in her direction. "Really?" he asked. "You worked pretty hard to earn that law degree and pass the bar exam and then build a resume. What would you do if you weren't a lawyer?"

As the alley between the Crocketts' and the B&B came into focus, toward the end of the block, cell memory must have kicked in, because Melissa felt the impact of her fall all over again, as if it had just happened.

"Interesting question," she murmured in response. Before the breakup, she and Dan had agreed on a general plan: she would take a few years off from her career when she felt ready, help raise his two boys, have at least one baby, try out some of the domestic arts, like cooking and decorating, à la Ashley. "And I don't think I know the answer."

And that was probably the whole problem, she reflected. She not only didn't know what she would do if she didn't practice law, she didn't know who she would be.

She'd been so sure that she loved Dan, wanted to make a life with him, but when it came time to set a date and to actually *get married,* Melissa had panicked. Dan, who'd been patient for a long time, had been coldly furious, and then he'd delivered an ultimatum; she had forty-eight hours to make a decision, one way or the other: marry him, or call it quits.

Melissa hadn't needed forty-eight hours, or even forty-eight *seconds*.

She'd called it quits.

Of course, she'd expected Dan to come around in a day or two—a week at the longest—with flowers and sweet talk, the way he had every other time they'd ever disagreed about anything, large or small, but that time was different. There was no soft music, no steamy makeup sex, no anything. Within a week, in fact, Dan was dating a waitress, the woman he'd since married.

"Well," Tom said, drawing the cruiser to a stop in front of the B&B. "We're here."

"Yes," Melissa said, squinting her eyes and peering at the front of her sister and brother-in-law's gracious house. "Let's get this over with."

Tom chuckled, unfastened his seat belt and got out of the car. Reaching the sidewalk, he opened Melissa's door for her, then released Elvis from the back.

Even from where they stood, the sounds of merriment coming from behind the house were clearly audible. There was spritely guitar music, laughter, cheering and loud, enthusiastic applause.

"Damn," Melissa muttered, shaking her head, as Tom opened the front gate and waited for her to walk through ahead of him.

"You can wait here if you want to," Tom offered, as Elvis trotted happily ahead, nose to the ground.

"It isn't as if I've never seen a naked man before, you know," she said.

Tom laughed. "Huh?"

Unwittingly, she'd just revealed her secret fear: that the B&B guests were naked again. "You know what I meant," Melissa replied, with a little snap to her tone.

Tom remained amused. "By the way," he went on, "what's the matter with you? You flinched every time I took a corner on the way over here, and I'd swear you're limping a little."

He'd taken the lead, following the walk that ran alongside the house and into the backyard with its high fences and sheltering trees, but he looked over his shoulder at her as he spoke.

Melissa raised and lowered her shoulders. Carefully. "I took a little spill when I was running this morning," she said. "It's no big deal."

Elvis, having reached the backyard, began to bark. The sound was the purest joy, and Melissa had to smile.

Tom stopped in his tracks as soon as he'd rounded the far corner of the house, and Melissa, bringing up the rear, almost collided with him.

"I'll be damned," he murmured.

She peeked around him.

And there was the Wild Bunch, the men dressed like matadors, except for their hats, the women in flamenco outfits and holding roses in their teeth, tangoing like mad across the wide stone patio.

The music, pouring from a boom box, was deafening.

Elvis stood near the edge of the patio, a delighted witness to the festivities, barking his brains out as he followed the action.

Spotting Melissa and Tom, John Winthrop hurried over to crank down the volume on the boom box. He was wearing one of those round hats trimmed with tiny pom-poms.

The other man in the group finished up the dance by dipping his partner.

Melissa, more impressed than she would have admitted to Tom Parker or anyone else, could only assume that osteoporosis wasn't an issue in this particular crowd.

Tom cleared his throat, then summoned Elvis to his side.

Melissa stepped up next to him, concentrating on one thing. Not laughing.

"Why, it's Melissa," said Mr. Winthrop, beaming, taking off his hat and bowing deeply. "How nice to see you again!"

"That's quite a costume," Melissa said.

"Rented," Mr. Winthrop replied. He drew in a deep, robust breath and let it out in a whoosh. "We got to talking about our trip to Spain—we went three years ago—and I guess we got a little carried away by all the memories."

"There's no costume-rental place in Stone Creek," Tom said, sounding suspicious.

"We called a shop in Flagstaff," Winthrop explained jovially. "They were kind enough to deliver."

"Oh," Tom replied, clearly at a loss.

"The neighbors are complaining about the music," Melissa told the gang. "It was too loud."

The women looked annoyed. The men were crest-fallen. Melissa felt like the original wet blanket.

"Well, I guess there's no harm done," Tom allowed. "If you'll all just keep the noise down a little, everybody will be happy."

"Not everybody," said the woman in the red dress, trailing ruffles behind her and fiddling with the Spanish comb in her hair.

"We'll behave," Mr. Winthrop promised.

The woman in the red dress harrumphed, arms folded.

"Fair enough," Tom said agreeably.

By then, Melissa was wondering why she'd come along on this mission, since Tom didn't seem to need her help. If asked, she would have said it had seemed like a good idea at the time.

She smiled apologetically at the croquet/tango team. Winced when Tom took a light grip on her arm.

"That does it," he said to Melissa, as they walked away, Elvis ambling along behind them. "I'm taking you over to the clinic in Indian Rock."

Melissa sighed. "I'm just fine," she protested. "In fact, I was thinking I might like to try the tango—"

Tom flashed her a grin as he opened the door of the

squad car for her and helped her to ease inside. "No way," he said.

"Why not?"

"Because," Tom said, with a wicked light in his eyes, "it takes two to tango, and I'll have no part of it, thank you very much."

Melissa groaned. "That was *such* a bad joke," she said.

But then she laughed.

Tom turned serious. "I still think you should see a doctor. I could run you over to the clinic in Indian Rock in no time—"

"I'm *fine,* Tom," she insisted. "And I'm not going anywhere but back to the office."

Tom didn't answer until he'd gotten behind the wheel again. "Not much going on there," he observed. "Andrea can probably hold down the fort. Why not stay home for the rest of the day, if you won't go to the doctor, and take it easy?" He indicated her purse with a nod of his head and another grin. "You could take care of all those phone messages. Reassure Bea Brady that you won't allow the toilet-paper contingent to get out of hand when it comes time to decorate the floats for the big parade. Tell Steven Creed you're hot for him and he's welcome to come by for supper anytime."

Melissa punched her old friend in the arm. *"I'm going back to work,"* she told her friend. "If I have to feel lousy, I might as well do it at the office as at home and, besides, my car is there."

"Never argue with a lawyer," Tom sighed, heading for the center of town.

"Maybe I *will* invite Steven over for supper again, though," she said, after musing a while. "Care to join us?"

Tom pulled the cruiser into the usual parking spot behind the courthouse and looked over at her. "I smell a setup," he said.

CHAPTER NINE

MELISSA GOT OUT of the squad car, opened the back door for Elvis, who leaped nimbly to the ground, and semi-hobbled toward the side entrance to the brick court-house. Tom's words echoed in her brain.

I smell a setup, he'd said, when she'd invited him to supper, moments before.

"You have a suspicious mind, Tom Parker," she accused.

"Part of the job," Tom admitted, holding open the heavy glass door for her.

It occurred to Melissa then, as it might have to Tom as well, that it was a shame their relationship had always been platonic. They'd have made a good couple, she guessed, but there was no spark on either side. Hanging out with Sheriff Parker was like being with her brother, Brad—easy, low-key and *safe*.

Keeping company with Steven, on the other hand, had the same charge as bungee jumping off a high bridge or riding a unicycle across the Grand Canyon on a tightrope.

"Taking risks is a part of your job, too," Melissa replied briskly, as they moved—man, woman and dog—along the corridor. "But when it comes to romance, you're nothing but a coward."

"So it *was* a setup," Tom said, with a note of triumph. "I knew it."

"I might have been thinking of asking Tessa Quinn to join us," Melissa answered, as they reached the outer door of her offices.

Melissa O'Ballivan, Prosecutor, read the faux-metal sign affixed to it.

She waited out a small rush of frustration. Once, she'd loved her work. Now, she was just marking time, it seemed, waiting for someone to break the law, so she could try them in court. Was that any way to live?

Tom frowned down at her, though there was a benevolent light in his eyes. "I'm looking forward to a platterful of Ashley's spare ribs," he said.

"You haven't won yet," Melissa pointed out. "In fact, the way you're dragging your feet—you've had plenty of time to ask Tessa out, it seems to me—you're looking more and more like the new chairman of the Parade Committee with every passing moment."

"I'll ask her," Tom said.

"Fine," Melissa retorted. "Let's see some action here. I'm not going to let you drag this bet out until we're all old and gray."

He huffed out a loud sigh. "Here's an idea," he said. "Why don't you just run *your* love life, O'Ballivan, and let me run mine?"

Melissa didn't have a reply ready, since neither of them actually had a love life, so she pushed open the office door and stepped inside, leaving Tom and Elvis in the corridor.

"As far as I'm concerned, the bet is off," Tom called after her.

"You wish," Melissa called back.

Andrea, though puffy-eyed, looked as though she'd rallied while Melissa was away. She smiled, pushed back her chair and hurried into the tiny break room, returning moments later with a steaming cup of coffee.

The fragrance was tantalizing.

"I made it myself," Andrea said, sweeping past her, into the inner office, and setting the cup down on Melissa's desk.

"I thought making coffee was against your principles," Melissa said lightly, extracting the stack of messages from her purse before putting the bag away in its usual cubbyhole.

"You're the one who said it wasn't in my job description," Andrea said.

Melissa smiled. "Nevertheless, Andrea," she replied, with a touch of irony that was probably lost on her assistant, "*thank you* for making the coffee. Did anyone call or stop by while I was out?"

For a fraction of a second, Andrea looked almost coy. "Mr. Creed was here," the girl responded. "About fifteen or twenty minutes ago."

Melissa's heart raced, though she was all-business on the outside.

Or so she hoped, anyway.

She sat down, reached for the cup, took a sip of coffee before saying anything at all. "Oh? Did he say what he wanted?"

Be casual.

"Lunch," Andrea said.

Lunch—an ordinary enough concept. When connected with Steven Creed, however, even the suggestion gave her that runaway roller-coaster feeling again.

Melissa merely nodded. She fanned the phone messages out on the surface of her desk, just to give herself something to do.

"I could get Mr. Creed on the phone for you," Andrea offered, her tone eager, almost breathless.

Melissa didn't look up from the messages. "I'll do that myself, Andrea," she said. "But thank you."

"He's pretty hot," Andrea commented.

Melissa sighed. Agreeing that Steven was hot would have been like agreeing that the sky was blue.

Andrea hurried out of the office and closed the door behind her.

Melissa picked up the telephone handset, squinted at the written message with Steven's name on it and dialed.

While she waited, a miniature *Cirque de Soleil* sprang to life in the pit of her stomach, performing death-defying spins and leaps and dives.

This was ridiculous. Maybe Steven Creed was attractive—okay, he was *definitely* attractive—but he was a mortal man, not a Greek god, for heaven's sake.

Then again, that was the problem, wasn't it? He was *all* man—too much man—maybe even more man than she could handle.

As if.

"Steven Creed," he said suddenly, startling Melissa. She realized she hadn't actually expected him to answer the call—she'd planned on leaving a message. Counted, inexplicably, on that little buffer of time.

"H-hello," she responded, all but croaking the word. *Get a grip,* she told herself silently. *You're a grown woman, dammit, not a teenager.*

"Melissa?"

"Yes." She cleared her throat. Squeezed her eyes shut tight. "It's me. I'm sorry—I was planning to answer your call earlier, but then something came up and I had to leave the office and—"

"I just wanted to invite you to lunch," Steven said,

with a smile in his voice, when she bogged down in the middle of her sentence. She'd have sworn he knew how rattled she was, and that only made her more so. "I'll understand, of course, if you're busy or something. It's pretty short notice."

Say you're busy, advised Melissa's inner chicken little. *He gave you an out.*

"I'm not busy," she said aloud.

"Great," Steven responded. "Meet you at the Sunflower Café at noon?"

Melissa checked her watch. It was quarter after eleven, so she had forty-five minutes to pull herself together. "Perfect," she said, sounding way more perky than she considered necessary.

Her "perky" quota was normally zero. Add Steven Creed to the equation, though, and she was about as sedate as a middle-school cheerleader at the first big game of the season.

"See you then," Steven said. "Bye."

"Bye," Melissa said, a few seconds after he'd hung up.

She took several sips of her rapidly cooling coffee, then squared her shoulders, raised her chin and started answering the messages Andrea had given her earlier.

A big believer in tackling the least appealing task first, she dialed Bea Brady's number. The older woman answered on the second ring, but not with a hello, or her name, the way most people would have done.

"It's about time you called me back, Melissa O'Ballivan!" she snapped, instead.

Melissa's temper surged, nearly breaking the surface of her professional composure, but she managed a pleasant tone when she replied. "I'm at work, Bea," she said. "Parade Committee business should probably be handled after hours."

"How do you know I'm calling about the parade?" Bea demanded, every bit as surly as before.

Melissa reread the message, hoping she'd transcribed Andrea's handwriting correctly. "It says here that you're concerned about someone purchasing toilet paper?"

"Adelaide Hillingsley bought a *truck load* of the stuff at one of those box stores in Flagstaff," Bea blurted. "She lives by herself. There's only one bathroom in her house. What would one woman be doing with so much tissue if she didn't plan on flouting the rules and using it to decorate the Chamber of Commerce float for the parade?"

Melissa closed her eyes, sat back in her chair and counted mentally until she was sure she wouldn't laugh. Adelaide *was* a force to be reckoned with; although she'd originally been hired as a receptionist, she'd been running the organization for years.

"Maybe you should ask Adelaide about that, Bea," Melissa said, when she dared to speak at all. "Since it's *committee business* and I'm at work—"

"Oh, don't give me that, Melissa O'Ballivan," Bea broke in. "Everybody knows you don't have anything to do most of the time anyway!"

Melissa counted again, but this time it was to keep from yelling.

"I beg your pardon?" she said, when she'd reached the double digits.

Bea backed off a little. "I didn't mean that the way it sounded," she conceded. She was a nice person, despite being a bit on the pushy side—as president of the local Garden Club, and an old-line Stone Creeker, she was used to being in charge, getting things done, that was all.

"I'm glad," Melissa said pleasantly, thinking the other woman's remark might not have stung so much if it wasn't so damn true.

"You'll speak to Adelaide? Remind her that the Parade Committee specifically voted *never* to use toilet paper in the construction of a float? It would be so tacky—"

"I'll talk to Adelaide," Melissa said, because she had other calls to make and she needed to move on to the next one. None of them were any more important or pressing than this one but, still. She *was* drawing a paycheck, and she was on county time.

"When? When will you talk to her?"

Melissa's cuts and bruises tuned up again, all at once, in a dull, throbbing chorus. "Tonight," she said. "Maybe tomorrow. But *soon,* Bea. I promise."

In those moments, Melissa went from wishing Tom would win their bet to wishing he'd *lose* and take over the Parade Committee.

Fat chance.

Bea was silent for a beat or two, but then she huffed out a sigh. "All right," she said. "But you mark my words, Melissa. Stone Creek will be the laughingstock of the whole state of Arizona if Adelaide has her way." She paused to sputter indignantly, then finished with "*Toilet paper,* for heaven's sake. That woman is obsessed with toilet paper."

Melissa bit the inside of her lower lip as a means of corralling the obvious response—that Adelaide wasn't the *only* one with an obsession—before promising to attend to the matter at the first opportunity.

By the time she'd made the remaining calls, noon

had rolled around and it was time to meet Steven for lunch over at the Sunflower Café. Because the small restaurant was close, and she thought the walk might be a remedy for some of her soreness, let alone her frustrations, she decided to leave her car at the office.

She and Steven arrived at the same time.

"I like the look," he said, taking in her skirt and sweater with a slow sweep of his eyes as they stood on the sidewalk in front of the café.

She let that pass. "Where's Matt?"

One side of his mouth kicked up in a grin. He looked better than good in his white shirt and well-fitting blue jeans. "At day camp," he replied, with a grin dancing in his eyes. "I spent the morning with an architect from Flagstaff. I'd like to have the house finished and the new barn up by fall."

Melissa looked down at the community dog dish, filled with clear water, and stopped just short of asking about Zeke.

Steven smiled again, opened the door for her, and held it wide. "Zeke's at home," he said, evidently reading her mind. "And he's fine."

It was disconcerting, the way this man could guess what she was thinking. What if he figured out that, even against her better judgment, just being around him made her want his body? She looked away quickly.

The café was crowded, as it usually was at that time of day, but Tessa seated them right away, at a corner table.

Melissa immediately reached for a menu, although her stomach was doing that nervous thing again.

"I had a great time last night, Melissa," Steven said. "So did Matt."

She looked at him over the top of her menu. Blinked

once. It should have been easy to come up with an answer—so why wasn't it?

"I'm glad," she said, after a long time.

Steven didn't take the other menu, which was tucked between the napkin holder and the salt and pepper shakers. He just sat there, across the table, within touching distance, looking all warm-eyed and amused. "I'm glad you're glad," he teased, lowering his voice and leaning forward slightly.

She blushed then, because the way his eyes caressed her made her feel as naked as any of the croquet-playing oldsters she'd seen in Ashley's backyard the other day. They were in a very public place, she and Steven, but, even though they'd already drawn their share of glances, the Sunflower was so full of noisy good cheer that no one could have overheard their conversation—although a few people were sure to try.

"The club sandwich is very good here," she said helpfully, giving the menu a little wriggle. "So is the beef stew."

Steven smiled at her again.

Tingly waves of—*something* rippled under her skin.

"Okay," he said, his tone husky.

Melissa gave him a level look. "Lunch?" she reminded him.

"Supper, too, I hope," he said, without missing a beat. "Six o'clock? My place?"

Her heartbeat quickened. "Your place?" she repeated stupidly.

"I'm afraid Matt won't be there, though," Steven said, sounding mildly rueful. "Meg and Brad invited him to sleep over tonight. He and Mac are already great buddies."

Melissa swallowed. If Matt wasn't going to be home, of course they would be alone, she and Steven Creed.

Say no, warned her practical side. *You know what could happen, and you're not ready for that.*

"Isn't this a school night?" she asked.

Wow. She was a veritable genius when it came to small talk.

"Matt goes to day camp," Steven pointed out, after indulging in another of those slow, lethal grins. "Not Harvard."

"Oh," Melissa said.

"Are you coming, or not?"

She blushed again. Had he worded the question that way on purpose? "It's a little soon," she said.

"For what?" Steven asked, clearly enjoying her discomfort.

"You know damn well *for what,*" Melissa told him. She'd lost patience with herself by then. All this waffling was so unlike her—she was a direct person.

His blue eyes twinkled with mischief. And the promise of sweet, hot, languid things. "Do I?" he drawled. And then he reached out, took the menu from her hands, and set it aside. Closed his fingers around hers.

"Yes," Melissa whispered. "You do."

Just then, Tessa reappeared, pen and order pad in hand. "What'll it be?" she asked, smiling at both of them.

Steven ordered the club sandwich.

Melissa opted for beef stew, even though it was a warm day.

Still smiling, Tessa nodded and turned away.

"You were saying?" Steven grinned. He hadn't let go of Melissa's hand; indeed, he ran the pad of his thumb over her knuckles, very lightly.

Flames shot through her. "I forget."

"Liar."

"It's too soon," Melissa reiterated. There was something feverish in her tone.

"Are you trying to convince yourself, or me?"

"Steven, *stop it*."

Tessa came back with their drinks then—both of them had ordered iced tea.

"You're okay, aren't you?" Tessa asked, giving Melissa much closer scrutiny than before. "Somebody at the counter just told me you were almost hit by a car this morning, while you were out for your run."

Small towns. Every incident, no matter how small, was grist for the mill.

"Just a little shaken up," Melissa said, aware of the change in Steven's face even though she wasn't looking directly at him just then. His grip tightened around her hand. "It was no big deal, Tessa. A miss is as good as a mile and all that."

"It could have been a *very* big deal," Tessa protested. "Did you see a doctor?"

"Tessa," Melissa said, with a smile and a shake of her head, "*I'm fine*. Really."

Tessa hesitated for another moment or so, then turned and walked away.

"You were almost run over by a car?" Steven asked. He was holding both her hands by then. And he no longer looked amused.

People were watching them.

Jumping to all kinds of conclusions.

She could *feel* it.

"I wasn't hurt," she insisted. It bothered her, how much she was enjoying his concern.

"What happened?" Steven asked.

"Nothing," Melissa answered. "That's why the word *almost* comes into play."

His fine jawline tightened briefly, relaxed again.

"Let's talk about something else besides accidents that didn't quite happen," she suggested, hoping to lighten the mood.

The grin was back, and it was as dangerous as ever. "Like what?"

"Well, not sex," Melissa said, and then regretted it.

He laughed. "I agree," he said. "It's better to just go ahead and *do* some things, rather than wasting time talking about them."

Melissa blinked. "Did you just say what I think you just said?" she demanded, whispering again. Leaning toward him.

"You were the one who brought up the subject of sex," Steven pointed out reasonably. "Not me."

He looked so damnably comfortable, sitting there, easy in his skin, with his glass of iced tea in front of him and his eyes that indescribable shade of blue-violet.

"Then I'm officially *un*bringing it up," Melissa said. "Forget I mentioned sex at all. It was totally inappropriate. A slip of the tongue—"

His grin flashed again.

She blushed even more. "I didn't mean—"

Mercifully, the food arrived then.

Since her stomach was still doing the circus thing, Melissa was surprised to realize that she was hungry. She picked up her spoon and focused on the delicious beef stew.

"What do you like to do, Melissa?" Steven asked, about midway through the meal. He'd made a pretty good dent in his club sandwich, and pushed away his plate to focus all his attention on her.

The feeling that gave her was exciting, in an unsettling sort of way. She was an attractive woman, and she knew it, but like many people, she felt invisible a lot of the time. "Do?" she echoed, confused. "I work. I read. And I jog."

"How do you feel about horses?"

"I grew up on a ranch," Melissa answered. "I rode a lot when I was younger. Not so much lately." And until she'd gotten over the effects of that morning's spill, she wouldn't be climbing into any saddles, thank you very much.

"I spent summers on the family ranch up in Colorado when I was a kid," he said. "Riding was about my favorite thing."

A picture flashed in Melissa's mind—she could imagine Steven as he must have looked growing up. That thatch of brownish-gold hair, those eyes, full of mischief. And probably a smattering of freckles, too. "Just summers?" she asked. "Where did you live the rest of the time?"

"Boston." That was all. Just "Boston." And the way he said it was clipped, almost abrupt.

"I've been there a few times," Melissa said. "To Boston, I mean. It's a great city. I especially love the Common, and the swan boats."

Steven relaxed then, but Melissa saw that it took an effort, and that made her wonder what the rest of the Creeds were like, specifically his parents. She'd met the Montana branch of the family—Logan, Dylan and Tyler—when they visited their McKettrick cousins on the Triple M, over near Indian Rock. Those three hadn't had the easiest of childhoods, that was for sure, but they'd turned out to be fine men.

It had been Melissa's experience that some adversity

made a person strong. She and Ashley, and certainly Brad and Olivia, were proof of that. Their mother, Delia, had abandoned them at a young age, and later on their dad, the classic man of few words but nonetheless the most solid presence in their lives, had been killed.

"Once my grandfather and my mother were both gone," Steven said, "that left my uncles running the show. Boston sort of lost its charm then."

It was a lot to absorb, and the café, however pleasant, surely wasn't the best place to discuss the things they were obviously destined to discuss.

Melissa figured things were getting too heavy. "Are we going to build our friendship around food, Steven Creed?" she asked. "We seem to be sharing quite a few meals these days."

Steven caught Tessa's eye, silently asking for the check.

Looking at Melissa again, he smiled. "I want to spend more time with you," he said forthrightly. "And out here in the countryside, that seems to include breaking bread together."

One of the waitresses brought the bill, since Tessa was busy with a fresh crop of customers, and Steven paid it on the spot, shook his head when the young girl asked if he wanted change.

Heads turned as they left the restaurant, as they had when Melissa and Steven came in, but Melissa was used to that. Stone Creek was, after all, barely more than a wide spot in the road, even a century and a half after the first settlers arrived.

"Thanks for lunch," she told Steven, when they were standing on the sidewalk again.

He looked around, probably for her car. "I could give

you a ride back to work," he offered. "My truck is just around the corner."

Melissa smiled. "That's okay," she said. "The walk will be good for me."

Steven didn't look convinced of that, but he didn't argue, either.

"I'll be expecting you around six," he said.

She nodded, wondering precisely when she'd gone around the bend. She decided it must have happened when she got her first look at Steven Creed, because she'd certainly been sane before that.

The hike back to the office was a short one, but it didn't make Melissa feel better any more than the walk *over* had done. If she'd been anybody but her stubborn O'Ballivan self, she'd have taken Tom's earlier suggestion, gone home, gulped down something for the pain and climbed into bed.

When she arrived, Adelaide Hillingsley was in the outer office, chatting with Andrea.

"I came about the toilet paper rumor," the middle-aged woman announced forthrightly, as soon as she spotted Melissa. Pudgy, with thin, reddish hair and bright hazel eyes, Adelaide was a cheerful soul, and her family, like Bea's, went way back in Stone Creek's history.

Melissa managed not to roll her eyes, but just barely. Did *anyone* in this town understand that this was the prosecutor's office, not the official headquarters of the Parade Committee?

Resigned, she gestured toward the entrance to her private space.

"Shall I bring in some coffee?" Andrea piped up, all chipper efficiency.

Melissa gave her a look.

"That sounds nice," Adelaide said, sweeping grandly into the inner sanctum. "I'd like mine with a little cream and two sugars, please."

"None for me, thanks," Melissa said, putting a little point on the words. And then she shut the door with a firm push.

Adelaide, dressed in her customary cotton print blouse and elastic-waisted jeans, sat down without waiting for an invitation.

"Someone really should persuade Bea Brady to go straight out and shop for a *life,*" she said. "My niece wore a toilet paper wedding gown when she got married, and she looked fantastic. The pictures were all over the internet for months afterwards."

Melissa sat down in her desk chair and tried to look serious. "I've gone over the bylaws for the Parade Committee," she began, with dignity, "and there *is* a ban on using bathroom tissue to decorate floats."

Adelaide waved that off. "What about creativity? What about being resourceful, and the wise use of our funds—which, in case you don't know, are shrinking with every passing year?"

Melissa drew a deep, deep breath and let it out slowly. "Adelaide," she said, "creativity is certainly a good thing. Ditto resourcefulness and good fiscal management. But this is an issue that should be debated within the committee itself—not here, during working hours."

"You've always been such a—lawyer," Adelaide remarked, without rancor.

She looked around, smiling. "I don't see any crooks standing around, waiting to be hauled before a judge."

Melissa allowed herself a small and very diplomatic sigh. She'd been raised to respect her elders and, besides, Adelaide had been her and Ashley's Girl Scout leader when they were kids. She'd mothered them both, after a fashion, after Delia left. "I think that's beside the point, don't you?" she said mildly. "I grant you, this isn't Maricopa County, where the courts see a lot of action, but I'm still sworn to uphold the duties of this office, Adelaide, and I'm determined to do that."

Adelaide gave a responding sigh as Andrea ducked in with fresh coffee for the visitor and handed it over.

"If you wouldn't mind," the young woman said, "I'd like to leave early today. Since things are so quiet and all."

Melissa pressed her back teeth together, but kept smiling. Andrea's timing was priceless. "Go," she said.

Andrea blushed slightly. "It's just that there was a cancellation at the dentist's office today. If I go in for my cleaning now, I won't have to do it Saturday morning."

Melissa glared.

Andrea ducked out.

Adelaide, in no hurry to get back to her receptionist's job, apparently, took a loudly appreciative sip from her coffee cup. "Did anyone mention how grateful we are, Melissa—the members of the Parade Committee, I mean—that you were willing to step in and take over for poor Ona Frame?"

"Now you're just trying to butter me up," Melissa said, smiling again. Irritated though she was, she liked Adelaide Hillingsley, and that was that.

Adelaide cast an eloquent glance toward the place where Andrea had stood just a moment before. "It seems to be the most effective way to deal with you," she replied, looking pleased with herself. "This job has made all the difference in the world to that girl. Heaven only knows what might have happened to her if she hadn't had the good fortune to wind up in Stone Creek."

"Right about now," Melissa confided brightly, "I wouldn't mind throttling her."

Adelaide took another drink of coffee, raised her eyebrows slightly. After swallowing, she ventured thoughtfully, "I hear she's dating that Cahill boy. Seems to me folks ought to be more concerned about *that* than whether or not any of the parade floats are festooned with toilet paper."

Melissa leaned forward in her chair. "The tissue issue," she said, "will have to be settled by the committee. I want no part of it."

"But you're the chairperson," Adelaide said.

Thanks to Tom Parker, Melissa thought.

"I'm also the county prosecutor," she said.

"Then we'd better call a special meeting and settle the matter," Adelaide decided, in her take-charge way. "How does tonight sound? We might be able to get the community room at Creekside Academy, but I'm pretty sure the quilting club's already reserved it and, besides, your place is central."

Here it was, Melissa reflected. An emergency meeting of the Parade Committee. Just the excuse—however thin—she needed to get out of being alone with Steven Creed in the close and luxurious confines of Brad's former tour bus.

Except that she didn't *want* to get out of it, fool that she was.

"I'm afraid I have other plans," she said. "But feel free to call a meeting anyway. Naturally, I'll go along with whatever the rest of you decide, as long as there's a consensus."

"Does this have something to do with that Creed fellow?" Adelaide asked bluntly. There was a twinkle in her eyes. "First supper, then lunch. My, my. It would seem you're over Dan Guthrie at last, and none too soon, either."

"I've been 'over' Dan Guthrie for a long time," Melissa said evenly.

And it was true. She still missed his kids, though. Missed the life she'd *expected* to have.

How crazy was that?

Adelaide gave a girlish giggle, set her coffee cup down on Melissa's desk with a thump, and rose from her chair. "And it's none of my business," she chimed sunnily. "I could get you the instructions for my niece's toilet-paper wedding dress, if you want."

"Thanks," Melissa said. "But I won't be needing one of those real soon." She stood up, too, and walked Adelaide all the way to the corridor.

As soon as Adelaide had trundled off down the hall and outside, into the parking lot, Melissa turned and strode toward Tom's office.

He was sitting at his desk, with his feet up, studying the contents of a manila file folder.

"I resign!" Melissa announced summarily.

"From what?" Tom asked, dropping his feet to the floor and standing.

"From the damn Parade Committee!"

Elvis, sprawled on his side over by the water cooler, gave a concerned little whine.

Tom chuckled. "I never figured you for a quitter," he said, folding his arms.

Melissa knew he was playing her, but her cheeks went hot with indignation anyway. "Well, maybe you'd better just 'figure' *again,* bucko," she snapped.

"'Bucko'?" Tom repeated, grinning now.

"I must have been crazy to let you talk me into this," Melissa ranted on, pacing now. Hugging herself to keep from flinging her arms out wide in frustrated emphasis. "Why can't Bea Brady run the committee? Or Adelaide Hillingsley? They both *give a damn,* after all, which is more than anybody can say for me!"

"Whoa," Tom said. "Calm down, counselor. If Adelaide headed up the project, Bea would raise hell, and vice versa. And for the first time in fifty-odd years, there wouldn't be a parade to kick off Rodeo Days."

"Then *you* do it!" Melissa steamed. With one hand, she made a slashing motion in front of her throat. "I am not going to spend the next few weeks arbitrating disputes over toilet paper!"

To his credit, Tom was trying hard not to laugh. He made a clucking sound with his tongue and shook his head.

"Melissa, Melissa," he said. "Stone Creek *needs* you."

CHAPTER TEN

"'STONE CREEK NEEDS YOU,'" Melissa muttered to herself, still riled from the conversation with Tom Parker that afternoon, concerning the Parade Committee. It was five-thirty, and she'd already showered, replaced her unaccustomed skirt and sweater with an even more unaccustomed black-and-white polka-dot sundress, and spritzed on cologne. "What a load of manipulative crap. And I fell for it!"

In the end, much as she'd love to resign as chairperson, Tom had been right. She wasn't a quitter and that was that.

Melissa studied her image in the mirror on the inside of her closet door and went right on talking to herself. "You're not fooling anybody, Melissa O'Ballivan," she told the reflected woman glowering back at her. "The real reason you're all bent out of shape is that you're about to do something you damn well *know* you shouldn't!"

That something, of course, was spending an evening alone, in a private and relatively small space—with Steven Creed.

The man was a sin sundae, and she was so tempted to dig in.

If she had any sense at all, she chided herself silently, she'd stay away from him until she stopped feeling quite so—well—*vulnerable*.

All right, it was true that she needed to get out of the house—and out of her own head. And it wasn't as if she didn't have options—Ashley, her favorite confidante, was still out of town, but Olivia would have listened without judging, and Meg, too. Her sister and sister-in-law were smart, savvy women, and if they gave any advice at all, it would be *good* advice.

On the other hand, they were both in committed, loving relationships with men they knew all about, not relative strangers like Steven Creed was to her. By now, they must surely have forgotten what it was like to be in her situation.

Bottom line, she wanted full-frontal contact with the delectable Mr. Creed, and that was that.

And so what if she did? Was that so wrong?

No, she reasoned, arguing the case in the courtroom of her mind, it *wasn't* wrong. Stupid, maybe, and probably shortsighted, but not wrong.

Having gotten exactly nowhere with this inner debate, Melissa slipped on a lightweight cardigan, not because she was cold, but because she had some bruises on her arms from biting the dust that morning, and she didn't want them on display. She found her purse, locked up the house and climbed into her car.

Melissa drove straight to Steven's demolition site of a place and parked behind the house, between two huge, overgrown lilac bushes. Stone Creek Ranch—and thus, Brad and Meg—were just down the road, and she didn't want either one of them to catch a glimpse of the car. A roadster sighting would lead to too many questions, ones she wasn't inclined to answer just yet.

While she was still thinking these thoughts, Steven emerged from the bus, cowboy-perfect in dark jeans and a spiffy white shirt, his hair a little too long and his boots showing just the right amount of wear.

He grinned in greeting.

The dog, Zeke, trotted over to her for a pat on the head.

"I thought you might back out at the last minute," Steven said, standing a few yards away, giving her space, his arms folded.

Melissa, who had been stewing over a variety of injustices ever since she'd left work, launched right in. "Just tell me this," she said, planting her sandaled feet and pressing her knuckles into her hips. "Why is it perfectly all right for a man to want sex and make no bones about it, say so right out, but a single *woman* has to come up with all kinds of reasons and excuses?" Not the most appropriate way to greet the man, she realized in retrospect, but the words had simply burst out of her.

Steven tilted his head to one side, and his grin was wicked, but he still kept his distance.

The scent of lilacs surrounded Melissa in a cloud, making her feel slightly drunk.

"I wouldn't say there were no bones about it," Steven drawled.

Embarrassment bloomed rose-pink in Melissa's cheeks. What was the *matter* with her? When had this—this alternate personality, perfumed and wearing a sundress—with a ruffled hem, no less—taken over her fine legal brain and caused her to forsake her tailored wardrobe?

In that moment, she couldn't think of a single sensible thing to say.

Painfully aware that she'd made a fool of herself—again—she actually considered jumping back into her car and zooming out of there. The problem was that just as quitting wasn't part of her constitutional makeup, neither was running away.

So she just stood there, feeling ridiculous.

Where were all her convictions about sex and the modern woman *now?*

Steven's grin softened, and he approached her slowly, the way he might have approached a frightened animal or a baby bird that had fallen from its nest.

When he was standing directly in front of her, he took her elbows into a gentle grip and looked down into her upturned and very flushed face.

"Hey," he said huskily. "You're calling the shots, Melissa. You can say 'now' or you can say 'never.' The whens and the ifs are entirely up to you. Meanwhile, why don't we just spend some time together and see how things go?"

Such a wave of relief passed over Melissa then that she was very glad Steven was holding on to her. If he hadn't been, she thought her knees might have given way.

"Thanks," she said, belatedly, breathing the word more than saying it.

He gave a low chuckle. Inclined his head toward the old dowager of a farmhouse; the paint was peeling away, and the flowerbeds were choked with weeds, but the blowsy old roses, splotches of crimson drooping under their own weight, gave it a singular appeal.

"Want a tour of the house?" he asked.

It was such an ordinary question. Such an innocent one. Melissa, who had grown up in an old house and loved them for that reason and a few others, nodded.

Steven released her elbows, but immediately took her by the hand, and they walked toward the structure.

The last dazzle before twilight turned the thick-glassed windows to pale purple.

They stopped just short of the back door, and Melissa looked up, shielding her eyes with her free hand.

"Don't you wish it could talk?" she asked wistfully.

Steven smiled. "I don't imagine all the folks who've lived here over the last several generations would consider that an entirely good thing," he said.

This man, Melissa thought.

One minute, he had her heart racing and her stomach doing flip-flops.

The next, he was soothing her, just by being who and what he was.

"I suppose not," she agreed. He stepped up onto the small, uncovered porch, and Melissa followed, trusting his lead. Suddenly, it was easy to talk to him. "This house has been here almost as long as ours, you know. The one old Sam O'Ballivan built, I mean."

"Sam O'Ballivan. The Arizona Ranger turned cattle baron."

Melissa nodded, mildly surprised.

"Brad told me a little about him," Steven said. "That's quite a story."

"The man from Stone Creek," Melissa replied, with another nod. "That was our Sam."

By then they'd entered the kitchen, and Melissa gravitated straight to the dusty, wood-burning cookstove in the far corner. "Wow," she said. "I'm surprised some antiques dealer didn't score this a long time ago. My sister Ashley would kill to have it at the B&B. She'd probably even *use* it."

Again, Steven smiled. "I take it Ashley's the domestic type," he said.

Melissa rolled her eyes. "You can say that again. That

was her cooking we had last night at supper, remember. *My* culinary repertoire is limited to deli salads and stuff from the freezer aisle at the supermarket."

"Mine isn't much better, I'm afraid," he told her. Sunlight streamed in through a dusty window and cast an aura around him. "We're having meat loaf tonight, you and I, but it's takeout from the Sunflower Café. Matt will probably be blown away by supper over at Brad and Meg's place—a decent meal, for once."

Melissa left the stove, overwhelmed by a strange, swift tenderness unlike anything she'd ever felt before.

She swallowed. So much for his being easy to talk to. "I think you take very good care of Matt," she said quietly.

"I try," Steven said, and she saw a flicker of sadness move in his eyes, quickly gone. "There's no denying that his mom and dad would have done a lot better job of raising him, though."

They were standing several feet apart, as they had before, out there in that bower of lilacs, but something electrical arced between them, undiminished by distance.

"What happened to them?" she asked. "Matt's parents, I mean."

For a moment, Melissa didn't think Steven was going to answer. When he did speak, he had to clear his throat first. "Jillie, Matt's mother, died of breast cancer close to two years ago," he said. "The grief got hold of Zack and it changed him. He was killed in a motorcycle wreck when Matt was four. I was named in both their wills as Matt's guardian."

"You must have been good friends, you and Jillie and Zack, if they trusted you to raise their child."

Pain moved in that handsome face, the features

rugged and aristocratic, both at once. "We were good friends," he confirmed, after a long time.

She wanted very much to touch him then, not sexually, but to offer comfort, one human being to another. She was careful not to move. "You legally adopted Matt," she said. Judge Carpenter had told her that, the first day. The day everything changed for Melissa.

"I figured it made sense," Steven replied, "and Matt was all for it."

"It can't be easy, being a single parent."

"Oh, believe me," Steven said, smiling again, "it isn't. But, just the same, I'd be hard put to think of anything more rewarding." He held out his hand once more, and she crossed to him, took hold. "This place will be a lot different when the contractor and his crews get through with it," he added.

Melissa's throat tightened. "Don't let them change it *too much*," she said, without intending to say any such thing. It was none of her business what Steven Creed did to his house.

Steven cupped her cheeks in his hands then, and she knew by the touch of his palms that, professional man or not, he was no stranger to physical work. "I guess I probably shouldn't kiss you," he mused, his gaze focused on her mouth.

"I guess not," Melissa agreed, but weakly.

He kissed her—lightly at first, and then thoroughly. She moaned and slipped her arms around his neck.

"It's too soon," she said breathlessly, when the kiss finally ended.

"I know," Steven rasped in reply.

After the longest moment of Melissa's life, he stepped back, away from her, let his hands fall to his sides. He was breathing hard, and a muscle bunched in his jawline, then smoothed out again.

They stood there, just looking at each other.

It was Steven who finally broke the silence, and what he said surprised her. A lot. "Tell me something about yourself, Melissa."

"Like what?"

Steven chuckled, standing there in a shifting mist of sun-speckled dust. Spread his hands. "What you love— what you hate—whether or not you believe in God. That sort of thing."

A smile tugged at the side of her mouth. She was relaxing a little—in spite of herself. "Oh, that," she said. She considered the question briefly. "Yes, I believe in God. I don't see how a person could help it, looking up at a sky full of stars, or in the early spring, when the grass comes up green, or watching a baby take those first few steps—"

So much for relaxing. Heat suffused Melissa's face. Why had she gone and blurted out a loaded word like *baby?* The man was going to think she was one of those women for whom all roads lead to marriage and children.

Steven was gracious enough to ignore her embarrassment, obvious as it was. "I agree," he said. "I'm convinced because of thunderstorms, the kind that seem to shake the ground itself. And because of the way little kids laugh, from way down deep in their middle, just because they're so full of joy they can't hold it in."

Melissa's eyes smarted, and her throat thickened, too. "Yeah," she managed to croak out, after what seemed like a long time.

Steven smiled, stretched out a hand to her.

Melissa hesitated only briefly, then took it. He led her

out of the house, with its benign ghosts and soft, musty shadows, into the deep grass that was once a lawn.

With a sweep of his free arm, he indicated the surrounding countryside. "Now it's your turn, Melissa," he said, his gaze resting gently on her face. "Show me the Stone Creek Ranch you remember, the parts of it you loved the best."

The request quickened something inside Melissa. "Okay," she said.

They took his truck, since there wouldn't have been room for Zeke in the roadster and neither of them had the heart to leave the dog behind.

She directed him to the pioneer cemetery first, the place where generations of O'Ballivans were buried, along with her dad and Big John, her grandfather.

"Olivia and I used to come up here on horseback all the time," Melissa confided, with a slight smile. "We were hoping to see a ghost and absolutely terrified that we might get our wish."

Steven grinned. "You and Olivia? What about Ashley?"

"She didn't care much for riding horses," she answered. "And even less for ghosts."

He laughed.

She loved the sound of his laugh.

"So," Steven began presently, looking around that peaceful place, "did you ever get your wish? See a ghost?"

She knew her answer would surprise him. "Once or twice, I thought I did," she said softly, remembering. "But it happened in the ranch house, not here."

Steven arched an eyebrow, ever so slightly, and the breeze raised tendrils of his hair, as if offering a mischievous caress. And he waited for her to elaborate.

"A glimpse of a figure, out of the corner of my eye, that's all it was," she said. She'd been comforted, rather than frightened, by the experience.

After a few moments, during which the two of them tacitly agreed that it was time to move on, Steven whistled for Zeke, who'd gone exploring amid the tall grass, sheltered, like the graves, within the cluster of flourishing oak trees.

Their next stop was the high ridge, with its spectacular view of both Stone Creek Ranch and, in the near distance, the town as well. Melissa had hoped for a sighting of King's Ransom, the legendary wild stallion that sometimes put in an appearance, but that day, he kept himself and his band of mares and foals well hidden.

"There's still the house, of course," Melissa said, once she was settled in the passenger seat of Steven's flashy truck again, figuring the tour was complete, "but since it's occupied, that part will have to wait."

Steven smiled, looked back at Zeke to make sure he was settled, and started up the engine.

Something had definitely changed between herself and Steven, Melissa thought. There was still tension, of course, but the strange sense of urgency had passed. Being together seemed only natural now, and easy.

Things just sort of unfolded after that, with no hurry and no fretting and no drama.

"What will it be, Melissa?" he asked her, very quietly and after a long silence, when they were back at his place, inside the tour bus. "Is it now, or is it never?"

"How about now?" Melissa murmured, realizing, as her heartbeat quickened and her breath caught, that she was completely lost. If the scent of lilacs had made her drunk, this man's close proximity affected her like opium.

Of course she could have cited chapter and verse on why she shouldn't go to bed with Steven Creed—they'd only been acquainted for a couple of days, and that was just the start of it. He could be six kinds of bastard and a few besides, for all she knew.

But she also knew—*had* known from the moment they met, actually—that making love with him, for better or worse, for heaven or for heartbreak, was as inevitable as the turning of the seasons.

Melissa had only been inside her brother's fancy bus a few times—Brad had expressly forbidden any of his three younger sisters to consort with his band—but she knew where the main bedroom was. And knew they were headed straight for it.

Steven laid her down on the bed gently, his eyes at once troubled and hungry. "Are you sure about this?" he asked.

Melissa nodded, swallowed. "I'm sure," she said.

Like hell.

He sat down on the edge of the bed, pulled off his boots, tossed them aside. Otherwise, Steven was fully dressed, just as she was.

Turning his head to look down at her, he smiled very slightly. "You knew this would happen," he said. The statement might have been a mere guess, it might have been an accusation.

It might have been both.

"So did you," Melissa replied, scooting over, so he could stretch out beside her, which he did.

"Some things," he agreed, in that same gruff voice, "are written in the stars."

She smiled up at him. "You're a poet on top of all your other charms."

He laughed. "Woman," he said, easing the skirt of her sundress up over her knees and then higher still, to the middle of her thighs, "poetry is the *least* of my charms."

She felt so crazy-happy, and the emotion was all the sweeter because she knew it wouldn't last. The *real* Melissa was hardheaded and practical, and wherever she'd gone, she'd definitely be back. With a vengeance. "And you're arrogant, too."

But his face had changed. He sat up, frowning, touching her with just the tips of his fingers.

Melissa remembered the cuts and bruises she'd sustained that morning, though she couldn't actually *feel* a single one of them. No, all she felt was Steven's caress, and the desire for more contact and then still more.

"This happened today?" he asked. "When you were *almost* hit by a car?"

Melissa bit her lower lip. "Yes," she said. "But—"

He met her gaze, his expression grave. "You're hurt," he said. And just like that, he was up and off the bed, moving away from her. He disappeared into the bathroom and returned almost immediately with a drugstore first-aid kit.

Still adjusting to the shift in mood, Melissa nearly laughed, out of pure nervousness, and started to shinny upright.

Steven stopped her, though, with just a look.

"You keep a first-aid kit handy?" she asked.

Stupid question, since he obviously did. But there it was.

"I have a five-year-old son," he reminded her.

He set the white plastic box aside, on the table next

to the bed, and that was when she noticed that he'd just happened to bring a small, easily recognizable packet along, too.

A condom. Anticipation returned, washing over Melissa in one great tsunami-like wave.

"Let's get you out of that dress," he said next.

And he simply whisked the whole thing right off over her head, without any sort of wasted motion.

Melissa had been undressed by a few men before, of course, but never in such a deft and matter-of-fact way. The yearning, strong before, pressed on her like a weight now, making it hard for her to breathe.

"That was—direct," she gasped, as a flush moved from her hairline to her toes. Goose bumps rose in its wake.

"I'm nothing if not direct," Steven said. Then he began applying some kind of medicine to her injuries, lightly and with skill.

"I've already used ointment," she struggled to say. Her body wanted to rise to him, to the touch of his hands, her back wanted to arch and her legs to part.

"Well, now you're getting more," Steven answered.

Oh, God, Melissa thought desperately, as his fingertips moved like a whispering breeze over the tingling flesh of her thighs and her knees, then her arms and shoulders.

He gave another of those raspy chuckles she was beginning to recognize as a hallmark of his personality. "Oh, lady, as roughed up as you are, you are *beyond* beautiful."

Apparently, they were past the first-aid stage.

Melissa suppressed a moan of pure need as she watched Steven stand up, unbutton his shirt partway, and then impatiently haul the garment off over his head.

His chest was broad, his muscle tone was good and a light dusting of hair, the color of brown sugar, caught the light.

"You're sure?" he asked again.

The longer she looked at him, the surer she was.

"Yes," she said. It was an ache, that simple word.

He didn't take off his jeans then, which was probably a mercy, Melissa figured, because she already wanted him so badly that she might have bolted right up off that bed and tackled him to the floor if she'd seen what was under them. Not that his erection didn't show, because it strained against that thin layer of denim.

The mattress dipped and he was beside her again, gathering her close, deftly unhooking her bra, so that skin met skin. Kissing her so deeply, so thoroughly, that she couldn't hold still any longer.

Her body flexed on the bed, already slick with need, and burning. Burning everywhere. She was on fire, and nothing had even happened yet.

She felt his thumb slide under the elastic on her panties, and then those were gone, too, as easily as if they'd dissolved under the heat of his hand.

His hand. It was between her legs now, stroking her, teasing her, subtly parting her.

He kissed his way down her neck, stopped to nibble at her left breast, then her right. She was squirming, even whimpering a little, by the time he left the nipples, wet from his mouth and so hard that they nearly hurt.

He reached her belly, tasting her skin, his fingers still plying her.

Melissa's whole body buckled in reaction; if he kept this up, she'd have an orgasm *way* too soon. She didn't realize she'd voiced this concern aloud until Steven laughed and shifted, kneeling between her legs now.

"Go ahead and let yourself go if you need to," he drawled, leaning forward now, his hands gently possessive on her breasts. "There will be plenty more where that came from."

Another groan escaped her, fierce, almost primordial.

And then he lowered himself to her, parted her with his fingers, flicked at her with the tip of his tongue.

Melissa's hips surged upward, and she made a sob-like sound, hoarse with lust.

He tempted. He teased. He feasted, and then withdrew, and then feasted again.

Melissa buried her fingers in his hair, frantic. Her body flew, but Steven stayed with her.

She began to quiver all over, and perspiration misted her skin, made wisps and tendrils of her hair stick to her neck and her cheeks and her forehead. Finally, she pleaded, in a scratchy rasp....

And the climax came, shattering, a thing of light and heat and fire, blinding her, wringing guttural shouts from her throat, causing her heels to dig deep into the surface of the mattress.

Steven held her afterward, until the trembling had eased, until she could breathe, and then got up, a haze at the periphery of her vision, and got out of his jeans.

She hadn't seen his shaft—everything was blurry— but she *felt* it all right, because he was soon on top of her. The length of him, hard and hot, pressed against her abdomen and belly, a physical portent of what was about to happen.

Melissa moaned again, as all the melted-honey satisfaction of her recent climax instantly morphed into something greedy and feverish and utterly wild.

Steven shifted his weight slightly, careful not to

crush her, and she knew he was putting on the condom. Even that move was graceful.

He kissed her again, then looked straight into her eyes and said, "Last chance to say no."

Melissa arched her back, inviting him inside her in that way as old as the human race, and now it was Steven who groaned. He was part of her in one swift, fiery stroke, sheathed to the hilt.

She reveled in the sensation of being conquered and, at the same time, conquering. By tacit agreement, they both lay still for a few long, delicious moments, simply savoring this most intimate of all connections.

As soon as he began to move, though, Melissa was lost.

She bucked under him, like a wild mare being broke to ride, and clawed at his shoulders and his back, and there was something so primitive, so freeing, in the joining that a terrible, consuming joy rose up inside her.

On and on it went, the delicious tension rising, rising—and then the peak. Melissa wept as she gave herself up to Steven Creed, completely, eagerly, without reservation or shame.

His whole body stiffened as, at last, he surrendered, his head thrown back, the muscles cording in his neck.

Then he collapsed beside her, one leg still sprawled across her thighs, and both of them lay gasping.

It was a long time—a very long time—before either of them spoke.

In the end, it was Steven who broke the silence.

Melissa's face was wet with tears, and he dried them with the side of one thumb, kissed the traces of them away.

"Did I hurt you?" he asked, and he sounded genuinely worried.

Melissa laughed softly. "*Hurt* me? Mister, if that was pain, bring on the next round."

His eyes, his wonderful blue eyes, remained solemn, and the chortling sound he made came out brief and a little raw. "Then why the tears?"

She crooned a sigh. She was soft everywhere, inside and out. And more deeply satisfied than she'd ever imagined it was possible to be. "Because it was so good," she said, tracing the line of his jaw with the tip of one index finger.

He ventured a smile then, shook his head. "Women," he said.

He got up, disappeared into the bathroom again, then came back.

Melissa looked at Steven, saw that he was hard again, and held out her arms to him.

THE MEAT LOAF was pretty good, in Steven's opinion, and after several hours with Melissa O'Ballivan, definitely the hottest woman he'd ever encountered, in or out of bed, he was ravenously hungry.

He was managing to keep his misgivings at bay, but he knew they were slinking around like wolves on the fringes of the light from a campfire, waiting to pounce.

She sat across the table from him now, fresh from the shower they'd just shared, wearing his T-shirt and nothing else. He felt downright overdressed in his jeans and the shirt he'd been wearing earlier.

Melissa picked up her fork, but instead of taking a bite of food, she looked around. Smiled.

"What?" Steven asked, amused, but feeling a touch of something else, too. Something proprietary, though he wasn't ready to call it jealousy.

"It's ironic," she answered, with a saucy twist of her

mouth and a twinkle in her beautiful eyes. "I've been inside this bus maybe three times in my life—Brad bought it for the guys in his band, while Ashley and I were still in high school, and Olivia had just started college. And none of us were allowed anywhere *near* it unless he was with us—he was that determined to protect our virtue."

Steven smiled. "Can't say I blame the man for that," he commented. "Looking out for three sisters—especially *kid* sisters—has to be a challenge."

Melissa took a few bites, looking pleasantly thoughtful. Then she asked, "Do you have sisters, Steven?"

He shook his head. "I'm an only child," he said.

"That sounds lonely."

"You know what they say. A person can be lonely in a crowd."

"That's true," Melissa admitted. "And I have to admit, there were times when I wouldn't have minded being an only child myself."

"Did you always want to be a lawyer?"

"No," she replied. "My first ambition was to reign as queen of Stone Creek Rodeo Days."

"Did you?"

"Sure did," Melissa answered. "When I was nineteen. Did *you* always want to be a lawyer?"

Steven paused a moment before shaking his head. "Nope," he said. "I planned on running a ranch, like my dad."

"What changed your mind?"

Steven was a little surprised to find himself discussing a matter he'd barely talked about with Zack, his best friend, or Brody and Conner, his cousins. "Ranching was in my blood," he said, "but so was the law, as it turned out. My grandfather founded one of the biggest firms east of the Mississippi. It was a family business."

"Was?" Melissa's tone was casual, but she was watching him closely.

"My uncles still run it. It wasn't the same after my mother and grandfather passed away."

"Wasn't there a place for you—afterward?" she asked.

Steven shook his head. "Not one I'd fit into," he said. "Zack—Matt's father—was a good friend of mine, from way back. He put in a good word for me where he worked, and I moved to Denver." He paused, looking back. It wasn't something he allowed himself to do very often; in his opinion, there wasn't much to gain by indulging in personal retrospectives. "Turned out I liked practicing criminal law a lot better than corporate. And I was good at it."

"But you didn't stay," Melissa said smoothly.

He grinned. "You must be pretty good in a courtroom yourself," he observed. Though the remark had been prompted by her subtle way of going after sensitive information, Steven meant what he was saying. Melissa wasn't just beautiful, she was smart, and most likely successful at just about everything she did.

Take sex, for instance.

Melissa smiled, and that was almost Steven's undoing. When the lady smiled, her eyes shone and her whole face lit up. "I do all right," she replied easily. Then she drew a deep breath, let it out, and squared her shoulders. "So," she went on. "What brings you to Stone Creek?"

"It's a great place to raise a kid," Steven said.

"So are lots of other places, like Denver. And Boston. And wherever else you've been in your travels."

Like Lonesome Bend, Colorado, he thought, with a touch of sadness.

He didn't see any need to tell Melissa about the experience that had soured him on the place. So he merely raised and lowered one shoulder slightly in what was meant to serve as a shrug. "As you probably know, your sister-in-law and I are distantly related. Turns out the founders of the McKettrick and Creed clans were half brothers. Meg tracked me down online, and we started emailing back and forth. The more she told me about Stone Creek, the more it appealed to me. I paid a brief visit, met Meg and the rest of the McKettrick family, saw that this ranch was for sale and made an offer."

Melissa bit down on her lower lip, her eyes luminous with worried curiosity. "Today at lunch, you mentioned spending summers on a Colorado ranch while you were growing up. Is that near Denver?"

Steven nodded. "It's outside a town called Lonesome Bend. My dad and stepmother still live there, when they're not traveling around the country in their RV. My cousin Conner runs the operation now."

"Your cousin?" She arched one eyebrow. The woman didn't miss much. "If the ranch was your home, at least part of the time, why not make a life there?"

He sat back, folded his arms. Tessa Quinn's meat loaf was fantastic, but he was satisfied. When it came to food, anyway. "Conner and Brody's father was the firstborn son in his generation. He inherited the ranch when my grandparents were both gone, and even though my dad stepped in and took over after his older brother died, there was never any question of ownership. Legally, the ranch passed to my cousins when they turned twenty-one."

"And your dad was just out in the cold after that?"

Steven grinned. "Hardly. The executors paid Dad a good salary for taking care of the spread, not to mention raising Conner and Brody, and he had some money of his own to start with. He's a master saddle maker—there aren't many of those left—and he fills custom orders for a pretty elite list of customers."

Melissa smiled. "When he's not RVing with your stepmother?"

"It's a big RV," Steven answered. "Dad does a lot of work on the road."

Melissa, also through eating, rested her forearms on the table and leaned forward a little way. "Does it bother you?" she asked.

"Does what bother me?"

"That your cousins each got a share of the ranch but you evidently didn't?"

"No," Steven said. "That was the deal. I knew it from the beginning. And, anyway, Conner and Brody offered me a third of the outfit. I turned it down."

"Because?"

"Because I wanted to build a legacy of my own," Steven said.

She spread her hands. "And here you are," she said, with another of those wrenching smiles of hers.

"Here I am," he agreed.

"Have you ever been in love?"

Steven chuckled. "Yeah," he said. "At least, I thought so at the time."

"But you were mistaken?"

"I guess you could say that."

"What was she like?"

"Beautiful. Smart. Tough as nails."

They were quiet for a few moments, while Melissa mulled over what he'd said. For his part, Steven was content just to look at her, though he wouldn't have said no to more sex.

"How about you?" he asked, in good time. "Have you ever been in love?"

As soon as he'd asked that question, he regretted it, because the atmosphere changed. He saw Melissa draw further into herself; her smile wobbled and the happy light in her eyes dimmed a little.

"I guess it's only fair, your asking me that," she said. "Since I asked *you* the same thing about two minutes ago."

His heart went out to her, and he wasn't sure it was going to find its way back where it belonged anytime soon.

He reached across the narrow table, took her hand, gave her fingers a light squeeze. "Another time," he said, watching her. Thinking he might just fall right into the blue of her eyes, tumbling head over heels forever, never hitting bottom.

"No," she said, shaking her head. "Fair is fair."

"If you don't feel like talking, Melissa, that's all right."

Melissa looked straight into his eyes, didn't move to pull her hand from his grasp, but it was a long time before she spoke. "His name was—*is*—Dan Guthrie. He wanted to get married, and he had these two great kids. I said yes. But every time we tried to go through with the plan and actually throw a wedding, I'd back off. Eventually, Dan got tired of that, and he—well—he's married to someone else now. They're going to have a baby."

Steven wanted to ask if she still loved this Guthrie

yahoo, but he figured there had been enough soul-baring for one night.

Besides that, he wasn't sure he could stand hearing the answer.

CHAPTER ELEVEN

PINK AND GOLD CRACKS split the dawn sky as Melissa rose from Steven Creed's bed, being careful not to wake him, crept into the bathroom for a hasty shower and slipped back into the sundress she'd worn the night before.

Common sense said to get out while the getting was good—she definitely didn't want Brad or Meg to find her there at that hour, if they had to bring Matt home early for some reason, for instance—but she couldn't resist leaning down to plant a whisper-light kiss on Steven's forehead before leaving. And when she did, he took her by the shoulders and eased her down beside him.

Startled, she gave a little shriek as she landed. Then she laughed and scrambled right back up again, careful to stay out of his reach this time.

Steven yawned luxuriously and cupped his hands behind his head, watching her with a glint of mischief in his eyes and a grin resting on his mouth. "Leaving so soon?" he asked, in a teasing tone.

"'Soon'?" Melissa echoed, pretending indignation. "I got here at six o'clock last night, and now the *sun* is about to come up. I should have left hours ago."

"I'm glad you didn't."

She couldn't help smiling; she felt so good. "I'm glad, too," she admitted. "But I've got to go. All the neighbors will probably see me pulling in at first light as it is, and I'm due at the office in a couple of hours."

"Right," Steven said, sounding resigned. Outside in the narrow hallway, Zeke gave an anxious little whimper. "Dog needs to go outside," he added, sitting up and starting to throw back the comforter.

Knowing only too well what was *under* that comforter, Melissa turned on her heel and rushed out. "Come on, boy," she told the waiting canine. "I'll let you out."

As she retreated, Zeke hurrying along behind her, she heard Steven chuckle.

Moments later, he appeared in the doorway of the bus, barefoot and shirtless, with his jeans misbuttoned. Melissa had been waiting for Zeke to relieve himself so she could let him back into the bus before starting for town. Seeing Steven shook her resolve a little, though.

Did he have to look so damn good, even five minutes after he got out of bed? He hadn't shaved or showered or even combed his hair, and he still made her ache for more of the same.

"Call you later?" Steven asked, shoving a hand through his hair.

Melissa could still feel the silken texture of that hair between her fingers. "Okay," she said. "Thanks for—" Heat surged into her face. "Thanks for supper."

He grinned. "Thanks for coming," he said mildly.

Another blush followed the first one, winding up at Melissa's hairline, where she could feel it throbbing in time with her heartbeat. She was *damned* if she'd say, You're welcome. "Okay," she repeated, heading for her car as the dog frolicked toward his master.

Melissa jumped into her car, started the engine and

drove away. Fast. Her face didn't cool down until she was almost at the town limits.

After that, she thought about how conspicuous her car was. If she'd been driving a normal subcompact, or some kind of sedan, she might have a chance of going unnoticed. In a bright red replica of an MG Roadster—not so much.

Melissa straightened her spine. Breathed in the fresh morning air, and tried to think sensibly. She'd had a relationship with Dan, after all, and the whole town knew it. Why was she so worried that news of her night with Steven Creed would get around?

She bit her lower lip. It definitely wasn't about shame or embarrassment—that much she was sure of. So *what,* then?

It didn't take her long to figure it out. Her time with Steven was precious and, therefore, *private.* She needed a while to process all that had happened, to make some kind of sense of things.

Good luck with that, she thought.

She was especially careful to stay within the speed limit as she cruised through town, because all she needed right then was for an early-rising Tom Parker to pull her over and give her a ticket.

At home, she parked the car in her tiny detached garage instead of leaving it at the curb or in the driveway, feeling grateful that none of the neighbors seemed to be stirring yet. She made a dash for the back door, keys in hand, and ducked inside like some fugitive two steps ahead of the law.

This morning, she was determined, would be like any *other* morning.

She got into shorts and a sports bra and a tank top, pulled on some socks and her running shoes, left again by way of the front door, pausing on the porch to lock up before slipping her ribbon-strung key over her neck.

The cuts and bruises from yesterday's fall hadn't been magically healed, but they didn't hurt the way they did before, either, so she warmed up as usual and jogged through the gate and down the sidewalk, following her favorite route.

Running always straightened out any tangles in Melissa's brain, and this run was no exception.

Mentally, she reviewed the situation. Fact: she'd slept with Steven Creed. Fact: she'd enjoyed the experience, and she wasn't one bit sorry. Fact: she'd better watch out, if she didn't want her heart smashed to bits all over again.

She dried a stray tear with the back of one hand and picked up her pace.

She jogged along Main Street, not stopping in for a bottle of deliciously cold water as she passed the Sunflower Café after lapping the town park three times, then headed for home.

All was quiet at Ashley's but, hey, she thought, with a small smile, it was early. The ancient ones were probably still snoozing away in their various beds, but who knew what they'd be up to after a hearty breakfast.

Minutes later, cooling down in her side yard, Melissa heard the phone ringing inside, and the tone seemed oddly urgent. She unlocked the door and hurried inside.

"Hello?" she sputtered. Not her usual way of answering.

"Hello," Tom responded. "Any chance you can come in early today?"

A prickle danced up Melissa's spine and then back down again. "I guess. Why?"

Tom was quiet for a moment. "It's the Carter kid—

Nathan," he finally went on. "One of my deputies ran him in last night for loitering—mainly so the boy would have someplace to sleep. This morning, Carter's claiming that Pete knocked him around, and he's got a shiner to prove it. Says he wants to press charges."

Melissa released a long sigh. Deputy Pete Ferguson, a solid citizen with a wife and four kids and a sterling reputation in the community. It was hard to imagine him abusing his authority in any way whatsoever.

"Great," she muttered.

"You're the prosecutor, O'Ballivan," Tom said, his tone light, but grim, too. "Ferguson is being accused of a felony. And he's beside himself over it. So you'd better get down here and decide whether or not the people have a case."

"I'll be there," Melissa confirmed. "Tell Pete to hold on."

She took a quick shower, got dressed and skipped the makeup, except for mascara and a swipe of lip gloss.

Melissa paused only briefly to check herself out in the full-length mirror before leaving the bedroom. Her tailored black slacks and peacock-blue silk blouse made her feel—and look—more like her old self. And that was important because, since last night, she hadn't been quite sure *who* the heck she was.

As soon as she set foot inside the municipal building, a sense of dread settled over her spirit. After pausing to steel herself for a moment, Melissa marched down the corridor to Tom's office, drew a deep breath outside his door, let it out again and went in.

Steven was standing by Tom's desk, all spiffed up for the day and yet still managing to look like a man who'd just enjoyed a night of lively sex.

Which, of course, he was. Moreover, he was a lawyer, there to represent *someone*—Pete? Nathan Carter?

It was anybody's guess, at that point, but one thing was for sure. Steven would inevitably side against her.

Melissa felt dazed, as though she'd collided with an invisible brick wall, crazy as it seemed.

Steven looked as cool as could be, in no apparent hurry to do anything.

His mouth crooked up at one corner when his gaze connected with Melissa's, after a slow cruise from her feet to her face. He was trying to unsettle her, of course, and it was working.

Melissa felt strangely *exposed,* as though Steven had X-ray vision or her clothes had turned to cellophane.

"Morning," he drawled. His eyes and that faint grin said it all.

He'd played her body the way Charlie Daniels plays a fiddle, during the night, and he wasn't going to pretend it hadn't happened, much as she wanted to do exactly that.

Melissa hoped Tom hadn't picked up on the note of intimacy in Steven's tone. He'd razz her mercilessly if he knew what was going on.

"Good morning," she replied stiffly, as though she and Steven were mere acquaintances instead of very recent lovers. She glanced past him, as dismissively as she could, toward the cells, where Nathan stood behind bars, smirking at her.

Pete Ferguson, who had been fidgeting at his desk, bolted to his feet. "It's a lie, Melissa," he blurted out. "You *know* I'd never rough up a prisoner—"

Carter simply pointed to his eye, which was nearly swollen shut, the flesh around it shot through with varying shades of purple and green as well as bruise-blue.

Nobody spoke for a few moments.

Then Steven cleared his throat and said, "In addition to the injury Mr. Carter suffered, there seems to be some question of Deputy Ferguson's reasons for detaining him in the first place."

Melissa felt as though she'd been kicked in the solar plexus. Hard. "You're representing Mr. Carter, then?"

Ferguson, tall and clean-cut, with a military haircut and pale blue eyes, looked sick. Tom just looked disgusted.

"It would be more accurate to say I'm advising him," Steven said. His tone was even, though a bedrock of resolve ran beneath it.

Melissa turned on Nathan Carter. He looked her over insolently, and the effect was quite different from when Steven had done almost the same thing. "What happened?" she asked.

"He was hanging around the park, and it looked like he didn't have any place to spend the night," Pete put in. "So I bought him a hamburger and let him sleep in the cell."

"You'll have your turn, Pete," Melissa said calmly. "Right now, I want to hear Mr. Carter's side of the story."

"I told the deputy I was fine with sleeping in the park," Nathan said. The smirk was gone now, replaced by a cagey narrowing of his eyes. "He said that was vagrancy and he had to take me in. When I argued with him, he put his fist in my face."

"That's not true!" Deputy Ferguson protested heatedly.

"Pete," Tom said, very quietly.

"But Carter already *had* that black eye when I approached him," Pete insisted. Color pulsed in his neck and his round, earnest face.

"I guess it's his word against mine," Nathan said, his tone dejected.

"Or not," Steven said mildly.

Melissa ignored him. "Were there any witnesses?" she asked, looking at Nathan.

Tom gave a derisive snort.

Melissa flashed him a look, which he returned in kind.

"Unless specific charges are being brought against Mr. Carter," Steven interjected, "I would suggest releasing him."

Melissa held her temper, while Tom made a production of jingling his keys, crossing to the cell and unlocking the door.

"You're free to go," he told the erstwhile prisoner.

"Whoop-de-do," Nathan mocked, waltzing through the opening and crossing the room to stand next to Steven. "How about locking up the deputy, there?" Again, he indicated his shiner. "I'm accusing him of police brutality."

Pete turned crimson.

Tom shut the cell door with a clang.

"Be quiet," Steven told Nathan, who remained in the sheriff's office.

Melissa turned to Pete. "What's your story?" she asked him. He was an old friend, like Tom, but if he *had* struck Carter without adequate provocation, there would be repercussions.

Miserably, Pete recounted the events of the night before. He'd been on routine patrol, he said, and spotted somebody skulking around the bandstand in the town park. He'd gotten out of his car and walked over, with a flashlight, to investigate.

Carter had flipped him some attitude, but it was nothing serious. The boy had ridden in the front seat of the squad car, without cuffs, and they'd both had burgers and fries from the drive-through at McDonald's. Pete added that he'd thought about taking Nathan home with him, letting him sleep on the couch, instead of parking him in a cell, but he'd decided against that because of the wife and kids.

"Are you going to arrest him or not?" Nathan barked, when the tale ended.

"No," Melissa said. "Not without a credible witness to verify that Deputy Ferguson actually struck you."

"Then I want to sue the Stone Creek County Sheriff's Office," Nathan said. "I want to sue the whole damn *town!* My rights have been violated here!"

Melissa didn't look at Nathan Carter, but at Steven. "Have at it," she said.

"Just go," Steven told the younger man, holding Melissa's gaze with no problem at all. He produced a wallet from the inside pocket of his spiffy suit coat and handed Carter some money.

Nathan hesitated, then snatched the bills from Steven's hand and stormed out of the sheriff's office.

Over by the water cooler, Elvis yawned loudly, making his presence known for the first time, and then shook himself hard, so that his ears made a loud flapping sound.

That broke the silence that had descended after Nathan's outburst.

"Go on home," Tom said to Pete Ferguson.

"I'm not suspended, pending some kind of investigation?" Pete asked, turning to the sheriff.

Tom shook his head. "No," he said.

Pete left, giving Melissa a wounded glance as he passed her.

Tom, meanwhile, focused on Steven. "I guess your work here is done, counselor, for the moment, anyway."

In other words, Melissa thought, *Get the hell out of my office.* She was inclined to agree.

Steven smiled, nodded politely and headed for the door.

Melissa would have waited until she was sure he was gone to duck out, but the fact was, she wasn't any more eager to deal with Tom than with Steven at the moment.

Steven was waiting in the hall. Melissa ignored him, walking on by. He stopped her by reaching out and taking a light but firm hold on her elbow.

Her temper flared. "I can't believe you would actually consider representing that scumbag!" she whispered, her fury at such a fever pitch that the words just formed themselves, seemingly independent of her brain, and came tumbling out of her mouth. "Pete Ferguson would step off the sidewalk and into the street before he'd *squash a bug* under his shoe, let alone manhandle anybody. And as for Carter—"

"Whoa," Steven said. "Everybody has a right to counsel. Or were you out sick when they covered the fundamentals the first week of law school?"

Melissa jerked her elbow free, in no mood to be reasoned with. "Yes," she agreed tartly, "everybody *does* have the right to counsel. But before you take on any more clients, you might want to take the trouble to find out what kind of people they are!"

"It doesn't matter what kind of people they are," Steven replied moderately. "The law is the law."

She took a step back. "Pete Ferguson's father was the

last sheriff," she said. "Before that, it was his grandfather, and before *that,* his great-grandfather. The Fergusons are some of the finest people in this community—"

Steven leaned in, so his nose was nearly touching hers. "*Beside the point,* counselor," he said. "If your friend, Deputy Ferguson, gave Nathan Carter a working over, I'll nail him for it."

For a long moment, they just glared at each other.

Then Steven turned and walked away.

Melissa didn't move until he'd disappeared through the outside doorway. It took her that long to calm down enough to set foot inside her office.

She was immediately met with a whole new Andrea. Gone were the jeans, the hair spikes, the too-tight T-shirts, the heavy eye shadow and the white lipstick. She was wearing a nice skirt, a white blouse and modest makeup.

Melissa couldn't help staring. "What happened to you?" she asked.

The girl straightened her spine and lifted her chin. The expression in her eyes was completely earnest, and she held Melissa's direct gaze without looking away. "I'm turning over a new leaf, that's all," she replied, with a little sniff. "Byron says it's important to look professional."

Melissa barely kept herself from smiling at that one. "Oh?"

Andrea nodded and then pushed back her chair and stood. "I even made coffee. It should be ready by now."

Melissa raised both her hands, palms out. "Sit down, Andrea," she said. "I was only teasing before. Making coffee really *isn't* in your job description."

"Can't a person do something nice for somebody?"

Andrea asked. Her lower lip was wobbling now, and her eyes misted over.

"Sit down," Melissa repeated, but gently.

Andrea sagged into her chair.

"What's this all about? This big transformation, I mean?"

"I almost ran over you yesterday morning," Andrea burst out, and a tear slid down her cheek. "I—I guess I'm just trying to—well—*make up* for what could have happened to you, at least partly, if—if—"

Melissa felt a burning sensation behind her own eyes now. "You've apologized," she reminded her assistant. "You've promised to be more careful in the future. You don't need to do anything more, Andrea."

Andrea absorbed that in silence, looking straight ahead. Her hands rested on the surface of her desk, fingers tightly interlaced.

Melissa waited a few moments, then asked, "Were there any messages?"

"Mrs. Brady called," Andrea said, turning her head. "So did Mrs. Hillingsley. They agree on *one* thing, anyway, that the Parade Committee meeting didn't go very well."

Meeting? It was a beat before Melissa recalled the great toilet-paper debate, and how she'd suggested that the committee gather right away to settle it.

"Oh," she said.

"Half of them want to let Mrs. Hillingsley decorate the Chamber of Commerce float any way she pleases," Andrea went on, a smile creeping over her mouth as she spoke, no longer gazing off into the beyond, "and the other half say there'll be hell to pay if she embarrasses the whole town of Stone Creek by decking the thing with miles of toilet paper."

Melissa muttered under her breath. If troublemakers like Nathan Carter didn't give her a migraine, the Parade Committee would. "Did anyone else call?"

"Mr. Blake left a voice mail," Andrea said. "It was so long that I thought it'd be better if you just listened to it yourself, instead of me trying to write it all down. You know how he rambles on."

Oh, indeed she did.

"More space aliens landing in his cornfield and scaring his sheep?" Melissa asked.

Andrea nodded, then gave a little giggle. "Sorry," she said, after a moment, clearly insincere.

Melissa heaved out a sigh. "Okay," she said. "That's everything, then?"

"That's everything," Andrea said.

Melissa practically dove into her office.

Concentrating on her work proved to be a challenge for the rest of the morning—she kept thinking about Steven, and the things they'd done together the night before, juxtaposed against the cold, hard reality of their separate philosophies concerning the practice of law.

She was a prosecutor.

He was a defense attorney.

There were similarities between them, of course, but just then, the differences looked a whole lot bigger.

CHAPTER TWELVE

JUST BEFORE NOON, Melissa saved a computer document to the file labeled "to be reviewed" and noticed for the first time that she was hungry. That morning's after-jog smoothie had definitely worn off.

Too bad the residual effects of Steven Creed's *lovemaking* hadn't—or those of the confrontation outside of Tom's office after Nathan Carter's release from jail. The occasional faint aftershock still rocked her—at once delicious and annoying.

Melissa decided to remain in the office over her lunch hour, although the day was lovely and it would have been a lot more fun to munch away on a half sandwich and a fruit cup from the little market down on the corner.

So, silently telling herself to *get over it* all the while, she had strawberry yogurt from her stash in the break-room fridge instead.

And she waited.

When she couldn't sit still for another moment, she stood up and walked out of her private office, past Andrea and into the corridor.

Tom was sitting at his desk when she walked in, scribbling away at some form on a clipboard. Seeing her, he pushed the paperwork away and got to his feet. His desk chair creaked in the process.

She didn't speak right away, so he spread his hands wide and said, "What?"

"Do you have any idea what kind of problems you've opened yourself up to?" Melissa demanded. "Maybe it was all right to throw someone into jail just to get them off the street back in the day, but it isn't anymore!"

Tom's eyes twinkled, though he looked weary, too. "Tell it to Pete Ferguson," he said, slowly sinking back into his chair. "*He* made the arrest."

"*You* tell him," Melissa snapped in response. "You're his boss."

Tom arched an eyebrow. "Are you through?" he asked, with a grin he couldn't quite suppress, though he did make a visible attempt.

Melissa began to pace. "Carter *could* sue the county for false arrest," she reminded her friend. "And even if Steven Creed didn't take the case, some ambulance chaser from Flagstaff or Phoenix would be thrilled to do it!"

Tom nodded toward the chair facing his desk. "Sit down," he said. "You're making me nervous."

She plunked herself onto the seat, arms folded.

"Speaking of Creed," Tom said, when she didn't speak, "what's going on between you two?"

"Who says anything is 'going on'?" Melissa countered, perhaps too quickly.

"Oh, come on," Tom said. "The air was *flammable* in here this morning. Good thing nobody smokes in public buildings anymore, because the whole crowd of us might have gone up in a blast if anybody had flicked a lighter or struck a match."

Melissa folded her arms. "I'm not discussing Steven Creed with you," she said. She wanted to discuss Steven with *someone*—Ashley and Olivia were both likely candidates—but not Tom. Definitely not Tom, because he'd tease her to death if she admitted anything.

Tom chuckled. "All right," he said, spreading his hands in a gesture of affable acquiescence. "But don't think you're fooling anybody, because you're not."

Melissa took a step toward him. Let her arms fall to her sides. "Speaking of not fooling anyone," she said, "remember our bet? You were supposed to ask Tessa Quinn out for dinner or a movie—or have you forgotten?"

He reddened slightly, under the jaw.

Elvis made a rhythmic thumping sound against the floor as he scratched under his chin with one hind leg.

"You said the bet was off," Tom told her.

"No, I didn't," Melissa argued. "*You* did. And that's as good as losing, as far as I'm concerned." She leaned in, tucked her fingers under her armpits and flapped her elbows like wings. "Cluck-cluck-cluck."

"Look, it isn't that easy, okay? Tessa comes from a different *world* than I do. She's beautiful. She used to be on TV—God only knows who she's dated in the past and—"

"Cluck," Melissa said. "Cluck. Cluck—"

"Stop it," Tom ordered.

"Arrest me," Melissa challenged.

"That is tempting," came the raspy reply. Tom hooked his thumbs under his belt. "And if you think all this jabbering is throwing me off, you're wrong. I'm a trained investigator, remember. I know there *is* something going on between you and Steven Creed. In fact, I'd go so far as to say you weren't even home last night."

"What makes you say that?"

"I might have driven past your place once or twice."

Melissa raised one eyebrow. Tilted her head to one

side. "Is that right? Well, let's assume, for one wild and crazy moment, that I *did* have something 'going on' with Steven. Why would that be any of your damn business?"

He smiled. "It wouldn't," he conceded. "But I'd be happy about it. The whole damn *county* would be happy, in fact."

Melissa's tone was dangerous, which was fine, since she wanted it that way. "Because—?"

"Because you don't have a life. Ever since you and Dan broke up, you've been—it seems like you're—"

"And I suppose *you* have a life?"

"I get by," Tom hedged.

"'Getting by' doesn't count. You're still a young man, Tom. You're nice-looking and honest and you have a steady job. *Lots* of women would be interested in you, and Tessa might just be one of them, for all you know. I can't believe that as brave a man as you are, you're afraid to risk one tiny rejection."

Tom didn't answer. He just stood there, looking like he was trying to think of a smart-ass comeback, but none was forthcoming.

"All right," Melissa said, "there's a dance at the Grange Hall Saturday night. Why don't you ask Tessa if she'd like to go?"

He let out a breath. "Tessa's always friendly when I stop by the café for coffee, or pick up something from the bakery side," he confessed, "so I get to thinking she might be up for dinner and a movie, anyway, but then at other times she seems pretty distracted, like a lot of things are worrying her. How do I know I'm not misreading the smiles and all that? After all, Tessa is nice to everybody, not just me."

Melissa felt a rush of sisterly tenderness and touched

Tom's arm. "It's a *dance,* Tom. Ask her. Either she'll accept and you'll both have a great time, or she'll refuse, and you'll be able to stop wondering and move on."

He turned stubborn then. "I'll ask Tessa if *you'll* ask Creed," he said.

The depth of her reaction to the suggestion startled Melissa. Suddenly, she wanted to run back to her office and hide behind her work again.

Which was completely crazy, considering the things she and Steven had done in bed together just the night before.

Weren't parts of her still humming with sense memories?

Tom pounced on her hesitation and jumped in feet first. "*Now* who's chicken?" he asked.

Melissa forced herself to relax. Tried for a throw-away smile. "How do I know this isn't a trick?" she asked. "I invite Steven to the dance and then you conveniently fink out on asking Tessa. Where would that leave me?"

"Dancing with Steven Creed?" Tom teased, a grin in his eyes.

"You go first," Melissa said. "And I have to be there when you ask her."

Tom pretended to be horrified. "You don't trust me?"

"Not when it comes to this," she replied, lifting her chin. "You've been waffling for a year, telling me you're going to make a move and then backing off again."

"You expect to *be there* when I talk to Tessa?"

Melissa nodded. Glanced at her watch. "Nearly two o'clock. It would be entirely reasonable for us to go out on a coffee break right about now," she said. "We'll head over to the Sunflower, and when Tessa comes to the table to take our order, you just say something like,

'There's a dance this Saturday night and I was wondering if you'd like to go with me.'"

Tom considered long and hard. It was a measure of how much he really liked Tessa, maybe even *loved* her, that taking such a small risk scared him.

"All right," he finally said. He whistled for Elvis, who got to his feet and crossed the office. Holding the office door open for Melissa, Tom added, "After you, counselor."

"I'm proud of you," Melissa said.

She ducked into her office for her purse—Andrea still wasn't back—and ducked out again.

"There's a catch," Tom informed her, when they were both strapped into the squad car and Elvis had taken up his post in back, behind the folding grill.

Melissa's stomach fluttered slightly. "What kind of catch?"

"Fair is fair," Tom said. "If you get to hang around when I ask Tessa to go to the dance, then the reverse is true. I have to be there when you ask Creed."

Awkward, Melissa thought. Her most recent exchange with Steven hadn't exactly been a friendly one. And, anyway, there was a big difference in situations here—she'd slept with Steven Creed. Recently. There had clearly been no such intimacy between Tom and Tessa.

Still, how could she refuse without explaining? And she certainly wasn't about to admit that she'd spent the night with the man, even though Tom had expressed his suspicions.

"You're on," she said finally. She'd think of a way out later.

Tom nodded and started up the cruiser, and they headed for the Sunflower Café and Bakery. Alice

McCoy was out front on her three-wheeled cart, putting tickets on windshields, and she waved merrily to Tom, one crime fighter acknowledging another.

Tom smiled and waved back, but he looked a little pale around the jawline, and Melissa knew he was nervous.

She felt fairly sympathetic toward him, even—until they walked into the café that is. There was Steven, sitting on the same stool as the first time she'd laid eyes on him, sipping coffee and going over plans with Alex Royce, an architect from Indian Rock.

Steven turned immediately to face Melissa, and his eyes sparked when he looked at her. The corner of his mouth quirked up, too.

Tom was so pleased to see Melissa put on the spot like this that he must have forgotten his own mission, at least for a moment.

"We're on a coffee break," Melissa said, perhaps a touch too loudly.

Conversation ceased all over the small eatery, and everyone looked in their direction. A few people smiled to themselves before going back to their late lunches, early suppers or afternoon snacks.

Steven spoke to Alex, who nodded, and then rose from the counter stool to walk over to Melissa and Tom.

"Have you calmed down a little?" Steven asked, unsmiling, gazing deep into Melissa's eyes. She felt as though she were being *undressed,* and her cheeks flamed.

She flushed, too tongue-tied to speak, while Tom grinned down at her, plainly enjoying her discomfort.

Steven's gaze held hers. "Evidently not," he said, apparently in answer to his own question.

Melissa glared at him. How was she supposed to ask

this obnoxious man out on a *date,* for heaven's sake, and in front of half the town, too?

"I'm fine," she managed.

"That's good to hear," he said.

At the same moment, Tom gave Melissa a light poke with his elbow. "Go ahead," he said, in a stage whisper that probably carried clear past the jukebox and down the short hallway to the restrooms. "Ask him to the dance."

Melissa tallied up her chances of getting away with murder and decided they weren't good. Too many witnesses, for one thing.

So she had to let Tom live. For the moment.

Steven's grin was even more crooked than before. He might have thrown her a lifeline of some sort, said *something,* but not a word came out of that highly kissable mouth. He simply stood there and waited.

Melissa cleared her throat, painfully aware that everybody in the place had an ear cocked that way. "There's a dance at the Grange on Saturday night," she said, because there was no way out. "And I was wondering if you'd like to go." She paused. "With me, I mean."

"Is it Sadie Hawkins' Day?" some redneck joked, from one of the booths.

"Say what?" someone else called.

Steven leaned in, not touching her, though his breath made her lips tingle. "Yes," he said. "I'll go to the dance with you, Melissa O'Ballivan, but only if you agree to pick me up in the roadster."

The tension subsided slightly.

"What's going on?" a customer yelled to a friend on the other side of the café.

"Melissa asked that Creed fella to the Grange Dance!" the friend boomed.

"It's about time she had a date," commented some-one else.

"Good," Melissa said. Then she turned on Tom and glowered up at him. At the edge of her vision, she saw Tessa coming out of the kitchen, looking lovely in her jeans, sleeveless white top and blue cobbler's apron smudged with flour. "Now it's *your* turn."

Steven, after one lingering look of sheer apprecia-tion, excused himself quietly and went back to the coun-ter, where Alex waited with the plans.

The clientele was still being unusually quiet.

"Have a seat," Tessa said, her glance moving ques-tioningly between Melissa and Tom. "Ella will be right with you." Ella was the other waitress.

Melissa flashed Tessa a bright smile. "We were hop-ing you could wait on us personally," she told her friend. "Would you mind?"

"Not at all," Tessa replied, dusting the flour smudge off her front with a few slaps of one hand. "On my way."

As soon as Melissa and Tom had seated themselves at a table in front of the window, Tessa was there, order pad in hand, pencil at the ready.

"Coffee for both of us, please," Melissa said.

Tom sat directly across from her, brooding. He wouldn't look at either Melissa or Tessa.

Melissa kicked him under the table.

Tom started, as though he'd been off in some other world and had just come in for a crash landing.

He looked up at Tessa, his hands so tightly inter-locked that his knuckles showed white, and blurted out, "I guess you wouldn't want to go out with me or any-thing."

Melissa sighed.

Tessa's cheeks turned pink. "I—I mean—"

And nobody in that café, except for Steven and his architect that is, made any pretense of minding their own business.

"See?" Tom said to Melissa.

"Are you talking about—a date?" Tessa faltered.

"Probably wants you to go to the Grange Dance with him on Saturday night," said that same helpful redneck who had spoken up before.

"Oh," Tessa said.

Tom's ears turned bright pink.

Tessa spoke again. "Tom Parker," she said, "look at me."

Surprised, Tom did as he was told.

Tessa leaned down, so that her nose was almost touching his, and said, "Now, say whatever it is you want to say. I want to hear it from you."

A sunburst of a smile broke over Tom's face, a mix of hope and cautious joy. "Will you go out with me? To the dance on Saturday night?"

Tessa straightened. Her face revealed nothing whatsoever.

Tom didn't move.

Melissa didn't breathe. If she'd thought for one moment that Tessa would turn Tom down, she wouldn't have opened her big mouth in the first place.

"Yes," Tessa said, at long last. "I think I *will* go to the dance with you."

The whole place erupted in cheers and whistles then, and Tom went even redder than before.

Melissa let out her breath and sneaked a sidelong look at Steven. By then, even he was caught up in watching the saga unfold, just like everybody else in the café.

"That's good, then," Tom said. Now that he'd made

his pitch, he seemed to be at a loss for titillating conversation. "That's real good."

Tessa smiled, her own color a little high, and turned to go behind the counter for the coffee order.

"Thanks for kicking me," Tom said to Melissa. "I think you broke my shin."

"She's going to the dance with you!" Melissa whispered, thrilled that her good friend hadn't been shot down, especially with the whole town looking on. It would have been her fault, at least in part, if that had happened.

"And you're going to the dance with Creed," Tom replied very quietly, grinning. "Not that I thought for one second that he'd turn you down."

Melissa looked toward Steven, just to make sure he was still out of range and, seeing that her Saturday night date was busy shaking hands and exchanging parting words with Alex, turned back to Tom. Raised both her eyebrows. "What made you so sure?" she asked, under her breath.

Tom bent toward her. His eyes sparkled. "Because you're already involved with him," he said slowly, and with a note of cocky triumph. "*That's* why."

"Says who?"

"Says you. Do you think I can't read simple body language, after all these years as a cop? Hell, Melissa, you might as well have hired a skywriter—the pulses in your throat and wrists are pounding so hard, they're visible." He paused, spread his hands in that way he had. "Case closed."

"Oh, shut up," Melissa said, just as Steven started toward their table.

She loved the way he walked, the way he moved, easy in his skin.

She loved the way he did a few *other* things, too, but that was beside the point.

He was trouble—the way they'd butted heads in Tom's office that morning should have been proof enough for anybody, including her.

So what was she doing?

"I'll be looking forward to Saturday," Steven said, when he reached them.

"Me, too," Melissa said, without intending to say anything of the kind. She definitely needed some space, a chance to figure things out, at least a little bit, but she also wanted to get up from that booth and follow him home.

Steven checked his watch. "Time to pick Matt up at school," he said.

Melissa's heart slowed and warmed at the thought of the little boy. "Tell him hi for me," she said.

"I will," Steven told her. Then he nodded to Tom and walked out into the midafternoon sunshine.

Melissa must have stared at the empty space where Steven had just been standing for a beat too long, because when she met Tom's eyes again, he was grinning like a fool.

She made a face at him.

Tessa brought the coffee. Along with two slices of fresh peach pie and forks rolled up in napkins. She blushed when she set Tom's down in front of him.

"Thanks," he said, turning shy all over again.

Tessa turned and hurried away.

Melissa unwrapped her fork. She'd had a carton of designer yogurt for lunch and it wasn't enough. Suddenly, she was starving.

GIVE HER SOME ROOM, warned a voice in Steven's mind, as he walked around to the side parking lot and unlocked his truck with the key fob.

He wanted to turn on his boot heel and go right back inside the café, grab Melissa by the hand and take her home with him. Smooth over the awkward stuff. Hear her laugh. Watch the late afternoon sunlight glinting off her hair. And, yes, he wanted to make love to her again.

Steven sucked in a breath and got into the truck, started it up. *Slow down, cowboy,* he thought.

She was a complex woman, that was for sure. In bed, she'd been a tigress. Ditto that morning, when she'd showed up at the jail. And yet asking him to a country dance had made her turn pink from her collarbone to her hair.

Easing out of the lot and onto the street, Steven shook his head, marveling at the things that were going on inside him just then. Not that he could identify any of them—the fact was, he'd never felt quite this way before. Never wanted to know everything there was to know about a woman, and more besides.

He reached Creekside Academy within a couple of minutes, and Elaine Carpenter brought Matt out, holding his hand as they came down the front walk.

Matt, a big piece of drawing paper in his free hand, glanced in Steven's direction then turned his attention back to Elaine.

Steven shut off the truck and went to meet them at the curb.

"I made a picture!" Matt crowed, as Steven leaned down to scoop the boy up.

Elaine smiled. "As first days go," she said to Steven, "this one rated an A-plus."

"Thanks," Steven said to her.

"Don't you wanna see the picture?" Matt all but shouted.

With a chuckle, Elaine turned and headed back into the school.

"Sure," Steven told Matt, "but let's get into the truck first."

He carried the boy to the rig and buckled him into his safety seat. Matt waved the piece of paper in Steven's face the whole time.

"All right, already," Steven said, laughing. He took the paper and looked at it.

Three stick figures—man, woman, little boy. A stick dog and a stick horse stood with them, in front of some kind of building leaning hard to the right.

Something fluttered in Steven's heart. It wasn't sorrow, exactly, but it wasn't happiness, either. If he'd had to put an adjective to the emotion, he would have said *bittersweet*.

"That's you," Matt said, stabbing an index finger into the chest of the stick man, but soon moving on to the woman. "And that's Melissa." He, of course, was the child, and the dog was Zeke. The horse was evidently there as a reminder.

"That's—great," Steven said, after a moment or two. He kept thinking he'd get used to things the boy said, but so far that hadn't happened. A glimpse inside Matt's mind always choked him up and, sometimes, like now, it made him afraid. He searched for the right words, a way to warn the little guy not to get his hopes up as far as Melissa was concerned without shooting down all that bright-eyed faith.

Nothing came to him.

"Next time I see Melissa, I'm going to give her this

picture as a present," Matt said, as Steven set him on his feet.

Steven's throat ached, and he couldn't quite look at the boy. "Matt—"

"I know, I know," the five-year-old broke in sunnily, "you and Melissa aren't married yet, and I shouldn't get carried away and make all kinds of plans—"

Steven could picture himself married to Melissa— though he hadn't really tried before now—but there was no telling what *her* take on the matter might be.

Sure, they'd had a great time in bed together, but he hadn't forgotten the hurt he'd seen in Melissa's eyes, during the interlude between bouts of lovemaking, when they'd sat at his table eating take-out meat loaf. The last guy she cared about had done a serious number on her, and she wasn't over it.

On top of that, she had a career, a house, a *life,* quite independent from his own. What would someone like Melissa O'Ballivan really have to gain by tying herself down at this point?

Sex? She didn't need marriage for that, any more than he did.

"Dad?" Matt jolted him out of the thought tangle by tugging at the fabric of his shirt.

Steven blinked, looked down at his son. "What?"

Matt was pointing in the general direction of the ranch house. "Whose truck is that?"

Seeing that old beater was like taking a punch in the gut. The black Dodge, dented and scraped and still sporting Wile E. Coyote mud flaps, even after all these years, belonged to none other than Brody Creed.

"Stay here," Steven told Matt, putting out a hand briefly to emphasize the point before striding off toward his cousin's truck.

The kid might as well have been born a Creed as get adopted into the family, because he never listened. Steven got all the way to Brody's truck, which sat in the high grass with its windows rolled down, before he realized that Matt was right behind him.

"Didn't I tell you to stay put?" Steven asked the boy.

Matt folded his arms and looked up at him, that stubborn glint in his eyes. "You might need some help," he pointed out manfully.

Steven sighed and shoved a hand through his hair in frustration. Then he stepped up onto the running board on the driver's side and looked in.

Brody lay across the seats, his hat over his eyes and his knees drawn up.

Steven jerked the door open, causing it to give way under Brody's booted feet, and he scrambled upright, ready to fight, as always. He shoved the hat back, so he could see, and an instant grin spread across his face.

"Dammit, Boston," he said, "you scared the hell out of me."

Steven was glad to see Brody—no question about it—but there was some anger there, too. The man disappeared for years at a time, with nothing but a ratty Christmas card, always arriving in mid-January, to indicate that he was still alive.

"You look just like Uncle Conner," Matt marveled, his piping voice a much-needed reminder that there was a child present and that meant no more swearing and no landing a fist in the middle of Brody's face. "But you're *not,* are you?"

Brody got out of the truck, resituated his hat, which, like everything else he owned, had seen better days. "Nope," he said, putting out a hand to Matt. "I'm his brother. Name's Brody. And who might you be?"

"Matt Creed," Matt responded, gazing wide-eyed up at Brody.

They shook hands solemnly.

"The rodeo," Steven said, "is still three weeks away."

Brody swung his ice-blue gaze to Steven. It was unnerving how much he looked like Conner, though it shouldn't have been. They were identical twins, after all. "Don't you worry, Boston," he said, in a slow drawl, tucking in his shirt. "I'm not here to stay—just passin' through."

"How come he calls you 'Boston,' Dad?" Matt wanted to know.

"I'll explain later," Steven said, ruffling the boy's hair and handing him the key ring. "You'd better go let Zeke out of the bus. He's probably crossing his hind legs by now."

Matt glanced once more at Brody, eyes full of curious interest, then dashed off toward the bus.

Once he and Steven were alone, Brody folded his arms. "Quite a spread you have here," he said.

It might have been a jibe, considering the state of the house and barn, but Steven didn't know for sure, so he let the comment pass with a quiet, "Thanks."

"Look," Brody said, rubbing his chin, which was bristly with dark gold stubble, "if you want me to hit the trail, just say so."

Steven laid a hand on the front fender of the truck, and he smiled as youthful memories rose in his head, brightly colored and glowing around the edges. "You're welcome here, Brody," he replied, "and you damn well know it."

Brody grinned again. "When did you get married?" he asked, with a gesture toward Matt, now bounding out of the bus behind the sheepdog-bullet that was Zeke.

"I didn't," Steven replied.

Brody arched one eyebrow, and his eyes danced. "I see."

"No," Steven told him, slapping him on the back to head him in the direction of the bus, "you *don't* see. And where the hell have you been all this time?"

CHAPTER THIRTEEN

MELISSA, JITTERY WITH SILLY, schoolgirl thoughts of what she would wear to the dance on Saturday night, decided as she left the office to steel herself and stop by the B&B to look in on the guests. Ashley would be back from Chicago soon, and Melissa wanted to be able to say she'd tended to business.

She smiled as she maneuvered the roadster out of the parking lot behind city hall. The breeze was fresh and the afternoon sunshine was glorious, and Melissa was glad she'd left the top down on the roadster that morning, even though the wind was playing havoc with her hair.

When she reached Ashley's place, there was a familiar SUV parked in front of the garage door, and Melissa's spirits rose even further at the sight of it. Ashley and Jack and little Katie were back from Chicago, at last.

Melissa parked hastily at the curb, maybe a shade too close to the fire hydrant, and barely remembered to grab her purse before dashing across the sidewalk, through the front gate and up the porch steps.

Ashley opened the screen door, grinning from ear to ear, two-year-old Katie balancing on one hip.

They were so different, Melissa and Ashley, that strangers were always surprised to learn that they were twins. Melissa's hair was dark brown, and she preferred to dress for success, while Ashley, a delicate blonde, generally wore pastels, gauzy skirts and ruffled things.

Their eyes, though, marked them as sisters, because they were precisely the same shape and the same shade of blue.

They hugged, Ashley's embrace one-armed because she was still holding Katie, and Melissa's eyes burned with happy tears.

"You were gone *way* too long," Melissa accused, when they were inside the entryway.

Katie, blond like her mother but with her dad's dark eyes, strained toward Melissa, who gladly took her and planted a noisy kiss on one pudgy—and slightly sticky—little cheek.

"And that goes for you, too, missy," Melissa told her niece.

"We missed you, too," Ashley said. She was barefoot, wearing white shorts and a matching top that showed off her light tan, and her hair was tumbling down from its Gibson-girl do in a way that was almost a signature. "Follow me to the kitchen," she said, and turned.

Melissa followed, carrying Katie and looking around for Mr. Winthrop and the rest of them as they passed through the long, cool hallway between the big living room and the equally spacious dining room.

Ashley's kitchen was the heart of the house, a welcoming place, cheerful and bright, always shining-clean and usually smelling of something delicious—as it did now.

Melissa sniffed. "Brownies?"

"Double Chocolate *Death* Brownies," Ashley replied, twinkling as she turned, took her daughter from Melissa, and gently plunked the child down in her playpen.

"And you're going to have at least two, because you've lost weight since we've been gone."

Ashley tended to mother Melissa. Also Brad and Olivia, when they allowed it. She was a born homemaker and a good businesswoman in the bargain.

"You, on the other hand," Melissa responded, tilting her head to one side as she looked her sister over, "are getting a tummy."

Ashley patted her abdomen. "Of course I am," she said happily. "I'm pregnant, remember?"

"Yes," Melissa answered, letting her nose lead her to the counter, where the batch of brownies was cooling, "but I don't have that excuse."

"You're too skinny," Ashley said, filling the electric teakettle at the sink.

"I am not," Melissa replied, good-natured bickering being pretty much their pattern. "And don't think I'm going to gain weight to keep you company for the next six months, either."

"We're twins," Ashley reasoned, hiding one of her sunshine-bright smiles. "The least you could do is pack on some sympathy pounds."

"In your dreams," Melissa said, but it was all she could do not to make quick work of that plate of brownies.

Ashley laughed, and inclined her head toward the table. "Sit down," she said. "And tell me what's been going on in Stone Creek over the last couple of weeks."

"Where do I start?" Melissa said, only partly in jest. She scanned their immediate surroundings. "Are your guests around?"

"They're in the backyard," Ashley answered, with a twinkle. "Practicing the tango."

Melissa shook her head. "I don't hear any music."

"They make their *own* music," Ashley said.

"You can say that again," Melissa retorted, recalling the nude croquet match. She wasn't sure she'd ever be able to put the shock of it behind her.

Ashley sighed. It was a happy, contented sound that made Melissa feel both love and envy, all in the same moment. "I like them," she said. "I wish they were staying longer. So does Jack."

"Where is Jack, anyway?" Melissa asked, looking around. Ashley's husband was one of those men who seem to fill a house with their presence, almost making the walls bulge.

Like Steven Creed.

"He went out to Brad and Meg's to fetch Mrs. Wiggins," Ashley said. "You know—our cat? The one you didn't want to keep at your house because she makes you sneeze?"

Instead of sitting down, Melissa went to the back door and looked out through the screen. Mabel, clad in plaid Bermuda shorts and a red T-shirt instead of the Flamenco dress she'd worn last time, held a rose in her teeth as she and Herbert tangoed their way across the patio.

"Amazing," she muttered. "I need to find out if those people take vitamins and if so, what kind."

Ashley laughed, moving to stand beside her. "They *are* pretty incredible," she agreed mildly. Then she nudged lightly with her elbow. "I hear your wild side has been coming out lately."

Melissa narrowed her eyes at her sister, who walked away to attend to the now-whistling teakettle. "Who told you that?" she demanded, though quietly.

Katie had curled up on the soft bottom of the playpen, and she was sleeping like an angel, with one thumb in her mouth.

Ashley poured hot water into the china teapot that had belonged to their grandmother on the O'Ballivan side, after scooping in some loose tea leaves. "I never betray my sources," she said primly.

Melissa chuckled. "Tom Parker," she said, making a not-so-wild guess. "He's been emailing updates all along."

"Texting," Ashley corrected.

"I swear he's a worse gossip than his aunt Ona," Melissa fretted. "What did he tell you?"

"That he thinks you're sleeping with somebody named Steven Creed," Ashley said, without missing a beat.

With anyone else, Melissa might have fibbed, and with a lot of protestation, too. But lying to her sister was just plain useless; they knew each other too well. "He has his nerve," she said, hedging. That didn't usually work, either, but sometimes she could pull it off.

Maybe Ashley was jet-lagged.

No such luck. "Is it true?" she asked.

Melissa double-checked to make sure Katie was sleeping and the white-haired guests were still tangoing to the music only they could hear before she answered, "Not in the *ongoing* sense, however Tom might have made it sound."

Again, Ashley giggled. She would have looked like a Victorian lady, standing there in front of the cupboard, waiting for the tea to steep, if it hadn't been for the shorts and top. "The 'ongoing sense'? What the heck does *that* mean, sister mine?"

Melissa sank back into her chair at the table again. She felt weirdly agitated and, at the same time, crazy-happy. "It means it happened *once,*" she said, in a whisper. "Last night. We've known each other for all of five days. He's a lawyer and his name is Steven Creed. Do you have any other questions?"

"Only about a million," Ashley said.

Outside, voices rose on the warm summer air, and a plaintive meow rang out. Jack was back, with Mrs. Wiggins.

"Guess they'll have to wait for a while," Melissa said.

"Guess so," Ashley agreed, pouring tea.

Jack opened the screen door and came inside, the family cat a fluff of white inside its plastic carrier, and Ashley put one index finger to her lips and pointed toward the sleeping toddler with the other.

The man's face fairly glowed with love for his wife and daughter, it seemed to Melissa. He nodded, kissed Ashley smartly on the mouth and carefully released Mrs. Wiggins from the carrier.

With all that, he still managed a brotherly wink for Melissa. He mouthed the word *hi.*

Ashley, an animal lover, stooped to pet the cat.

Mrs. Wiggins, no doubt indignant over her people's long absence, twitched her tail, gave one petulant meow and vanished through the dining room door.

Melissa sneezed.

"Oh, for Pete's sake," Ashley said. "You're *not* allergic."

Melissa sneezed again.

Jack, a dark-haired, outdoorsy type, agile and fit, cocked a thumb over one shoulder, evidently indicating the backyard. "Mamie Crockett just waylaid me in the driveway," he told Ashley in a be-quiet-the-baby's-sleeping voice. "She said our guests have been raising three kinds of hell ever since they got here."

"Mamie," Ashley said, "is a sweet old thing, but she's also a curmudgeon."

"It's true," Melissa said.

Jack grinned admiringly and shook his head. "I sure hope *I'm* still getting into that much trouble when I hit my nineties," he said. "If somebody calls the cops because the tango music is too loud, I'll count that as a real accomplishment."

"Not to mention just *making* it to that age," Ashley added, slapping Jack's hand when he reached for the brownies and grabbed three of them in one swoop.

"I wonder if they skydive," Jack teased. "And ride mechanical bulls."

"I wouldn't be a bit surprised," Melissa replied.

Just then, Katie awakened, hauled herself upright by gripping the rails of her playpen, and let out a wail. "Potty!" she yelled.

"Your turn," Ashley told Jack, helping herself to a brownie before carrying the plate to the table and setting it down in the middle.

Jack swept the toddler up and kissed her on the cheek. "Too late," he said, after patting Katie's diaper-cushioned bottom.

With that, he and Katie disappeared through the dining room doorway, headed upstairs.

It was hard to believe that Jack McKenzie, able diaper-changer, had so recently headed up a top-notch security company, personally rescuing men, women and children from South American jungles and other politically volatile environments. Although he still owned the firm, and occasionally met with clients and with his key employees, always somewhere far from his wife and child, he seemed content to live in Stone Creek. Riding the range with Brad and Tanner, Olivia's husband, seemed to be all the adventure he needed these days.

"Now we can talk about the new man in your life," Ashley said to Melissa.

"He's *not* 'the man in my life,'" Melissa insisted. "I barely know Steven."

Ashley, sitting across the table from her now and nibbling at one of the brownies, raised an eyebrow. "You know him well enough to *sleep* with him," she said.

"Be quiet," Melissa whispered, as the screen door creaked open and the first of the guests entered into the kitchen.

"I smell brownies!" Herbert whooped.

THEY'D WALKED THE property, checked out the ramshackle old house and the ruins of the barn, now partially removed by the work crew that had been there earlier, but Brody still hadn't answered Steven's question. Still hadn't said where he'd been since he and Conner got into a fistfight in a parking lot in Lonesome Bend one night, two weeks after graduating from college, and parted ways.

Brody hadn't even gone home to pack up any of his belongings, as far as anybody knew. His old dog, always riding shotgun, was with him, and the two of them just lit out without so much as a "Go to hell" to the rest of the family.

Now, watching as Matt and the dog played tag in the softening afternoon light, Brody hooked his thumbs in the belt loops of his threadbare jeans and smiled to himself. "You gonna tell me how you happened to come by a kid, Boston?" he asked, his voice low-pitched and gruff with some private emotion.

Steven explained about Zack's and Jillie's deaths, and how he'd adopted Matt when they were both gone.

"That's doing things the hard way," Brody commented, and Steven couldn't be sure whether he was referring to Zack and Jillie, for dying, or Steven himself, for stepping up to raise a child.

But sympathy flickered in Brody's eyes as he watched the boy and the dog playing their games. He was one tough cowboy, and that was as true a thing as any statement ever had been, but deep down, he was a sucker for kids and critters. Always had been.

He slanted a glance at Steven, slapped him hard on the back. "I figured you'd be married by now," he said.

Steven laughed. "Why?"

Brody gestured toward Matt. "Because you're the marrying kind," he said. "Unlike me."

"'The marrying kind'?" Steven repeated. "Excuse me?"

"Face it," Brody said, and another grin splashed across his face. "You were born to be a husband and a father."

"Unlike you?" Steven prodded lightly.

"Unlike me," Brody affirmed. "No good woman would have me, and while I might sleep with a bad one, I'd never put a wedding ring on her finger."

Steven couldn't stand the wondering any longer. "Brody," he said, his tone firm now, his gaze direct. "Where have you been?"

"It's like that old Johnny Cash song," Brody said. "I've been everywhere, man."

"Not good enough," Steven challenged. "Do you have any idea how much Dad and Kim worry about you?"

Something changed in Brody's face; he looked older

than his thirty years, and sadder than a man that young ought to be. "I thought about going home a million times," he said gruffly. "But my pride always got in the way, and I couldn't seem to find a way around it."

Steven thought of Zack and Jillie as he watched their child, and of how unlikely it seemed, even now, that they could be gone. "You gonna wait until somebody dies, Brody? Trust me, if that happens, you'll be a long time regretting it."

Brody's look was sharp as he turned his head toward Steven. "Is one of them sick—Davis or Kim, I mean?"

Steven shook his head. Was Brody implying, by deliberately omitting a third name, that it would be just fine with him if *Conner* were sick? "No," he said. "And neither is your brother. But you ought to know as well as I do how fast things can change."

Before Brody could reply, Matt rushed them, head back and arms out like airplane wings, as good as flying. Zeke ran, barking, behind him.

"I'm *starved!*" Matt declared loudly.

Brody reached out and ruffled the boy's hair. "Me, too," he said. He looked at Steven again. "What's for supper, Boston?"

"Leftover meat loaf and canned ravioli," Steven said, leading the way toward the door of the bus.

"How come you call my dad 'Boston'?" Matt piped.

"'Cause that's where he's from," Brody said. "*Steven*'s too formal for me—can hardly bring myself to say it—and he won't answer to Steve. So I call him Boston."

They were inside now.

Matt picked up Zeke's empty bowl, ready to hike back to the little room where the water heater and the washer and dryer were, that being where the kibble was kept. So far, he'd kept his promise to look after the dog.

"I'm from Denver," Matt said to Brody, "that's where I was born. But nobody calls me that."

Brody pretended to size up the little boy, take his measure the way he might do with a grown man.

It made Matt throw back his shoulders in pride and puff out his chest a-ways.

"I don't reckon *Denver* suits you all that well," Brody said, after some time had gone by. "Nope. If I was going to give you a nickname, I'd pick the Colorado Kid."

Matt's face lit up. "Like *Billy* the Kid?"

"Yeah," Brody said, grinning. He'd never met the man, woman or child he couldn't charm straight into next week.

"Feed the dog," Steven told Matt.

Matt nodded and started down the hallway, followed by said dog.

"Do me a favor," Steven said to Brody, keeping his voice down.

Brody's grin faded. "What?"

"Don't set Matt up for a fall, okay?"

Brody took offense, which was more like him. "What the hell do you mean by that?" he rasped, glaring at Steven.

"You said it yourself. You're just passing through. So go easy on the avuncular charm, because I don't want Matt to get too attached to somebody he might never see again."

Brody didn't get the opportunity to respond, because Matt and Zeke reappeared. Matt set the bowl down in its accustomed place and the dog began to crunch loudly on his supper.

Steven, who could do with some supper himself, washed his hands and then went to the full-size refrigerator and took out the leftover meat loaf. There was a lot, because Melissa hadn't eaten much and, as for him, he'd wanted second helpings of something else entirely.

"This is quite a rig," Brody said, looking around.

"It belongs to Brad O'Ballivan," Matt said. "And he's *famous*."

"I figured that," Brody replied, "from the big head painted on the side, along with his name airbrushed in letters three feet tall."

Steven put the meat loaf in the microwave and took a family-size can of ravioli, the old standby, out of the cupboard. He was annoyed, and he was worried, but he couldn't help the grin that tugged at one corner of his mouth.

"It's just like a house," Matt said, raising his voice to be heard over the dog chomping on kibbles. "There's even a washer and dryer. And I've got my own room, with bunk beds."

Brody gave a low whistle of appreciative exclamation. "Is there a shower? Because I've been on the road for a while, and I could sure use a good sluicing off and a close shave."

Steven opened the ravioli can and dumped the contents into a saucepan. Turned on the gas underneath.

"Yep," Matt said. "There's a shower. Did you know Brad O'Ballivan is famous?"

Brody grinned. "Yeah," he said. "I like his music. Looks like you and him must be pretty good buddies."

"He's a *grown-up*," Matt responded, as though that precluded friendship. "His son, Mac, is my friend, though. I slept over last night, at Mac's, I mean. We rode on his pony before and after supper."

It was the first Steven had heard about the pony ride; Matt hadn't mentioned it that morning, on the way to day camp. He smiled at the thought.

"I see," Brody said.

The timer on the microwave dinged. Steven let the meat loaf sit while the ravioli heated up and he put three plates and some silverware on the table. Surveying it, he realized he'd forgotten to buy milk again. Good thing there was melted cheddar on top of the meat loaf.

Brody went off to wash up for supper, and Steven hoisted Matt up so he could soap his hands and rinse them off in the kitchen sink.

"I like Brody," he whispered to Steven, as though imparting a confidence.

"Me, too," Steven answered.

Brody came back, and they all sat down to supper.

Brody told stories about his life on the rodeo circuit, both in the States and north of the Canadian border, all of them noticeably devoid of personal information. His cousin might have been an alien from another planet, posing as Brody Creed, for all the connection Steven felt. Once, they'd been as close as brothers, the two of them.

Except for Brody's looks—even in need of a shave and a haircut and decent clothes, he was still a dead-ringer for Conner—he was practically a stranger.

It bruised something in Steven, even thinking that.

Brody. A stranger.

How was that possible?

After supper, Matt reluctantly agreed to take his shower and get into his PJs.

Brody cleared the table, and when everything was in the sink, he paused to pick Matt's drawing of the stick family up from the desktop, pondering it solemnly.

"Everybody wants the same thing," he murmured, holding the sheet of paper as though it were somehow sacred. "A family."

Steven's throat tightened. "Yeah," he managed, when he could get the word out. He went to check on Matt next, because his eyes were burning, and while the boy probably wouldn't notice, he couldn't risk letting Brody see.

When he came back, after toweling Matt off and digging out the pajamas he'd forgotten to bring into the bathroom with him, the door was standing open and Brody was gone.

Had he left again, already, without even a goodbye?

Considering the possibility, Steven felt his heart skip a beat or two before common sense overtook him. The dog was outside, and Brody was with him.

He went to the doorway.

Brody was hauling a suitcase from under the tarp in the back of his truck. That piece of luggage looked like it was bought at a thrift store, beaten with a tire chain and then dragged down five miles of rough road behind a tractor.

But, then, so did Brody. Life had used him hard, that much was clear.

He might want to talk about it eventually, or he might never say a word. Cussed-stubborn as he was and, conversely, unpredictable, it might go either way.

Brody brought in the suitcase, along with a couple of tattered blankets, the kind they sell cheap in the markets of Tijuana and Nogales, and set everything down on or near the couch.

Steven didn't say anything. He just went to the door and whistled for Zeke, who was chasing some kind of flying bug around the yard. It was a comforting sight, somehow, a dog playing in the twilight, with the old house standing watch in the near distance.

"I'm done with my shower!" Matt announced turning up at the end of the hall. "And I brushed my teeth, too!"

"Good deal," Steven said.

"I don't need a story tonight," Matt added manfully. "You probably want to talk to Brody and everything."

Steven smiled. "There's always time for a story," he said. Ever since Matt had come to live with him, scared and small and confused, clinging to his blanket and his toy skunk, they'd read out of a book every night. Even when Steven wasn't home, he'd made sure the babysitter kept up the ritual.

"I'd just like to look at my picture for a while," Matt said. He sounded mighty philosophical, for a short guy.

My picture. The photo of Zack and Jillie, skydiving on their honeymoon, Steven thought. He was about to say it was right where they'd left it, on Matt's bedside table.

But the boy scampered across the living-room– kitchen and claimed the drawing he'd made at day camp.

That's you, and that's Melissa, and that's me.

Steven's eyes started burning again. "If you change your mind about the story," he said, his voice hoarse, "just let me know."

Matt nodded, then gave a wide grin. "'Night, Dad. 'Night, Brody."

Steven just nodded.

"Good night, Colorado," Brody said seriously.

Matt beamed at that. Summoned the dog. "Come on, Zeke," he said. "It's time for bed."

Zeke, who had been sniffing at his empty kibble bowl, obediently trotted over to Matt, and the two of them vanished down the hallway and into the second bedroom.

"All right if I take a shower?" Brody asked Steven when they were alone again.

"Of course it's all right," Steven said, maybe a touch more abruptly than he should have. "You need anything?"

Brody grinned. "You mean, like a toothbrush, Boston? Hell, I haven't sunk *that* low."

"You're not going to tell me about the time you've been away, are you?" Steven asked, already knowing the answer.

"Not yet," Brody said, with sadness in his eyes, briefly resting a hand on Steven's shoulder. "You asked me for a favor earlier. Now, I'm asking you for one. Let me get around to talking in my own way and my own time. I'm still sorting through things myself."

Steven nodded in agreement.

Brody left the room without another word, and a few seconds later, Steven heard the shower running.

FOR THE NEXT four days, Melissa's life ran smoothly.

She worked. She gained two pounds after having supper with Ashley and Jack and the one-time flashers on several nights. The tenants, meanwhile, remained on their best behavior, probably because, one, there was a child in the house and two, Jack clearly wasn't the sort to put up with any nonsense.

After work, she happily weeded her little patch of garden. She mediated more disagreements, thankfully minor, between the members of the Parade Committee, and ran into Steven fairly often—in the post office, in the grocery store, once at the Sunflower Café, when she stopped for a bottle of water during her run, and another time at the dry cleaner's next door to his new office. He introduced her to his visiting cousin, Brody.

These encounters, mundane as they were, both un-
nerved and excited Melissa, but she'd said it herself:
Things had been moving pretty fast between her and
Steven. She was grateful for a breather—and equally
grateful that she saw him almost every day.

On top of all this, the weather was flat-out perfect.
Warm, but not hot. Sunny, but not glaring.

Happily, there were no confrontations with Velda and
no calls from Eustace Blake, lodging his interminable
complaints about space visitors.

Nathan Carter had apparently left town again, because Melissa hadn't seen him around, which was a
weight off Deputy Ferguson's mind, and hers, too.

Her cuts and bruises healed, and the last of the soreness faded away, although she could still feel ecstatic
little catches of physical pleasure sometimes, when she
allowed herself to remember how it was, making love
with Steven Creed.

Rummaging through Ashley's closet one evening,
she even found a killer dress to wear to the dance on
Saturday night—an aqua-blue sundress with thinnest-
of-thin vertical silver stripes shimmering through the
silky fabric.

Life was downright idyllic, all things considered.
Which was precisely why she should have been prepared, she would think later.

On Saturday morning, she met with the members
of the Parade Committee, as agreed, for the walk-
through—a sort of rehearsal, but without the costumes
and the floats.

Bea Brady and Adelaide Hillingsley were still on the
outs over the toilet-paper question, but the ice was broken when Tessa Quinn and a few assistants showed up
at the meeting place in the park with coffee and a big

bag of fresh doughnuts, her contribution to the community effort.

Melissa, suitably clad in blue jeans, sneakers and a T-shirt, her hair pulled up into a Saturday ponytail, her face bare of makeup, shepherded everybody into line—Tom had temporarily closed Main Street by placing a sawhorse at each end—and appropriate gaps were left for the high-school band and drill team, the sheriff's posse, and the annual offering from over in Indian Rock.

Stone Creek and Indian Rock tended to be a little competitive, as far as their town floats were concerned, but that only served to up the quality of the event.

Oscar Vernon, who owned a used-car dealership and salvage yard outside the city limits, always put the Stone Creek float on the road, and he was invariably secretive as far as colors and subject matter were concerned. He was keeping his mouth shut this year, too—wouldn't give so much as a hint of what he planned—but since he'd done the place proud every year since 1978, nobody really pushed him for answers.

Everyone was poised to begin when Steven and Matt sprinted across the grassy expanse of the park to join in.

Melissa's heart did a thing her granddad Big John would probably have called a twenty-three-skidoo, whatever that was, and she wished she'd bothered with lip gloss and mascara and maybe even a little perfume.

"We're here to help," Matt informed all and sundry, in a piping voice. "What are volunteers supposed to do, anyhow?"

Steven chuckled and ruffled the boy's hair, but he'd locked gazes with Melissa as soon as he came to a stop, and he wasn't letting go.

"Well," Melissa fumbled, reminding herself that Steven had graciously offered to help out on the Parade Committee, managed to shift her eyes to Matt's up-turned face, "you could walk where the sheriff's posse will be riding on the big day. That'll give us a better sense of—spacing. Between the floats, I mean."

Steven smiled, well aware, obviously, that she was disconcerted and enjoying the fact. Someone pointed out where the posse went, and Matt ran to the area, earnest and eager.

Before joining him, Steven moved closer to Melissa and gave her a heated once-over, very private.

Her nipples pressed hard against the fabric of her bra, and things warmed and softened inside her.

She blushed.

Steven grinned down at her. "You haven't forgotten about our date, have you?" he asked.

Melissa bit her lower lip and rummaged up a smile, for the sake of curious onlookers—of which there were many—rather than Steven. "I haven't forgotten," she said. Then she looked past his shoulder, pretending to search for someone. "Where's that drop-dead gorgeous cousin of yours?" she asked, just to take some of the smugness out of the man's grin.

It didn't work. Steven Creed looked every bit as cocky as before; maybe even more so. "Brody left yesterday," he said. "He had to be up in Oregon for a rodeo by tonight."

"Oh," Melissa said.

Steven turned, mainly because Matt was calling for him to do his part holding the gap for the sheriff's posse, but he looked back at her over one shoulder and his smile was so intimate that she felt as naked as any member of the infamous croquet team over at Ashley's B&B.

CHAPTER FOURTEEN

"Now, don't go wearing a three-piece suit on your hot date, Boston," Brody warned, via cell phone, at around four-thirty Saturday afternoon. He'd called, as ordered when he left, to let Steven know he'd gotten to Oregon with no mishaps along the way. "You're going to a dance with a pretty lady, not arguing a case before the Supreme Court."

Steven laughed, standing there in his bedroom in Brad O'Ballivan's tour bus and grimly assessing the limited wardrobe he'd brought along from Denver. Most of his clothes, like the furniture and the lion's share of his and Matt's personal belongings, were in storage until the farmhouse was ready to live in. "Point taken," he said. "What *do* guys wear to a country dance these days, anyway?"

"Well, *that's* a dumb-ass question if I've ever heard you ask one—which I have, of course," Brody responded, his tone jocular. The way he talked, nobody would guess that he'd turned his back on the whole family almost a decade before and cut off all communications except for a once-a-year greeting card. "Wear jeans. Pretty new, if you have them, along with a halfway decent Western shirt and good boots, polished to a shine. You can dispense with the hat—you look like a dude when you wear a hat. Oh, and iron the jeans and the shirt, too."

Steven pretended to be aggrieved. He and Matt had both missed Brody since he hit the road. "Are you through?"

Brody chuckled. "OK," he conceded, "you looked all right in a *real* hat, back when you were rodeoing and punching cattle, but don't try to get away with anything fancy, because it won't work."

"Got it," Steven said. Then he asked if Brody had signed up for his events yet, and when he thought he might be rolling back through Stone Creek.

During Brody's visit, they hadn't discussed the past much. Only a few words about Davis and Kim had passed between them, and they hadn't talked about Conner at all. Steven felt a prickle of guilt, wondered if he shouldn't tell Brody that his brother was planning on coming to Stone Creek's rodeo, and then clue Conner in, too. But since he knew neither one of them would show up if they so much as suspected the other would be there, too, he kept that knowledge to himself.

It was a little like being the only person in the world who knew that, at a certain hour, on a particular day, a colossal meteor would strike the planet.

Steven had considered warning his dad and Kim, in case they decided to change their travel plans and swing by in their RV for that visit Kim had mentioned. They'd be more than ready to spend some time with Matt, whom they missed sorely, and they had to be curious about the new place. He was still undecided on that score, because he knew Kim, the eternal optimist, might not be able to resist telling Conner. She would naturally think the twins' long overdue reconciliation was a sure thing.

Steven knew it was anything but. In fact, it might be a replay of that long ago summer night, when Conner and Brody had lit into each other with fists flying and blood in their eyes. Some risks were worth taking, though—there was always the chance that Kim was right.

"Tell the Colorado Kid I'll be seeing him again soon," Brody finished. He'd already established a bond with Matt, but would he hold up his end of the bargain?

No telling.

Steven swallowed hard. "I'll do that," he said, and rang off.

Matt was spending the night over at Brad and Meg's again, with Mac, because of the dance, and Zeke had gone with him.

That left Steven feeling a lot more alone than he cared to.

He dropped his cell into his shirt pocket, ran a hand through his hair and sighed. Not surprisingly, he had Melissa on his mind. He wondered if he ought to go for more sex, or keep on giving her the space he sensed she needed. In the end, he decided he'd have to play it by ear.

He got out his best pair of jeans, the only ones that were still clean as a matter of fact, and chose a shirt with snaps instead of buttons and a Western cut to the yoke. He poked around the bus until he found an iron and a fold-down ironing board, and he managed not to scorch the duds while he pressed the wrinkles out and the creases in. Then he showered and dressed and polished his good boots with spit and a wad of paper towels, since he hadn't bought a tin of the waxy stuff he normally used to shine up his shit-kickers.

Even with all that done, it was only 5:30 p.m., and he wasn't supposed to pick Melissa up at her place until 7:15. Too restless to stay home, without even a dog for company, he grabbed his keys, fired up the new truck and headed for town. Once there, he'd find some way to kill time, and he wanted to track down a nice bouquet for his date.

He shook his head and chuckled as he began the short drive down to the road. When had he ever been this excited about spending an evening with a woman? Hell, not since high school—if then.

And since he wasn't all that crazy about dancing in the first place, there were some serious implications here.

She's a prosecutor, he reminded himself. Just like Cindy. And, just like Cindy, Melissa had worked hard to carve out a career for herself. She'd loved Dan Guthrie, loved his kids, too, but she hadn't been willing to give any ground at all to save the relationship.

Briefly depressed, Steven shook off those thoughts and moved on to new ones. Work on the house and the new barn would begin on Monday—he had the contractor's word on it, and the guy had a solid reputation for honesty and hard work. Matt was settling in just fine at school, and Stone Creek was already proving to be a good place to call home.

In an unpredictable world like this one, that was enough.

Reaching the edge of town, Steven glanced down at the gas gauge and decided to fill up. That would use up the better part of fifteen minutes, he calculated.

He pulled in at the combination convenience store–gas station, where there were exactly two pumps, one of which dispensed diesel. He shut off the truck, got out and read the handwritten sign taped to the paper-towel dispenser.

"Machine broke. Pay inside."

Steven started for the door, passing a rusted-out Bonneville with cardboard in place of the glass that should have covered the rear window. Besides his truck, it was the only rig around.

Business must be slow this time of day, he decided.

A plump woman stood behind the counter, in front of the register, and her nametag said "Martine."

Steven glanced to one side, spotted the probable owner of the Bonneville over by the cooler, evidently shopping for beer. The guy was young—maybe under the legal drinking age—and nobody he recognized, but that didn't mean much. After all, Steven was new in Stone Creek; there were still a lot of people he didn't know, small as the place was.

He said hello to Martine, who smiled at him as she returned the greeting, and ran his debit card through the machine to make advance payment for whatever a full tank of gas wound up costing.

"Well," Martine responded, "welcome to Stone Creek. It's nice to see somebody moving into this town instead of out. Seems like there was a mass exodus after the mill closed down."

"Thanks for the welcome," he said. He knew she'd read his name off the credit card, but he offered it up just the same, since that was the polite thing to do.

"You got a wife, Mr. Creed?" she asked.

Steven wasn't exactly pressed for time, so he lingered longer than he might have done otherwise. "No, ma'am," he said. "It's just me and my son, Matt."

Martine tilted her head to one side and studied him, a mischievous light dancing in her clear-as-creek-water eyes. It crossed Steven's mind that she might know all about his rendezvous with Melissa, that being typical of a small town like Stone Creek.

"We can always use another eligible bachelor," she said finally. "Not that you'll be on the market long, a good-lookin' cowboy like you."

The remark made Steven feel uncharacteristically shy. "Thanks," he said, for the second time, feeling his earlobes burn a little. Now, he fled.

"I've got a daughter!" Martine called after him. "Her name is Jessica Lynn and she's going to be a full-fledged dental assistant in another six weeks!"

Steven pretended not to hear the pitch, but he couldn't help chuckling as he took the nozzle off the fuel pump and stuck it into the tank's opening.

He'd been so busy trying to figure out Melissa O'Ballivan, it hadn't even occurred to him that he might be the subject of some matchmaking. How many other mamas, besides Jessica Lynn's, were eyeing him through the matrimonial crosshairs, right at that very moment?

Since the tank was nearly empty, it took a while to fill it. Steven washed the windshield, checked the tire pressure and wiped a few bugs off the grillwork.

When the gas pump shut down, he went back inside to sign the credit slip and get his receipt.

Martine had acquired some more customers by then, and she was too busy at the register, ringing up jugs of milk, lottery tickets and cigarettes to try to sell him on Jessica Lynn again.

Thinking ahead to that evening's dance at the Grange Hall, which would probably be attended by just about everybody in Stone Creek and maybe Indian Rock, too, he couldn't help wondering just what he might be letting himself in for.

He grinned to himself as he drove away.

Maybe he'd attract enough attention to make Melissa a little jealous.

Wouldn't *that* be something?

MELISSA STOOD IN front of the mirror on her closet door, scowling at herself. Now that zero hour was approaching, she didn't like the aqua dress half as much as she had before.

She sucked in her stomach. "There they are," she said, pointing at her reflected backside. "The two pounds I gained eating *your* food."

Ashley, sitting on the bed and holding Katie on her lap, smiled and shook her head. "Please. You could gain ten *more* pounds and still fit into every pair of jeans you own."

"As if I'm going to let *that* happen," Melissa said, with a little sniff.

Ashley laughed softly. Her eyes shone with contentment and good humor. Once upon a time, she'd been pretty tense herself, but since Jack's arrival in her life, and then Katie's, she'd mellowed considerably.

Which was sometimes annoying.

"Are you planning on spending the night with him?" Ashley asked.

Melissa turned and made a big deal of cupping her hands loosely over Katie's little pink ears. "What a thing to say in front of a *child,*" she said.

Ashley rolled her twinkly blue eyes. "Katie is *two,*" she reminded her sister. "And anyway, you're just trying to stall."

Melissa uncovered Katie's ears, sighed. "I don't know," she said.

More twinkling. Happiness looked wonderful on

Ashley, just as it did on Olivia and Meg. "You don't know if you're stalling?" she teased.

"I don't know if I'm going to—" Melissa glanced down at Katie, who was holding Ashley's long, golden braid in both hands and gazing at it in wonder, and lowered her voice, "sleep with him."

"What's the holdup?" Ashley asked.

Melissa plunked her hands on her hips and mimicked, "'What's the holdup?' Easy for *you* to ask, Ashley O'Ballivan McKenzie, when you have the whole rest of your life laid out like a path between two rose gardens!"

"Stalling," Ashley repeated, singing the word.

Katie giggled and sang her own version.

Melissa stumbled over her answer. "It's just—well—we hadn't known each other very long when—"

"Maybe," Ashley reasoned, "it's a matter of knowing each other *well* enough, instead of long enough."

Melissa arched an eyebrow, her hands still resting on her hips. Which felt slightly wider under her knuckles, though that was probably an illusion brought on by concern over consumption of her sister's incomparable lasagna. "Whose side are you on, anyway?" she asked.

"There are *sides?*" Ashley countered, raising her own eyebrows. "Who knew?"

Melissa let out a big breath and sat down beside her sister on the bed. "I'm trying to be sensible, here," she said.

"Love isn't sensible," Ashley informed her.

"Who said anything about love?" Melissa countered. "This is a case of lust. If I were in *love* with Steven Creed, don't you think I would have noticed?"

"Not necessarily," Ashley chimed. "For such a smart woman, you can be pretty obtuse when it comes to men."

"Obtuse?" She took a slow, deliberate breath, in a bid for patience. "Just because you're married now, Ash, you're suddenly an expert on men?"

"I'm an expert on *one particular man,"* Ashley responded, a little smugly. "That's all I need to be."

Melissa studied her twin in silence for a long moment. Then her shoulders slumped slightly. "Don't you ever get scared?" she asked, very softly.

Ashley took her hand, squeezed lightly. A slight furrow appeared in her forehead. "Scared?"

"Caring so much," Melissa murmured. "It's, well— it's *dangerous."*

Ashley's entire countenance softened, along with her face. "Oh, honey," she said. "Is this about the breakup with Dan? That's why you think it's dangerous to care too much? I know you were hurt, but honestly, what are the odds of something like that happening twice in one person's lifetime?"

Melissa sighed again. "Have you checked the divorce statistics lately?" she asked. Her stab at humor fell flat.

"Statistics are statistics," Ashley said. "And people are people. Every couple is different, Mel. It's all about finding someone who wants the same things out of life and has similar values, and then both partners trying like hell to make it work. There aren't any guarantees, obviously—not for any of us."

"So you never get scared. Never worry that something could happen to Jack or, God forbid, Katie or the baby?"

"Of course I worry sometimes," Ashley replied. "I'm only human, and I have some of the same abandonment issues as you do, because of Mom leaving and Dad dying so young. But I try never to dwell on all the things that could go wrong. Melissa, so many things go *right,* every single day, for everybody, but nobody notices that."

Melissa leaned closer and let the side of her head rest against the side of Ashley's. "You're amazing," she said.

"Yes," Ashley replied, with comical primness, "I am, rather, aren't I?"

They were quiet for a while, content just to be side by side.

Then, perhaps because she'd missed Ashley so much while she was away visiting Jack's family, Melissa asked a question she might have kept back, saved for another time.

"Ash, did you ever feel as though your own life didn't fit you anymore?"

Ashley squeezed Melissa's shoulders. "Before Jack, I did," she replied quietly. "I had everything I'd ever thought I wanted—you and Olivia and Brad, this house, my own business, all of it. But I finally had to face facts after Jack turned up again. Something was definitely missing, and that something was a man to love and be loved by." She paused, sighed happily, and kissed the top of Katie's head. "A man I could make babies with. Share dreams with. Even argue with."

Melissa sighed, too, but it wasn't out of contentment. She felt confused, as though she'd reached some kind of crossroads and didn't know which way to turn. "We're so different," she reflected, "despite being twins. You've always been old-fashioned, baking pies and wearing aprons with ruffles on them, seemingly glad to stay right here in Stone Creek until the end of your days, while I always wanted to take on the world, prove I could hold my own against the best of them."

Ashley smiled, but her eyes were serious, and full of tender concern. "Maybe we're not so different as you'd like to believe," she said. One corner of her mouth quirked mischievously, which meant there was a zinger coming, for sure. "You'll probably never be a decent cook," she went on, "but I think you'd really *like* to have a home and a husband and some kids."

"I *have* a home," Melissa said, thinking of her tidy, mortgage-free cottage.

"You have a *house,*" Ashley corrected her gently. "That isn't the same thing at all."

"Ashley O'Ballivan McKenzie," Melissa challenged good-naturedly, "are you saying a woman can't live happily ever after without a man in her bed and a gold band on her finger?"

"Of course not. Lots of women thrive on being single. Men, too. But that's them and this is you, Mel. Olivia and Meg and I have been worrying about you for a long time—since you and Dan called it quits, especially. You put on a good show, sister mine, but we—your nearest and dearest—are not so easily deceived."

"All right, so I get lonely sometimes," Melissa retorted. "Who doesn't?"

"*I* don't," Ashley said. "And I don't think Olivia and Meg do, either." She paused again, looking thoughtful. "In my opinion, you've gotten so used to being lonely that you think it's normal to feel that way."

Melissa huffed out a sigh, ready for the conversation to be over. Ashley's comments struck a little too close to the bone. "What would you suggest I do?" she asked, going against her own decision to change the subject. "Shall I just cut some poor, unsuspecting guy out of the herd, throw him down on the ground and hog-tie him?" She pretended to ponder the plan. "He'd have to be a pretty slow runner, of course."

Ashley gave a soft hoot of laughter at that. The

woman twinkled all over, like a tree bedecked with fairy lights. Was it even *legal* to be that happy?

"Do you know what your problem is, Melissa?" Ashley challenged, with a note of smugness in her tone.

"A twin sister with a penchant for minding my business instead of her own?" Melissa teased.

Ashley stopped smiling then, and the fairy lights dimmed a little. "Your whole life is geared to wins and losses. No gray areas for you—and you *really* don't like to lose. When your relationship with Dan went under, you saw it as a personal defeat. After that, you were scared to try again."

"Nonsense," Melissa said, but her tone was decidedly hesitant.

"I was always the old-fashioned type," Ashley maintained gently. "And you were always competitive. Because you weren't the one to put an end to the whole thing, instead of Dan, you counted it as a rejection."

Melissa's throat tightened, and she swallowed, but it didn't help. She didn't have the words to contradict Ashley, or the conviction, either.

On some level, the breakup with Dan *had* left her with the idea that love worked for other people, but not for her.

Still holding Katie, Ashley stood, bent to kiss the top of Melissa's head. "Just have a good time tonight," she advised.

And then she and Katie left the room.

ONCE HE WAS through at the gas station–convenience store, Steven drove around town for a while, marveling at his own sense of blithe aimlessness, and finally realized he was hungry. He headed for the only drive-through burger place in town, ordered a cheeseburger and a cola, and ate in the driver's seat, being careful not to spill anything on his clean shirt or his best jeans. He'd pressed them both, and he wanted to stay spiffy as long as he could.

Even when the burger was history, there was lots of time to go before he could reasonably knock on Melissa's front door.

He found a flower shop, after some searching, but it was closed. From there, he proceeded to the supermarket. He'd seen roses and various houseplants in the produce sections of grocery stores lots of times. He'd have preferred something a little fancier, a big bouquet with exotic blossoms and ribbon tied around the vase, but for tonight anyhow, he'd have to make do.

Inside the store, Steven chose between daisies, rosebuds just opening up, and what was probably some kind of lily. He considered buying several bunches and putting them together, but he wasn't sure which colors went with which. So he settled for a dozen yellow roses, stuck them, stems dripping, into their vase-shaped plastic bag, and headed for the checkout counter.

All the lines were long. Folks with shopping carts filled to overflowing, toddlers wailing with boredom or fatigue or some combination of the two. A few last-minute Louies—like himself—who'd stopped in for flowers.

Steven waited patiently. After all, a line was a line and he had plenty of time, anyway. He was caught off guard when another cart in front of his rammed into his from the side, lightly but still with a startling crash of metal.

Tessa Quinn, from over at the Sunflower Café, was standing there, grinning at him. "Oops," she said. "Sorry. I wasn't watching where I was going."

"Hey," he greeted her, with an easy smile.

She took in the yellow roses. "Nice flowers."

Steven sighed. "Yeah," he said.

Tessa blew out a good-natured breath. "Not another man of few words," she lamented cheerfully. "We've already got a surplus of those in this town."

He chuckled. "Looking forward to the dance tonight?" he asked, having decided to make more of a social effort. Up on the ranch, outside Lonesome Bend, Kim was forever claiming that she'd trade the whole bunch of quiet Creed men for someone who spoke in complete sentences.

Tessa's smile dazzled. "Oh, yes," she said. "I thought Tom Parker would *never* ask me out."

The line moved, and Steven held back to let Tessa go ahead of him. "And I thought Melissa would never ask *me*," he joked. No matter how things turned out between them, he figured he'd never get tired of the memory of that woman swallowing her formidable pride, right there in the Sunflower Café, in front of half the town, to invite him to a dance.

Tessa laughed. "That *was* a surprise," she said. "Tom must have tricked her into it." The expression on that well-known face was priceless as she realized how the remark must have sounded to Steven. She even blushed. "It's just that—well—the two of them have been buddies since they were little kids. After Dan Guthrie broke Melissa's heart into about a million pieces, people thought she and Tom might finally get together—" She fell silent again, looking miserable.

"But they didn't," Steven said, trying to help the poor woman off the hook.

Tessa shook her head. "No," she confirmed. "They didn't."

He might have asked her to tell him a little more about Melissa's broken heart if the time and place and circumstances had been different, but the clerk was waiting none too patiently to ring up Tessa's purchases and the line behind them stretched clear back to the freezer aisle.

When Tessa had finished with her transaction, she grabbed her grocery bags and almost *ran* out of the store.

Thoughtfully, Steven paid for the flowers and headed for his truck.

Once there, he got in, snapped his seat belt into place and then just sat for a while, staring through the windshield.

So Melissa had some emotional baggage, he thought. Didn't everybody, himself included?

Cindy had done a number on him, back in the day. So had a few other women, though to lesser degrees. And as much as he loved Kim, he'd spent a lot of time wishing, as a kid, that his stepmother had never entered the equation in the first place. Why, he'd wondered privately, couldn't his mom and dad have gotten married, and raised him together, like normal people, instead of shunting him back and forth between two very different worlds until he was old enough to make his own choices?

Finally, Steven had been forced to accept the pertinent facts. Life was messy. It was unpredictable. And 99.9 percent of the time, it didn't make any damn sense at all.

For all that, it was still good.

It was a gift.

The trouble arose, he reasoned, when he tried to swim upstream, against the flow.

He sighed.

It was a warm summer night. He was going to a country dance with a beautiful woman.

He decided to let that be enough, for the time being.

MELISSA FELT A little quiver of excitement in the pit of her stomach when she opened her front door to find Steven Creed standing on the porch, a bouquet of yellow roses clasped in one hand.

For a moment, she was a teenager again.

Wishing Ashley had stayed to meet Steven, instead of taking Katie home, she stepped back to let him in.

His gaze drifted over her in an appreciative way that didn't rankle, as it would have with some men. "You look fantastic," he said.

Melissa smiled. *You don't look so bad yourself, cowboy,* she thought, letting her eyes speak for her.

Steven shifted, looking somewhat uneasy. "I'm probably a little early," he said.

Still smiling, she took the flowers. "I'll just pop these into a vase and we'll go," she told him, leading the way into the kitchen.

There, she filled a vase with water and clipped an inch or so from the end of each of the rose stems, so they'd last longer.

"They're from the supermarket," Steven said, from somewhere behind her. He wasn't touching her, but he was close enough that she could sense the hardness and the heat of him.

Or was that her imagination?

"The florist's shop was closed," he added.

She turned, holding the vase full of yellow roses, and said sincerely, "All roses are beautiful. Thank you, Steven."

A spark of something—possibly relief—lit his blue eyes. "You're welcome," he said, and his voice sounded hoarse. He crooked an elbow at her. "Shall we?"

Melissa laughed. "Let's."

Outside, he hoisted her into the passenger seat of his pickup, his hands strong on the sides of her waist, stirring up all sorts of deliciously uncomfortable sense memories.

They kept the conversation light during the drive—Steven said his barn would be going up fast, because the contractor had talked him into a prefab, and the concrete foundation was scheduled to be poured on Monday. The house would take a little longer, he told her, but it would be livable in a couple of weeks.

"I guess that tour bus is starting to feel a little cramped," Melissa said, and instantly regretted the remark.

Talk about sense memories.

Out of the corner of her eye, she saw the slightest grin flicker across Steven's mouth. "Actually," he said, "it's pretty comfortable."

Melissa was relieved to see the Grange Hall up ahead. The building was historic, dating back to Sam O'Ballivan's lifetime, and the never-painted walls were weathered by a century of hard rains, deep snows and long, ground-cracking dry spells. Thanks to Brad's generosity, the place was much sounder than it looked, the roof solid, the dance floor level, the small stage equipped for live music and the productions of the local amateur theater group.

Tonight, cars and pickup trucks jammed the gravel parking lot, and there was a buzz of anticipation in the air. The twang of electric guitars spilled into the sultry evening, a nearly tangible vibrato, and the whole scene reminded Melissa, in a bittersweet flash, of a time long past—back when she and Ashley and Brad and Olivia were kids, their mom not yet gone and their dad still young and vital.

How Delia had loved a community dance—looked forward to it all week long. Wore her freshly shampooed hair up in rollers all day Saturday, and often squeezed the cost of a dime-store lipstick out of the grocery budget because, as she put it, a new shade always made her feel prettier. Delia had favored dresses with full skirts, the better for twirling, and she'd primp in front of the mirror on top of her bureau, as if she was practicing her smile for the upcoming occasion.

Or maybe she wasn't practicing for the dance at all, but for the men she'd meet after she got on the bus one day and left Stone Creek—and her family—behind for good.

Melissa sighed. Delia was gone now; she'd died of hard living and the effects of long-term alcohol use a couple of years ago. By then, the woman had been a stranger for so long that the loss felt impersonal; Melissa had done the bulk of her grieving as a small child.

Back then, Melissa's dad, a quiet man, thoughtful and maybe a little shy, had watched Delia's antics with smiling admiration glowing in his eyes, as if he'd never seen a more beautiful picture than the one his wife made, spinning to make the hem of her dress fly out around her shapely legs.

Whole families had attended the dances in those days—not just the mothers and the fathers, but babies and kids of all ages, and old folks, too. Melissa recalled running wildly around the Grange Hall, inside and out, with her brother and sisters and a flock of other local children, until they all finally ran down.

As the evening wore on, the younger kids would collapse from sheer delighted exhaustion, one by one, and, lie down to rest on a makeshift bed, usually consisting of horse blankets or suit coats, to be carried out to the family rig around midnight, when the festivities ended.

For a moment, Melissa was back there—she could smell her dad's aftershave and the fresh-air scent of the jacket he wore for dress-up, feel the warmth and strength of his shoulder, where her head rested. He'd carried her in one arm and Ashley in the other, and remembering brought a lump to Melissa's throat and a sting to the back of her eyes.

Steven paid the modest price of admission—the money collected went partly to the band and partly to the local historical society—and she knew he'd picked up on her mood by the way his eyes narrowed slightly when he looked at her.

He moved nearer to her and, since the noise was intense, leaned close to her ear to ask, "You look a little peaked. Are you okay?"

She nodded, swallowed. She felt a little deflated, though, the way she always did when she remembered the demise of her parents' marriage and the vast emptiness left behind when it was over. "I'm fine," she told him, but it was herself she wanted to convince.

It was a long time ago, she thought. *Let it go.*

Melissa was good at shaking things off—and it helped when she spotted Olivia and Tanner waltzing on the other side of the hall, lost in each other's eyes, seemingly oblivious to the fast song the band was thrumming out and the dancers spinning and gyrating around them.

Her sister and brother-in-law were happy together, as were Ashley and Jack and Brad and Meg. There was no antilove curse looming over the O'Ballivan family.

When the band struck up a slow tune, Steven drew Melissa into his arms and claimed a space for them on the crowded dance floor.

Melissa drew in the delicious, fresh-air-and-green-grass scent of his skin and hair. Reveled in the hard heat of him, though the sensation wasn't about sexual attraction—though God knew there was plenty of that—but instead came from a sense of being protected and even cherished.

Steven's breath was like a balmy breeze against her ear. "I'm issuing a blanket apology, in advance," he told her, with a note of laughter in his voice. "I've never been much of a dancer, and if I step on your feet, please assume it's unintentional."

She smiled, tilted her head back to look up at him. She could see the underside of his chin, the strong line of his jaw, but only part of his face. By then, the memories of her youthful parents had been carefully folded and tucked away in the softest places in her heart.

"You're doing just fine," she said.

He drew back just far enough to look her full in the face. She saw tenderness in those periwinkle eyes of his, and something that glowed like light. "Thanks," he replied.

And they danced.

Dan Guthrie passed, with Holly in his arms, and Melissa waited for the pang she usually got when she saw them together, but it didn't come.

When the song ended, the crowd parted, women laughing and fanning their flushed faces with their hands, men looking relieved to get a break from dancing.

Dan and Holly, hands clasped, came right through

the path that had opened for them and straight to where
Melissa and Steven were standing.

"Hello, Melissa," Dan said, his tone solemn, his eyes
fond as they rested on her for that first moment. His
gaze almost immediately shifted to Steven, and he put
out a hand, the way men do when they introduce themselves to a stranger, and added, "Dan Guthrie."

Steven accepted the handshake. "Steven Creed," he
replied. "Good to meet you."

Holly, a pretty thing, skinny except for the prominent baby bump pushing out the front of her cotton sundress, wore her blond hair pulled up into a ponytail that
night. It bobbed near the top of her head. She couldn't
seem to stop smiling.

Dan slipped an arm around Holly's waist and said,
"This is my wife, Holly."

Steven smiled and said hello.

It was all so ordinary, Melissa thought. So comfortable.

She and Dan might have been old friends, perhaps
one-time classmates, instead of former lovers.

"How are Michael and Ray?" Melissa asked, as Steven took her hand.

Dan grinned proudly at the mention of his young
sons. "They're growing like weeds," he said. "I swear,
a bunkhouse full of hardworking cowpunchers couldn't
put away more food at a sitting than those two."

Melissa laughed, felt a whisper of tenderness deep
in her heart, not for Dan, but for what they'd once had
together, and for his children. She opened her mouth to
make some comment she wouldn't remember two seconds later, but a burst of happy laughter from near the
entrance stopped her.

Tom and Tessa had arrived, Tom looking handsome

in civilian clothes—jeans and a nice Western shirt—
Tessa exquisite in a sundress with a blue print and ruffles.

Seeing Melissa, Tom grinned and pointed an index
finger at her before pulling Tessa through the throng
of Stone Creekers to approach the group.

Dan and Tom shook hands, and the music started up
again, compelling Dan and Holly to drift off into the
swirl of sweaty noise and motion.

Melissa and Tessa chatted briefly, but since conversation was almost impossible, they soon gave up.

She sighed, looking up at Steven, as the other pair
moved away. "They make a great couple," she said.

Steven responded with a nod and then they, too, were
dancing again.

After an hour or so, they stepped outside to get some
fresh air and admire a sky full of stars. As the strains
of a romantic ballad spilled from inside, Steven took
Melissa into his arms and they waltzed in the shadows
of the old building.

His smile was tender as he looked down at her. "I
warned you about my dancing, didn't I?" he drawled.

She laughed, enjoying the sheer masculinity he ex-
uded, the controlled strength, the hard muscles of his
arms and chest, the clean, woodsy scent of his cologne.

"You're doing just fine," she told him.

And they continued to dance, even between songs.

For Melissa, it was a time out of time. They'd
stopped, and she'd just tilted her head back for the kiss
she knew was coming, when someone drove into the
lot at top speed, tires flinging gravel in all directions.

"What the hell—?" Steven muttered, still holding
Melissa's shoulders in his hands, but distracted now.

She peered through the darkness, saw Martine, who

worked over at the Stop & Shop, jump out of her beat-up sedan.

"Help!" Martine yelled. "Somebody, *help!*"

The music drowned out her voice, but Steven and Melissa heard her plaintive cry, and they rushed toward her.

"Martine—" Melissa sputtered "—what on earth?"

"There's been a robbery!" Martine choked out. "A man wearing a ski mask—he took all the money in the till and made me open the safe—he had a gun—"

"Breathe," Melissa ordered, taking Martine's hands.

"I'll get the sheriff," Steven said from somewhere at the fringes of Melissa's awareness, and she nodded without looking at him.

"Are you hurt?" Melissa asked, and Martine shook her head, still half-hysterical.

"No—I did what he said—there was nobody else in the store, thank God—"

Melissa steered Martine, who was trembling violently by then, back to her car. Seated her on the passenger side.

Tom arrived quickly, with Tessa and Steven and several other people following. Melissa moved aside, and Tom crouched next to Martine's car, looking up into her pale face.

"Tell me what happened," he said gently.

Martine repeated what she'd told Melissa. A man had come into the store, waving a gun and wearing a ski mask. She'd been so scared—certain he meant to kill her, he was so jittery—and she'd done what she was told. Given him all the money she had access to, including the contents of her own wallet.

Tom asked if she'd recognized the man.

Martine shook her head, bit down hard on her lower lip.

"What?" Tom prompted, very quietly. "Tell me, Martine."

"I was practically out of my head with fear, but—but something made me look out the window—I guess I wanted to make sure he wasn't coming back—and I saw him get into a car and drive off." She paused again, looking miserably uncertain. "I can't swear to it, Tom, but it sure looked like that old heap of Velda Cahill's."

Melissa felt a tightening in the pit of her stomach.

Dear God. *Byron?*

Tom straightened, turned to Tessa. "I'm sorry," he said, his voice gruff.

Tessa nodded, reached out to touch his arm. "I can get home on my own," she said. "You be careful."

Call it a premonition, call it common sense. Whatever the feeling was, it washed over Melissa like ice-cold water.

For now, maybe forever, the fun was over.

STEVEN AND MELISSA took Tessa home, pulling into the alley behind the Sunflower Café, where an outside stairway led to the apartment upstairs.

Leaving Melissa in the truck, Steven saw Tessa to her door, waited while she worked the lock, leaned inside to switch on the living room lights. A visible shudder moved through her as she paused on the threshold.

"It's creepy," she said. "Knowing a criminal might be running loose in Stone Creek, I mean."

"We could wait," Steven offered. "Until your brother and his wife get here, at least."

"I'll be all right," Tessa replied quietly. "Olivia and Tanner won't be long—they just wanted to go by their place and make sure the kids were okay."

Tessa might have been a lot of things, but "all right" wasn't among them. She looked scared to death.

"We wouldn't mind hanging around for a while," Steven reiterated.

Tears glimmered in Tessa's eyes. She sniffled and shook her head once, as though to fling away her fears. "This guy threatened Martine with a *gun*. What if— what if something happens to Tom—?"

"He strikes me as the type who can take care of himself," Steven said truthfully. "And, besides, he has deputies to back him up."

"If anything happened—" Tessa fretted, more to herself than to Steven.

Steven didn't answer. He wasn't about to throw out a flippant "Don't worry, everything will be all right" since experience had taught him that that wasn't necessarily so. Nor did he feel right about leaving quite yet.

"I've never told Tom that I love him," Tessa said, looking directly into his eyes. "What if I don't get a chance to tell him?"

Steven touched her arm. "What if you do?" he countered gently.

Just then, another truck appeared in the alley below, sitting headlights-to-headlights with his own rig.

"Looks like Tanner and Olivia are here," Tessa said, with obvious relief.

Melissa had gotten out of Steven's rig to speak to them. The two women were embracing, while Tanner took the stairs two at a time.

Steven nodded to him and stepped back, and Quinn pulled Tessa in for a quick, brotherly hug.

"I'm all right," Tessa insisted. Then she made introductions, and the two men shook hands.

"Thanks for looking out for my sister," Tanner said.

Steven merely nodded, then headed down the steps. At the bottom, he met Olivia, Melissa's sister, for the first time.

Not a word passed between him and Melissa until they'd both gotten back into his truck and he'd backed out of the alley and onto a side street, coming to a stop at the only traffic light in Stone Creek.

A right turn, and they would be headed for her place. A left, for his.

Steven was torn. He didn't want to leave Melissa alone, but suggesting that she spend the night with him didn't seem right, either.

"Where to?" he finally asked.

"The courthouse," Melissa said, not looking at him.

She didn't offer any further explanation, but Steven knew all too well why she wanted to go there. She meant to wait, either in her office or in Tom's, until there was some kind of news.

"Okay," Steven agreed, and when the light finally changed, he turned neither left nor right, but drove straight through the intersection, headed for the parking lot behind the courthouse.

The whole building was blazing with light, and Tom's cruiser, along with two others, sat at angles from the main entrance, as though quickly abandoned. One of the motors was still making a ticking sound, in fact.

A group of onlookers stood watching.

"Showtime," Melissa said, under her breath, without even a semblance of humor.

Steven kept pace with her, nodding to various locals as he passed them.

They reached the large glass doors, and he opened one of them, then waited while Melissa crossed the threshold.

"You don't have to stay," she told him, when they were inside the corridor.

Noise spilled from Tom's office at the other end of the hallway—a woman was alternately sobbing and shrieking, and a dog, probably Elvis, was barking.

Steven made no response.

Melissa gave a small sigh of apparent resignation, and they walked toward the sheriff's office.

VELDA CAHILL REELED, wild-eyed, when Melissa stepped through the doorway, but the woman was looking past her, to Steven.

"You've got to help my boy!" she cried. Word that he was a defense attorney must have gotten around.

Melissa stiffened slightly, but that was the only outward indication she gave that she knew what was going to happen. In some strange way, she'd known it all along.

Byron Cahill hadn't lasted long on the outside. Most likely, she'd be filing charges of armed robbery against him by morning, if not before then.

Steven spoke quietly to Velda; Melissa didn't attempt to listen in. She exchanged glances with Tom Parker and then swung her gaze toward the old-fashioned cells at the back of the office.

Byron sat on the cot in one of them, his head down, his hands hanging between his knees, fingers loosely intertwined. Elvis peered in at him, through the bars, reminding Melissa momentarily of one of the scenes in the Pirates of the Caribbean ride at Disneyland.

"What happened?" Melissa asked, speaking to Tom but still watching Byron. She had a sinking feeling in her middle, and she knew the trouble went beyond the sure and certain knowledge that she and Steven would be on opposite sides of the coming fight.

They were emotionally involved so, technically, anyway, she and Steven could not legally oppose each other in a courtroom.

She could handle the prosecution, or Steven could defend Byron Cahill, but not both. One of them would have to withdraw.

And it wasn't going to be her.

CHAPTER FIFTEEN

STANDING BESIDE MELISSA as she gazed at Byron Cahill through the bars of the cell, Tom explained what had happened after he'd spoken to Martine in the Grange Hall parking lot. He'd started for the Stop & Shop, intending to begin his investigation where the crime had taken place, and had nearly been hit by the Cahill car as it shot out of an alley.

Tom had stuck his portable light on the roof of his personal vehicle and set it flashing, wishing he had a siren, too.

The driver hadn't slowed; in fact, if Byron hadn't swerved to miss a cat running across the road in front of him, and pitched his mother's car into the ditch in the process, the chase would still be on.

"I didn't do anything wrong," Byron said, lifting his eyes at last, looking out at them with an expression so hopeless that Melissa felt that drowning sensation again, like a swimmer going under.

"You didn't stop when I pulled in behind you and turned on the light," Tom reminded him calmly.

"I was scared," Byron answered. "I knew you wouldn't believe me!"

"Know why I don't believe you, Byron?" Tom inquired, his tone smooth. Even. "Because on top of trying to outrun me, you happened to be carrying a ski mask and a backpack full of $5, $10 and $20 bills in the trunk of your car."

Melissa folded her arms. She didn't want it to be true; if only for Andrea's sake and for Velda's, she'd hoped Byron would keep his nose clean. Make a new start.

But the evidence was stacked against him.

"If you didn't rob the Stop & Shop," she ventured, watching Byron's faced closely, "who did?"

Elvis made a slight whimpering sound, full of sympathy.

Byron looked away. "I don't know," he said.

Years of taking depositions and reading juries had taught Melissa to spot a lie, and Byron Cahill was definitely not telling the truth now.

"Do we have a case?" Tom asked Melissa.

It was a rhetorical question, of course.

"I'm afraid so," Melissa answered wearily. "I'll file formal charges in the morning. In the meantime, since Mr. Cahill did his best to evade you when you tried to pull him over, it would be best to keep him here."

Byron was on his feet, knuckles white where he gripped the bars with both hands, looking past Melissa and Tom. "Can they do that?" he demanded. "Can they hold me when no charges have been filed?"

Steven joined the group in front of the cell. Melissa slanted a sideways glance at his face, through her lashes, but said nothing.

"Depends," Steven answered.

"I can always file charges tonight," Melissa told Byron crisply, "if that's what you want."

Steven sighed.

Byron spun away.

"That went well," Tom observed, leaning down to pat Elvis on the head.

When Melissa turned around, she was surprised to see that Velda had left.

"I asked Mrs. Cahill to wait in my truck," Steven said. "I'm taking her home."

"That's very nice of you," Melissa said, without inflection.

"You might as well go on home," Tom interjected. "Both of you. There won't be much going on here for the rest of the night."

Cautiously, Steven touched Melissa's elbow. "I'll drop you off at your place," he said.

"No, thanks," Melissa replied lightly, but with an edge. "I'll call someone."

A look passed between Steven and Tom. Tom walked away, whistled for Elvis, who remained in front of the cell, keeping watch over the prisoner.

"I'd like a word with you, in private," Steven told Melissa.

Melissa gave one abrupt nod and followed Steven out into the corridor.

She surprised herself by being the first one to speak. "You know damn well you can't ethically defend Cahill," she said, glaring up at him. "Not while I'm the prosecutor."

"And you do intend to prosecute?"

"Of course I do," Melissa answered impatiently. "It's my job."

"Has it occurred to you that the kid might be innocent, just as he claims?"

"He'll have a public defender," Melissa pointed out.

"No," Steven argued, his tone and his eyes stone cold. "He won't."

"You can't defend him, because—because of—"

"Us?"

"Yes," Melissa said, fighting a humiliating urge to break down and cry.

"You're right, counselor," he said, maintaining the chill. "You and I can't oppose each other in court. But I know some other lawyers who'll be willing to take the case pro bono."

She blinked. "Why are you pushing this?" she asked.

"Because I think Cahill is innocent," Steven answered.

"He was caught with the mask and the money! How *could* he be?"

"Ask the dog," Steven said.

And with that, he turned and walked away, leaving Melissa standing alone in the corridor outside the sheriff's office.

Ask the dog, Steven had said. What the hell did that mean?

She opened Tom's door quietly and slipped back into the office.

Elvis was still sitting in front of Byron's cell. The prisoner was sprawled facedown on his cot. And Tom was seated at his desk, entering data into his computer.

Melissa approached, sank into a chair nearby. Glanced at Elvis.

"What's up with your dog?" she asked, after a long time.

Tom sighed. "I'm not sure," he said, so quietly that Byron wouldn't have heard. "I've never seen Elvis behave like that before." He paused. "I don't mind admitting that it bothers me a little, though."

"Why?" Melissa asked, wishing she were at home, in her own bed, that the night hadn't happened.

That *Steven Creed* hadn't happened.

"Well," Tom said, at some length, "Elvis has always been a pretty fair judge of character."

IT WAS HIS night for walking women to their front doors, evidently.

Steven squired Velda Cahill along the dirt path leading to her rusted-out single-wide. A plastic gnome stood guard on a little porch jerry-rigged from mismatched scraps of lumber.

The trailer door swung open, and Melissa's assistant, Andrea, stood framed in the light from inside. Even with her face in shadow, Steven could see that she'd been crying.

"Where's Byron?" she demanded.

"He's in jail," Velda said. She'd been frantic earlier in the evening, but now she seemed beaten down.

Andrea gave a little wail of despair.

"You'll help him, won't you?" Velda almost whispered, turning to look up at Steven. "You'll make sure my boy doesn't go back to prison for something he didn't do?"

"I'll do what I can," Steven answered, just as a young man replaced Andrea in the doorway, easing her to one side.

Steven had never seen the guy before.

"Nathan Carter," he said, stepping aside long enough to sort of steer Velda into the trailer, then putting out a hand.

"Steven Creed," Steven answered.

"Somebody's got to look after these women," Nathan said, although no one had asked what he was doing there. He sounded regretful as he spoke, but his eyes told another story. On some level, he almost seemed to be enjoying the excitement.

Steven hesitated a moment, reluctant to leave and, at the same time, eager to be gone. He finally nodded to Carter and turned to descend the three rickety steps to the path.

It was late, so, as he and Meg had agreed earlier, he didn't stop at Stone Creek Ranch to pick Matt up. By now, the boy would be sound asleep.

Back at the tour bus, Steven let Zeke out into the yard, waited while the dog made good use of the front yard and followed him inside.

Zeke stood looking up at Steven, wagging his tail. For a dog, he sure was expressive.

And so was Sheriff Parker's four-legged deputy, Elvis.

"Things don't look real good for Byron Cahill," Steven told Zeke, leaning to pick up the mutt's nearly empty water dish to refill it at the sink. He set the bowl down on the floor and watched as the animal lapped up a drink. He remembered the expression on Melissa's face, there in the corridor outside the jail. "Come to think of it," he added, falling just short of a smile, "they're not looking all that good for me, either."

It was Tom who drove Melissa home that night.

She was thoughtful during the ride.

He and Elvis walked her to the front door, waited until she was safely inside and left again. She knew Tom planned on spending the night on the couch in his office, rather than leaving the prisoner unattended until morning.

Melissa locked up, then wandered into her bedroom and stood in front of the full-length mirror, shaking her head at the bedraggled figure staring back at her.

The aqua dress, which had made her feel so pretty

and so feminine earlier in the evening, seemed to mock her now.

Her hair drooped, her mascara made faint shadows under her eyes and she'd long since chewed off her lipstick.

With a sigh, she grabbed her robe and headed for the small master bath just off her bedroom. There, she stripped, stepped under a hot shower and scrubbed until her skin squeaked.

After that, she dried off, put on the robe and headed for the kitchen. What she needed, she decided, was a nice cup of herbal tea.

Or a shot of whiskey.

She decided on the tea, and was sitting at the table near the windows, sipping from a mug, when someone pounded on the back door.

"Melissa!" yelled a familiar female voice. "I know you're in there—let me in!"

Andrea.

Melissa went to the door, turned the dead bolt and then the knob. She didn't ask what Andrea was doing there, at that hour of the night no less, because she already knew.

The young woman was obviously upset; she'd been crying, hard, and her eyes were so red they looked raw.

"Sit down," Melissa said gently.

Andrea collapsed into a chair at the table and, after locking the door again, Melissa prepared a second cup of tea and set it down in front of her midnight visitor.

For a moment, Andrea looked as though she might send the mug and her tea flying with one angry swipe of her arm. Fortunately, she seemed to think better of the idea in the next instant and carefully lifted the cup to her mouth, her hands shaking.

"Were you with Byron tonight, when he held up the Stop & Shop?" Melissa asked.

Andrea flung a beleaguered look in her direction, but she retained her composure.

"I was with Byron tonight," she said. "But he didn't rob the Stop & Shop."

Melissa merely waited, her own tea cooling, forgotten, on the table.

The set of Andrea's jaw was obstinate, but only for a moment or two. Fresh tears brimmed along her lower lashes, and one trickled, zigzag, down her cheek. She wiped it away with the back of one hand, but only after the fact.

"I'm telling you, Byron didn't do anything wrong," the girl insisted.

"You know," Melissa said carefully, when Andrea lapsed into another silence, "I keep hearing that. From you. From Velda. But Byron was heading out of town at top speed when Tom caught up with him, and later, the money from the robbery was found in the trunk of his car, along with a ski mask like the one Martine described when she reported what happened."

"We were in bed," Andrea said, in a broken whisper. "Byron and me."

"Where?" Melissa asked. She still suspected her assistant of making up an alibi for her boyfriend, but she was willing to listen.

"His place," Andrea said, meeting Melissa's eyes only with an effort.

"Velda must have loved that," Melissa commented.

Andrea bristled. "She was at work," she said. "Byron and I had the place to ourselves. Velda called from the cocktail lounge around nine-thirty and said she didn't feel very well and she needed to come home, and would

Byron pick her up. That's when he found out the car was gone."

"Gone? You mean, stolen?"

"Byron knew who'd taken it. It was that loser, Nathan. He's been hanging around the Cahills' place lately—he and Byron ran around together when they were younger—said he needed someplace to stay. I guess Byron felt sorry for him or something." Andrea tossed her head slightly; a good sign. She was turning back into her old, spirited self. "That Nathan, he's a sneak. He tried to borrow money from me a couple of times—I turned him down. And he bragged that he had a case against Deputy Ferguson because of that black eye, and the county would have to give him some kind of settlement to keep the story out of the news—" She stopped, took a shaky breath, and then rushed on. "Deputy Ferguson didn't give Nathan that shiner. Velda did."

The tale was just crazy enough to be true. "Velda?" Melissa asked, intrigued and more than a little uneasy. "Why?"

"She said she caught him going through her purse," Andrea said. "Byron and I weren't around at the time. She told us later that she slugged Nathan because he gave her some back talk, and then she kicked him out." Another sigh. "Of course, he came back, and Velda decided the cops were out to get him and so she'd let him stay at the trailer a while longer."

"Were you planning on mentioning this to me at some point?" Melissa asked archly. "The accusation Nathan Carter made could have ruined Deputy Ferguson's career—or even his life."

"We didn't know he'd accused anybody of anything until he started bragging about it," Andrea said, sounding miffed. "I wouldn't have let Deputy Ferguson be blamed, and neither would Byron. He's a good person, Melissa."

"I really want to believe that," Melissa said slowly.

"But you don't?" Andrea challenged, and the tears were back again.

Melissa didn't answer.

"Don't you see?" Andrea pressed, looking and sounding desperate now. "*Nathan Carter* robbed that store, not Byron!"

It wasn't beyond credibility, but there was one obvious problem. Nathan hadn't been trying to get away from Stone Creek with the money taken at gunpoint from the Stop & Shop—*Byron* had been the one at the wheel when Tom caught up to him. And Byron probably wouldn't have stopped at all if he hadn't run off the road.

"Then why wasn't he driving Velda's car, Andrea?" Melissa asked, after taking a few moments to collect her own composure. "If Nathan went into that store, wearing a ski mask, and stole that money, why was Byron the one who tried to get away?"

"I don't know," Andrea said.

"You don't know," Melissa repeated, absorbing that.

"After Byron realized his mom's car was missing, he told me to go back to my apartment and stay there. He said there was going to be trouble, he could feel it, and he didn't want me to be involved."

"And you went home? Just likc that?" Melissa was skeptical. The Andrea she knew wasn't fond of taking orders.

"*Yes,*" Andrea replied. "Byron was really upset, and I was scared. Not of Byron, but of whatever had scared him so much."

"So you've been home, in your apartment, since Byron sent you away?"

Andrea bit her lower lip, then shook her head. "No," she answered, after a few beats. "The Crockett sisters heard about the robbery over their police scanner, and they couldn't wait to tell me that Sheriff Parker and all his deputies were out hunting for Byron. I panicked and went over to Velda's, and Nathan was there. He told me Byron was in big trouble, that he'd pulled a heist with a deadly weapon and Velda had gone to the jail to try and do something to help—"

A chill trickled down Melissa's spine. "And after that?"

"Steven Creed brought Velda home. She's a basket case. Nathan's making like he's all caring and everything—he made her a hot toddy and everything."

"And you decided to come and talk to me." It was a statement, not a question. Melissa's mind was racing, but she knew she appeared calm on the outside. She'd had a lot of practice at that.

Andrea nodded hard, glanced nervously in the direction of the door. "I knew Byron thought Nathan had taken the car, and when I heard about the robbery and headed over to Velda's, and Nathan was there, I knew what had *really* happened. I sneaked out while he was making a fuss over Velda, making her a drink and everything, and then I was scared to go home, because Nathan knows where I live."

Melissa rose from her chair, crossed to the wall phone, and picked up the handset.

Tom Parker answered on the first ring. "Stone Creek County Sheriff's office," he said. "This is Tom."

Melissa launched right in, telling Tom everything Andrea had told her.

He didn't interrupt, but simply listened.

"I'll check it out," he said, when she'd finished. "Keep Andrea there with you, and make sure all the doors and windows are locked up tight."

"Tom," Melissa said, after catching her breath. "Be careful, okay?"

"Always," he promised, with a smile in his voice. "I'll leave Elvis here to guard the prisoner."

Melissa didn't comment. "Call me," she said.

"Lock up tight," Tom responded.

And then he hung up.

Melissa checked the front door and all the windows. She brewed more tea, and she and Andrea moved to the living room, where there were draperies over the windows.

Melissa was definitely creeped out, and she knew Andrea was, too, although neither of them said much. Andrea seemed exhausted, and little wonder, after the night she'd put in.

Eventually, Andrea fell asleep on the couch.

Melissa covered her with an afghan Ashley had crocheted for her years ago, as a Christmas gift, and sat down in her easy chair again, huddled inside her bathrobe.

The clock on the mantel ticked ponderously. Every passing second seemed like a full minute to Melissa, every minute an hour.

At some point, she nodded off.

ANDREA AWAKENED HER with a cry of alarm. "My car is gone!"

Melissa straightened, blinking, surprised to find herself in a chair instead of her bed.

Andrea was standing by the window, holding back

one of the drapes. Cold light spilled over her puffy face, and her cheeks were streaked with mascara and last night's tears.

"Wh-what?" Melissa said, bumbling to her feet. Yawning.

"My car!" Andrea wailed. "I parked it right out there, at the curb, last night. And now it's *gone!*"

"Are you sure?" It *was* a stupid question, but, despite years of getting up at the crack of dawn to go out and run, in actuality, Melissa wasn't a morning person.

"Of course I'm sure!" Andrea replied. "It was there, and now it's gone!"

Melissa sighed. Time to put in another call to Tom.

She picked up the cordless handset in the living room and punched in his office number.

"Stone Creek County Sheriff's office," he answered.

"Andrea's car has been stolen," Melissa blurted.

Tom was quiet for so long that Melissa spoke up again.

"Tom? What's going on?"

He gave a raspy sigh. "I'll tell you when you get here," he said. "In the meantime, put Andrea on. I'm going to need as much information about her car as she can give me."

"But—"

"When you get here, Melissa," Tom repeated, sternly patient. "Oh, and fair warning. You're bound to run into Steven Creed. He's on his way here right now, to oversee Byron Cahill's release."

"You're letting him go?" Another stupid question.

She needed coffee. Pronto.

"Yep," Tom said.

Melissa turned to find Andrea standing wide-eyed

at her elbow. "The sheriff wants to ask you some questions about your car," she said to the girl.

"They're letting Byron go?" Andrea asked softly.

Melissa nodded. "Sounds like it," she said.

While Andrea was trying to remember her license-plate number and other pertinent details, Melissa hurried off to her room.

She dressed quickly, donning a black pantsuit, pulling her hair back and fastening it in place with a barrette. She applied minimal makeup and rejoined Andrea in the living room.

The girl was still standing there, looking dumbfounded with joy. Sure, her car was gone, possibly for good, but Byron was getting out of jail.

For Andrea, it was all good.

They both hopped into Melissa's roadster, keeping the top up because it was a misty morning, and headed for the courthouse.

As fate would have it, the first person Melissa encountered was Steven Creed. He was dressed for lawyering, as Big John would have said, in a tailored suit and shoes polished to such a sheen that they almost made her blink.

Andrea dashed past him, anxious to see Byron.

Steven's expression was just short of smug, but something in his eyes made Melissa wary.

"What?" she finally whispered, standing there in the corridor, looking at him.

He straightened his tasteful tie—pale blue silk with very thin gray stripes running diagonally—and even though his mouth didn't shape itself into a smile, he looked amused.

"So this is your evil twin," he said, taking in her mean-business pantsuit, slapdash makeup job and prim, no-nonsense hairstyle. One of his eyebrows rose slightly. "I must admit, I like the other Melissa better, the one with no hard edges."

Evil twin? Hard edges?

"Get out of my way," Melissa said.

Steven didn't move except to shove his hands into the pockets of his perfectly tailored trousers and cock his head to one side. "Temper, temper," he scolded, with syrupy insolence. "Your edges are showing."

She tried to go around him, but he blocked her way.

"Before you go in there, there's something I need to tell you."

Again, Melissa felt that quiet alarm. She drew a deep breath, let it out slowly, and silently instructed herself to calm the heck down. It was downright unprofessional, letting this man rattle her the way he did.

And even worse that he knew exactly what he was doing.

"All right," she said, finally. "What is it?"

His face tightened almost imperceptibly, and he actually averted his gaze for a moment. "Velda Cahill was assaulted last night."

"What?"

Steven relaxed a little, took a light hold on Melissa's shoulders. "She'll be fine in a few days," he assured her. A muscle bunched in his cheek, and she saw a combination of anger and regret flare up in his eyes, gone as quickly as it appeared. "Carter knocked her around some last night, when he realized Andrea had slipped out of the trailer behind his back. He stole Velda's watch and the contents of her tip jar and took off."

Melissa felt cold all over. "Poor Velda," she said. "That woman cannot catch a break."

"She's an inpatient at the clinic over in Indian Rock.

I thought I should let you know ahead of time because Byron hasn't been told yet. He's bound to be shaken up, not to mention furious, and I figure he'll want to go after Nathan Carter himself. If he does that, obviously, he'll be back in jail for sure."

Melissa nodded slowly. "Do you have a plan?"

"If it weren't for Matt, I'd have Byron stay at my place until he settles down or Carter is in custody, whichever comes first. There are too many unknown factors in the equation, of course, and I'm not about to risk Matt's being hurt. Tom and I talked it over, and he's willing to take the boy in, since it's just him and Elvis. God knows whether Byron will agree or not."

Melissa pondered the idea. Given Byron's history with the sheriff, it didn't seem likely, but stranger things had happened.

"Thanks," she said stiffly, and this time when she moved to enter Tom's office, Steven didn't get in her way.

BYRON WAS OUT of the cell and back in his civilian clothes, plunked sullenly in a chair next to Tom's desk. Andrea stood behind that chair, her hands resting on Byron's taut shoulders.

Following Melissa into the large, open room, Steven shifted his focus from her shapely posterior to the tasks at hand.

His gaze snagged with Tom's.

"You must be out of your mind," Byron blurted, glaring at the sheriff.

Elvis slunk over, placed his muzzle on the young man's blue-jeaned thigh and made a soft sound full of sorrowful affection.

Byron automatically stroked the dog's head, but he

went right on trying to bore a hole through Tom Parker with his eyes.

Tom, perched casually on a corner of his big desk, looked unflappable. Initially, Steven had pegged the man for a rube, but he'd since revised his opinion. "I reckon three-quarters of the people I know would agree, since I just invited you to bunk on my screened-in sun-porch for a while."

"Why would I want to do that?" Byron snapped. Andrea's fingers tightened noticeably, and he shrugged her off.

Tom glanced in Steven's direction, and Steven nodded in response. Cleared his throat.

"Byron," he said, "your mother has been hurt—"

Byron leaped to his feet and whirled around so fast that his chair toppled over and both Elvis and Andrea had to jump out of the way. "What happened to my mom?" Byron demanded. "How bad is—?"

Steven held up both hands, palms out. "She'll be *fine*, Byron. They're keeping her at the clinic a day or two, mostly for observation, but she's going to be all right."

Byron reddened, and clenched both fists at his sides. "*He* did it, didn't he? That son-of-a-bitch Nathan Carter hurt my mother!"

Melissa went to stand beside a trembling, wide-eyed Andrea, putting an arm around the girl's shoulders, giving her an encouraging squeeze. Essentially, holding her up.

Tom spoke next, quietly and with authority. "That's what she told Deputy Ferguson when he took her to the clinic last night," he said, watching Byron. Like Steven, he was poised to land on the kid if his temper got any further out of hand. "Velda has some cracked ribs, two black eyes and a split lip. And if there's one thing your mother *doesn't* need right now, it's for you to get yourself into trouble all over again."

Byron calmed himself a little, but not quite enough for Steven and Tom to let down their guard. He swore under his breath and thrust a hand through his rumpled hair, and his eyes filled with angry tears.

"You must have known it was Nathan who robbed the Stop & Shop," Steven said reasonably, watching Byron. "Why didn't you tell me, or Tom?"

Byron seemed to deflate, like a balloon two days after the party. He groped his way back into his chair. Glanced up at Andrea with an expression of such profound concern that Steven himself was moved by it. "I would have, when the time was right," he finally replied, "but I was in here and Carter was out there where he could do anything he wanted, and I was afraid for the people I care about."

"Are you ready to tell me where you were headed last night, when you wrecked your mother's car and Sheriff Parker hauled you in?" Maybe Tom had gotten an answer to that question in the interim, but Steven was still in the dark.

Byron's shoulders sagged, and he spent a few moments petting Elvis before he made his reply. "I just panicked, that's all," he confessed. "I didn't know where I was going. I just wanted to get away and hide out someplace, so I wouldn't have to go back to prison."

Tom's response surprised everybody. "I can see why you'd freak out," he said. He paused, gave a sigh, but his gaze was steady on the younger man's face. "There's an APB out on Carter," he went on, "and we'll get him. But it's my job—mine and the department's—to bring him in, not yours. You try to take matters into your own hands and you *will* go to jail, for violating your parole at the very least."

Byron swallowed, nodded again.

Andrea moved away from Melissa and approached Byron's chair. Laid a hand on his shoulder, like before. "You ought to stay with Sheriff Parker," she said, very softly. "It's good of him to offer, Byron. He's trying to help you."

A smile crooked the corner of Tom's mouth. "Elvis is all for taking in a roommate," he said.

Byron didn't move for a long time. Then he put his hand on top of Andrea's, gently squeezed her fingers.

"Okay," he said.

And one matter, at least, was settled.

Now, Steven thought ruefully, *to settle everything else that's gone wrong lately.*

As though reading his mind, Melissa looked at him and narrowed her eyes, in a like-hell sort of way. She told Andrea to take the day off, asked Tom to keep her posted on the statewide hunt for Nathan Carter, and breezed past Steven like he wasn't even there.

The door snapped shut behind her.

Steven immediately followed. He knew he was probably making bad matters worse, but he damn well couldn't help himself.

He caught up to her at the door of her office.

"Melissa," he ground out. "Wait—"

"Go away," she said. "I don't want to deal with you right now."

He steered her inside the room where Andrea normally worked, and closed the door. "Well, that's just *tough,* counselor, because you are going to deal with me."

She glared up at him, folded her arms. Her words

flew like well-aimed bullets, staccato and dead on target. "It was all a mistake. You and me, I mean. I should have known better. Case closed."

"Melissa," Steven heard himself say, "that's crazy."

She was on a roll. "You do criminal defense. I'm a prosecutor. We don't think the same way."

"Of course we don't think the same way," Steven countered easily. "Why would two intelligent, independent adults even want that?"

"Do the math," Melissa persisted. "We might as well be from different planets."

"Mars and Venus?" Steven teased.

"Very funny," she replied. But she didn't look or sound all that amused.

Steven tried again. "What I meant was—"

"I don't *care* what you meant, Steven."

"I can see that," he answered calmly. "So, what happened, Melissa? Was your mother scared by a member of the Dream Team when she was pregnant with you?"

"Ha-ha," Melissa said.

"Can't we just agree to disagree?"

"Yes," she said, after swallowing visibly. "We can agree to disagree. How about forever?"

Steven whistled, long and low. "Hello? Don't you think you're overreacting just a little here?"

"All we have to do is pretend nothing happened—"

"No," Steven interrupted flatly. "We aren't going to do that."

"Why not?"

Damn, she was stubborn. Too bad he found that quality so attractive in a woman. Or, at least, in *this* woman.

"Because it *did* happen."

"Now you're just nitpicking," she protested.

Steven rolled his eyes. "We went to bed together," he said slowly and with emphasis.

"Keep your voice down!" Melissa retorted, glancing toward the door.

He flung out his hands. "I give up."

"Good," Melissa said. "It's about time."

He leaned in, so their noses were almost touching. *"For now,"* he clarified. Then he left her standing there, and strode out into the corridor, headed back to Tom's office.

He had business to attend to—and he'd better put Melissa O'Ballivan out of his head.

CHAPTER SIXTEEN

"THIS IS AN INTERVENTION," Olivia announced solemnly, a week and a half after Melissa's last conversation with Steven Creed.

Melissa looked around Olivia and Tanner's living room, sweeping Meg and Ashley up in an indignant glance.

"You tricked me," she said, in an accusing tone. Olivia had suggested that all four of them meet at her place that Thursday evening, after Melissa got off work, to discuss the parade, which was scheduled for the following night. Ostensibly, her devoted sisters and sister-in-law were supposed to assist her with last-minute logistics.

What a sucker she was.

"We had to do something," Ashley said earnestly, near tears. "You've gone around the bend."

"You're definitely not yourself," Meg added, plainly concerned. She took in Melissa's outfit. "Since when do you go to work in sweats and sneakers?"

"Without makeup," Olivia pointed out.

"And look at your *hair*," Ashley all but wailed.

"Plus you haven't been running," Olivia contributed. This whole confrontational thing had probably been her idea—she'd always been the bossy big-sister type.

"Maybe I'm a little depressed," Melissa admitted,

feeling defensive. "It'll pass as soon as they catch Nathan Carter and this damn parade is over."

"Even after you and Dan parted ways, you didn't let yourself go like this," Ashley pressed, waving off Melissa's words as she spoke. "We're worried about you."

"You're falling apart," Olivia said.

"I think this *mood* you're in has something to do with Steven Creed," Meg insisted. "You've been different ever since he hit town."

Olivia and Ashley nodded in unison.

"No, it does *not* have to do with—him," Melissa lied. The truth was, she couldn't seem to get the man out of her mind, even for her own good.

"Level with us," Olivia urged, her eyes softening. "We want to help you."

"I need help with the parade," Melissa said. "Not my personal life."

Olivia, Ashley and Meg all looked at each other, exchanging unspoken messages.

Melissa stood up.

"Sit down," Olivia said firmly.

Melissa sat. "This is silly," she said.

"Are you in love with this Steven Creed person?" Ashley wanted to know.

"No," Melissa said, hoping she sounded convincing. By then, she was so confused, she didn't know *what* she felt. Was wanting somebody—not just physically, but emotionally and mentally and even spiritually, for pity's sake—the same as loving him? "It was just a case of temporary lust." She waved one hand dismissively, much as Ashley had done earlier. They were, after all, twins. "Anyway, it's over."

"What happened?" Meg asked.

"That," Melissa said, "is none of your business—any

of you—but I'll answer anyway. Yes, there was an attraction. But Steven and I are both lawyers. Worse yet, we have very different viewpoints, since he's Defense, and I'm Prosecution. While that may not seem like a big deal to *most people,* it constitutes irrevocable differences in our private philosophies. When it comes to our philosophies of life, we're polar opposites."

Ashley shook her head, marveling. "What a lot of gobbledegook," she said.

"I'd call it BS," Olivia interjected.

"Now you know why I didn't want to talk about this," Melissa said loftily. She stood up again, and this time she meant it. She was leaving. "I knew none of you would understand. And why should you? All three of you have children, and happy marriages—"

"Melissa—" Ashley said.

Melissa picked up her purse, ferreted inside it for her car keys and headed for the Quinns' front door. There, she paused and turned to assess—very coolly— the three other women who had summoned her on false pretenses. "The parade starts at six tomorrow night," she said. "We're gathering at four, in the parking lot behind the high school. If any of you actually want to *help,* be there."

Nobody said anything.

Naturally.

Slinging the strap of her purse over one shoulder, Melissa left with a flourish.

It HAD BEEN over a week since he'd seen Melissa, except at a distance, and Steven did his damnedest to carry on as if nothing had changed.

Every morning, he fed Matt and the dog breakfast, made do with stale, reheated coffee himself. At night, he slept heavily, mired in mixed-up dreams he couldn't remember two seconds after he opened his eyes, and he sure as hell didn't feel rested—more like a wino, hung over after a three-day binge.

Quite a trick, since he hadn't had anything to drink since before Brody left.

Leaving the tour bus that Friday morning, locking it behind him, Steven was mildly pleased to see that the renovation crew had already arrived to put in another day's work. The barn, a nifty-looking prebuilt structure, already had walls and a roof and, by Monday, the stalls would be in, as well. He stopped to confer briefly with the foreman, who told him they were putting up drywall in the bedrooms that day, and they'd start installing the kitchen and bathroom fixtures tomorrow.

"If you don't watch it," Steven said, only half kidding, "you're going to give the contracting business a good name."

The foreman smiled at the comment, puny as it was, and informed Steven that the company was family-owned, had been in business for four generations and there had been at least one member of the clan on one crew or another from the first.

The watchword, Steven thought, was *continuity*. It was a way of life with most of the Creeds—the Mc-Kettricks and the O'Ballivans, too. And it was what Steven wanted for Matt, for himself, and for any descendants inclined to live out their lives on a ranch.

He hadn't reckoned on Melissa when he'd decided to put down roots in Stone Creek, but life was full of things nobody had reckoned on, wasn't it? A man had to do the best he could with whatever hand he was dealt, press on, take the good with the bad.

Some family histories just happened. Others were deliberately created.

Steven intended to build a dandy one, and to do that, he'd need a wife. Eventually.

Things would turn out just fine, he assured himself, while he was buckling Matt into his safety seat in the truck, as long as he stayed away from lady lawyers— Cindy aside, he'd never been able to get along with them, outside the office or the courtroom, even when they played on his team.

Insanity, the saying went, was doing the same thing over and over again and expecting to get different results.

Melissa was beautiful and funny and smart, everything he admired in a woman, but when push came to shove, she had the prosecutorial mind-set: The accused was guilty until proven innocent, not the other way around. And Steven, to the roots of his being, was *all about* the other way around.

Matt brought him out of his reflections with a jolt, his tone worried. "You look really sad."

"Maybe I am a little," Steven said, once he'd helped Zeke onto the seat, next to his pint-size master.

"Because you're not going out on dates with Melissa anymore?"

"Partly," Steven replied. He never lied to the boy, but he wasn't inclined to burden a five-year-old with adult problems, either. He just wished Matt hadn't developed a shining sct of high hopes as far as the Stone Creek County prosecutor was concerncd.

In Matt's mind, Steven was sure, Melissa was on the fast track to becoming his new mommy. His drawing of the stick-people family was still taped to the refrigerator door, and he wouldn't hear of taking it down, except to pore over it and add a detail here and there, with a pencil or a stub of crayon.

"I guess it's grown-up stuff?" Matt asked, with a certain resignation.

Steven grinned, though he felt hollow inside. "Grownup stuff," he confirmed. "Nothing you need to worry about."

"Okay," Matt agreed, but he didn't seem convinced.

Steven shut the door, walked around the truck and hauled himself up behind the wheel. He was only thirty-five, but he felt about eighty that morning.

The dreams he couldn't remember still weighed on him.

He shoved a hand through his hair and started the engine.

Matt was quiet during the drive into town; Steven could almost hear the gears grinding in that little head.

When they pulled up at Creekside Academy, Matt didn't seem happy to be there, as he usually did.

Kids, Steven reassured himself, as Matt dawdled along the sidewalk, delaying entering the building for as long as he could, are resilient.

Must be nice, he thought, trying to remember what it felt like, being good at bouncing back.

He watched until Matt was safely inside the building, then turned and got into the truck again. Zeke, still in back, craned his neck and laved the side of Steven's face once with his sandpaper tongue.

Steven chuckled, checked all the mirrors and backed out of the parking space.

The Stop & Shop was back to business as usual, had been since the morning after the robbery.

Talk about resilience.

On impulse, he turned into the lot and parked.

Martine was back at work, as he'd hoped—she'd taken some time off after the robbery, and Steven hadn't wanted to bother her at home.

After adjusting the windows and telling Zeke he'd be right back, he walked into the store.

Martine was there, looking a little pale around the gills, but otherwise she seemed pretty cheerful.

A plain young woman standing at the counter paid for her purchases—a half gallon of milk and two lottery tickets—and nodded to Steven as she passed him on her way out of the store.

Steven nodded back, waited until he and Martine were alone, then reintroduced himself. They'd already met, of course, but she'd been through a trauma and he figured she might not remember.

"Hello, again," Martine responded, with a wan smile, proving him wrong. He recalled last time's reference to her unmarried daughter. "What can I do for you, Mr. Creed?"

"Steven," he corrected, approaching the counter. "I'd like to ask you a couple of questions about the other night, if you wouldn't mind."

Martine looked reluctant, almost pained, but she nodded. "You and half the cops in the state of Arizona," she sighed. Evidently not one to be idle, she wiped ineffectually at the glass countertop with a cloth as she spoke. "It started out as a normal night. Things were quiet, so I went back to the storage room to call my boyfriend on my cell. We've been having some trouble lately, him and me. Anyhow, when we were finished talking, I was too antsy to finish my break, so I headed for the front of the store. And the guy with the ski mask was standing there, right about where you are now, with a gun in one hand—" She paused to point, blanching as the experience replayed itself in her mind.

"And you recognized Byron, even with the ski mask covering his entire head?"

"I recognized Velda's car," Martine stressed. "I was too scared to identify anybody, notice eye color or height or anything like that. I just wanted to give the robber whatever he wanted so he'd get out of here— without shooting me."

Steven nodded. "Any customers in the store right before your break?" Steven asked moderately.

But Martine shook her head. "As I said, it was quiet. Everybody in town was over at the dance." She paused, gave a husky, rueful chuckle. "Everybody except George and me, anyhow."

George, Steven assumed, was the boyfriend, the one she'd been on the outs with on the night in question. He didn't pursue the subject. "No strangers came in? Say, early in your shift?"

Another shake of the head. "Last strangers I recall seeing were an older couple traveling in an RV, and that was at least a couple of days before—before it happened."

Steven didn't respond directly. Since he hadn't gotten around to having cards printed yet, he helped himself to a stenographer's notebook resting on the countertop, along with the accompanying pen, and wrote down his cell and office numbers. "I'd appreciate a call if you remember anything else," he said. He started to turn away, but Martine stopped him with a remark meant to sound offhand, most likely, but falling a ways short.

"I hear you're serving as Byron Cahill's lawyer."

"Not exactly," Steven said, after an inaudible sigh.

"As you know, Byron is no longer a suspect. I'm just trying to help out in whatever way I can."

"It was good of Tom to take the boy in for a while," Martine said. "Byron and Velda haven't had it easy, that's for sure. Do you think they'll catch Nathan Carter anytime soon?" She stopped for a breath, shuddered slightly. "It gives me the heebie-jeebies, knowing he's still out there. What if he comes back and tries again, since he didn't get to keep the money last time?"

"I don't think he will," Steven said in parting.

It wasn't much, but at the moment, it was all he had to offer.

Feeling as if he'd made no progress at all— what else was new?—Steven left the Stop & Shop and drove to his office, passing the Sunflower Café on the way. The place was doing a brisk business, as usual, the parking lot packed with cars, motorcycles and pickup trucks.

Steven cruised on past the courthouse next, casually stealing a glance in that direction, as he did every time he came into town for any reason. Melissa's roadster was parked in its usual place, with the top up and a reflective shield across the inside of the windshield.

He considered stopping by to say hello—*hello?*—but soon discarded the idea.

What was there to say? Melissa had made up her mind about him, and about what he did for a living. She was an intelligent woman, a practicing attorney; at least in principle, she definitely understood that under the American judicial system, faulty though it was, everyone—guilty or innocent—has the right to counsel.

It seemed more probable that she was merely using that difference of opinion as an excuse to avoid anything remotely resembling a lifetime commitment. She'd admitted to caring a lot for Dan Guthrie, once upon a time, and Steven had seen what could only be called regret in her eyes when she spoke of Dan's children, the two boys she'd expected to raise as her own.

She was clearly fond of Matt—a point in her favor, of course. Unless she'd been attracted to Steven *because* of the child, and only because of him.

He parked alongside his building, got out of the truck and almost forgot Zeke in the backseat. A cheerful yip reminded him that he wasn't alone, so he retraced his steps, hooked a leash to Zeke's collar, and lifted the dog out of the truck, setting him on the ground. Waiting.

Zeke sniffed the gravel for a while, checked out various thatches of weeds at the edges of the lot, then lifted a hind leg in front of the weathered log marking the boundary of the property on the Main Street side. Steven was still stumbling around in his own thoughts, too distracted, by his own reckoning, to be good for anything much—that day, at least.

He rubbed the back of his neck with one hand, remembering the wild time he and Melissa had shared in his bed. Male egotism aside, he knew she hadn't been faking her responses—he'd felt the subtle flexing of her body as she'd reached one orgasm and then another, felt the moisture of exertion on her silky skin and thrilled to her uninhibited cries of pleasure.

Steven shifted uncomfortably. Tried to turn his thoughts in another direction.

Zeke finished up and they headed for the side door.

Inside, Steven unsnapped the leash and left the dog to wander around the inner and outer offices until he'd found just the right place to curl up for a morning snooze. This involved some circling, some pawing at the carpet, and a couple of big sighs, but Zeke finally settled himself in a patch of sunlight in front of the window to the street, dropped off to sleep and began to snore.

Steven checked his messages.

Zip from Melissa, of course.

Two from Velda Cahill; she'd been calling regularly since her release from the clinic in Indian Rock a few days back, wanting to know what was being done to find Nathan Carter and making a lot of noise about how Byron ought to come back home ASAP.

Byron, on the other hand, seemed happy enough bunking with Tom Parker and Elvis—the kid did his share of the yard and household chores to earn his keep, according to the sheriff, and although not much was said, they all got along just fine. In his spare time, Byron helped out over at the animal shelter, and there was talk about his getting hired steady, bringing home a paycheck, however modest.

So far, so good.

Except that Carter was still at large, of course.

Settled at his desk, Steven booted up his computer, checked his email for the first time that day.

Conner was on his way, he learned, and Davis and Kim were coming along, too, bringing their RV. Everybody was up for a visit and a good old-fashioned rodeo, according to Conner's brief message.

Steven sighed. Brody was headed for Stone Creek, too, planning on competing in the bronc-riding events, both bareback and saddle.

His twin cousins were about to meet up, after all this time, though neither one of them knew it.

Once again, Steven wondered if he'd made the right decision by keeping the impending collision of Creed tempers under his hat, so to speak.

It was the hope—however frail it might be—that

Brody and Conner would finally work things out and get on with being brothers that prevented Steven from issuing a storm warning. Those two were both stubborn to the bone, and if either found out that the other one was going to be in Stone Creek for the rodeo, *neither* of them would show up.

Therefore, Steven thought, as he tapped out a response to Conner's email, revealing nothing, the chips would have to fall where they may.

MELISSA WENT FOR a run on Friday morning—something she hadn't done for a few days—and took special care with her hair, makeup and clothes when she got back home.

It *wasn't* because of that stupid "intervention" Olivia, Ashley and Meg had sprung on her the evening before, though. No, sirree. She would be leaving her office early to put the finishing touches on the parade that would kick off Stone Creek Rodeo Days that night, and after that, the whole thing would be over.

Looking good was her way of celebrating, that was all.

The morning went by quickly, for once.

She skipped lunch, feeling too nervous to eat, and, conversely, loaded up on coffee. At three forty-five, leaving her assistant to hold down the fort for what little remained of the workday, Melissa headed out.

Ferociously hungry all of a sudden, and telling herself that relaxing her dietary standards a little didn't mean she was on a greased track to hell, she downed a burger from the drive-through place and then, after steeling herself, drove over to the high school, where the Parade Committee had gathered, together with the parade participants and their various floats.

Horses were arriving in trailers, all of them on loan from Stone Creek Ranch, since the sheriff's posse didn't actually ride much, except for occasions like this one. They definitely didn't saddle up and chase outlaws into the hills, as Sam O'Ballivan and his pals had back in those thrilling days of yesteryear.

Brad and several of his ranch hands were supervising, while members of the posse—all of them honorary deputies—argued over who'd put on the most weight since last year's parade.

Although some of the floats hadn't lumbered in yet, there were nearly a dozen crepe paper–bedecked monstrosities in evidence. The standout float was the Chamber of Commerce's contribution—a massive replica of a nearby ski slope, made almost entirely of toilet paper. It even had trees, the branches weighted down with white tissue "snow," and spangles of glitter made the whole shebang sparkle in the sun.

Adelaide Hillingsley and Bea Brady, both wearing their best polyester pants suits and sporting fresh perms, were already nose to nose.

"You're just mad because our float is better than yours!" Adelaide challenged.

Bea looked as though she might be getting ready to throw a punch, so Melissa maneuvered herself between the two women.

"Ladies," she said, "let's remember that we're all friends here."

"Not anymore," Bea scowled.

Adelaide gestured toward the toilet-paper extravaganza. "It's beautiful and you know it!"

The thing really *did* look good.

Over the course of the holiday weekend, folks would drop slips of paper, their vote for the best float in that year's parade, into a mammoth plastic raffle drum set up in the middle of the fairgrounds. On Sunday afternoon, the votes would be tallied and Bill Norman, who always emceed the rodeo, would announce the winner.

A trophy would be presented.

And Melissa had figured out this much, anyway: Both Bea and Adelaide wanted the honor.

Melissa cast an imploring glance in her brother's direction, but Brad didn't look her way, though even from a distance she could see a little grin resting lightly on that famous mouth. Unless she missed her guess, he was pretending that he hadn't noticed what was going on.

"It's too late to do anything about the float now," Melissa said to Bea, in what she hoped was a sympathetic tone. "Let's have a look at yours, shall we?"

Bea looked apoplectic, but she led Melissa away from the offending mobile ski slope to show off the Garden Club's entry, a giant bouquet of colorful papier-mâché flowers of all types and sizes, the whole display perched precariously on top of somebody's farm tractor.

"It's lovely," Melissa said, and she meant it. Enormous amounts of thought, effort and plain old hard work had gone into the construction of that float, and the others, too.

Bea was still upset. "Rules are rules," she exclaimed. "Adelaide Hillingsley thinks they apply to everyone but her!"

By then, cars were pulling up, spilling out uniformed members of the Stone Creek High School marching band.

Melissa thought quickly. "We have to set a good example in front of the children," she said. "So let's keep things as dignified as we can."

Bea huffed at that, but her temper seemed to subside a little.

Melissa patted her back, cast another admiring look over the Garden Club float. "You've outdone yourselves, you and the Garden Club," she said. "As always."

The band kids began to toot on horns and beat on drums right about then. Mercifully, conversation was impossible.

Melissa fled, taking care to avoid Adelaide Hillingsley and her float as assiduously as she meant to avoid Bea.

Just get through this, she told herself. One crisis at a time.

She sought Brad out next, found him still over by the horse trailers, making sure the animals were unloaded properly.

"Thanks for all the help," Melissa said, putting a sharp point on the words in case her brother failed to notice the irony in her tone *and* in her expression.

Brad grinned at her. "There was a problem?" he asked innocently. "I guess I missed it."

Melissa punched him in the arm, but it was a halfhearted move. If there had been a *real* problem, she knew, her big brother would have been the first one to jump in and help.

"I see the intervention worked," he said, when she didn't say anything.

She gave a derisive little snort. "That wasn't an intervention," she said. "It was just plain *meddling.*"

"You know Meg and Ashley and Liv love you," Brad told her. His eyes were still twinkling. He went through the motions of looking at the watch he wasn't wearing. "They ought to be here anytime now," he added. "Meg said you needed their help with the parade."

"If I don't keep Bea and Adelaide apart until this is over," Melissa replied ruefully, "I may need help from the *National Guard*."

Brad laughed, laid a hand on her shoulder, but his eyes had turned serious. "You all right, shortstop?" he asked her.

The childhood nickname, familiar as it was, made Melissa's throat tighten a little. "Not you, too," she managed to say.

"When Meg worries, I worry," Brad replied gently. "It's part of my job description as a husband-father-brother."

"I'm fine," Melissa insisted.

"Not so much," Brad said.

Ashley showed up then, dressed in jeans and a short-sleeved yellow blouse, her fair hair falling in a long braid down the center of her back. Joining her brother and sister, she smiled. "I *told you* I would be here to give you a hand with the parade," she said brightly, rubbing her palms together in anticipation and ignoring Melissa's somewhat impatient glance. "What needs doing?" Before Melissa could answer, Olivia and Meg arrived, Meg standing on tiptoe to kiss Brad on the cheek. He slid an arm around his wife and held her against his side for a moment.

"This had better not be another intervention," Melissa warned. She was still a little insulted by the whole concept, frankly.

Olivia was, as usual, completely undaunted. She'd once treated a wild stallion for injuries, up in the hills, and it took more than an irritated younger sister to throw her off her game.

"The last one must have worked," she said, after

looking Melissa over. "Your hair has been combed and you're wearing makeup."

Melissa made a face, but then she had to laugh.

"You're impossible," she said, addressing Olivia, Meg *and* Ashley, all together.

"Looks like the ice cream shop's float is in trouble," Ashley said, shading her eyes as she watched the giant cone, made of cardboard and crepe paper, teeter wildly to one side.

Meg pushed up the long sleeves of her fitted blue T-shirt. "Let's go see what we can do to help before that thing falls over and spooks one of these horses or something," she said to Ashley and Olivia. There were at least a dozen of the animals nearby, waiting to carry the sheriff's posse on a triumphant sweep along the relatively short length of Main Street.

"Good idea," Melissa said. And they were off.

The horses, as it happened, were doing just fine—Brad and his wranglers had brought them to town and unloaded them early for the express purpose of giving them time to get used to being off the range and in a fairly unfamiliar environment.

"They mean well," Brad told Melissa, watching the three women march over to take charge of the giant ice cream cone and the overwhelmed junior management type trying to contain the thing.

"I know," Melissa said, with a little sigh. Then, as a farewell, she added, "Later."

"Later," Brad confirmed.

It was surprising, Melissa discovered over the next couple of hours, how many things could go wrong with one small-town parade.

The convertible that was supposed to carry the mayor of Stone Creek, that year's grand marshal, threw a rod.

The tractor supporting the Chamber of Commerce's infamous toilet-paper float stalled out, and the teenage rodeo queen had to borrow a horse from Brad, because her own turned up lame.

And those were the *easy* things.

Nonetheless, Melissa found herself enjoying the distraction. At least, being so busy, she wasn't brooding over her life in general and Steven Creed in particular.

By five minutes to six, all the participants had taken their proper place in line. The high-school marching band was in formation, tuning up their instruments for the umpteenth time. The sheriff's posse, led by Tom Parker, of course, were all safely mounted on patient horses—the kind Meg and Brad generally reserved for inexperienced dudes.

The oversize ice cream cone had been stabilized.

Another convertible had been found to replace the one that had broken down earlier, so the mayor was riding high and all set to wave to the crowds on the sidewalks, and the rodeo queen was sporting a dazzling smile and plenty of sequins.

Ona Frame, well along the road to recovery after her gallbladder surgery, looked on from a place of honor.

It was all good.

"Melissa!"

She turned at the sound of her name and saw Matt Creed about half a block farther along Main Street, perched on Steven's shoulders. They were clearly part of a group, Steven and Matt; a good-looking couple in their fifties, dressed Western, stood close by.

The man had to be Steven's father, Melissa thought, distracted in spite of her better intentions. Same build, same hair color, same innate sense of quiet confidence. The sight of them all made her throat catch, for some reason, and caused the backs of her eyes to tingle slightly. She smiled and waved to the little boy, pretending not to notice the man, and turned to give the signal that would start the parade rolling.

Folks along the way cheered, their faces alight with pleasure in this simplest of all small-town-America celebrations. Many of them were people Melissa knew, lifelong residents of Stone Creek and Indian Rock and the surrounding areas, but others were strangers, passing through. The annual rodeo, with its customary trimmings, always drew plenty of fans, along with competitors from all over the country.

Melissa felt as though she'd been swept up in something, and was being carried along, watching that parade pass. She was, in those moments, ridiculously proud of her hometown, and the stalwart people who inhabited it. She was even a little proud of *herself,* for sticking with it, for seeing the task through to its fruition.

Not that she ever intended to get roped into heading the Parade Committee again, as long as she lived, because she most certainly didn't. Next year, someone else would have to oversee the project, keep Bea Brady and Adelaide Hillingsley from coming to blows, and make sure no one wound up pinned beneath an enormous cardboard ice cream cone.

She looked over toward the fairgrounds—the rodeo would start at noon the following day and run well into the night, and the festivities would be repeated on Sunday, the Fourth, with a finale of spectacular fireworks. Meanwhile, the Ferris wheel loomed neon-pink against the darkening sky. As the parade noise subsided, the tinny music from the carousel and all the other rides and games would settle over the town like a blanket.

Once the last float had wobbled down Main Street, people would head over to the carnival, kids in tow, to fill up on roasted corn, served on sticks, barbecued meat and chicken, cotton candy and plenty of other nutritional disasters as well.

Some of Melissa's first memories were of that carnival and the big rodeo, before the family had splintered apart. The old sequence played out in her mind, yet again. Delia had left them, getting onto a bus one day and never coming back. Not long after that, their dad was killed. Then Big John died, too.

A strange mix of sadness and gratitude overtook Melissa, right there on Main Street, with friends and strangers all around her. She'd lost a lot in her life, but she still had Brad and Olivia and Ashley, their spouses, and all her nieces and nephews.

She was part of a close and ever-growing family, and that was more than a lot of people could say. So why wasn't it *enough?*

STEVEN KEPT TRACK of Melissa as best he could, given how crowded the sidewalks were. He'd lose sight of her, then get onto the balls of his feet and crane his neck to find her again, all the while trying to look like he wasn't looking.

Kim was beside him; she and Davis had rolled in that afternoon, their new RV almost as fancy as Brad O'Ballivan's tour bus. Brody was still missing in action, and Conner, apparently, had been temporarily detained up in Lonesome Bend. He'd be there by morning.

For now, it was just the four of them.

"Where's Melissa?" Kim asked, nudging Steven lightly in the side when there was a lull between the high-school marching band and the sheriff's posse on horseback. "Point her out to me."

Steven was a little taken aback—as far as he could recall, he hadn't mentioned Melissa to his folks—and while he was still trying to come up with a response, Matt leaped into the conversational breach.

"That's her!" he fairly shouted, shifting excitedly atop Steven's shoulders to point. "That really pretty lady with the twisty curls in her hair!"

Matt's voice carried far and wide, and Melissa, looking country-delicious in her well-cut jeans and peach-colored off-the-shoulder blouse with lots of little ruffles, reappeared from the throng and turned her head in their direction.

"Melissa!" Matt called out, overjoyed, it seemed, to see her. By then, he was waving so wildly that Steven had to tighten his grip on the kid to keep him from tumbling to the sidewalk. "Melissa! Over here!"

Steven watched her scrounge up a smile, and then crank up the wattage for Matt's sake.

"Nice parade!" Matt complimented her, when she entered their small family circle. "You did a *great job,* Melissa!"

"Thanks, cowboy," she said, with tenderness in her voice as well as her eyes, as she reached up to tug at Matt's "rodeo" hat. It was one of several presents Kim and Davis had brought along.

"I'm Kim Creed," Steven's stepmother said warmly, putting a hand out to Melissa. "And this is my husband, Davis."

Davis's eyes twinkled as he shook hands with Melissa. "Well, now," he said, giving a tug at the brim of his own hat, a larger version of the one Matt was wearing, but otherwise a near duplicate. "It's nice to meet you in person, though I will admit that I feel like I already knew you."

Melissa blinked at that, and her cheeks turned almost the same enticing shade of peach as her blouse as she darted a confused glance at Steven, looking as though she might be wondering if he was the type to kiss and tell.

So to speak.

"Matt's been talking about you pretty much non-stop," Kim explained, smiling at Melissa.

"I showed them the picture I drew," Matt piped up. "You're in it. It's you and me and Dad and Zeke and my pony, looking like a family."

Inwardly, Steven groaned. Outwardly, he managed to keep his cool.

If Melissa had any reaction at all to the boy's remark, it didn't show.

"Not that I *have* a pony," Matt added, when no one else spoke up right away. "Even though Dad promised we'd both have horses as soon as the barn was finished."

Davis chuckled at that. "Give your dad a chance, boy," he said easily, looking up at Matt. "It was just yesterday that the shavings were put down in the stalls and the water supply was hooked up."

Steven was grateful to his father for saying something, because his own tongue still felt like a twist of rusted barbed wire. Though he couldn't stop staring, he hoped Melissa would be too distracted by Matt and Davis and Kim to notice.

I love you, Melissa O'Ballivan, said something inside him.

Steven was, oddly, as shaken by that silent voice as

Melissa and the others would have been, if he'd said it out loud. Thank God, he hadn't. Had he?

She looked up at him, her expression curious. Somehow unsettled.

Then she recovered, smiled a brilliant smile that skirted over him but took in Davis, Kim and especially Matt.

"I'd better be going," she said. "Once the parade wraps up, I'll be expected to offer my congratulations to one and all."

With that, she walked away.

Steven didn't make a sound. He couldn't see where Matt was looking, but it wasn't hard to guess.

Davis and Kim, of course, were watching Melissa hurrying alongside the last straggling remnants of the Independence Day parade.

"I want Dad to marry Melissa," Matt said, with so much enthusiasm that more people than just his grandparents heard the statement and turned to grin as they registered it. "But I'm not getting anywhere with it."

Steven reddened, starting with his neck and ending somewhere above his hairline.

Kim smiled, and reached up for Matt with both arms. "The parade's almost over," she said, as the boy went to her, readily. "Let's head over to the fairgrounds and get a jump on the line for the Ferris wheel."

Matt nodded eagerly.

"And you," Kim said to Steven, holding the child comfortably in those strong, ranch-woman's arms of hers, "can probably find something constructive to do while your dad and I spend a little time with our grandson."

Davis chuckled again, and slapped Steven on the back.

And then all three of them walked away and left him standing there, looking like a damn fool who hadn't figured out that the parade had already passed him by.

CHAPTER SEVENTEEN

STEVEN FELT LIKE a stalker, but he trailed Melissa to the supermarket parking lot at the other end of town, where the parade was already breaking apart into colorful segments, like some snake undergoing a mysterious rite of renewal.

There was a lot of hugging and hand-shaking, and then more hugging. The kids from the marching band stripped right there in the open, shedding uniform coats and creased pants to reveal the shorts and T-shirts underneath. Then they tossed the discards, including their hats with the spiffy gold insignia above the brim, into the backseats of various minivans and SUVs. They were off to the carnival, traveling in noisy packs, thinning the crowd as they went.

Steven tried to stay out of sight, but, as luck would have it, Brad O'Ballivan, there with a few ranch hands and several large horse trailers, spotted him and called out. Which made Melissa turn her head toward him and then away again. Quickly.

Feeling like an idiot, Steven managed a grin he hoped looked easy and unconcerned, and walked over to where Brad was standing.

"Need some help loading these horses?" he asked.

"Sure," Brad replied. His gaze, while not unfriendly, seemed a little more intent than usual.

Steven busied himself with work he could do without

thinking, removing saddles, replacing bridles with hal-
ters, leading weary critters up hoof-scarred ramps and
into trailers that smelled pleasantly of hay and horse,
securing them there, so they could make the trip home
in safety.

All the time, he thought about Melissa, though he
didn't dare look in her direction. Stupid, he decided,
since she was the whole reason he'd followed the parade
to this parking lot in the first place. But there it was.

By the time the last of the animals were loaded and
the doors on the trailers shut and bolted, she'd vanished. Brad approached and said thanks, and the two
men shook hands.

"Looking for Melissa?" Brad asked, after a few moments of awkward silence.

"Was it that obvious?" Steven countered, discour-
aged.

Brad grinned. "Oh, yeah," he said. "It was that obvious." Then he sobered again. "This is the part where
I ask you if your intentions are honorable, as far as my
sister is concerned."

"And if they are?"

"I'll be real pleased," Brad answered affably. Then
he leaned in slightly and commenced to using John
Wayne's voice in place of his own. "On the other hand,
Pilgrim, if it turns out that you're just looking for a good
time, I'll have to personally feed you your own ears,
one at a time. And after that, I'll hurt you."

Steven laughed. He reckoned if he'd had a sister, he'd
have felt much the same way. "Fair enough," he said.

"Melissa caught a ride back to the other end of town,
where she left her car before the parade," Brad went
on, back to being himself again, though his imitation
of the Duke had been more than passable. "She's worn

out—plans on going straight home, as I understand it, and heating canned soup for supper."

After a short hesitation, Steven nodded, said thanks, and turned to walk back to the center of town. He'd left his own rig parked beside his office, and he hurried toward it now, cutting between buildings instead of taking a more direct route, which would have led him past the courthouse. He still felt the pull of habit, even though he knew she hadn't gone back to work.

He didn't know what he'd say to Melissa once he caught up to her, but as he reached his truck, got inside and started up the engine, he felt a peculiar sense of urgency, as if there was no time to waste.

That, of course, was crazy. Brad had told him what Melissa meant to do—collect her car from the parking lot behind the high school and then go home. She probably *was* exhausted, after all the rigmarole of making sure the Fourth of July parade came off with no notable hitches, and the wiser course would almost certainly be to leave her alone.

Steven couldn't do that, for whatever reason. Something compelled him to find her and say—what? What, exactly, was there to say?

Damned if he knew, but he had to see her, without Matt and his parents around. When he looked into her eyes, the words would come to him—or not.

He pulled out onto Main Street, now dappled with horse manure the clowns with brooms had missed, multicolored bits of confetti and the remains of the wrapped pieces of hard candy the mayor had tossed from his perch in the convertible, and was gratified to see Melissa one intersection over, at the wheel of her roadster.

She'd put the top down, since the weather was good,

and even from that distance, Steven could see the last spangles of daylight catching in her hair.

There wasn't another vehicle in sight, in either direction, and the effect was eerie, almost postapocalyptic. He'd missed the green light, since he wasn't paying attention, and watched with some surprise as Melissa turned right, instead of left, which would have taken her in the direction of home.

She cruised past Steven, and he pulled out behind her.

Sure, she'd see him, but he was tired of skulking around like some character in a bad spy movie. He'd defended a stalker or two in his time, but he'd never expected to be one. He did have a little more insight into the nature of obsession than most people, which he wryly supposed was a plus.

When she signaled her intention to turn in at the Stop & Shop, Steven got that spooky feeling again, as if he ought to stay close by, keep her in sight.

Melissa stopped at the gas pump, got out of the roadster to swipe her credit card and fill up.

Steven drove right past her, to a parking space in front of the store, which looked deserted, like the rest of town, feeling ridiculously self-conscious again.

She looked up, smiled vaguely and went back to fiddling with the nozzle on the pump hose. Her brow creased into a frown as she clicked away at the starter lever, getting no response.

Steven sighed, turned, and forced himself to walk casually toward her.

"Hi," he said.

"Hello," she responded. She didn't sound unfriendly, just distracted, as though she knew they were acquainted, but she couldn't quite place him.

Oh, yeah, he imagined her saying, as realization hit, tapping her forehead with the heel of one palm, *that guy I went to bed with.*

"Where's Matt?" she asked. There was a certain distance in her tone, and they might as well have been facing each other from opposite sides of an electric fence—with razor wire strung along the top.

"He's over at the carnival, with my parents," Steven answered, in a perfectly normal tone of voice, which was amazing because on the inside, he felt as though he'd swallowed a hive full of bees, all taking flight, all buzzing.

"Oh," Melissa said, averting her eyes.

Something had to give. Break through the barrier, get them talking like adults instead of feuding teenagers. "Melissa—"

"What?"

"I—we need to talk."

One of her perfect eyebrows rose slightly. "About—?"

"About us, dammit," Steven said.

Her voice was sugar-sweet. "And what 'us' would that be?"

Exasperated, Steven gestured toward the gas pump. "Maybe you've noticed that that thing isn't working," he told her.

She sighed, sounding put-upon. "I guess I'll have to go inside to pay," she answered. "Get Martine to flip the switch."

With that, she walked away, moving toward the glass doors of the entrance at an impressive clip.

Steven followed, double-stepping to catch up. "I can't stop thinking about you," he was surprised—and mortified—to hear himself say.

Melissa favored him with a winning smile, waited while he held one of the doors for her, and whispered, "Try a little harder, then."

She was inside in the next moment, Steven right behind her.

"There has to be a way around this lawyer thing," he whispered back, nearly colliding with Melissa when she stopped abruptly.

The store was silent, and yet the air seemed to vibrate.

Martine was indeed behind the counter, and Nathan Carter was right beside her, with the barrel of a pistol pressed up hard under her fleshy chin. Her eyes were round with fear and they flitted between Steven and Melissa, begging for help.

Steven acted instinctively; caught Melissa by one arm and fairly threw her behind him.

"Put the gun down," he told Nathan, his voice calm.

Melissa was back, and she tried to edge around him, but, with one arm, he eased her behind him again.

Carter merely cocked the pistol, a flashy move, like he'd watched a lot of old Westerns on TV or something, and then practiced endlessly.

Oddly, it struck Steven then, and certainly not for the first time, that if criminals put the same effort into honest work as they did taking illegal shortcuts, they wouldn't need to turn to crime.

Martine made a small, whimperlike sound. "The armored car service came today," she said weakly, her eyes awash in tears now, "picked up most of the cash we had on hand. All I have is a couple hundred dollars, so I can make change."

"Shut up," Carter rasped, poking Martine harder with the gun.

"Easy," Steven said, in a tone he usually reserved for spooked horses and unfriendly dogs. "You don't want the kind of trouble you'll be in if Martine gets hurt. Believe me, you don't."

Carter was sweating, and his pupils seemed to be spiraling in the centers of his eyes. He was high, or drunk, maybe both. Very bad news. Drugs, alcohol and stupidity didn't make a good combination.

"She's lying about the money," the thief growled. "She won't tell me where the money is!"

"I just have what's right here in the till," Martine insisted, in a frantic squeak. "We've been selling a lot of gas and beer and soda and stuff, with all these people in town for the parade and the rodeo, and the boss wanted most of the money in the bank—"

"I *told* you to shut up," Carter said. Then, quicker than Steven would have thought anybody could move, especially when they were stoned, he turned the pistol in his hand and used the butt of it to whack Martine hard in the side of the head.

The sound was like a baseball bat striking a watermelon.

Melissa screamed, more in objection than fright.

And Steven pitched himself over the counter at Carter, who, in that split second, was fumbling with the weapon.

A shot ripped through the air, shattered the glass in the front window.

The alarm began to shriek.

Steven landed on Carter and they both went down, in a tangle, not far from where Martine lay, perfectly still and bleeding.

The quarters were close behind that counter. Carter still had the gun—Steven could feel it pressed sideways between him and his adversary, knew the other man was groping for the trigger, and if he managed to get a finger around it—

Sirens sounded in the distance—too *far* in the distance.

The struggle for control of the gun seemed never-ending, although it couldn't have lasted more than a few seconds. When the pistol went off, Steven froze, waiting for the bullet to tear through him.

But it was Carter who'd been hit.

He looked up at Steven, smirked and then closed his eyes.

Steven raised himself slowly, got as far as his knees, then took the gun from the dead man's fingers—there was blood everywhere by then, some of it Carter's, some of it Martine's.

Melissa scrambled, half crawling, around the base of the counter, her eyes huge, her face chalk-white. Her gaze found Steven, clung to him for a fraction of a moment, skittered over Nathan Carter and fixed itself on Martine, who was beginning to stir. Moaning a little.

"Are you hit?" Melissa asked. And when she didn't get an answer in the next second, she repeated, *"Steven, are you hit?"*

"No," he said. The bloody pistol made a thunking sound as he reached up and set it on the counter.

She wriggled past him, and Carter, to reach Martine. "Hold on," she murmured to the other woman. "Please, hold on. Help is coming. Do you hear the sirens? You're all right now, you're safe—"

The sirens were louder.

Closer.

Steven hauled himself to his feet, dazed.

Flashing lights swiped at the windows, a slap of red, a slap of blue.

He blinked.

Melissa was still on the floor, trying to comfort Martine.

Tom Parker burst in, gun drawn, still wearing his fancy parade uniform. "What the hell—?" he said.

"You can holster that thing," Steven told him, in a remarkably calm voice. "The shooting is over."

Tom hesitated as two deputies piled in behind him, their own service revolvers out and ready.

Tom raised a hand, evidently a signal that any immediate danger was past, and ordered, "Tell the EMTs it's okay to come in, and make sure—make *damn sure*—nobody else sets foot in here. I don't want this scene messed up."

The deputies obeyed.

Things had been happening at warp speed right along, but now time seemed to move even faster.

The EMTs appeared.

Steven took Melissa's hand, and pulled her out from behind the counter, held her close while the medics worked to stabilize Martine.

"I'm all right," Martine said, over and over again.

Steven tightened his arms around Melissa when she began to cry.

Martine was carried out on a stretcher, and loaded into a waiting ambulance.

Tom rounded the end of the counter to look down at Nathan Carter, who was so obviously dead that the paramedics hadn't bothered with him.

"What happened?" Tom asked, in the thunderous silence.

Outside, the world was still a noisy place, a thrumming void, threaded through with panicked shouts and carnival music and the screech of tires on asphalt as the ambulance sped away. Instead, that store was like the bottom of a lake. Or an ocean.

Melissa buried her face in Steven's shirt, avoiding the blood for the most part, and trembled against his chest.

Slowly, Steven recounted what had happened.

The State Police arrived, along with their crime scene techs. The store was secured, and Tom told Melissa and Steven to go on home, because there was nothing more to be done here.

"You can't let Matt see you with blood all over your clothes," Melissa said, when they were outside in the warm night.

The statement reassured Steven that she was all right. She was coming back to herself. Back to him.

"I know," he said, weary to the core of his soul.

Bystanders shouted questions to them, questions Melissa fielded with an upraised palm and, "Tom will make an announcement when that's appropriate. In the meantime, I hope you'll all cooperate and let the authorities complete their investigation with no interruptions."

"Is Martine gonna make it?" someone called out.

"Yes," Melissa said, her arm around Steven, just as his was around her.

He wasn't sure who was supporting whom.

The roadster was still parked at the pumps, its paint job shining under the outside lights.

Steven steered Melissa in the direction of his truck— whatever happened, he wasn't ready to let her go—and they were almost to the driver's-side door when a man in a hat stepped out of the shadows.

"Boston? Does all that blood belong to you or somebody else?"

Brody. Steven felt a rush of emotions, but at the moment, relief was the only one he recognized.

"I'm all right," he said.

Brody swept off his beat-up old hat, nodded politely to Melissa. "How about you, ma'am?"

She simply nodded, leaning into Steven a little.

"Dad and Kim are over at the fairgrounds, with Matt," Steven said to his cousin. "Find them and bring them out to the ranch, will you?" He paused, looked down at his clothes. Tom hadn't said so, but the police would probably want them as evidence, and he'd be questioned, without a doubt. This was likely to be a long night.

Brody nodded. "I'll do it," he said. He took Melissa's arm and escorted her to the other side of the truck, helped her into the passenger seat.

He could be a gentleman, when he chose.

Steven was behind the wheel by the time Brody returned to look in at him through the open window.

"Maybe you'd like a little time to get out of those duds," Brody observed gravely. "If Kim and the little guy see you looking like you lost a gunfight, they'll freak for sure."

Steven nodded. "Give us an hour," he said.

He shifted into gear, backed the truck out, shifted again.

"Do you want me to drop you off at your place?" he asked Melissa, as an afterthought.

Steven was more than relieved when she shook her head no.

They drove to the ranch in relative silence; both of them were probably in shock. When she saw that there were lights burning in the old house, and Brad's tour bus was gone, replaced by Davis and Kim's RV, she sat up a little straighter.

"You've moved into your house?"

"It's more like we're camping out," Steven answered, smiling. It felt good—and strange—to smile, as if he'd forgotten how to do it and then suddenly remembered. "But it's shaping up. Matt's in his room and I'm in mine. The kitchen works, and so do the shower and the bathtub."

She looked down at her clothes, when Steven stopped the truck and shoved open the door, causing the interior lights to come on.

"I'm a mess," she said.

"You can borrow something of Kim's," Steven replied, getting out.

Before he could go around and open the door for her, Melissa had alighted on her own.

They met behind the truck.

"You're—you're really okay, Steven?" she asked.

He started to touch her, drew back his hand at the last moment. "You might say I've seen the light," he said, after giving a nod.

She moved to his side, slipped an arm around him, and they started toward the house.

Inside, Zeke was barking his head off, waiting to greet them.

Eager to greet *anybody*.

They entered the house, and Steven acknowledged the dog, then crossed the kitchen and plucked a couple of garbage bags from the box under the new stainless steel sink. He offered one to Melissa, pointed her in the right direction. "You take the first shower," he said. "There's a robe on the hook on the back of the bathroom door."

"What about you?" she asked, her voice quiet, worried. "Matt would be beside himself if he saw you—"

"Brody will make sure he doesn't," Steven said. His cousin was about the least dependable person he knew, but when it mattered, Brody always came through.

"Still," Melissa argued.

Steven put a hand on the small of her back and steered her to the bathroom door.

"Go," he said from behind her and close to her ear. "I'll go out to the RV and swipe something for you to wear. Put your clothes in the garbage bag—there's a good chance the forensics people will want them."

She nodded, without turning around to look at him, then pushed open the door and disappeared into the bathroom.

He waited until he heard the shower running, then retraced his steps to his bedroom. He stripped and stuffed his clothes into the second bag, and pulled on a pair of sweatpants he'd been meaning to throw away. After one last hurrah, their time would come.

Steven got out a shirt, socks and sneakers. He heard the shower stop, and imagined Melissa stepping naked out of the stall, drying off quickly, reaching for his robe and shrugging into it, cinching the belt up tight. The thought made him smile.

It also made him want to hold her. Skin to skin, yes. But the desire was more about knowing that Melissa was safe than it was about sex.

They met in the hallway.

"I'll make coffee," she said.

"Good idea," Steven replied.

Fifteen minutes later, when he joined her, she was sitting at the kitchen table the movers had brought from his condo in Denver—it looked too modern for a ranch house and too small for that kitchen—but Melissa looked just fine.

She turned her head and he knew by the look in her eyes that her brain was in top gear.

Amazing, considering what she'd been through earlier in the evening.

"Hold on," he said, sounding gruff. "I'll be back in a minute." He took the keys to his parents' RV from the hook beside the back door and headed outside, taking Zeke with him. While the dog sniffed around and lifted his leg against an old wagon wheel half buried in the dirt, Steven unlocked the fancy RV and went in.

There were a couple of suitcases on the bed in the master space, both open, but Davis and Kim hadn't unpacked yet.

Steven helped himself to a likely looking pair of jeans and a T-shirt with "Lonesome Bend Pioneer Days" imprinted on the front, but he didn't touch the bras and panties. He didn't know for sure, but he figured it was a fairly good bet that women didn't like wearing each other's underwear any better than men did.

No, Melissa would just have to go without. The thought made him smile again. And that was remarkable, considering.

He returned to the house, Zeke frolicking happily at his heels, and offered the jeans and T-shirt to Melissa.

Still sitting at the table, she accepted the neat little pile of clothes without comment, got up from her chair and went back to the bathroom to put them on.

She returned in time to drink the fresh coffee Steven had just poured into her mug. She reached for the cup and breathed the aroma in gratefully.

Kim was taller than Melissa, so the jeans and T-shirt looked a little big on her, but she didn't seem to care.

"What happens now?" she asked, after dropping back into her chair.

Zeke walked over and laid his muzzle in her lap, as if to offer comfort.

"Tom calls us in for questioning," Steven said, though he was sure she'd only asked rhetorically. "Maybe tonight, probably tomorrow." He turned a chair around, sat astraddle of it, with his arms resting across the back. "We're witnesses, counselor."

And I killed a human being, Steven thought.

A brief flash sparked in her eyes. "I *know* that," she said. "I was talking about—I meant—what happens between us?"

A grin tugged at the side of his mouth. "Not too long ago, a lady told me, with some emphasis, that there *is* no us."

Melissa sat up straighter, one hand curled around her cup, the other stroking Zeke's head. "That was before she—I—came face-to-face with my priorities. That happens, when you think you might die."

Steven nodded. His heartbeat quickened, but she had no way of knowing that, of course. A good thing, to his way of thinking. "What are *your* priorities, Steven?" she asked.

He took his time replying, even though the answers lived in the very cells of his body, little holograms, each one containing the whole. "Matt. His health and happiness and freedom, my own, my family's, and everybody else's. Knowing, when I'm about to fall asleep at night, that I did what I thought was right that day, even if things didn't turn out the way I hoped they would." He allowed himself a measured pause. "What about you? What are your priorities, Melissa?"

"The people I love matter most," she said, after taking a few sips of coffee. Her gaze was fixed on the far side of forever. "The law matters, because without some kind of social order, we're all in trouble." She looked down at Zeke. Smiled tenderly. "Animals mean more to me than I ever realized—they're so devoted and so loyal."

"Thinking of getting a pet?" Steven asked, when another silence fell.

She smiled, shook her head. "Not right away," she said. "But I think I'd like to work for Olivia's foundation, once my term as prosecutor is up. Livie and I used to talk about it a lot, how I could serve as a kind of animal advocate."

Steven took that in, along with a few sips of coffee. Tried not to look too pleased by what she'd just revealed. He would have bet his best saddle that this woman would remain the Stone Creek County prosecutor until her hair was tinted blue.

"That's—interesting," he said.

Zeke lifted his head off Melissa's lap and started barking again.

They heard the sound of an engine, the slamming of a door.

Brody poked his head into the kitchen a few seconds later. "Is the coast clear?" he asked.

"It's clear," Steven said.

Brody's smile broke over his face like a summer sunrise, full of light. "Good," he replied. "I'll go get Kim and Davis and the boy."

As quickly as that, he was gone again, and Zeke went with him.

Zeke had long since appointed himself the official welcoming committee.

Melissa bit her lower lip. "I know I should ask you to take me home, but—"

Steven closed his hand over hers. "But?"

"But I don't really want to be alone, and my family would make such a fuss over all the things that *could* have happened—I don't think I can face that, tonight, anyway."

"Stay with me," Steven suggested, husky-voiced. "I'll hold you. Nothing more than that, I promise."

Tears filled her eyes as she searched his for any sign of deception.

"Okay," she said, just as Matt burst into the house, with Kim and Davis and Brody and Zeke close behind.

MELISSA NOTICED THE picture taped to the refrigerator door only after Steven had given Matt and the others a watered-down version of that night's events. Kim and Davis and Brody all listened intently.

He left several pertinent details out of his account— the fear they'd all felt when Martine was struck down with the butt of Carter's pistol, the struggle for that weapon, the shot that ended the robber's life—but he still managed to convey a lot.

Yes, someone tried to rob the Stop & Shop. Yes, Melissa and I were scared. Both of us. No, I wasn't a hero.

"Yes, he was," Melissa disagreed, pulling her gaze away from the drawing of the stick-family Matt had mentioned earlier, in town, when the parade was about to end.

Kim smiled and tugged Matt onto her lap. "Why don't you get your pajamas and your toothbrush and come spend the night in the RV with your grandpa and me?"

The boy's eyes widened. He looked tired, but the things Steven had said had apparently calmed his fears.

"You'll be okay, Dad?" he asked.

"I'll be fine," Steven promised.

Matt turned to look up at Kim. "Can Zeke come, too?"

Davis answered for her. "Sure, he can," he said, his gaze moving to Brody, who was leaning against the counter, with his arms folded, watching them all. "There's plenty of room out there," he added.

Brody grinned, gave a little salute as an answer.

He was good-looking, Melissa thought, strangely detached.

"Will you still be here in the morning?" Matt asked, coming to stand next to Melissa's chair and looking up at her with what she read as a combination of concern and hope.

It was a tricky question. Melissa looked to Steven for help, but he said nothing.

Suddenly, Matt dashed over to the refrigerator and fetched the drawing, bringing it proudly back to the table to show Melissa. Tape still clung to its now ragged edges.

Steven cleared his throat. "Maybe you ought to go and get your pajamas and your toothbrush, as your grandmother asked you," he said to his son.

The glow in Matt's little face barely flickered. He nodded in response to Steven's words, but he was focused on Melissa and on the drawing.

"See?" he said. "It's the one I told you about, at the parade. There's me, and there's my dad, and there's Zeke. And there's you."

Melissa's throat ached. Her crayon image wore her hair up, and she had on what looked like a suit and carried either a very large purse or a briefcase.

"And this?" she said, indicating an equine-shaped creature.

"That's my horse. I'm getting one any day now. Grandpa Davis says if Dad doesn't get me a pony, *he* will."

"Is that right?" Steven asked his father, in a low drawl.

"Let's all get us some shut-eye," Davis said, with bluster, exaggerating the yokel-speak a little. "There's a rodeo tomorrow, and I don't know about the rest of you, but I plan to be there in time to get a good seat in the bleachers, and that means I need my sleep."

Reminded of the rodeo, Matt forgot about the drawing and dashed for his room, returning pronto with the things he would need for the impromptu sleepover.

Melissa felt a little guilty, knowing she was the reason Brody and Matt were sleeping in the RV instead of the house. Given what had happened, Matt might *need* to be close to his father tonight, if only for the reassurance that Steven was safe.

That *he* was safe.

Brody and Davis went outside, engaged in some quiet conversation of their own. Steven and Matt had gone back to Matt's room to get a clean pair of pajamas to replace the ones the little guy had chosen first.

"Steven seemed to think you wouldn't mind if I borrowed some of your clothing," Melissa said to Kim, when it was just the two of them, even more embarrassed than before.

Kim patted her hand and smiled. "Don't you worry," she said. Her gaze moved to the drawing, still in Melissa's hands.

Matt's voice echoed in Melissa's head. *There's you... there's you...*

"Are you sure you're all right, Melissa?" Kim asked.

Melissa tried hard to smile. Shook her head. "I don't think so," she confessed. "It was so awful, especially when the gun went off a second time and I thought Steven had been—I thought he was dead or badly hurt—"

Kim rested a hand on Melissa's shoulder; her touch was light, but firm enough to be comforting, too. Out of the blue, Melissa thought of her mother, who had never really been there for any of her four children, and couldn't be there for her now, and a stab of regret and resentment hit her so hard that she nearly bent double.

"Maybe you should see a doctor," Kim suggested.

"No," Melissa said. "I'll be fine in the morning."

Just then, Steven returned with Matt, who was now outfitted in a pair of cotton PJs covered with tiny covered wagons, cacti and tepees.

"I'm the Colorado Kid!" he exulted, raising both hands as if the pajamas represented proof of his preferred identity.

"You're a nut," Steven said, with affection, ruffling the boy's hair with one hand.

Kim stood, after giving Melissa one more concerned look, and made a big production of yawning and stretching.

"We'd better turn in soon, Colorado," she told her grandson. "It's getting late."

"Good night," Steven said to his stepmother and his son.

Melissa sat at the table, and Steven stood where he was for long moments after everyone else, including the dog, had left the house.

Melissa, who had spread the stick-family drawing out on the table in front of her, looked down at it. Her eyes were burning, and her throat felt thick.

Steven finally crossed to her, took her hand, raised her to her feet. Then he cupped her face in his hands and tilted her head back so he could look straight into her eyes.

"All I want to do is hold you," he said. "But if you'd rather spend the night in Matt's room, that's fine, too."

"I want to hold *you,*" Melissa replied.

He smiled. "Then we're on the same page," he told her.

His room, like Matt's, was on the main floor.

The bed was huge, and oddly modern-looking, given the rustic nature of the ranch house, and brass lamps shed pale gold light onto thick pillows. The linens were Egyptian cotton, unless Melissa missed her guess, with a very high thread count.

Was she channeling Ashley?

No, Melissa nodded. She was nervous, that was all. And it was silly to be nervous *now,* when she was perfectly safe.

As calmly as if they slept in the same bed every night, Steven left Melissa to her hesitation and disappeared into the adjoining bathroom. By the time he returned, she'd appropriated a T-shirt from a chest of drawers and pulled it on. She'd left Kim's clothes folded and resting on the seat of a chair.

Her eyes widened when she saw Steven—he was totally naked. *Gloriously* naked.

Melissa reddened as all sorts of things quickened inside her.

"I sleep like this," he explained.

"Oh," she said.

He got into bed on his side and, after a few more moments of silent debate, Melissa joined him. They lay far apart, staring up at the ceiling.

Then Steven stretched to flip the switch on his lamp, and both lights went out, leaving the room dark, except for a skim of moonlight that made the bedding glow white.

"Still okay?" Steven asked, after a long, long time.

"Still okay," Melissa confirmed. "You?"

"Better than okay," he said. And he drew her into his arms, held her close against the hard warmth of his body. "What would you say if I told you I think there's a very strong possibility that I love you?"

A terrible joy spread through Melissa before she had a chance to raise her usual defenses. Long moments had passed when she was finally able to answer. "I'd say," she replied, snuggling close to him and soaring inside, "that you're probably just shaken up by everything that happened tonight."

"Suppose it's more?" Steven suggested, propping his chin on the top of her head. "What then?"

Melissa started to cry. "I'd say it was a good thing," she told him.

A chuckle moved up through his chest, and his arms tightened around her. She couldn't remember when she'd last felt so safe.

"Which means?" Steven prompted.

Melissa sighed, sniffled. "Which means," she answered, "that I'm 99 percent sure I feel the same way about you."

"But you wish you didn't."

"Don't you?"

Steven considered before countering, "Not much use in that now, is there?"

"It is what it is," Melissa responded.

"Think you could maybe work up a little more enthusiasm?" Steven teased, turning now, so his lips hovered just over hers.

She smiled, slipping her arms around his neck. "Yes," she said. "But I'll need some encouragement."

CHAPTER EIGHTEEN

STEVEN DID NOT make love to Melissa during the night; he'd promised to hold her, and he kept his word. But when dawn broke, and the first pinkish light of a new day tickled her awake, everything in Melissa seemed to catch fire.

It was a slow, smoldering burn, all the hotter for that.

Last night, she'd been in shock and vulnerable.

Some men would have taken advantage of her—but not Steven Creed.

She slipped out of bed, scurried into the bathroom and returned with an empty bladder and, thanks to a bottle of mouthwash she'd found in the medicine cabinet over the sink, fresh breath.

She stood looking down at Steven, willing him to open his eyes.

"I know you're awake," she finally said.

A grin crooked the corner of his mouth and, just as he raised his eyelids, Melissa peeled off the T-shirt and tossed it aside.

Steven muttered an exclamation.

"Did you mean it?" Melissa asked, enjoying her brief moment of power. Once Steven got her under him, she knew full well, the balance would shift; he would be in command.

Mostly.

"Did I mean what?" Steven hedged. He scooted upright, sat with his bare back against the headboard, the pillow fluffed behind him.

"When you said you thought there was a good possibility you might be in love with me," Melissa said. "Did you mean that?"

He grinned, and his whole face changed, seemed to light up, like the world beyond the bedroom windows. "Actually," he said, reaching out with lightning speed, clasping her hand, and pulling her down onto his lap, "I understated the matter considerably."

She blinked, still breathless from being yanked, however gently, off her feet. "You mean—?"

"I'm sure of it now," Steven said, his gaze holding hers, direct and unflinching. "I love you, Melissa. I have from the first—it just took me a while to admit it to myself, that's all."

"Are you just saying that because you want sex?" Melissa challenged. She was sitting on his lap and therefore had proof positive that he wanted sex.

He leaned forward, kissed her. The faker, he'd just been pretending to be asleep. He smelled tantalizingly of toothpaste and soap, and his hair was faintly damp. He'd been up well before Melissa.

"I can't deny that I do want sex," he said with a smiling acknowledgment of his arousal. "However, the fact remains, counselor, that I do. Love you, I mean."

Melissa wanted it to be true, was so afraid it wasn't. "How can you be so sure?"

He grinned again, stroked her hair with one strong, calloused hand. "I'm sure," he said, as the same hand moved down, skimming the bare flesh of her shoulder, setting it to tingling, and then curved around her breast. With the side of his thumb, Steven chafed her nipple.

It tightened deliciously, ready for his mouth, and Melissa groaned.

Steven turned her, so that she was straddling him, and tasted her with just the tip of his tongue.

Fresh heat surged through her.

He suckled at her breast, gently at first, and then with a growing hunger.

Melissa whispered something senseless, let her head fall back, offering herself to him.

The night before, he'd shown restraint. This morning, he was all over her, attending to her breasts at leisure, rolling her onto her back, burying his head between her legs after kissing the length of her inner thighs.

He nibbled. Teased.

Melissa cried out and plunged her fingers into his hair, unsure whether she wanted to push him away or pull him closer still. The pleasure was excruciating, almost beyond her ability to bear.

"What about—?" Her question came out as a strangled croak.

"Let—go—" Steven assured her, between flicks of his tongue. "We're—alone—"

Melissa moaned, pleading incoherently. She needed the tension to end, and to *never* end.

Steven took his time, taking her to the verge, then withdrawing. Finally, though, he gave her what she wanted.

Or she took it.

The orgasm seemed to unspool, like gossamer thread, wild and glittering loops of incomprehensible satisfaction.

Melissa held nothing back, and by the time she'd stopped responding, her body flexing and easing and flexing again, in the throes of helpless release, Steven, too, had lost control.

He must have had a condom ready, because he'd put it on and entered her, deeply, in almost the same motion.

Melissa, having just descended from the heights, didn't expect to be aroused again, especially so quickly, but with that first thrust, she was flung back into the same ecstatic desperation as before.

Only more so.

They climaxed simultaneously, Melissa's body arching under Steven's. Steven driving deep inside her and thrusting his head back as he uttered a low, guttural shout of relief.

The recovery took a long time, but hearing Zeke barking outside set them both scrambling. Melissa got the first shower, as she had the night before, and it was a good thing, because when she got to the kitchen, Matt and Davis and Kim and Brody were all there. And so was Tom Parker.

Melissa blushed, tugging at the waistband of her loose, borrowed jeans.

Seated at the table, a cup of fresh coffee steaming in front of him, Tom favored Melissa with a saucy grin that said, "So," long and drawn out, as clearly as if he'd spoken the word aloud.

"Fancy meeting you here," he drawled, his eyes dancing with amusement.

"Just imagine," Melissa said, but she kept her tone moderate, because Matt was there, and Steven's folks, and his cousin Brody. And all of them were watching her.

"Did you sleep over?" Matt asked Melissa, with frank innocence, his voice carrying all over that big kitchen.

The adults hid their amusement with coughs or by turning away. Except for Tom, of course. He was enjoying Melissa's discomfort *way* too much.

"Yes," Melissa told the child, because she knew Steven's policy toward his son didn't include lying. "I did."

Matt, still wearing his Southwestern pajamas, ran over and threw his arms around her. "Will you stay for breakfast? Please?"

"Blueberry pancakes," Kim said, patting the reusable shopping bag in her arms. You had to like a woman who brought her own ingredients *and* was willing to cook. "You're welcome to join us, Sheriff," she added, for Tom's benefit.

He agreed readily. Tom might have been quiet, but he wasn't shy. Except as far as Tessa Quinn was concerned, that is.

"We'll be having bacon and eggs, too," Davis Creed said.

"*You* won't," Kim replied, leveling a look at her husband. "I want to keep you around for a while, if you don't mind."

Something crackled between those two, Melissa would have sworn. They loved each other, without a shadow of a doubt. Loved each other deeply, passionately—and permanently.

It *was* possible, then, for a marriage to last through good times and bad, not just over a few years, but over the ups and downs of decades.

Theoretically, Melissa had known that, of course. But emotionally, because of her parents' experience, and her own, she hadn't quite dared to believe it.

Melissa helped Kim by setting the table, enjoying the talk, the laughter, the wonderful smells of breakfast cooking.

The meal was noisy and delicious, a family affair, for sure.

Steven seemed on edge, though; his gaze kept straying toward the windows, or the back door, and when a horn honked out on the country road that ran past his property, he actually started slightly.

"What's the matter with you, Boston?" Brody asked, from behind a stack of pancakes that rivaled the Leaning Tower of Pisa.

Melissa watched with interest, out of the corner of her eye, as Steven's neck reddened, the color climbing into his face. He stabbed at his food with his fork, but he wasn't actually eating.

"Nothing," he said, and his glance held a warning for Brody: *don't push this*.

Surely Steven wasn't worried about Tom's presence, Melissa reasoned. It was true, of course, that both of them would have to answer a million questions, and testify in court, too, eventually, but the case itself was pretty straightforward.

With his training and experience in criminal law, Steven had to know he wouldn't be blamed for Nathan Carter's death—so what was bothering him? She studied him closely.

Tom's cell phone buzzed before anyone could speak again, though Brody certainly looked as though he'd meant to do just that. Defiance flashed in his blue eyes, and his mouth was pressed into a hard line.

Brody Creed, Melissa concluded, didn't like being told what to do. Big surprise there.

"Tom Parker," the sheriff said, into the mouthpiece of his phone. "Yes? That's good. That's *really* good. Sure, I can stop by the office in a little while, but I have to pick Elvis up at home first. He loves the rodeo."

Melissa smiled, though her stomach was tight with sudden tension. *What,* she wondered, was "really good"?

"Thanks," Tom said, ending the exchange by shutting the phone and dropping it back into his shirt pocket.

Everyone was watching him, and *nobody* was even pretending to eat.

"That was a doctor at the hospital in Flagstaff," the sheriff explained, taking up his fork again. "Martine will be fine. They're releasing her today."

Melissa choked up again. Now that she didn't have to hold thoughts of what had happened to the other woman at bay to keep from panicking, relief rushed in, bringing tears to her eyes.

"Thank God," she said.

"It's not that you're not welcome, Sheriff," Steven said, when some of the emotional energy zipping around the table had subsided, "but you must have had a reason for driving clear out here on a Saturday morning."

Tom glanced at Matt, who was busy trying to sneak a piece of bacon to Zeke, and therefore distracted from the conversation between the grown-ups. "I'll need the clothes you were wearing," he said, looking directly at Steven now. "As well as Melissa's. The—er—interviews can wait until Monday, when the rodeo is over and the dust has settled a little."

The hard line of Steven's shoulders seemed to soften slightly. "Okay," he said. And he glanced toward the window again.

Who was he looking for?

Melissa didn't get the opportunity to ask until the meal was over and the dishes had been put away and everybody was ready to head into town, including Tom.

And by then, she'd forgotten she'd had a question in the first place.

STEVEN WAITED IN Melissa's living room while she disappeared to exchange Kim's clothes for an outfit of her own. She returned looking five kinds of wonderful in black jeans that fit her only slightly more loosely than a second skin, and a blouse just like the peach one she'd had on the day before, except that it was turquoise. And not soaked in blood.

To complete the look, she'd pulled on a pair of superfancy boots, also turquoise, and decorated with shining silver conchos and a few rhinestones for good measure.

"Wow," Steven said. She wouldn't be mucking out any stalls in those boots, that was for sure.

"The last time I wore these," Melissa replied, "I was Queen of Stone Creek Rodeo Days."

Steven cleared his throat. "They've held up well," he said, sliding his gaze upward from the boots, past all the hidden places where he'd touched and kissed her in bed that morning, until he reached her face. "And so have you."

She laughed. "Nice save," she said.

Steven shifted. "We can do this, can't we?" he asked.

Melissa crossed to him, slipped her arms around his waist, stood on tiptoe to kiss the cleft in his chin. "Do what?" she countered softly, her eyes twinkly and warm.

For a moment, he felt as though he might tumble right into those eyes, and fall end over end, forever.

"Make it work," Steven said. "You. Me. Us."

"We can make it work," Melissa confirmed gently, splaying her hands over his shoulder blades now. "All we have to do is keep trying, Steven. If we give things time, and we don't give up, we'll be fine."

He smiled, bent his head to nibble at her lips. "Spoken like someone who comes from sturdy pioneer stock," he teased.

"Just like you do," she breathed, against his mouth.

"We could be a little late for the rodeo," he suggested.

"What rodeo?" Melissa asked.

At that, Steven scooped her up in his arms and carried her to bed.

MELISSA COULDN'T STOP SMILING, which was crazy, since she'd nearly been killed the night before, in the Stop & Shop. Steven's lovemaking, in his bed and later in hers, had left her feeling as though every step she took was part of a dance.

Was it a risk, letting herself love a man so completely?

Of course it was. But, just as Steven said, she was descended from pioneers, people like Sam and Maddie O'Ballivan, and generations as strong as they were. They hadn't been afraid to open their hearts to that special person, and Melissa wasn't, either.

Nor were Brad and Meg. Or Olivia and Tanner. Or Ashley and Jack.

All of whom, as it happened, were sitting in the same part of the bleachers as Davis and Kim and Matt when Steven and Melissa arrived, holding hands. Matt, in fact, was playing chase with Mac, in the aisle between rows of seats, waiting out the lull between events.

Olivia, Ashley and Meg were immediately on their booted feet, rushing Melissa, each of them hugging her in turn, all of them crying and saying over and over again how glad they were that she was safe.

The men, Melissa noticed, despite the onslaught of sisterly love, just shook their heads.

When the emcee announced the bareback bronc-riding event, they all returned to their seats. Brody was competing in this round.

Or was he? Melissa blinked at the man coming up the aisle, his hat in one hand, a grin spreading across his handsome face. He looked exactly like Brody.

But he wasn't.

Melissa felt Steven stiffen beside her.

The stands were packed, and a roar went up as the emcee announced the first rider. "We have an out-of-towner with us today, folks," the familiar voice boomed out, over the loudspeakers. "Let's hear a real Stone Creek welcome for #32, Brody Creed, out of Lonesome Bend, Colorado!"

The roar intensified.

Melissa missed the whole eight seconds of Brody's ride, because she couldn't tear her eyes away from the man in the aisle.

Not a vestige of his grin remained, and his hands were clenched into fists at his sides.

"Uh-oh," Davis said, low. Then, by some tacit agreement, he and Steven both got to their feet.

"Who *is* that?" Melissa asked Matt, who had stationed himself in her lap.

"That's Conner," Matt said. "Him and Brody are twins, just like you and your sister. Only they're the kind that look alike."

Conner, his face hard with anger, looked at Davis and Steven and turned to head back down the aisle.

Melissa looked to Kim, and saw that the other woman was worried.

Davis and Steven followed Conner, and soon, all three of them were out of sight.

"What's going on?" Melissa asked Steven's stepmother.

"World War III, probably," Kim answered, but there was a flicker of something in her eyes, despite her serious expression. On some level, she was *pleased* by this development.

"Are we just going to sit here?" Melissa asked, fretful.

"Yes," Kim replied firmly. "For Matt's sake, if no one else's."

"Where did Dad and Grandpa go?" Matt asked.

"They're getting hot dogs," Kim said, without missing a beat.

Melissa looked at her in surprise.

But Kim just smiled and turned her attention back to the rodeo, where Brody's score was just being posted on the big board above the announcer's booth.

The numbers were impressive; he'd be hard to beat.

But a whole bunch of other cowboys were ready, willing and able to give it a try.

CONNER WAS ABOUT to climb back into his dusty black truck and speed away when Steven and Davis caught up to him.

Davis reached out and spun his nephew around, thrust him hard against the side of the rig. "Didn't you get the memo, Conner?" he asked, through his teeth. "A Creed doesn't run. From anything."

"Tell that to my twin brother!" Conner spat furiously, his eyes shooting azure-blue flames.

"Why don't *you* tell him?" Steven asked, folding his arms. His boot heels were planted hard in the gravel of the fairgrounds, and he'd widened his stance slightly, too, just in case Conner threw a punch.

Stranger things had happened.

"I'm not telling him anything," Conner said, the

words raspy and raw, like they'd scraped their way past his throat. He glared at Steven. "But I've got something to say to *you,* that's for damn sure. You set this up. You knew, cousin. And I don't know if I can forgive you for that."

"Grow up," Davis told Conner. A few stragglers, late for the rodeo, glanced in their direction, but nobody looked like they were fool enough to interfere in what was obviously a matter between close kin. "Whatever happened between you and Brody, it's time to get past it and move on. Dammit, we're *family.*"

Conner ran the back of his hand across his mouth. He was still pissed off, but out of good sense, respect for his elders, or both, he didn't speak his mind to Davis.

Then again, he didn't *have* to. It was written all over him. He was mad from the top of his hat to the soles of his battered boots, and he wouldn't be over it anytime soon. If ever.

He turned to open his truck door, and this time Davis didn't make a move to stop him. Neither did Steven.

It took them all by surprise when, before Conner could start up that truck of his and drive away in the proverbial cloud of dust, Brody appeared, thrusting his way between Steven and Davis and lunging at Conner.

The whole scene reminded Steven of two bucks in rutting season, circling, preparing to lock antlers.

It was unclear whether Brody pulled open the truck door, or Conner pushed from the other side, but the next thing anybody knew, the brothers were rolling around on the ground, throwing punches, grunting and obviously bent on killing each other.

Steven sighed and started toward them, but Davis caught hold of his arm. The old man might have been in his fifties, but he was still strong.

"Let them settle it," Davis said.

Conner and Brody were so equally matched that Steven figured the fight would run into the middle of next week. Instead, they both wound up exhausted and rolled onto their backs in the dirt, breathing hard and cursing like a pair of old salts with seawater in their veins.

Davis grinned.

One of Tom Parker's deputies rushed over, red-faced. "We don't allow fighting inside the city limits," he blustered. An older man, significantly overweight, the deputy probably should have retired years before.

Brody hoisted himself upright and, beside him, Conner did the same.

"This isn't settled," Brody gasped out.

"You're damn right it isn't," Conner retorted, just as short of breath.

Brody got to his feet. "I've gotta go," he said.

"You scared I'll kick your ass?" Conner asked, rising, too.

"No," Brody bit out, "but I paid good money to compete in this rodeo, and I've got another event to ride in."

"I'll be waiting," Conner told him.

"You'd be one chickenshit son-of-a-bitch bastard if you weren't," Brody retorted. He bent to retrieve his hat from the ground and whacked it against one thigh, making the dust fly.

Conner made a move toward Brody, but Davis put out his hand again, making contact with the younger man's chest this time.

"Go make your ride," Davis told Brody, though he was smiling warmly at the deputy the whole time. "Everything's fine now, officer. We won't trouble you again."

Brody strode off toward the arena.

Conner swore and picked up his own fallen hat, punched the inside of the crown back into shape with so much force that Steven half expected his cousin's fist to break through. He rolled his broad shoulders and then glared at Steven before plunking his hat back on his head.

"You don't know what you've started," Conner bit out. There was sadness in his eyes now, along with the lingering anger. "If you did, Steven, you'd have left Brody and me alone."

Steven ached inside. As kids, the three of them had been close. Their summers were almost magical back then, straight out of *Huckleberry Finn*.

When had that changed? What had gone so wrong between Brody and Conner that they couldn't even look at each other without tying in with fists flying?

"I guess I was hoping you'd gotten over whatever it was that came between you," Steven said quietly.

"Or *whoever*," Davis put in.

Steven turned to look at his father, suddenly wondering if Davis had known what the trouble was all along.

"She's long gone," Davis went on, still watching Conner. "Isn't it time you and Brody put that whole business behind you and moved on?"

A woman, Steven thought. He should have guessed that much but, back when the split happened, and Brody and Conner went their separate ways, he'd been too wrapped up in his own problems to really put his mind to it.

He'd been reeling then, from his granddad's death, following so quickly after his mother had passed away unexpectedly. He'd been embroiled in a battle with his maternal uncles over his inheritance. Busy mak-

ing a name for himself in the Denver firm where Zack
worked.

In those days, he'd believed that Brody and Conner would simply work out their differences. After all,
identical twins or not, they'd always had *plenty* of differences.

Instead, a decade had gone by, with both of them
holding their grudges, unwilling to give so much as
an inch.

The waste made Steven grind his back teeth. All
those Thanksgivings and Christmases, when Brody's
chair at the big dining room table was empty. All those
weddings and births and deaths. All those years when
they could have been, *should* have been, a family.

When tragedy struck Jillie down, and then Zack,
Davis and Kim and Conner had been there for Steven.
But he'd missed Brody sorely during those days, just
the same.

Now, he felt a strong and sudden—or maybe not so
sudden—urge to throttle Conner, right then and there,
then find Brody and do the same thing to him. To keep
himself from doing just that, Steven turned on one boot
heel and headed back to where Matt and Melissa were.

His cousins could do whatever they damn well
pleased—they always had—but Steven was through
wasting time. He was through waiting and hoping, and
being scared of getting things wrong. He knew what he
wanted, and he meant to get it. Soon.

MELISSA TOOK STEVEN's hand when he sat down beside
her in the bleachers, his face still flushed with temper.
"Where's Conner?" she asked, whispering because even
though Matt had moved up a few rows to sit with his

buddy, Mac, she didn't want to take the smallest chance of his overhearing.

"I don't know," Steven said coldly, "and I don't care."

"I don't believe that," Melissa said.

His shoulders, tense before, loosened a little as she reached up to rub Steven's back with her palm. He gave her a sideways glance and grinned, albeit wanly.

"I love you," he said softly.

She smiled. "Well, that's convenient, cowboy, because I love you right back."

"I wish we could leave—right now."

Her eyes sparkled. "And miss the rodeo? Sacrilege! Besides, my sisters and Meg would know *exactly* what we were up to."

"I'm thinking they know already," Steven pointed out.

"Let me stay in denial as long as I can," Melissa said.

Steven laughed, and she laid her head against his shoulder for a moment, and he forgot, at least for the time being, what it meant to be unhappy, or lonesome, or scared.

All he felt then was a quiet joy, the kind that weathers every kind of sorrow, the kind that lasts.

Forever.

"Will you marry me?" he asked quietly, his hand tightening around hers.

She smiled sweetly. "Eventually," she answered.

And Steven kissed her, right there in the stands at the Stone Creek Rodeo, in front of God and everybody.

Let 'em look, he thought.

EPILOGUE

One year later...

MELISSA AWOKE TO Steven's kiss, and his hand moving gently over her pregnancy-distended belly. The birth was still two months away, and she could feel their twin sons moving within her, wondered if they were already at odds, like Conner and Brody.

After the rodeo, Steven's hardheaded cousins had gone their separate ways—again.

Conner returned to the ranch up at Lonesome Bend, as did Davis and Kim.

Nobody knew for sure where Brody had gone. He'd been conspicuously absent from the wedding, held in Ashley and Jack's spacious front room at the B&B, barely three months after Steven and Melissa had first met. Even though it had been a wonderful, happy day, Melissa knew Steven missed having Brody there.

Now, Steven's hand was moving lower on her belly.

Melissa caught hold of it and stopped his progress, which would inevitably lead to serious delay. Also, alas, serious *pleasure.* They didn't make love in the usual manner these days, since she was well along with the twins, but Steven had his ways. Oh, yes, he definitely had his ways.

"There's a wedding today, remember?" she said. "And it *starts* at noon."

Tom Parker and Tessa Quinn were finally tying the knot, in the First Congregational Church, and the whole town was thrilled. Like her sisters and Meg, Melissa was involved in the preparations.

They still had crepe-paper streamers to hang in the reception hall, and folding chairs to set up, and programs to fold for the special service preceding the wedding itself. There was simply no time to waste.

Steven caressed her.

Melissa moaned. "Steven Creed," she murmured.

"What, Melissa Creed?" he asked.

"You know damn well I can't resist you when you do that—"

He chuckled, the sound throaty and innately masculine, and kissed her neck. And he intensified his efforts.

"Think of it this way," he murmured, against her flesh, already kissing his way down her body. "You'll be glowing with—happiness—"

Melissa groaned. *"Steven—"*

He kissed her belly, one hand playing gently with her breast, the other parting her, preparing her for pleasure.

"Do you want me to stop?" he asked.

Melissa's back arched slightly as he worked her with easy circles of his fingertips. "I'll—be—*late*—" she protested, forestalling the inevitable. When it came to sex, her husband always got his way, and she always wound up glad he had. Still.

"Melissa?"

"What?"

"Do you want me to stop?"

Melissa swallowed and finally gave in. "No," she gasped. "Damn you, *no.*"

Steven chuckled at that, and went on about his business, and five long minutes later, Melissa was in the throes of a glorious orgasm, the first of several.

ELVIS WAS SPORTING a little kerchief, made to resemble a tuxedo front, and his coat gleamed with a recent grooming. Byron Cahill, the dog's fast friend, crouched beside him, stroking his ears, offering encouragement. Matt was nearby, too—during the ride to town, he'd beamed up at Melissa and said, "Now Tessa and Tom will be a family, like us!"

And her heart had melted into a warm pool of love for the earnest little boy, the one she already loved as completely as if she'd borne him herself.

Now, Melissa smiled. Only in Stone Creek, Arizona, would a dog serve as best man at a formal wedding.

"I hope you made sure he's—comfortable," Melissa said to Byron, who was now a fixture at the animal shelter and also training as a veterinary assistant, under Olivia's guidance. She saw him practically every day, now that she was working for her sister's foundation.

Byron flashed a grin at Melissa as he stood. "We were just outside, weren't we, Elvis?" he said.

Andrea came to his side, and he slipped an arm around her, squeezed. Since Melissa had finished out her term as county prosecutor and declined to run for a second one, the office was held by a seasoned attorney from over in Indian Rock, and Andrea worked for him now.

Tom appeared, wearing a real tux, fiddling with his string tie. He was clearly nervous, and glanced down at Elvis, who seemed eager to take their places in front of the altar and wait for the wedding march to begin.

"Relax," Melissa counseled, fixing her friend's tie for him and then kissing his cheek. "The fuss will be over soon, and you'll get to spend the rest of your life loving Tessa."

The sheriff's face lit up at the reminder. "Thanks," he said.

Melissa turned him bodily in the right direction and gave him a little push. Tessa, resplendent in her wedding dress, was already on her mark in the church's entryway, on the arm of her brother, Olivia's husband, Tanner, who would give the bride away.

"Go," Melissa ordered.

Tom looked back at her, then down at Elvis. He grinned.

"Showtime," he said.

* * * * *

PART TIME COWBOY

Maisey Yates

To Haven. I've dedicated a lot of books to you, but in truth, you deserve them all. You're the reason I get anything done, and the reason I believe in love and happily-ever-afters. I'm so grateful that I've got you.

CHAPTER ONE

WHOEVER SAID YOU couldn't go home again had clearly never been to Copper Ridge. The place hadn't changed. Not in the ten years before Sadie Miller had left town, and not in the ten years since. It probably wouldn't have changed much in another ten years.

Well, it would change a little bit now. The population sign would increase by one, adding back the resident she'd taken away when she'd left town at eighteen. And it would also contain at least one more bed-and-breakfast.

So, in an unchanging landscape, she would be responsible for two changes in a very short amount of time.

She deserved a medal of some kind. Though she doubted anyone in this town would ever give her a medal. She was just the wild child from the wrong side of the tracks. Not many would be welcoming her with open arms.

But that was fine with her. She wasn't here for them. She was here for her.

She looked across the highway, at the ocean, barely visible through the trees on her left. She could remember walking there as a kid. A long hike in the sand, through gorse and other pricklies, around the lake and across the road.

A walk she and her friends had always made without their parents. Because the main perk of getting out for an afternoon was getting away from their parents, after all. At least it had been for her.

It was strange to see something familiar. She'd spent so many years moving on to the next new place. She never went back anywhere. Ever. She went somewhere new.

This was the first time she'd ever been somewhere old. And she wasn't sure how she felt about it.

She looked at the gas gauge on her car and sighed. The little yellow light was reminding her that she hadn't made a pit stop since she'd gone through Medford, nearly three hundred miles ago. She was going to have to stop somewhere in town before she went out to the ranch. She wasn't exactly sure where the Garrett ranch was, just that it was on the outskirts of Copper Ridge.

She'd never been invited onto the property before.

The fact that she was leasing a business on it now would have been funny if she didn't just feel horrible, stomach-cramping nervousness.

But then, she figured facing past demons was supposed to be scary. She wouldn't know for sure since she'd spent years avoiding them. Six months ago, that had changed.

Working with people dealing with grief and loss was always impacting—there was no way around it. But one very grumpy older woman who'd lost the house she'd been in since the 1940s had forced her to think about things she'd always avoided.

"Home is wherever you are," Sadie had told her.

Maryann, whose every decade on earth was marked clearly in her snow-white hair and the deep lines etched in her face, had scowled at her. "Home is where I raised my children. Where my husband breathed his last breath. I don't know who I am outside those walls."

"You're still you. I've spent a lot of my life moving from place to place, and I take my essence, my soul, or whatever you want to call it, with me wherever I go."

The other woman had waved her hand in dismissal. "You can't know, then. You're a vagrant in your own life. If nothing matters to you, how can you sit there and tell me that something I poured the past sixty years of my life into is meaningless?"

And that was when she'd realized...as a crisis counselor she'd helped so many people deal with loss. Either the loss of a loved one, the loss of a marriage or, very often, the loss of a home, and she'd realized that all that advice had been thin. Rootless, because she was.

Because nothing was permanent in her life. Because not one thing had the kind of deep resonance and meaning for her that Maryann's home had for her.

She'd never before been quite so conscious of the transient nature of her life. But in one blunt sentence her patient had reduced the past ten years to a tumbleweed in her mind's eye, while Maryann's own past had risen up like a redwood. Towering, significant. Rooted.

After that she'd felt so aware of how alone she was. That she'd let every friendship she'd left behind wither on the vine and die, that she'd done a crap job of making new friends since she'd moved to San Diego. That her last boyfriend, Marcus, hadn't been missed from the day she'd rolled him out of bed and out the door for the last time.

Those revelations had led to online perusals of Copper Ridge. Which had led to an ad she hadn't been able to get out of her head.

Long-term lease. Perfect for a private residence or bed-and-breakfast.

From there, she'd examined her savings, done estimated profit and loss based on exhaustive research of similar businesses, and before she'd quite realized what she was getting herself into…she'd committed. Committed to leaving the career she'd spent more time in school for than she'd spent actually practicing.

For the first time in ten years, she'd agreed to an extended time frame in one location. And for the first time in ten years, she was headed back to the one place she'd ever called home.

Of course, now she felt like she was approaching doom. Which she didn't think was at all dramatic. Since she was never dramatic.

Except for when she was dramatic.

From the backseat, she heard Tobias, more commonly known as Toby, let out a plaintive meow. The entire road trip had been endured with growing indignation by her cat. But then, she paid the rent, so he had to deal.

"Sorry, bud," she said. "I have the thumbs, I man the can opener. That means you have to stick with me. And if that means moving up the coast, it means moving up the coast. At least I didn't fly and throw you into cargo." Which, during their many moves together, had been a necessity on occasion. Toby wasn't a fan of air travel.

The cat didn't respond to her attempts at mollifying him. Which didn't really surprise her. In many ways, she was much more dependent on him than he was on her.

Sadie looked out at the expanse of evergreen trees that lined the road, a rich, velvet green that she hadn't found anywhere outside of Oregon. California was sun and palm trees, deep blue ocean and heat. It was beautiful, but in a different way.

Copper Ridge was all majestic mountains, shades of green and steel-gray sea. Not the kind of beach you hung out on in a bikini unless you were a local. The wind was cold and blew the sand up hard and fast, the grains biting into skin like little teeth.

It was its own kind of beauty, that was for sure. She'd been all over the United States. From the Deep South to the East Coast and back west again, and nothing had ever been quite like this. She'd never thought she'd be back.

But she was. And the dread was ever encroaching.

Suddenly, the car engine started to growl, and she pushed down the gas pedal, hoping to feel it rev again, only to be disappointed.

"Oh, frickety frick," she muttered as she pulled to the side of the road and the engine went totally silent.

Gas had apparently been needed sooner than expected.

She leaned forward, pressing her head against the steering wheel. "I knew it was doomed. I knew I was doomed!" She straightened up and looked backward at Toby. "Don't start. Don't get judgey."

Toby did nothing but stare at her with green eyes that were extremely judgmental despite her command. "You suck, cat," she said, reaching down and digging for her purse, then feeling around for her phone.

She pulled it out and saw one bar of service. Oh, right. Because that's what you got for moving away from civilization and settling in the absolute sticks.

She tapped her fingernails against the side of the phone and contemplated who to call. She didn't really know anyone in town anymore. Her own parents had moved away ages ago, and she wouldn't call them even if they hadn't.

Thankfully, she could get roadside assistance, but what a freaking pain.

She pulled up the browser on the phone and typed *tow trucks* into the search engine, then grimaced as she watched the little wheel up in the top left-hand corner of the phone spin, and spin and spin while it tried to grab hold of a satellite signal for long enough to pull up some results.

"Oh, Copper Ridge, you've bested me before, you aren't allowed to do it again." She kept her eyes on the phone and then growled at it, setting it on the passenger seat while she leaned over and pulled a stack of papers out of the glove box. She had to have a number for her insurance on hand at least.

Somewhere. It had to be somewhere.

A loud rap on the glass behind her shot a shock wave through her and she whipped around, releasing her hold on the stack of papers, sending them flying through the car, where they settled in both the front and backseats.

She looked around at the mess, then at the knocker. On the other side of the glass was a man in a tan uniform, a gold star on his chest, sunglasses over his eyes. What she could see of him was...well, hot. Which was the last thing she expected, because she'd been living in San Diego for a few years, the land of the beautiful, and rarely, if ever, was she so overcome by a man's face that all she could think was "hot." But maybe that had to do with the recent startle. She was just a little dazed, that was all.

He pointed downward, an authoritative gesture that took her a minute to attach meaning to, mainly because something was pulling at the back of her brain. A memory that was attempting to come to the forefront.

She blinked and tried to get herself together, tried to get herself back into the present. She pushed the button on the door and the window slid down, removing the barrier between herself and Officer Hottie.

"Hi," she said. "I'm out of gas. But I have roadside assistance so... I mean, I'm okay. Except I don't have very good cell service. So I was looking for... Well, anyway, did you stop for a reason?"

"To check on you," he said, the expression on his face strange. He looked like he had a memory tugging on his brain, too, and that made her own memory pull even harder.

"Yes...because...distressed motorist." She looked around at all of the scattered papers. "Right. But I'm not really distressed. I'm fine."

Wow, but he really was hot. Chiseled jaw, short dark hair. He created a response, low and deep in her body, that felt familiar in a very disquieting way.

He bent down in front of the window and she caught the name on his badge.

E. Garrett.

Oh, no. No no no no. There were not enough swearwords in the English language to express all of the bad in this situation. She was stranded on the side of the road, and she'd just encountered one of the chief demons from her past. In a uniform. The welcome committee from hell. Not that she'd imagined she'd be able to avoid him forever, considering her B and B was situated on his family's ranch, but she'd imagined she might avoid him for at least ten minutes after hitting the city limits.

She was not in the mood to deal with him. She was

revising his nickname. Not Officer Hottie. Officer Stick-Up-the-Ass. That's who he was.

Not only that, he was a reminder of a whole host of things she would rather just forget.

And then his expression changed, and she knew he was catching up.

"Sadie Miller," he said.

"Well, damn." She smiled at him as best she could, but her palms were starting to sweat. Authority figures did that to her in general, and authority figures who had once fingerprinted her were an even bigger issue. "You do have a good memory."

"You never forget the first woman you put in handcuffs," he said, his voice low and firm, giving zero impression of a double entendre, and yet, it hit her that way.

Hit her and ricocheted around to parts inside of her that had gone ignored for a long time.

She cleared her throat and straightened her shoulders, trying to look arch and serious, and everything she'd spent the past ten years turning her life into.

Eli Garrett wasn't allowed to make her feel like a scroungy teenage girl, because she was not a scroungy teenage girl anymore. Similarly, he was not allowed to make her feel hot and bothered like he'd done back then, either, because…well, because she wasn't the same person she'd been then.

"Indeed," she said.

"What brings you back into town?"

He didn't know? She looked at him, studied him. He didn't know. Well, that was just peachy. Connor Garrett had neglected to tell his brother that he'd offered her the lease on the house. She had a feeling that was going to go down with Eli like a live leech in his breakfast cereal.

"Am I, um…am I being detained?" she asked, fidgeting in her seat.

"No," he said.

"Then am I free to go?"

"Where? You're out of gas."

Point to Officer Garrett. "Yes. I am. Maybe…maybe you could help me with that?"

His lips, which were far more interesting than they should be, didn't smile, didn't lessen their tension. They simply remained in a flat line. Uncompromising. Unfriendly. Like the man himself. "Just a second." He turned and walked back toward his squad car and she started picking up the papers she'd strewn all over the car.

Her heart was beating so hard she thought she might have a medical event. What were the odds that he was the first person she saw when she came back to Copper Ridge? It was a bad omen. A very bad omen.

Of course, her first thought, still, was that he was hot. She'd thought that at seventeen. But then, to a rebellious kid with an affinity for underage drinking, a man who was part of the sheriff's department was sort of the ultimate fascination. The ultimate no-go. So of course, even when she'd resented his presence, she'd gotten a little kick out of checking him out.

She let out a long breath. She'd sort of hoped that he'd gone on to law enforcement in another town. Or that maybe he'd given up wearing a uniform altogether and discovered a passion for pottery…maybe in the south of France.

But no. Eli Garrett had done what most people from Copper Ridge seemed to do. He'd found his place in the little community and stayed in his carved-out niche.

You should judge. Since you're back and all.

Yes, she was back.

At this point in the game, Copper Ridge had seemed as good a place as any to give her demons the big middle finger.

And hey, she was facing one of them a little bit early. But, considering he had a gun strapped to his lean hips, she thought maybe giving him the finger wasn't the best idea.

"I put a call in for you," he said from over her shoulder.

"Gah!" She startled. "Could you not sneak up on me like that?"

"Do I make you nervous?"

"No. Why would you make me nervous?"

"Criminals *do* seem to get nervous around the badge."

She frowned. "I am not a criminal. I am a licensed therapist in eight...no, *nine* states."

"With a criminal record."

"I was a minor."

"No arrests since then?" he asked.

"I ask again, am I being detained?"

"No."

"Then... I'm free to go."

"Except that you're out of gas," he pointed out. Again.

"Well, *you're* free to go, then."

He lifted a shoulder. "Yeah, I could. But I feel like it's my mission to make sure you don't get into any trouble. Or light anything on fire."

"Okay, look, I didn't light anything on fire on purpose. I knocked over a lantern."

"Which is why arson wasn't on the list of things you were arrested for."

"Do you forget anything?" she asked.

"Public drunkenness. Disturbing the peace, resisting arrest. Not arson, though. And that's not even mentioning the number of times we had to come and ask you and your friends to leave a store, or stop loitering where you didn't belong."

"Good lord, what a sad small life you must lead to remember my rap sheet. *I* barely even remember it."

"As I said, you don't forget your first."

She screwed up her face. "That sounds possibly more sexual than I think you mean it to."

"How does it sound sexual?"

She squinted. "Really?"

She waited for a full four seconds while it registered. She could see when it did because his humorless, impassive face had a slight shift before going back to being total granite. He still had his sunglasses on, so she couldn't see his eyes, only her own reflection. Which looked flushed and flustered. And not from heat, that was for sure.

"Why are you here?" he asked.

"I didn't say," she said.

"I know. I tend to remember conversations that happened less than five minutes ago."

"Yeah, well, I don't see how that's any of your business, since I'm not being detained for questioning."

"For someone who hasn't been arrested more than just the once, you have the lingo down perfectly."

"I'm a therapist. I work with some troubled souls. I've seen more than one arrest."

"Hmm," he said. A noise halfway between a word and a grunt.

"What?"

"I'm surprised you became a therapist, is all."

"Why?"

"Because."

She knew what that because meant. *Because you're such a mess.* That was what it meant. And she was not a mess. She wasn't perfect, but she wasn't a disaster, either. Anyway, thankfully, having your crap together was not a requirement for being able to help others get their crap together. So there. She didn't say that last part, though. Because…well, gun. Badge. Handcuffs.

"I like to fix things," she said. That was honest. "To fix people, actually. I don't just arrest them and throw away the key. I try to make an impact on people's lives."

"Well, it takes both types, I guess," he said.

"Yeah. So anyway, don't you have some teenage miscreants to harass? I seem to recall that being your MO."

As soon as she said it, an old red pickup truck eased into the space in front of her and an old man, one who looked familiar, got out, holding a gas can the same color as the truck.

"Well," the other man said, a smile on his face, "if it isn't Ms. Sadie Miller."

Apparently she was wrong about not having anyone in town who still knew her. It was like these people had nothing better to do than remember every single soul who was born in this burg. For all eternity.

In fairness, though, she remembered Bud, too. She had no idea what his real name was. Or if he had one. Hell, that could be it. There was more than one Bubba in town, and they went by it completely un-ironically, so there really was no telling.

"Yes," she said. "Yes, it's me."

"What brings you back to town?" he asked. "Your parents aren't back, are they?"

"No," she said. "They're still down in Coos Bay."

Not that she spoke to them. For all she knew they could be somewhere else entirely by now, but she didn't care. Not anymore.

She couldn't watch their dynamic, not now that she had a choice. She'd moved away from her father's rages. She wasn't going to expose herself to them again.

And her mother wouldn't leave. No matter how many times Sadie begged, her mother wouldn't leave.

"I see. Well, it's good to have you back." He put his hand on the bill of his ball cap and tugged it down sharply before heading to the back of her car and opening up the gas tank.

Just like that. Like her presence mattered. Not like she was some hooligan who'd accidentally started a little barn fire and gotten herself arrested. Not like she was the child of a wife-beater or a disturber of the peace.

Like he was happy she was there.

Darn. She felt a little emotional now.

She unbuckled and got out, standing next to the car and watching Bud, bent at the waist and pouring gas into her car. "Hey, whatever I owe you, I'll bring it by the gas station. I don't have cash, but…"

Bud straightened. "Don't you worry about it," he said. "Consider it a welcome home."

She couldn't fathom why he was being so nice. She'd barely had any interaction with him. Back when she'd been a kid she would often go into the store that was adjacent to the station, after she and some friends had gone swimming in the river, and buy candy bars for fifty cents. Shivering in wet bathing suits in the cold, air-conditioned building.

But she hadn't really thought of him as someone who would know her. Or…care. "I appreciate that." But she would still be going down to the gas station to pay him back as soon as she could.

Maybe even before she went to the Garrett ranch.

"Thank you. Both." She wasn't going to let Eli Garrett get to her. She wasn't going to let this stand as some sort of sign of how the rest of her venture here was going to be.

Nope. Just because it began with a vehicular disaster and Eli Garrett did not mean it would continue on that way.

Her eyes clashed with Eli's and she looked down at the ground before realizing that was more awkward than just looking at him like he was a normal person. And not like he was a very handsome person who had once handcuffed her.

Even though he was.

She cleared her throat. "I'm going to go now. I have… places to be." Eli would find out what those places were eventually, but hopefully that didn't mean they would have to actually see each other.

She got back in the car and shut the door, and saw in her rearview mirror that Eli had done the same. Good.

She took a deep breath and started the engine, then put the car into gear. She was on to new things, reclaiming an old past and stealing its power.

And a little run-in with Eli Garrett wasn't going to change that.

CHAPTER TWO

THE CATALOG HOUSE was even more beautiful than advertised. Rough around the edges, yes, but Sadie had been warned about that.

The lawn needed replanting. Or sod. But she wasn't sure she had the budget to lay down a grass carpet. Which meant she might be stuck with seeding, and patience. She hated being patient. She didn't like sitting around. And she had never waited for the grass to grow.

She leaned back against her car and studied the house. From the rocks that went halfway up the facade, to the solid, original wood paneling and the cut-glass windows, it was something that spoke of a different time.

It was hardly a rough-hewn cabin. It was almost too elegant to be out here, buried in the trees at the base of the mountains. But she knew, from what Connor had sent in his email, that the house was one his great-great-grandfather had ordered for his wife from a Sears and Roebuck catalog around 1914. Something to make the wilderness of Oregon seem a little less wild, compared to their old home in Boston.

Sadie imagined that, in a land of log cabins, this had been the most modern dwelling in the area.

Not so much now, but it had charm. And really, that was what a bed-and-breakfast needed. Connor had said renovations would be up to her, but she had permission to do what she wanted to the place, so long as she paid for it and—per her lease—left it in better condition than when she came. Which meant, according to him, "no stupid shit like shag carpet."

She took in a deep breath, let the smell wrap itself around her. The sharp tang of salt from the sea, wood that was heated by the sun, and pine all lingered in the air.

It was familiar, but different, too. She'd been away from this air for a long time, and when she'd left, there was nothing about Copper Ridge that had felt special to her. She hadn't been able to see the beauty anymore. It had all shrunk down to a little house on the wrong side of the highway, and the smell of dirt, blood and booze.

There hadn't been a lot of moments where she'd stopped and smelled the forest. If she'd ever gone into the forest it had been to hide out, in a little alcove not far from the Garrett ranch, and smoke a cigarette. Which sort of negated the fresh clean air aspect of it all.

It struck her then that she was within walking distance of the place. That if she wanted to, she could leave her half-unpacked boxes and see the haven she'd gone to with her friends all those years ago.

A strange ache filled her chest, a feeling of longing and homesickness that was unfamiliar to her. There was weight in that clearing. Roots. And, she strongly suspected, a high probability of ghosts of bad decisions past.

She and her friends had been nothing more than children then, angry at life. Determined to do whatever they could to take back some control. Which had taken the form of drugs, alcohol and sex. Because those little rebellions felt like an achievement.

But she was an adult now. And she had the control.

The life she made here would be hers. More than just a reaction to what was happening in her family home.

She didn't need to see the clearing. And there were no ghosts.

With that final thought, she picked up Toby's pet carrier and strode up the front porch and lifted the lid on the mail slot by the door. Connor had said he'd put a key in there for her. She had the impression he intended to interact with her as little as possible.

Which suited her just fine. She had the money she needed to do the remodeling on the house, and she was sort of looking forward to spending a few weeks in relative solitude handling all of it before she got things up and running.

Maybe then she'd look up her old friends. Or not. That would be…well, it would be too close to revisiting times that hadn't been fun for anyone. Maybe she would meet a guy. Go on a date.

Lately she'd been out of the habit of both dating and making friends.

The moves made it hard. And if she was honest, starting fresh was her preference. She didn't like bringing old places with her into the new ones. Not that there weren't friends and boyfriends she had cared for. She had cared. She did. It was just that she liked them as happy memories. She didn't like letting a relationship stretch on to the point it started to show wear and tear.

She pulled the brass key out of the box and put it in the matching lock, turning it hard before it gave. "All right, Toby," she said. "Welcome home, whether we like it or not, because we can't back out of the lease, and after I remodel this place, we'll officially be broke."

She walked them both inside and looked around. It was dark, but it was clean. The wood floors were definitely in need of polishing, but nothing was seriously wrong with them. There were some threadbare rugs that needed replacing, light fixtures that needed updating. But it didn't smell like mold or anything, so that was a bonus.

"It really does have to work out," she said, setting Toby's carrier up on the kitchen table. "Because otherwise you'll be reduced to standing on a street corner and offering kitty head scritches for money. And none of us want to see you stoop that low."

She opened up his cage and he wandered out, looking around and sniffing the air, his tail twitching. She ran her hand over his gray striped fur, then scratched him behind his ears. "Really, though, you could charge for this service," she said. "You give me instant Zen."

Toby just looked at her, as though to say he would be much more Zen if they were back in their bright, white apartment in sunny San Diego.

But then, Toby was used to following her around at this point, so she knew his indignation would be brief.

First order of business was to get Toby's litter box out of the car. The second was to start making this place habitable.

Like it or not, ready or not, she'd made a five-year commitment, and she had to see it through.

"All right, Toby," she said. "It's time to do this thing."

"THERE WAS A car over at the Catalog House. I saw it when I pulled in," Eli said.

"Yeah."

Eli glanced at his brother, who was at the kitchen table looking more sullen and antisocial than usual. Which was saying something.

"And there was a light on," Eli continued, pushing for an explanation.

"Yeah."

"You don't sound surprised."

"No shit. I thought you were the law enforcement around here. You'd think you could put two and two together."

Eli was tempted to hit Connor over the head with something, but it was June. And June was a bad month for Connor, since it was his anniversary month. But then, March was a bad month for Connor, too, because it was Jessie's birthday. And April was a bad month because it was the month she'd died three years ago. August was when they'd started dating, ten years ago. December was when they'd gotten engaged.

So basically, there were a lot of bad months for Connor. And Eli got it, and he hurt on his behalf. But it didn't mean he didn't want to hit his brother for his obnoxious surliness sometimes.

"Would you care to explain?"

"Sure. We need some more revenue. I leased the house. Long-term."

"What? Don't you think we should have talked about this?" he asked.

"No," Connor said. "Because while I respect that this ranch is yours, too, you have to respect that it's more essential to me. It's my only job, Eli. You and Kate have work outside this place, but I don't, because someone has to run it full-time."

"I know that, but you didn't think about telling me you were going to lease out a house on our property?"

"I did think about it. I decided against it. Because I thought, at the end of the day, it was my damned decision."

"Dammit, Connor, I say this with love, please get drunk and pass out. You're impossible when you're like this."

"I'm always like this," Connor said.

"Yeah, and you're always impossible."

"Why are you all growling in here?" Kate, the youngest of the Garrett clan, walked into the kitchen, her dark hair in a low ponytail. She looked like she'd been working hard all day, and it was probably because she had been.

"Because Connor's in the room," Eli told her.

Kate smiled and crossed to Connor, planting a kiss on his cheek. Connor grunted.

"I love you, too," she said. "Did anyone make dinner?"

"No one made dinner," Eli said. "We all have jobs. But I did bring a pizza, just in case." Eli turned and put the box of pizza on the granite countertop. Kate started getting plates out of the cupboard.

This was Connor's house, the main house on the property, which he'd shared with Jessie during their years as a married couple. He stayed because this was the family ranch, going back generations. Because he was the one who worked the land, and the one least likely to leave. This was his rightful place.

But Eli often got the feeling he hated it.

"I will take a beer now," Connor said.

"Get it yourself," Kate suggested. "I'm already dishing up your dinner, and I am not a waitress."

"You wouldn't get a tip if you were one," Connor grumbled, getting up from his spot at the table and wandering to the fridge, jerking it open.

Eli noticed that there wasn't much in it beyond beer and cheese. He wasn't sure he liked what that said about his brother's mental state. Or maybe it was just that Connor hadn't had time to go shopping recently. That could be it.

"You should get a housekeeper," Eli said.

Connor grunted, which was something he seemed to do a lot lately. "I don't want a stranger rifling around in my stuff."

"Then hire someone you know."

"No."

Eli took a piece of pizza out of the box and set it on a plate, doing his best to ignore Kate, who wasn't using her plate, but was standing, arched over the bar, dripping sauce onto the otherwise clean surface.

Eli didn't like that. He liked things in their place. He liked things clean. He'd spent too many years putting things in order to let them slide now.

When they'd been kids, cleanliness hadn't just been a preference, it had been survival. Connor keeping things going on the ranch and Eli making it appear that there was a functional adult managing the household had been the only way to keep Child Protective Services away.

Order had been the only thing keeping them all together.

"So, Connor was just telling me about our new tenant."

"We have a tenant?" Kate asked, her mouth full.

"Yes, we do."

"Get me a beer, Connor," Kate said.

"Do I look like a damned waitress, Katie? Do I?" he growled, while he stalked back to the fridge and got out two beers, handing one to each of his siblings.

"Guess so," Kate said, taking the bottle and popping the top on the counter.

Sometimes Eli wondered if Kate had suffered a bit for having nothing but men in her life. But if he mentioned that to Kate she would probably spit on him. Which just proved his point.

"So," Eli said, leaning against the counter. "The tenant."

Anything to get his mind off the events from earlier today. Sadie Miller. He remembered her as a little blonde ball of trouble. Dressed in all black, ripped jeans, she'd been a stereotype of social rebellion. His least favorite kind of brat to deal with. She'd also been feisty as hell. Resisting arrest was putting it mildly. It had been his first summer with the sheriff's department, and they'd broken up a big party in an empty barn. Drunk, freaked-out teenagers had made the whole thing a nightmare. Basically, all hell had broken loose.

And he had ended up handcuffing and booking seventeen-year-old Sadie, making her the first person he'd ever arrested. Though ultimately she wasn't charged, as he'd said, with ill-advised word choices today, you never forgot your first.

"I drew up a long-term lease so that the Catalog House could be used as a bed-and-breakfast," Connor said.

"A what?" he and Kate asked the question in unison.

"You heard me. With the renovation of Old Town, and the fireworks show on the ocean getting bigger every year, tourism is a big deal. And I want in on that industry."

"How is your going behind our backs us being 'in on the industry'?"

"Income from the lease, and a small percentage of profits. And like I already told you," he said, directing his words at Eli, "some of us only get money from the ranch, so the more profitable I can make it, the better."

"And you're sure that your lessee isn't going to destroy the place?"

"She's a local. Or at least, she was."

The hair on the back of Eli's neck stood on end. "Is she?"

"Yeah. Younger than us, older than Kate, so I don't think any of us would have known her in school."

He would have laughed if there were anything remotely funny about it. "I have a good guess about who it might be," he said, setting his beer on the counter. "Sadie Miller?"

"Yeah. How do you know her?"

"I arrested her once."

Connor's eyebrows shot up.

"Well, damn, I didn't know she was a criminal."

Eli let out an exasperated breath. "She's not a criminal. At least, I don't think she's a career criminal. Granted, she committed a crime, that's why I arrested her, but she's not going to make a skin suit out of anyone."

"Bleah." Kate stuck out her tongue.

"I'm just saying. I arrested her for being drunk and disorderly about ten years ago. It wasn't exactly organized crime. And before that she was the kind of kid you'd see wearing too much eyeliner, smoking cigarettes and looking angry at the world. A bigger danger to healthy lungs than to society at large."

"Well, that's comforting," Connor said.

"I take it you didn't do a background check?" Eli asked.

"I did. But apparently not a thorough one. Credit check, though. Because her rental history reads like an epic novel. I needed to make sure she wasn't dodging. But she wasn't. She just likes to move."

"Well, I can't have any of this interfering with my campaign," Eli said.

He'd thrown his hat in the ring to run for the position, with the blessing of the current sheriff, who was now retiring. And since he'd decided to do it, it had become more and more important daily. Especially after he'd won a top two spot in the primary, his lead over the other man running substantial enough that a win in November looked almost certain. But that didn't mean he was resting on his laurels. No.

There were spreadsheets. Lots of spreadsheets. Because he couldn't help himself. Anything worth doing was absolutely worth doing right.

"It's not going to mess with your campaign. She's going to run her business, and you'll take care of your business. While I increase some of my profits."

"So how long do you think she'll stay here?" Eli asked, hoping the answer was "not long." She disturbed his sense of order. All of this did, but the fact that Sadie Miller was involved only made it more disturbing. And he did not need disturbing. Not right now. Not ever, really.

"She signed for five years."

"Five years?" he and Kate spoke together again.

"Will you stop repeating my answers back to me in question form? Yes, five years. It's going to take time to get a business going. There's some updating that needs to be done on the house. She's agreed to pay for it, and orchestrate it all."

"You're crazy. You're going to let someone else, a stranger, live on our property for five years without even…meeting her first?" Eli asked.

"It's over. It's signed. I'm not discussing it any further," Connor said.

Eli leaned back against the counter and took a long drink of his beer.

Kate shrugged. "It might be nice to have a woman around again."

"She's not going to be around," Eli said. "She's running a bed-and-breakfast, apparently. There's a difference between that and her being around. This is a big property."

"I was just saying. And maybe I'll go visit her," Kate mused.

"Eli's right, Katie," Connor said. "Everything is going to be kept separate."

"That's fine." Kate picked at the top of her pizza. "But I do think it would be nice to bring her something. A housewarming something. Foodstuffs. Small-town hospitality in action and all."

"Feel free to deliver foodstuffs," Connor told her. "I don't give a sh—"

"Yeah, yeah, I know," Kate said. "You don't. About anything. I get it. You're a grumpy codger and you aren't going to be sociable. Ever. Again. I won't make you."

"Good," he said.

Kate turned to Eli, her brown eyes wide.

Eli put his hands up. "Don't look at me," he said. "I'm not joining your small-town welcoming committee."

"Fine. I'll be the representative for this family. And try to prove we weren't—" she took a bite of her pizza and spoke around a mouthful of cheese "—raised by fucking wolves."

"Well, we'll leave that up to you," Eli said. "I have faith in you."

"Gee, thanks."

"I'm going to head home," Eli said. "I'll leave the pizza."

That earned him a thanks from Kate and a grunt—no surprise—from Connor.

"I've got the afternoon off tomorrow," Eli added, "so that means I'll be by to help out. Do you have anything big going?"

"Not a lot. We have to tag the calves this weekend, though. Are you free?"

"Yeah," he said. "I'll be around for that."

He was in law enforcement by choice, but he was a rancher by blood. He, Connor and Kate all did some local rodeo events now and then, too, though Kate was by far the most successful and was looking to turn pro when she got the chance.

Of course, the fact that he was either working for the county or working on the ranch was a big part of why he had no social life. But he didn't really miss it. Unless he was horny. Then he kind of missed it.

"Great," Connor said. "See you tomorrow, then."

"See ya." He turned and walked out of the kitchen, through the entryway and onto the porch. He stood for a minute and looked out at the property, and at the light in the distance. The light that was coming from the Catalog House.

Sadie Miller was in there. On a five-year lease. Damn it all, it didn't get much more disrupting to his sense of order than that. Of course, the past couple of years had been one big, giant disruption for their family.

They all felt the loss of Jessie. And they all felt the hole that her death had carved into Connor. He wasn't the same. He never would be.

But then, that was the way this place was. Or at least,

that seemed to be the way love was for their family. You got it, you lost it.

It had started with the first generation of Garretts on this land. His great-great-grandfather had ordered that house and had it built. His great-great-grandmother had lived in it for only two years before getting pneumonia and dying.

Then there were his great-grandparents. His great-grandmother had died in childbirth, leaving her husband a shell of a man, barely capable of keeping the land going, and not entirely managing to keep track of his children. His grandfather had run off with a woman from town, leaving his grandmother to raise her kids alone. And then there were his parents.

Their mother had gone when Kate was a toddler. Off to God knew where. Somewhere warmer and sunnier. Somewhere with men in suits instead of spurs.

A place without needy kids and the smell of cows.

But it had left her husband to sink into a mire of alcoholism and despair.

It had left Connor to grow up at fifteen. And for Eli to follow right along with him.

And all that pain had started in the house that now sheltered Sadie Miller. It seemed fitting in some ways. Since she was a pain in his butt.

He walked down the steps to the driveway, then headed down the path that took him the back way to his house.

Sadie Miller wouldn't be a problem, because he wouldn't let her become one.

He was the law around here, after all.

CHAPTER THREE

Sᴀᴅɪᴇ ᴡᴏᴜʟᴅ ᴠᴇɴᴛᴜʀᴇ down into town today at some point. Grab some supplies. After she'd taken inventory, of course. She knew there were some tools in the shed, per the typed-up—and very brief—note Connor had left on the kitchen counter.

But until she had some clue about what sort of work she might need to do, the tools were fairly useless. She had some basic information on the minor flaws in the house, but there were other things she wanted to tackle.

Most of the place had the original wood paneling. Wainscoting that went halfway up the walls, which were painted a deep cream. The wooden detail was echoed on the ceiling, crossbeams forming a checkerboard over the plaster ceiling.

It looked like the crown molding in a few of the rooms had been replaced at some point, and it didn't match. Which meant she was going to need to take it down, and then mount some new stuff.

That wasn't a part of her original plan, but she had a little cushion for some surprises. And money set aside for some major projects, like the addition of a back deck. And since structural issues were Connor's problem, she didn't anticipate running into anything that would absolutely kill her budget.

Some people might call her a flake, but she was

a well-educated flake with a basic understanding of money management.

She walked into the kitchen, and to the walk-in pantry that was larger than some bedrooms she'd had in her years of apartments. The solid wood shelves had a fine layer of dust over them. A mop and broom standing in the corner were the only residents, except for a few daddy longlegs hanging on the ceiling.

She made a mental note to take care of those guys later and walked back out into the kitchen, opening up cabinets that were mainly empty. There was one cabinet filled with mismatched teacups, and she counted that as a good find.

A quirky touch to add to the place. As inspiration went, it was a good place to start.

She wandered back through the dining room, which was nearly dominated by a large wooden table that was scarred from years of use. Refinishing that would go on her list of to-dos, but not for a while. She'd throw a tablecloth on it for now.

Out in the hall, the old wooden floor squeaked under her feet. Weirdly, she liked the sound. Liked the reminder of the age of the house.

The boards on the stairs were the same, her fingertips leaving a light trail on the banister as they cut through the thin film of dust. The house had obviously been cleaned when the previous tenant had left; it had just been a couple of years since anyone had been back inside.

She walked down the hall and pushed open the doors to each of the four bedrooms. They all had gorgeous four-poster beds. They would need all-new linens and drapes, but she'd been expecting that. The two bedrooms on the backside of the house faced the thick, undeveloped forest, and the other two provided views of a bright green field, dotted with cows.

All the rooms needed blinds to block the light so guests could sleep as late as they liked, and do whatever they wanted with no privacy concerns.

Two rooms had private bathrooms, while two others had to share one in the hall—not ideal, but given the age of the house, that it was as well-appointed as it was was sort of a miracle.

All it would take was a bit of scrubbing, polishing and the addition of matching molding. Also, some knickknacks, new furniture and a carload of linens.

The shopping would be the fun part. She would try to keep it local so that the finished product reflected Copper Ridge. She was really getting into this whole concept of community.

For now, she was going to go and hunt for those tools Connor said were in the shed. What she would do with them was up for debate, but she had a kind of driving need to do whatever she could.

Sadie tromped down the steps and into the yard, the bark-laden ground soft beneath her tennis shoes, dew from the weeds flinging up onto her pant legs and sending a chill through her.

It wasn't warm yet this morning, but the wind was still, the trees around her seeming to close in tight, sheltering her and her new house from the outside world.

She whistled, the sound echoing off the canopy of trees, adding to the feeling of isolation. She liked it. And even more than that, her guests would like it.

Well, they'd better, anyway, since she was committed to five years here. Claustrophobia's icy fingers wound their way around her neck when the thought hit. Five years. In one place. In Copper Ridge, no less, the keeper of her hang-ups and other issues.

You're confronting your past. It's what you'd tell a patient to do.

Her inner voice was right. But her inner voice could go to hell. She wasn't in the mood to confront things. She was just…trying to feel a little less wrong. A little less restless.

A little less like she was a rolling tumbleweed. Or a running-at-full-tilt tumbleweed.

She'd given so much advice that she'd never once followed. Facing fears, facing the old things that held power over a person. Going back to a point of trauma and seeing that it held no magical properties.

Well, she was following it now.

She zipped up her hoodie, fortifying herself against the general dampness that clung to the air, and walked down the path that should lead her to the shed.

An engine roar disturbed her silence, and she turned to see a black truck barreling down the long, secluded drive that led to her house.

She stopped and watched, trying to catch a glimpse of the driver. She failed, but she figured it was too grand an entrance for someone who wanted to Freddy Krueger her, so she was probably good.

She shoved her hands into the pockets of her hoodie and headed back to where the truck had parked. "Hello?"

"Hi."

The feminine voice that greeted her wasn't what she'd been expecting. Neither was the petite brunette who dropped down from the driver's side, wearing a flannel shirt and a pair of Carhartts. Her braid flipped down over her shoulder as her boots hit the ground, and she looked up and smiled.

Sadie vaguely remembered that there was a female Garrett, but she'd never known her. Unsurprising, really, since this girl looked wholesome and shiny, and all the things Sadie had never been.

"Kate," she said, extending her hand. "Kate Garrett. The sister."

"Nice to meet you," Sadie said, shaking the other woman's hand.

"I didn't want to drop by last night because I thought it would be rude, but I thought I'd stop in today just to say hi. And to ask what all your plans are."

There was something wide-eyed and sweet about Kate, something that stood in contrast to her firm handshake and confident manner. She was strength, and openness, and for a moment, Sadie envied that. The bravery it must take.

"Well, I have plans to turn the house into a B and B that will hopefully be ready for guests in about a month and a half." She put her hands on her hips and let out a long breath. "Enough time to get things arranged, and to settle in, hopefully."

"If you need any help, or anything, I'm happy to give it. I work at the Farm and Garden, and I know a lot about plants, animals, general repair stuff."

It stunned her, yet again, how nice people had been to her—exception being Eli—since she'd shown up. She'd imagined...she didn't know. She'd turned Copper Ridge into such a dark place in her mind that she'd been sure people would all but greet her with torches and pitchforks. And yet, no one had.

Facing your demons, and finding out there aren't quite as many as you thought?

"That's really nice, but I don't want to take any of your time," Sadie said.

"Really, I don't have a whole lot happening right now. Just work. And it's very male around here, so it's nice to have a more feminine influence."

It occurred to her then that it was time to stop resisting connections. *Five years, remember?*

"If I need something, I'll take you up on that," she said. "You'll be better company than a random hired hand."

Kate laughed. "I try. What are you after today?"

"Trim. Light fixtures. I might look at new hardware for the cabinets."

Kate wrinkled her nose, then looked at the house, and at Sadie's car. "If you have renovation stuff to buy, you aren't fitting it in there. Ten pounds of potatoes, five-pound sack. But if you want, you can come in with me and use my truck to make deliveries back to the property. You just need to be able to pick me up at closing time."

Sadie hadn't had a firm plan for the day, but she couldn't deny that the use of a truck had a very high chance of coming in handy.

Her immediate gut response was to say no. Because accepting help meant the possibility of needing to pay someone back. Sadie was fine giving help, and expecting nothing in return. But she'd always been afraid of leaving town owing a debt.

But you're staying here. At least for a while.

"Thank you, Kate," she said. "That's so nice of you. I would really appreciate your help."

"WELL, SHIT," CONNOR SAID, looking around the field. "I think we missed a calf."

Eli straightened and wiped the sweat off his forehead. It hadn't seemed too hot earlier, but now the sun was high in the sky, beating down on them. The middle of the field provided no shade, and the work they'd been doing wasn't easy.

"You think?" he asked, looking around the field and spotting a red angus, one of the few reds who had ever popped up in their herd, who he knew full well had been ready to birth a while back. "Oh, yeah. She calved already."

"And I don't see baby. Which means she's got him hidden somewhere, or he's dead."

"Dammit." Eli tugged his T-shirt up over his head and mopped the sweat off his chest before chucking the shirt on the ground and getting up onto his horse. "Let's go find him."

Eli spurred his horse on. "Got her number?" he asked, meaning the identification number on the mother cow's ear.

"Yeah, I know it."

"I'm going to guess he's under the trees somewhere." Eli gestured to the back of the field that led toward the houses. It was still heavily wooded, providing the herd with a place to escape the weather.

Connor followed him, the horses' hoofbeats the only sound as they galloped across the field. Eli kept an eye out for a carcass in the grass, but the absence of crows and buzzards had him feeling optimistic.

Death was a part of ranch life, but it wasn't one he enjoyed.

Sure, they raised cattle for beef, but they took care of them. They had value to his family that ran deep. It was hard to explain to someone outside of the ranching community, but those in it understood the connection without him having to voice it.

Hell, with a job this demanding, you had to love all the elements of it, or you'd never choose to do it. It was really why he chose to do it only part-time. Maybe that made him a fair-weather cowboy, but he was okay with that.

He still got his job done. Both his jobs, in fact.

He tugged his horse's reins and slowed her down when they got to the edge of the trees and Connor dismounted.

"Oh, great," he said, looking back. "We got mama's attention. But then, I guess that means we're close."

But the last thing they wanted was to be on a twelve-hundred-pound mother cow's radar while they tried to run down her three-day-old calf and give him a piercing.

Eli got off his own horse and followed Connor under the trees. "Okay, Con," he said, "make this fast because I don't want to deal with mom cow's attitude, all right?"

Then he saw it, spindly and wobbly, under the trees. Black as night, obviously not inheriting his mother's coloring.

"Okay…" Eli said. "Let's do this thing."

Connor crossed his arms over his broad chest. "Get in there, part-time cowboy. You're on shift." He handed Eli the applicator, which was already clean and ready.

Eli took it, then flipped Connor his middle finger before wading into the foliage.

He looked over his shoulder. The mother cow was jogging now, heading toward them, not happy to see them getting closer to her baby. And they couldn't blame her. But he needed to get the baby's tag on so they could match him up with his mother later. Easy enough to figure it out now, but harder later in a field of black calves.

"Hurry up, man!" Connor called.

"Right," Eli said, tossing the word over his shoulder as he battled through the brush, sticks breaking beneath his boots as he headed toward the calf, who was attempting a getaway. "I'll just speed this along."

"I don't want you to get your ass trampled."

"Well, neither do I," Eli growled.

Eli lunged for the calf, and as he did, the mother started to charge in their direction.

"Hell!" Connor dodged to the side and the mom nudged at him with her head, bellowing and generally trying to intimidate him. He sidestepped her next attempt at butting him.

Eli turned his focus back to the calf and grabbed him, fitting the applicator to his ear and punching as hard and secure as he could, holding the animal's neck and head still with one arm while he finished the job with the other.

"Got him!" He released the little black calf, who now had a yellow tag on his ear and seemed none the worse for wear.

"Then haul ass," Connor said, moving through the trees and back to his horse. Eli did the same, and fortunately the cow was now just focused on her baby, who was making a low bawling sound.

"He's playing it up now." Connor wiped his forearm over his brow. "Trying to make his mom even madder."

"I don't think she could possibly get much madder," Eli said, trying to catch his breath.

"Probably not. I'm going to ride back out for a minute," Connor told him. "Just to check everything over. You want to meet me back at the barn?"

"Yeah, sure."

Eli mounted his horse again and rode back toward the barn. One of the ranch hands, a high school kid Connor had hired to help with menial stuff, looked up from mucking stalls as he entered.

"Hey, Mike," Eli said. "Mind taking care of Sable for me?" He got off the horse and patted her neck.

"Got her," Mike said.

"Great, thanks." Eli walked around the barn, Connor's most prized acquisition. They'd poured all the money from their father's life insurance settlement into it.

Eli braced one hand on the solid wood wall, arching backward. Damn. He had a hitch in his back. He was too young to get old.

And he had to work a shift for the force in the morning, which meant he didn't have time to be sore. Double duty was a bitch. But he couldn't ever give up either job.

Connor lived and breathed the ranch, but Eli appreciated the break.

Because, when it came right down to it, he'd rather chase bad guys than be chased by a damned cow.

Though, being sheriff potentially meant doing a lot more paper pushing, and a bit less bad-guy chasing. But it also meant the chance to effect some good change in the county. Sure, some of it was down to the fact that he was a control freak, and the chance to take total control of the filing system was almost irresistible, and some of it was even ambition, but mainly he wanted to be sheriff because he loved Copper Ridge and the surrounding areas. And serving in law enforcement was the best way he could think of to show that love.

He heard a loud crash, followed by several more crashes and a shrill curse word. He started toward the noise without even thinking, because that was what he did. If there was something wrong, he went toward it, not away from it.

He walked down the path toward the din. Toward the Catalog House. And he already knew that whatever he was going to find there was going to make him very, very grumpy.

When he came through the trees he saw her, across the driveway in front of Kate's truck. Sadie was standing at the end of it, holding a bundle of crown molding or trim of some kind that had to be ten feet long at least. And in front of the tailgate, down by her feet, were various pieces of hardware and what had probably been a light fixture before it had met an untimely demise on the gravel driveway.

And here was the distraction he just didn't need.

"What are you doing?" he asked.

"Oh." Her head whipped up, her blue eyes wide for a moment, before they narrowed, her expression turning into a scowl. "You have to stop sneaking up on me. I've been in town less than twenty-four hours and I think you've scared a grand total of twenty-five minutes off my life."

"Somehow I think you'll be fine without them."

"Says you. That's an entire sitcom's worth of life you just cost me. Now my plans of watching one final episode of *Friends* before I go to meet my maker are completely dashed."

"Do you need help?" he asked patiently.

"Do you ever laugh? Because that was funny."

"Rarely. Not as rarely as my brother. But rarely."

"Maybe it's a male Garrett thing. Your sister is more fun than you are."

"So much fun that you stole her truck? Are you already adding to your list of felonies?" Eli asked, making his way over to the truck and surveying the small disaster around Sadie's feet.

"You of all people should know I was never charged with a felony, Deputy Pedantic, so let's not be dramatic."

"Just looking out for my sister." And he meant it. Because Kate was too sweet. Too trusting. And Sadie was someone he couldn't predict. The combination made him nervous.

"Kate stopped by and offered her pickup truck. Because she's very, very nice."

"Too nice," he said, still looking over the items that had spilled out onto the ground. "And you figured you'd unload this all by yourself?"

"Well, the trim isn't heavy. It's just unwieldy. But I didn't realize the guys had packed my bags up against the gate, and they had one tangled in the trim and... Anyway, I had a momentary disaster, and I have a broken pendant light. But it will be okay."

"I could help."

"Helping me wouldn't make you burst into flame?" she asked.

"Depends. Are you planning on lighting something else on fire?"

She let out a growl. "I told you. I did not light anything on fire. I knocked a lantern over. There is a difference."

"You started a fire. It was an accident, but you did, in fact, light an entire barn on fire."

"I feel like intent should matter here."

"All right, then, I intend to help you. Maybe you could stop trying to make everything so difficult and let me get to it."

SADIE WATCHED, AND tried not to let her mouth hang open, as Eli came closer, shirtless and muscular and just im-damned-possible not to stare at. He had dirt on his chest. His hairy, masculine, muscular chest.

He'd looked so clean in that uniform of his. Like he ironed it directly onto his body so that it would form straight to his physique and never wrinkle. And he looked good in it.

But never had she imagined that there was something so raw and manly underneath it all. He was downright... rough and uncivilized beneath all that law and order.

She suddenly realized she was staring. Pretty much at his nipples. It didn't get more horrifying than that.

She cleared her throat and looked back up at him. Met his brown eyes, which was the socially acceptable thing to do.

"Thank you," she said.

And all her good intentions fell like a Jenga tower when he grabbed the middle of the trim and crown molding bundle she was holding and lifted it up, out of her hands, to hoist it over his shoulder.

"Where do you want it?" he asked.

Her brain was taking in too much stimulus to compute the exact question. He was standing there, every muscle outlined to perfection by the stance and the weight of the items he was holding. He just looked so damned capable. Standing there and holding things that had been almost impossible for her to manage, like they weren't anything at all.

Actually, that part was really freaking annoying.

But it looked great. And she couldn't refrain from letting herself have a little moment. One where she admired the strength in his chest, the sharp, defined lines in his stomach. And down beneath those abs, a perfectly flat plane with deep grooves on either side of it that disappeared beneath the low-slung waistband of his jeans.

She almost had to bite her own fist to keep from whimpering.

What the hell was wrong with her? She didn't lust after guys she didn't like. Anymore. Sure, she'd lusted after him—mildly, until he'd arrested her. But she'd grown up since then.

She liked it simple, she liked it happy. She liked nice men who wanted a sweet, easy relationship, and when that wasn't easily available, she did without.

She'd been without for a while, so she was clearly just having a weak moment on the physical desire front. And hey, that happened. But that didn't mean she was going to do anything about it. Most especially not with Eli Garrett. No, thank you.

She wasn't a fling girl anyway. Mainly because the idea of getting naked with a total stranger was not at all appealing. She always got to know a guy before she hopped into bed with him. And getting to know the guy made it not a fling, but a relationship.

And if relationships were not, at present, a happening thing, flings weren't a happening thing ever. Ergo, sex was not a happening thing for her.

Ergo his abs had just killed 65 percent of her brain cells.

"Just…the porch is good," she said, walking backward, her eyes still trained on him. She grabbed one of the plastic bags, which was lying, tipped and spilled, on the tailgate, and bent, her eyes still on Eli as he turned and started walking toward the house.

His butt.

Oh, my.

Yep. She'd just crossed over into shameless ogling

and she didn't even care. Didn't mind even a little bit that she didn't even like the guy.

Why not look at him for a minute? The fact was, thrills were few and far between for her. Connor might be just as hot. She might ogle him next.

But he wasn't here. So for now she would just take a moment to note the way the denim cupped Eli's muscular, rounded...

"So...you gonna nail this up or what?"

It took her a full second to realize "nail this up" wasn't a euphemism for a sex act.

"The molding?"

"Yes," he said, setting it down across the porch.

She scrambled to pick everything up, avoiding the broken pendant light and gathering the rest of her odds and ends. "That was the plan. There's a nail gun in the shed. At least, I think Connor had that on the list. He left me a list."

"Decent of him."

"He's been sort of the invisible man since I arrived. He left instructions, but I haven't seen him."

"Yeah, well, he's like that. Actually—" he bent down to straighten up one of the trim pieces and she cocked her head to the side and watched the muscles on his back shift and bunch "—he didn't tell me anyone was coming to rent the place." He straightened. "Let alone signing a long-term lease and spending the next five years running a bed-and-breakfast on my damn property."

"It's sort of a shared property. If you want to be technical." She scurried up toward the porch, her bag in hand.

"Right. So how is it you're going to install all this? And why are you installing all this?"

"I want the trim to match. Obviously over the years

some things were replaced at different times and some
of it doesn't match. The wood in here is beautiful and
I don't want anything detracting from it."

"But even the replacement molding is older than...
we are. It might as well be original."

"Well, no, it might as well not be, because if it were,
it would match. It gets accolades for age but I'm still
replacing it."

"So you're going to put this cheap-ass stuff in there?"

"It is not cheap-ass! Look at how much of my budget
is devoted to this and you will see just how not cheap-
ass it is. It's very nice, actually. And if all you're going
to do is insult my molding, then...get off my porch."

He crossed his arms and leaned against the railing. "I
don't think I will. It's my porch. You're just leasing it."

"I have rights!"

"It's a bed-and-breakfast. What if I want to make a
reservation?"

"It's not open yet."

"It could open faster if you didn't want to replace
perfectly good molding."

She sputtered, her comebacks all jumbled around
because...biceps. And forearms. And things. Why was
he so distracting even while he was annoying? Why
did it seem like the annoying only made it all more interesting?

She had no idea what was wrong with her. She
needed some wine. A bottle of wine. And for him to
go away. She was done with her thrills. She was on
thrill overload. She was clearly giddy with the thrills
and had crossed over into crazy town.

"What else do you have in the bag?" he asked.

"Things," she said.

His dark eyes narrowed. "What kinds of things?"

"Things of a home-improvement nature. Which I will use to improve this home."

"What the hell does it need improving for?"

She huffed and stalked to the front door, fishing the key out of her purse before pushing the door open. "Come in and see for yourself."

She walked in ahead of him, trying not to be overly conscious of just how big and masculine and *there* he was.

"Look," she said. "And by that I mean really look, like someone who's never seen this place before, and not like someone who loves it because it's sentimental."

"Who said it was sentimental?"

"Obviously it's sentimental. You're attached to molding."

"I just don't like change," he said, the words coming out stilted.

"Oh, really?"

"There's an order to things," he muttered. "It's easier to keep track of them that way."

She waved a hand. "Well, I love change. It's what makes life interesting."

"Which begs the question why you're back here. Committed to five long years…"

"Because there's no place like home. I've been all over the country and I've never been anywhere that felt like Copper Ridge."

He paused, studying her far too intently for her liking. "How long did it take you to get that response down so perfectly?"

Anger sparked through her. Because he had her number. "Are you saying my response seems rehearsed?"

"Yes. Very. Why are you really here?"

Oh, damn him. "Because. It was time. Because... I was tired of feeling like I was running away."

"From?"

She lifted a shoulder. "Things."

"Same things you got in that bag?"

"Yep. Nuts, bolts and other assorted crap."

Toby chose that moment to come padding down the stairs and into the kitchen.

"You have a cat," he said, "in the house."

"Yes," she said. "Where else am I going to keep my cat?"

"The barn."

"You don't keep a friend in the barn. Well, maybe *you* keep your friends in the barn. That could be why you don't have any friends."

"I have friends."

"I haven't seen any."

"You've seen me at work and at home."

"And I've seen nary a friend. Are they in the barn now?" She made her eyes round and looked at him in mock horror.

"None of my friends shed. And they don't leave dead animals on your carpet."

"Neither does Toby. I don't think he'd kill a mouse. He's too civilized for that."

"A cat that won't kill mice? That just sounds worthless to me."

She shot him a dirty look and scooped Toby up from his position by the table. "You can't have it two ways. Either it's bad for him to leave dead animals lying around, or it's bad for him to not kill things."

"I like it when cats kill things. Outside."

"Then have your cats the way you want them. I'll have mine the way I want him. And I will have matching molding. We're just going to have to disagree on the fundamentals of life. Big surprise there, right?"

"Good point."

"Well. Good. Glad we've come to that…conclusion." She set Toby on the table. "So…now I need to get back to work."

"You honestly think you're going to do all this alone?"

"Yes. I am. I'm a hard worker and I'm not afraid to get my hands dirty."

"I thought you were a therapist."

"Was."

"Didn't you listen to people for a living?"

She blew out an exasperated breath. "Listening is hard work, I'll have you know. It's why so few people do it. And anyway, I have the desire to finish all this work, and one thing you should know about me is that when I set out to do something, I get it done, okay?"

"Well, I'll look forward to seeing you get this done."

"Yeah, well, I look forward to you putting a shirt on," she said.

The words hung between them and she tried not to pull a face and reveal just how embarrassing they were to her. Because, damn it all, she was trying to pretend that she hadn't noticed. And she was pretty sure she'd been managing to hide the whole I'm-helplessly-checking-you-out thing from him, too. Except now she'd gone and shown she was disturbed by it.

Bah.

He cocked his head to the side. "This bothers you?"

"No."

"Then why did you say…?"

"Because. Because this is a place of business."

"I thought you weren't open."

"I'm not, but…still."

He leaned in and she caught his scent—sweat and skin. Man. And the want, the need, grabbed her around the throat and shook hard, unwilling to let her go. She should move. She should stop breathing him in.

But she couldn't think about what might come next. Because her brain was totally blank.

All she could do was stare. At his lips. At the square cut of his jaw. It was dusted with stubble now, not clean like it had been yesterday. Yes, today he looked more out of order in every way, and she had to admit, it was interesting. Fascinating. Dangerous.

Something crackled between them, and he seemed to feel it, too. Because his expression wasn't granite like usual. There was heat there. Even fire. It flickered, quick and hot, in his dark eyes, and then it was gone.

"I think I've imposed on you a little too long," he said. "I have my own work to do."

"Right," she said. "Go on, then."

"If you need anything…"

"I'll call Kate."

"Call Kate." His words came at the same time hers did.

"Right," she said. "I'll do that. I'm picking her up… soon, actually. So. Okay, then."

He ran his hand over his hair, and she felt a little zip of attraction hit her low as the motion highlighted his biceps. Yet again. There was something wrong with her. It must be all this fresh air.

"I think we'll be okay, Sadie," he said, his voice rougher than it had been a moment ago.

"You…do?"

"Just stay out of my way, and I'll stay out of yours. And try not to change too many things."

CHAPTER FOUR

SADIE MILLER, IT turned out, was incapable of following orders. She'd done nothing but change things in the two days since she'd breezed onto the Garrett family ranch, and she showed no sign at all of stopping.

First of all, she'd had a crew there reconditioning the wood, stripping paint. Then she'd followed behind, repainting trim. She was like a little blonde windup toy, and every time Eli drove on the road to Connor's house or the main part of the ranch, he caught glimpses of her working outside the house. He could always resolve to hole up on his end of the property. The road to his own house ran the opposite direction, but that would mean no visiting with his family, and no ranch work. And he wasn't that desperate to avoid her.

Still, he didn't want to catch glimpses of her. He didn't want her there. And dammit, even he knew that verged on curmudgeonly. But he couldn't be bothered to care. He had things happening in his life. Important things. And he didn't need her wandering around the place like a breeze-blown hippie.

Shit, he was uptight. But even so, he hated the feeling of an interloper on Garrett land, and yeah, dammit, he was totally a curmudgeon. There was no denying it. But it just felt...invasive.

He didn't like change. He didn't like people crowding. It was a habit from childhood. They didn't have friends over, well, friends other than Jack Monaghan, and they didn't invite company in past the front porch. They didn't let them see what was inside. They didn't let anyone know the extent to which things had fallen apart.

It was a habit that died hard. Or not at all.

Eli pulled his car past the Catalog House, determined not to look again. Determined not to care. He'd promised Connor and Jack an evening of poker and beer and he planned to deliver. Connor would probably be happy as hell if they canceled, which was one reason he was determined not to.

He parked in front of the porch and looked up at the house. When Jessie had lived there, it had looked nicer than it ever had in Eli's memory. And everything had slipped since losing her.

Connor's muddy boots and other random castaways from a day's work were spread out on the wooden deck, which was in bad need of staining. The windows, vast and prominent, were spotted with water drops and splattered with dirt. Even the door had dirty handprints. Like a very large child lived here. A man child who'd crawled down into a bottle of whiskey the day his wife had been put in the ground.

A man who echoed their father a little too much. Not that Eli had a right to judge, considering that he'd never loved anyone. Not the way Connor had loved Jessie.

He'd never lost like that as a result, either, and he planned to keep it that way.

He got out of the car and noticed Jack's F-150 was already parked in the muddy driveway—which badly needed to be graveled, Eli would handle that—and he walked up the steps, knocking his boots against the top stair to get some of the mud off before pushing the front door open.

He could hear Jack's voice already—animated, loud, the same as he'd been since they were a bunch of skinny preteen boys. Jack was a year younger than Eli, but had always been close to both Connor and himself. If Eli had gotten in trouble as a kid, Jack was the reason. As much as Eli liked order, Jack liked disrupting it. Eli couldn't help but foster a strange admiration for Jack's total disregard for rules.

He couldn't partake, but he could admire. From a distance.

"The police are here," Eli said drily, walking through the entryway and into the dining room, where Connor and Jack were already seated, a stack of cards and poker chips in the middle of the table.

"Sadly," Jack said, "we haven't had the chance to do anything illegal yet."

Connor just sat there looking long-suffering. It was painfully obvious they were trying to pull him out of the pit he was in, and as always, he was so damned aware of it that he'd dug his heels in and was clinging to rock bottom for all he was worth. Stubborn ass.

"And now you won't get a chance. Are we ready to play? And drink? Thankfully, I'm within walking distance so sobriety is not a necessity."

"Public drunkenness?" Jack asked.

"Private property."

"Fair enough."

"Liss is coming," Connor said.

"Then why isn't she here?" Eli asked.

"I invited her," he ground out. "But she's not off work yet."

"So now we have to wait, I take it?"

"She's bringing the good alcohol," Connor said.

"Well, in that case," Jack said, relenting.

"Where's Kate?" Eli asked.

"Home, I expect," Connor told him.

Kate lived in another house on the property. It was small, and designed for two people at most, but it was perfect for her.

"Does she know Liss is coming? She might want to see her." Liss was one of Connor's best friends, and had been a very close friend of his and Jessie's, both before and during their marriage. And Kate seemed starved for female companionship, as evidenced by her obvious desire to wrap Sadie Miller up in a blanket like a little stray kitten. But he was not having that. There would be no adopting of Sadie Miller.

He grabbed a beer from the center of the table, out of the bucket of ice emblazoned with the Oregon Ducks O on the side, and popped the top off.

"We don't really need Katie hanging out and listening to us talk," Jack said.

"Don't call her Katie," Connor said. "She hates that."

"You call her that exclusively," Eli reminded him.

"Yeah. I'm her older brother. I can." He jabbed a finger in Jack's direction. "He can't, though."

"Oh, for God's sake, Connor. Isn't it hard work being this unpleasant all the time?" Jack asked.

"You're still here," Connor said. "The door is open. There are plenty of other men for you to play cards and drink with. Though they'll never satisfy you the way I do."

Eli almost choked on his beer. "You have to warn people before you break out random acts of humor, Connor. It's unexpected."

"I hate to be predictable."

"Yeah," Jack said. "You also hate puppies, rainbows, and I'm pretty sure if compound bow season ever opened on unicorns you'd be first in line."

Eli heard the front door open, and the sound of feminine shoes on the hardwood floor. Which meant it wasn't Kate, because she wore boots, just like the rest of them.

"I'm here!"

It was Liss. She breezed into the room, tugging her auburn hair from its bun and shaking her head. "Gah. Nightmare of a day. Going through financial records for…a place. Confidentiality, sorry."

"Yeah, I know something about that," Eli said.

"I'm sure you do. But accountant work doesn't show up on a police scanner." She set a brown bag on the table. "I come bearing Jack. Daniel's, that is."

"Then you can sit down," Connor said, already reaching for the bag.

Liss frowned.

"Stop it," he said. "Don't give me the sad eyes." He looked around. "This isn't an intervention, is it?"

"Does it need to be?" Eli asked.

"No. I'm fine. Let's play cards."

"Strip poker," Jack said. "Because Liss is here."

Liss looked him over, then looked at Connor and Eli. "I'd win that game, Jack. No matter how you cut it."

"No strip poker," Eli said.

"You're just still mad because the last time I talked you into taking your clothes off, when we were about twelve, I think, we ended up getting caught skinny-dipping by that group of high school girls," Jack said.

"And that was the day I quit listening to you."

"Less talking. More betting," Liss said, pounding the table.

"Fine. Fine."

There was a knock at the door that sounded border-line frantic. And Eli knew that Kate wouldn't knock.

Connor got up. "Just a sec."

He walked out of the room and they all watched after him, listening. "Oh! Thank God you're home." A woman's voice.

"I'm always home," Connor said, his flat tone carrying into the dining room.

Connor. Full of charm as always.

"I'm having a slight disaster." Oh, no.

"Come in." Damn.

More footsteps, then Sadie Miller walked into his brother's dining room.

She was a mess. Her hair was wet and hanging in twisted, yarn-like strands over her face and down her shoulders. She wore a baggy gray sweatshirt that had damp spots spreading wherever her hair touched the fabric. "I'm having a problem," she said a little bit sheepishly, looking around the table at everyone.

Jack and Liss both looked confused.

"This is Sadie Miller," Eli said. "Our new tenant in the Catalog House."

Liss's eyes darted from Connor back to Sadie. "Oh. Hi. You're the one doing the B and B?" For some reason, her friendliness sounded forced. And of course Liss knew about the bed-and-breakfast. In fact, Eli had a feeling she'd been involved somehow.

"Yes," Sadie said. "That would be me. Though, right now the B and B is doing me. So to speak."

"What happened?" Connor asked, crossing his arms over his chest.

"Pipes. Burst. And I was trying to—" she brushed wet hair out of her face "—stop it. To a degree. But I couldn't. So I...uh...wrapped the pipes as best I could and changed and came here. I'm not sure where this falls under our tenant agreement. Technically this had nothing to do with my renovation and everything to do with me trying to shower in the upstairs bathroom."

Connor's brows locked together. "Well...hell if I know. I didn't really anticipate having to be involved."

Sadie blinked. "Well, we signed a whole...agreement. And there are certain things...as the...the landlord...and..."

Eli sighed. "Would you like me to go and take a look, Connor?"

Connor nodded once. "If you don't mind."

I mind. I mothereffing mind. "Nope," Eli said, sliding his beer toward the center of the table and pushing his chair back to stand.

Sadie was eyeing him warily. "Thank you," she said, and he could tell she minded about as much as he did. But she had no place to be irked in all this. She was the one who'd chosen to rent a place on his family property.

She was the one with really quite nice breasts, thank you very much, that were causing him some problems currently.

Getting laid in a small town was problematic. Which made breasts that were actually probably no better than average more noticeable than they should be.

She didn't look hot right now. She looked like a wet hen. He should remember that. He sent a meaningful message below his belt, but he had a feeling it was going to get lost in translation.

Mainly because his body never seemed to want to translate those kinds of messages. But then, what guy's did?

Especially not when the only company said body

had enjoyed for the past six months was that of his right hand.

"All right," he said, "let's go check out your disaster. I'll sit this round out," he told Jack.

Jack swept the deck of cards to the edge of the table and leaned back, shuffling expertly. "All right, kids, get ready to lose your hard-earned money."

"Sorry," Sadie said, as they walked out of the room. "Obviously I'm interrupting."

"It's not a big deal. It's a thing that happens a lot. Poker. I'm not going to miss one game. And the sad fact is, Jack's right. We're all going to lose our hard-earned money to him. And he'll continue the grand tradition of having non…hard-earned money."

"I bet there's a story there," she said.

"Isn't there always?" he asked.

She nodded. "Yeah, in my experience, there is. Speaking of—" she pushed the front door open and he followed her onto the porch "—what's Connor's story?" The end of the sentence was hushed.

He closed the door, feeling a little uncomfortable having a stranger digging for information. Mainly because he was so used to family junk staying in the family. Because it was still ingrained in him. To keep the exterior looking shiny, no matter how bad the inside was.

But Connor's deal wasn't really a secret. A cursory visit to Copper Ridge's cemetery would tell his story in full.

"I don't know if you remember Jessie Collins."

"Vaguely. I might. Did she work at the Crow's Nest?"

"I think so," he said, trying not to picture his sister-in-law too clearly. Because it was too sad, even for him.

"Well, she was Jessie Garrett for about eight years. But, uh…she was killed in an accident."

It was a night Eli would rather forget. He could remember the scene clearly. A dark two-lane highway, and a car wrapped around a tree. He'd known it was too late for whoever was inside. That it had been from the moment of impact. He'd seen too many accidents like that, and not enough miracles.

The car had been so messed up he hadn't recognized the make or model. Hadn't realized it was Jessie's until one of the volunteer firefighters, who'd been first on the scene, had come charging back from the car yelling at him not to come closer.

They'd been trying to spare him because of who it was. But in the end, he'd looked. Because he had to be sure.

And then he'd been the one to officially notify his brother. And nothing in all of his life, in all of his training, had prepared him to stand on the front porch in his uniform and tell his older brother that his beautiful wife wasn't coming home. Not that night, not any night after.

Damn trees. Damn road. Two people they'd loved lost that way.

Though in their dad's case, he'd been at clear fault. Alcohol had caused his crash. Jessie had probably swerved to miss a deer, but they'd never know for sure.

"Oh," Sadie said, her voice muted.

"So he comes by his attitude honestly," Eli said, walking down the stairs to the driveway. "You want to ride in the patrol car?"

She looked at him, a brow raised. "It's a short walk. Anyway, I don't want to have any flashbacks."

"Emotionally traumatized?"

"Completely."

"Good. I probably kept your ass out of trouble."

"Ugh," she said. "Do not act like you did me any favors. What helped was getting the hell out of this town."

"Is that what helped?"

"Yeah. There's not enough options here. And there's way too much free time. I badly needed to escape."

"So why are you back?"

She sighed loudly. "Can I get away with repeating what I told you earlier?"

"No."

"Well, fine. That is just a damn good question." She took a big step and her foot landed in a pile of sticks that crunched loudly beneath her boot, before she shifted, her other foot making contact with soft dirt as she continued on toward the Catalog House.

"And you don't have the answer?"

"You know…you have to live somewhere. And I've had a hard time finding a place that didn't…suck. So I'm back here. Because—" she turned partway and offered him a shrug and a sheepish smile, the setting sun igniting a pink halo around her pale hair "—well, I am. And currently, all I've achieved is drowned-rat status."

"Don't go near the barn. Connor has rat traps."

"And cats, I hear," she said, tromping through the tree line and into the driveway of her…his…house. He followed, frowning involuntarily as he caught a glimpse of the bare flower beds. Sure, all that had been in them before was overgrown weeds, but she had them completely stripped now.

"Those are the rat traps I was talking about."

"Don't talk about cats that way in front of Toby. He's sensitive."

"He's probably been talking to you about his feelings too much."

"Was that a therapist joke?" she asked, moving ahead of him and up the stairs to open the front door.

"Yeah, it was. Excuse me, I'm out of practice with jokes."

"Obviously."

Her cat was there, on the kitchen table, looking at him pointedly. As if he sensed that Eli had absolutely no use for him, and he was greatly offended by it. Except Eli knew that wasn't it because it was a cat, and cats had no higher consciousness, as evidenced by their reaction to string.

He stared back at the cat.

"He is unimpressed with you," she said.

"The feeling is mutual. Now hang on a second while I try to figure out where the water shutoff is."

"That would be helpful," she said. "Water shutoff valves would be helpful."

"Connor should have left you a list of that stuff. Where it all is. Fuse boxes and water mains. Though I'm betting he doesn't even know where it is here."

"How long has it been since anyone's lived here?"

"A couple of years. An older lady rented it for about ten years, until she died."

"This place is kind of full of sad history," Sadie said.

"Yeah. Welcome to the Garrett Ranch, where the motto is, if it doesn't kill you…just wait."

"That is distasteful. I'm sure."

"Completely, but also the story of our lives. Now, I'm willing to bet your shutoff is somewhere inconvenient, like…maybe the shed outside?"

"I haven't looked."

"All right, come on. If we find it, I can show you how to shut it off."

"Maybe I know how to shut it off," she said, following him back out the door and down the stairs. "Maybe I'm a water-valve expert."

"But you aren't," he said, opening the door to the shed.

"Fine. I'm not. But I usually have nearby landlords who…do this for me. Which is sort of what's happening now, except you're involving me. Although, I have to say, I have never had a pipe just…explode all over me before. Not a euphemism."

"How could that be…?"

Her eyes widened and she looked at him meaningfully. "Pipes…burst…liquid all over the… Oh, wow. Think about it. Please don't make me say it. And I'm going to stop talking now. Please shut my water off."

Suddenly, he got it. Heat shot from his face down to his groin. This was what happened when he spent six—okay, honestly, it was closer to seven—months without sex. His mind was completely void of anything that went beyond boobs and the innuendo that had just popped up. So to speak. It was enough to…well, as she'd put it, *explode his pipe*.

He did not have time for this. He didn't have the patience for it, either.

"Fine," he growled, stalking to the pipe that was sticking out of the ground in the back of the old building, wrapped in a thick swath of insulation. He reached down and pushed the valve up. "So now your water's off. Direct me to your flood and I can see if there's a quick fix that won't require you to go without water all night."

"It's in the upstairs bathroom. So…back to the house. And I hope you're enjoying this tour of…things that are not finished in the yard," she said, leading them both back to the house.

"What are you doing with the flower bed?" he asked, looking at the bare dirt.

"I don't know… Something. I was hoping someone could tell me which plants you…plant here this time of year. I don't know anything about flowers or grass or… I'm going to do some investigating tomorrow."

"Haven't you planted flowers before?"

She shrugged. "There's never been any point. I leave before anything grows. Or…when I was in San Diego I had an apartment and I had, like, a little pineapple plant in a pot. But some asshole stole it off the balcony. So I figured unless I wanted chains on my potted plants I'd just forget it. This is nice. I don't have to chain things to the porch." She opened the front door and walked in, then paused at the base of the stairs. "Up that way. The one off the master bedroom."

He sighed and walked upward, toward his watery doom. Or something like that.

He could hear her following behind, her footsteps softer and off rhythm to his own.

He walked into the bedroom and saw a few damp footprints on the wood floor, then he looked into the bathroom, where there was a sizable puddle by the sink.

He sighed heavily and got down on his knees, the water seeping through his uniform pants, then he opened the cabinet doors. "What the…hell?"

"I had to improvise," she said, her voice small.

He leaned in and examined the makeshift stopper she'd wrapped around the pipes. A shirt, a pair of sweat-pants and…a black lace bra winding it all together.

"I was about to get in the shower, so I was already naked, and then there was water and so I had to stop it, and then I had to…tie it off. With something. I think that bra is toast."

He cleared his throat. "Probably." He reached out and started unwinding the bra, and tried not to think about how this was the first time he'd touched a woman's underwear in seven—okay, maybe it was more like eight—months.

It was Sadie Miller's bra. He should focus on that. On the fact that he remembered what a gangly, hissing little miscreant she'd been back when she was a teenager. All long limbs and blond shaggy hair, smelling like booze and cigarette smoke as she kicked at him while he'd tried to put her in handcuffs without breaking her slender wrists.

Sadie Miller's bra should hold no interest for him. And neither should her breasts. Or her innuendos.

ELI UNWOUND THE strap a little bit more and the rest sprang free, spraying his face with water.

Sadie bit her fist to keep from whimpering as she watched Eli Garrett, on his hands and knees, fiddling with her bra. She was so mortified she wanted to flush herself down the toilet. It would be preferable to this nightmare.

She was just one giant explosion of embarrassment after the other tonight. The whole pipe euphemism? What was her problem? Why did she say things like that around him? Good gravy.

She was good at talking to people. She did it for a living. Spoke with calm authority and with self-control, and with carefully chosen words.

And here she was pointing out every innuendo and dying a million tiny deaths—not in the good French way—like some extra awkward high school geek she'd never been.

What was it about Eli that caused regression? It was

a mystery to her. He made her feel flaily. And kind of…
horny. And that was just stupid. Cracking lady-wood
over a cop said nothing good about her deep emotional
issues. She was a therapist. She really should have a
better handle on this.

Though she wasn't really a therapist at the moment.
She was a bed-and-breakfast owner who was sinking
her life savings into a place with leaky pipes, populated
by grumpy, muscular men. Who said she didn't make
good life choices?

He unwound all of her clothing—thank God she
hadn't used her panties. She was just really, really
thankful. Then he stood up, the sodden garments in
his very large hand, his dark brows drawn together.
"This isn't a quick fix. You will need a plumber. Which
my brother will pay for."

"He said he wasn't sure where all that fell in the
agreement." She reached out and took the ball of
clothes, water dripping onto the floor.

"But I am," he said, his voice hard. "It's BS to act
like he won't pay for a burst pipe. Obviously that had
nothing to do with your improvements. My brother is
just being a lame landlord. Trust me, he's not doing it
on purpose. He's just…nonfunctional right now."

Sadie's heart squeezed tight. "I'm sorry about his
wife. I… If he ever needs to talk…"

"He would rather shove barbed wire under his fingernails. And I'm being literal."

"Okay, then, so maybe vouchers for my services
wouldn't go over well in exchange for this debacle."

"Connor isn't a talker," Eli said.

"Well, big surprise," she retorted, dumping the wet
clothes into the sink and walking out of the space that

really was way too small to be sharing with a man of his stature.

"What is that supposed to mean?"

"It just seems like it runs in the family, that's all."

"Meaning?" he asked.

"You're a little uptight," she said, walking near the bed and feeling a sudden surge of heat and self-consciousness. Dear Lord, it was like she wasn't even an adult anymore. Internally jittering because she was standing near both a man and a bed and they were alone.

"If by uptight you mean responsible for a shit-ton of stuff, sure," he bit out, "I'm uptight. Do you need water?"

"I have some," she said. "All over my floor."

"That isn't what I meant," he said, his civility clearly almost at an end. "You're going to need…coffee in the morning at least, I assume, and you need to shower."

She lifted a shoulder. "It wouldn't hurt."

"Either Connor will get his ass in gear and try to fix this tomorrow, or we'll want to call out a plumber. Either way you don't have water tonight, because the main has to stay shut off since the pipes are so old. And it means you don't have water until midmorning tomorrow. So, would you like to come to my place and shower and get a couple gallons of water?"

She blinked. "I…uh…"

"It's a simple question."

"I just didn't expect you to extend me hospitality," she said.

"I'm not a complete asshole."

"Oh. Okay."

"You say that like you don't believe me."

She shrugged. "I don't know, Eli, but whenever you're around I get a tension headache. Or I end up in handcuffs. So, suffice it to say, I'm not entirely convinced that you aren't a total asshole. Sorry."

And she also wasn't convinced she wanted to go to his house and get naked when he was in a nearby room. And run her hands all over her wet, slick skin, which would inevitably feel really good. And with his image so very large in her mind…

Yeah, well, again, she regressed in the company of this man. What grown woman worried about this stuff? It was…prurient. And juvenile. And things.

She needed both a shower and some water and the man was offering. So she should stop sweating, and stop insulting him, and just go with it.

"That would be great, actually," she said. "And I'm sorry about the asshole thing."

He put his hands on his lean hips and she took a moment to admire him. His uniform conformed to every muscle in his body; the tan shirt and dark brown tie, along with the gold-star-shaped badge honest-to-coffee did things to her insides that were unseemly.

Obviously she needed to buy batteries for her long-neglected vibrator. Dammit, how sad was it that her *vibrator* was neglected. A sex life, sure. People had crap to do. Who had time to go around hooking up and sweating and making walks of shame? She certainly didn't.

But she barely took the time to orgasm anymore. And when she did, she had to kick Toby out of the room, because it was awkward, and then it sort of felt like she was announcing her masturbatory intentions to her cat, which felt even weirder. There was something unspeakably sad about the whole thing.

But that was the reason Eli's presence had her so shaken. That was her story, and she was sticking to it.

"Whatever," he said. "Come with me."

He certainly didn't make a big song and dance about graciousness. He almost seemed burdened by inescapable chivalry, which was sort of hilarious, or would be if she wasn't so busy marinating in her embarrassment.

"Let me get some clothes," she said. "You can wait downstairs." Because she would probably fizzle into an ash ball and blow away in the wind if he watched her pull a new bra out of a drawer.

"Fine," he said, walking out of the bedroom and swinging the door partway closed. She waited until she heard his footsteps on the stairs before rummaging for new clothes. She pulled out a long-sleeved thermal shirt and a pair of black yoga pants, and a new bra and panties. And then she got a duffel bag to conceal it all in.

She stuffed the clothes inside and walked downstairs to where Eli was waiting, standing there staring at Toby, who was still on the table, looking defiant.

"I'm ready," she said. "Do you have jugs at your place?"

"Yes," he said. "We always save a bunch for target practice, so that won't be a problem."

Holy hell, she really wasn't in San Diego anymore. She was in Oregon, no question at all. "I should have guessed."

"What's that supposed to mean?" he asked, holding the door for her.

"Nothing. I just forgot the kinds of things you good ol' boys get up to in your spare time. I've been living in a city, if you recall."

"You've been gone for how long?" he asked, walking down the front porch steps. She followed him closely, clutching her bag to her chest. Looking at his dark brown pants, which seemed to be giving his butt a hug while shouting, "Look at it! Look at it!"

"Ten years."

"And where have you been in those ten years?"

"Polite conversation?" she asked.

"Why don't we try it?"

"I'm game if you are. Okay, I went to three different schools in four years. I started in Tampa, because, parties and the beach. Which is nothing like the beach here. Turns out, I hate college parties and breathing in Florida is like inhaling soup. So I lasted a year there. I basically toured the South." She increased her pace to keep up with Eli's long strides, following him down the darkened driveway. He pulled a flashlight off his belt and used it to light up the bark-laden ground. "Louisiana, North Carolina, and after I graduated I went to Texas, which you really don't want to mess with, just ask the locals."

"After that you went to California?" he asked.

"Nope. After that there was New York, Chicago and Branson."

"Branson?"

"Missouri. It's Las Vegas for families, Eli. Incidentally, I also lived in Vegas, but not for long. Then I went to the Bay Area and quickly discovered I couldn't afford to live there unless I wanted to donate a kidney to science, and then I went to San Diego. And now I'm back…here."

He stopped walking, the flashlight beam still directed at the ground. "I can't imagine picking up and moving that much."

"No?"

"I've got too much to pack up and bring with me.

You know, Connor, Kate, all their stuff. The cows. Plus, there's this land. Our family land."

"Yeah, well, it's just me and Toby. We travel light."

He started walking again, continuing on straight down the drive. "I'll regret asking this, because... I shouldn't care. But what the hell did you expect to find moving from place to place?"

She lifted a shoulder. "I don't know. Everywhere is so different. I managed to trick myself into thinking that I'd find a place that made me different. And to a degree, it's true. Every place changes you a little. When I was doing therapy, I was a crisis counselor, so I always dealt with people going through the worst things possible. Every patient I spoke to changed me in some way. Every home I lived in, every restaurant I ate at... But...the one thing I've never done is go back to a place. I've only ever gone somewhere new. I thought I would see what it was like."

"And?"

"No magic yet. But I do think I've finally realized that it doesn't really matter where I live. I'm not going to find a perfect place that makes me perfect. So I figured I'd come back here and wrestle demons."

"What kind of demons are you wrestling?" he asked.

It was said drily. Insincere. And yet she found she wanted to answer. She found she wanted to talk to him about the demon she'd met head-on the night he'd arrested her. The night she'd nearly been killed.

She didn't blame him for that. Not really. She knew dimly that some people might. But she'd never put her father's actions onto Eli Garrett's shoulders. Because it had started long before then. Because she had a feeling that night was inevitable. Regardless of what date it fell on, regardless of what triggered it.

And it had been the reason she'd gotten into her car and driven away. And never once looked back. Until now.

"This way," Eli said, pointing his light toward a cluster of pine trees off to the left. "We can cut through here. It's faster."

She followed him through the trees and into a clearing. There was a house up the hill, surrounded by trees, the porch light on as if someone inside the two-story wooden cabin was waiting for them. Wide steps led up to a wraparound deck with a glass door, and large windows dominated the front of the place, making the most of the location, set deep into the trees and far away from any roads.

"No wonder you've never left," she said.

"Well," he said, "not much point when you have a house ready and waiting for you, is there?"

"Sure there is," she said. "If my parents had given me their house I still would have run. Happily for me, they never offered. I think the house ended up with the bank when they went to Coos Bay." She felt like the statement was a little more revealing than she might have liked, but oh well.

"Well," he said, obviously uncomfortable. And obviously unwilling to say more, even though the *well* held a wealth of meaning. He was really, at his heart, a decent man, even if he was reluctant in his decency.

"Well," she said, matching his tone, "my parents' house was essentially the crap cherry on top of a landfill, so for that reason alone I wouldn't want it. Thank you for being too nice to say that." She hopped over a tire rut that was filled with muddy water and continued following him down the road.

"I wasn't thinking it."

"Bull, and ten points if you can guess the word that follows."

"I wasn't, Sadie. I've been to a lot of houses like that. I've seen a lot of things. People have hard circumstances. And I don't like to think of their living situations that way."

"Why not?" she asked. "They do. Trust me. I mean… we do. We know."

"I don't judge people based on where they live."

"Is that honestly how you feel? Or are you just throwing out some…good-guy line?" she asked, as they came to the end of the road, where it narrowed and led up to his house.

"Honestly?" he asked, turning to face her. "I care about this place. I care about Copper Ridge. And I care about Logan County. This is my home. And the people here are my responsibility. It's not my job to look down my nose at anyone. It's my job to protect the people here." He continued walking, turning away from her again, his broad back filling her vision.

Her heart jammed up against her sternum. Anger mixed with a strange kind of longing that she didn't want to apply to him. That she didn't want to apply to anything or anyone, really.

"And you do a damn fine job, I'm sure," she said, following him up the steps and waiting for him to unlock his door. The man locked his door. In Copper Ridge. Dear Lord.

"I know," he said. "I haven't exactly been hanging out for the past ten years so my first arrest could tell me that, but now that you have, it's sort of nice and circular. I could use it for my campaign."

"Hold up," she said. "Campaign?"

"Yes. I'm running for sheriff." He bit the words out as if sharing them with her was a monumental task.

"Oh, really?" she said, eyes widening. She couldn't help but be…intrigued by that. Maybe *intrigued* was the right word. Because Eli Garrett seemed to be a few things to her, and none of them were overly diplomatic. And it seemed to her, not that she was an expert, that a person running for any sort of elected position needed to behave, at least some of the time, like he didn't have a stick lodged in his rear.

But that was just her take on it.

"Yes," he said. "Really."

"Well, color me intrigued. What all does this entail?"

"Right now? I was the top finisher in the primary, and the final election is in November. My lead was pretty strong, but I still need to keep campaigning. Make more signs. I have a few months to prepare for a community Q & A," he said, pushing the door open. "This is the house." He swept his hand in a broad gesture across the living space. It was open, and neat, very different from his brother's place, which had an air of sad neglect about it, every bit of dust and dirt a fingerprint of grief. Eli's home had no fingerprints at all. Which, in and of itself, she found fascinating.

"Wow. Connor should hire you," she said.

"Because I'm not at all busy," he said. "I mean, obviously I'm not. I'm here getting water for you and letting you use my shower."

"Because you care for the members of the community," she said. "Which I am, at this moment, grateful for. Much more so than that time you cared for the community by handcuffing me and putting me in the back of your patrol car."

"That seems to come up a lot."

"It's our cute meet, meet cute, whatever they call it. It's part of our story," she said, watching the tension between his brows intensify with each word. There was no doubt, she disturbed him. And he was growing even more disturbed having her in his house.

"Right. So, the bathroom is upstairs. Feel free to take as long as you need in the shower. I'll get the water ready for you to take back."

She cleared her throat, annoyed with herself for finding sincerity so hard. She was a basket case. Why anyone took her advice on anything was a mystery to her, particularly when she acted like this. "Thank you. Honestly. I know that I've sort of crashed into your life sans finesse here, and I appreciate you...well, I'm glad you haven't found a reason to arrest me again and I'm very grateful for the chance to shower."

He nodded slowly. "You're welcome."

"I'm going to go and...shower now." And she was going to hope that she could do it without thinking too much about his proximity. Or without thinking about him at all. Yes, not thinking about Eli Garrett at all—in the shower or out—would be the ideal thing.

If only she could manage it.

CHAPTER FIVE

ELI GRITTED HIS teeth and hunched his shoulders, trying to ignore the sound of the running water. Trying to ignore any and all thoughts of Sadie in the shower.

It was hard, no pun intended, because there hadn't been a woman in his house, in his shower, in…possibly ever. It had been so long since he'd had an actual relationship, he couldn't remember. Longer still since a relationship had mattered, since every actual girlfriend he'd had sort of faded into the distant past like a soft hazy dream.

The kind he had no desire to revisit. Because girlfriends were a whole level of responsibility he didn't want or need. At this point, with Kate still unsettled and Connor deep in his grief, Eli couldn't fathom taking on much more.

Which is why it's obviously the best time to increase your workload.

He pinched the bridge of his nose and took a deep breath, before dropping his hands back to his sides and stalking to the fridge. He was going to drink a beer. And he wasn't even going to bother to go back for the poker game. They'd all do fine without him.

He pulled a cold bottle out from the back and popped the top off with the magnet opener he kept stuck to the freezer.

Yeah, it was a terrible time to take on more. Connor

needed help on the ranch, and he always would. It was their legacy, and Eli had to take part in it. Then there was the emotional aspect of dealing with his family.

On top of that, Sadie being in residence was adding another layer to his to-do list that he did not need. Because for all Connor said he was going to handle it, here *Eli* was, freaking handling it.

Not a huge surprise and not much he could do about it, either. Five years. Five years of Sadie and foibles that would undoubtedly be similar in nature to this. Sometimes he wondered if he'd been an ax murderer in a past life and he was destined to spend this one atoning.

But then he remembered reincarnation was bullshit and took another drink of his beer.

And reincarnation was not the only thing that was bullshit. That there was a naked, wet woman in his house whom he could not and would not touch was also bullshit.

He'd had a permanent frown etched into his face since Sadie had shown up. He didn't even feel like trying to fix his attitude. It was just one more thing to add to his list of things to worry about. One more thing that he had to add to an increasing, unwieldy pile of Things For Eli to Manage.

Things he knew without a doubt wouldn't get taken care of if he didn't do it. Because that was life. It was his life.

Which he was normally not so bitter about. But something about the addition of a woman whom he wasn't allowed to touch, a woman he shouldn't even want to touch, naked in his house was like jamming an injured thumb into the center of a lemon. Grabbing two empty gallon jugs from under the sink, he began to fill them for the woman he was trying not to picture naked.

He heard soft footsteps on the stairs and turned to see bare feet come into view. Bare feet with shocking pink nails. Followed by baggy black pants and a very soft-looking shirt, molded to breasts that he should not stare at—but did anyway—and then the rest of Sadie appeared.

Her blond hair was wet and piled on top of her head, tendrils falling down the sides of her face, her cheeks flushed from the hot water. Her makeup was gone. Lashes that had looked dark and heavy were now spiky and pale.

She looked damp and warm and he had no business wondering about her body temperature, or her level of dryness.

"Thank you," she said, her feet hitting the floor. She walked to the kitchen counter and slung her bag, and her shoes, onto the granite surface. "I feel more like a human and less like a mole person, so that's always good." She was smiling now, effortless, friendly.

As if she hadn't been pissy and sulky with him only a few minutes ago. As if they had no history between them whatsoever.

Fine, it didn't matter to him. She was just a problem to check off his list. He was not going to waste time overthinking her. He didn't have the time to waste.

"Shoes," he said, the muscles in his back tensing from his belt line to his shoulders.

"What?"

"Take your shoes off my counter, please."

"Sorry," she said, pulling them from the surface that would now have to be disinfected.

"Yep," he said. "I'll grab your jugs for you."

Her blue eyes rounded. "Oh, really?"

"What?"

"You're going to…grab my jugs for me… I don't… You've *had* sex before, right?"

Heat assaulted him, starting in his face and burning a line straight down his chest to his cock. "Yes. What does that have to do with anything?"

"You seem to be operating on a frequency wherein sexual innuendo doesn't exist."

Jugs. Suddenly an image of him putting his hands over her breasts and, well…grabbing them…flashed through his mind. "Because I'm not a fourteen-year-old boy," he shot back. "And I don't call women's breasts jugs." He said the last part through gritted teeth, trying to figure out how in the hell he'd gotten into a conversation about breasts with the woman whose breasts had been tormenting him from the moment she'd crashed back into town like a blonde tornado.

"Well, that's mature of you. I don't typically call them jugs, either. I prefer 'the girls' or 'sweater bunnies,' but even I went there."

He about choked on the sip of beer he was trying to take. "Don't you have work to do back at your place?"

"Nothing pressing," she said.

He gritted his teeth. "Do you want a beer?" He didn't want her to stay for a beer. Why was he so compulsively appropriate? Especially when she was standing there talking about *sweater bunnies*.

"Thank you," she said, "that would be good."

He laughed, even though he found nothing about any of this funny, and turned back to the fridge, tugging another bottle out, and opening it before sliding it across the counter toward her.

In spite of himself, he found he was curious about her plans for the Catalog House. Because maybe if he

knew about the changes, they wouldn't feel quite so in-
vasive. A long shot, but worth a try.

And anything was better than talking about her
breasts.

"What's next on your list for the place?" he asked.

"I have to make the downstairs back bedroom livable. That's going to be my room. It's small, and part
of an addition. So it's a little damp and chilly, but with
caulking and some oil heaters I won't die. And since
we're headed into summer it won't be bad at all. Then
obviously I need to make sure the plumbing is better
than it is. Flower beds are a priority, and linens and
blinds. And after that, barring menu creation, I should
be good to start advertising and getting special events
scheduled."

"Wait...special events?"

"Yes! I thought it would be fun. Ranch tours. Picnics.
And I'm thinking on Independence Day a community
party would be great."

"People. Here?"

"Yes, people. I'm opening a bed-and-breakfast, for
people and not, despite what you may have thought,
cats. And if I want to attract people, it seems like bringing visibility to the place is the way to do it."

"What's the point of attracting locals?"

"Uh, locals go away on romantic weekend getaways
to local places. And also, their family members come
and visit. And people from surrounding areas might
come to the parties and think of me. And honestly,
maybe they'll think of Garrett specifically when they
go to buy beef."

"How do you know about what we do on the ranch?"

"I Googled it. Because I am interested in helping

you. And me. It's all…symbiotic helpfulness. And what's wrong with that?"

He felt like he was losing control. Like she had come along, grabbed his control and was running around holding it over her head, laughing maniacally as he tried to reclaim it.

"What's wrong with that is you're proposing to turn this place—*my* place—into a fun fair. We live here. We work here. This isn't a carnival."

"I never said it was! But what's wrong with a few special events? It's not like I have to take over the barns. I mean, I would, but I can keep it contained."

"Have you run any of this past Connor?"

She shrugged. "Not…specifically, but he did agree to let me bring a certain amount of the public onto the property when I initially sent over my business plan, so I didn't see why this would be a problem."

"You didn't see why it would be a problem?" he asked.

"No. I didn't." She took a drink of her beer. "I'm running a business, and it benefits Connor, benefits Kate and you. I have a five-year lease agreement, and it seems to me that we should all be into ideas that will make things more successful. Right?"

"Not ideas that include my ranch crawling with a bunch of random people. I don't like that kind of disorder."

"You are the singularly most frustrating, uptight, obtuse… No one makes me mad, Eli. No one. I am not an angry person. I like to smile. And every time I'm around you, no matter how cheerful I determine to be, I end up irritated."

"That's funny, Sadie, because I feel like I end up irritated every time I'm around you."

"I just think your irritation is contagious," she said.

"Maybe you're so irritating you irritate yourself."

"Oh! Bah! What are you, twelve?"

"I thought you were the one acting like an adolescent boy, not me."

"No, I am the one acting like I have a sense of humor. Because I do. And you," she said, drawing her beer against her chest, "are ridiculous. And humorless."

"If you think that barb is going to wound me, you obviously don't know me very well."

"I don't know you very well. And I'm content with that. I think I will spend the next five years not knowing you very well." She grabbed her shoes from the stool and plopped onto it, bending over and fidgeting while she put them on her feet. She straightened, a clump of wet hair falling out of her bun. "I'm going to go now. And I'm taking the beer. And the water. Thank you. Again. I'll try not to bother you anymore."

He snorted. "Good luck."

"Oh, I don't need it. I don't mind bothering you. You are clearly the one who is bothered by being bothered. So…you're the one who needs the luck, not me."

She stood up, collected her bag and managed to grab the water jugs as well, then turned on her heel and stormed out toward the entryway, out the front door, slamming it shut with her foot and rattling the windows.

She had no right to be angry. He was the one who had every righteous reason to be pissed. She was a tenant, not a part owner. She had no right to be making decisions that affected his life and his business.

Tomorrow, he was going to talk to Connor about her. And very definitive boundaries. After he was done with work anyway. He groaned and shoved his beer back. It was officially getting too late for him to stay up and drink. Sadie Miller had ruined his entire evening, and now he was going to have to go shower in a shower still wet with water that had been on her body. And then he was going to have to sleep with visions of sweater bunnies and strangers doing the hoedown on his porch dancing in his head.

Which meant he was better served getting on the computer and working on campaign plans. At least planning would help make him feel like he had some control.

Yes, tomorrow, he would talk to Connor about what needed to be done.

And tonight? Tonight he would just have to deal with his annoyance. At least annoyance was better than sexual frustration.

ELI TOOK A sip of his coffee and walked out of Copper Ridge's coffee shop, The Grind, and onto the main street. Connor gave him endless grief about the fact that he cut his coffee with steamed milk. And that he ordered lattes. But he wasn't a fan of the black sludge his brother poured down his throat all day.

Eli needed caffeine, and he would get it in the way he found most palatable, even if his older brother called it Bitch Coffee.

Besides, he needed his coffee extra bad today because of his encounter with Sadie last night.

He'd been so annoyed that he'd barely been able to sleep, thanks to the images of his property being overrun with civilians. And he knew that it shouldn't bother him. But he also knew that if it really did happen, he would be putting caution tape all around his portion of the property and shouting, "Get off my lawn!" to anyone who got too close.

Old habits died hard, and things like that.

Anyway, that kind of behavior wouldn't be good for his campaign. And he had to think about that kind of thing now.

He let out a breath and headed toward the crosswalk. He waited for the signal to change, then started to cross, heading back toward his patrol car. A breeze came in off the waves. Salt, brine and moisture filled his lungs.

He needed to get his head on straight and stop worrying about Sadie. Though if there was a magic way for him to just stop worrying he would have found it a long time ago. But it seemed like the day his mother had walked out the door, she'd taken his stability and shoved a knot of anxiety straight into his chest that he'd never been able to get rid of.

He put his uniform on every morning and took it off at night, and the worry didn't go on and off with it. It was in him. Part of him. He'd more or less accepted it. And accepted that the only way to really deal with it was to make sure things were taken care of.

"Deputy Garrett!"

He looked to his left and saw Lydia Carpenter signaling him. He really didn't have time to field any issues from the Chamber of Commerce today. Lydia always had something to talk to him about. From obtaining proper licensing for an event, to dealing with complaints from home owners about "noise pollution" during one of her carefully planned summer concerts.

Everything in him screamed, *Not my problem*, but on the outside he just smiled and nodded. Because, most especially, when someone was hoping to gain the good favor of the voting public, one had to be pleasant.

"Ms. Carpenter," he said, "nice to see you. I'm on patrol so this has to be quick."

"Oh, fine, fine, fine," she said, tucking a strand of

dark hair behind her ear, spitting the words out rapid-fire. "It will be. I just wanted to tell you I had a chance to meet with Sadie Miller today."

"You what?" he asked.

"Sadie came by the Chamber with a list of ideas for community events hosted on the ranch."

"She did what?" he asked, the words coming out a bit terse.

Lydia didn't shrink under his terseness. She didn't react at all. Her petite frame was unshaken, her smile firmly in place. She was young to be in the position she was in, possibly a bit younger than he was. And when he thought about it, he had to concede that the woman must be almost entirely composed of efficiency and stubbornness to achieve what she had, even in a town so small.

Her smile broadened, which he would have thought was impossible. And he had to admit that she was actually very pretty. But it didn't make this less annoying.

"She stopped by and we had a lovely chat, Eli." Suddenly he was Eli and not Deputy Garrett. "Her ideas for the Independence Day community barbecue are so good. She's talking about canvassing all of Logan County with flyers. I suggested we get it listed on the nightly news Community Chalkboard and on the Chamber's website. I think it's the kind of thing that could really benefit Copper Ridge. The coastal fireworks on the Fourth are already such a big draw, adding events that extend tourists' stays will only be good for everyone."

He was afraid, honest to God, that a blood vessel in his eye was going to burst. Sadie'd circumvented him and Connor, and now he was effectively roped around the balls by the president of the Chamber of Commerce.

If he tugged too far the other way, he could find himself neutered. And if not anything half that dramatic, he could at least find himself out of the running for sheriff.

"Thank you, Eli, so much for allowing this to happen on the ranch. I can't think of a better place, or a better man to host. All things considered, I mean. I'd love to help with anything I can," she said, looking at him with large eyes. "I can help plan games. I could come by your place and look at different areas that might be of use for the event."

He cleared his throat, hoping it would help dislodge the rage ball that was blocking his ability to breathe. "I'll get in touch with you, Ms. Carpenter," he said, very purposefully not using her first name, because for some reason he just had a feeling that was asking for trouble. "Now, if you'll excuse me, I need to get on with my day."

He turned around to face his patrol car, which was parked against the curb, to see Sadie two blocks down, exiting one of the little shops on the corner, a small paper bag in one hand and a coffee in the other.

Before he could even think through his next move, his feet were propelling him toward her. And he was pissed.

She lifted her head and froze when she saw him walking toward her, her eyes widening, before she schooled her expression into an easy smile. "Why, hello, Officer Garrett," she said.

"Deputy," he bit out. "And do not give me that overly innocent face, Sadie. I know what you did."

"Do you?"

"Yes, I spoke to Lydia just now," he said.

"Ah," she said, nodding. "Yes. Lydia. She was so excited about the ideas that I had. And very keen to come over and help me get everything in order. And very, very excited to talk to you about it."

"What does that have to do with anything? What does it have to do with the fact that you have, yet again, overstepped?"

"Nothing. I was just making an observation that you have a big fan there."

"What?"

"She likes you," Sadie said, taking a sip of her coffee. "A lot. And I'm not really sure why, but I sort of assumed you have to possess something that looks like a personality when you're not around me, or you wouldn't have half the people in your life that you do. Which leads me to the conclusion that you just don't like me. But back to Lydia… Yeah, she likes you."

"What the hell do you mean she *likes* me? Who says that anymore?"

"Fine. She wants your body. Do you approve of that assessment?"

"No," he said, frowning. "No, I don't. She's just friendly because she's president of the Chamber of Commerce, and it's her job to be friendly."

Tourism was an emerging industry in Copper Ridge, and it was quickly becoming the heart and soul of the town, which was, in his opinion, the jewel of this section of Oregon coastline. The coastal Old Town section had been totally revamped half a decade earlier, and what had once been dilapidated was now made charming.

With that had come vacation rentals, small motels and a smattering of bed-and-breakfasts, similar to Sadie's.

In addition there were now candy stores, boutiques and shops specializing in crap made of salvaged flotsam that were destined to collect dust on mantelpieces up and down the West Coast.

The rest was mill and timber towns, run-down fishing communities, all banded together under the header Logan County, so named for its surplus of loganberries that lined the highways and tangled around the trees in the forest. All his responsibility. A responsibility that was starting to feel a little more burdensome just at the moment.

"Sure. I'm not going to argue the point with you," Sadie said. "But...you're a little oblivious."

"I find that ironic coming from a woman who seems oblivious to the fact that I don't want to host a community barbecue...picnic...pie eating contest or whatever the hell it is you're—"

"Oh! Pie eating! That would be great!"

"Sadie," he said, his tone warning.

"What? You're being a stubborn cuss," she said. "I am working hard to establish my B and B as something special. Yes, there are several in town, but they're just that—*in town*. Which, I grant you, provides the ocean view, but if you want solitude, a chance to be surrounded by the mountains. To just...be on a ranch? Well, that's what I provide. I want people to come and see it. I want people to *want* to be there."

"And you're going to accomplish that with pie eating."

"Argh! I genuinely don't understand what your issue is."

"Because I didn't tell you what it is," he said. And he didn't plan on it. The bottom line was, he was uncomfortable opening the ranch up to the public, and that was all she needed to know.

"Well, maybe you should."

"Do you want me to talk about my fucking feelings?" he asked, the language, in this context and while in uniform, not something he would normally use. But the woman was standing on his last nerve and grinding it beneath the heel of her impractical sandals—and yes, he'd noticed them, since the top of her head was now just above his shoulders, rather than at the middle of his chest. "Because we're not in your office, and I would not pay for that level of torture."

"I would refer you to someone else," she said. "A specialist of some kind. And anyway, I'm not practicing here. I'm just opening a bed-and-breakfast and trying to bring cheer—and pie—to the community." Her pale brows locked together, a slight crease forming between them. "Do you hate pie and cheer?"

"I like both, in the appropriate place, at the appropriate time. I assume you still haven't run any of this by Connor."

"Not as of yet."

"Well, his *hell no* will be even more emphatic than mine."

"What about Kate?" she asked.

"If you use my sister against me I am throwing your cat out into the barn with the rest of the rat traps," he said.

"Okay, then, note to self, speak to Kate about this, because she will clearly side with me."

"I have work to do," he said. "Work that does not include playing house on someone else's property. We'll have to resume this at another time."

"Okay," she said, lifting her chin in the air, "we will."

SADIE WATCHED ELI's retreating back and fought the urge to throw her coffee at him. She imagined it, though.

Imagined the cup landing smack in between his broad shoulders and spraying that uniform with dark brown liquid.

She would mourn the loss of such a gorgeous, well-fitted garment, but it would be a small price to pay for how satisfying it would be in terms of venting her frustration.

No, she hadn't talked to Connor yet, but when they'd discussed the agreement—granted, over email—and come to an understanding about the percentage of her income he would be entitled to, they'd also discussed taking steps to ensure that it was a very profitable venture.

Connor wasn't the friendliest guy, even via email, but one thing he had talked about was the ranch, and why he was interesting in leasing the house. Ranching was hard and increased restrictions made it even harder. Selling their product wasn't as simple as it had been when the ranch had first started, and the cost of getting cattle to official USDA stations wasn't negligible.

One thing she'd picked up about Connor was that the ranch was the most important thing to him. And she felt like he would be on board with her plans when he saw the merit in expanding what they used their property for.

Of course, the chance remained that he was as unreasonable as his younger brother.

She huffed and headed down the street, the opposite direction from Eli, toward the Farm and Garden, where Kate Garrett was currently working her shift. And no, Sadie was not above using the youngest Garrett in a bid to get her way.

She pushed the door open, a bell tied to a string resting above the entryway signaling her presence with a soft, pleasant sound.

Being back in a small town was jarring and strange, but comforting in a million little ways she hadn't let herself imagine it might be. From gas station attendants who knew your name—and pumped your gas for you, welcome to Oregon—to little bells in doorways.

"Hi, Sadie, what brings you in today?"

Sadie smiled at Kate, who was behind the counter, her dark hair in a simple braid, her figure disguised by a plaid flannel shirt that was tucked into a pair of tan Carhartts.

The urge to strangle your brother is what compels me today, thank you very much.

"Flowers, actually. I need to get the front flower beds in order and I know absolutely nothing about anything leafy or petally."

"Well," Kate said, coming out from behind the counter, "you've come to the right place. Because I know a lot of things about plants."

"Good. So…you sort of know where I'm talking about, right?"

"Just the boxes in front of the porch?"

"Yeah, um…what can I plant there?"

Kate laughed. "I'll help you out. Just come out to the back with me."

Sadie tucked a strand of hair behind her ear, adjusting the paper bag she was holding as she did so, then took a sip of coffee as she followed Kate out through double, automatic glass doors to the back patio. Plants were hanging from metal scaffolding overhead and more pots were on pallets raised up from the ground. Flats of flowers were stacked into racks, and against the chain-link fence in the back rested bags of potting soil and fertilizer.

"I'm going to have to have you load up a cart for me, because I don't know what I'm looking at," Sadie said, surveying the plant life.

"I'm more than willing to do that. And I will even give you my employee discount." Kate looked around, her expression shifty. "Just don't tell."

"Don't do it if you'll get in trouble. Otherwise, please and thank you, because I'm not *that* well-off."

"It'll be fine. It's for Garrett land, after all." She grabbed the handle of a flat metal cart and turned it, then stuck a flat of dark purple flowers onto it. "This will get you started. And…" She started hunting through the displays.

"So," Sadie said, feeling ridiculously adolescent for what she was about to say, but unable to stop herself from saying it, "what is your brother's deal?"

"Which one?" Kate asked.

She could always deflect now, and say it was about Connor, which should in no way make her feel less awkward, but it did. Probably because, as handsome as he was, in that grieving, several-weeks-old-beard kind of way, she just didn't want to look at Connor's butt. Eli's, on the other hand…

"Eli," she said, grimacing at her honesty and thankful that Kate was still eyeballing plants.

"Uh…" Kate straightened and flipped her braid over her shoulder. "I'm not sure he has a deal."

"He doesn't seem that happy to have me around. Furthermore, he got a little…testy when I suggested we might have some events on the ranch."

"Oh, well…he's private. I guess. I mean, I never really thought about it, but it's not like we have parties or anything at the ranch. Birthday stuff we do at Pappy's Pizza, and for stuff they don't include me in they go to Ace's. So…yeah, maybe that's it. Maybe he just doesn't like to have people out. I never do, but that's not really a choice. More of a happenstance. Because…you know, this town is really small and everyone knows I have a brother with the power to arrest them. And one who would probably shoot and bury someone with no blip of conscience." She frowned. "Anyway, I'm sorry about Eli. Usually it's Connor we all have to apologize for."

"No, don't…apologize for him. But…is there, like, a plant I could get him?" she asked. Maybe a peace offering was the way to go. Right now she seemed to just be going the Purposefully Ruffle His Feathers Route, which was honestly really stupid and wasn't going to solve anything.

"Well, sure…you could get him an azalea," Kate said.

"An azalea?"

"Yeah, it's a flower, but they grow native here so it's less…groomed and more…manly. A manly flower."

"Okay," Sadie said. "A manly flower. I'm down with that. I'll get him an apology azalea. And then maybe we can try to talk again. Like adults instead of sniping children."

Kate winced. "Was it that bad?"

"I don't know. But some of it was my fault. We just… rub each other the wrong way." And she had a feeling that a lot of her annoyance boiled down to the strange tightening in her stomach whenever he was around.

Of course, putting it like that made it seem like she didn't know what that was, when she knew full well what it was. It was just…unusual in this context.

Usually she felt that level of excitement, that sort of low, giddy tug, when she was about to have sex. A brief little flash of anticipation. If she remembered right. It *had* been an awfully long time.

She was not used to it in regards to a man she wasn't interested in. Was not used to it being connected to a man she didn't like, much less a man she wasn't in a relationship with.

She was something of a serial monogamist. She'd meet a guy, they'd go on a few dates and they'd have fun while it lasted. And when things got...un-fun, they'd stop. There was no second-guessing, or yelling at each other. There were no question marks. She liked it straightforward and simple.

Her most recent ex, Marcus, was a classic example of that. They'd met at her gym. He was hot. He was fun. They'd gone on some dates, and then slipped easily into a physical relationship. And then, he'd gone and screwed it up by asking for a drawer. The man had never spent the night, and he wanted a *drawer in her dresser*.

It had been, to Sadie at least, a clear sign that they wanted two different things. And while her instinct had been to placate him or string him along, she knew that it wouldn't benefit either of them. And a lovely time in their lives would only be remembered for the discord in the end. She said a big no-thank-you to that.

It was always better to let someone go too soon than to hold on too long.

She liked it clear. And she liked it *simple*.

There was nothing simple about the way Eli made her feel. And there was nowhere for it to go. So, it could just stop.

But then, even when she'd been a teenage miscreant, loath to deal with his presence, she'd found him hot. So, if she knew anything about herself, it was that her body was die-hard stupid for Eli.

"Well, Eli really is a decent guy," Kate said, adding a plant with fuchsia flowers to the cart. "So I'm sure once you get on the same page he'll be reasonable."

"You think?"

"I don't know. But I'm just his sister. So often he's not reasonable with me, but I tend to think that's genetics at work."

"Right. Well, I'm an only child, so I'm not really up on the dynamic."

"That must have been lonely," Kate said.

For some reason, her words hit a sore spot. "Uh..." Sadie cleared her throat. "I had a lot of friends." Friends she hadn't spoken to in a decade. Were they here? Were they gone? She had no idea.

She didn't hold on. It wasn't healthy. And she was a bastion of positive mental health and good feelings. And stuff.

"Well, that's nice. I have...minimal friends, actually," Kate said. "But you know, the ones I have are good. People who love horses as much as I do."

"Hey, that's important. And it's better than lots of crappy friends anyway." Her friends hadn't really been crappy. Sure, they'd been terrible influences on each other, but they'd all had sucky lives. Smoking in the woods, drinking beer and making out were the best they could do since their homes were in such a sorry state.

"Yeah, I'm sure that's true," Kate said, putting a few leafy greens onto the cart. "Do you want some basil or mint or anything?"

"Oh, yeah!" she said. "Any. All. Can I put those in the windowsill in the kitchen?"

"Yep. I'll grab herbs on our way back inside and you can wait for me at the counter."

"Thank you," she said. "For your help and the discount and…not hating me."

"Eli doesn't hate you," Kate said, shoving the cart in through the door, her petite frame obviously a lot more muscled than it appeared at first glance. "He doesn't hate anyone. He's really very decent down to his core."

Sadie went to the front of the counter and set her coffee on the rough-hewn wooden top, digging in her back pocket for her credit card. "He seems like he is."

"He took care of me for most of my life. Our mom left when I was little. You probably knew that. Everyone knows that." She reached around and tugged on her braid, the gesture so childlike and sad it made Sadie ache a little bit. "Anyway…" She flipped her hair over her shoulder and went about grabbing the scanner and checking the plants. "Our dad… Things were hard for him after that and someone had to take care of the ranch—that was Connor. And someone had to take care of me and the house. And… Eli did that."

Sadie cleared her throat, strange, aching emotion pressing in and making it feel tight. "Well, then it's a good thing I plan on extending an olive branch. Apology azalea. Whatever. I mean, since he's such a good guy."

The total flashed up on the screen, and Kate tapped away on the ten key, bringing the amount down by almost half, and Sadie sighed in relief. "Really. Really, thank you."

"Really, no problem. Maybe…maybe we could hang out sometime?"

"Yeah, maybe. I think… I probably won't get to plant these until tomorrow. But if you're around, maybe we could work on it together?"

Kate brightened. "Sure! And actually, if you don't need them now, if you want I could put them in the bed of my truck and bring them home tonight. Then you wouldn't get dirt in your car."

Kate's offer gave Sadie serious feelings in the region of her heart. She wasn't sure she deserved the other woman's friendliness. But she wanted it. She wanted a friend, darn it. "Thanks. I'll take the apology azalea, though, since I need to talk to Eli and I'm not doing it without reinforcement."

Kate grabbed the largish potted plant from the cart and handed it to Sadie. "Here you go."

Sadie wrapped her arms around it, holding both her coffee and the bag of knickknacks she'd purchased earlier. "Great. Well. See you later." She turned and headed toward the door, pausing when she realized she had no available hands.

"Sorry!" She heard Kate scurry around the counter, rushing to hold the door for her.

"No problem," Sadie said. "I'll see you."

She walked out into the warm afternoon, wind kicking up from the ocean, blowing her hair across her face and into her mouth as she walked back up the sidewalk toward where she'd parked her car. She did a little cursory scan for Eli's patrol car but didn't see it.

And she tried not to think too much about the sinking, vague sense of disappointment she felt over that.

CHAPTER SIX

BY THE TIME Eli clocked out, he was ready to sink onto the couch and zone out. Maybe watch whatever sport was on. He wasn't picky. Hell, he'd take tennis at this point. Just something that didn't require thought.

But when he pulled his car into the dirt drive that led up to his house, it didn't take long for him to see that was not going to be in his future. There was a shiny black sedan in his space. Which meant there was a person here. Which meant he had to be on still. Which had him cursing internally in a variety of interesting combinations.

He groaned and pulled his car to the side, so that whoever owned the sedan could easily get out again once their business with him was done.

He put the car in Park and killed the engine, unbuckling and getting out, letting out a long-suffering breath as he did.

He took a few steps toward the house and saw the back of a dark-haired woman, long hair, shiny and curly, swinging down to a slim waist. She was facing…well, off into the vague distance as far as he could see.

He frowned and moved closer, then he noticed that there was another woman kneeling down in the dirt, her face partly blocked by a curtain of blond, straggly hair. He could see one pale, dirt-splattered arm. And for some reason, the sight of the bedraggled woman on her hands and knees gave him a jolt that the back of the glossy brunette hadn't.

Then the brunette turned, and revealed both her identity and that of the blonde. And suddenly everything, including his reaction, made very irritating sense.

Because Lydia Carpenter belonged to the glossy dark hair, and the gritty mess in his dirt was, of course, Sadie Miller. Of. Course.

He and his dick needed to have a very serious conversation about appropriate reactions to women who were very annoying.

"What's going on here?" he asked, realizing, in some dim part of his brain, that this was not a socially acceptable way to greet people.

"Eli!" Lydia said, smiling broadly, taking a few steps toward him, her tan legs on display in a very short summer dress she had not been wearing earlier. She was also wearing red lipstick, which he didn't remember from earlier, either.

Sadie looked decidedly less happy to see him from her position on the ground. She looked up, squinting against the sun, offering an approximation of a smile that looked a little bit like she was baring her teeth at him.

"Hi. Did we have a…meeting I forgot about?" he asked, looking from Lydia to Sadie.

Lydia's smile suddenly went a little snarly. "Uh. No. Great minds, I guess. Though I feel like I should have brought a plant."

"What?" He took that moment to look a little more specifically at what Sadie was doing.

There was a mound of fresh dirt around an azalea plant, bright pink buds mocking him with their cheeriness on the ends of the branches.

"Surprise!" Sadie said weakly.

"Uh…" And he had nothing to say after that, so he just let it hang there.

"Eli," Lydia said, and he wondered, yet again, how they'd gotten all first-name basis all of a sudden, "I wanted to let you know that I ran the barbecue idea past everyone on the board and the response was massive. We're so thankful to have someone running for Logan County Sheriff who has such a vested interest in the well-being of Copper Ridge's economy."

Oh, dammit. This was like his worst nightmare come true. He was being railroaded. By two petite, smiling, *evil* women.

"Well… I… Of course I care," he said, and Lydia's expression changed to something else entirely. Something that he couldn't quite identify, but that terrified him down to his soul.

"I knew you did," she said, walking toward him and putting her hand over his. "And it's so greatly appreciated. By me. And…of course, the whole town. And county."

"Of course," he said, drawing back slowly. He looked down at Sadie, who seemed frozen, her eyes wide with a combination of amusement and horror.

"Well, I have to go," Lydia said, "but we should discuss this further. Over coffee." She reached into her purse and dug a card out, pressing it into his hand.

"Okay," he said, curling his fingers around it.

Lydia turned and smiled at Sadie, and again, he had a feeling it was a smile meant to convey something other than happiness. There was a lot of strange emotional subtlety happening here, and he basically needed to be bludgeoned over the head with feelings to have any idea of what was going on, so he resigned himself to confusion, and relief when Lydia walked back to her car and started the engine.

He turned back to Sadie, who was still on the ground. "What is happening here?"

"I brought you an azalea."

"Why?"

"To apologize," she said, blinking as if she was suddenly realizing that her idea might not have been the best. "And to extend…goodwill."

"Some people just say they're sorry. They don't go planting unsolicited shrubbery in front of someone else's house."

"Yeah, well, some people lack imagination." She straightened and brushed her hands off on her jeans, leaving a trail of light dust streaked over the dark denim.

"Or have a greater grasp of social boundaries."

She made an indignant sound in the back of her throat. "That's also a possibility. I mean, maybe. But your sister assured me this was a manly plant. And also didn't seem to think it was a terrible idea."

"It has pink flowers."

"Honestly, the whole gendered colors thing is extremely ridiculous to me. Colors are colors. How can one be masculine and one be feminine?"

"I'm going to skip over this part of the conversation if it's all the same to you."

"It is."

"Great. What was Lydia doing here? Was she part of the plant installation?"

"No. Our missions were separate and coincidentally intertwined with each other."

"She's really into your barbecue idea. Congratulations on your evil plan working, by the way."

"I don't think it's the barbecue she's into."

"Are you still gnawing on that bone?"

"You don't need to whip out that much leg to talk community barbecue. Also, she was a little chilly to me."

"Why?"

Sadie rolled her eyes and crossed her arms. "She's threatened by me. Me and my azalea."

"She has no reason to be," he said.

"You like her that much?"

"I like you and your azalea that little."

"Dammit, Sheriff, right in my soft white underbelly. I'm trying to be nice to you."

"You've put me in a position I don't want to be in. Now I'm going to have to advocate for your little circus."

"Why?"

"Because. You heard her. The whole Chamber of Commerce is really excited, and it's an indicator of my commitment to the community. And my votes are riding on this stupid crap that I don't want to do."

"Oh. Ouch. Public opinion is a new concern for you, isn't it?" She didn't look at all sorry. She looked downright gleeful.

"Not exactly," he said.

"You have to join forces with me," she said. "Assimilate or die."

"You don't have to enjoy this so much."

"But I do!" she crowed. "I really do. And anyway, it's not going to be that bad. No one's going to make you participate or smile."

"I need boundaries," he said. "And a plan. If it's going to happen, I'm going to oversee it."

"Control freak much?"

"Yes," he said. "Much. And I'm fine with it. Now,

if you're going to do something on my property you have to be okay with it, too. You don't have to like it, but the bottom line is, you will do as I say, or it doesn't happen at all."

"Oh, really? I thought you acknowledged that I had you over a barrel." She tucked a strand of blond hair behind her ear and arched her brow as if to say, *Gotcha*.

No. Way.

"Oh, no, baby," he said, not sure where the endearment had come from or why it had rolled off his tongue, but he didn't stop to try to figure it out. "You may have me in a position where I have to be willing to consider your idea, but make no mistake, it's you who has the most to lose. I don't *have* to do a damn thing, and I'm the one with his name on the title for this chunk of earth. So if you want to play, you'll play my way."

SADIE FELT AN unfamiliar surge of raw, unmitigated anger course through her veins. This was not her style. It was not her game. She didn't do toe-to-toe shouting matches. Not with men, not with anyone. No. She did yoga. She meditated. She had a pottery wheel somewhere. That she never used, but still, she had outlets. Outlets that were not screaming like a child. Or hitting people with your fists until the anger beast cooled in your chest.

She didn't believe in giving free rein to negative emotions. It was healthy to acknowledge feelings, yes, and to talk about them in a safe space. But to let them explode out of your mouth and through your chest and let them take over all of everything? Which was what was happening right now, whether she wanted it to be happening or not.

She was...seething. And it was overflowing. Onto

her, onto him, onto everything. And sure, maybe planting the azalea had been a step too far. But Lydia had
shown up when she was dropping it off. And something
about the other woman made her feel…competitive.
Which was annoying.

But somehow she'd told Lydia that she was supposed
to be there. Planting the azalea. And Lydia had lingered.
Her mere presence a challenge. So plant it Sadie had.

And he was rejecting it. Honestly, even if her gesture was weird, it was nice. And he was being an ass.

"I bought you a motherfucking azalea!" she said, the
words shooting out hard and short, intense like gunfire.

"And I didn't want it," he said, taking a step toward
her. "I don't want it here. I don't want you here."

"Why?" she asked, moving nearer to him, compelled
forward by the kind of deep, negative emotion she
hadn't even known she possessed. "Because I'm getting
my dirty, been-arrested, other-side-of-the-tracks, poor-
girl filth all over your hallowed Garrett walkways?"

"Because," he said, "you are a mess. And I spent
most of my life managing a giant-ass mess, and I don't
see any reason why I should willingly subject myself
to another one. I have things just the way I want them."
He moved closer, a muscle in his square jaw ticking,
the cords on his neck standing out. "And I do not need
you coming in and ruining anything."

"Oh, really?" She moved nearer to him, so close she
could feel the heat of his breath on her face. "I guess
you are awfully neat and tidy," she said, her gaze flick-
ering over his uniform, so perfectly pressed and…sexy,
in spite of everything that was going on between them.
"It would be a shame if I got my mess on you." And
before she could police herself, she'd reached out and
grabbed his tie, her dirt-encrusted hands sliding over

the fabric, leaving a pale dust streak and tugging his face down closer to hers.

Her heart was pounding so hard it was making her light-headed. Her blood pumped to parts...more southerly. She had no idea what was happening to her. This was no sexual attraction as she knew it. It wasn't anything as she knew it. She was angrier than she'd been in recent memory, and a hell of a lot more turned on, and she genuinely didn't know how to process the two together.

She also didn't know how to process that she was inches from his face, his tie clutched tight in her hand, as his dark eyes blazed rage into hers. Rage and something else. Something hotter. Something that looked a lot like the fire burning in her belly felt.

And then...and then he dipped his head, his lips crashing into hers. And that's what it was. A collision. It wasn't a testing, or a tasting, or anything tentative at all. It wasn't nice, or fun, or easy. It was gasoline on a lit match. An instant conflagration that had gone from spark to out of control at the moment of contact.

She had no idea what was happening, only that she didn't want it to stop.

She tugged tighter on his tie and angled her head, parting his lips beneath hers and slipping her tongue into his mouth. He groaned, rough and raw and not anything like the good guy he seemed to want the world to think he was.

He locked one arm around her waist, drawing her tightly against his hard body. His lips were firm and sure. And everything about him, about this, was so much more intense than she'd imagined it could be.

She released her hold on his tie and cupped the back of his neck with her hands, holding him to her. She

shifted, breaking some of the contact, and he growled—
an honestly feral growl—and bit her lip, drawing her
back in close.

Pleasure rocketed through her, her nipples tightening
into hard points, desire settling low in her stomach, an
iron fist gripping her inside and tugging hard, sending
a shock wave of need straight down to her core.

She wanted… She wanted it to go on forever. This
need that wrapped her up in a cocoon and held her to
him. That blocked out everything. All the worry, all the
anxiety, all the anger, and turned it into something…
Good seemed too insipid a word. And she wasn't sure
if this was good at all.

But it was necessary.

Suddenly, it was so very necessary.

She arched her hips against his and felt the very hard,
irrefutable evidence of his own investment in this explosion of need. She wanted everything all at once with an
intensity that defied anything she'd ever experienced.
And she wanted it with all of herself.

Her heart seized tight, a painful spasm, and suddenly she felt herself move away from him, jumping
back like a startled cat.

She was shaking. Her hands, her knees and everywhere in between. And kisses did not make her shake.
And she didn't kiss men she didn't like. She didn't kiss
men in uniforms who had a fetish for order and cleanliness.

She didn't yell at people, either, but right now the
yelling was lower on her list of sins than the kissing.

"What did you… I don't even… I'm going to go."
She turned, her shoulders stiff, her heart hammering
in her ears.

"If I'd known a kiss would have gotten rid of you, I

would have kissed you the moment I saw your car sitting on the side of the road."

Oh. That. Did it.

She whirled back around, anger gaining traction in her again. "Well, sure, your kiss got rid of me. Congratulations. Now who's going to help you get rid of the hard-on it gave you? Your right hand?"

He lifted a shoulder, his expression stone, the dull red color on his cheekbones the only indicator that he was affected at all. That the casual manner was a lie. "My right hand suits me just fine. And it's a hell of a lot quieter than you."

"Oh, sure, the masturbation reference you get. You must spend a lot of time alone."

A muscle in his jaw ticked, the color in his face deepening. Embarrassment or anger? For some reason, she felt compelled to find out.

"No comment on that?" she asked. "Hugely shocking to me that women aren't flocking to you." But honestly, his body was stupid sexy and there were, in fact, women who seemed to flock to him. Or at least, one woman. That she'd seen. But, whatever, she was trying to make him mad, so truth didn't have to come into it. Petty meanness was the only thing that mattered. "I mean, you're a jerk. And you don't like anyone in or around your house. You don't even like flowers."

He crossed his arms over his broad chest, and she had to fight to keep herself from looking below his thick utility belt down to where she was sure she would be able to see evidence of his arousal. She was so, so tempted. Because she'd felt it, and it had felt so good. And she was curious beyond reason about how it looked. How he would feel in her palm...

No. Stop it.

"I'm not fighting with you," he said. "But I'm not changing my stance. My way, or no way. It's up to you."

So he wasn't even going to acknowledge the kiss? He wasn't going to fight back and feed her anger and make her feel justified and...and... That bastard.

"Fine," she bit out. "I'll work with you. But if you kiss me again, I'll bite your tongue off."

"Don't worry," he said. "I don't think I'll be tempted again."

That stung. And she had no idea why. Because they shouldn't kiss again. They shouldn't have kissed once. So that meant there was no reason for her to feel upset about him not wanting to kiss her again.

But she was.

"We'll discuss this more tomorrow," she said, straightening her shoulders, trying to maintain dignity she knew she no longer had. "And if I come back tomorrow and my azalea is maimed, uprooted or otherwise denigrated I will vandalize something on your porch."

Then she turned and walked away, trying to calm her pulse, trying to calm the racing of her heart.

She just needed to go back to her place, calm down, and—now that the plumber had been in—get herself a cold shower to help recalibrate her stupid body.

And then everything would be fine. Tomorrow morning, she would be over this thing that had flared up inside her, and she and Eli could get on with planning the community barbecue.

Yeah, that was a very nice lie. And it was one she was going to keep on telling herself until she couldn't anymore.

"THAT WOMAN IS a menace," Eli said, pacing the length of his brother's living room, all the blood in his body still heated to boiling since he'd gone and done the most stupid thing imaginable and kissed Sadie Miller like she was oxygen and he was suffocating.

"I don't know, she hasn't caused much trouble other than bursting the pipes, but even with paying for that, her rent is bringing in enough that we're still coming out ahead on the agreement this month."

"Assuming she doesn't cause any more disasters," he said.

"Well, sure, assuming that," Connor conceded, sinking deeper into the couch, his legs sprawled out in front of him, his arms spread out across the back.

"Which is a big assumption, all things considered."

"Untwist your panties," Connor said. "You're just still pissed because I did this without consulting you. And you don't like change. And you don't like feeling out of control."

Well, dammit, was he that obvious?

"This isn't about me. It's about her."

"Sure," Connor said, resting his head on the back of the couch and drawing his hat down over his eyes.

"Will you stop that?" Eli asked.

"What?"

"Stop being so damned disengaged all the time."

Connor straightened, pushing his hat back. "Sure, Eli. You going to arrange to have my wife returned to me?"

Eli's chest seized up, his heart squeezed tight like it was locked in a vise. "You know I can't."

"Then maybe fuck off and stop commenting on how disengaged I am."

It was rare for Connor to acknowledge that he was still grieving Jessie. But then, it was rare for Eli to call Connor on his bullshit in a serious way.

"Fair enough," Eli said, his voice coming out tight.

"Now, I believe you were ranting about our tenant." Typical of Connor. Get really pissed, then pretend it hadn't happened.

"I was. She has plans. And dammit, Connor, I sort of have to side with her on them."

Now Connor's body registered some tension. "What kind of plans?"

"Community barbecue plans," he said.

"And how does this concern me?"

"Because she wants to host things here," he said. "Particularly, she's planning on having a county-wide Independence Day celebration here on our ranch."

Connor had the decency to look perturbed about that. "Here? On the ranch? I won't have to do anything, will I?"

Eli let the implosion happen internally. He hadn't imagined his brother would actually propose that he help out with things, but then, it would have been nice if everything that wasn't cows didn't fall to him.

Which was maybe really unfair of him, but at the moment he didn't care.

"We'll have to clear things with you and your schedule. And I would guess base some things around what fields you want your cows in at a given time. Also, if any barns are going to be used, that needs to be cleared with you."

"Right. Fine. Just…when plans get more advanced, run dates and things by me and I'll see what I can do."

The fact that it made Connor look so damn tired brought Eli back from annoyance to pity. "Great. Sounds like a plan."

Connor frowned. "What happened to your tie… and…all of you?"

"What?" Eli looked down and saw the streak of dirt on his tie. It screamed *feminine handprint* to him, but he was pretty sure that to the unknowing observer it looked like a streak of dirt. Still, it made him feel a lot more like a kid caught with his hand in the cookie jar than he would like. And it made him think about what had happened between him and Sadie, which, in all honesty, he hadn't stopped thinking about since he stepped onto Connor's porch, but now he just felt like his face was projecting the words so Connor could read them easily.

He tried to remind himself that Connor wasn't that perceptive. And then he wondered what was wrong with him because any normal man would feel some sense of pride over kissing a woman as pretty as Sadie.

But then again…what they'd shared wasn't exactly a kiss so much as an explosion that happened to be detonated by the meeting of their lips.

"You look like you rubbed up against the side of a barn."

Eli looked at the rest of his uniform, heat making his face sting. He could see where every inch of her had been pressed against every inch of him. "Something like that," he said.

Connor narrowed his eyes. "Something like that?"

"I wasn't paying attention."

"You pay attention to everything. Which means… you paid extra close attention to whatever happened to your uniform, because obviously you're lying."

"Why the hell have you chosen to get engaged with what's happening right this moment?"

Connor raised a brow. "I think this is the first time I've ever caught you doing something you weren't supposed to do."

"I'm an adult. As long as it's inside the law there's nothing I'm not supposed to do."

"But let's be honest, Eli, the laundry list of things you think you can't do is longer than your arm."

"You don't know everything I do."

"No, but I know everything you don't do. We live too close to keep secrets."

"Fine. I brushed up against the barn."

"Giving it a hug because you were so happy to see it?" Connor asked.

"Okay, you caught me," Eli said, keeping his tone dry. "I found two women mud-wrestling just outside town and when I went to make sure they had a permit for it, they couldn't keep their hands off me."

"Now I believe you hugging a barn before I believe that."

"Well, pick one. Because they're the only two stories you're going to get. Now, if you'll excuse me, I have to go and start organizing this disaster of a party, because frankly, I just didn't have enough to do."

"You know you don't have to do everything, Eli. There's a certain freedom in just giving the world the middle finger."

"Yeah, but since you do it so expertly, someone has to get in there and care." Eli turned and walked out the front door, feeling like a total ass.

Grab a woman who hates you and kiss her? Big fat check next to that box. Insult your grieving brother? Check.

He was on a roll today. There was no denying it.

He sort of wished the mud-wrestling story was true. That would have been fun at least. There was nothing fun about what had passed between him and Sadie. Hot, yes. But not fun. And certainly nothing he could strut around feeling proud of.

When she'd pulled away from him…*appalled* wasn't a strong enough word for the look on her face. She'd looked completely horrified that they'd touched. And he'd just wanted to grab her again. And kiss her more.

What the hell was wrong with him?

When he had…affairs, relationships…whatever you wanted to call them, he was careful about his selection. He found women out of town. He found women who weren't needy or close in proximity. He found women who wanted sex and some easy, occasional companionship.

With the notable exception of Brandy, the last woman he'd been seeing, they were all very casual and very nonintense. Brandy had turned out to be something of a secret badge bunny and about the time he found her naked in the back of his patrol car begging him to put her in handcuffs, he'd known that relationship had to end.

And one thing was certain—he didn't pursue women who didn't want him. Sex was easy. Attraction was easy. It wasn't…whatever this was.

And now he was officially too wound up to enjoy his downtime. Now he was on the verge of an extreme hard-on that would have to go unsatisfied. And now he was officially way past rest and relaxation, he realized during his walk through the property.

What he needed to do was focus on Sadie's event plans. Yes, that was what he needed. He needed the control. Which, when he thought about it, was probably what the kiss was about. Some unevolved part of himself was trying to seize control through sex.

It had nothing to do with reality. Or with Sadie. Or

with him genuinely wanting to shove her top up and her bra down so he could get a look at her breasts.

No, that had nothing to do with it. It was the power struggle. But there was another way. He changed direction abruptly, heading toward the Catalog House as quickly as he could, determination making each step hit the ground harder than was strictly necessary.

He took the steps up the porch two at a time and then knocked on the door.

SADIE CHECKED THE reheating quiche in the oven and smiled. She'd put it in just before getting in the shower. It was looking perfect. And it had taken her only a few tries over the past few mornings.

She'd done it before, but she usually used a premade crust and she'd decided that wasn't going to cut it at Chez Sadie once she had guests. She took her oven mitts off the cabinet door and opened the oven, pulling the quiche out and putting it on the stove top.

Yes, it looked like heaven. And she was self-satisfied to a ridiculous degree. There was something she liked about all this. Building a business from scratch. Building…quiche from scratch. It was awesome any way.

There was a sudden, impatient pounding on the door that nearly made her jump out of her skin. But almost immediately, she knew who it had to be, without even looking. Because no one else seemed to have emotions strong enough to merit knocks that were quite that intense.

Unless someone had been involved in a terrible wood-chopping accident and was knocking on her door with what remained of their arm. In which case, she should hurry and answer it.

She felt bad for hoping it was someone with a bloody stump, but it seemed oh so infinitely preferable to Eli.

"Coming!" she shouted, pinning her damp hair back and reaching for the door handle, feeling her expression contort to one of horror when she saw who was behind it. "Oh, it's you."

"Who did you think it was?" he asked, his dark eyes intense and far too interesting for her own good.

"I was sort of hoping it was someone who'd been gravely injured and was in need of help."

"Sorry to tell you, it's just me."

"Are you in grave danger? Missing any appendages?"

"All body parts present, accounted for and attached," he said, his tone dry.

And now all she could think of was the body part that had most certainly been present and accounted for during their kiss. And she needed to think of anything else. "Well, damn."

He leaned in and for one moment, she had the fleeting thought that he was going to burst through that door, throw her onto the table and finish what they'd started earlier in the garden.

Which was ridiculous because she didn't want him to do that. And because she was not the kind of person who had crazy, throw-down-on-the-table sex. Because that required a certain amount of insanity that was just not a part of her physical relationships.

She was into relationships where you kept your head on straight and had sex at the end of a nice meal. She was well-adjusted about things. She wasn't an animal.

"I have to work for the next few days, so I don't have time to entertain you, or help you plan your little barbecue. But the minute that I'm off for the week? You and I have some talking to do."

So, he was not here to ravish her. Which was good. It really was. She was relieved. Almost as relieved as she would have been to see someone with a severe wound at the door.

"You make it sound like I'm in big trouble," she said, the words sounding a little softer and a whole lot more flirtatious than she intended.

Her body, it seemed, hadn't realized what her mind had—which was that the ravishment was off the table, so to speak—and had gone into Mae West mode accordingly.

She tried to tell her inner hussy that he could *not* come up and see her sometime, but her heart was still beating at hyperspeed.

"That all depends on your definition of trouble, Miss Miller," he said.

Oh, Lord, why did the way he said those words make a shiver of something rattle through her bones? *Why?* Why did she sort of wish she could go back to being in trouble with him?

She needed another shower. A colder one this time.

"Not really," she said, her words terse. "It kind of depends on yours since you have legal backing."

"I just want to give you a tour of the place. And discuss what is reasonable for the barbecue, and what isn't."

"Okay," she said, feeling a little blindsided by his darn reasonableness. "But I'm not really sure what inspired you to play nice."

"Must have been the azalea. And if you'll excuse me, it's my time off, and I'm going to go unwind."

She really wished she could stop herself from imagining what all him unwinding might entail. She remembered the presumptively thick erection from earlier and imagined him settling down and unzipping his pants…

No. Bad Sadie!

"Well, you go…do that," she said, forcing herself not to look down. Forcing herself to look only at his eyes and nowhere else, which, frankly, she felt she deserved a freaking medal for. His hardness had been pressed right up against her today and never—not once—had she given in to the urge to visually explore it.

"I will. And I'll be here on Thursday morning. Very early. Be ready."

"Bring coffee."

He arched a brow. "All right. I will."

And for some reason, that easy agreement before he walked down off the porch and into the fading light made her more nervous than any fight ever could have.

CHAPTER SEVEN

THE LAST TIME someone knocked on her door this emphatically, it wasn't because of an ax wound, and she had a terrible feeling it wasn't this morning, either.

Sadie wiped her hands on her apron and then untied it, draping it over a chair as she walked to the door. "Coming!"

She smoothed her hair, then jerked the door open with a smile pasted onto her face.

And there was the man himself, the cause of the past four sleepless nights, looking awake and far too sexy for a man in a simple pair of jeans and a black T-shirt. And far too tempting.

She looked down at the mug of coffee in his hand. "So thoughtful of you," she said, reaching out and snagging the bright blue-and-white-spotted tin mug and lifting it to her lips. "Mmm."

"That was mine," he said, pushing past her, "and are you going to invite me in?"

"You're in," she said, feeling warmed both by the coffee and by the implication that his lips had been on it. Which was juvenile in the extreme. She'd kissed him. What was the point of getting warm and sweaty over her lips touching a mug his lips had touched?

"So I am."

She took another sip of coffee, fully aware of the awkwardness that was building as they stood in the doorway, making eye contact and with her drinking his drink. Her nipples prickled and she shifted, the motion seeming to draw his eye right down to the place that was currently feeling quite perky and obvious.

"Do you want to come sit at the table?" she asked. "I actually have more coffee. Lucky thing, since you didn't bring any extra as instructed. And happily for you, my quiche of the day is ready."

"You have coffee and you took mine?"

"It's rude to turn down gifts, Eli. Didn't you ever hear not to look a gift azalea in the mouth? Oh, no... you must not have heard that."

"And gift quiche?"

"Same. It's spinach. And salmon."

He lifted a shoulder. "Well, I might be able to have some."

They moved into the kitchen and she fought to breathe right. She went to the counter and got a knife, slicing a generous piece of quiche for Eli, before getting him coffee, and delivering both to his seat.

"You're my guinea pig," she said, watching him expectantly.

"You're staring," he said, looking at the food, then at her.

"Yeah, I want to see if you like it."

"That's...disconcerting."

"Sorry. I'll look the other way." And she did. Obediently. Until he made a borderline orgasmic sound that sent a thrill straight down through to her midsection and...beyond. She looked back and watched his jaw working while he chewed. So weird, but she found the motion sexy. What the hell was wrong with her?

She wanted to make an excuse about needing to change her top or something since she'd been cook-

ing. Just so she didn't have to sit and eat with him. And
stare at his weirdly sexy mouth motions. But that felt
self-conscious. If she ran off before he was done, she
would look like she was doing it because she was uncomfortable around him—which she was.

Oh, to hell with pride.

She stood up. "I'll be right back. I have to... I got
flour on my top and I'm gonna...change."

She turned and scurried out of the kitchen, moving to
the back room, where she'd just gotten all of her things
organized last night.

It was part of an addition made to the house in more
recent years. By which she meant the 1940s or so. The
room was skinny and rectangular, set slightly lower
than the rest of the house, matching the incline of the
property, with windows covering the entire back wall
and a slanted, wooden ceiling that had been painted
white at some point.

It was weird, and quirky, and she was sure guests
wouldn't like it very much. But it suited her just fine.

She opened the top drawer of her dresser and retrieved a new top. She tugged it over her head quickly,
then hovered by the vanity, wondering if she should
put makeup on. No, she shouldn't put makeup on. That
was stupid. It was why she hadn't applied any after her
shower this morning. They were just going out on the
ranch, after all. And putting makeup on implied she
cared about how she looked. And she totally didn't.
At all.

While she was thinking, she picked up a blush brush
and dashed it through the pink powder before swirling it over the apples of her cheeks. There. She looked
awake now anyway.

She frowned and picked up her tube of mascara,

brushing some over her lashes quickly. There. In the interest of looking awake.

She slicked some pink gloss over her lips next. That wasn't vain. That was just…upkeep.

She grabbed a rubber band from the little porcelain hand statue on top of the bright yellow vanity and re-strained her hair as best she could.

Okay. So that was done. And not to impress Eli but just because…it was basic hygiene. Right. She didn't care what he thought. At all.

She walked out of the bedroom and into the kitchen again, waiting to see the look on his face when he registered the change to her appearance. And…nothing. He just sat there drinking his coffee. She'd put makeup on and *nothing*.

Which was fine, because she didn't care. But…she'd expected a little better than that. From the guy who'd hate-kissed her once.

Okay, nothing about Eli and her attraction to him, her preoccupation with him, made sense. So maybe she should just stop trying to excuse the weird things she seemed to do in his presence.

She tried, for a second, to figure out what she would say to a patient in this situation, and couldn't find any readily available wisdom. Because when it came to at-traction, her philosophy was simple. Pursue it and, if there was no returned interest, release it. If there was, continue on with it until it was no longer mutually sat-isfying.

But there was nothing about that philosophy that ap-plied to this situation.

She didn't like him. She didn't want to be attracted to him. And he clearly didn't want to be attracted to her. If he even was.

Well, she knew he was, because boner.

But was that actual attraction or just some testosterone-fueled rage thing? And if it was, then why did the idea make her feel hot and twitchy and not angry?

Nothing about this man, or her response to him, made sense.

"So, what's the plan, then?" she asked, leaning against the door frame and staring down at him, where he had made himself very at home in one of her kitchen chairs.

"I'm going to show you around. We're going to talk about your ideas, and I'm going to tell you which parts of those ideas are absolutely impossible."

"Or, to make it not sound dire and negative...you're going to tell me what will work?"

"Honestly, I have a feeling we'll be talking a lot more about what won't work."

"You are a ray of freaking sunshine, Eli. Has anyone ever told you that before?"

He looked over his mug and arched a dark brow. "No."

"Well, that's just shocking."

"You don't sound shocked."

She smiled. "That's because I'm not."

She reclaimed her coffee cup, but didn't rejoin him at the table. She hovered back, taking her caffeine hit before putting the mug back on the table. "Did you want to run this to your house or car or...?"

"I'll pick it up later." He tilted his cup back and finished his coffee in one deep drink before setting it back down and pushing himself into a standing position.

"Great. Then let's go tour." She turned and walked back out into the entryway and out the door, pausing just outside. "We're not taking the patrol car?"

"No," he said, walking past her. "I drive the truck around the ranch. And around town. I only drive the patrol car when I'm on duty. And today, I'm playing the part of cowboy, not the part of lawman."

Both of those things sounded so much hotter than they had a right to.

"Well, yee-haw," she said, following him over to the truck. It wasn't a new truck. It was one of those big, growly monsters with big tires and metal runners to assist in getting inside. It was square and boxy, a dull, faded red with mud splatter fanning out around the tires.

She pushed the button on the door handle and tugged it hard, before heaving herself up and onto the bench seat. There was a blanket over the original upholstery, and it made her wonder just what sort of things the man got up to in here.

She could certainly think of a few things that might be fun…

She was really starting to get concerned for her sanity. The mistake, she feared, was that she hadn't had a lover in…a while. Like, since pre-California, which put her at two years of celibacy and that was crazy.

She hadn't really accounted for needing sex when she'd moved to Copper Ridge, but she most certainly did, and the size of the town was going to make everything much more complicated.

Slow down, tiger.

Of course, she hadn't been worried about it at all until Eli. Now she was hyperworried about it.

She settled into the seat and closed the door, her elbow butting against the armrest, her shoulder against the window, anticipating just how intense it would be when Eli joined her in the enclosed space.

He climbed into the driver's side and, just as she'd

feared, the moment he shut the door, she felt like all the oxygen had been sucked out, replaced by a heady mix of hormones and the scent of Eli's skin.

And yes, he most definitely had his own scent, one she was suddenly very keyed in to. It made her think of the kiss. Made her think of how he'd tasted. Salt, skin and man. And she really, really wanted more.

But that was crazy and she knew it.

He started the truck and it growled to life, vibrating beneath her in a way that was sort of perilous considering her current thought process.

"What is the first stop, then?" she asked.

"The largest barn seems like a good place to start," he said, putting his arm across the back of the seat as he put the truck in Reverse and backed out of her driveway, taking them to the main road that ran to the different houses and fields on the property.

"So you raise…?"

"Cows," he said. "And we have a hell of a lot of them. Connor deserves the credit for that. I give him a hard time, but if it weren't for him this place wouldn't exist."

"Why do you give Connor a hard time?" she asked, slipping into the easy, question-asking mode that she'd always used with patients.

"Because he's my older brother," Eli said, rolling his shoulders upward, his grip tightening on the steering wheel. "And it's what we do."

"Well, yes, but the way you said it implied something deeper than the natural brother-to-brother expression of affection via 'busting chops.'"

"Are you charging me for this session?"

"What?" she asked, like she was surprised, even though she was fully aware that she was both distracting herself and distancing herself by becoming Therapist Sadie, rather than being Sadie the bag of flail who was marinating in her own lustypants.

"You know. Don't play innocent. It doesn't suit you."

"Is that a value judgment based on the fact that I have a criminal past, albeit a very uncolorful one?"

"Yeah."

That was it. Just yeah. No apology. No attempt to explain. He didn't even seem at all apologetic for the fact that he was some kind of a relic from a bygone era. With his angry kissing and generally judgmental attitude, who even needed him or his kissing or his judging? She didn't. Well, for anything other than getting this whole community events thing started.

"Well, you know, some people might say that the way you judge other people says a lot more about you than it does about them," she said, sounding annoying to her own ears. Pious, even.

"Yeah," he said. "I'm sure it does. It says that I've spent so much time cleaning up the crap that other people just leave around that I'm short on patience for it. That I've spent my whole life being cleanup crew, which means I know people can do better than they do, because I do better. So yeah, it is about me. And I'm judgmental and I don't care to change it."

"Well," she said, "okay."

She was used to very postmodern men. Men who believed in the exploration and articulation of their feelings. Or men like Marcus, who had liked smoothies and telling her about his day over a light dinner.

She was not used to this kind of Neanderthal he-man thing. Well, scratch that, she was. And she'd walked away from it ten years ago. She wasn't going to willingly put up with it now.

She didn't say anything, though. Instead, she just

let the silence grow between them until it filled in all the free spaces in the cab and pushed against her throat until she didn't think she could bear it anymore.

Because she didn't do the walking on eggshells thing now. She didn't take the path of least resistance, because she didn't have to. When people were asses, she walked away. No one got to insert their judgments into her life without her permission.

Not even when the person trying to do so was a badge-carrying, gun-toting deputy. Not. Even. Then.

"Listen, I don't care what you think," she said. "And I'm not going to let you try to put me down because of some kind of moralistic—"

"I know you don't care what I think," he said. "And none of this has anything to do with being moralistic. You know full well you were trying to psychoanalyze me, and then you went and played dumb about it. And now what? You're going to get all pissy because I said you weren't innocent? Because you're going to apply that statement way further than it was ever intended to go? And you're going to try to do it while feeling all self-righteous? Hell no, baby, that's not going to happen."

She sputtered. "I don't… You don't…"

"Tell me I'm wrong, Sadie."

"You're wrong."

"Liar," he said, putting the truck in Park in front of a giant barn that she wouldn't have even guessed was a barn at first glance. It had a dark brown tile roof and honey-colored wood siding, glass-paned windows and sliding doors of varying widths. It was more what she'd associate with a high-end stable, not a cattle ranch.

"I'm not a liar," she said, unbuckling and marveling at the severe…neatness of everything. Sure, it was dusty and there was hay all over the ground, but it was neat and tidy. There was no denying that. It was such a sharp contrast to Connor's house, and the lack of organization there.

"You are. And if you don't think you are, you're at least lying to yourself." He got out and slammed the door behind him. And she sat for a moment before scrambling out after him. "Thing is," he said, looking over his shoulder, "it's not that big of a deal. The original thing I called you on. I think you just like fighting with me."

"I don't like fighting," she said. "With anyone. And I went a very long time without doing it at all before you came back into my life."

"Correction, honey, you came back into mine."

"Call me honey one more time, and I'll dip your fist in honey and shove it in an anthill."

"My point stands."

"Okay, sweetie pie," she said, "the point is that except for you, I never fight with anyone. So I think it's pretty safe to say that you're the damn problem. Not me."

"Is it?" he asked.

"Yeah," she said, crossing her arms beneath her breasts. "It is."

"Or do you just not talk to anyone who dares to disagree with you?"

He strode toward the barn and left a hissing and spitting Sadie standing there, stunned for a full thirty seconds before she took off after him.

"Why don't we get back to business," he continued. "Since I don't really want to get to know you, and I'm betting you don't want to get to know me."

"Yeah," she said, "fine." She reached behind her head

and tugged the end of her ponytail. "I don't want to know you. I want to know your barn."

"Get ready for the excitement," he said, his tone dry. "And I'm assuming *barn* isn't a euphemism for my... for anything."

"How could a barn be euphemistic?"

"I don't know. But you're always accusing me of missing those kinds of things so I figured I'd take pre-emptive measures."

"Right. Well. No. A barn is just a barn. Though, may I say, this is a particularly fantastic barn. Have you ever had weddings here?"

"No," he said.

"You should. Weddings and parties and—"

"No."

"You are the boringest man."

"I thought we were letting go of personal things and getting on with business?"

"Well, I was, but then you started talking about the possibility of barns being something dirty. Which made me think of your—" *don't say anything dirty* "—exasperating nature."

"Just look at the barn." He walked to the side door and released a wrought-iron latch, pushing it open, muscles in his thighs flexing, his biceps and forearms straining just enough to make everything in her tense up to match.

She stepped inside, the wood floor hollow-sounding beneath her feet, the expansive, empty section cleaner than most of her apartments had ever been. "Wow," she said. "I'm serious, you could host events here. And you could charge lots of money for them."

"It's nothing special. Just a place to keep equipment and hay."

"So…just a place to keep your entire livelihood? Yeah, you're right. It's not that special."

"Well, it's a serviceable barn. And it cost a hell of a lot of money. But the old one was run-down, and after we ended up with moldy hay one winter…it was pretty clear things had to change. After Dad died, we got a good chunk of change from his life insurance, and Kate and I gave our share to Connor to invest."

"Well, he did it in a very serious way," she said.

"Yeah, he did. But this place is our family legacy. Connor's the keeper of it, sure, but when…when there's another generation, I guess they'll all have a part of it. Though I'm sort of skeptical about any of us managing another generation."

"Okay," she said. "You, sure, because… I can see that you're not the open-your-home-up-to-chaos-and-crazy kind of guy. But Connor could find someone else."

"He doesn't want to. He seems to think cracking a smile's some kind of hanging offense."

"And Kate?"

"She's a kid."

"She has to be in her twenties."

"Twenty-one," he said. "She's way too damn young to be thinking about that stuff."

"Well, I agree on one level. A husband and kids? No way. Not at her age. But I assume she's dating and otherwise showing a normal interest in that sort of thing."

"Uh…not so much."

"Oh." Sadie's face heated, embarrassment washing through her. "Sorry, I was making assumptions. I should have said partner."

"What? Why?"

"Oh, just the way you said that I thought maybe I'd made a very broad assumption about her sexuality, is all."

He winced. "Can we please not talk about sexuality and my sister in the same sentence?"

"I just meant, if she's a lesbian I have no problem with that and I would hate for it to seem like I was passing judgm—"

"She's not," he said. "Considering the number of times I found torn-out magazine pages of...what's his name? Zac Efron?"

Sadie laughed. "Okay, but you realize that's an indication that she does have a sexuality."

"I refuse to have this discussion."

"All I'm saying is, don't give up on the next generation yet. You're such a cliché," she said, shaking her head and laughing.

"Maybe," he said. "But I sort of raised her from the time she was two years old, so I reserve the right to be a little insane."

The admission hit her somewhere around the heart. Which made her very uncomfortable. "Oh. Right. I wasn't...thinking."

"Our mom left before Kate turned two. Dad might as well have left. Someone had to work, someone had to take care of the baby. Connor and I were an old married couple before we could drive."

"Eli..."

"Hey, look, I'm over it." Except he so obviously wasn't. He wore it as sure as he wore his uniform. His need for order. His need for control. "But the thing is... I think that's why this place means so much. And why I'm an overprotective crazy person. Because it was all down to Connor and me. And when you have that much responsibility that early, it becomes a part of you in a way it never would otherwise."

She turned and looked at the barn, at the care that had so clearly gone into it. Evidence of money that could have taken them away from here. That could have taken the Garrett family on to other things. College, maybe. Had any of them gone? Kate was twenty-one and working, so she clearly wasn't in school.

They had given their all for this place. To hold it together. Because it was what they'd done all of their lives and it was what they continued to do.

For a woman who hadn't lived in one place for more than a couple of years, it was a level of commitment that was...hideously daunting. It was sticking something out through thick and thin, rain and shine. Old barns and new.

It was choosing to keep on staying even when there was an out. And suddenly all that history, all that intensity, made it feel as though the walls were closing in.

And you're here for five years.

"Wow," she said, taking a deep breath. "Anyway, this is great. I mean, if we could do tables, lots of tables in and around here, that would be...excellent. Just so very excellent." She started to walk back out, quickly, trying to escape the weird, oppressive weight that had settled onto her stomach.

"I'll have to clear it with Connor. Farmwork getting done is going to be the top priority. But I think we can arrange to have the field just over here cleared for parking, which should make things easy. It'll all have to be roped off and...well, it's going to be a big deal."

"I know," she said. "But the city is willing to kick in for some funds. And I think I might be able to entice some vendors. Local beers, wines, cheese. And you know, if you wanted to kick in some beef, I think it could end up being really great for the business side of the ranch."

"Again, I'll talk to Connor about it. I may need to get him drunk first."

"He doesn't have to hang out if people…bother him."

"Everything bothers him. To be honest, I'm not sure if he'd be any more miserable in a crowded bar than he is alone."

"I'm sad for him. Your brother seems like a nice guy."

"No, he doesn't."

Really, he didn't. But she'd been searching for something to say and the blanket, insincere words had rolled off her tongue easily. "Fine. He doesn't seem that nice. But I'm still sorry for him."

"That makes two of us."

"Anyway, it doesn't sound like the worst idea, does it? We'll get pies donated from the diner. We'll get… fried pickles from Ace's. We'll make it a whole thing!"

"You're really embracing this local spirit. Surprising, all things considered."

"Yeah, no one is more surprised than me. But I was ready for a change, and at this point, putting down roots is kind of the only way to feel like something's changed."

"And change is…"

"Good," she said, getting back into the truck. "Healthy. I mean, people should change things around them every so often. Especially when life isn't gelling the way it should." Practiced lines she'd told herself over and over. "So, why don't you take me to see that other field?"

"You want to see the potential parking lot?"

"Sure. And anyway, I thought you were supposed

to tell me why all my harebrained schemes wouldn't work."

"Well, I haven't come up with a single damn reason why what you're asking for won't work," he said, slamming the truck door. "Do you have any idea how annoying that is?"

"I have a fair idea of how annoying that must be for you. It must really suck."

"It does."

But somehow, even he didn't seem unreasonable right now. He seemed…understandable. Here in this vast, wild place, so carefully tamed by the hands of his family, by him and Connor, she could see what a huge job it had been. Two boys who had been essentially alone in the world, with a sister to care for. She could easily see how much grit and strength it would have taken to hold things together. She wondered if that impossible task was what had built the solid man she saw in front of her. The man who was still doing the same thing. Still trying so hard to hold the pieces together.

Dammit. It made her heart all achy, and that was much more disconcerting than being horny.

They didn't get very far up the road before Eli stopped the truck again. "Right there," he said, "we'll move the cows to another pasture and open up the gates."

She looked over to where he was pointing and shaded her eyes as she studied the bright green fields, dotted with glossy black animals, their heads down, the sun casting a ripple of light and shadow over muscle and sleek hair.

Yellow flowers popped like little sunbursts across the grass, standing in sharp contrast to the dark green and fading blue of the mountains beyond.

It took her breath away. It reminded her why this place was home.

Which was so strange, because she couldn't remember ever really feeling like it was before, but sitting in the truck, looking out at all this, she felt it. Not like something new, but even better and more rare for someone like her, it felt familiar.

"Parking lot doesn't really do this justice. Will it be okay to...drive on it?"

"Yeah, it's fine. We cycle the cows through the fields anyway and they're about done here for now."

"I can suddenly see why none of you ever left."

"It's beautiful," he said. "Some days I kind of forget to look at it. But the expression on your face just reminded me."

Something warm shot through her, across her face and down into the pit of her stomach. She swallowed hard, fought against it. It was a good feeling, but weird. Deeper than the kinds of feelings she was used to.

And she wasn't sure she liked it.

"Anyway, I have to get out and help Connor for a while, so I'll drive you back."

"I'm fine walking," she said, suddenly feeling the need to escape again. To feel a little sunshine on her face and some wind in her hair. "I mean, really, I want to walk."

He shrugged. "All right. Suit yourself. See you around."

She climbed out of the truck and tried to ignore the somewhat fuzzy feeling his casual, and not at all hostile, goodbye carved out in the pit of her stomach. Right in the middle of all the warmth.

"Yeah," she said, "see you."

She hopped out of the truck and breathed in deep, the

air sweet from the flowers and salty from the nearby sea. She looked up and closed her eyes, letting the sunshine wash over her. And even though she wanted to, she didn't look back at Eli. Not even once.

CHAPTER EIGHT

NEVER HAD ELI been so glad for Jack to draw the short straw. That made him the designated driver for the evening, and it meant that Eli could drink some beers. Because he really, really wanted to drink some beer tonight.

Not that he would drink to the point of public drunkenness, since he had a reputation to uphold. And the legacy of being a worthless drunk's kid. But something to take the edge off the Sadie Miller knife that was digging into his gut would be nice.

Just a little haze. That was all he required.

Jack was still sulking because he had to stay sober, Connor had already gone to the bar to order beer and Eli was leaning back in his chair, enjoying being in town in plainclothes. Enjoying sitting back and watching people do things without feeling like he was on duty at a day care.

The bar was packed, but it was Saturday night and there were a limited amount of activities in town. There were average-quality restaurants, very expensive seafood restaurants, a movie theater with five screens and a local dinner theater. The bar was one of the more popular choices for obvious reasons.

Alcohol, darts and pool being some of the most obvious.

"Don't sulk, Jack," Eli said. "It's not a good look on you."

"Drunk isn't a good look on you," Jack returned, his arms crossed over his chest.

"I haven't been drunk since I was twenty-one. On my birthday. And never again."

"You're such a cliché."

Since this was the second time he'd been accused of this recently, he was starting to wonder if it was true.

"Aren't we all?" he asked. "We're in a bar on Saturday with nothing better to do."

"Looking to get laid," Jack said, turning and taking a Coke out of Connor's hand as he returned to the table with drinks.

"Speak for yourself," Eli said.

"Oh, right, you don't shit in your own yard."

Eli grimaced and took the pale ale Connor was offering him. "Not my favorite way of putting it, but the principle is sound."

"Liss isn't coming?" Jack asked Connor.

"Not tonight. She said something about painting her toenails and watching old movies. And that is where having me as her best friend tends to not pay off."

"You don't want to put the little toe separators in for her and blow on her feet until the polish dries?" Jack took a drink of soda to disguise his smile.

"I thought I'd come here and see if you wanted to throw darts at my balls instead," Connor said, tipping his beer bottle back and taking a long drink.

"If I were drinking, I would absolutely take you up on that," Jack said.

"Remember the time we were hanging out at the house," Connor asked, "and we thought we'd play darts? But there was nothing to hang the board we found…

and you, you put the board in your lap? And told me to hit the bull's-eye?"

"I still have a scar on my thigh," Jack said. "So yeah, I remember."

"We did really dumb stuff."

"You two did dumb stuff," Eli corrected. "I mainly watched."

And told no one because there was no one who would have cared. Jack's mom was too exhausted from work to look his direction more than once a week, and the Garrett patriarch was usually passed out in his own vomit by 6:00 p.m.

They used to joke that if their parents got married they could be the world's most fucked-up version of the Brady Bunch.

That hadn't happened, because their individual parents had been too busy wallowing in their problems, but Jack basically lived at their house anyway, simply by virtue of the fact that it was bigger and there were more places to find trouble.

Jack liked trouble, and trouble liked him. Typically, female trouble.

He had no issue shitting where he lived, so to speak.

"We were badass," Connor said, a wistful look on his face. He took another sip of beer. "And you," he said, pointing at Eli, "were not blameless. You're the one who thought to build a ramp that went off the hayloft. And ride your bike down it."

"Ah…how did we not die?" Eli asked.

"Hell if I know," Connor said, tapping the side of his beer bottle. "But then, I'm sort of mystified by how those decisions are made." And just like that, the brief light on his face dimmed again.

Dammit. It was way too easy to say the wrong thing when someone had a ghost following them around.

"We all are," Jack said, slapping Connor twice on the back. "And when we're too mystified, we drink and talk crap at the bar."

"Damn straight," Eli agreed, knocking back another drink.

"With friends like you guys... I'll have a hangover in the morning," Connor said, making a weak attempt at a smile.

"You could have been painting Liss's toenails. You're paying for your own awesome choices," Jack told him.

"And you could have had beer," Connor said. "But you drew the short straw."

"It's a stupid tradition. We should just take turns."

"And you'd bail every time it was your turn," Eli said.

Jack smiled and shrugged in the boyish manner that got him out of situations that would have seen lesser men castrated. "Probably."

"And that's why we draw straws. Because one out of three men at this table is a piss-poor friend," Connor said.

"Guilty." Jack looked over Connor's shoulder and frowned. "Isn't that your hot new tenant?"

"What?" Connor asked, turning around completely unsubtly. The motion would have made a bull look graceful.

Eli looked up and saw that it was definitely Sadie, blonde, petite and, yeah, very hot, walking into the room and over to the bar. She leaned in, and he couldn't help but look, really look, at the way her jeans fit her rather fantastic ass.

"She really is hot," Jack said, his eyes getting that keen, focused look that he got when he was on the hunt.

"Not in this lifetime, Monaghan," Eli said, the words coming out a whole lot more threatening than he'd intended them to.

Jack sat back, dark brows shooting up. "Oh, really?"

"Damn straight," Eli said, hooking his hand around his beer and tugging it back, holding it against his chest.

"You're not for real," Jack said. "Sleeping with a woman who lives on your property is almost the same as marriage."

Marriage. That was the last thing he wanted. A little sex on the other hand...

Heat streaked through Eli's gut. He hated that his desire was that transparent, especially when he was still trying to pretend that he wasn't attracted to her at all.

He looked over at Sadie again. "I wasn't even thinking of it."

"Liar."

Connor was noticeably silent during the exchange. Eli managed to tear his eyes away from the view to look at his brother.

Connor looked up, his expression hostile. "What?"

Jack looked at him, too. "You're not commenting."

"Didn't notice she was hot," Connor said. "I was thinking about it, trying to decide if she was or not. Then I realized my dick is fucking broken."

Hell, maybe Eli's was, too. Because this was a total departure from his usual rules. He hadn't fully realized it until Sadie had pointed out the sheer volume of sexual innuendo he missed on a daily basis when he was with her, but his normal course of action was to just shut his libido down until he was ready to do something about it.

He had great luck with women—when he was pursuing one. Otherwise...otherwise he lived his life with blinders on. And it wasn't by accident.

He kept his life classified in very careful segments. And maybe the problem now was he'd left one segment neglected for too long. And now things were... intertwining that definitely shouldn't be intertwining.

And beyond the intersection of his personal life and his love life, the fact that it was Sadie whom he wanted when she was the most infuriating, irritating woman... well, that just proved that his dry spell had reached Saharan proportions.

"She is hot," Jack said. "But I have a feeling Eli is marking his territory."

"I am not," he said.

"You don't like her," Connor pointed out. "She's a criminal. You arrested her."

"She's not a criminal," Eli said, gritting his teeth. "And it was ten years ago."

"Yeah," Jack said. "Marking his territory."

"Don't say it like that. She's a woman, not territory. And she's definitely not mine. You sound like a jerk."

"I *am* a jerk," Jack said. "It's like you haven't known me since I was twelve."

"As you so eloquently put it, or...as you should have put it, I keep my sex life away from here. Far, far away. I'm not going to pursue a woman who has a five-year contract to live on my property. That's a degree too close to marriage for my taste."

Jack laughed. "Okay, I get that. So does that mean I can...?"

"No," Eli growled. "You can't. Mainly because I don't want to catch sight of your bare ass through any open windows. That is guaranteed to get you shot."

"You're not allowed to shoot my friend, Eli," Connor said. "I only have two of them. I can't afford to lose any."

Eli looked at Sadie and watched as she cocked her head to the side, blond hair spilling over her shoulder, the fluorescent lights from the Mirror Pond Ale sign behind the bar casting a yellow-and-blue glow over the pale strands.

Ace was behind the bar, big and bearded and wearing flannel, which women seemed to be giddy over these days. And Sadie was obviously no exception, with the way she was giggling and smiling and…dammit, touching the guy's forearm with her delicate hands. Hands that were, incidentally, not covered with soil from planting an azalea.

Annoyance coursed through him. She'd just kissed him last week, and now she was in here flirting with Ace.

And so what?

So, it pissed him off. Which made him even angrier. Because he shouldn't care. He wasn't jealous. He was never jealous because jealousy implied that he cared, and he never cared.

Not that he didn't like the women he had relationships with, but he didn't quite care what they did when he wasn't around.

This Sadie thing was messing with his head. Not only was wanting her simply a bad idea, he was sitting here pondering ways to remove Ace's arm.

"Excuse me," he said, getting up and pushing his chair back, leaving his beer on the table. He could feel Connor and Jack staring after him, and he knew that they were probably ready to discuss conspiracy theories about whether or not he'd been brainwashed or body-snatched.

And he didn't really care. Because right now he had Sadie in his sights and he was going to walk over to her and do...something. He would figure it out when he got there.

Hopefully.

His feet hit the wooden floor harder than necessary with each step and he knew that people were looking at him, because he was Eli Garrett, current candidate for county sheriff, walking across a bar like he had sex and murder on his mind.

Both of which were strictly true.

"What brings you into town, Sadie?" he asked, leaning against the bar next to her.

She jumped and turned, blue eyes wide. "What brings you here to talk to me voluntarily, Eli?" she asked, her expression schooled into something casual now, covering up the moment of shock.

Ace looked at them both and turned away from Sadie, pulling a drink from the tap and walking down to the other end of the bar.

"Curiosity," Eli said.

"It's not that weird that I'm at the bar," she said.

"But you're alone."

"Who would I be with? Anyway, I was just stopping by because I wanted to feel out the best local brews and find out if Ace had any contact info for me. For the Fourth of July thing."

"Right," he said. "You're on a first-name basis with Ace?"

"I remember him vaguely from school. Also, I called in earlier."

"Okay," he said, sounding a lot more uptight than he would like.

"Why do you care?" she asked, tilting her head to the side like he'd watched her do earlier.

"Honestly? I don't know," he said. *Honestly?* Why

had he been honest? Honesty in this situation was a terrible idea. Because it was ceding the upper hand. It was admitting he was out of his depth and that was not acceptable.

Her expression changed. Not wide-eyed shock or practiced casualness. She lowered her lashes, her lips more relaxed, her gaze falling to his mouth. Each shift almost imperceptible, and quick. And yet, he saw it. Was so painfully aware of it, as if he could hear each change like the cocking of a gun. It was clear, it was intentional. And the only thing he wasn't sure of yet was if she was shooting to kill.

"Is it because you want to kiss me again?" she asked.

She was shooting to kill. This shot had hit square in his gut, radiating down to his groin. He'd only had a half a beer, so he couldn't even blame that.

"It's more because I don't want *him* to kiss you," he said, leaning in, his palm flat on the bar. "I don't want to kiss you. I wish I hadn't kissed you the first time and trust me, Sadie Miller, I sure as hell don't want to do it again." He angled his head and moved in closer, conscious that they were being watched by almost everyone in the bar. Aware that he had to be close enough to make his point, but far enough away that no one would be planning their wedding by tomorrow. "But I'm starting to wonder if I will. If it's inevitable."

She drew back, her breasts pitching sharply with the harsh breath she drew in. "I'm not sure how something like that could be inevitable. I mean, either you want to kiss someone or you don't. If you do, you do. If you don't, you don't."

"I thought it was that simple. Until you. You've completely screwed up my kissing theory." Damn, maybe he *was* drunk.

"That's more than thirty years of kissing theory messed up by one woman," she said, her voice sounding lower, thicker all of a sudden. "That's…a lot of power."

"It is," he said, his own voice following the same path hers had.

"Are you drunk?" she asked.

"I wish."

"Wow. You really, really know how to turn a girl on." Sarcasm tinged her tone, but the huskiness in her voice told him that he actually was turning her on, and he had no idea how to feel about that. "Telling me you don't want to kiss me and you wish you could excuse your being over here with your being drunk."

"That's because I'm not trying to turn you on," he said. And that at least was true.

"I wish I could say it was working."

"Me not turning you on?"

"Yes," she said, looking down at the bar.

"Are we flirting?"

She looked back at him, her pulse beating hard at the base of her throat, hard enough that he could see it. "I don't think so."

"You're probably right. I don't think I know how to flirt."

"You're just trying to keep me from getting flirted with."

"Sounds about right."

Ace came back over to their end of the bar and crossed his arms over his broad chest. "He's not bothering you, is he, Sadie?"

Oh, for God's sake.

Sadie looked at Ace, her lips quirked into a funny smile. "You know he's a deputy sheriff, right?"

"I know who he is," Ace said.

Oh, great, the jackass was in the mood to be tough, and Eli wasn't in the mood to compete for Sadie because he didn't even want Sadie. Or at least, he didn't want to want her.

But there was no way he was going to be able to let it slide. He knew that there was no way because he'd crossed the room to stake a claim on a woman he shouldn't want just because she'd put her hand on another man's arm.

He already knew he was too far gone for common sense. He already knew his head wasn't in charge of this one.

"Then you know that I'm more likely to protect her than drag her off and throw her into my trunk," Eli said.

"What is it they say about cops and the domestic abuse rate?" Ace asked.

"Cute. Did you take an online class?" Eli asked.

Sadie giggled and they both looked at her. "I'm sorry," she said, her smile barely suppressed. "Please go on. I'm enjoying the novelty of two men warring for my affections."

"Outside," Eli said.

"I'm sorry, are you ordering me around? Do you honestly think I'm going to obey like a lapdog? I, sir, am a cat person, and I'll probably just bite your hand."

"Out. Side," he repeated.

She arched a brow but slid away from the bar and started to walk toward the exit. He turned to Ace and shot him a look before he dared glance at Jack and Connor, who were staring at him openly. Connor looking a little annoyed. Jack looking annoyingly impressed.

Bastard.

He turned away from them and followed her out the front door, rounding on her as soon as it swung shut behind them. It was dark outside, the waves crashing against the shore nearby the only sound, the moon glinting on the water like silver fish swimming over the surface. Every pitch of the surf casting white light over Sadie's face.

She was so beautiful it hurt. A real ache that started in his head and pulsed through his teeth, all the way down through his gut and to his cock. Just from a little light across the bridge of her nose. The bridge of her *nose*. He needed his head examined.

But not by Sadie. Because the little therapist was the person causing all of his mental and physical unrest.

"What is going on?" she asked.

"I'm…not sure," he answered, pacing the sidewalk in front of her. "I'm really not sure. I came out to drink and maybe eat some fish-and-chips and definitely not to talk to you, or see you, or think about kissing you."

"Hey, I came down here to talk microbrews, not to deal with you and your chest-beating, rawr rawr, he-man routine!"

"Then why are you dealing with it?" he asked.

"Why are you talking to me?"

"Hell if I know," he said.

"Then consider that *my* answer. Hell if I know!"

He moved toward her and she backed up, the wood-shingled wall of the bar stopping her. Eli took a breath and pressed his palm flat to the wall, just by her head, his eyes locked with hers, heat arching between them. He couldn't have looked away if he wanted to. And he didn't want to. He wanted to keep looking at her. He wanted to kiss her.

And then some.

He wanted her more than he could remember ever

wanting any woman. More even than his first, on a spring night after prom.

Right now he was beyond himself. Beyond control. And Eli Garrett was never beyond control.

Somewhere, in the depths of his thoroughly bent brain, it registered that that was a problem. That he shouldn't have ever let it get this far. That he needed to get a grip on things and stop it before it went further.

Dammit. He didn't want to.

He gritted his teeth against the rising tide of arousal. So intense it just hurt.

He took a breath through his nose and closed his eyes, lowering his head. If he just didn't look at her for a second…he could get a handle on things. On himself.

He breathed in again, slowly, and let it out through his mouth. Then he opened his eyes and looked back up at her. "Here's what we're going to do," he said, his voice almost unrecognizable.

"What?"

"We're going to go back in the bar. And you're going to go back and talk to Ace about local beer. And if he asks you on a date? I think you should go on it."

"What?"

"Yep. I'm going to go back to my table and drink at least two more beers, eat something fried and play darts. And I'm not going to look at you. I'm not going to talk to you. I'm not going to kiss you. We're going to start this night over, like I never walked over to you and opened my mouth."

"Eli…"

"And when we interact on the ranch it's going to be because we have tenant-landlord type business to deal with that Connor's pawning off onto me."

She bit her lip and nodded, a crease appearing between her eyebrows. "I'm even more confused now," she said.

"This ends one of two ways," he said, his throat getting tighter. "Either we keep this up," he said, thinking the *this* in the statement was fairly obvious, "and it goes too far. Or we stop it now. But I have a feeling if we keep it all accidental, then..."

"Right. And what would...be so bad about that?" she asked.

Her simple, nonexplicit words sent a slug of lust through him that was so intense he could hardly breathe around it. "Let me tell you something about me, Sadie. I'm a good man. I pride myself on that. But I'm not a very nice man. And I'm not the kind of man who does relationships. This is my town and I care about the people in it. When I want sex, I go outside the city limits for it because I know before I ever get in a woman's bed how it will end. Quickly. I don't want to bring that here. I don't want to run into old lovers while I'm crossing the street or when I'm making routine stops. And I sure as hell don't want to run into an old lover every time I cross my driveway." The very thought offended his sense of order in every way.

"I see," she said. "But...what makes you think I want any more than a little harmless sex?"

"Because sex is never harmless when it's this complicated. It's like setting fire in a barn instead of a fireplace."

She blinked and nodded. "Great. Fine. Whatever. I don't even see the point of banging a guy who wouldn't know fun if it got on its knees and sucked his..." She looked down, so pointedly that he felt it. "Well, you get the idea. Ace seems like he might be more the type I'm after. So I'll go in before you. I'll talk to him. Maybe I'll leave with him. We'll see."

You will not. His inner he-man, as she'd called it, growled.

"Sounds like a plan," he said instead. Because this was crazy. And it had to be stopped.

She forced a smile, her eyes meeting his quickly, a brief flash of electricity shooting straight through him before she turned away.

He watched Sadie walk back into the bar and waited for the tightness in his stomach to recede, for the ache to go away.

He had a feeling he was going to be waiting for a long time.

CHAPTER NINE

Driving into Copper Ridge the next day, Sadie decided to take a left instead of a right at the last minute. She'd been headed toward the main street of Old Town to visit Rona's Diner and see about pie, and something had pulled her the other way.

A ghost, maybe. The same one she'd been afraid she might find in a clearing. Or maybe just what normal people would call memories. She obviously wasn't normal.

But here she was, driving on the road that led away from the ocean. Away from the picturesque portion of the little town. This was where the other half lived. The poor half. The half who worked in the logging industry and at the mill, or didn't work at all.

The half she came from.

And on this road was her childhood home. Her throat tightened as she shifted her suddenly slick hands on the steering wheel.

She'd never imagined, ever, that she would come back here. In fact, she'd actively intended not to. What the hell was all this? Why was she here?

Who knew why she did anything these days? Coming back here, kissing Eli, almost kissing Eli again last night...

There was no point in thinking about that right now.

She took a deep breath and eased her car to the side

of the road as she stopped in front of a blue house with shingle siding.

She took her hands off the wheel and looked out the window. The knot in her stomach eased. It looked different.

It was cleaner. The grass was cut. There was grass. When she'd been there, it had been nothing but a carpet of dandelions punctuated by groups of star thistle.

It was smaller, too. Brighter. She was sure it wasn't actually smaller, but it seemed that way.

A white minivan drove by her car and turned into the driveway of her old house. She watched as it parked and a woman got out. Gently taking her toddler from the backseat, along with a brown grocery bag.

They opened the front door and a small dog ran out to greet them. Sadie hadn't been allowed to have a pet.

Maybe this was what they meant when they said you couldn't go home again. The home that loomed large in her mind, *her* home, didn't exist. It hadn't since the Miller family moved out.

She thought of her patient Maryann, and how much she'd loved her home. How losing it had devastated her, because her memories had sunk into the wood. The love her family shared.

It wasn't like that for Sadie. Not for her family. Nothing of them was still here.

And thank God.

There was no power in this place.

She put her car in Drive and turned back around, shaking her hair out of her face. She felt like maybe things should seem momentous, but instead she just felt deflated.

Whatever she'd thought she might find there, she hadn't. Good or bad, really.

"You're getting weird," she said to herself as she turned onto Old Town's main street and drove to the far end, pulling into the driveway at Rona's Diner before killing the engine.

She didn't have time to be sentimental about a pile of wood, bolts and insulation. She had a pie mission to see to.

Sadie took a deep breath and wrapped her sweater tightly around herself. It was June, but the Oregon Coast had no respect for summer. Even when the sun was shining, the wind had to undermine it with a chill that cut straight through the warmth, and her sweaters, apparently.

She clutched her paper coffee cup a little bit tighter and walked into the diner at the end of the main drag, out near the jetty. She'd been informed that they had the best pies in the county, and she wanted the best for the barbecue.

It was two in the afternoon and the diner wasn't very crowded, the lunch crowd long since dissipated, the dinner crowd not yet arrived. There were some middle-aged men sitting in the corner with cake and pie on plates and coffee all around. Fishermen, Sadie guessed by the look of them.

That was one of the unique things about this place. It was a coastal town, with deep traditions tied to the sea. With fishermen, and crab shacks, seagulls and amazing fish-and-chips. But just inland were the cowboys and ranchers. Sheep, cows and beautiful stables with high-priced horses.

Copper Ridge was the melting pot of everything good in Oregon. Trees and waves, forests and beaches. In that regard, her hometown was a lot more special than she'd realized until she'd been away from it for a decade.

Old Town had changed, too. Where before things had worn a coat of neglect and salt from the sea, they were repainted, revamped and attractive to tourists now. Which was a very good thing for her.

"Can I help you?" a waitress called to her from behind the counter.

There was a glass display case beneath the countertop, laden with the very same pies and cakes the fishermen in the corner were indulging in. There were also doughnuts, giant cinnamon rolls and cupcakes that Sadie was thinking needed to go with her coffee right now.

"I'd like a cupcake. And to talk to whoever does the baked goods."

The woman blinked and something about her expression sent a flash of memory through Sadie. "That's me."

"Oh, well, great."

"What kind of cupcake?"

"Your favorite. I'm not picky."

"I like the chocolate peanut butter."

"Sounds perfect." Sadie watched as the other woman bent to get the cupcake from the bottom of the display case.

Familiarity nagged at Sadie, but she still couldn't quite place her. Obviously she had to be someone she'd known here. Someone from school?

When the waitress rose back up, the motion stiff, a grimace on her face, it hit her. "Alison?" Sadie asked. "Sadie! Sadie Miller. From school. And other things that weren't school-related."

The other woman's eyes widened for a moment and something sad passed through them before there was recognition and then, finally, a small smile. "Oh…oh, Sadie. I didn't recognize you."

"Well, I wear less black eyeliner these days. Clearly, so do you."

She laughed nervously. "Yeah. A bit."

"So, what have you been up to?" Sadie asked, dimly realizing that there was something uniquely wonderful in seeing faces from your past.

"Nothing much, really. Working here. Baking. I got married."

"Congratulations."

"Yeah," she said, forcing another smile that looked distinctly sad.

Alison had been part of her tight-knit crew. They'd caused a bit of trouble together—the barn incident being one of them—and mainly spent time in the woods near the Garrett ranch or on the beach, because for them it had been better than being at home.

They were the misfits of Copper Ridge, and even if no one else had fully realized it, they had. They knew they were different. They knew they were wrong. Broken families, poverty. Abuse.

There was only one elementary school, one junior high and a high school that sat squarely between Copper Ridge and Tolowa, making the most out of the shared student population. That meant they'd spent a lot of years circling each other like wary strays, slowly forming a group. A bond that had been, at the time, thicker and stronger than the bond with their families.

Alison, Damian, Matthew, Kelly, Sarah, Josh and Brooke. A few other people rotated in and out, but that was the core.

And she'd left them behind. She'd never contacted them.

In that moment, she felt ashamed.

"Not married," Sadie said, holding up her bare left hand for emphasis. "I've been...moving a lot. Being a crisis counselor. And now a proprietress at a bed-and-breakfast. So... I still don't make a whole lot of sense."

"Sounds nice to me. You escaped," Alison said.

That was how she'd felt at the time. Now she wasn't so sure.

"I'm back. This place has that way about it. It even called *me* back eventually, and I like moving on a lot more than looking back. Historically speaking."

There was a disconnect happening. Something so fundamentally defeated in Alison's eyes, something so familiar, that it hurt Sadie to look at it. And she couldn't nail down what it was or why. Maybe just fatigue from a long shift.

"Do you ever... Do you talk to anyone else from school?" Sadie asked.

Alison looked down. "Not really. Matt's still here. He fishes. Brooke owns a shop up the road, but we don't... I don't have a lot of time. Everyone else moved like you. Josh went on and made all kinds of money... I'm just still here."

"Oh." She made a mental note to track Brooke down later.

"Yeah."

"Well," Sadie said, filling in the silence, which she was professionally good at. "I heard that you had the best baked goods in town. And the thing is I'm organizing a community Independence Day barbecue on the Garrett ranch, which is, not incidentally, where my B and B is. And I wanted to have a dessert booth. Possibly a pie eating contest. So I wanted to talk to you about what you have, what is possible production-wise and if the owner of the diner might be interested in donating a certain number of pies for the contest in exchange for advertising space."

"These are the best pies!" one of the men shouted from the corner. "Alison makes the best everything." There was a round of agreement from the other men at the table and that pulled another smile out of Alison.

Getting a smile out of her, Sadie was coming to realize, was as difficult as pulling Toby out from the back of the lazy Susan cupboard when he was annoyed about the vacuum cleaner.

"There, that's all the validation I need," Sadie said. "So if you're up to it, I'd really like to involve you. And if the diner owner isn't super into it, I'm happy to purchase pies directly from you. Or maybe you'd be interested in manning the dessert booth? You could sell pie by the slice. It'll be a great bit of advertising for you. And hey, since I think you're probably a million times better than me at baking, pies might be a great thing for me to have in the B and B anyway."

Sadie wished she could stop the tumble of words now, because Alison looked wary, and it hit a warning button deep inside Sadie. But the ideas were rolling off her tongue now without her permission. Possibly because of that internal warning signal.

For a therapist she was awfully useless in out-of-office people situations.

"I'll have to check with Jared. If he can spare me for that much time," Alison said.

"The diner owner?"

"My husband," she said, blinking rapidly. "He may not want me getting so involved in something like that. It's already hard with how much I do here."

"Right. Well, I mean, only if you want to. Don't feel an obligation to me or anything."

"I do want to," she said.

"Then I'm sure your husband will be happy for you. It'll be good for you and all."

Alison didn't look so sure and that right there sent Sadie's instincts from warning bells to the desire to maim the guy in the testicular region.

"Right. Yeah. Just the cupcake?" she asked.

"A marionberry pie, too, actually. I'll have it after dinner."

Alison bent and pulled a pie out and put it in a white box before ringing both items up.

"Great," Sadie said. "And now I know where to get my goody fix, and where to see an old friend. So all in all, this was a productive day." Sadie reached into her purse and pulled out a crumpled receipt from the coffee stand she'd gone to earlier, and wrote her cell phone number across the back. "Call me. If you ever need anything, or want to hang out, or have questions about the barbecue."

"Sure," Alison said, taking the receipt. "I will."

Sadie had the feeling the other woman was lying. And again, she couldn't quite place why. But everything seemed wrong. Well, the statement about the husband not wanting her to be gone too much seemed off to Sadie, but then, Sadie knew there might be other factors. Even though her gut response was that it sounded awfully controlling.

"Thanks for the goodies. If I slip into a sugar coma, don't be too surprised." Sadie waved and walked out the door, back down the sidewalk toward where she'd parked her car.

She was happy about the pie, but uneasy about everything else.

And this was the problem with coming home. There

were so many emotions tied up in things. She didn't like it. Before leaving Copper Ridge she'd had a whole lifetime of heavy. Of bad feelings and worry and outright terrifying crap, and she just didn't like to feel things that were even close to that anymore. It wasn't healthy to dwell, after all.

But Copper Ridge made her dwell, dammit.

And just like that, the magic of returning home was gone.

IT WAS DECK DAY. And Sadie had a bevy of shirtless construction workers off the back of her house, putting down posts and cement blocks in preparation for the building of the massive deck she'd designed for the B and B.

She had big plans for it. Tables. A barbecue. No, a barbecue wouldn't strictly be breakfast, but she could fix other meals.

Her one serious question, though, was whether or not a group of construction workers was a bevy.

Perhaps they were more an assemblage. Or a herd. A pack. That sounded nice and manly. Very sexy. She sipped on her lemonade and watched them from her living room window, privately pleased that she was perving on them rather than the other way around.

"Yeah, baby," she said, tilting her glass back and catching an ice cube between her teeth. "Show me what your mama gave you."

She was determined to get some visual enjoyment out of these guys. It was a way better idea than thinking about Eli and how much she would rather see him shirtless and sweaty.

There was a knock at the front door and she jumped, splashing lemonade onto her hand. She shook her head, walking to the door. She supposed it served her right. Getting caught being a dirty peeping Tom. She still didn't feel guilty, though.

She tugged the door open and saw Kate standing there, schooling her expression into something almost comically casual. "There are a lot of work trucks out here."

"There are indeed," Sadie said. "Because I'm having a deck built. And the guys are doing it without shirts on if you want to come in and watch."

"That was what I was hoping," Kate said, her cheeks flushing pink.

"Never apologize for being a connoisseur of the male form, Kate. And never blush about it."

Kate blushed deeper and followed Sadie into the living room.

"Dear Lord," she said, and Sadie had the feeling that only the barest hint of decorum was keeping her from pressing her face to the glass like a frustrated window-shopper.

She recalled what Eli had said about feeling protective of Kate, or rather, being content to deny she had a sexuality altogether, and she wondered if Kate ever got to do anything more than window-shop.

"Not bad at all," Sadie said. "Makes me feel like a lady of leisure. Sipping cool beverages and ogling the slick sweaty men. And I'm not sorry about it."

"My female intuition told me that this might be happening over here."

"The force is strong with you. Would you also like a cool beverage? Lady of leisure status could be yours, too."

Kate smiled. "Sure. That sounds great."

Sadie went into the kitchen, humming as she did,

and took a glass out of the cabinet before pouring some lemonade from the pitcher on the counter.

She returned a moment later and handed it to Kate. "Get your leisure on."

Kate took a sip and let out a long sigh, her eyes glued to the activities outside. "It's too bad this isn't a transferable skill."

"Not so much a big market for ogling while indulging in cold drinks, no."

"My goal is to make money doing things with horseflesh. Not manflesh."

"Doing what?"

"I barrel race. I'm looking to turn pro, but I haven't quite earned enough points to get my card. I didn't get to compete as much this year because I needed to work more hours at the Farm and Garden. Focus on saving. I won a decent-sized pot a while back, but not much since and I need money if I'm going to travel with the rodeo."

"That's incredible. You really barrel race? Like…you ride horses around barrels and wear sequined jackets and things?"

"I'm light on the sequins, but yeah."

"And you're good enough to go pro."

Kate took another sip of lemonade and smiled broadly. "I think I am. And my winning streak concurs. But it's just getting everything to line up. And feeling like Eli won't implode when I leave."

"Ah. Eli."

"He's a nervous hen."

"I can definitely see that," she said, thinking of him and his do-gooder complex.

I'm a good man but I'm not a nice man.

Oh, no, she didn't need to replay that scene.

Because it made her shivery in…places. Which was

silly because that should be off-putting. She liked nice men. She did not like scoundrels. Or men in uniform with hella-bad attitudes and control-freak tendencies.

She could not be controlled or contained. She was the mothereffing wind.

"And he needs me more than he thinks," Kate said.

Sadie had a feeling that was a lot more insightful than Eli would think it was. "Sure," Sadie said slowly. "But you can't live your life for other people, Kate." She knew she was playing therapist again. But she was licensed, so it wasn't really *playing*. She was unsolicited, but she was a professional at least. "It only builds resentment, and in the end it destroys more bonds than honesty will. If you want to go, then you should be free to go."

"You make it sound really simple."

"It is," Sadie said. "It's what I do." She realized dimly that insinuating anyone should do what she had done was edging into bad-advice territory, so she attempted a redirect. "But it isn't as though you'll stay gone. It's just that you may need a bit more independence."

"And more shirtless men in my life that I don't share genetic material with," Kate said. "We're country, but not that country."

Sadie laughed. "Uh, I don't suppose you are."

"But yeah. I need to get away. Small town. Same places. Same jobs. Same guys. Take those guys, for example. I either went to high school with them, and they showed no interest in me. Or they went to high school with my brothers and wouldn't dare touch me."

Sadie figured it was better not to mention she hadn't had that problem with guys in high school. But then, she hadn't given off the salt-of-the-earth vibe Kate did. And she also didn't have two giant older brothers.

There was also the fact she doubted Kate had the knack for finding trouble that Sadie did. Which was probably for the best since Sadie had managed to find serious, life-threatening trouble thanks to the smaller trouble she'd found.

Not that anyone in Kate's family would ever hurt her. She could say that for Eli and Connor. She knew they would never hurt women, or anyone who didn't really deserve it.

And she was thinking about unpleasant things again. Ugh.

This place had a way about it. Good and bad. And both a little more intense than she'd been prepared for.

Though, if she was totally honest, she was never really prepared for intensity.

"That is a problem," Sadie said, keeping an eye on the guys. "Which ones did you go to school with? I feel like they're probably off-limits to me."

"Are you really going to...talk to them?" Kate asked, sounding awed.

She should. She should offer them cold beverages while wearing a bikini top. And get numbers. But she wasn't going to.

And she had a horrible feeling it was stupid Eli's fault.

Why she was still thinking about him in those terms was a mystery to her because he'd made it very clear he didn't want to find her hot. Even though he obviously did find her hot. And he'd turned down her very clumsy, ill-advised, sort-of offer of casual sex, too.

In that moment, if he'd agreed, she really would have hopped into the nearest bush with him and ridden him until she was saddle sore.

Had she ever wanted a man this much?

She didn't think she had, and that made her feel relieved he'd put a stop to it. Well, maybe not relieved. She felt twitchy and annoyed, and super horny.

She scowled and looked more determinedly out the window, trying to decide which guy had the nicest butt, and from there trying to decide if she would enjoy smacking it.

She could not decide. And she did not want to smack *any* of the denim-clad asses, truth be told.

She was broken, and it was Eli Garrett's fault.

There was a knock on the front door, which was still slightly open since she'd let Kate in. "Come in," she shouted.

The door opened and she heard footsteps on the hardwood in the entry, and then in walked the man himself. The new owner of her libido. Who had rendered her mainly useless when it came to ogling. It was all very upsetting.

"Hello, Eli," she said. "Is this your version of avoiding me?"

"Why were you avoiding her?" Kate asked.

"I'm not," Eli said, lying neatly for a man with an honor complex. "I came looking for you."

"How did you know I was here?" Kate asked.

"Your truck is in your driveway, but you weren't, and your horse was in his paddock. You weren't with Connor, so I thought I would see if you were here, and lo…" He looked past them both and out the window. "Are you kidding me?"

"We're learning how to build a deck," Sadie said, arching a brow and swilling her lemonade, the ice clinking against the glass. "By observation."

Eli looked at Kate.

"The human mind is an amazing thing," she said, on the verge of giggles.

"Just watching all the nailing and screwing," Sadie said. "It's so sweaty." She took the glass and pressed it to her cheek, giving Eli a very meaningful look.

He swallowed visibly and shifted. Well, he'd obviously taken *that* innuendo on board. Good. He deserved to suffer. He deserved to suffer as she was suffering. He deserved to watch beach volleyball and get no joy from the bouncing. Which was mean-spirited, she knew. But she didn't care.

"I was looking for Kate," he said, his words very pointed as he turned back to his sister. "Carl Ames came by and was looking for someone who could possibly board a horse for his daughter. I said we had the space, but the thing is they might need someone to ride him on days they can't make it out. And I didn't want to volunteer you without asking. Of course, you would get the boarding money."

"All of it?" she asked.

"Yeah. I mean, if you took responsibility for the horse, I don't see why you shouldn't get paid."

"Paid to ride a horse. You know I have no problem with that."

"Great. Well, here's his number if you want to call. They'll probably have him by next week." Eli handed her a card and Kate smiled, set her lemonade on the sideboard, then waved at Sadie and dashed out of the house. Obviously construction workers still ran second to horses in Kate's world.

Eli probably loved that.

"That's going to leave a ring," Eli said, indicating the glass Kate had just discarded.

Sadie picked it up. "How did she turn out to be thoughtless of coasters with you in charge?"

"I blame the missing coaster gene on Connor. Anyway, I see you're being a bad influence on my sister," Eli said, but there was no venom in his words.

"Your sister heard the work trucks a mile away and came running for her chance to gaze upon some prime, Grade A man muscle. Don't blame me for her actions."

"I don't really," he said.

He should leave because there was no reason for him to be there. Not when they were avoiding each other.

"So, you're having a deck built?" he went on.

She nodded. "Yes. Connor approved that plan before I moved in. I'd seen pictures of the place in the online ad and knew I wanted something more than just the front porch."

"Online ad. Liss must have helped him with that."

"Was she the woman who answered the phone call I made?"

Eli lifted a shoulder. "I would guess so."

"His…girlfriend?" Sadie asked, knowing it was nosy but not really caring.

"Friend. You met her at the poker game," Eli said. "She's one of the only people he listens to. Incidentally about the only person who can put up with his bullshit for more than a very short amount of time."

"I see. And who puts up with yours?"

"No one. I put up with everyone else's."

"Right," she said, looking back at the construction workers. "Men and tools are a marvel."

"What about you? Ace putting up with yours?"

She laughed. "Uh…not currently."

"Interesting."

"Why?"

"I'm surprised he didn't ask you out."

Dammit. "He did," she said. "But flannel isn't really my thing. Beards are so…scratchy. You have testosterone, we get it. So much that hair is growing from your face!" She waved her hands, the ice clanking against the glass again. "Just so…obvious."

"You prefer nonobvious men?"

"Just, you know, maybe I don't prefer any man right now. Or any one man. I have a fine assortment right out there. Why would I tie myself down to a date with one bartender, when I could stand here and look at the variety behind the glass, so to speak."

"You're making an awful lot of excuses about turning down a date. To a man you profess not to like."

"I don't like you," she said. "And may I say, you're loitering a lot in the house of a woman that you profess to be avoiding." She looked pointedly at him.

"I guess I am."

"And so…"

"Nothing. I'll go." He turned and she felt instant regret, which was more annoying than anything else. More annoying than not being able to enjoy checking out other guys. More annoying than all the darn emotions this place made her feel.

"I just… I ran into Alison," she said, not really sure why she was prolonging the conversation. He turned back toward her. "Used to be Brown. At the diner. She's the one who makes the baked goods there. I was just wondering if you knew anything about her. Like…if she's okay. I knew her in school and she seems… I don't know. Something felt off."

He nodded slowly, a shadow passing over his face. "Yeah. I know her. From the diner mostly. Her husband, Jared, is a logger. I know him because I've arrested him once or twice for after-work fights with coworkers. And yeah, I think something seems off. But she's never said a thing to me, and I've never seen anything... There's only so much you can do."

Her stomach tightened painfully. The memories from ten years ago were way too close to surfacing. Such familiar words. Familiar regret.

Only so much we can do. If you weren't an adult we could send child services in. But you're eighteen. Your mother is telling a different story. You could always call the police in...

She shook it off. Forcing the memory back into dark, dusty, unused corners of her mind.

She didn't need this. Not any of it.

"Right," Sadie said. "That...sucks. That sucks."

"I'm sorry for her."

Anger built up in her, more familiar now than she would like it to be, and all connected to Eli Freaking Garrett.

"If you were sorry, if you were paying attention, you would do something instead of just apologizing to me."

"What?" he asked.

"That's all people like you do in situations like this. Talk about how it's sad and unfortunate and regrettable—that's when you're not acting like you just don't see it at all." She ignored the guilt that lodged in her chest because that had been the first thing she'd done. Her first instinct. To think she was paranoid, and that it could be other things.

And sure, it still could be. But in the interest of her own comfort she'd been completely dismissive, and she knew the kind of pain that caused. Knew that that attitude could be utterly devastating to the people being shoved into the shadows for the convenience of others.

"The thing is, Sadie, I haven't seen anything. Except that I know the guy is a dick. On the job site and off. But being a dick isn't a crime. Now, when he has committed crimes? It's been handled. But he hasn't recently, and I swear to you I have nothing but supposition about how he treats her."

"But can't you investigate—"

"No," he said. "I can't. Because as much as I would like to sometimes, adults have a right to privacy. If there has not been a crime, then there's nothing I can do. I can't assume someone has committed a crime and go in after them. There are lines, and I can't cross them."

"Whatever. You're a chronic do-gooder. You're all up in your family's life. You feel like you're all up in mine, because here you are in my house again, and you're talking to me about boundaries?"

"I'm sorry, but the girl who runs from everything is going to talk to me about getting involved in people's lives? When was the last time you were involved in anyone's life besides your own, Sadie? When was the last time you took the time to help someone with their problems?"

"I did it for a living, jackass."

"And that helps you sleep at night, doesn't it? It helps you feel like you talk to people and like you've done something, but you never have to stay around, day in and day out and see the same people. See the same struggle. Know that all the help you've offered has meant nothing in the end."

"What are you talking about?" she asked, crossing her arms under her breasts.

Eli turned away from her and stalked toward the entryway and she followed him, her heart raging. "Hey, you just impugned my character, now stick around and explain it," she said.

"People don't change, Sadie. If I've seen one thing in my life, it's that. But to realize it you have to stick around. You got to sit in an office and listen to people talk, for money, but I won't even go too deep into that because, yeah, I take care of this community for money and I don't think a paycheck negates caring. But the thing is, I'm here. Year in, year out. I arrest the same kids over and over again. The same street people, the same addicts. The same abusers. And I wish to God they would get it. That something would reach them, but nine times out of ten, it just doesn't."

"I try, Eli. Even if I don't stay for twenty years, it doesn't mean I don't try," she said, the ball of fury growing hotter, bigger.

"You get to feel superior," he said, "and that's damn convenient. Because you get to judge me for what you think is me refusing to make a difference, and the view from your high horse tells you that you have made one. But it's only because you're all wrapped up in this fuzzy, fake reality blanket you knitted for yourself. You get to say that it's real, that what you do is real, and you get to look around this place that hasn't changed and say that what I do isn't. But it's because you've never bothered to look behind you."

"That is…" she said, searching for words. But it was hard when they were all mired in anger. "That is completely unfair."

"Is it? You're standing here telling me I don't care when, honestly, the thing is, I do. But caring doesn't do a damn thing. You have to act. I act according to the law. I keep things in order, using real rules and guidelines. I don't deal in the subjective, because I can't afford to make irrational mistakes."

"I see. So emotions are irrational."

"Hell yes," he said. "Emotions are damned irrational."

He took a step toward her, the tight space of the entryway growing smaller. "You know what else is irrational?" he asked.

"What?" She shouldn't ask what. Because she shouldn't want to know. Because the answer was going to lead to something stupid, and she knew that better than she knew just about anything at this point.

"Attraction," he said, his voice getting deeper.

Oh, no. That was definitely the wrong topic.

Everything slowed down, except her pulse, which sped up, beating hard in her neck, her wrists and, noticeably, at the apex of her thighs.

"Sure," she said. "Attraction is…you know, not logical, because it originates in your pants and not your brain. Which is not strictly true, actually. Your brain definitely plays a part in attraction…" Which begged the question why her brain and body were conspiring against her.

"It's a nuisance," he said.

"Get off my lawn, sexy feelings," she said, shaking her fist and trying to laugh.

But before she could finish the fake giggle, it was cut off by Eli's mouth over hers, by the fierce strength of his body propelling them both backward until they hit the wall. She dropped her lemonade, hearing it hit the floor, hearing it splash upward and spill the ice. It would be sticky and slippery and she just didn't care right now.

He pushed his pelvis against hers, the hard ridge of

his erection evident against her softness. She rolled her hips against him and he groaned, the sound reverberating through her.

She didn't know why anger and lust were all tied into one thing with this man. She didn't know why she couldn't control her emotions or her body around him. She didn't know why she wanted him even when he drove her crazy.

Even when she didn't like him. At least, she was pretty sure she didn't like him.

It was hard to parse the finer feelings just at the moment.

He growled, a kind of deep, low sound. A sound that spoke of both satisfaction and hunger as he moved his hands to her waist to hold her, slid them down to her hips and held her tight.

She wrapped her arms around his neck and pressed herself more firmly against his body, and she found herself backed more tightly against the wall, the kiss intensifying.

She bit his lip and he returned it, his teeth leaving behind a stinging impression that burned all the way down. She was past thinking. She was past anger. She was past caring whether or not they could ever go out to dinner together without fighting.

Because what did that matter when there was this? Nothing else mattered. Not the construction workers outside, not her pride, not anything. Not in comparison with the heat that was burning between them, white-hot and insistent. Perfect.

This was sexual need in its purest form. Undiluted. A straight shot of alcohol that buzzed right through the brain and turned everything on the periphery gauzy. Consequences didn't matter. Eli mattered. While the rest of the world faded, he remained. Sharp and present, perfect. Necessary.

She released her hold on him and ran her hands down his chest, over the thin black T-shirt that seemed to be his out-of-work uniform. She could feel the muscles underneath, the hard ridges, defined peaks and valleys.

And she couldn't stop herself from dragging her fingertips all the way down to the edge of his shirt and pushing her hands beneath the hem. She hissed when her fingers made contact with hot skin and rough hair.

This might kill her. He might kill her.

She didn't know if she had the fortitude for this. Because it was definitely like nothing she'd ever experienced before.

This wasn't a pleasant tightening in her stomach and a bit of slickness between her thighs. It was all-over need. Warmth that bloomed low and spread to all of her extremities, that infiltrated her veins and heated her blood, making it flow hotter, faster, went straight to her heart and sent it into overdrive. Left her shaking and weak and *needy* in a way that should terrify her.

Scratch that, it *did* terrify her. But the arousal drowned out the fear. Mayhem was crashing around her, but it didn't matter because lust was a giant hand holding her head down beneath the waves. Where she was insulated, and at the same time in terrible danger.

But that only made it better. More exciting. More desperate.

She moved her fingertips up over his stomach, over abs that could be played like a washboard in a country band and toward that broad, perfect chest.

"Oh, just take your shirt off," she muttered against his lips, pushing upward while he tugged the end and hauled it over his head.

Her heart stuttered for a second before racing ahead again as she took in the overwhelming hotness that was Eli Garrett. She'd thought of him as Officer Hottie on first sight, but she'd had no. Freaking. Idea.

Tanned and toned with just a smattering of body hair over his chest and down the center of his abs. Like the path on a map, leading to buried treasure. And she could tell, based on the feeling of his hardness against her, that he was packing some serious treasure.

He pushed the straps on her dress down, exposing the thin, peach-colored bra she was wearing. He swore, harsh, breathless, and moved to cup her, sliding his thumbs over her nipples. She leaned her head back, banging it on the wall. And she didn't even care.

He lowered his head, pressing a hot, openmouthed kiss to her cleavage, the desperation in his actions spurring her on, bringing her closer to orgasm with each touch of his lips, his tongue, his teeth on her tender flesh.

Kissing, touching, had never brought her so close. He hadn't even put his hands between her legs—where she was wet and aching for him—and she was still right on the edge, ready to go over with the slightest touch. Another flick of his thumb over her cloth-covered nipple, another calculated slide of his tongue against hers.

He didn't do either. He lifted his head and looked at her, dark eyes meeting hers. His brows were locked together, his lips pressed into a line. He looked like a man trying with everything he had to cling to his control. A man who was losing. The moment jarred her, gave her body just enough of a reprieve that she didn't feel so close to the end.

She moved her hands behind her back, shaking, and unclasped her bra, throwing it onto the ground.

A flame burned hot and dark in his eyes and she could see the moment that all that control snapped. As sexy as it was to see Eli Garrett in full command, seeing him unleashed was even better.

He moved back to her, lowering his head and sliding his tongue around the center of her nipple before sucking it in deep as he moved his hands around her back, slipping them beneath her dress and cupping her butt.

He inched one hand lower, his finger dipping between her thighs. She gritted her teeth in a futile attempt to hold back a hoarse moan as his fingers slipped under her panties, over her wetness, and one pushed deep inside her.

She moved her hands to his back, nails digging in deep as she arched into his touch. Between his hands and his mouth, she was going to lose her ever-loving mind before this was over.

You already have. Might as well enjoy the ride.

That was the truth. But it was hard to regret losing her mind when it had led to the discovery of *this*.

He shifted his attentions to her other breast while he withdrew his finger, then slipped two fingers across her slick folds, over her clit.

She dug her nails into his skin, and she was pretty sure she might be drawing blood, and she didn't even care.

He slipped his fingers back, teasing her entrance with partial penetration before he pushed both inside of her. A ragged curse word escaped her lips as her orgasm crashed through her, as she held tight to him and rode out the storm.

When the waves stopped moving through her, he withdrew, shoving his pants and underwear down his thighs, revealing his body to her.

"Damn," she said, the word tinged with awe.

He smiled for a second, before the expression was replaced with one of total intensity and concentration. Then he bent and grabbed his jeans, fumbling through the pockets for his wallet, and then fumbling through the wallet for a plastic packet that was a more welcome sight than water in the desert.

"I will never mock your sense of responsibility again."

He opened the condom and rolled it onto his beautiful, considerable length, then he closed the distance between them. "Sadie?"

"Yes?"

"Shut up." He bent his head and kissed her, pushing his hand back between her legs and tugging her panties to the side before gripping her thigh with his other hand and tugging her up against him, the thick, blunt head of his cock testing her.

Then he thrust in fully, a raw sound escaping his lips, the sudden, intense invasion leaving her breathless, leaving her on the verge of begging for more. On the verge of coming again, even though she'd just had an orgasm strong enough to render her whole two-year man hiatus forgotten.

She held tight to his shoulders and lifted her other leg up over his hips, her ankles locked behind him as he pushed her back hard against the wall, his hands holding her hips tight as he withdrew and thrust deep inside her.

"Yes," she breathed against his ear, biting his neck gently, then licking it as he pounded into her. Driving her back toward orgasm so much faster than she would have imagined possible.

He captured her mouth again as he thrust in deep

and she felt the first ripple of a new climax starting to move through her.

Then he put one hand on her breast again, squeezing gently and flicking his thumb across the tightened bud at the center, and she was consumed by it. Pleasure tore through her, and on its heels was a rough, feral growl from Eli as he lowered his head and gave himself up to his own climax, his erection pulsing inside her as he came.

He collapsed against her and her legs slipped down his lean hips, her feet making contact with the floor, her shaky knees making it impossible to stand straight.

She pressed her shoulder blades against the wall, suddenly very aware that her sundress was tugged down beneath her breasts and pushed partway up her hips, her undies askew. And her lemonade had spilled all over the floor, the ice cubes melting on the hardwood.

So many bad choices made in such a short period of time. And it was hard to regret them when her body was still buzzing, her breath was still MIA and she just felt so thoroughly satisfied that for the first time in her life she didn't feel on the verge of running somewhere else and never returning.

But all of that lasted only a moment.

"Fuck," he said, straightening and pushing off from the wall, walking back and forth for a second, looking down at the condom, which he was still wearing, a crease appearing between his brows.

"The bathroom upstairs," she said. "You can use it without walking by open windows."

He bent gingerly and grabbed his jeans, picking them up and climbing the stairs, and in spite of encroaching regret, she paused to admire his muscular calves, thighs and butt as he made his way to the bathroom.

She was high. On pleasure. On him. And with every step he took away from her, she sank a bit lower. Until her stomach was in her feet.

She wasn't needy after sex. It was not her thing. But she needed something more than this. Something more than a curse and his naked back as he left her.

The bastard. He was post-orgasmically uptight, which was a commitment to crabbiness that seemed almost impossible to maintain.

But Eli was incredible that way.

And in other ways.

The man was built. He'd just proved that the size of the boat had a lot to do with how the motion of the ocean felt, that was for sure.

Under normal circumstances she would feel…triumphant. He was, without a doubt, the single hottest guy she'd ever been with. Not that there had been a lot, but she'd never been too worried about it. It was all casual.

The trade-off with Eli seemed to be that nothing about it felt casual. Amazing, cataclysmic sex, with a side of angst.

Gah, and no thank you.

She preferred no angst to multiple orgasms.

Lie, lie, you lie. That was the best sex of all time. It'd be worth waxing both your eyebrows off in their entirety to experience that again.

Meh. Why did her internal voice have to know her so well? She heard footsteps on the stairs again about the time she realized she was still standing there half-dressed. She scrambled to get her dress pulled into place, kicking her bra into the corner.

Then she reached beneath her skirt and adjusted her panties and straightened, hoping she looked a little less epically tumbled.

Sadly, she didn't feel less epically tumbled. She was hypersensitive and tingly, and her mouth felt like she'd gotten it too close to a flame.

She turned, and all those feelings got worse. He was walking toward her, down the staircase, jeans low on his hips, very low, no underwear band visible because his underwear was still on the floor and not on his fine body. His chest was bare, his ab muscles rippling with each step.

His mouth was grim. And it still looked kissable. His lips looked extra kissable when they were grim, which was some sort of sick joke her hormones were playing. Because everything in her took it as a challenge. To soften his mouth. To make him relax. To make him groan.

To make him shake and sweat and come.

Bad road. Her mind had gone down a bad road.

"So, that was…fun," she said, clearing her throat.

He shot her a glare that could only be described as evil and bent to get his T-shirt, tugging it over his head, and over her happy fun times ab show.

"I take it *fun* isn't your adjective of choice," she said, knowing she was making it worse, unable to stop herself from warding off the awkward silence with even more awkward words.

He took his underwear off the floor and stuffed them in his pocket. She would have laughed if it wasn't all so horrible. Actually, she might have laughed anyway because anything so singularly hideous had to be a little bit funny.

But she didn't laugh because she didn't want Eli to kill her with those very angry brown eyes of his.

Though, they were starting to make her angry, since

it wasn't like she'd assaulted him. He was the one who
had kissed her.

He had kissed her and now he was glaring.

And just like that she went from tingly to uncon-
tainable rage.

"Please don't stalk around here like I compromised
your maidenly virtue. You kissed me. You pushed me
against the wall. You were complicit in the screwing.
So get over yourself."

His nostrils flared and a muscle jumped in his jaw.
"I am well aware that I'm at fault here."

And that made her bristle, too. "At fault? You make
it sound like we had a fender bender. It was sex, Eli.
There doesn't have to be a guilty party."

Color slashed over his cheekbones and she knew that
he felt…ashamed. Of her. Of wanting her. And that just
made her feel like garbage. All the glow was gone. All
the good everything. And the anger, too.

It just left her with a sharp sinking sensation, a feeling of aching uncertainty. And just like that, the fear,
the knot of terror that seemed to be a constant companion, was back in her chest.

And she wanted to run.

Not just from the room, or the house. But from the
town. The state. She just wanted to leave it all so far in
the rearview mirror that she couldn't see it. That she
wouldn't be able to remember this regret.

"Why don't you just go," she said.

He nodded once and walked out the door, closing it
firmly behind him. And she realized they hadn't even
locked it. They'd screwed in the entryway of a place
that seemed to have revolving doors on every structure
and they hadn't even locked up.

"I wish I could go," she said, pressure building in her chest, tears stinging her eyes.

She cried. Of course she did. At the end of books, during commercials for life insurance and movies with intense acts of bravery that were sure to end in death but were performed anyway.

But she didn't cry over real-life things. Because she kept negative space, negative emotion, out of her life. And she didn't feel it. She didn't let it get down beneath the surface when it did run out to confront her.

But Eli had managed to get inside her, and not just in a sexual way. It was…terrible. She leaned against the wall, her heart slowed down to a dull thud that resonated in her ears, her stomach turning, making her feel sick.

Okay, she was not going to wallow. She was *not*. Wallowing didn't solve anything. And repeating the same mistakes twice didn't solve anything, either.

One good thing about growing up with her abusive asshole of a father: she'd learned about human nature in a harsh and real way. Had seen what happened to the optimistic when they believed a bad situation could change with love. With lying to yourself.

She'd come out of that with eyes wide-open. And with a ruptured spleen, but that was another matter entirely.

She sucked in a deep breath and managed to hold back the tears. She wasn't going to cry over Eli. It was a spilled-milk situation. Or rather, spilled lemonade. She just needed to wipe up the mess and carry on.

She heard the soft thump of four paws hitting the kitchen tile, and then Toby wandered into the room, rubbing against her bare legs, his gray tail twitching up above his head.

She bent down and scratched him between his ears.

"I messed up," she whispered, because her voice didn't seem to want to function on any other level. "But I guess that's par for the course, right?"

Toby meowed and pushed his head harder against her hand, angling so that she hit a particular spot just behind his left ear.

"How do you put up with me?" she asked, and was met with nothing but a request for more head petting. Which in many ways was just fine. "Kitty before man-titty," she said, moving her hand beneath his chin and scratching.

This was just a onetime thing. A moment of insanity. She should be grateful it had happened. Yes, grateful. Because the intensity brewing between them wasn't healthy. And it had needed some diffusing. That was what today had been. She could draw a line under it and call it good.

What was sex like with Eli? Question answered. What did he look like naked? Question very much answered. There was no more burning curiosity. None.

And that meant the tension between them should be somewhat relieved. So there.

She took another breath, some of the tightness in her chest easing. There was no reason to be upset. They were adults, and they could handle this. Eli would be fine next time she saw him. He'd just been suffering orgasm hangover and hadn't handled things well.

But everything would be fine.

It had to be.

CHAPTER TEN

IT WAS PIZZA night for the Garrett family, and it should have been somewhat enjoyable. Usually, Eli liked the routine of them assembling in the main house for an evening.

Even though there weren't a whole lot of sunnier times for their family to be reminded of, they'd always had each other.

The three of them, and sometimes Jack, against the world.

But tonight he wasn't enjoying it to the degree that he should, and all because of Sadie. Because of Sadie and the fact that, only four hours ago, they'd had sex against a wall, which he'd never, ever done in his life.

Because that spoke of a lack of control he didn't even think he was capable of. Never before had a kiss just turned into sex.

When he had sex with a woman, they both knew it was on the agenda and things followed careful steps. Living room couch to bedroom. And then out the door again because he didn't spend the night, but it was okay, because they didn't expect him to.

It did not just…happen like that. Almost against his will, and certainly against his better judgment. But one minute they'd been shouting at each other, the next they'd been kissing, and then…then he'd been about knocked on his ass by the intensity of his orgasm.

Before he knew it he'd been upstairs in her bathroom, totally naked, pouring cold water down his neck so that he could get back downstairs and out the door again without popping wood when he saw her.

He'd spent the rest of the day riding his horse around the pastures, doing essentially nothing but trying to pound his balls into submission with tight jeans and a punishing day in the saddle.

Unfortunately, he'd just ended up replaying the scene in Sadie's house over and over.

"Why are you scowling?" Connor asked from his position at the counter, where he was sitting on a bar stool and inhaling his pizza. "Scowling is kind of my thing, and I feel like you're edging in on my territory."

"Scowling is your thing? I thought the Robinson Crusoe look was your thing," he said, indicating Connor's beard and hair, which were both starting to get a little long.

"I can have more than one thing."

"What's my thing?" Kate asked, leaning forward on the counter, speaking around a mouthful of cheese.

"Bad table manners and objectifying construction workers, apparently," he said, his words a little testy since, in fairness, it was Kate's fault that he'd gone looking for her in Sadie's house. It was his sister's damn *sex drive* that had put him in this position.

Her cheeks turned pink and she looked down. "Thanks for ratting me out, bastard."

"Objectifying construction workers?" Connor said in mock horror. "That's shocking. Did you whistle at them and say, 'Hey, baby! Why don't you drop that hammer so I can watch the view'?"

"I did not," she said, looking like she was about to fold in on herself.

"Missed opportunity," Connor said.

"Whatever," Kate said, pulling a piece of pepperoni off her pizza and putting it in her mouth. "You would lock me in my room if I ever did that." She stuck her thumb in her mouth and sucked the grease off it loudly.

"Honestly," Connor said, "I don't worry much about you and men."

Kate looked genuinely offended by that. "Why not?"

"I have my reasons," Connor said.

Relationships, or hookups, which was the veiled content of the conversation, were not Eli's favorite topic just now, so he was keeping his mouth shut.

"So what happened the other night?" Connor asked, his focus on Eli now. As if his older-brother sense told him that Eli was clamming up to avoid talking about something.

"Which night?" Eli asked.

"You dragged Sadie out of the bar and returned ten minutes later. She looked like she'd been scolded. You looked like you'd accidentally branded your own ass instead of a calf's. What happened?"

"Why are you choosing this moment to start paying attention to what I do?"

"I always pay attention. It's just you don't usually have anything happening. And I want to know what's happening with Sadie."

He thought about earlier. Soft skin under his hands, her full breasts…what it had been like to take one of those perfect nipples into his mouth. How wet she'd been.

Mind-blowing, cock-busting sex.

"Nothing," he said.

"Yeah, I don't believe you."

"They're avoiding each other," Kate said, looking at

him almost apologetically. "Well," she continued defensively when he shot back a mean glare, "it's what she said when you were at the house earlier. When you busted us creeping on those guys."

"I'm avoiding her because she's a pain," he said.

"And yet you told Jack to keep his hands off."

Kate's head whipped around to Connor. "Jack is interested in her?"

"Jack," Connor said, "is interested in tits. Whether they're attached to Sadie or not is immaterial. They are the new breasts in town, and therein lies the attraction."

Kate lowered her head and mumbled something that Eli didn't understand.

"What was that, pumpkin?" Connor asked.

"Gross," she said, a little louder, and a little crisper.

"Men are. Your life lesson for the day," Connor said.

Seemed like it was Eli's lesson for the day, too. Since he'd done a fantastic impersonation of a pig today.

"To be fair, Connor," Kate said. "I appreciate a man's ass in a pair of Wranglers."

Connor looked like Kate had hauled off and slapped him with her meat-greasy fingers. "Sure," he said.

"I just meant Jack's attitude is gross. Sex isn't gross at all." Kate was looking mutinous now, and Eli's blood pressure was rising because he didn't need sex talk just at the moment. And he needed sex talk from Kate never.

"That's enough," Connor said.

"I mean, if a guy wants to look at my tits I'm not going to—"

"Did someone spike your Diet Coke?" Eli asked.

"I'm just sick of this overprotective crap you guys always pull. 'Boys are gross,'" she said, in a bad imitation of Connor's voice. "'You'll get cooties if you touch them.'"

"I *never* said that," Connor said.

"You told me penises had teeth," she said, deadpan.

Eli's head whipped around to face Connor. "Did you really?"

"I don't remember," Connor said.

"You did," Kate said. "I spent the next two years concerned for the health and safety of the inner thighs of every boy I knew."

In spite of his mood, Eli laughed. "I'm sorry, that's just funny."

"Brothers are horrible," she said.

"I know, but we're also the best you have," Eli said. Poor Kate. They were all she had, and they fell short in so many ways it verged on tragic.

"You're good for some things," Kate said. "Not as much for others."

"The same could be said for anything," Connor pointed out. "Badgers. Great for being kickass in the woods. Bad for sharing a shower."

"Connor…" Kate groaned.

"Krazy Glue. Good for sticking things together. Bad for personal lubricant."

Kate scrunched her eyes shut and stuck out her tongue.

"I rest my case," Connor said. "Men are gross."

"*You're* gross," Kate said.

"Your mom is gross."

"My mom's hygiene is open to interpretation because no one has seen her in nineteen years."

"Sorry," Connor said. "Bad joke."

"Sure," Kate said, looking dismissive, "but she's your mom, too."

"Barely," Eli said.

She was the woman who had left them all to drown

in chaos. His father slipping away on a wave of alcohol while the kids were left to pull themselves up from the wreckage of glass bottles, unwashed clothes and garbage.

To say that Eli had come out of it a little bit of a neat freak was an understatement. Order and control had become essential to survival, and bleach had been a weapon he'd employed early on.

If Connor had become the man of the house, Eli had become the housewife. No thirteen-year-old boy wanted that job. But they had Kate to worry about. And dammit all, worry didn't even begin to cover it.

But Eli and Connor were both old enough to realize that if rumors about their dad's drinking got passed around, there was a high likelihood CPS would step in. There had been too much loss for them to be split up. For Kate to be taken away from them. For them to be taken from the ranch.

And so they'd done whatever they'd had to.

School days had been torture for a while. He'd been in hell wondering if his sister was being cared for while he was trapped in a classroom, Kate in a crib while his father drank the day away.

Fortunately, Connor did more with the ranch as a fifteen-year-old than their father had ever done, and they'd earned enough money to put Kate in full-time day care.

So Connor would get up before school and do what needed to be done on the ranch, and Eli would get up and wake Kate. Give her a bath, wash and braid her hair. There was too much to do for him to allow chaos, too much at stake to ever let Kate look like she was less than lovingly cared for.

Connor and Eli had kept up appearances until the old bastard had driven off one of the winding Copper

Ridge roads five years ago, drunk as hell, and nobody had been in the dark after that.

In so many ways, it was easier with their dad dead. At least they didn't have to take care of him now, too.

Well, you did a terrible job of taking care of him in the end.

He shook that thought off. What the hell was wrong with him today? Sex against a wall and this stupid stuff.

He didn't like reflecting on the past, and he wasn't really sure why he was doing it now. Maybe just because today sucked like that.

But did it really suck? Because, be honest, you've never had sex that good.

No, he hadn't. And that made it even worse.

Because no matter how bad of an idea he thought it was, he wanted more. The temptation to shove her down onto the floor, hook her legs over his shoulders and have his way with her had been way too big, which was why he'd stormed out of there as quickly as he could.

Because he didn't trust himself. He almost didn't know himself, and for a guy like him, that was a terrifying admission.

"Well, genetically," Connor said, "I think we can all agree that other than in the looks department, we lost the parental lottery."

Eli almost laughed at that since Connor was currently looking shaggy enough that it would take a very close inspection to decide whether or not he was good-looking.

"But seriously," Kate said, "brothers are actually good for a lot of things. So… I've never felt like it was so bad."

Eli cleared his throat. "Dammit, Kate, why'd you have to get all sincere?"

"You have to warn a guy, Katie," Connor added.

"Call me Katie again, and I won't say anything nice to you for the foreseeable future." And it was all back to normal already.

Okay, he'd screwed up earlier. No denying that. And things were going to be weird for a while. And hard for a while, which was a potential double entendre Sadie would have enjoyed. But he still had Kate and Connor. And his run for sheriff. So most areas of his life were fine. He was just going to rope off that little disaster labeled Sadie and avoid it for the time being. Pay attention to the good and ignore the wreckage.

The incredible, mind-blowing wreckage.

He took a bite of pizza, even though he wasn't hungry. Tomorrow he was back to work. And with any luck, that would help keep his mind off things he had no business thinking about.

CAMPAIGN SIGNS AND posters weren't enough, it seemed. Not for the general election. TV ads and radio spots were needed. According to Lydia at least.

He knew those things were probably necessary, and he'd done some checking into it already, but there was something about the way Lydia talked about the election, filled with spark and enthusiasm, that made it seem like a very daunting reality.

Made him fear it was just too damn much to take on. The feeling he was sinking beneath a pile of endless work was one he'd had for most of his life, so it wasn't new. But it didn't mean he had to like it.

He ought to slap a campaign manager button on her chest and hire her right here in the coffee shop. But that would mean constant exposure to this level of energy and ideas, and he wasn't sure he could handle that now.

Not with hurricane Sadie encroaching on his borders.

Eli was starting to think he needed to buy coffee somewhere else. But other than The Grind the closest place with decent caffeine was fifteen miles away and it wasn't his usual assignment. And he basically had no reason ever to drive there for a latte, even when it meant avoiding Lydia's too-keen eyes.

After what had happened with Sadie it felt exposing, and made him feel a little guilty. Which was stupid, because if Lydia was interested in him, he'd never given her a reason to be. And he shouldn't feel at all like he'd somehow led her on.

But he did. And he felt even worse because she was helping with the Independence Day Community Whatever and because she seemed so invested in his campaign.

And if she found out he'd slept with Sadie...well, the help would likely be withdrawn from both endeavors. Which, when he thought about it, was more tempting than it should be.

"I think you should do a full-color spread," Lydia was saying now.

"Excuse me?"

"Like...put your picture on the posters and the signs. I feel like you have the looks to really grab voters."

"Is that...a thing?" he asked.

She smiled. "It's always a thing. I mean, when you're as kind and dedicated as you are, handsomeness shouldn't matter. But it certainly enhances things. It's part of charisma."

He was so rarely accused of having that.

"Well, the other guy running certainly has a lot of good qualities, and has years more experience than I do."

"He isn't from Copper Ridge, though. And since this

is the largest town in the county, that matters. They just work here. It's different."

It was in his mind, too. Man, it would be so much easier if he found Lydia attractive. Ferret-like levels of energy aside, she was pretty amazing. They could work together on his campaign, and hell, in spite of his gut opposition to a wife and family, he could eventually settle down with someone like her and they could be the unofficial king and queen of Logan County.

Too bad a stick in the eye sounded more appealing.

He looked away from Lydia, across the street, and saw a messy blond bun bobbing on the far side of the cars parked against the curb. And he knew, instantly, who the bun belonged to.

He'd avoided her for three days. Three days without seeing her and kissing her, or putting her up against the wall and banging her.

It had been a successful, if not entirely fun, three days.

The identity of his visual target was confirmed when she appeared through a gap in the parked cars, turning away from the street and facing the wall of one of the shops. She set a stack of papers on the ground and held a staple gun up. Pressing one sheet of paper to a bulletin board and holding the gun against it, she efficiently shot a staple into each corner, before bending and picking up the flyers again and moving on to the next shop.

They were maybe fifteen feet apart, but that didn't stop her from adding a flyer to that board, too.

"Sorry," he said to Lydia. "I have to...law enforcement business."

He walked to the end of the sidewalk, to the crosswalk, and moved quickly across to where Sadie was.

"What are you doing?" he asked.

She turned, her expression fierce as she pressed the trigger on the gun and shot a staple through the paper and cork board. "Posting posters," she said.

She lowered her hand to her side and lifted her eyebrow, the staple gun menacing in her dainty hold.

"I can see that."

He looked behind her head and read the words.

Logan County Community Barbecue
Independence Day
Come to the Garrett Ranch for food, fun and games.
Horseshoes, pie eating contest, live music
and a barbecue battle.

"Well, this is…firming up."

She looked down below his belt pointedly, raising her arm, and the staple gun with it. "Is it?"

He frowned. "Sadie…"

"Give the guy a little sex and suddenly he gets the dick jokes."

"Are you mad at me?" he asked.

"Did you expect me to be super thrilled with you?"

"I expected you to do the socially acceptable thing and pretend nothing happened while you brooded silently. That was my plan."

"Too bad for you, I've never excelled at the socially acceptable."

"Look, let's talk about this," he said, indicating the poster. "Not…the other thing. This is good. The other is bad."

"The other was actually *quite good*, if I say so myself. I am apparently not only good in bed, but good against the wall. Adding it to my résumé."

"Why are you so difficult?" he asked.

"I don't know. Character flaw? Asset? You be the judge."

"And I'm trying to be nice."

"Not doing a very good job." She propped her chin on the staple gun handle.

"So why don't you try to play nice for two seconds. Why don't you go ahead and not keep bringing up what I think is sort of an awkward moment for both of us."

"I don't think *awkward* is the word I would use," she said, frowning.

"It's not?"

"It was actually really athletic. I thought we were kind of awesome."

"Yeah, I guess we were," he said, taking a sip of his latte as an involuntary smile tugged at the corners of his mouth.

"Ah, the male ego," she said, giving him the squinty eye. "So susceptible to praise. Now suddenly The Sex exists."

"I know it exists. I just don't see the point of doing a postmortem on something that we both know can't happen again."

"Why not?" she asked.

"Because. Because it can't," he said, feeling the conviction leak out of his words as he spoke them.

"Because why?"

"Because we don't get along. And I'm busy running for sheriff."

"Yeah, well, I'm busy, too."

"And I'm busy with cows."

"Moo," she said.

"That is absurd."

"Yep."

"And cute," he said, trying to get a handle on the heat firing through his veins.

Then her cheeks turned pink, a smile curving her lips. "Aw, you think I'm cute."

"I think puppies are cute, too. Don't go getting a big head."

"And cats?"

He shook his head. "You know I don't think cats are cute."

"Which is another reason we shouldn't have sex, is that right? Because I love cats. Not just Toby. I love every kind of cat."

"Yeah, no."

"Also, you're humorless."

"Untrue."

She crossed her arms beneath her breasts and leaned back on her heels. "Is it? Tell me a joke."

"I'm not going to tell you a joke."

"So you are humorless."

He paused for a second, genuinely considering telling her one just to get her off his back and prove that he had humor, dammit. But then for some reason, he could think of only one joke. And it was…well, not the kind of joke he should tell.

"Well?" she asked, cocking her head to the side.

"Fine," he said through gritted teeth. "What's the difference between snow boys and snow girls?"

"What?" she asked, smiling wide.

He sighed heavily. "Snowballs."

"Ha! You said balls. Also, that is a terrible joke."

"It's the only one I could think of."

"I don't think that counts toward proving your point."

"Of course you don't, because if it does, I win."

"I don't think a bad joke constitutes as a win for any

involved. Are you going to stand here all day? Because I have posters to hang."

He frowned. "And I have a job to do."

"Are you not patrolling the streets?"

"I should be out doing traffic stops."

"Doesn't that just make you feel like a dick?"

"No," he said. "I've lost too many people to road accidents. If I make someone mad because I pull them over or give them a ticket, that's not really my problem. Or my concern. My concern is that they live to drive another day, as do the other people they share the highway with."

He was annoying himself with how obnoxious he sounded, how serious and in general downbeat. Especially when talking to Sadie, who seemed to be all smiles and laughter, except when he messed with things. He was the bad guy in this scenario and he didn't particularly like it.

"Fair enough," she said, her voice softening. "I'm sorry, that was kind of insensitive of me."

"Why would you ever connect doing traffic stops with the people I've lost? It's my own particular issue. It has nothing to do with you."

"We all have issues, right? And I get that you want to take care of everyone," she said, biting her lip. "It's pretty obvious that you really do care a lot for the people in your life. And the people here, which I think I owe you an apology about, but more on that later."

"When later?"

"When I feel like eating dirt. Right now I don't really want to because I'm hanging posters and I feel bad enough for saying what I did about the traffic stops."

"Don't feel bad," he said, and he meant it.

She looked at him expectantly.

"What?" he asked.

She blinked. "What do you mean, what? I said I owed you an apology for saying bad things about you. Don't you owe me one?"

"I think you've said a lot worse things to me than I have to you," he said, frowning.

"Oh, really?"

"Yeah, and anyway, most of what I said was true."

She blinked rapidly. "Excuse me?" And she was pointing the staple gun in his direction, with what appeared to be intent.

"Sadie..."

"You said that I ran from things. And that I was on my high horse. And that the work that I do is worthless. And you're going to stand by all of that being true?"

"That's not exactly what I said."

"It's pretty much what you said."

"I'm sorry," he said. And he was feeling pretty sorry for most everything that had happened since Sadie had come to town. He'd screwed up with her. Way more times than he wanted to count. And now she was standing here calling him on it. All of it.

She huffed out a growl. "You're just saying it now."

"So?"

"So it doesn't mean anything now."

"I give up, Sadie," he said, turning away from her and walking back in the direction of the crosswalk.

"Wait," she said.

He stopped. "What?"

"Don't leave. I'm mad at you. And I feel like we haven't resolved anything."

"Do we need to?"

"I'd like to."

He turned to face her again. "Okay, what is it you want resolved?"

"I was wondering something."

"What?"

"Do you want to keep having sex?"

CHAPTER ELEVEN

SADIE COULD HAVE immediately bitten her own tongue off. Where the heck had that come from? Oh, okay, she knew where it had come from.

Sleepless nights, endless erotic dreams about his strong body, his hands, his lips, his...well, his everything. She couldn't forget him. Couldn't forget how amazing it was to be with him. How much she wanted him.

She was so annoyed with herself, too.

She didn't do the physical obsession thing. She just didn't. And here she was basically burning up her sheets alone, waking up all sweaty and tangled up in the bedding like a dolphin in a tuna net.

On the verge of orgasm and with no desire to finish the job herself. And now this. This had come out of her mouth. On a public street, during a lovely sunny day. With children most likely playing at a nearby park.

Eli had been walking away, she'd looked at his butt, a butt that was so perfect and masculine and muscular and begging for her to touch it, and the words had just fallen out of her mouth.

He was just standing there, his expression stone, his lips pressed into a firm line.

Now she was filled with regret. Swollen with it. And she was still holding a staple gun.

It was a weird moment. There was no denying it.

"What did you say?" he asked.

"Oh, you know what I said. Why do people do that? Ask you to repeat something they heard but was totally crazy. Do you think I actually want to repeat that?"

"I have to be sure you said it," he said. "Because honestly? My mind could be playing tricks on me. It's entirely possible."

"Yeah, I said it."

"Then I have to be sure you meant it."

He was frozen, every line in his body hard and firm, on high alert. Was he interested? All of his talk about how crazy it was—and it was—and the way he'd stormed out after... But maybe it was just because it was all making him feel as insane as she did.

Maybe it was because he wanted it but didn't want to want it.

Well, he could join the club.

He just kept staring at her, waiting for her answer. And dammit, she didn't know the answer. She wanted it, yes, but was she willing to engage in a purely sexual, no-strings fling with a man who made her want to pull her hair out?

"Yes." Apparently she was. "I meant it."

She could see his hard swallow, his teeth grinding as his jaw shifted. And she hoped, a good portion of her *really* hoped, that he would say no. That he would make her angry. Walk away again and say something insulting on his way down the street that would be so vile all the lust she felt for him would be knocked out of her system.

"Okay," he said. "But I need rules."

"I..." She couldn't believe he'd agreed. She'd been counting on him to be the voice of reason. That was what he did, who he was, except for that time against the wall. And she'd been counting on him to make the smart choices here, since she was very obviously not going to do it. "What kind of rules?" she asked.

If he couldn't be the voice of reason, maybe, just maybe, there was still time for him to piss her off so she'd change her mind.

He looked to each side and then walked toward her, apparently satisfied that there were no prying eyes. "Just sex," he said.

"Yeah, that's what I said."

"And no one knows about it."

She rolled her eyes. "Well, obviously. I'm not going to print it in the paper. Or march over to your brother's place like, 'Hey! Been banging Eli. Here's your rent.'"

"I'm serious. I don't like complications. This is more complicated than I like it already, so it needs to stay clean."

"You don't strike me as a player."

"I'm not."

"But these are player rules."

"They're the rules of a man who generally doesn't date women who live within walking distance of his house. Or even the same town. Or really…a man who doesn't date much at all. But I'm still not a player. I'm just a guy who has too much to do. I don't want a wife, kids or exes all over where I have to patrol every day, so that means I do the best I can to keep things separate."

She hadn't really thought of it like that. Eli moved around town, around the whole area, all the time. Talked to random people, responded to calls. Having exes right in town had the potential to be a mess. She tended to move states away from hers, and she was never all that attached to any of them, so it wouldn't have much mattered anyway.

"Okay," she said. "And ultimately it doesn't really matter to me one way or the other. I like it casual, and no, I don't normally go in for sex only. In fact, I never do. But my relationships have all been very...nonserious."

"I just don't want you to get hurt," he said.

"Pfft. Eli, I've yet to fall in love with any man who touched me. Good in bed or not. Even if the guy is prone to giving me flowers and taking me out, I tend to remain fairly distant. It's hardly going to change with you. Remember? I don't even like you. I just want your body. And that means that this will be the best sex-only relationship ever. Plus, we live close. Late-night booty calls will be a breeze and there will be no temptation at all to develop finer feelings."

He lifted his coffee cup and took a drink. "Okay, I have to get back to work. Then I have to bring Connor food to ensure he does more than ingest alcohol today."

"Sure," she said, feeling a little like shrieking or scurrying in circles or something. Not with joy or anything, but with...panic, excitement and a pulse of adrenaline that seemed more appropriate for scaling a mountain than propositioning a guy for no-strings sex.

"I'll see you after."

"My place?" she asked, her throat dry.

"Probably for the best."

"Bring condoms," she said, looking around, suddenly concerned people might have started milling around since Eli last looked. "I am lacking, currently. And that would be a shame."

He nodded. "I'll come prepared." The black radio on his shoulder buzzed and he put his hand up over the top of it. "I have to go. See you tonight. Good luck with the posters."

Then he turned and walked away. Like some badass action movie star with a surprisingly poor exit line.

Oh, dear Lord, what had she done?

She bent and picked up her stack of posters again, holding them to her chest, the staple gun braced against the back of them.

There was no reason to panic. None at all. She'd propositioned Eli Garrett. And he'd said yes. They were going to have a no-strings fling that would result in many orgasms for both of them.

Putting it like that, it didn't seem like a big deal at all.

No, it sounded awesome.

A slow grin spread across her face and she turned and started walking down the sidewalk, beneath the covered walkway that ran along the row of little shops.

She paused at the next bulletin board, her heart beating fast, excitement building now.

Things had just gotten a whole lot more interesting.

"Dammit, Eli. There's mustard on this."

"What?" Eli looked at his brother for a full ten seconds before he processed what he was saying.

"My burger. There's mustard. You know I don't like mustard."

"Sorry," he said, taking a French fry out of his carton and eating it, looking across the kitchen counter at his brother, who was looking grumpier than normal.

"How the hell do you forget something like that?"

Oh, good, Connor was hell-bent on being an ass. This would be fun.

"I just did," Eli said.

Because his mind was on Sadie. Because his brother could starve for all he cared, except he couldn't really let that happen.

So he was here, pretending like he was invested in the meal he'd brought in for the two of them, listening to Connor bitch about condiments.

"Ace knows I don't like mustard," Connor said, glaring and getting up from his seat, going to the counter to get paper towels and a knife.

"He didn't ask if the burger was for you."

"Who else would it have been for?"

Fair question. "Kate. She likes mustard."

"And you remember that, apparently," he said.

"Shut up, Connor," Eli said, watching him flick the bulk of the mustard off the top bun with a knife before wiping it, seriously wiping it, with the paper towel, then scraping it thoroughly with the knife.

"You don't normally forget."

"If you want a flawless hamburger order, have Liss do it, since she actually likes taking care of you. Or better yet, why don't you go and order your own damn food."

Connor took a bite of the hamburger. "Because you do it for me," he said.

"I should stop," he said, putting another fry in his mouth.

He heard footsteps in the doorway and for a moment, his heart leaped up into his throat, his body tensing as he wondered if it was Sadie with a disaster of some kind, or… Sadie for any reason, really.

But it was Liss, speaking of, walking around the corner, holding a big white box. "Pie," she said, smiling.

Connor looked at Eli. "See, I bet she got it without mustard."

"If you put that pie down in front of me I'm going to squirt mustard all over it, Liss," Eli told her.

"Connor doesn't like mustard," she said, setting it down on the counter.

"Yes. We know."

She dropped her purse onto the counter and her keys with it, sighing heavily. "Is there anything for me?" she asked, turning and facing the fridge, jerking the door open.

Liss had a tendency to act like she lived here, which didn't seem to bother Connor at all. But then, Liss had been a fixture during his marriage, since she'd been close to him and Jessie both. "Dear Lord, Connor, you need to go grocery shopping."

"Still?" Eli asked. "I told him to go two weeks ago."

"I did. I went out to fill up my truck and stopped and bought beanie weenies and beer."

Liss gave him the evil eye. "That doesn't count."

"Why not?"

"I'm eating your fries."

"That's healthy."

"Fries before pies," she said, reaching over and snagging a handful of them out of the container.

And now that Liss was here, and would probably manage to keep Connor from drinking himself into a coma before bed, it was time for Eli to leave.

"I'm going to take off," Eli said, standing, shoving another French fry in his mouth and pushing the carton forward.

"Are you going to finish your burger?" Liss asked.

"No."

She reached out and pulled the carton over to another stool and sat down. "Thank you."

"You're welcome."

"Where are you taking off to?" Connor asked.

"Tired," he said, lying his ass off.

Connor gave him some serious side eye. "Okay. If, say, I were to send our younger sister to your house on a random errand in about an hour she wouldn't be emotionally scarred by activities conducted with female visitors, would she?"

No, because he wouldn't be at his house.

"No, but she'll wake me up and I'd be forced to come over here and shove your head in a toilet."

Connor smiled. "Interesting. Well, fine, I won't send her over. And I won't bug you."

Eli grunted and walked out of the house, feeling very much like he'd already been caught with his hand in the cookie jar. But he didn't care. He was going to go eat his damn cookies anyway.

SADIE WAS A ball of nervous energy. Adrenaline pumping through her veins, heat pooling in her stomach, arousal throbbing between her legs.

She was expecting him soon. And she'd been waiting all day. No, she'd been waiting for this all week. This was what she wanted, and now that she was finally embracing it she was free to appreciate how much she truly craved him.

She wanted more than against the wall. She wanted him naked. All the way naked. In bed. For hours. Subject to her exploration and any twisted desires she might have. She didn't usually have desires she'd consider twisted, but she hadn't ruled anything out with Eli.

Because he made her feel like a giant ball of want. Like a ticking time bomb of need that was ready to explode all over her living room—which was currently spotless, because after she'd done any and all planning she could do for the barbecue alone, and after she'd ordered bedding online for all of the bedrooms in the house, she'd had nothing better to do but clean.

You know. The floor, the wall, the kitchen counter. Just in case he wanted to bang her on unconventional surfaces. She did not need a nasty kernel of cat food right by her head while Eli was trying to satisfy her on the living room rug.

"Oh…cat," she said aloud.

Toby might not allow for sexual spontaneity.

He was currently sprawled over the blue armchair in the living room, looking like the tragic victim of a train collision, his paws out straight, head cocked back and to the side, his back legs up and spread.

"You're a sophisticated beast, Toby."

He didn't move. But of course, it was because it didn't suit him to move. If Eli started making out with her on the couch Toby would probably wake up and decide the only place in the world he wanted to be was on Eli's lap.

And she wasn't going to go locking him in the bathroom or anything just so she could have a good time in the room of her choice. The thing with Eli was physical. Toby, though he couldn't speak actual words, was her friend. Who had stuck with her through it all, mainly because his other choice was a life on the streets as a mouser and he wouldn't engage in anything so gauche.

Either way, she wasn't prioritizing her hookup over her cat's comfort.

Besides, she was having soft, luxurious bed fantasies. And that was better anyway.

The heavy knock on her front door had her scrambling toward the entryway, her heart bouncing around in her chest like a rubber ball that had been thrown at a wall as hard as possible.

She stopped for a second and looked down at the scoop-neck dress she was wearing. Then she leaned forward, reached down the front of the dress and cupped her breast, tugging it up in her bra before doing the same to the other one.

She took a breath and examined her improved cleavage. "Okay. We're good. We can do this."

She shook her head, her hair falling over her shoulders, then walked to the door, grabbing the handle and opening it.

"Hi," she said, going for casual.

"Can we not do the talking thing?" he asked. "You just get mad at me when we talk." He shifted, the bag he was holding rustling with the motion.

"I'm okay with that."

He walked into the house without waiting for her to invite him in, his presence dominating the entryway, filling it. He was a solid wall of man, and now that she'd been naked with him, she knew just how solid.

Knew how his skin felt beneath her hands, how his lips felt on hers, how his stubble felt against soft skin.

And she didn't want to talk, either.

"I want you naked," he said. "Now."

"Should we go into the bedroom…?"

"No," he said, slamming the door shut, shrugging off his jacket and hanging it on the peg.

That made her smile, because even in his dark intensity he couldn't bring himself to make a mess. Even now, he was still conscious of order.

But that was okay, because it was part of what made him him.

And no matter what she said about not liking him, she had to like him at least a little bit, or any male body would do. There was something special about this male body that went past muscles and body hair and…well… generous physical attributes down below the belt.

And that was the soul that was in the body.

The thought made her chest feel tight. Made it hard to breathe. But then, that could just be because he was looking at her like a starving man might eye a piece of very chocolaty cake.

She took a breath, banished the nerves and made eye contact with him as she reached around behind her back and tugged the zipper on her dress down.

She folded her shoulders in slightly and let it fall to the floor, left herself standing there in nothing but a lacy black bra and matching panties.

She'd never been insecure about her body. She had one small scar from her laparoscopic surgery, but nothing too noticeable. Which was good, because she rarely had to explain it, and she barely thought about it, since it was so close to invisible.

Also, she'd never seen the point in being inhibited. If a man had shown interest when she had clothes on, he wouldn't get less interested once her clothes were off. And if he did, that was about him, not her.

But right now, she cared. She really, really wanted to see interest flare in Eli's eyes. Wanted him to be crazy with desire because she felt that way about him.

Because he wasn't another naked man, as good as any other. He was the best-looking man she'd ever seen. Because just looking at him got her hotter than twenty minutes of foreplay with any of her exes. So it felt much more important that he find her more than passable.

She watched him closely, watched the color across his cheekbones heighten, watched his chest pitch with hard breath, his hands clenched into fists at his sides.

It was safe to say she had a captive audience.

She arched her back and reached behind her, putting her hands on her bra clasp and carefully separating the hooks and eyes before letting the garment drop to the floor, her black lace flag of surrender.

He kept his gaze on hers. He didn't look down at her breasts, not right away, and for some reason, that was unspeakably hot. Watching the tension increase in his frame, watching his dark eyes burning with heat, determinedly fixed on her face.

She smiled. "Are you trying to earn an award for not being too obvious?" she asked, sliding one hand up her stomach, just beneath the curve of one breast, before drawing her fingertips over her nipple, a small gasp escaping her lips.

That broke his concentration.

His eyes dropped then and she ran her hand over her other breast, pausing to tease the tightened bud. His jaw was clenched tight, his arousal pushing aggressively against the zipper of his pants.

Oh, yes, she had nothing to worry about.

"You aren't done," he bit out.

"Am I not?" she asked, stilling her hands and glancing at him, trying to look innocent. Knowing she was failing, because she wasn't innocent at all. She was a woman who knew exactly what she wanted. And she knew how to get it.

Knew she was going to get it.

"The rest," he said, the words a hard command that sent a shiver through her.

She pressed her palms against her body and slid her hands down to the waistband of her panties. Then she pushed her fingers below the lace, in the front, cupping herself as she pushed them down, watching as his breathing increased, the pulse beating so hard in his neck she could see it.

She shoved them down her legs and kicked them to the side, leaving one hand where it was, sliding her fingertip over her clit. She gasped, white-hot pleasure firing through her. She was a whole lot more sensitive than she expected to be. But a day of anticipation, combined with how it felt to have his attention, was a hell of a lot more intoxicating than she'd anticipated.

"I'm wet," she said. "If you were curious."

"Bedroom," he said. "Now."

She turned away from him and walked slowly through the house, through the living room, casting a quick glance at Toby, who was still asleep, because obviously he couldn't be bothered to care about humans and their shenanigans.

She could hear Eli's heavy footsteps behind her. And she fought the urge to look back. But not looking was so much better than looking. Feeling his hot gaze on her without seeing him. Knowing he was watching her butt as she walked. That he was as tense with need as she was.

She led him to her bedroom. "Watch your step," she said, taking the small stair that dropped down at the entrance to the room.

She heard his boot hit the carpet behind her and she turned, her heart kicking hard against her breastbone as she looked at him.

"Can you close the door?" she asked.

"Why?"

"Trying to avoid Cattus Interruptus," she said.

"Right." He turned and shut the door behind them, setting the bag, which she assumed contained contraception, on the dresser. "This is another point in favor of keeping animals outside," he said.

"Yeah, yeah. Your anti-cat platform has no momentum here, might as well drop it. And while you're at it, drop your pants, Sheriff."

"Deputy sheriff."

"Why is that hot?" she asked, sitting on the edge of the bed and leaning back, propping herself up with her elbows. "Why is you being obnoxiously pedantic sexy? I don't even get it."

"Hell if I know."

"I mean, I know why the rest of you is sexy. Dayum."

He smiled as his hands went to his shirt collar. "Sorry about this," he said, tugging his tie from his shirt collar in one easy snap, the whole thing intact.

"Clip-on?" she asked.

"Standard issue. You can't take it off without looking like an idiot."

"All right, I'll let the tie go. But only because I'm already naked over here. And very, very horny."

"Points for me," he said, setting the tie on the edge of her vanity. Then he moved his hands to the first button on his shirt and released it, undoing it quickly, revealing a plain T-shirt the same color as his uniform underneath. "This is less of a strip show than bachelorette parties might have led you to believe," he said. "Didn't have time to go home and change."

"Are you embarrassed?" she asked.

He stilled with his hands on his belt. "No. But you went to a lot of... You had on matching underwear."

She nodded. "I did, it's true. But I am way less interested in your clothes than I am in the removal of them. So carry on."

He undid his belt and shrugged the tan T-shirt over

his head. Beneath that was a thin black vest. Kevlar, she assumed. And something hit her in the stomach, a sharp pang. A realization of who he was and what it was he did on a whole new level. He wasn't just a man who cared about his town. He was a man who put his life on the line. He was a man who backed up his word.

And tonight? He was all hers.

He took the vest off, laying it neatly with everything else.

"Oh, yesss," she said, the breath hissing through her teeth. "That's what I'm here to see."

He looked at her, one dark brow arched.

"What?" she asked. "Women don't usually sing the praises of your body?"

"In my experience, it's expected for me to sing the praises of theirs." He turned to face her, working at the clasp on his pants, the muscles in his chest shifting, his abs rippling with the motion.

"Well, by all means, sing my praises. But it has to be said that you are one hell of a man."

He shoved his pants down and proved her point and then some, his erection thick and enticing and, right now, just for her. He folded his pants carefully on top of the rest of his clothes.

"Come here," she said.

"You think you're giving the orders?" he asked.

"If you want to play," she said, raising a brow, "you might want to follow them."

"What sort of game do you want to play?" he asked, his voice rough.

"One we're both going to like. I want to taste you." His eyes darkened, his expression getting tense.

"Come on, Deputy Sheriff," she said.

He walked over to the bed and wrapped his hand

around her head, gripping her hair tight and leaning down, kissing her hard on the mouth before straightening, putting all of *himself* right at eye level.

She licked her lips and looked up at him, bracing her hands on his lean hips. She wanted this. Had wanted it since well before the first time they'd been together. They'd only had urgency then. No thought, no finesse and very little time for exploration.

Now she wanted to explore.

She leaned in, gripping his shaft in her palm and squeezing tight. He groaned, his head falling back, his hand returning to her hair, tugging slightly, the stinging sensation sending a shot of pleasure down between her thighs. Making her hotter. Wetter.

Then she leaned in, blazing a trail over his hard length with the tip of her tongue, her heart hammering fast as she explored him from tip to base and back again before taking him deep inside her mouth.

He was beautiful. He was incredible. And he made this a pleasure. A gift that was truly more blessed to give. Though based on the shivering of his thigh muscles he was very happy to receive.

She pleasured him with her hands, her lips, her tongue, reveling in this strong, solid man's loss of control as he cursed and shook beneath her touch.

She'd never felt more powerful.

She'd never felt more wanted.

Such a dangerous game, but she wanted to play as long as she possibly could. To hold her hand near the flame until it burned her.

She shifted and took him in deeper and he tugged her hair hard, pulling her head up. "Not like that," he said, his words a growl.

She looked at him, at the fierce, untamed light in

his eyes. Eli Garrett was never anything less than civil. He'd once put her in handcuffs while she'd clawed and spit like a mad cat, and he'd never been less than a gentleman.

That was probably where some of the strange conflicting anger-desire had come from back then. Even when she was angry at him, she'd sensed somehow that he was the closest thing to a real-life superhero. Truth, justice, the American way and all that.

Yes, civility was second nature to him, and now it was stripped away. And he was reduced to nothing more than a man who desired a woman. Desired her. Restraint folded up on the floor with his uniform.

"What do you want?" she asked, moving away from him, leaning back on the bed, conscious of how her posture displayed her breasts, of how her relaxed thighs gave him a view of everything else.

"I need to be inside you," he said, moving to the dresser and getting the bag, tugging out a box of condoms. He opened it, took out one condom, then threw the box to the bed, where it landed next to her. "You can put those in your nightstand."

"Generous of you."

"They're only for me," he said.

And she knew then that she'd only teased him at all to hear him say something like that. To hear him get proprietary and possessive and all the things she usually hated.

But being with Eli seemed to be an exploration of everything she'd previously labeled off-limits. Everything she'd always called a bad idea.

This was her chance to dip her toe into some fantasies she'd never given breath before. A man who would take charge. A man who would give as good as he got.

A man who wouldn't shrug and say, "Yeah, whatever," if she called it off.

She put the box in the nightstand, not wanting to push him now. Someday she would. Just for fun. Just to see what would happen. But not now.

He tore open the packet and she watched, rapt, while he rolled the condom onto his thick length. She liked seeing that big, masculine hand wrapped around his cock. She'd love to watch him bring himself off sometime. And she'd never wanted to do that before, because what would be in it for her?

But with Eli…watching him was one of the best things she could think to do with her time.

He moved to the bed and she smiled, kissing his lips, then pushing against him with all of her weight so that he was on his back and she was straddling him, the slick entrance to her body touching his hard length.

"What are you doing?" he asked.

"Going for a ride," she said, smiling.

"Not just yet."

He angled his head up and took one nipple deep in his mouth, sucking hard. A sharp groan volunteered to be the soundtrack to her pleasure, and there was nothing she could do to stop it as his hand teased her other nipple, while he slid his other palm down over her ass, his fingertips delving into the elegant line there, sending a shock wave of sensation through her.

Then he gripped her butt hard, tugging her into position, lowering her down onto his arousal, every thick inch filling her slowly. Perfectly.

"I'm supposed to be in charge here," she said, when he was buried in her to the hilt.

"Sorry," he said, his voice rough. "Missed that memo."

"No, you didn't."

He slid his hand over her bottom again, squeezing her. "What are you going to do about it?"

"Ride you until you can't speak anymore. Until you don't have the energy to challenge me."

"We could be here all night," he said.

"Oh, I hope so."

He gripped her face, tugging her head down so he could kiss her hard, his other hand still firm on her bottom, keeping her pressed tightly against him as he flexed his hips upward, stealing her control, stealing her breath.

He was amazing. Perfect. Everything.

And never before had she assigned those adjectives to a man.

But they fit him, just like he fit her.

She pushed her hips forward, butting up against his, sensation rocketing through her. He released his hold on her chin, his head falling back, his hands moving to a more relaxed position on her hips as he let her take the lead.

She braced her hands on his shoulders, moving in time with his breathing. Slow and measured at first, then faster, harder, more intense. Her orgasm started to build, a low ball of pleasure and intensity in the pit of her stomach, pulsing down to her core, her internal muscles tightening around his hard length.

She squeezed his shoulders tight, her nails digging into his skin. She hoped he felt it. The pain and pleasure. She hoped she marked him, because he was damn well marking her. This didn't feel like a game now. Not the light power struggle it had been. The fun flirtation. This was something raw. Pleasure walking a knife's edge. One wrong slip and it would cut deep. Wound. Destroy. And scar forever.

She closed her eyes, her heartbeat pounding against the backs of them, blood roaring through her ears. "Oh... Eli..."

"Not yet," he said, his voice harsh, pulling her through the haze, pushing her climax back.

He removed his hand from her hip and put it between her legs, just near where their bodies were joined, his fingers tracing her clit, sharp, hot need assaulting her as he did.

"I want to give it to you," he said, his eyes intense on hers as he continued to stroke her. The combination of his touch along with the feeling of him inside her was almost too much to bear, but now she was fighting her orgasm.

Because she wanted to stay like this. On the edge. In this moment of beautiful torture.

He took his hand away and she gasped, then lifted his fingers, the tips touching the edge of her lips. Then she looked at him, leaned forward and sucked both deep into her mouth.

He swore, short and hard, never looking away. She ran her tongue along the edge of his forefinger and he pulled her down, hard, thrusting up inside of her as he did. That was enough. To push her from the edge into the abyss.

She shuddered, leaning forward, palms braced on the bedspread as she rode out the climax, waves rolling through her, leaving her breathless, shaking and on the verge of the kind of emotional breakdown she never allowed herself. Ever.

He let out a harsh breath, his grip on her tightening, his muscles shivering as he found his own release, his stomach muscles contracting and expanding beneath her.

She waited until it was over. Until he was relaxed. Then she rolled away from him, lying on her back, her arm over her face, her eyes shut tight behind it, trying to gain her balance. Trying to find her center or whatever. But she was firmly…off center, so that just wasn't going to happen.

He'd tromped all over her center. Left his big, standard-issue boot prints all over it.

She was wrecked.

He wrapped his arm around her and pulled her close and she moved her arm, blinking, shocked by the fact that he was touching her, that he wasn't halfway out the door. But no, he was leaning in, his head pressed to her breasts, his breath hot against her skin.

She lifted her hand and traced his jaw with the tip of her finger, his stubble rough. There was something undeniably male about it. Undeniably sexy.

What was it about him? Why did he make her feel so *much*?

She shook all that off, trying to catch her breath. Trying to pull herself out of the emotional well she'd fallen into. This wasn't like her. She didn't get moony and weird. And she didn't sleep with guys after sex. She was too busy getting dressed, saying goodbyes and getting back to her own space. Or pushing them back to theirs.

Well, she wasn't going to sleep with Eli. She was just going to rest for a second while she got her bearings, and then she would remind him that he needed to get back to his place stat.

He moved his hands over her curves until she could feel herself melting into the sheets like a candle pressed into a flame.

Man, she was pathetic.

And all she wanted to do was sleep. Or turn over and lick him. All over. Oh, yes, that was what she wanted to do. Lick every inch of Eli Garrett until he was shaking. Until he was hard again. Until...

There was a fearsome-sounding scratch and a sound that was closer to a caterwaul than a meow at the door.

She jumped, the sound breaking hard through her fantasies.

There was more scratching, this time on the carpet beneath the door, followed by more angry feline noises.

"Oh, you damn cat!" she growled, wiggling out of Eli's hold and sitting up. And she was almost grateful Toby had come to the rescue then, because it had saved her from revealing her fairly intense neediness.

She stood and looked down at Eli, who was staring at the ceiling, all naked and muscle-y and as hot as ever. Then she turned and went to the door, flinging it open. "What?"

Toby sauntered in, and his eyes seemed to go straight to Eli. "Don't judge," she said to Toby. "You don't have balls. You don't know what this kind of drive does to a person."

Eli laughed, a deep, male sound that was much more relaxed than he generally was. "Do you always talk to your cat?" He sat up and swung his legs over the side of the bed and she was sort of struck dumb by the whole display.

His body in motion, regardless of the motion, was a beautiful thing. And naked? It was mouth-dryingly, pantie-dampeningly beautiful.

"Yes, yes, Eli, I do talk to my cat. And please be advised," she said, crossing her arms beneath her bare breasts, "that I won't allow for anti-cat speech in this house."

"Anti-cat thoughts?"

"Forbidden. The thought police are here. Assimilate or be destroyed."

"I didn't understand any of that."

"It's a good thing you're nice to look at."

"Nice to touch, too, I hope," he said, standing and walking toward her.

Her heart stuttered. "Do you have to ask?"

"Doesn't hurt to be told."

"Touch. Taste. All of the above. I very much enjoy the many attractions your body has to offer."

"Possibly the strangest compliment I've ever received."

"Well, that gives me a new target to aim for. Something weirder than that."

"I look forward to it." He bent down and picked up his clothes, shaking them out, tugging his underwear and pants on.

Her heart sank. She was so much more disappointed by the fact that he was leaving than she should be. She'd just been thinking she needed to get rid of him. Reclamation of space and all that.

But now he was vacating her space. And that was different.

At least it felt different for some reason.

He tugged the tan shirt on over his head and collected the overshirt and tie, and put them into the bag the condoms had come from. Then he went for his boots. And she just stood there naked and watched, which was hugely stupid but she couldn't really bring herself to stop watching him. Or to move and get dressed.

She didn't want her lacy underthings or her dress back anyway.

She wanted jammies. And she wanted to cry a little bit.

She felt like an alien being with way too many feelings had crawled into her ear and then chewed his way from her brain stem, down her neck and into her chest, where he'd made a comfy home and decided to force his emotions on her.

Yes, that was what she felt like. Foreign, and completely out of her depth. And she just wasn't used to feeling that way. She kept herself out of situations that made her feel this way for a reason.

"See you tomorrow," he said, all casual and like his skull hadn't been cracked by the thundering pleasure that had just rolled through them both.

"Uh…okay."

"I can't stay," he said, not looking at her.

"No," she said. "No, I know. I mean, I wasn't going to ask you to. I was going to ask you to leave, actually. But I didn't have to because of the cat, and then you got up, and now you're going so I didn't have to."

Sure, Sadie, ramble. That's convincing and doesn't sound at all weird.

"Okay," he said slowly.

"Don't say it like that. I'm fine. I don't sleep with guys. I like my space, just like you do. And we made rules. Rules on the street corner. In front of God and everyone."

"I'll see you tomorrow, Sadie."

Two days in a row. That was intense. It was, she realized in that moment, a violation of her usual relationship conduct. She'd never been in a relationship where she felt the need to have sex that often. It was healthy and good to have nights alone, and to have time to herself and…and…he was talking sex tomorrow. Probably the next day, too.

And she was going to say yes.

"Okay. Tomorrow. Do you work?" she asked.

He nodded. "Yeah. I'll be patrolling the highway mainly, but I always come to town for coffee and lunch."

"I was going to stop in on Alison again. So I'll be in town tomorrow, too."

"Maybe we can run into each other when I get coffee," he said.

"Elevenish, right?"

He nodded.

She shouldn't be making a coffee date with the guy. She shouldn't even have made an immediate follow-up sex date with him. And now there would be an additional meet-up. But she wasn't going to tell him no. She might not show up to coffee, though. She might not.

Toby started rubbing against her legs and she looked down at him. "What?" she asked, and got nothing but a blank cat stare in return.

"See you," Eli said.

"Yeah, bye."

He walked out of her bedroom without even kissing her goodbye, and she stood there, naked, until she heard the front door shut behind him. And she became acutely aware that she was standing naked in a room with a cat leaning against her legs, watching the blank space where Eli had been.

She shuffled to the bed and flopped onto her stomach, then shrieked when Toby followed, jumping onto the bed and walking across her back, the pads of his feet cold on her skin.

"Boundaries!" she shouted, mainly at Toby but also partly at herself.

If this Eli thing was going to work there would have to be boundaries. Because he'd left her feeling hollow and emotional. She rolled to her side and curled her knees up to her chest, her heart thudding dully.

It was all because she'd been celibate for too long. She was out of practice. The sex had been easy. More than easy, it had been so much better than she'd ever remembered it being. But the surrounding stuff all seemed harder. Deeper. Weirder.

But she would work it out. They would work it out. Because this was way too good to give up.

But she was not meeting him for coffee tomorrow.

SHE COULD NOT believe she was meeting Eli for coffee. Sadie frowned deeply so that she would appear as angry with herself as she felt and tugged on her sweater sleeves, crossing her arms beneath her breasts as she stormed across the street and into the coffee shop.

Where he was not.

Well, eff him and his effing coffee break. Was he not coming? Was that the game? Make Sadie think you were coming to coffee and then not come to coffee the day after you banged her senseless and left her curled up alone in bed with a cat?

As if he could make her feel more pathetic.

No, she wasn't pathetic. And he wasn't allowed to make her feel pathetic because she forbade it. She withdrew permission. She was the keeper of her own life, blah blah blah.

She leaned against the counter, tapping her fingertips together while she looked over her shoulder at the closed door, then into the empty dining room.

There was a girl who had to be in high school working behind the counter, pulling espresso shots and chatting with another boy who really was no more than an infant. Or…sixteen, but whatever.

They were flirting. Ugh. Well, someday he would leave her standing in an empty coffee shop. So flirt away, little children.

Bah.

Sadie didn't know how Cassie, the owner of The Grind, could stand to be around the heady teenage hormones all day. But there she was, smiling away at the register and seemingly un-annoyed by her employees.

It was because Cassie was in love herself, probably, as Sadie had learned during her frequent visits to get coffee. Because Cassie was so in love, she radiated joy and spent much of her time talking about her man, Jake. That love nonsense seemed to blind otherwise rational people to related stupidity.

The door behind her opened, the wind rushing in. She turned and the breath rushed out of her. Eli. He was here. He hadn't stood her up.

And it shouldn't matter.

Feeling a bond with him post-sex is okay. It's not like you've ever done it quite like this before.

Ah, yes, her running internal monologue had a point.

Before him she'd always been in an actual dating relationship with the men she slept with. And with that had come companionship and coffee dates and nice talks. And it had all gone a long way in reinforcing her and her ego.

But this was different and so the fact that she didn't have a firm handle on it really was understandable.

There, pep talk managed. And now she would just enjoy her coffee.

"You came," she said.

"I'm on time."

Yes, dammit, he was. And she had been flailing around for no reason at all.

"Of course," she said. "Coffee?"

"That's what we're here for." He walked to the counter and Cassie smiled.

"Deputy Garrett, the usual?"

"Yep," he said. "And whatever Sadie would like."

Her eyebrows shot upward but she didn't say anything. He was buying her coffee in public. That seemed like a…thing. Like a public declaration, even. Or maybe it was just coffee. Probably it was.

"I'll have just a coffee. Room for cream. Two raw sugars," she said.

Eli pulled out his wallet and paid with cash and she almost laughed. He, and everything about the town, was about eight years behind everything else. In fact, now that she looked, she didn't think the store was set up to take a debit or credit card. Good thing he'd treated, because she didn't have any cash.

"And how has your day been?" she asked.

"Good. Gave out some speeding tickets, so the answers of those I've encountered could be different."

"I would say," she said. "I've gotten a lot of speeding tickets."

"Have you?" he asked.

"What can I say? I'm a rebel." Too late she realized she was making jokes about not driving safe again. Bah. She should have gotten a biscotti to gnaw on so her stupid mouth would be occupied. Talking to Eli wasn't safe.

And why was that? Why was she such a mess with him? She was usually really good with men. All small talky and light and flirty like the barista babies behind the counter.

But not now. And not with him.

"Here you go," Cassie said, handing the cups to Eli. "Have a nice day, Deputy Garrett. You, too, Sadie." The other woman's expression was far too meaningful for Sadie's liking.

"Same to you, Cassie. Tell Jake hi." He turned and started to walk out of the shop, her coffee in his hand.

"Wait! I need my cream." He stopped and handed her the cup, which she took from him before turning to face the little bar, popping the white lid off and picking up the thermos to dump a healthy amount of half-and-half into her drink.

She put the lid back on, managing to avoid spilling and looking like a total dork, which, with her shaky sweaty hands, had been a distinct possibility. "Okay, now we can go."

He shook his head slightly and pushed the door open, holding it for her. It should not have made her stomach feel warm and fuzzy, but it did. She had a serious fuzziness issue where that man was concerned.

"So," she said, once the door closed behind them. "How did *you* sleep last night?"

He turned, his shoulder stiff, his cup paused midsip. "Fine," he said.

Fine. Well. Fine. She'd been fine. Totally fine. Not at all shivery or lonely or horny. "Oh, good. Me, too."

"The way you said it made it seem like maybe *you* didn't sleep well."

"That's a lot of…meaning you read into my very simple question."

"Your very simple question with what sounded like specific emphasis."

"Fine," she said. "It had emphasis. Specific emphasis. But you're lying."

He raised a brow and stopped walking, the wind ruffling his short dark hair. "Really?"

She wasn't going to stand there and wallow in indignation. She was going to take a chance. To take a chance on the fact that last night had been as amazing for him as it had been for her.

"Uh-huh. Lying. You didn't sleep well." She leaned in. "You slept terrible. Naked. Sweaty and tangled up in your blankets. Wishing I was there to touch you. Wishing it was me putting my hand around your cock instead of you."

She could see the tension work its way through his body, tightening his shoulders, tightening his jaw. The gamble had paid off.

"That's enough," he said.

"Oh, no, it's not nearly enough."

"I am on patrol."

She winked. "Yeah, you are."

"Euphemism?"

She lifted her shoulders. "Could be."

"For what?"

"Just messing with you."

"Don't you have somewhere to be?"

"Well, sort of," she said. "I was going to swing by the diner to talk to Alison about pie."

And also kind of to check in on Alison, since Sadie was feeling twitchy about the entire situation. Unless someone came into her office to talk touchy situations, she didn't normally seek them out. But Alison used to be a friend. And this was different.

Though she felt she could be talked out of involvement very easily since it sorely tested her comfort zone.

But then, just about everything she'd done for the past couple of months—signing a long-term lease, sleeping with a man who gave her feelings and dealing with spiderwebs in a house that had been long empty— had tested her comfort zone.

So why not continue the theme?

"Right. You were going to, but...?"

"What is your stance on ride-alongs?" she asked, looking at his patrol car parked down the street.

"It depends on who the person is."

"Me. Me is the person."

"Heavily against."

"Why?" she asked, knowing she sounded whiny, knowing she was using him to help her avoid the Alison thing.

"Because. I'm not going to let a known criminal sit in the front seat of my car."

"Ha-ha-ha," she said drily, "you are a clever, clever man. And fine. I'll go off and do my actual stuff instead of forcing you to spend any more of your precious time in the presence of my adorableness."

He let out a long breath. "Fine. Come on."

"I can go?"

"If you promise not to mess with things."

"I can't promise that, Eli."

"Why?" he asked, looking long-suffering now.

"Because if there are buttons, I may not be able to resist the urge to push them."

"I'll dump your ass on the roadside and leave you to hitchhike back to town."

"No, you won't," she said, breezing past him. "You're too nice."

"I am not."

"Sure you are," she said, waiting by the passenger-side door of the car. "You're so nice you're letting me come on a ride-along."

He opened his door and unlocked hers from that side, then got in without waiting for her. She opened the door and climbed in. There was a laptop mounted to the dash, and in the center console were all the buttons, radios and things she generally wanted to mess with, but didn't, because the car wasn't moving yet, and at this point he probably would still kick her out.

"That is not evidence of any particular niceness," he said, starting the car and putting his drink in the cup holder.

"You don't like it that I think you're nice?"

"I don't want you to get the wrong idea," he said.

"You're just annoyed because I have the right idea."

He pulled the car away from the curb and onto the mostly vacant streets. It wasn't quite lunchtime and it wasn't peak tourist season, so the main street of Copper Ridge was quiet.

"So how did you sleep?" he asked. "Real answer this time."

"Like a baby."

"So you woke up every few hours crying?"

"Meh," she said, taking a sip of her coffee.

"Or maybe just…wet and aching and wishing it was my hand between your legs instead of your own."

She snorted, coffee spurting over the hole in the cup lid and down her chin. She lowered the cup and wiped at her face.

"What?" he asked. "Was that not a nice question?"

She was wet and throbbing now. And not just from the slight dribble of hot coffee on her chin.

"No, it was not nice. Or polite. Or gentlemanly."

"I warned you. Good, sure. Nice, no. Also, not a gentleman."

"I feel like I'm learning a lesson about still waters running deep. And a little dirtier than expected, to be honest."

"Are you sad about that?"

She thought back to last night. To his much-better-than-average bedroom skills. "Uh, no. Can't say that I am."

"I thought you seemed to enjoy it."

"Are we allowed to talk about this on a ride-along? Shouldn't we be talking official sheriff's department business?"

"We could. Do you have questions?"

"Funniest call you've ever gotten?"

"Concerning piglets who scattered in the elementary school."

"Wow. That is…way to break small-town stereotypes, Copper Ridge."

He laughed. "A student had brought them in for show-and-tell. And I happened to be there for a Say No to Drugs assembly. So when all hell broke loose I took the call over the radio. So I was the official first responder to the pig debacle."

"Legend," she said.

"Pretty much."

"Did you always know you wanted to do this?"

"Sort of. I mean, at first I thought maybe I'd do state police. Or head up to Portland and work there. Do something in the city. But I always had my eye on law enforcement because I liked the idea that I could…make people follow the rules." His voice halted a little on the last part.

"You wanted everyone to behave?" she asked.

He cleared his throat. "When I was a teenager I thought… I thought maybe if I were a cop I could make my mom come back. Make my dad quit drinking. It was power to me. Authority that I didn't have. I mean, I got over the fantasy really quick, but the desire to be able to change things stayed with me."

She clutched her coffee to her chest, her eyes on the thinning buildings and the increasing trees, the waves in the distance. Something about his words had made her feel raw. Like the admittance of his own childhood fantasies, of change and control, had scratched against hers.

Interesting how those two desires had put them on such different paths. She'd thrown up her hands and let it all go. Walked away and never looked back because when she'd realized that nothing in her family would change, she'd realized that she couldn't stay. That she couldn't even tempt herself to try.

And yet Eli had stayed. And he'd made changes here that were concrete. He'd done what he'd always dreamed, in many ways. Even though he still hadn't saved his family. It made her feel like the flake she'd been accused of being more than once.

Especially next to this solid man who had dug his heels in and stayed, even when it was hard. Even when it seemed like there was no point.

But then, she had no brothers and sisters. She'd had no one to stay and fight for.

What about your friends? Alison?

But then they would have known. They would have known what had happened to her and the simple fact was, she hadn't been able to take the humiliation.

She'd lost her spleen and her family, so it had seemed a bit much to also lose her pride by letting everyone know that her dad had beaten the shit out of her and her mother had sided with him.

No, thank you. Internal bleeding was enough.

Man, what a massively horrible train of thought that was. She was done with it in three, two…

"I think it's amazing you did what you set out to do," she said.

"And what about you?" he asked.

Well, darn. She wasn't in the market to talk about her.

"What about me?"

"Did you always want to be a therapist?"

"No," she said. "I'm not even sure I wanted to be one when I was one. Which is why I typically did other things on the side. Painting, working part-time in coffeehouses, that kind of thing."

"Then why did you do it?"

"I was able to get financial aid for school with the help of a guidance counselor." That counselor and Jenny, her therapist, were the only two people she'd ever talked to about her dad. "And then from there it was recommended I see a therapist. And it was part of being a student at the school, so I went. Jenny listened to me. It made me feel good. I realized that having someone to listen was important."

She'd never spoken with honesty before. Not even to her high school friends. They'd spoken in veiled terms about how bad it was. Some had unexplained bruises. Some had drugs they'd stolen from their parents' dresser drawers. They were all escaping, supporting each other, but none of them had ever wanted to detail what their home life was like. If they spent their time away doing that, what was the point of leaving?

She cleared her throat. "Anyway, it was different

with Jenny. She made me feel like my words had value. Like I mattered. Like my experiences mattered and like I'd solved something by talking about them. I wanted to do that. And I had to choose a course of study so… I ended up getting a master's in social work. I figured I would find a way to help people."

"And you chose crisis counseling."

"That's partly because I move so often. It makes more sense for me to work with people who are dealing with a sudden, isolated event, rather than people who need long-term care. I like to help people. But it's not an easy job. I mean, people in crisis are…well, they're in crisis. And hearing about those problems isn't always the most fun." She drummed her fingers on the door handle. "Though I imagine I'm preaching to the choir."

"Yeah," he said. "Law enforcement isn't all locking up bad guys and being the hero. It's a whole lot of sad reality."

"Reality is lame. It's basically my least favorite."

"Too bad there's so much of it around."

"Man, I feel like you *get* me," she said, laughing and letting her head fall back against the seat. She was happy being with him. And she didn't want to examine that too closely.

"We're going to park up here," he said.

She sat up straighter, her heart thundering. "And make out?"

"And wait for speeding cars to go by."

"Uh. Boo. I like mine better."

"This," he said, waving his hand between them, "has to stay in your bedroom."

"Then why did you meet me for coffee?"

"Why did you meet me?" he asked, pulling over and turning to look at her.

"Because it seems like I should know you a little. And that we should talk without fighting. If we're going to sleep together."

"I thought the same thing."

"Well, so then this makes sense," she said, biting her lip.

"Yep."

"And we're not making out in the patrol car."

"No," he said. "Please tell me you aren't a badge bunny."

"A badge bunny?" She turned to face him. "Is that a thing? Tell me that is not a thing."

"It's a thing."

"Wow. You sound so regretful about it. It's like a badge-related groupie, right?"

"Yes, yes, it is."

"And you don't sound thrilled."

He let out a sigh. "It's weird. I'm not a rock star or anything. Women who are hyper into the whole uniform thing...it's weird."

"Most guys wouldn't question it."

"Jack wouldn't. Jack doesn't," Eli said. "The other bunny we get is the buckle bunny. They like cowboys. They go after Jack and Connor."

"Connor obviously doesn't go back."

"No. He was never much of a player. And he's less of one now. Jack, on the other hand..."

"That's your friend. The one I met briefly the night I burst the pipes. And he was with you in the bar, too, right?"

"Yeah. That's him. He's more like a degenerate brother. But he's never taken anything half as seriously as Connor or I do. Which is probably why he's happier."

"If more sex is equal to more happiness, then sure. Though you should be bucking up by now."

"We've only had sex twice," he said.

"We probably could have doubled that if you would have stuck around for a while last night."

"Not the best time to have this conversation."

"Well, just don't go scuttling off into the cold tonight and you're likely to get a little more action."

He cleared his throat. "I didn't want to assume."

"Oh, I can go all night, buddy," she said. Which wasn't a theory she'd tested. Because usually one and done for the evening was fine with her. One orgasm basically put her under the table. She was a sexual lightweight in that way.

"Good to know," he said, sounding a little strained.

She liked that she could affect him this way. Because he was so solid. So stoic and serious and *good*. She liked that a little naughtiness got him hot under the uniform collar. And clip-on tie.

"So now we wait in semi-camouflage," she mused, looking into the woods on the passenger side of the car, "for an unsuspecting speeder to go by?"

"Basically," he said.

"I'm drunk with power," she said. "And I don't even have ticket-writing powers. How the hell do you do this without succumbing to the urge to abuse your authority?" She wiggled her eyebrows.

"Humorless response coming, beware."

"I expected nothing less," she said, rolling her eyes.

"If I abused my power, my entire reason for wanting it wouldn't be the same. I want to fix things, remember?"

"So you're not going to go breaking them further."

"Not exactly."

The radio buzzed and Eli held up his hand, putting his hand on the black button. A woman's voice filled the car, along with a decent amount of feedback. "Disturbance at Oak and Scotchbroom. Suspect appears to be unarmed but is threatening diner patrons."

"Copy. En route."

He put his hand back on the shifter and put the car in Drive, flipping a U-turn before turning on the lights and heading back toward town. "More than you bargained for?" he asked.

"Yes," she said, hanging on to the door handle. "The diner."

"Yep."

"We would have been meeting up even if I hadn't gone with you," she said, suddenly very glad she was on this end of the call, and not the other. Because men—violent men—did scare her. There was a place down in her soul that went cold when she saw violence in a man's eyes. That same part curled up in a ball and cried like a little girl getting kicked, over and over again, by her father.

A memory that was never buried as deep as she wished it were.

Suddenly she felt tense. Tense and transparent. He would know that she was afraid. That heading toward whatever was happening was like walking back into a fractured memory she never wanted to revisit.

Calm the hell down, Sadie. It's a man creating a disturbance and you're with a man who has a gun.

She took a deep breath and let her internal pep talk bolster her a little.

"Everything will be okay, right?" she asked, in spite of herself, looking over at him.

"I have a 100 percent success rate on making it

through the day. I don't expect today to be any different."

She didn't argue with him about how everyone on earth had the same success rate he did, right up until they didn't. Because it was too nice to hear him say that. Too encouraging. And it made her warm all the way through. Banished that ice-cold fear. And for now she was going to let it, because it was so much better than being afraid.

They entered the town and her tension rose, metallic fear flooding her mouth, like her internal thermometer had broken, poisoning her with a wave of mercury. Or possibly she was being overdramatic. Hard to tell, what with the fact that she was panicking.

He pulled into the lot of the diner and she saw a group of men standing in the parking lot, and Alison on the fringes, wringing her hands.

"Stay in the car," Eli said.

"But Alison—"

"Stay. In. The. Car," he repeated, his words terse as he got out, his hand resting on the top of his gun.

ELI SURVEYED THE CROWD, assessing exactly what was happening. It was what he suspected—a late-morning drunken dispute, which was something that shouldn't happen, but did—and he doubted anyone's life was in danger today.

But then, those kinds of thoughts got people killed, and he well knew it, which meant his hand was staying on his gun. He didn't want to come in looking like a threat, but he wasn't going to be passive, either.

He knew these guys. Loggers mainly, and unsurprisingly, at the center, Alison's husband, Jared. He was the

drunk one from the looks of things, and the one causing trouble.

"What's going on here?" he asked, walking over to
the knot of men.

"Jared being an asshole," said Randy, a middle-aged
man with a long beard and a tobacco habit that had
taken a toll on his teeth.

"Typical day, then," Mark, a fisherman, added.

"I'm just defending what's mine," Jared growled, his
expression mutinous and unfocused.

"Jared..." Alison said.

"Shut up. Shut the fuck up," Jared spat in his wife's
direction. "I wouldn't have to be down here if you
weren't acting like a slut. So shut your whore mouth."

Eli let out a long slow breath. Because otherwise he
would be tempted to get violent. And that wasn't what
he was here for. But the temptation to move in and shut
Jared's mouth with his fist was a lot stronger than he'd
expected.

"There's no need to talk like that," he said, his tone
hard.

"Free speech, Deputy," he said.

"We could take a vote on whether or not we like your
kind of speech," Bud, not the one from the gas station,
said. "I, for one, would cast my vote with my fist."

"That's enough," Eli said. "Is anyone hurt?"

He looked around the group. There was no blood
or visible bruising. But there was no way he could say
there was no harm done. Alison was ashen. Terrified.
And it churned his gut.

"Is anyone wanting to press charges?" he asked.

"Nah," Mark said. "No one got hurt."

Dammit.

He could escort Jared home, but that was about it.

State laws regarding public drunkenness were essentially nonexistent. A public health concern, not a misdemeanor. And given that no punches had been thrown, he was back at sending Jared back to his house, where Alison would be later. And that gave him no small amount of concern.

"Jared, I'm going to make sure you get home okay."

"No, thank you, Deputy," he spat.

"Oh, well, see, that's not your choice. Get in on your own, or get in in handcuffs." He turned back to his car and opened the passenger door. "Out, Sadie, I have to make a delivery, and I'd rather you weren't with me."

She looked at him with big worried eyes and it made something in his chest twist. She'd been afraid on the way to this call, and he'd dismissed it as normal, civilian fear, but right now he had a feeling it was something different.

Especially when she got out of the car without argument and headed to the side, not approaching the crowd.

"Stay here and eat pie, I'll be back for you," he said.

"I… I could walk to my car."

"Wait for me," he said. "You'll be fine."

He looked pointedly at Jared, who chose that moment to obey him. "Backseat," Eli said, then he walked over to Alison. "Call me," he said. "Call someone if he gives you any trouble, do you understand me?"

She shook her head. "He doesn't."

"You're lying to me," Eli said, his voice low and soft.

"I'm not." She met his gaze, her brown eyes defiant.

And he wanted to punch something again. A wall. Jared's face. Why did she protect him? Why did they always protect them?

"Well, even so…" He reached into his jacket and took out his card. "Call me."

He walked back to the patrol car, back to his drunken, asshole backseat tenant. He would drive Jared home. The guy would sober up for a while. And the cycle would go on and on.

He knew it would. It was what he saw in a town this size, over and over.

Times like this he could understand why Sadie didn't stay.

CHAPTER TWELVE

SADIE SAT IN the booth, a cup of coffee and a piece of pie in front of her. The fishermen were back in their corner booth, and Alison was pacing behind the counter.

She took a bite of the lemon meringue. "It really is good pie," she said, loud enough for Alison to hear.

Alison tried to smile. "Thank you."

"Could I get more coffee?" She didn't need more coffee, but she needed Alison to come to where she was sitting, and to stop hiding.

So yeah, this wasn't her favorite thing, but obviously she wasn't avoiding Alison, or the facts about Alison's life today. Fate had handily intervened even when she was trying to jump ship.

She felt a little like Jonah. Thrown overboard, swallowed by a giant fish and vomited into the diner, the very diner she'd been avoiding. Yes, it was an analogy of Biblical proportions, but appropriate, she felt.

Alison walked across the diner and looked into Sadie's full cup.

"Just kidding. I lied. Sit down."

"I'm working," Alison said.

"Yeah, and I'm eating pie. Sit."

Alison did, her hands folded tightly in her lap, the carafe placed in front of her on the table.

"So, hi," Sadie said. "It's been a while. Or since last week. But you know."

"Yeah," Alison said.

"I feel… I feel like I should apologize."

Alison looked startled by that.

"For dropping off the earth after high school. For never calling. For never coming back. Because we were a team, in some ways. We laughed together, and I don't think we laughed very much when we were apart. You spent all those years sticking by me. All of you did. Josh Grayson was my first kiss. Hell, my first…everything. And I just left you all. Without looking back. I had to leave… I had to. But I should have thought of you."

"Sadie…we never knew what happened to you really. Your mom just said you'd run off. And…"

"You believed her because I used to say I would," Sadie finished. "And I did run off. It's true. I mean, I ran off to college. And a career and things. It's not like I was pole dancing, not that there's anything wrong with that. It's just…the long and the short of it is, I ran."

"We missed you," Alison said.

She looked so tired and sad. A sharp contrast to the Alison whom Sadie remembered. A girl in black clothes, with a fierce light of determination in her eyes.

A girl who'd looked ready to fight.

The fight was gone from her now. Drained out of her slowly over the years. Years when Sadie had been gone.

But if Sadie had stayed…the same thing might have happened to her. She and Alison had started out in the same place. A couple of teenage girls who'd never had innocence. Who'd always seen the hard, ugly side of life. Neither of them had illusions about love.

And still Alison had ended up with that man. Sadie was very aware that it could very well have been her sitting there, sad-eyed and defeated.

Sadie sucked in a sharp breath, feeling like something had cracked in her chest. "I... I didn't expect to be missed."

"I don't think any of us would have," Alison said.

"That's a problem," Sadie said. "It's not...healthy, that's for sure. So... Josh left?"

"Yeah, he's doing business somewhere. Washington first, and I haven't heard anything about him in a while."

"Hmm." Sadie allowed herself a brief, nice memory of him. He'd been hot, at least in her teenage estimation. But the memory of him didn't make her shiver or anything. Not like Eli.

"You stayed," she said, turning her focus back to Alison.

"I thought about leaving, but my mom's health wasn't good. Then right after she died, I met Jared."

"Ah, yes," Sadie said, the ache in her chest inverting, splintering and sinking down to her stomach. "I believe I met him today."

Alison cleared her throat and looked determinedly at the carafe. "I know it looks bad."

"It is bad," Sadie said. "Don't BS me. I'm a therapist by trade, when I'm not renovating bed-and-breakfasts. I see women who have come out of abusive relationships all the time. I see men who are afraid they might be abusers. And more than that, I lived with a man who solved problems with violence for my entire childhood. So, I repeat, do not BS me. I am the wrong person to try that on."

"He's not that bad."

"We can skip that part. We can skip the part where you tell me why you make him do it. And he's a good guy. And his past was hard. Because I've heard it. Just... five months ago maybe, I saw a woman who was in the hospital. Recovering from the wounds her husband had inflicted on her. I've seen where it ends, Alison. Unless you make the decision to leave."

Alison grabbed the napkin to her left and started twisting it, her hands shaking.

"I'm not talking to you as a therapist," Sadie said. "I'm talking to you as an old friend. As someone who knew you before him. You're not the only one. And you don't have to be embarrassed."

"I don't have to be embarrassed?" Alison asked. "I think I do, actually. Because…because I think you have to be pretty stupid to get pulled into something like this."

"That's not true," she said. "It's not. It doesn't matter how smart you are. It's not your brain making these decisions. It's your emotions. It's the things he's done to you. The things he's told you. The stuff he's twisted all up so slowly over the years you barely realized what was happening."

The other woman shook her head. "It's too late for me," she said. "I don't have anyone else. I don't have anything else. Just this job. And that man."

"Then get more," Sadie said, frustration burning through her. "Want more."

Alison stood up. "I don't remember how. Coffee and pie are on me. Thank you," she said. "Just…thank you."

Alison turned, slight shoulders hunched, and walked back to the counter, just as Eli walked through the door.

Sadie stood, not having any of the appetite to finish her pie, even if it was free pie, and walked toward him, shepherding him back out the door before he could ask why.

"Did you get him home?" she asked, barely meeting Eli's eyes when they were out in the parking lot.

"Yeah," Eli said. "Do you see what it's like?"

"He deserved to be hit. He deserved to have his head shoved into the pavement."

"Yeah, and I can't do that, Sadie. The minute I act like I can, I'm not a whole lot better than he is. Because I have authority and I have to be careful never to abuse that. But I might have let Mark and the other guys off with a warning if they would have done it. Or if someone would have…said anything."

"Given you a reason to arrest him," she said.

"That's the problem with situations like this," Eli said, putting his hands on his lean hips and looking back toward the diner. "She's an adult. I can't drag her out of that house any more than I can put handcuffs on him for something I suspect but have never seen." He turned and hit the top of his patrol car with his open palm, a rough growl escaping his lips. "Sometimes the more power you have the less powerful you feel."

"She won't… I tried to talk to her," Sadie said. "But…"

"I know." He took a deep breath. "Listen, I'm on for a while longer. I'll take you to your car."

"Okay. We'll see each other tonight?"

He nodded slowly. "Yeah. I think I need to."

SHE WASN'T LESS nervous than she'd been the night before. If anything, she was more nervous. Because now she knew for a fact the intensity between Eli and herself wasn't a fluke.

Because she was kind of going all in tonight, knowing full well what she was getting herself into. It was a dangerous game and she liked it. That surprised her more than anything.

But today had been beyond upsetting and she was

looking forward to something just as strong to help take away some of the unsettled feelings that remained.

At least for a while.

You can't fix things for people when they don't want them fixed.

She'd reminded herself of that countless times over the years. Every time she hadn't called her mother. Checked in on her to see if her father was still ruling the house with a fist of iron. Because she'd tried to help. And her mother had chosen to stay. Her mother had chosen the man who'd put her daughter in the hospital. So Sadie had accepted that she couldn't change things for her mom and had set about changing them for herself.

She was going to have to let this go, too. Even though it sucked. It was a lot harder when you couldn't physically let it go by driving into another city and never looking back.

"Bah." She stalked into the kitchen and hauled herself up onto the counter, her knees planted firmly on the granite surface as she rummaged through one of the cabinets for a bottle of wine. Probably she would have to get a real fancy-ass wine rack for when guests were here. Luckily, she had a little time.

She took two glasses down, along with the wine, because in all honesty, Eli probably needed a drink, too.

She wondered if he would get more relaxed if he had a glass or two. If she could get him to smile. If his lips would taste like merlot and sin and the *smile* that was the rarest thing she could think of.

She licked her own lips in anticipation and carried the objects she now considered her fantasy aids into the living room.

She was still in the same clothes she'd been wearing earlier—sad for Eli, no matching bra and panties for him today. But after the incident at the diner, she'd thrown herself into B and B things, including looking at website proofs, which were fan-freaking-tastic, and choosing the stain for her deck, which was very nearly done because a whole team of burly men could handle decks like no one's business.

She hummed as she set the glasses on the old-fashioned captain's trunk she was using for a coffee table and sat on the couch, her feet tucked up under her.

And for one heart-crinkling moment she really wanted Eli to just come and sit next to her. To release his stress while she let go of hers. To share in a calm moment.

She blinked. No. That wasn't what this was about. It wasn't supposed to be about sharing emotions. It was supposed to be about sharing nakedness and orgasms.

The heavy knock on her front door saved her from her thoughts. "It's open!" she shouted.

She heard the door open, then close, the heavy shoes on the wood floor, and finally Eli appeared in the living room entryway.

"Hiya," she said, surveying his tall, lean frame. He'd changed. Dark jeans conforming to muscular thighs, a tight black T-shirt giving hints of all the fun that lay beneath the fabric.

"Hi," he said.

"You can come in," she said, patting the empty spot beside her.

"Right." He cast a long look at a sleeping Toby, who was in the chair he'd claimed as his own, before walking across the room and joining her on the couch, keeping a healthy distance between them.

"Wine?" she asked.

"I don't really care for it."

Well, dammit. There went her merlot-flavored fantasy. She'd just drink enough for both of them. "Well, I hope you don't mind if I drink," she said, tugging the already-popped cork out. She poured herself a generous amount, then picked the glass up and clinked the edge against the empty one still sitting on the trunk. "Cheers to me, then." She took a sip and sat back, feeling distinctly broody now. Because she'd gotten a picture in her head that shouldn't have been there, and now she was disappointed for him not conforming to said ill-advised picture.

"Are you mad at me now?" he asked.

She looked up over her glass and at him, at serious brown eyes that made her stomach do tricks. "A little."

"Why?" he asked, the corners of his mouth turning up.

There was her smile. A small one, but she'd gotten it. "Because you were supposed to drink wine and be cozy with me."

"That doesn't sound like what we agreed on," he said, his tone gentle. Why was he being so nice? She was trying to be peeved.

"No, I know it doesn't. But I was sort of hoping for it. Because I am a fickle and difficult creature."

"Yeah, you are."

"You weren't supposed to agree so readily."

"Sadie," he said, his dark eyes burning hotter now. He reached out and gently touched her glass, lowering it. "You know what this is."

"I know," she said. "You don't need to worry about me."

"Then why are you angry?"

"Because," she said, setting her wineglass down on

the trunk and standing, moving over to where Eli sat and standing in front of him, "I had a little fantasy."

"Did you?" he asked, his focus sharpening.

"Mmm-hmm." She put her knee on the couch, next to his thigh, and then the other one, straddling his lap. "It had to do with getting you to relax a little."

"This is not the way to relax me," he said, putting his hands on her hips. "You realize that, right?"

"I was going to relax you," she said. "Lick the wine flavor off your lips." She leaned in and traced the outline of his top lip with the tip of her tongue. "But I have to say you taste pretty good all on your own."

He took a deep breath, his hold on her tightening, his head falling back. "You're dangerous. Do you know that?"

"I've never been accused of being dangerous." She planted her hands on his chest and leaned forward, kissing him hard. "Flaky. Fun. Fluttery. Lots of *F* words, none too naughty. Never dangerous."

"Then the men you've been with before were blind."

"Or maybe we just didn't have this kind of chemistry. It's definitely a little bit more combustible than the norm."

"True," he said, sliding his hand upward, forking his fingers through her hair, his thumb teasing the edge of her lips. "You still mad at me?"

"Not really," she said.

"Good. Because I didn't come here to fight."

"I'm hoping you came for another one of those *F* words."

"Yep," he said, "and I stand by my original statement. You, Sadie Miller, are dangerous as hell."

"You're not exactly a kitten, Deputy Garrett." She arched her hips forward and gasped as she came into contact with his erection, rock-hard and obviously ready for her.

Really, she was becoming less and less disappointed in the loss of her brief domestic fantasy.

He tightened his hold on her hair and tugged her face down to his, kissing her deep and long. Leaving her gasping for breath. "Not exactly," he said.

Just like that the intensity was back. The need that hit hard like a punch to the stomach and made it hard to breathe. The desire that verged on pain, her core already so slick with need for him, so sensitized, one more calculated move against his cock would send her straight over the edge.

But the releases Eli offered weren't easy. Not a sweet relief like the opening of a flower, they were like going through a storm. And she was charging in willingly, knowing full well how it would be. Knowing that this time might be the time that saw her washed overboard, completely adrift.

It was worth the risk. Every time it was worth the risk.

She kissed him back, bit his lower lip as she tugged his T-shirt up over his head. Then she put her hands on his chest, all that hard, hot muscle for her to explore. Just for her.

"You, too," he growled.

And she hastened to obey, tugging her shirt up over her head, undoing the front clasp on her bra. She leaned forward, a short, sharp sound escaping her lips when her nipples came into contact with all that hot bare skin.

He moved his hands over her back, his touch firm and sure. He touched her with the kind of authority she had no issue with at all.

He tightened his hold on her and picked her up,

switching their positions so that she was lying sideways on the couch, on her back, with him over her, his hands on the snap of his jeans. Heat flooded her face, her body, anticipation coursing along her veins as she waited for him to get his pants off.

She undid her jeans and pushed them and her underwear down her legs. "Come on," she said, "you're going to kill me."

"I don't think you're going to die," he said, leaning in, tracing the outline of her nipple with his tongue.

"Yes," she said, the breath rushing from her lungs, "I really think I might."

"I didn't realize you were so fragile," he said, kissing her lightly on the breast before moving downward, pressing another kiss to her stomach.

"I am not fragile."

"You sure, baby? Another one of those *F* words."

"You turn into such a bad man when your dick is hard," she said, her voice shaky.

"And you like it," he said.

"Hell yes, I like it."

"Then we don't have a problem." He took hold of her leg, his fingertips sliding along her inner thigh, her muscles quivering in response.

"Except the little problem where I die because you won't give me what I want."

"What do you want?" he asked, pressing his lips along the path his fingers had just traced.

"Oh… I… You know."

"You want this," he said, leaning in, hot breath blowing across her clit.

"Oh…yes. Please."

"You're going to have to ask me by name."

"Please, Eli," she said. She wasn't above taking orders. Hell, at this point, she was so desperate for release she wasn't above begging. "Oh, please."

"Please what?"

"Please do...you know."

"You want me to lick you until you scream?"

Heat shot through her, her face burning hot. She was not a prude, but she'd never had a man talk to her like this before, either. And the fact that it was Eli, straight-arrow Eli Garrett who didn't get double entendres and who'd once put her in handcuffs in an un-fun way, made it feel all the more illicit and shocking.

"Eli..."

"Do you?" he asked.

"Yes," she said.

He curved his hands around both of her thighs and tugged her down hard, his lips meeting her tender flesh, his tongue stroking her clit. She threw one arm over the back of the couch, putting the other one on his shoulder as he teased her, as he pushed her, mercilessly, straight over the edge into a climax she wasn't even remotely prepared for.

Pleasure poured through her, threatening to drown her, and all she could do was cling to Eli. Cling to him and hope she survived the storm.

"Turn over," he said, his voice rough.

"What?"

"On your knees, babe," he said.

She sat up and obeyed, resting part of her body against the arm of the couch, her knees pressing into the cushions.

She could hear him getting his wallet out, tearing the condom packet. Her throat was dry, her body throbbing. She could not need to come again this bad less than a minute after that last orgasm. It wasn't even possible.

But it was happening.

She was shaking, she needed him so bad. And shaking with fear because this level of need was terrifying. But she couldn't stop him. Which only made it scarier. Because she didn't want to. She should be running. She should be in her Toyota and halfway to the Washington border. But she was here, bracing herself on the couch, waiting for Eli. Needing Eli.

She didn't have to wait long.

He pushed inside her, and she lowered her head, her forehead pressing against the arm of the couch, the brocade pattern biting into her skin.

He gripped her hips and established a steady rhythm, his hand drifting between her thighs, stroking her clit, making her shiver. She was powerless in this position, at his mercy. And she loved it.

It was so different from the last time they'd been together, when she'd ridden him until they both lost their minds. This was his game. He set the pace, and he had total control. She'd never liked this, submitting to a guy like this. But she liked it with him.

She more than liked it.

He pulled her back against him and increased the intensity, her whole body tightening up, pleasure twisting around her, reaching that unbearable point where she knew something had to give.

He pressed down hard between her thighs, the added pressure the final straw that snapped the tension, sending waves of release pounding through her.

He put both hands on her hips, his fingers digging into her skin as he rode her hard, chasing his own release. He found it on a harsh growl as he stiffened against her, then relaxed, his head resting against the curve of her back.

He moved away from her, her skin prickling in the cool air after he removed his warmth. "I'll be right back," he said.

She lay flat on her stomach, her knees and arms like wilted kale. She tried to catch her breath, to catch a thought, before he came back. So she didn't do something dumb and needy like crawl into his lap and bury her head in his chest.

But she kind of felt dumb and needy. Which was really aggravating.

She pushed herself into a sitting position so that she would look a little less pathetic upon his return.

He walked back into the room, beautifully naked, his eyes most definitely focused on her breasts. "Hi," he said.

"I'm having déjà vu. Except you were wearing clothes last time you walked in and said that."

"So were you."

"Yes, well. Not now."

"Obviously."

"Don't leave," she said, and she could have bitten her tongue off.

"I won't," he said. "Just yet."

"Yeah, that's what I meant. Just not…right now. We could… We could go into the bedroom, and…"

Toby chose that moment to jump onto the floor between them and look at them both, judgment gleaming in his golden cat eyes.

"Oh, you," she said, "go make yourself useful. Catch vermin!"

"You said he didn't catch vermin," Eli said, a smile curving his lips.

"He needs a hobby. One that is not staring at us after we have sex. Over it, cat. I'm over it."

Toby meowed and walked over to Eli, rubbing against his bare legs and winding his tail around his calf. Eli looked pointedly at Sadie, his eyebrows arched.

"He can smell your disdain. It's…well, it's like catnip to him. He feeds off hatred."

"Why do you like him again?"

"Don't take this the wrong way, but I think for reasons similar to the ones I like you for."

He looked back down at the cat, who was winding himself around his ankles, then back at her. "Excuse me?"

"We don't always get along. You can be grumpy. Standoffish. Judge-y as hell. But there is just something about you."

"You're really selling my personality."

"Hey, I know what I like. Grumpy, judgmental cats and…grumpy, judgmental men in uniform."

"I'm not judgmental," he said.

"Sure you're not."

"I'm not."

"You seem upset. Are you going to punish me to the fullest extent of the law?" She wiggled her brows and stood up, her legs wobbling beneath her.

"I might," he said, his voice getting deeper, huskier.

Oh, yes, this was better than the alternative. Desire was better than that other stuff. The intense aftershocks of sex with him. The deep need that it seemed to expose, without ever satisfying it.

"I think it's time for us to go to bed."

And for once, he didn't argue with her.

CHAPTER THIRTEEN

IT WAS EARLY. It was cold. And it was fence repairing time.

All things that, in many ways, Eli found enjoyable. All right, so fence repair wasn't the most fun thing he could think of to do on a Saturday, but it was quiet work. And he and Connor had thermoses of coffee set on the fence posts, their breath putting out bursts of condensation in the cold air, and there was something about it that was familiar. Constant.

Of course, his brain was back in bed with Sadie. He'd gone to her place every night that week. He hadn't slept there any of the nights, but last night he'd stayed until the sky had started to lighten, slept for an hour, and now, here he was out in the field.

It was jarring. To go from this sort of out-of-reality experience with Sadie, in her arms, in her bed. He had the kind of sex with her he'd barely even fantasized about. Because he hadn't thought it was real. Or even a possibility.

What they had was hot, on a level he hadn't known existed. He wasn't used to sex consuming him like this, but he sure as hell wasn't arguing.

But yeah, the transition from there, to sleep, to this had him a little off his game.

"Hand me the wire cutters," Connor said, his voice still rough from sleep.

"Sure," Eli said, reaching out and taking the cutters from the ground, and placing them in Connor's outstretched hand.

"You're quiet this morning," Connor said.

"And you appear to have woken up with an estrogen surge."

"What the hell?" Connor asked.

"Seriously, what was that? 'You're quiet this morning.'" Eli knew he was being a jackass, because he *was* tired, because he'd been up all night having sex. Which he felt kind of smug about, but also which he didn't want his brother to know about. "Only women say crap like that."

"You seem to have woken up on the asshole side of the bed this morning and stepped in a pile of sexist on your way out to the barn," Connor said.

"You make a similar trek every morning. Why should it bother you if I'm trying to speak your language?"

"Because you don't normally. You are normally very well-adjusted, which actually kind of pisses me off, because you're my younger brother and your shit is way more together than mine. In fact, no matter what's going on, it all seems together for you. Which makes me very suspicious of why you're acting this way." Connor straightened and tugged off his glove, leaning against the wooden fence post and picking up his thermos, unscrewing the cap. "Yeah, very suspicious." He poured himself a cup, black, no sugar. "Either you're still mad because you want to screw Sadie, or...oh, no," he said, a smile curving his lips. Eli groaned internally. "No, that's not it. You said you weren't going to sleep with her, so even if you were in full monk vow of celibacy mode you wouldn't be grumpy like this. You did sleep with her. And you're mad because you broke your little vow."

Wrong. He was not mad about sleeping with Sadie. He loved every minute of it. He was, however, more than a little pissed that his brother had guessed so close to the truth.

"Shut up, Connor," he said, reaching for his own thermos and pouring himself a cup, with cream and sugar.

"You did. You slept with her."

"I *am* sleeping with her," he corrected, his tone hard. He hadn't intended to admit it, because it just wasn't Connor's damn business. It felt like something that was just for him and Sadie. And it felt wrong to talk about it. Like it violated what they had. Like it violated her.

"Well," Connor said, pushing his hat back on his forehead. "I did not expect that."

"What?"

"To be right, for you to admit it if I was, and for it to have happened more than once."

"I can't even count how many times it's happened." And there he was putting male ego over decency, which he rarely did, but he was only human.

Connor shook his head and took another sip of his coffee. "For a second, I was jealous of you," he said.

"Only for a second?" Eli asked.

"Yeah, then I remembered how much I don't want to screw with any of that stuff ever again."

Eli let out a long, slow breath. He didn't want to have this conversation with Connor, but they were apparently having it. "You're never going to sleep with anyone again?" he asked.

"Not planning on it." He took another sip of coffee.

"That's not… You're thirty-four years old, Connor. That's not healthy."

"You don't still believe in blue balls, do you?" Connor asked.

"No. Look, I just…" He swallowed. "I don't like to tell you how to deal with this. To deal with Jessie, and the loss of her, because who am I? I've never loved a woman, Connor. I don't plan on ever marrying one. It's just not in the cards for me. But *you* have to move on."

Connor shook his head, his jaw tight. "No, Eli, I don't. I don't have to move on. I don't have to do anything I don't want to do."

"So you're going to be like this forever?"

"Maybe. I run my ranch. I get the work done. What the hell else do I need to do?"

"Be okay?" Eli asked.

Connor laughed. "I'm not okay," he said. "Why should I bother acting like I am?"

Eli looked down. "It's been three years," he said, his tone soft.

"And it was supposed to be a lifetime." Connor put the lid back on his thermos. "When is the appropriate time to get over the loss of your whole life? Answer that question, Deputy."

"I can't," Eli said.

"Yeah, I didn't think so. You don't want to get married."

"Give me one reason why I should," Eli said, leaning forward on the fence, propping his boot up on the bottom slat. "Love comes here to die." It seemed a weird thing to say, with the pine trees in the distance tipped in gold from the sun, and the breeze coming in from the sea, mixing with the scent of earth, trees and livestock. With all these things that made the ranch look like heaven, it was hard to see it for what it was.

But the simple fact was, no one in his family had ever managed to hold on to love. The house, the Catalog House that he was starting to think of as Sadie's, was the original monument to that. A gift for a woman who wouldn't stay.

And on it had gone, all the way to Connor.

No, Eli had no plans to get married. He'd never seen a good reason to want love, and he'd seen plenty of reasons to avoid it.

"Yeah," Connor said. "Sometimes it feels that way. But my point is, you already don't want marriage. With the way things were for Dad after Mom left… I did, and look where it got me? Don't you think I have enough of a reason to not want to get married again?"

"Sure, but not to never have sex again."

"Let me worry about that."

"Yeah, I promise I'll never think about it again. Or ask you about it again."

"Sounds like a plan. So there. You had the talk with me. You said the thing that's been brewing. And I spoke my piece. You can call your brotherly duty done."

"Good," Eli said, but none of it felt good.

"The sex good?" Connor asked.

"What?"

"With Sadie. Is the sex good? Tell me that at least."

"Damn good."

Connor groaned. "Okay, well, we got that out of the way, too. World's most awkward conversation?"

"Very."

"Did you want to talk about religion or politics next?"

"I'll pass," Eli said.

"I guess we just fix the fence and mind our own business, then."

"I'm okay with that."

Eli went back to work, his eyes on the pale blue sky extending above lush green mountains. He tried not to replay the conversation he'd had with Connor. Tried not to remember the bleakness in his brother's eyes. It was everything he'd been afraid was in him, said out loud. That Connor wasn't okay at all.

And he couldn't fix it. Dammit, he hated when he couldn't fix it.

It was like his dad all over again. Watching somebody drown in sorrow, doing their best to manage their addiction until just once…just once you weren't there to stop them. To care for them.

At least Connor wasn't drinking as much as their father used to. But Eli worried. His brother sure as hell drank more now than he had before Jessie's death.

The thought gave him heartburn. More than that, it made him want to get back into Sadie's bed. At least there things were good.

Mind-bendingly good.

There, he didn't think so much about the things he needed to fix that couldn't be fixed. He could just think about himself. Just a hell of a lot more length of fence to fix, some calf vaccinations to deal with, and he'd be back with her.

That would be his happy thought for the day. It was rare he had a happy thought, and no one was more surprised than he was that today Sadie Miller was his.

"THANK YOU FOR COMING, Kate," Sadie said, standing with one hand outstretched, an apron dangling from her fingertips.

Kate looked from side to side. "I see no half-naked deck builders."

"You're not here to ogle, sweetheart. You're here to bake."

Kate crossed her arms beneath her breasts, her dark eyebrows shooting upward. "I am?"

"Yep. We're going to make dinner rolls. I mean, if you want to. I thought we could hang out. And since I'm trying to learn how to get some recipes perfected I thought this might be fun." Sadie really hoped this might be Kate's idea of fun. Otherwise she feared hanging out with Kate might involve intensive horseback riding, or something equally outdoorsy. Not that Sadie was opposed. She just needed to work up to it.

Much to her relief, Kate brightened and took the apron. "Sounds great." She started putting the apron on. "Not that I really need to protect my clothes," she said, indicating her plain white T-shirt and high-waisted jeans.

"Better than wearing flour for the rest of the day."

Sadie started getting out mixing bowls and ingredients while Kate stood in the center of the kitchen, obviously slightly out of place in the environment.

"Let me guess," Sadie said. "You don't have much cooking experience."

"Not really. Eli's always done that. Throw meat on the grill, bring home pizza or whatever. Why are you cooking rolls for a bed-and-breakfast?"

"Well, I have to eat so I thought I would offer additional meals for an additional price a few days a week," Sadie said. "Anyway, I like cooking."

"Oh." Kate moved in closer and stood at the counter. "You sound surprised."

"Eli never seemed to like it. But, I mean, he did it. And his food is edible. Unlike Connor's…"

"So Eli did all the cooking for you guys?" Sadie asked, unbearably curious and slightly guilty. She should not be interrogating Kate about her brother. Especially because Kate's brother was her secret lover. And if Kate knew that Sadie and Eli were sleeping together, she would probably make a horror face and run screaming from the room and never speak to Sadie again.

And thus, Sadie would lose one of the very few friends she had.

"Yeah. He did. Connor kept the money coming in, and, I mean, Lord knows that was important, but… Eli was the one who made sure I was ready for school. He learned to braid my hair," she said, her hand going to the hairstyle she still wore.

Sadie's stomach squeezed tight, her eyes stinging. Eli's strength was sexy, no question, but this? This was even sexier. It was a part of the strength, really. A part that most people wouldn't see.

Braiding a little girl's hair.

Sadie saw it, though. An older brother, a teenager, getting his little sister ready for school. Cooking meals. All things that would never be public, but that had shaped Kate into the woman she was.

Eli was all that had stood between Kate growing up to feel safe and secure…and growing up feeling like Sadie had. Like no one cared. Like she was better off cutting ties and leaving parents who didn't want her anyway.

It was Eli who'd protected Kate's trust. Her openness. Eli who'd given her her strength.

Sadie couldn't help but be envious. And she realized

then that the little fascination she'd had for him when she was a teenager hadn't been about a bad girl wanting a cop. It had been about wanting a man with that kind of strength to protect her. Care for her.

Well, he didn't. No one did. Deal with it.

"That's...really sweet," she said, grabbing a measuring cup and pushing it down into the flour bag, a white cloud rising up around them.

Kate smiled. "Well, don't let him hear you say that. But then, if he's still avoiding you, that shouldn't be a problem."

Sadie felt a twinge of guilt, which made a sucky companion to the envy. "Yeah," she said. "Not sure when I'll see him again. So, let's make rolls."

"POTATO SACK RACING."

"Lame," he said, lying back on the bed, keeping his focus on Sadie, who was sitting next to him, completely naked, her hair tumbling over her shoulders.

"It is not lame. Not for kids."

"Three-legged race is better."

"Unless you have to run with a boy who is stupid, doesn't listen and stinks."

"But what if you get to run with the cute girl that you have a crush on?" he asked, leaning in and kissing her shoulder.

"Did you have crushes?" she asked, cocking her head to the side.

"Sure, didn't everyone?"

"I don't know. Sometimes I kind of picture you like you sprang out of the ground wearing your uniform and a frown."

"Your flattery is almost embarrassing."

"Sorry if it didn't sound complimentary," she said.

"I wouldn't be here if I didn't like you. Scratch that, I would be here, you wouldn't be. And I would be alone."

"Well, I wasn't born in uniform."

"And I wasn't born running," she said, smiling faintly.

"Life has a lot to answer for."

"Sure does."

She flopped backward, raising her arms above her head, and his eyes fell to the little silver scar on her side. A surgical scar. Sometimes he wanted to ask her about it, but ultimately, her medical history wasn't really his business. So he didn't ask.

"Where are you at on your big barbecue plans in terms of booths? We'll put three-legged races to the side for now," he said, shifting so that he was lying on his side.

"I've got pony rides. Cookie decorating, face painting. John from the Farm and Garden is going to bring over one of those mini-sheds that looks like a playhouse for the kids. And the pie eating. There will be pie eating."

She ran her fingers through her hair and the temptation for him to do the same was too much. He wanted to pull her close. Play with the silky blond strands. Braid it. Which was not something he'd ever done for his lovers, but something about the idea appealed to him.

He wanted to take care of her.

He wrapped his hand around her hair, about to separate it into three separate sections, but she turned her head. He dropped his hands back down to his sides, the strange tightness in his chest dissipating a little.

He'd had a moment of temporary insanity. Sadie was good at doing that to him.

"What are you going to do about Alison?" he asked.

"Nothing," she said, chewing her lip. "What can I do? I can buy pie from her. Hope she feels proud of her accomplishment. Hope she wants something different for herself, but really, there is nothing else I can do."

He moved his hand over her breast, down over her stomach, his conscience tugging at him. "I told Connor," he said.

"About Alison?" she asked, frowning.

"About you and me."

She sat up, blinking. "Why?"

A damn good question. A weird impulse, as weird as the one he'd just had to braid her hair.

"I just… He sort of asked. Well, he tried guessing. He guessed I slept with you once, and I…corrected him. I'm not a very good liar."

She leaned forward, covering her mouth, a giggle trapped behind it. "Oh, my gosh. No, I bet you aren't." She looked down at him, her hair sliding over her shoulders, over her breasts, covering pale pink nipples. She was such a tempting picture. Naughtier because she was smiling, because she was covered. He wanted her again. So soon. And it didn't even shock him anymore. "You're way too straitlaced."

"I'm straitlaced?" he asked.

"Yeah, you kind of are."

He pushed her onto her back and she shrieked, then he kissed her neck, feeling her pulse quicken beneath his lips. "How many straitlaced men do you know who can make you come so hard?"

He never talked to his lovers like this. Ever. Hell, he never really talked in bed at all. But she brought it out in him. He didn't worry. He didn't overthink. He told her what he wanted. And she loved it. And that did things to him. Things he hadn't known he wanted to have done to him.

In truth, he'd never been this consumed by sex. Because his mind was always somewhere else. Because taking care of things was still in the forefront, but here, there wasn't room for anyone but her and him.

"None. But then, I think this might be colored by the fact that I haven't exactly tested the sexual prowess of every straitlaced man I've known."

"Fair point."

"I like that you don't lie," she said, her blue eyes on his. "I like that when I look at you, I feel like I really see *you*. Not just the man you want the world to see."

That made him feel a little guilty. Since, in so many ways, he felt like he did just put on a good front. The man who seemed unruffled on the surface, hiding the festering pool of worry beneath. The gut-churning terror all the responsibility he took on built in him.

"Sadie…"

"No. If you're going to tell me you have secrets, just don't. Because I want to think I know. What's the harm in thinking that for now? It's not like this is forever."

"No," he said. "It's not."

For some reason, her words and the agreement made his chest feel like it was full of lead.

"So let's have the fantasy. You be the straitlaced badass who rocks my world. I'll be comfortable here with you, trusting you. All well-adjusted and stuff." She smiled and kissed his chin, wrapped her legs around his calves.

"Are you saying you aren't well-adjusted?"

"Shh. In the fantasy, I am."

"Are you drunk?"

"A little," she said. "You won't share the wine with

me so it's not my fault I have to drink more than normal."

"Connor won't tell anyone," he said. He was sure of that. Because the information Connor had given in exchange was too precious. Connor wouldn't want anyone to know how bad he was hurting. How hopeless he felt.

Eli didn't even really want to know, but he did. And now he had to try to fix it. Make it right.

He could never escape that feeling.

He pushed it aside, though, because Sadie was beneath him, and devoting everything to that sensation was, right now, more important.

"It's for the best. We don't need everyone all up in our business. And besides, Lydia is a good ally. She keeps the Chamber of Commerce on my side. And I have a feeling she might cut me if she knew I was sleeping with you."

"Really?"

"She's very smiley. I find that concerning."

"Maybe she's friendly."

"Maybe," Sadie said. "You are just something else."

"Am I?"

"How have you seen so much of the crap you have, and still… How are you so good, Eli Garrett?"

"I have to be," he said, the words slipping out before he had a chance to think them through.

"Why?" she asked, pushing his hair off his forehead.

"If I'm not…who will be?"

"Not enough people," she said.

"You are," he said.

"Me? You mean me, who runs away from everything and everyone?"

"I should never have said that to you. I'm sorry." Regret tightened his stomach.

She shook her head. "You weren't wrong. And the more I see you here, the more I realize how much harder it is to deal with people when you have to watch them not learn. And not listen."

"Regardless, it doesn't mean that you haven't helped people. You listen to people."

"For money," she said.

"So? Some people would pay to *not* listen to people's problems."

She laughed. "Okay, so maybe we're both okay?"

"Sure. We're both okay."

"Right now anyway." She arched against him, sending a shock of pleasure down his spine.

"Right now I'm more than okay."

SADIE CLOSED HER laptop and looked out the window at the row of buildings across the street. The sky was bright blue, clear, the breeze pushing waves over the American flag that rose up from the two-story restaurant behind the main street, just off the harbor. She imagined it was creating matching waves on the sea beyond the buildings, too.

She'd managed to touch base with Alison, awkwardly, about the pies and confirmed that she would make some for the contest and sell some in the booth. But it didn't really make her feel much better about the situation as a whole.

She'd spent most of the day in the coffee shop approving the mock-up of the B and B's website. She'd ventured out briefly to go to the Wagon Wheel, a local home store, and special order curtains for the house, and some quilts. Then she'd stopped in at the glass studio Brooke, her old friend from school, now owned.

Brooke's life seemed to be going better than Alison's.

So that was a comfort at least. She'd been enthusiastic about the barbecue and had asked for brochures for it, and for the B and B, to put in her shop. They'd parted with plans to do lunch, and unlike most times vague lunch plans were made, Sadie had a feeling they really would get together.

She tapped her fingers across the top of the computer. Eli was off today. Well, working on the ranch. Putting in his part-time cowboy hours. Which was his definition of a day off. And she'd decided to leave the ranch and come to town because it was better and less embarrassing than hanging out and hoping to catch glimpses of him walking around all sweaty and sexy and *everything* that a man should be.

Yeah, she needed an Eli hiatus. Which was why she'd asked Kate to drop her off at the coffee shop this morning, so she could do all her online work for the B and B from a remote location.

She wouldn't be taking a hiatus from him at night, of course, because heaven knew how many nights they had left together. And she would not be skipping a single night of orgasmic bliss. Apparently, pleasure was the price she'd willingly pay for her sanity. And she couldn't even be bothered to feel bad about it.

Nope. All she felt was pleasantly aroused, thank you very much.

But the issue with being around him all day was that he made things other than her lady parts fluttery. He made her chest area feel fluttery. And that was not something that needed to be indulged.

In fact, quite the opposite.

It was harder still after nights like last night. Where they'd sort of wound around each other, naked, and talked, and laughed. And he'd told Connor about them.

That had made her breath hitch. Made all the questions about what that could possibly mean float to the forefront of her brain. The logical part of her knew it meant that he was too honest to lie to Connor. But then there was this weird, previously dormant girlie part of her that seemed to want to pull it apart further to assign labels and meaning to every little piece and part of what he'd said.

This was not a good time to get all freaky about that stuff. Well, okay, there was never a time for that. She sighed and stood up, tucking her laptop into her purse, chucking her cup into the trash can and waving at Baby Barista Number One before stepping outside.

She shook her head and lifted her face toward the sun, taking a deep breath before crossing the street and cutting through two buildings on her way down to the wharf.

The water was a deep gray blue, pitching and rolling against the rocks on the jetty. She turned and looked down toward the bar, and saw a patrol car, parked across the narrow street in the do-it-yourself car wash.

"He's at the ranch," she said to herself. "And not on duty, so that isn't him." She was already walking toward the car, her internal commentary not doing anything at all to deter her.

She got closer, and her view shifted, and then she saw him. In blue jeans and a T-shirt, washing the patrol car in one of those do-it-yourself car wash spots. It was like some sort of fantasy delivered to her at a very unexpected time.

All that was left was for him to spray his chest with the water so the shirt stuck to his muscles...

"Hello, stranger," she said, feeling like a total dork the moment it left her mouth. "I mean, hi, Eli." She knew the amendment hadn't done much to cover up the original silliness, but oh well.

His eyebrows shot up. "What are you doing here?"

"I am a hallucination," she said. "Your subconscious mind brought me to you."

"Oh, really?" he asked.

"Yes. Don't you want to know what I mean?"

"I suppose you're going to tell me."

"I mean that you're extremely—" she wiggled her brows "—randy. And you're feeling sexually frustrated. Taking it out on your car, too. Wax on, wax off. Very suggestive."

"Is that all, hallucination Sadie?"

"No. I'm also here to warn you. You're in graaaave danger."

"Is that all?"

"And I would like a sandwich?"

"Do you evaporate soon?" he asked.

"Nope." She approached the car and him, her heartbeat speeding up a bit when she got near him. "Because I'm real. Surprise."

He smiled then, and her heart did a full turn in her chest. "In that case, what are you doing here?"

"I was in town working. Your sister dropped me off."

"Are you ready to head back?"

"Sure. Are there sandwiches?"

"There could be sandwiches," he said.

"What kind?"

"Get in the car."

There was something about that authoritative tone that made her shiver all the way down to her toes. He was magic like that.

"Only because you asked so nicely." She opened the

door and got in, and he did the same. "So, you wash your car on your days off?"

"Yes," he said. "It's either that or leave for shift early, or leave late. And I keep the car parked at the house, so it gets a lot of stuff dropped onto it from the trees."

"You are so cute," she said.

"I'm not sure how I feel about that."

"What? I like that you don't lie and you take care of your things. My gosh, except for your lack of inhibition in bed, you're like a flashback to a black-and-white film."

"And what is my lack of inhibition like?"

"A flashback to spam emails often found in my inbox. But, like, in a good way."

He smiled, started the car engine and pulled forward through the car wash, and around, out toward the street. "I haven't really been to the beach since I've been back," she said, looking out at the ocean.

"Do you want to go?"

"Eh. Sand has its place. It also gets in *places*, so there's that."

He snorted. "What the hell sort of things do you do on the beach?"

"Not *that*. *That* we saved for the woods. It's more private. Actually most of my teenage shenanigans were saved for the woods. We conducted very few on the beaches."

"Likely why you got away with them. Especially back when I worked nights, I did a lot of drive-by spotlighting on the beaches."

"Oh, man, that would have been awkward."

They needed to change the conversation topic since she was starting to get a bit hot around the shirt collar talking sex with him in an enclosed space.

Something about the car turned her on. And granted, she'd been existing in a perpetual state of arousal since Eli had first kissed her, but this was different. It had an edge to it. Maybe it was the fact that, while she was sure it wasn't this exact car, he'd put her in the backseat of one very similar to it ten years ago, her hands in cuffs.

And maybe it had something to do with the fact that the memory had morphed into something sexy since she'd begun sleeping with him.

Strange, since before it had been such a horrible one. Not because of what he'd done, but because of what had happened after.

Something about the car fantasy seemed like a reclamation of that night. And maybe that was assigning too high of a purpose to her sexual fantasies, but she kind of liked it.

"So you've never had sex in your car?" So much for changing the subject.

He whipped his head to the side to look at her. "What? That's…random."

"Not really. We were talking about my sex life…in the woods, not on the beach, thanks. And I was wondering about you."

"No. That's edging into… Like I was saying, I was with a woman once who was a badge bunny. Which was fine in some ways, but in others got really weird. And…no, I haven't."

"So it only seems *weird* to you?" she asked, biting her lip, feeling disappointed. "Not even a little hot?"

"I feel like you're leading me somewhere."

"I want you to do it with me in the back of your car."

He applied the brakes, hard, sending her jerking forward, the belt catching her. "Ow. Glad to know I succeeded in shocking."

"I didn't expect that."

"I guess not." She looked over at him, his jaw clenched tight, his knuckles white on the steering wheel. "What are you doing?"

"Thinking of all the places I could pull over and not get caught. I know where I have caught people having sex in cars before, so I'm trying to be original."

"Are you serious?" she asked, eyes wide.

He took his hand off the wheel and curved it around her arm, drawing it over to his lap, to his erection, hard and thick beneath his jeans.

She moved her palm over him. "Serious indeed."

That he was doing this for her, that he wanted to do it when it had put him off before, was a thrill she hadn't realized it would be.

"You have that effect on me."

He turned away from town, onto a service road that led out into the forest. It wasn't the preferred location she and her friends had used, but it was similar, she imagined. A pocket deep enough in the woods that people rarely bothered to drive in, especially when it wasn't hunting season.

Her stomach tightened and she squeezed his cock through his jeans.

"It'll be over before it starts if you keep doing that," he said, his teeth gritted.

"Well, we can't have that. I want my reward."

"Your reward?"

"I was arrested by you, and put in the back of a car. And it was one of the least fun backseat experiences I've ever had." They were driving over dirt and pine needles now, the pavement ending abruptly as the trees thickened. "Scratch that, it was the worst backseat experience I've ever had. Given all that, don't you think you owe me a better one?"

"I damn well think I do," he said, pulling into an alcove of trees just off the road. "Get in the backseat."

She unbuckled slowly, keeping her eyes on him as she did, before opening the door and getting out of the car. It was so quiet the silence seemed to close in around her, around them. It was a strange, intimate openness. Somehow much more public than being in a bedroom, but also much more secluded.

She closed her door, then opened the back door, climbing inside before closing herself in.

He got out of the car and she watched him through the windows as he moved to the back and opened the door, his hands on his belt, sliding it through the loops before joining her inside, closing the door.

"This is way more like it," she said, leaning back, resting her head on the window.

"Yeah?" He moved over her, leaning in and kissing her deep.

"Mmm. Yeah. Much better than being back here all by myself."

"I'm surprised you remember it," he said, and this time, there was no judgment in his voice. No disdain.

"I was pretty drunk, right?"

"Yeah, you and everyone else. They kind of scattered and left you to it." He brushed his knuckles over her cheeks. "I never thought that was very fair."

"I survived," she said. "The charges didn't stick anyway. My rap sheet remains somewhat mythical."

"Well, you left town anyway. Probably would have ended up getting charged with failure to appear."

"I needed to leave," she said, her heart tightening.

His dark eyes turned serious. "I'm sure you did."

She looked over to the side and saw a glint of silver in the center console of the car. She knew what they were, remembered what it had been like to wear them in the back of the patrol car. Feeling trapped. At his mercy. How different that thought was now. How different it was with Eli, the man as she knew him now.

"Are those handcuffs?" she asked, reaching out and snagging them. "Well, indeed. You just leave these lying around?"

He took them out of her hand. "Not usually."

"You put these on me that night."

Emotion passed over his face. Something like regret wrapped in horror. "I had to."

She smiled. "I know. But in the interest of re-creating things…"

ELI LOOKED DOWN at Sadie, his heart thudding dully in his throat, making him feel like he might choke. He was so turned on he couldn't see straight, and somewhere, in the middle of just trying to remember to breathe, he was trying to parse exactly why when his ex had done this, it had turned him off. And why now, with Sadie, it didn't just seem sexy, it seemed impossible to resist. And heavy with some kind of meaning he was having trouble guessing.

That again had to do with body parts shifting. Heart to throat, blood to cock. Things like that.

And then the handcuffs.

"You really want me to handcuff you?" he asked.

She bit her lips, the action so unconsciously sexy it sent a jolt through his body and down to his dick. "I really do."

"Why?"

"Do I have to know why something turns me on?"

she asked. "If so, I like the idea of putting myself here, of my own free will. Letting you keep me, because I want you to. Because that first time I didn't have a choice…well, I didn't have a choice once I'd made the several bad ones I made that got me arrested in the first place."

"That's a little twisted," he said, even as his gut tightened.

"And what's your point? Isn't it a little twisted that I came back to town and fell into your arms?" She traced his jawline with her forefinger, a wicked smile on her face. "To tell you the truth, I think you like twisted a little bit."

He wrapped his arm around her waist and tugged her down so that she was lying flat on the seat, then he gripped her hands, deftly putting the cuffs on. In many ways, he was more confident in his ability to handcuff a woman than he was in seducing her. He'd just never wanted to combine the two.

"Maybe I do," he said, his words rough.

She saw things in him. The dark things. The secret things. And he couldn't deny, something in him liked it. Because it meant he didn't have to hide. Didn't have to try so hard to be upstanding.

Very few people would call what he was doing now upstanding, and he knew that. But they didn't matter. Nothing mattered but her.

"Now what?" he asked.

"I think you're the one in charge," she said, blue eyes wide.

"I guess I am." He traced her lower lip with the edge of his thumb, his eyes intent on hers, watching to make sure she wasn't nervous or afraid. "You okay with that?"

Her mouth curved upward beneath his thumb. "It's kinda what I asked for, right?"

"I promise to make it worth it."

He lowered his hand to her stomach, pushing her shirt upward, watching the muscles contract as she took a short, sharp breath. He pushed it up higher, his fingers brushing the rounded underside of her breast before sliding up farther, the fabric of her T-shirt folding over his hand as he moved his thumb across her tightened nipple, barely covered by her whisper-thin bra.

Her head fell back, her hands lifted upward, bound by the cuffs.

"Good?" he asked.

"Mmm."

"I'll take that as a yes."

He moved his hands to her jeans, unsnapped them, cursing the stiff denim as he hauled it down her thighs and pushed it, and her shoes and socks, off her legs.

"This was just an excuse to get me to do all the work, wasn't it?" he asked.

"Ah, darn," she said. "You're onto me."

He looked at her, her top pushed up, barely covering her breasts, bright blue panties low on her hips, standing out against her pale skin. "I'm finding it hard to be too upset about it."

He slipped his finger beneath the waistband of her panties, his breath hissing through his teeth as he felt the soft hair beneath the silken fabric. As he moved lower and felt how wet she was for him. How much she liked this game.

Well, he liked it, too. It was everything he never thought he'd do, things he'd never thought he'd want, and now he was all in, shaking with need. Unable to turn back.

He didn't even want to.

He leaned in and pressed a kiss to her stomach, her skin soft beneath his lips. He breathed in deep, taking in the scent of her arousal, the scent of *her*.

He lifted his head and looked at her, at her flushed cheeks, her blond hair tumbling over her shoulders. This was not his life. This was not the kind of thing that happened to him. Not the kind of beauty he was allowed to indulge in.

He almost couldn't breathe. Everything in him was bound up, suspended in the moment.

He reached into his pocket and took out a condom, shrugging his pants and underwear down his legs while holding tight to the plastic condom packet. "I did this out of order." He tugged his T-shirt up over his head, fighting with the tight space of the car.

She giggled. "I'm suddenly remembering why, since becoming an adult with my own bed, I haven't revisited my backseat days."

"I never had to use one."

"Oh, am I your first?" she asked.

"You are. My first for quite a few things in this particular instance. And now, my first woman in handcuffs in more than one way."

He tore open the condom and rolled it over his cock, his chest muscles seizing up as his fist squeezed his aching flesh tight.

She arched her hips upward and he positioned himself, pressing his arousal against her cloth-covered sex, heat shooting up through his teeth when he made contact with her. He rocked against her and she gasped, arching upward, pressing her breasts to his chest, the metal handcuffs clanking against the window.

"Oh...please," she said.

He didn't need any encouragement, not when he felt like he needed to be inside her five minutes ago. But he loved to hear her beg. Loved that she was at his mercy.

Who the hell was he?

Right now, he didn't know, and he didn't care.

All he knew was that watching her, seeing how much she wanted him, making her wait, was the best damn feeling he'd ever had. This was for him. It wouldn't fix anyone, it wouldn't save a damn thing. But it would feel good. And he wanted it.

Wanted her.

"Take my panties off," she said, her words coming out short, harsh.

"Not yet," he said, rocking against her, watching the color in her cheeks deepen.

"You bastard," she said, and wrapped her legs around his hips, tugging him down harder.

"I think you called me that last time I had you in handcuffs."

"It was true then, it's true now." She shifted. "And you didn't make me come either time."

"We still have time." He slipped his hand around beneath her and cupped her ass, tugging her hard against him.

She whimpered, her breath hot on his neck. "Please… I need you."

He shifted his hand and tugged her panties to the side, positioning himself at her entrance and sliding in slowly. He cursed, short and sharp. She was so slick and tight, he thought he might go over the edge the moment he was buried inside her to the hilt.

"Eli," she whispered, his name broken on her breath, the splinters lodging deep inside him, burning his soul. Branding him.

"I've got you, baby." Her eyes clashed with his, wide and…shocked? Almost afraid? It made his stomach clench tight. "Hey, hey, I've got you."

She nodded wordlessly, her eyes never leaving his. He leaned in and kissed her lips, long and slow, withdrawing from her body, just an inch, before pushing back inside.

Then he was lost completely, chasing the liquid heat that was raging through him, building, bringing him closer to the edge. His blood roaring through his ears, canceling out everything, his vision going dark, nothing remaining but the hot, hard bite of pleasure, twisting and turning in his gut, ready to savage him, ready to squeeze everything inside of him into dust, the pressure building, threatening destruction if he didn't find release soon.

"Come for me, Sadie," he said, the words hard-won, almost impossible to push through his tightened throat. "Baby, I'm on the edge. Come for me."

She arched against him, flexing her hips, the motion twisting everything in him even tighter. He tightened his hold on her ass, his other hand braced flat on the window behind her head as he circled his hips slowly, grinding against her clit.

Finally, he felt her give, heard the hoarse cry escape her lips, felt her internal muscles squeezing him tight. And he let himself go.

His release roared through him like a wildfire, scorching everything that had been contorted inside him, hollowing him out completely and leaving him devastated in its wake.

He tried to catch his breath, his muscles shaking, sweat rolling between his shoulder blades. He felt like he'd just run five miles in the desert. And found an oasis at the end of the race.

Sadie.

He let out a harsh breath and moved away from her. "Well," he said, leaning back against the seat, dimly aware that sitting bare-assed in his patrol car was probably not the most professional thing, but he didn't think he could move much farther right at the moment. "I didn't think the condom thing through," he said, looking down, feeling vaguely embarrassed that he hadn't quickly dealt with it out of her sight, like he would normally do.

"Oh, dear," she said, wiggling slightly then giving him a hard stare. "I need releasing."

"Oh, sorry," he said, leaning forward and pulling the key out of the cup holder, undoing the handcuffs as quickly as possible.

She smiled, almost shyly, which was unusual, if not unheard of, for Sadie. She rubbed her wrists, looking around. "Yeah, I think you have to bury it."

He let out a long breath. "This is more complicated than I thought."

"Well, you can't litter. That's a crime and you're, like…running for sheriff. Can you imagine the scandal?"

"You're right. We can't have that," he said, opening the passenger door, one bare foot hitting the pine-needle-covered ground. "This is the most awkward thing I've ever experienced."

He heard a giggle behind him and turned and gave her a hard look.

"The view is good anyway," she said.

He rolled his eyes and shut the door, hurrying, naked and in broad daylight, into the trees, where he dug a small hole in the soft dirt and disposed of the condom. Then walked as quickly as he could back to the car, taking light steps, trying to avoid majorly sharp rocks and any particularly crunchy sticks.

When he returned to the car, Sadie was sitting there with the door open, her legs sticking out, jeans back on and T-shirt tugged back down. And she was smiling. Far too broadly.

"You look all back to normal," he said.

She stood, her legs wobbling. "Looks can be deceiving. Are you ready to head back?"

"Well, I'd like to get dressed."

She swallowed visibly and nodded slowly, moving to the side so that he could reach in and grab his clothes. He shrugged his underwear on, making sure none of the pine needles that were sticking to his feet flaked off inside the underwear, then grabbed his jeans, tugging them on as quickly as possible.

And now he felt at least marginally less ridiculous. He turned back to Sadie, who wasn't smiling anymore. She had her arms folded beneath her breasts, a blank stare on her face, her lower lips trembling.

He flashed back to that moment she'd looked at him. That calm before the storm when she'd looked almost terrified in his arms.

"Sadie? Did I… Did I hurt you?" he asked, regret slamming into him, making his face feel numb and his stomach sick.

"No," she said, shaking her head, "I'm fine." A tear trailed down her cheek, leaving a streak of glitter on her skin.

"You are not fine," he said. "What did I do?"

"Nothing," she bit out. "It's just… I don't know, it was more intense than I anticipated, is all."

"I should never have agreed to this. To the handcuffs and…"

"No, it's not that. Well, it is that. It's just… I can't stop thinking about what happened that night."

"I'm sure it's scary to get arrested," he said, feeling like he was treading on thin ice, unsure of what to say next. "I'm sure…"

"Not the arrest," she said. "It's what… Eli, that night after I left the police station…my father picked me up." She leaned against the patrol car and picked up a twig that had fallen onto the trunk. She gripped it, pushed on it with her thumb and snapped it in half, the sound echoing in the dense silence around them. "And when we got home…he beat me so badly I ended up in the hospital."

CHAPTER FOURTEEN

OH, DAMMIT, SHE was crying. And not just a few tears, but the honest-to-God beginnings of a flash flood. She could feel the dams eroding, so much emotion building, pressing against the already-compromised structure, and she knew the minute it gave way, she was going to cry until she was dry inside.

Because it had been building for years. And now it was all falling apart in front of the man she...the man she'd spent a long time blaming in so many ways. The man who'd just taken her to heaven and back in his car, with what could very well be the same handcuffs on her wrists.

It was fitting he was the one to witness this. When he hadn't witnessed it then.

Why didn't you protect me, Eli? You protect everyone. Why couldn't you see I needed it?

But she didn't say that out loud. Instead, she continued on, ignoring the tears that slid down her cheeks.

"He was angry at me. For the arrest. And...oh, he said I'd been daring him for a long time. And he wasn't wrong about that," she said, swallowing hard, imagining how her father had looked that night. His face red, the vein in his forehead standing out as he'd screamed at her. As he'd landed his first blow, knocking her to the ground. And after that she hadn't seen him at all. She'd just wound herself into a ball while it continued.

Unable to defend herself. Unable to move. While she heard nothing. Nothing but the sound of his knees, boots and fists hitting her body.

When she'd imagined him doing this, she'd heard her mother screaming for him to stop.

But in reality, she hadn't. In reality, her mother had been silent.

"Anyway," she said. "It was the last straw. I'd finally set him on me. After years of watching him go after my mother I finally managed to turn it onto myself. She didn't call 911. So you would never have heard it over dispatch. She drove me to the hospital in Tolowa. We were far enough out that it was just as close as the one on the other end of Copper Ridge."

"Sadie," he said, his voice rough. "I had no idea…"

"I know," she said. "But please let me finish. I had to go into surgery. I know you've seen the little scar." So funny that it was so small, when the scars beneath were so massive. "My spleen had ruptured."

"Shit," he said, the word harsh in the silence of the forest, so much heavier with emotion than her own blank retelling.

"My mother told them I had gotten into a fight. She didn't tell them my father had done it. When I was alone with the nurse she said that I could press charges. But that it was going to be difficult because my mother was adamant I'd gotten into a fight with a group of boys," she snorted. "She said if I were a minor I could be removed while investigations were done, but I was eighteen and that meant there was nothing they could do. So she asked me what I wanted. My father had come to pick my mother up. My car was in the parking lot. My mother had left the keys. And that was when I realized that people don't change. So I figured… I'd just change everything around me."

He covered his mouth with his hand and took a step back, his complexion waxen. "Sadie, I don't—" He dropped his hands to his sides. "That happened because I arrested you?"

"Don't," she said. "Don't do that. I've done that. I… I do it still sometimes. It was my choice that got me arrested. It was his choice to beat me. It was…"

Suddenly she was pulled tight against his chest, all of the resistance pulled from her by his tight embrace, all of the emotion wringing out of her, tears falling down her cheeks.

He moved his hand over her back, warm and comforting. And way too much.

She buried her face in his chest, the tears hot now, angry. "Why didn't you protect me?" she asked, the words slipping out before she could process them. Before she could analyze just how unfair they were. He didn't know. He couldn't have known. But it was the question that had screamed inside of her for ten years, even when the pain was buried so far beneath years of rocks and rubble and dirt she'd thrown on top of it in an effort to keep it quiet. In an effort to blot it out.

He tightened his hold on her and she curled her hands into fists, pressed against his bare chest as she let him hold her. Her shoulders jerked upward on the sob that filled her throat, forcing her to suck a sharp breath of air.

"You said it's your job to protect everyone," she said, the words muffled by his chest. "Everyone in your town. But you didn't protect me."

He gripped her shoulders tight, tugging her backward and looking down at her face, his dark eyes sincere, intense. She wanted to look away from him. Hide her weakness, her emotion. Every insecurity and stupid thought.

"Never mind, it's not your fault..." she began again.

"Sadie, listen to me," he said. "I would never have given you to him. Ever. I would never have let you go home. If I'd had any idea..." He shook his head. "I should have seen it."

"Why would you?" she asked, stepping back, feeling so embarrassed she wanted to crawl under the patrol car and curl up into a ball.

"It's my job. And...sometimes I think I don't look long enough or hard enough. Because...well, like with Alison. My hands are tied because she won't tell. She won't ask for help. She won't leave. I hate knowing that. That, no matter what, I can't help. But I could have helped you. If I had asked...you would have told me, wouldn't you?"

She studied his handsome face, the deep grooves around his mouth that spoke of years of frowns. The lines between his brows that told the story of just how many nights he'd sat up worrying. "I was angry, drunk and belligerent. There was no reason for you to offer me anything. I deserved to be arrested and I—"

"You said something to me when you first came to town," he said, interrupting her.

"What?" she asked, feeling gritty and watery at the same time, and not really enjoying either sensation.

"You said that...that there were people like me who just put people away, and people like you who listen, and try to change things. You're right. I wouldn't have listened, not then. I didn't listen. I figured I was doing the right thing. The legal thing was all the protection that was needed, but it wasn't."

"Eli, don't. Don't take it on yourself. You wouldn't have listened, but I wouldn't have told you. I wanted him to do it. For years... For years and years I watched him hit her. And then I finally decided I was sick of walking on eggshells. That I was going to go ahead and dare him to do the same to me. Because in my head I figured I could take it. Because I figured she would stop it. Well, it turns out I'm not as tough as I thought. And it turns out she didn't care as much as I thought, either."

"Sadie, you said—"

"I shouldn't have said it. But I needed to say it," she said. "I don't... I've thought it before. I... Look, I really hate talking about this but I needed to tell you because, well...hello, post-sex emotional breakdown, and you did need to know why. I've... I was hammered that night, okay? But when you grabbed me and put me in the car, all I could think was you were really strong. The kind of guy who could put a jackass like my dad in his place. The kind of guy who would. You were good, Eli, and I knew it then. I know it now."

"I'm sorry I didn't stop him."

"I'm sorry I ever blamed you."

"Don't apologize to me," he said. "Not for that." He looked grim, and she knew she'd pushed the worst button she could have ever pushed.

Other men might have shouted and said there was nothing they could have done, and they would have had a right. She'd given Eli a new sin that didn't belong to him, to add to the long list of other people's transgressions he seemed to be trying to atone for.

He released his hold on her and turned back toward the car and she just stared at his broad back, his strong shoulders.

All the better to carry the weight of the world on them.

She moved over to him and wrapped her arms around him, resting her head against his bare skin. "Don't carry this," she said, kissing the deep groove beneath his shoulder blade. "Please don't."

He lifted his hand and covered hers with it, pressing it against his chest. "No one's going to hurt you again," he said. "I promise."

Another tear trailed down her cheek. Because it was everything she'd ever wanted to hear from someone, and it terrified her how much it meant to hear from him now.

Even more terrifying was just how much the words meant, and how cold she felt in her chest when she had to acknowledge that the only person who really had the power to hurt her was him.

No matter how much she'd wanted to keep her feelings for him neutral, he'd burrowed beneath her protective layer. At some point "just sex" had become a hell of a lot more. And she had no idea how that was possible.

She'd had relationships with men, whole relationships based on more than just sex, that hadn't been like this.

At least, she thought that was what they'd been. They'd gone on dates and chatted, and some nights they hadn't even slept together, which proved that they had a deeper connection than just the physical. Or that's what it was supposed to prove.

But this was supposed to be sex. Hot, sweaty, ill-advised cop-cowboy sex. Like some kind of alpha-male female fantasy on steroids. With handcuffs. On a horse.

So why hadn't it stayed that way? Why did she feel like things were changing? How in the hell had a romp in the backseat of a patrol car turned into the most exposing, soul-baring experience of her life?

"I guess we should get back," she said, stepping away from him, wishing that separating the feelings that she had for him from her heart was as easy as breaking contact with his skin.

"Yeah," he said, bending down and retrieving his shirt from the backseat of the car and tugging it on.

Something had changed between them. It was good and bad. She could feel it. He was all tension now, and she couldn't blame him. But at the same time she felt like the bond had tightened between them.

Because he was the only person who knew. The only one who knew the whole story. Who knew that she wished, more than anything, she'd had someone to protect her.

She hadn't even let herself in on that, not really, until the moment she'd told him.

"That was fun," she said, wiping the moisture from beneath her eyes.

"Yeah," he said, slamming the back door shut before jerking open the front door. "Fun."

ELI SLAMMED THE maul down on the splitter and two pieces of wood went flying onto the dirt, the physical energy doing very little to relieve the raging...whatever the hell these feelings were that were roaring through his veins.

He didn't know what he was feeling. So he was chopping wood instead of feeling. Or at least, that was the plan. And if that didn't work, eventually he would be exhausted enough that he would just forget he had feelings that didn't involve his screaming muscles.

Barring that, he'd drink them away, but considering

that was the way most other men in his family handled Unpleasant Things No One Wanted to Handle, he was averse. But not entirely opposed. Desperate times, et cetera.

"You have enough wood to keep all of Copper Ridge toasty through the wet season. Why are you chopping more?"

Eli turned and saw Kate standing just behind him, her hands on her hips, her weight resting on one leg. "Because," he said, bending over and picking up one of the log halves, "I'm expecting it to be a cold year."

"Oh, okay. Hey, have you talked to Sadie lately?"

Oh, good, that was what he needed. To talk about Sadie with his sister when he was trying to forget the woman via manual labor. In that way that he just wanted to forget about her for long enough to make himself feel comfortable again.

Enough to make himself forget the look on her face. The way she'd shivered in his arms.

Why didn't you protect me?

He bent and picked up the other log half, scowling deeply. "I talked to her this morning. Why?"

"I wanted to tell her that I made rolls."

"What?"

"I made rolls by myself. And they're edible. She showed me how yesterday, so I was... Hey, how are you?"

"Fine," he said, gritting his teeth and walking over to the wood pile to stack the pieces on top.

"You don't seem fine," she said, frowning. "Is this about the people coming for the barbecue next week?"

Weirdly, that bothered him a hell of a lot less than it had in the beginning. In fact, in a very strange way he was looking forward to it. Looking forward to seeing Sadie's vision come to life. To seeing her hard work become a real, tangible thing.

He shouldn't care. He did.

Don't carry this.

Too damn late, Sadiepants.

"Nope," he said. "I am fine."

"You are growly."

"And?"

"That's Connor's job. What is up?"

"Just thinking about things," he said, putting another log on the stump. "Dad."

"Oh," she said, looking down.

He positioned the splitter, then lifted the maul again, bringing it down hard. "It's that time of the year."

"Yeah, I guess it is." She bit her lip and looked down, then back up, her dark eyes fierce. "I don't think about him very much."

"You don't?"

"No."

He looked at Kate and fully realized—maybe for the first time—that she had never, ever known the good parts of their mother or father. And they had existed. Their mother hadn't always been despondent and unable to cope. Their father hadn't always been a man viewing life through an alcohol haze.

He'd gotten to know the people they were. So had Connor.

"He was a good man at one time, Katie," he said.

"That's fine," she said. "For him. For you and Connor. But I never knew that man. I never saw him any way but falling on his ass drunk. You and Connor loved me. Then Jessie, when she married Connor. Jack was there, and Liss, our friends who always made our house feel less empty. But I can't miss the person who made the house seem sad."

She didn't understand, because she didn't realize what really made him think of their father. She didn't know that he was trying to cope with the feelings Sadie's words had triggered.

That they had brought to mind all he'd failed to protect.

And that was the crux of the problem. He wanted to protect the people he loved, the people of Copper Ridge. And his track record was hit or miss at best.

"Hello." He turned and saw Sadie standing in the driveway, her hands in her back pockets, tugging the T-shirt she was wearing tight across her breasts, her expression sheepish. "Hopefully I'm not interrupting anything."

"Not anything important," Kate said, forcing a smile.

She looked a whole lot like him when she faked okay, and he wasn't sure what he thought about that.

"How is everything, Kate?" Sadie asked, smiling. Sadie's smile, regardless of her feelings, always seemed genuine. And that was even more concerning. He was starting to realize that everything about Sadie, all of her ease and lightness, wasn't what it seemed.

Ruptured spleen. Hospitalization. Her mother wouldn't defend her...

He couldn't imagine it. Couldn't believe this bright, amazing woman had been subjected to horrors that topped the Garrett Ranch's Greatest Hits by a mile. He hadn't even guessed at her pain, and today she'd poured it out onto his chest.

And he felt it now. The weight of it. Of what he hadn't done. Of what he always left undone.

"Good," Kate said. "I was actually just asking about you."

"Well, here I am! Things are really moving along for the barbecue. Though I wanted to ask you, and I know it's really last minute, but are you interested in doing any type of rodeo demonstration?"

Kate brightened visibly. "Yes. I'd love to. I could do some barrel racing in the arena, or even some calf roping."

"Both if you want."

"Maybe Jack will be interested in helping out," she said.

"That would be great."

"I'll go and call him," Kate said. "See you." She waved and then bounded off in the direction of her little cabin.

"She is quite something," Sadie said, moving in closer to him.

"She is. Sometimes I'm afraid she really lost out having to be raised by us. We're not exactly a soft touch."

"No," Sadie said, "but you're a pretty darn satisfying touch if I say so myself."

"Well, thanks for that."

"Actually, that's what I'm here to talk to you about."

"Oh?" he asked, feeling the scowl forming from the inside out. He'd come to cut wood and escape her and here she was.

Wanting to talk about the feelings he was pretending not to have.

"I'm sorry about what I said. I wanted to make sure we were okay."

She didn't meet his eyes when she said any of that. And he knew she really was sorry, and that she was afraid that she'd overstepped. But he also knew she'd meant it all. And it had hit its mark.

"We're fine," he told her, because it was the thing he had to say to get sex. And whatever he felt, he knew he still wanted that.

"Good. I don't normally spill my guts like that. Normally I listen to other people do it. That's kind of why I do it. Did it."

"Therapy?"

"Yes. Because I got to give it to other people and sort of turn over their own issues and never think of mine. I mean…it hurts. That memory hurts. I think it always will. And I'm projecting. I know that. I…wished someone would have seen, Eli, and in my head, because you were so tangled up in that night, something in me made that person you. My patients do the same thing and I know better. But you know…it's a 'doctors are terrible patients' kind of a thing."

He could hear what she was saying, and he even believed her to an extent. But it didn't change the way that heavy mass of emotion felt in his chest. Didn't make breathing easier or his throat less tight.

"Let's forget that it happened," she said. "You know. You're basically the only person who knows. And… I think we should just…go to bed."

"It's six o'clock."

"So?" she asked.

They were standing outside his house. And he'd never had her in his house before. But he'd had her in his patrol car. And that was, in some ways, more intimate.

"I guess I can't think of a reason." Mainly because the blood had all rushed down south of his belt. A chronic, Sadie-related issue.

"Oh, good," she said, looking relieved. "I don't want things to change."

Neither did he, but he was afraid that they had.

"We're on the same page, then."

"Your house or the car?"

"House," he said.

"Probably for the best. In hindsight, it was a pretty poor use of the people's property. Doing it in a county-owned vehicle."

"Excuse me," he said, the tension in his chest easing slightly, though not the tension in his cock, "you started it."

"True. But then," she said, putting her hand on his chest, a smile curving her lips, "I am a criminal. A very bad girl. And you are so good."

He wrapped his hand around her wrist and drew her fingertips up to his lips, sucking one into his mouth, swirling his tongue around the tip. Then he closed his teeth lightly over her skin and released her. "Am I?" he asked.

He didn't feel good. He felt like a failure. Like a man who'd let another man beat this woman near to death. Like a man who couldn't protect the weaker people around him, even though he tried with everything in him.

There were tons of people who never let their fathers drive off in a drunken stupor and die. And those people probably didn't try half as hard as he did.

Sometimes he wondered if he was destined to fail everyone around him, no matter how hard he tried to be acceptable. To be good enough.

So if he was going to be bad, maybe he should just embrace it.

"I think you're underestimating me," he said. "Still. And I've had you in handcuffs."

"I don't know, Eli."

"Sadie," he said, gripping her chin, kissing her firmly on the lips. "Get your ass in my bed."

CHAPTER FIFTEEN

SADIE WASN'T SURE what was happening, or why it felt so different. It wasn't about sex. She knew that much. Well, it was about sex, but it was about something more, too. Something deeper. Something she really didn't want to guess at.

Eli had only let her in his house that night she'd used his shower when she'd burst the pipes. Never since.

They had sex at her house. And then he returned to his space. His neat and ordered space.

She walked through the front door, her heart hammering hard. Everything was like she remembered, identical, really, to the only other time she'd ever been here.

Neat, clean. Verging on shiny.

For a man who worked with farm animals and criminals, he sure kept his space spotless.

Maybe that was why.

"You know where my bedroom is," he said.

"Yes."

"Get upstairs." There was a hard, determined light in his dark eyes. Like a switch had been flipped. There was so much electricity arching between them. So much heat. And so much intense meaning.

Things had changed. She'd changed them by telling him her story. By telling him he should have protected her.

She wasn't sure yet if she'd made things better or ruined them, but she was sure she'd changed them. She'd felt it then, standing isolated in the woods with him, and she felt it now.

"Okay," she said, because whatever was happening she wasn't going to tell him no.

She turned and headed up the stairs, her footsteps loud on the wooden floor, her heart hammering louder in her ears, sounding over her feet.

"I like to watch you walk," he said. "Though I like it better when you aren't wearing anything."

She heard him behind her, following her, his voice rough. "Well, I'm hardly going to walk through your kitchen naked," she said.

"I walked through the woods naked for you," he said. "And that's not my usual thing."

"No," she said, tossing a look over her shoulder, her stomach knotting tighter as she saw the hungry look on his face. "I don't suppose."

"But I don't do any of the usual things with you," he said.

She pushed open his bedroom door and tugged her shirt over her head, ditching her bra just as quickly before crossing one arm over her breasts and turning, giving him her best saucy smile. "Oh, really?"

"No," he said, his voice lowering. "I don't."

"Well," she said, spreading her fingers, giving him a slight peek at her nipple, knowing that she was driving him crazy, "maybe we can see what else I might tempt you to do."

He advanced on her, his expression dark. He extended his hands and cupped her face, tilting her head backward, his fingers forked through her hair. "Don't make this a joke, Sadie."

"I'm not," she said, her heart tightening, like he'd grabbed hold of that instead of her face and squeezed tight.

"You're trying to make light of it so you don't feel it. I can't do that. As you pointed out, I'm a pretty humorless bastard." He traced the edge of her lower lip with his thumb. "So no more talking. Don't try to make it funny. I have to feel it. So you damn well have to feel it, too."

Her heart lurched into her throat, made a response impossible. But it didn't matter because then he was kissing her, his lips hard and firm on hers, stubble scraping her chin, her cheeks, as things intensified between them.

Their little love scene in the car had been intense, driven by her need to wash something out of the past. To make it different. But this was different still. He was different.

And he was right. She wanted to do exactly what he had accused her of. She wanted to do a striptease and laugh and make it fun. She wanted it to be the kind of sex she knew, the kind she could control.

But Eli was in charge now. And for some reason, she felt more helpless now than when her wrists had been in handcuffs.

Because that had been her idea, her plan. But this was about his demons, not hers.

He pushed her back onto the bed, stripping her jeans, underwear and shoes from her body before he shoved his jeans down his hips, leaving him naked, bare for her.

"I'll be right back." He turned and walked into the bathroom and returned a moment later, rolling the condom onto his length as he moved back to the bed.

He positioned himself between her thighs, kissing

her deep. There was no foreplay, no preamble at all, but she didn't care. She was ready. She'd been ready since the last time he was inside her.

There was just something about him.

He pushed inside of her, deep, thick, filling her completely. A sharp gasp escaped her lips as he pushed his hips forward, going impossibly deeper. She wrapped her legs around his thighs, opening herself to him, allowing him better access.

She smoothed her hands over his hair, down his shoulders and back, her eyes never leaving his, the impact hitting her deep, sparking off the protective shields she'd built up around her chest, making her burn. Making her feel like she was on the verge of an attack that might bring the walls down forever.

He ground himself against her, pleasure rushing through her, her orgasm taking her by surprise, taking her over completely. Rushing through her and eclipsing all of the emotions that had been knotting up in her chest, leaving her feeling clean, new.

Relieved.

Above her, Eli lowered his head, his body shaking as he shuddered out his own release. He let out a hard breath and moved away from her, rolling onto his back. She just stayed where she was, staring at the ceiling, at the slats of wood, knotted and imperfect, but somehow orderly. Like the man himself.

The only sound was his harsh breathing. Probably hers, too, but for some reason she was much more aware of him than of herself. Possibly because she didn't want to be aware of herself, all things considered.

The things considered being the fact that it felt like there was a potential avalanche of feelings about to crash down inside of her. A veritable rock slide of emotions.

No, thank you, sir.

She closed her eyes and tried to capture the post-orgasmic warmth that she was counting on coming to the rescue. She felt decidedly less glowy than normal.

She was far too aware of everything. The burn on her cheeks from his whiskers, the blood still throbbing hot through her body, her heart beating unevenly. How cold her breasts felt now that he'd moved away from her.

The shifting of the mattress as he got up and the sound of his feet slapping on the wood floor as he headed back into the bathroom. She shivered, then looked around the room, pushing herself into a sitting position.

He didn't have pictures on the walls. The wood-paneled walls were broken up by large windows that overlooked the dense trees that backed the house. The sun was sinking outside, golden rays filtering through the green, casting everything in a hazy filtered light.

She suddenly felt completely exhausted, her eyelids ready to sink like the sun. She crawled up to the head of the bed and slipped beneath the covers, lying on her side, watching the tree branches outside wave in the breeze. She heard Eli walking back through the room, felt the mattress sink just across from her.

The covers slipped down and she felt his warmth beneath the covers. Wordlessly, he wrapped his arms around her and pulled her close. She relaxed, head resting against the solid wall of his chest.

She would just close her eyes for a second.

Then she would go.

WHEN SADIE OPENED her eyes, gray light was bathing the bedroom, and Eli's arms were still wrapped tightly around her.

She scrubbed her eyes, rolling onto her back, his hands drifting over her breasts as she did. Then she craned her neck to look over him, and at the bedside clock.

It was five-thirty, and she sure as hell knew she hadn't gone back in time, which meant she'd slept here all night.

She sat up, pulling the covers up to her chest. Eli made a deep noise, then rolled over.

Her heart was hammering, her hands a little sweaty. She'd never done that before. Never slept beside another person like that. There was something so impossibly intimate about it. Something sort of terrifying.

She waited for her muscles to spring into action, for her legs to get her out of bed and her feet to run her out the door.

But it didn't happen.

She breathed in deep, and the panic started to subside, her breath normalizing. She didn't want to leave. That was the most startling revelation that came from her subsiding panic. Other startling revelations included that she actually felt happy that he'd let her stay the night. That he'd invited her into his home and his bedroom.

He'd shared something with her last night. Like she'd shared with him after they'd made love in the car. But he'd done it wordlessly, and she had no idea what exactly she was supposed to extrapolate from it, but she still felt it.

She slipped out of bed and hunted for her clothes, tugging them on before she went downstairs and helped herself to Eli's mugs and his coffeemaker, humming absently as she did.

She remembered that he ordered lattes and pulled

some milk out of the fridge, nuking it in the microwave, then whisking it while the coffee brewed. Then
she added a generous helping to his coffee, along with
some sugar. Leaving her own coffee fairly underdressed
with a dollop of warm milk and a little sugar. When
she got back upstairs, Eli was out of bed, standing in
the center of the room, naked and looking a little lost.

"You're still here," he said, when she walked in.

"Yes, I am. And I come bearing caffeine."

"Well, then, I'm very glad you stayed," he said.

"Is that the only reason?"

"No."

"Well, good. A woman hates to be wanted only for
her bean-brewing skills. Though mine are legend. And
no man has ever benefited from them. But they will at
the B and B."

Eli frowned and set his mug on the nightstand, grabbing his black boxer briefs and T-shirt from the ground,
throwing both on, then retrieving his mug. "What do
you mean no man has ever benefited from your skills?"

"I'm not into sleepovers," she said, smiling, trying
to keep it a little lighter than things had been between
them. She turned away from him, and he caught her
arm, turning her back.

"What does that mean?"

Oh, damn Eli. Why did he always want to know what
something meant?

"It means that I like to sleep alone, which I've told
you before. And it means that I've always slept alone.
Whiz, whir, thank you, sir, if you will."

"Why, Sadie?"

"Because I don't do close, okay?" she said, realizing
as the words slipped out of her mouth, cranky, curt and
very pre-coffee in attitude, that they were true.

It was easy to pretend she was fine. That she had normal relationships and let them go when they weren't working because she didn't need conflict, because she wasn't going to submit to a life of unhappiness and violence under the guise of sick, twisted love, like her mother had done.

But the simple truth was, she didn't do heavy, because she didn't want to get close to anyone. She didn't let her boyfriends spend the night for the same reason she lived in a place for only a couple of years at a time.

She didn't want to bond with anything. She didn't want to need anyone.

She blinked, standing there frozen in the middle of Eli's bedroom having an epiphany. "I don't like to let people get close to me," she repeated, the words making the back of her neck prickle.

"Why?" he asked.

"Because people hurt you." That was true, too. She was filled with truth. She needed to be filled with coffee, so her truth could stay in. In and buried, like it normally was.

He nodded slowly and walked toward the French doors, undoing the latch on one and opening it out, and onto the deck that wrapped around the second floor of the house.

"Care to take your unheard-of morning-after coffee out on the deck?"

"Oh, why not?" she said, lifting a shoulder and following him outside. He set his mug on the railing, and she did the same, resting her elbows on the rough wood and looking out at the view.

She tried to see through the trees, past the closest branches, to see what was beyond, but they were like a dark blot of green ink, bleeding together to cover the blankness.

"I'm sort of mad at you," she said, looking down into her coffee, listening to the wind rustle through the trees, to the birds that were just starting to wake up.

"Why?"

"I thought I was really well-adjusted before I met you."

"Did I...maladjust you?"

"No, you just had the balls to point out that I'm a total head case. No man before you has dared."

"Every man before me got the boot out the door too quickly."

She waved her hand. "Eh. Granted. All right," she said. "Why is your house so clean?"

"Because otherwise it gets chaotic. And out of control. And I've lived that way before. I won't live that way again."

"Your dad?"

"Yes. He was a mess, Sadie. I took care of Kate, but my dad was like another child at a certain point. He made bad decisions, and it was up to me to clean it up. Cover it up. Before my mom left he was okay."

"He never got over your mom?"

He lifted a shoulder. "Probably at some point he was just an alcoholic who liked booze. Probably there was a point where he'd forgotten why he ever started drinking. But that's just a theory. There was always so much to take care of."

"It explains you."

He looked at her, his eyes blank. "I failed him, though. In the end."

"What?"

"The night he died. Whenever Dad got drunk, I used

to take his keys and hide them. That was my routine. Dad was drunk every night, for the record, so I knew to hide his keys every night."

"Eli, you should have never had to deal with all that."

"But I did. We don't get to choose our lot, we choose what we do with it. Except…the night my dad died I decided not to go home after my shift. I was out. Connor and Jessie lived in the cabin Kate lives in now. My dad and I were in the main house. I hadn't moved out because he needed someone. And I knew he needed someone. But that night, I figured he was probably passed out so I didn't need to go home. Went out with a bunch of guys from the department instead. And a call came in over the radio."

"Oh… Eli."

"Yeah, well…it's been a long time. And my dad was not a father to me, not really. But that doesn't change the fact that I let him down. He was impaired, always. And he needed someone to help manage his decisions. I wasn't there and he died."

"You can't honestly blame yourself…"

"You blame me for not saving you from abuse I didn't even know about. Of course I blame myself for this."

"Eli, I don't really blame you…"

"You do," he said. "And I understand. It's because I've promised to protect people. If I just said screw it like…like Connor does, then I wouldn't expect better. And no one else would, either. But if I say I'll take care of it, I better. And I haven't always. I've failed a lot of people."

"I'm sure you've helped more people," she said, her stomach clenching.

"But I failed where it really matters."

"But it was his fault."

"Does it matter?" he asked, turning his back to the view, leaning against the railing. "Does it matter if you know you should feel a different way about it?"

She thought about how she'd felt when her blame had poured out of her back in the woods. About how she'd been carrying that feeling around, buried deep and low, for years.

"I guess not," she said. "But...you shouldn't feel that way."

He lifted a shoulder. "Sure."

"Do we get some sort of...accolades for exposing just how screwed up we both are?" she asked. "Because I figured this just-sex thing would involve a lot less talking."

"Then why are we talking?" he asked.

"Because. I spent a lot of years listening for a living and never met anyone I wanted to talk to. And... I want to talk to you. But I don't always like the things that get said."

"Neither do I."

"Maybe we should stop talking, then," she said, moving to him and curling her hand around his neck, kissing him.

"I have to be at work in an hour."

"I can get a lot done with twenty minutes. Just you wait and see."

SADIE WAS ACTUALLY NERVOUS. Like...upchucking nervous. The barbecue was today. Booths were being set up. Volunteers were on hand, paid workers were on hand, individual vendors were on hand.

Over the past week she'd finalized everything for the barbecue, bought new linens for the B and B, and perfected her menu, and also during that past week, she'd been sleeping with Eli, either at his place or hers.

She liked to think that had something to do with how well things were going. If for no other reason than being with him made her feel very good.

She paced the open field area where everything was being set up. The good thing about getting local businesses to participate was that everyone basically saw to their own booth once she directed them.

Barbecues were already being fired up for the cook-off, very large pots of beans and potato salad were either heating or chilling. Beer on tap was at hand. Kate and Jack were in the large uncovered arena ready to do some rodeo work and to show some basic roping techniques.

And Jack was even coordinating a round of mutton busting, with prizes donated from the Farm and Garden. She wondered if Connor had checked with his insurance about that. She imagined not.

Jack and Kate had proven to be enthusiastic additions, and their passion for the events was contagious. It was also enticing a whole new segment of the county to the barbecue.

The only booth that was empty was Alison's. And it was starting to make Sadie wring her hands in despair. Well, she could get pies from the grocery store for the contest if she had to. But she doubted it would make for as special a dessert booth as she'd planned. In fact, without the homemade stuff, it felt like a "why bother."

But considering what had happened the last time she'd seen Alison, she wasn't that surprised.

"Sadie!"

Sadie turned and saw Lydia, her favorite intrepid Chamber of Commerce representative and fellow admirer of Eli's butt. "Hi, Lydia. You're out early."

The other woman smiled. "Yes, I am. I thought I would see how it was all shaping up."

"Nicely," Sadie said, surveying the grounds. "It just might not fail."

"Eli would never let it fail," Lydia said. "Not to say you would," she quickly amended. "Only that I've known Eli for the past six years and he's always been so stable and organized. Just one of the many reasons I'm wholeheartedly endorsing his bid for sheriff."

Sadie scanned the field, looking for Eli. She didn't see him. "Yeah, I definitely think he's the man for the job," she said.

She thought back to last week's conversation on his porch. About how he felt like he failed when it came to caring for people.

She couldn't understand it.

Maybe because you suck and you threw a bunch of your issues at him?

Maybe because I really feel that way, she argued back with herself. *Because maybe...if I ever thought there was such a thing as a knight in shining armor, it would have been him.*

She didn't even bother to push the thought away.

Didn't bother to pretend there wasn't more swirling around inside of her than simple lust.

Somehow, in the space of a month and a half, she'd gone from disliking Eli immensely to...well, whatever this thing was where she felt like the sun hadn't really risen until she saw his face.

Whatever you called that.

"Sadie." Lydia interrupted her train of thought. "I was wondering if you wanted to get brochures for the B and B down to the Chamber. And also, I was wondering if we could put some brochures in the B and B for some other businesses. Tourist attractions, whale-watching excursions, things like that."

"That would be great!" Sadie said, feeling strangely warm toward Lydia at the moment. Not that she was cold toward her normally, but it was a little awkward to talk to the woman you knew had a thing for the guy you were semi-secretly sleeping with.

"Beneficial for all," Lydia said. "Oh, there he is!" Her smile broadened when she saw Eli, and Sadie felt a sliver of guilt push its way beneath her skin. Lydia was more Eli's type. They made sense. She was organized, passionate about the community. Caring.

She wasn't terrified of interpersonal connection and more likely than your average startled house cat to tear off and hide under the furniture than forge any kind of meaningful relationship with someone.

Except…she and Eli did have a meaningful relationship. She could feel it. She was carrying it around in her chest, and it weighed a ton. And it was effing inconvenient.

"Eli!" Lydia called, waving.

Oh, man. Like it couldn't get more awkward. Because she and Eli were not a couple, and when she stood near him in front of the general public she didn't know what to do with her hands. Because they were itching to touch him but she knew she couldn't.

He walked over to them, looking generally awkward, as awkward as you would expect the guy to feel in the situation.

"Hi," she said, shoving her hands into her back pockets so they wouldn't get all feelsy with him.

"Sadie," he said. "Lydia. How are things going?"

"Great," Sadie said. "And on your end?"

"Parking area is set. Connor is sober. I consider that a win."

Sadie winced. "Is Connor going to come?"

Eli shrugged. "I don't know. I kind of doubt it. Families and things...he doesn't handle this stuff well."

"Man," Sadie said. "I didn't think of it from that angle. I feel like crap now."

"Don't," he said. "Connor objectively realizes the value in this. Okay, he didn't say that, but I know he does. He'll hide away. It's his deal. Though Liss might be able to draw him out for a while when Jack and Kate ride."

"I can't wait to see them," Lydia said. "Really exciting. It'll be very fun. We've had a lot of calls about this down at the Chamber."

"That's great," Sadie said. "And goes a long way in eliminating my deep fear that I will end up here alone, eating all of the food myself. Which is, in many ways, not a bad fantasy, but...you know. People are investing a lot of time and money in this, and there has to be a good turnout or it just won't be worth it."

Eli surprised her by putting his hand on her shoulder. "There will be a big turnout. Because you've done an amazing job. And I know I was kind of grumpy about it for a while, but this is great. You did great. And people have already started pouring in." He slid his palm down her arm, the gesture going from casual encouragement to something that revealed a deeper level of intimacy between them.

And Lydia noticed. Her smile faltered for a moment, and Sadie inwardly cringed.

"Thank you," Sadie said. "Thank you both for all your help and thanks... Eli, for saying that. I really...

tried." And in spite of herself, she had bonded with this place.

She looked around the picnic area, at the people there. Bud from the gas station sitting with his wife and smiling. Cassie from The Grind was with a very nice-looking man Sadie assumed was the same Jake she talked about with a dreamy smile on her face.

The group of fishermen from Rona's were there with their families, and their beer. Her old high school friend Brooke with a group of women dressed in cutoff shorts and American-flag T-shirts.

It wasn't just this place. It was these people.

This man.

And if she was going to do this, be here, she wanted to do it right. She wanted to do it all well.

She sort of hated the pressure that came with it all. The crushing need. So different than a life that wasn't tied to anything. No anchors holding you back. Nothing to entice you to try. She missed it, in a way. But then, going back to it seemed impossible.

Because...big, cowboy-in-a-uniform-shaped anchor. No matter what looked better or easier, it would never really be easy again. Cutting ties with Eli would be something she regretted. But being with him was damn hard. Because he called her on her BS and made her be serious, made her look in his eyes when she climaxed. Forced her not to joke about her pain, but to speak about it honestly.

He added an uncomfortable level of depth to her life. Discomfiting when she'd tried for so long to stay in the shallows. Bastard.

"You did more than try," he said. "You succeeded. Now we just need to wait for the place to fill up."

And it did fill up. It was unbelievable. By the early

afternoon they had people everywhere. Eating, laughing, talking. There was a band playing. Ace, the sexy bartender, was serving beer from the portable tap. The barbecues were going strong and adults were laughing while kids danced in the grass with bare feet.

Eli's three-legged race was a serious hit, and everyone was anxiously awaiting the official barbecue judging, and Jack and Kate's demonstration.

She noticed Eli standing on the perimeter and walked over to where he was, jabbing him lightly with her elbow. Since, you know, she probably couldn't kiss him in public.

"You hungry yet?" she asked.

"Starving."

"Let's get food. There's obviously enough. And we earned it."

"We did," he said. "Well, you did."

"Stop it," she said, leaning into him again and shoving him with her shoulder. "This is your place. And you've been a big support. Stop being so nice to me. It's freaking me out."

"Am I not nice to you?" he asked.

"You are," she said. "I think you've officially crossed over into being mainly nice to me. Which, considering where we came from, is kind of a huge deal."

"Well, I know you now. Instead of just thinking I know about you."

"Same," she said. "Shall we get our barbecue on?"

They walked through the crowd, Eli periodically smiling and waving at those who called out a greeting, and all she could do was just walk next to him in awe of all that he was to these people. He was a cornerstone, her man. The kind of guy who did good all the time. The kind of guy who'd affected many of the people here in amazing ways.

It was daunting. Daunting that a man like him could have clearly done so much and still feel like he hadn't done enough.

It was extra daunting because she wasn't sure if she'd ever made half that impact, even if you cobbled together the things she'd done across all the places she'd lived.

"Chicken or beef?" she asked, when they approached the barbecue line.

"Any," he said. "Any and all."

"All right, we'll fill your plate with meats."

He smiled and right then she didn't really care about impact and other deep things like that. Because Eli was smiling right at her, and that meant a hell of a lot.

"What about you?" he asked.

"I want steak, and I hear it's fantastic because it's Garrett beef. And I want copious amounts of potato salad because who doesn't love a mayonnaise and starch party in their mouth?"

"Well, you obviously do," he said.

She smiled at him, then had to look away to avoid kissing him. She noticed that Alison was at her pie booth, looking harassed and serving pieces of pie onto plates as quickly as possible. Then she noticed that Jared was standing right next to her, his large arms folded over his chest, looking every inch the threatening, Neanderthal jackass he was.

"Uh-oh," she said, "I think we might have a problem."

Eli frowned, then followed her line of sight over to the pie booth. "Oh. That asshole."

"Yeah."

A muscle in Eli's jaw ticked. "I'm feeling pretty short on patience with him."

"I know. But I do understand that there's…" Suddenly Eli was moving out of line and heading toward the booth. "Oh," she said, hurrying after him.

Jared was leaning in near Alison, saying something, and Alison was looking increasingly distressed. And Eli was starting to walk faster.

"Do we have a problem here?" Eli asked.

Jared was a big guy, and scary enough if you were a woman. But Eli stood about four inches taller and had to outweigh him by thirty pounds of pure muscle. Even without the badge and the gun, Eli was an intimidating sight.

In many ways he was more terrifying without the uniform than he was with it on. Because in the uniform, you could see his boundaries. Clearly. Deputy Garrett was a lawman. He was a man who would see justice done in accordance with the legal system.

Right now in his cowboy hat, tight black T-shirt and jeans he looked more likely to dispense a different kind of justice entirely.

And she didn't really know what he might do.

And that was funny because he was predictable and good. Except…except he wasn't all that predictable, not really. When they were in bed, he was a different man, a dangerous man.

When they were together he was something a lot more authentic.

Just now, as he was standing there ready to do God knew what, she realized that the man he was in bed wasn't an anomaly. It was him.

"No problem, Deputy Garrett," Jared said, not drunk today, just hella mean, apparently. "Just talking to my wife." Alison's shoulders shrunk in when he said the word. "That's not a problem, is it?"

"It depends on what words were being used."

"Eli…" Alison said. "It's okay…"

"You on a first-name basis with him?" Jared asked, his tone hard. "Is that why he always seems so worried about you? Are you sleeping with him, you stupid whore?"

And that was when Eli moved.

He leaned in and grabbed Jared by the back of his neck at the same time he brought his fist in to meet the other man's nose. Then he shoved him downward, bending him at the waist while he brought his knee up into Jared's stomach.

Before stepping back and letting the other man fall to the ground at his feet.

People were looking now, craning their necks, wide-eyed. Sadie just stood frozen, almost unable to believe that Eli had done it. And yet, at the same time…she wasn't shocked. No, she wasn't shocked at all.

But she was proud.

"I don't take kindly to the words *bitch* and *whore*," Eli said, keeping his voice low so that the families nearby couldn't hear him. "Especially not when you're talking to your wife. Now stand the fuck up." He gripped the back of Jared's neck and brought him to his feet. "You want to hit someone, why don't you hit me? Or is it not as much fun to go toe-to-toe with someone who outweighs you? I'll bet you're okay with hitting women. But that's not going to play today, so why don't you go ahead and hit me instead?"

Jared spat and blood dribbled down his chin. He wiped it with the back of his hand. "You prick," he said, his eyes blazing.

"Yep," Eli said, "and let me tell you something, this prick is not on duty today. Today, I'm just the owner of this property, and you're the bottom-feeder who isn't welcome on it. You're not welcome in my town, either, but there's nothing I can do about that. But I'll tell you this. I'm going to be looking for you to make a mistake. And then I'll lock your ass up. You put one finger out of line?" He gestured to Alison. "You touch her again? I will see that you stay in a jail cell for a very, very long time. So step carefully. And right now? Step. The hell. Off my property."

Jared stumbled forward and headed away from the stand. Then he turned to Eli, shouting obscenities that all ran together in a blur, before he stopped, like he intended to come back. Until Connor walked into view, from the direction of the main house.

He wrapped his hand around the back of Jared's neck, holding him steady. Eli was pretty big. Eli was threatening. But bearded Connor, who was broad and thick, every bit of him heavily muscled and with rage pouring off him, was terrifying. "I think my brother asked you to go," he said. If Eli hadn't been deterrent enough, Connor was there for backup.

Jared looked back at Eli one more time before turning and walking away, spitting profanities as he went.

Connor moved forward and joined the group. "Well, what an asshole. Sorry." He directed the apology to Alison, who was wide-eyed and shaking. "But seriously."

"Are you okay?" Sadie asked Alison.

Alison nodded, then shook her head, closing her eyes. "I don't know."

"Fair enough," Sadie said.

"I'm embarrassed. I'm so embarrassed that I'm still

married to him," she said, her voice breaking. "But it's…"

"I know," Sadie said. "And trust me, I have spoken to a lot of women who've dealt with this, professionally. And unprofessionally…my mother has never left, Alison. She's stayed and stayed. For more than thirty years. I've seen what it does to someone. I've seen what they can make you think about yourself. But you have to know, whatever he's said, it's a lie."

She nodded. "I know. I do."

"Please don't go back to him. Don't go home tonight."

Connor shifted his stance. "Especially don't go home tonight. He's a coward with us, and that means he'll take it out on you."

"Is there somewhere you can go?" Eli asked.

She nodded. "My…my mom and dad live in Tolowa. I can go there. Not sure what they'll think when I show up, since I don't really… I've been so embarrassed."

"You can call them if you like," Sadie said.

Alison shook her head. "Right now? I just want to serve pie. Because that's what I'm here for. And now that… I have a feeling I'm going to need this. This business. The pie."

"Well, I'll buy a few a week at least for my B and B," Sadie said, determined. No matter how good her cooking skills were, she wasn't going to produce a pie as amazing as Alison's. "And I'll be around. Whatever you need."

"And if he ever comes near you again," Eli said, "if he hits you or threatens you…"

"I'll report him," she said. "I promise I will." She took a deep breath and straightened, and for the first time, Sadie saw an echo of the girl she'd known in the

woman who stood before her. Someone a little scrappy.
A lot angry. Someone who was ready to fight. "Now,
I have pie to serve."

She turned and went back to slicing her pies and Eli,
Connor and Sadie moved away.

"What are you doing out?" Eli asked Connor.

Connor shrugged. "Liss is going to meet me to watch
Kate ride. You know I like to watch her do her thing."

"Yeah," Eli said. "She's great."

Sadie looked behind Connor's shoulder and saw red
waves bouncing just before Liss came into view, jogging up behind him. "I made it. I'm late but I made it."

"You're chronically late," Connor said, turning to
face her. "It's an illness."

"I'm bizay, Connor," she said, poking him in the
side. "You don't know anything about that, obviously."

"No," Connor said, "I just run a whole fricking
ranch, Liss. I know nothing of your busyness. I bet all
that paperwork is a real strain. Wanna trade?"

"Eff no. I am not roping cows."

The ghost of a smile touched Connor's lips when he
looked at his friend. "The cows don't like you much,
either, honey."

"Glad to know it's mutual. The cows and I can go
on giving each other the evil eye. Then I'll eat a burger
because I'm human and I win."

"Come on, then, let's go," Connor said, putting his
hands in his pockets and jerking his head in the direction of the arena.

"We haven't eaten yet," Eli said, and his referring to
them as a "we" made Sadie feel a little warm and fuzzy.

"Go get some food, then. We'll see you over there,"
Connor said, eyeing them both, and Sadie felt her
cheeks heat a little.

"So that was Connor in a good mood?" Sadie asked, when he and Liss were out of earshot.

"Pretty much. He got to threaten bodily harm to someone so I fail to see how he could have had a better day."

She started back over to the barbecue line, chewing on her lip. "Are you worried?" she asked. "About how all that might affect your campaign?"

He frowned. "I didn't even think of that. Which is… weird. I usually think of everything."

"Well, I don't want to add concerns that you don't really need."

"No," he said, "I think it's interesting. I don't care," he said, meeting her gaze. "I just don't care. Because I still want to be sheriff. I still think I'd do a damn good job, but I do a good job at what I do now. And… whether or not it was a popular thing or easy thing or good thing…punching that asshole in the face was the right thing to do."

She wrapped her arms around his neck and hugged him, then quickly stepped back, embarrassed by her public demonstration. "It was," she said.

"Somehow, knowing that, believing that, makes me not care very much what the consequences are."

"I think you're amazing," she said, looking ahead, smiling. "I mean, if that matters."

"It does," he said.

"And…thank you. Because she's my friend. Because she reminded me too much of my mom. And… I'm always afraid people like that will never leave."

"A lot of times they go back," he said, his voice rough.

"I know. But we'll help her."

"Yes," he said, "we will."

Yet again, she didn't know what to do with him. She felt so close to him right now, and she couldn't kiss him here. She wanted to ask him to hold her. She wanted to tell him something about herself. Wanted him to decide that, much like punching a guy in front of the whole town, she was okay, too.

And right then, she thought of the one place she hadn't been yet. She'd driven by the house where she'd grown up, but she hadn't been back to her clearing. Even though it was within walking distance of the B and B. She'd avoided serious thoughts of it since the first day back.

Again, a prickling sensation dotted the back of her neck.

There are no ghosts there. And if there are...maybe this will put some of them to rest.

She let out a long, slow breath, trying to gather her nerve. "Can I show you something?"

"My mom warned me about girls like you," he said, a smile teasing the corners of his lips.

"Did she?"

"No, my mom wasn't here."

"That's a dire punch line."

He lifted a shoulder. "Sometimes life is so dire you have to make a joke about it, right?"

"I think you've learned too much from me."

"Or not enough," he said.

"Hey, I'll get our food. Can you get a blanket for us to sit on?" she asked.

"Yeah."

She finished waiting through the line and got small portions of everything on offer, making small talk with the men and women manning the grills and scooping up sides. It was hard to do, though, since she was all jittery and fluttery inside over what she was about to do.

And there was no real logical reason why. Just that it seemed like a big deal. Bigger in some ways than what she'd shared about her father.

Because this was something she'd avoided. The last bit of Copper Ridge she hadn't revisited. And she wasn't going to test it alone to be sure she was okay. To be certain she could visit it without betraying her emotions.

She was going to let him see. All of it.

She wandered over to where he stood on the edge of the lawn, where people were sitting at the tables that had been set up, and on blankets spread out like a rainbow patchwork over the green grass.

"Okay," he said, "what do you have to show me?"

"I hope you're ready for a hike."

IT WAS ONLY a five-minute walk, through the trees behind the B and B, just over the Garretts' property line. But the path was thick with brush and branches, the narrow trail overgrown in the years since Sadie and her friends had used it.

She and Eli wound through the evergreens, needles reaching out and grabbing her T-shirt. Then the grove thinned out, and beyond that was her clearing.

It was overgrown now, moss covering the ground, ferns encroaching. There was still a fire ring. Stumps, some on their sides, some still positioned like stools.

It had definitely been used by other people in the past decade, but not, it appeared, very recently.

"This," she said, "was my home away from home."

Her chest swelled up with emotion just looking at it, being in it. She wasn't sure why. She wasn't sure why this felt so big. Why she felt so naked.

But, like all her big feelings concerning Eli, the flip side was that as much as it hurt, she wanted him to know this part of her.

She wanted him to know her. There wasn't, she realized, another person on the whole planet—except Toby—who did.

"Alison, Matt, Josh, Brooke and a few others and I all hung out here in the afternoons. Sometimes when we were supposed to be in school. Usually on weekends."

"Doing what?" he asked.

"Drinking. Smoking…things of varying degrees of legality. Like you do. Well, not like *you* do, but like a lot of teenage ne'er-do-wells do."

He looked up at the canopy of trees overheard, then back at her. "I bet it was a great place for that."

'Perfect," she said. "You never arrested me here."

"I didn't."

"But then, in fairness, I never lit the woods on fire."

"That is true enough."

He set the blanket down in the middle of the clearing and they sat, putting their food in front of them. Sadie sat on her knees and started to poke at her potato salad.

"I lost my virginity here." Next to her Eli made a choking sound and she laughed. "Sorry," she said, "just a Sadie fun fact." It wasn't, though. She was minimizing it again. Minimizing why she'd told him. She always did that. So that if what she'd offered was rejected, she could pretend it didn't hurt.

She shoved her plate to the side and took a deep breath. "Sorry." She started over. "I told you because it seemed… This is where I learned to run," she said. "Where I learned to escape. None of us could handle the things that were happening at home and so we came here. Did a bunch of things that made us feel good. Sex was just another thing to do. But that's changing for me. All the way until I met you, sex was just a part of the logical steps in a relationship. A way to pretend that I was intimate with someone without ever really having to be. And this? Telling you this, showing you this, it's more intimate than anything I've ever done. But that's fitting, because when we're together…when we… It was never part of a logical step. It was just a thing we couldn't *not* do. And that's different, too."

"You're…different for me, too," he said.

She wanted him to say more. And she didn't know what more, but she did. She wanted to say more, but again, she wasn't sure what else. Wasn't sure what she could say that wouldn't scare her off.

She was a flight risk of the highest order, putting herself in a situation that scared her to death.

"Eli… I…" She wanted to say something big. She wanted to try to express what she was feeling but she couldn't even quantify it to herself.

The thing she wanted to say was the thing she couldn't say. Because to say it was too much. And way more than this was ever supposed to be.

The one thing she knew for sure, and the thing that terrified her to her bones, was that she wanted to have him here. In this place. The moments of weighted silence, punctuated by heavy sighs and long drags on cigarettes. Days when they'd come and sat in the rain and talked and swore as loud as they wanted, because screw the world. They were in their own world. When she'd come alone with Josh and kissed him and, eventually, taken things further because they'd both just needed someone to touch.

In this place where she'd been with her first guy, she wanted to be with Eli. The last one.

Shock skittered over her skin in an electric current. At the weight of the thought, the depth of it, the truth of it.

So she just said what she could.

"I want you."

"I thought you wanted potato salad."

She tried to laugh, shaking from the inside out. "No. Just you."

He seemed to sense the shift in tone. Another luxury of being with him. Of having him know her. He seemed to know what was happening inside her without her having to say it.

He set his plate off the blanket, too, cupping her cheek and leaning in for a kiss. She returned it, her chest filling, swelling, making it impossible to breathe. But breathing seemed secondary at the moment. Because of Eli.

She wrapped her arms around his neck and he slipped one hand down her back, holding her waist tight as he lowered her to the blanket, his body solid and warm above her. They sat together, his hands stroking her face, her hair.

He kissed her deeper and she laced her fingers through his hair. She felt everything happening on the surface of her skin. The scrape of his stubble against her neck as he kissed her there. As his hands moved over her T-shirt, the warmth of his touch seeping through to her skin.

But it was the echo beneath the surface that really hit. That anchored her to him, to the world. It was like a deep bass note that resonated through her, vibrating along every vein, moving deep to the core of her being.

They broke the kiss, looking at each other, and her

eyes met his, emotion building in her chest, bigger and stronger than any sexual climax.

It was painful and beautiful. She didn't think she could stand it for another moment, and she didn't want it to end. In that moment, she felt it all, the good, bad and scary, bound together, inescapable.

She was drowning in it, drowning in *him*. In what he made her feel. She couldn't run from it, couldn't make light of it. Couldn't shove it to the side.

All she could do was embrace it.

She held on to him, hoping his strength would hold her together because at this point, she didn't trust her own. And that was a damn scary place to be. But she was with Eli, so it had to be safe, too.

"When I'm with you, I don't want to be anywhere else," he said, moving his hand over her hair, sliding his fingers through the strands.

"Me, either," she said.

It was true. And for a woman who was always so keen to move on to the next place, the next thing, it was a huge and frightening admission.

He shifted their positions so that she was sitting between his thighs, her back to his chest, his fingers gentle as he laced them through her hair. She closed her eyes, a tightening moving from her chest, up her throat, making it hard to breathe. Making her ache.

"Is this what you used to do here?" he asked.

She laughed, a shaky sound that didn't do anything to loosen the knot of emotion inside her. "Not exactly. I've never done anything quite like this."

"Me, either."

He tugged lightly on her hair, once, then again. She turned and looked at him, and he kept hold of her. "What are you doing?" she asked.

He cocked his head to the side, a rueful smile on his face. "Braiding your hair." He kept his eyes on hers as he wove another section together. "Is that okay?"

She looked at his face, at the sincerity in his eyes. Sincerity and caring she'd never had directed at her before, and that she'd never hoped to deserve. The walls inside her cracked and she had to fight to keep the tears that welled up in her eyes from spilling down her cheeks.

Because when he said that, what she heard was *I'm taking care of you.*

"Yeah," she said, the word a whisper. "It's okay."

She closed her eyes while he finished, focusing on breathing. On not breaking down completely over this moment. On not betraying everything she felt.

He slid his thumb down the side of her neck, his touch gentle. "Done."

She turned back to him again. She wanted to say so much. And nothing, and everything.

He leaned in slowly, his breath fanning across her cheek. Then he kissed her, and she let herself get lost in it. In a kiss that wasn't meant to start anything, wasn't meant to arouse. A kiss that was meant to forge a connection. An outpouring of all the emotion their joining had brought to the surface.

Panic clawed at her as she realized the kiss would have to end. This moment would have to end.

She didn't want the kiss to end, because when it did, they would have to deal with what happened next. And part of her was already panicking about that. Part of her was feeling the need to run.

This was deep. And it was real. And the most terrifying four-letter word she could think of was pushing into her consciousness, hovering on the edge of her lips, burrowing into her heart.

And that was the one thing she hadn't wanted. The thing she feared more than anything.

But the kiss had to end. And it did. When they parted he slid his thumb over the edge of her lip. "Sadie…"

"We should go," she said, terror gnawing at her. Terror that he was going to say what she was trying not to think. That he wouldn't say it. That he would never say it. Or that he would now when she wasn't sure she could deal with hearing it.

She reached back and touched her hair, ran her fingertips over the imperfect braid. "We really should go," she repeated.

"Uh…yeah," he said, letting out a big gust of air. "You're right. The barbecue. It's your baby. You…you should be there for it."

"Well, yeah," she said, wrapping her arms around her midsection. "I kind of should. Sorry about… Not much of a seduction, I guess."

He met her gaze, his eyes intense. "I don't know if I'd say that."

She breathed in deeply through her nose, smoke burning her nostrils, and frowned. "I would have thought they'd be powering down the grills about now. It's getting dark."

"Maybe that many more people showed up," he said, sounding slightly grim and serious, and it was probably her fault. For cutting him off. For bringing him out here and spilling her guts and then basically telling him nothing of what she was feeling because it all scared her too much.

"We can hope," she said, rounding up the blanket and holding it tight against her chest. Like she was trying to apply pressure to a wound, and in some ways, she felt like that's exactly what she was doing.

Eli picked up the uneaten food, and Sadie mourned it slightly, because she didn't feel like eating at all now. She was too full. Of feelings she didn't want to sort through. Emotions she didn't want to have.

They headed back toward the ranch, cutting through the trees, Sadie taking the lead and not walking hand in hand with Eli, like she sort of wished she could.

You can't bolt if he's holding on to you.

The smoke got thicker as they got closer to the ranch, the wind bringing a wall of it their direction. "What the hell?" he asked.

"I don't know," she said. "That's not... That's not normal."

Eli picked up the pace, passing her, before he moved into a dead run. She followed after him, clutching the blanket against her pounding heart.

She was saying things. Worried things. Things with swearing. But she couldn't really make sense of them. They were just pouring out of her mouth without any kind of specific order or reason. Fear, irrational at this point, but intuitively driving her on.

She knew something had gone wrong. She knew it as certainly as anything she'd seen with her own eyes.

And she knew it was bad.

They crossed the dirt road and back into the Garrett property line to see flames rising up above the trees.

"Oh, no. Oh, no," she said, running after Eli, releasing her hold on the blanket and letting it fall to the ground as she picked up her pace.

They ran back to the main area to find the picnickers standing facing the barn. The beautiful barn that Connor had poured his money into. Now on fire. A wicked blaze that was eating through the beautifully stained wood, the newly shingled roof.

"The horses," she said, gasping for air. "Animals?" She couldn't think. She couldn't remember the layout of things, not now. Her brain was just swimming.

"No animals in there," Eli said, his brow creased, his mouth turned down. "Just the equipment. The feed. All Connor's equipment," he repeated. "Did someone call the fire department?" Eli asked.

"Yeah." Sadie turned and saw Liss standing there, a tear rolling down her cheek. "I did."

"Is there anyone inside?"

"Not as far as we know," Liss said, her eyes not on Eli, but on Connor, who was standing nearer to the blaze than anyone else, his posture stiff, staring right at it. Watching so much of his livelihood burn.

"There's insurance," Eli said.

"Of course," Liss said. "It'll be okay." She didn't sound convinced, not at all.

A group of boys, who must have been twelve, walked up to Eli, their faces ashen, their eyes wide. "We didn't mean to, Deputy Garrett," the smallest one said. "But it's a Fourth of July thing and we were messing with fireworks..."

"In the barn?" Eli asked, his tone hard.

"Well, yeah, because we didn't want our moms to see. And we didn't think..."

"About the hay," Eli said.

"We thought," one of the other boys said, "that we'd gotten all the sparks doused and we left..."

And they'd left a smoldering firework in the hay, to burn it all from the inside out so that by the time anyone realized, the blaze inside had consumed the fuel and moved on to the structure.

Sadie was starting to shake. It was too similar to her last night in Copper Ridge. Too close to sins she'd already committed. Eli hadn't wanted this on his property, Connor hadn't wanted it and she'd pushed. She'd come onto their property, into their lives and destroyed their order.

And this was the result.

This is what happens when you try. You can't fix it. You never could.

She was watching the Garretts' world burn in front of her. Her handiwork. No, she wasn't going to fall prostrate to the ground and take total fault. She wasn't an idiot. It had been little boys with firecrackers, not her with a match. Not her at a party knocking over a lantern.

But it didn't change how horrible she felt. Didn't change the way it was unfolding. Or the fact that the boys were only here because of her.

"Eli…"

"Not now, Sadie," he said, his voice rough.

"I'm so sorry… I…"

"I said not fucking now, Sadie," he bit out, forking his fingers through his hair, his eyes on the scene in front of them. Sadie's heart curled in tight around the edges, like it had been set on fire, too.

She took a step back from him, her head swimming. She wondered if she should do something with the crowd? Try to manage? But everyone was frozen, staring at what was happening, and she just felt useless. Helpless. Like she'd been as a child in her home growing up. Watching sick, unending horror playing out before her eyes while she cowered, powerless to stop it.

The fire department came, en masse, sirens rising up over the sound of the blaze. And when it was over, there was no question as to what was left: nothing.

Nothing but a charred husk. Unusable, unsalvageable. The crowd had thinned by then, families with small children taking them away from the upsetting scene. They'd all moved on to the main fireworks display down at the beach. Though mainly they'd left so quickly to escape the smoke and debris. Sadie wished she could get carried away from it, too, but she had to watch, her own eyes gritty with ashes. She felt honor bound in so many ways.

Finally, all that remained were Liss, Jack, Kate, Eli, Lydia, Ace, Bud and the fishermen.

And Connor. Who stood alone, silent and in sharp contrast to the blackened ruins in front of him. Unmoving.

Liss was the one who broke from the small crowd and went to him, her hand going to his shoulder. He jerked away from her and walked back toward the main house, leaving Liss standing there with her arms folded beneath her breasts.

A moment later she took a deep breath and marched after him, a stubborn set to her jaw and shoulders, and for a moment, Sadie could only admire the other woman's strength. Liss was a woman who stayed. A woman who went the tough rounds.

It made Sadie feel painfully inadequate, standing there in the semi-darkness, with cooling ashes just in front of her.

"Whatever you need, Eli," Ace said. "You know we're here to help out."

"I know," Eli said.

"Anything," Lydia said. And Sadie knew she was ready to offer comfort as well, and Sadie couldn't even be mad because she felt so unequal to the task.

"Probably we all just need sleep right now," Eli said, forcing a smile.

Kate was standing silent, tears streaming down her cheeks, her shoulders shaking. Sadie moved nearer to her and put her arm around her. Feeling so inadequate to do anything to stanch the flow of grief around her.

"Of course," Ace said. "We'll get out of your hair. I'll come by tomorrow if you want, help assess the damage?"

"Thanks. I imagine we'll just be making an insurance claim. And they'll have to send someone out. Best we leave it untouched for now."

"Fair point. Come by for a drink, though," Ace said, touching the brim of his ball cap before walking away.

"Guess I better let you get rest, too," Lydia said, putting her hand on Eli's shoulder in a decidedly nonsisterly way. "I'll come by and check in on you tomorrow."

Eli didn't protest.

Lydia squeezed Sadie's shoulder, too, as she walked by her. "I'm happy to check in on you, too."

That tipped her over into utter misery. Because she didn't deserve that kindness. Not at all. "Thanks," she said, her throat raw.

"I'll go talk to the firemen," Jack said, "see if there's anything we need to know. I'll report back."

"I'm going to go find Connor," Kate said, her voice thick as she pulled away from Sadie and walked in the direction of the main house.

That left Sadie and Eli, and a pile of glowing, charred wood, alone in the darkness.

She swallowed and tried again. "Eli, I…"

"We have to be done," Eli said, cutting her off.

"What?"

"This. Us. It has to… I can't do this," he said.

ELI'S HEART TWISTED into a knot in his chest, but it had to be said. It had to be done. Because yet again, while he'd been out enjoying himself, the whole world had fallen apart. All of this, the time spent with Sadie, had been an illusion.

When he didn't keep control, the world burned. In this case, literally.

It was just too damn close to his other failures. Too damn close.

"When I'm with you, I forget what I'm doing. I forget other people. I forget myself. No, I don't forget myself, because myself is all I think of. Myself and my dick, and it can't happen like this. There is a reason that I've lived my life the way that I have. A reason that I can't ignore for good sex."

Sadie blinked rapidly, her eyes glossy in the dim light. And his stomach twisted, sick regret forming. But there was nothing else he could do. He needed to stay on top of this stuff and he wasn't doing it.

His sister had just stood there in tears, his brother watching the one thing he'd held on to since losing his wife burn to nothing.

It was all way too reminiscent of the night when he hadn't taken the keys. Of the last time Eli had let himself become distracted.

And it didn't matter what Sadie said, because in the end, this was the result. It didn't matter if he shouldn't feel at fault. He did. And it didn't change the fact that when he wasn't holding up the world around him, it all seemed to fall apart.

For a second today, he'd thought he could be something different, have something different. And then all this had swooped in and reminded him just why that wasn't possible.

Why he had to forget their moment in the woods, and every moment before. Why he had to stop wanting more, when more would never be in the cards for him. He knew that. He'd known that before Sadie Miller had blown into his life like a windstorm and rearranged his existence. Made him think that maybe everything he'd believed about his life, about himself, had been a lie.

Which was a whole lot crueler than never having hope had ever been.

For one moment, he'd thought he could do it. Thought he could punch the hell out of a guy who deserved it, thought he could sneak into the woods for a moment alone with the only woman who'd ever driven him that crazy.

Thought he could go to sleep with her every night and wake up with her every morning.

"Good sex, Eli?" she asked. "Really? Good sex? Because I think, I mean, I pretty freaking well think what we have is a lot more than that. I mean, I think we'd both had good sex before we ever met each other, and that…this is something else entirely. What we share is something else."

"It doesn't matter," he said. "It can't happen." He wanted to lash out. To blame someone other than himself. He was so tired of carrying it all. And this was just another failure. "It seems like when you're around barns tend to burn down," he said. "You have a knack for spreading disaster, I guess."

"Eli, please don't do this. Not now, not… Please."

"Sadie, I can't afford any more distractions," he said, the words scraping his throat raw. "And that's all this was. All you are to me is a distraction."

She stumbled backward and he felt like his heart lurched through his chest to follow her, leaving nothing but a bloody, vacant hole behind. This felt like he thought dying might. But he couldn't take the words back now.

He wouldn't.

It was the right thing to do. Other men could have wives and kids. Other men with other lives.

Not him. Never him.

"Well," she said, her voice thick as she put distance between them. "Don't let me distract you any longer."

She turned and walked back in the direction of the B and B, which he only thought of as hers now. What a difference a few weeks made.

But he couldn't afford the difference, and neither could any of the people who depended on him.

CHAPTER SIXTEEN

SADIE DIDN'T SLEEP at all. She spent the whole night out on her newly stained deck, a mug of coffee clutched tightly in her hand, tears rolling down her face as she slowly accepted what had happened. As she slowly accepted what she'd let herself do.

She loved Eli Garrett.

He was the first person she'd loved since she'd lost hope in her family a decade ago and run out of town.

He was the first person she'd been close to in as many years, if not more. If not ever.

She stayed on the deck, wrapped in her blanket and her misery, Toby snuggled in her lap, until pink started to bleed into the sky, extending up above the tree line.

Well, damn. There went her theory about the world stopping because she was devastated.

She deposited Toby gently onto the deck, then went into the house with him following behind her. She went upstairs, undressed and stepped into the shower, letting the hot water wash away the stiffness, the misery.

In the end, some of the stiffness got worked out, but the misery remained.

She brushed her teeth, which were fuzzy after an evening of nursing coffees, then made herself another in her single-serving brewer, bought especially so that her guests could have a fresh cup at any point in the day.

She let out a heavy sigh. Her guests. She'd had several people get in touch since the night before, inquiring about availability through her website. So soon there would be guests. She had a five-year contract.

She lowered her head, feeling very much like she was sinking into the mire. A mire she couldn't just cut and run from.

And suddenly she felt claustrophobic. She wanted to claw her clothes off, claw her skin off, step out of her body and just run from all of it.

Get away and start fresh. Away from that man, away from the feelings he made her feel.

She looked around the B and B, at her attempt to build something permanent. To make something stable. She should have known it was never about her surroundings. It was about her. It always had been.

She couldn't sign a five-year lease and expect it to make her different.

The simple truth was, she'd never been important enough for anyone to change for her. That was the painful heart of it. Her mother would rather spend her life being beaten by a man, the same man who beat her child, than leave him for the good of them both.

Her love for a husband who dealt out pain and misery was stronger than her love for Sadie. And that made it impossible to imagine anyone changing their life drastically for the sake of her love.

And Eli was proving that no one would.

This was why she always left. Because if she left first, if she never let anyone close, if she never asked anyone to know her and accept her anyway, she couldn't get hurt.

But she'd come back to Copper Ridge. She'd given of herself. She'd fallen in love and dared to hope for it back.

And now she was broken. And she had no idea how long it would take to glue the pieces back together.

One thing was for sure. She couldn't do it here.

"Toby," she said, looking at her little gray friend, the only friend she really had, "I think it's time for us to go."

ELI PACED THE length of the living room, eyeing his brother, who was passed out on the couch. He was going to hate life a whole hell of a lot when Eli woke him up.

Which was going to be now, because Eli hated life, so Connor might as well join the living.

In hell.

"Wake up, Connor," he said, clapping his hands and watching his brother go from blissfully conked out to awake and in a world of pain in an instant.

"Dammit all!" he said, then winced, his hand on his forehead. "Ow."

"Yeah, I would think *ow*. You drank roughly the amount of alcohol it would take to cleanse all the wounds on a frontier battlefield."

"Oh…shut up, Eli. Honestly."

"We have things to do."

"Like?" he asked. "Work? Because I think all my tools are gone."

"You have animals that might want to get fed."

"I don't have hay," Connor mumbled.

"So get off your ass and get some," Eli said, feeling angry. At himself, mainly, but yelling at Connor was more convenient than dealing with that.

"What the hell is your issue this morning?" Connor asked, moving into a sitting position, running his hands over his beard.

"Maybe I'm tired of watching you wallow while I

take care of you," Eli said, resentment flaring up, rage burning hot in his chest.

He'd resigned himself to this last night.

To caring for other people and putting himself on hold. But this morning? This morning he'd woken up alone. And it hurt worse than he'd imagined it could. Thirty-two years of it. He should be used to it. But this morning his bed had felt so empty it had mimicked the damn hole in his chest.

And he was forgetting already why a burned-out barn had mattered more than Sadie next to him.

"What?" Connor asked.

"You are my older brother. You're a grown man."

"I never asked you to take care of me," Connor said.

"You expect it," Eli bit out.

Connor shook his head. "Look, man, I don't know what the hell your problem is, but I've never asked you for anything. I'm glad you're here, I won't lie, but if you weren't? I would be happy to just stay drunk and live in filth. You're the one who—"

"And it's things like that, Connor, that mean I can't leave you to it. Because you don't think I know you'd sink in it? I do, and I won't let it happen."

"And so what, Eli? I'm supposed to get myself together the way you see fit so you don't have to deal?"

"Yeah," Eli said. "Yeah. Just…could you? Because I can't work a job, and work on the ranch, and run for sheriff, and file your insurance claim and not lose my fucking mind. I can't… I can't do it all."

That was the first time he'd ever admitted that. To himself. To anyone else. That he couldn't shoulder everything. That he didn't even want to.

"I didn't know, Eli," Connor said, looking straight ahead. "I've had a hard time caring about anything other than myself. For the record, I mostly still don't care about anything else, but... I'm damn sorry you felt that way."

"It wasn't ever just you," Eli said. "But you know you've added to it."

"Well," Connor drawled. "I do what I can."

"You make me feel like a dick for complaining since you've been through hell."

"Yeah. Still in it most days," he mumbled. "But I guess I don't have to bring you with me."

"Sometimes I think I brought myself on purpose."

"Well, stop," Connor said.

"What?"

"Stop. Being unhappy is stupid. If there's any way you can fix it? Fix it. I can't bring my wife back. I can't...fix anything that happened. I can't make my life better just by making a different choice."

"I'm not sure I can, either," Eli said.

"Does it have to do with Sadie?"

Eli breathed in deep. "Yeah."

"She's not dead, is she?"

"No," Eli said, his voice rough.

"Then there's still hope."

CHAPTER SEVENTEEN

SADIE FINISHED PILING her personal belongings into the car. She was violating her lease agreement and she knew it. It sucked, but she just… She couldn't stay. She didn't know much about what would happen next, but she knew that much.

She sighed and put Toby's cat carrier in the backseat, safely on the floorboards, before shutting the back door.

She heard a car driving up the driveway and swore copiously under her breath. She didn't want to deal with a crestfallen Kate, a pissed-off Connor or…worse than them all, an Eli, in whatever form he chose to present.

But instead of a Garrett vehicle, it was a shiny black car making its way down the driveway.

"Lydia," she grumbled, leaning against her car and looking down. Oh, well, the other woman could give her a send-off. Hell, she'd probably be thrilled to do it.

Lydia stopped her car and got out, a stack of brochures in her hand and a frown crossing her fine features. "What's going on?" she asked.

"I'm heading out," Sadie said. "It's…kind of what I do. Don't be alarmed."

"Too late," Lydia said. "I am. Eli didn't tell you to—"

"Oh, no, he's too much of a gentleman for that." Not too much of one to break her heart and say she wasn't important, but he'd never ask her to violate a lease agreement. That shit was legally binding.

"Does he know you're leaving?" she asked.

"No, I didn't tell him. Though it's really more relevant to Connor since he's the one who sort of headed up the lease thingy…"

"Oh, what a bunch of baloney," Lydia said. "It is not more relevant to Connor than it is to Eli if you go. And I think you know it."

She averted her eyes. "Do you know it?"

Lydia sighed. "I'm not stupid. Possibly a little bit… mmm…too hopeful? But yeah, not stupid. I've seen the way you look at each other."

Sadie cleared her throat. "But have you heard the way we talk to each other? Because that might be a better indicator of where we're at."

"Do you love him?" she asked.

Sadie's heart squeezed tight. "It doesn't matter."

"It matters. Eli Garrett is the best man I know. The best man I've ever known. And you know, I realized he's not that into me. Sure, it's sort of been a die-hard crush, even with that in mind, but pretty much the minute you showed up I knew I was screwed." She smiled, the expression tinged with sadness. "Not in a fun way, either. But ultimately, I know I won't be happy with a guy I have to coerce into a relationship. And I have a sneaking suspicion he won't be happy *without* you."

Sadie laughed. "Tell him that. He told me he didn't want me."

"He's lying," she said. "You realize that, right?"

"I don't think Eli knows how to lie."

"Well, maybe not on purpose. But he's lying even if he doesn't know he is. One benefit of watching someone more closely than you should, you get to know them. The way he looks at you? That's special. If I were you? I wouldn't walk away from that. I'd fight for it. And I'll be honest, Sadie, I took you for kind of a badass, so...if you run now, I'm going to have to retract that."

"I'm not a badass," Sadie said. "I'm basically whatever is the opposite of that. And I've never pretended to be much more. I'm a runner. And it's my cue to go."

"That sucks, because I think if you stayed, and if we weren't competing for the same guy, we could be friends. And I think if you stayed, and you married him, eventually, we would be friends. You know, after I got over my seething jealousy."

"You don't seem to be seething all that much," Sadie said.

"It's a quiet seethe. Like I said, I know he's not mine." She smiled a little more genuinely now. "Kind of bummed I never got to..."

Sadie coughed. "Yeah...that's kind of... He's good at the sex."

Lydia cleared her throat, her cheeks turning pink. "I was going to say kiss him. But sure."

Sadie winced. "Well, he's good at that, too."

"I can't decide if it sucks to know that or if it's gratifying to realize my fantasies were on track."

"It sucks to know. Because I know it sucks that I know. Because it's over. And I wish it weren't."

"So fight for it, badass," Lydia said. "Fight for *him*."

"I don't think there's anything to fight for."

"Well, then, maybe you should go. Because I happen to think he deserves someone who will fight. I thought that might be you."

"Maybe you should fight for him," Sadie said, feeling mean, small and not at all in the mood to watch another woman fight for the man she loved. But not brave enough to go and get him herself.

Lydia looked at her sadly. "It was nice to meet you,

Sadie. I hope you find whatever you're looking for. And I really hope that you don't realize it was here when it's too late for you to come back."

Sadie watched Lydia toss the brochures on her passenger seat and drive away and felt a whole hot ball of rage grow in her chest. Who was Lydia to tell her what she should do? Seriously. She hadn't been there. She hadn't heard the way Eli talked to her. What he'd said.

Lydia probably had no idea what it was like to be certain that the only way attachment could end was rejection.

And hell, he'd rejected her. Why subject herself to it twice?

Because for the first time, you felt complete. Because for the first time you want to stay. Really, really.

Well, it didn't really matter. Because he'd pushed her away.

You're just too pathetic to fight for him. Too afraid.

Yeah, well, because what if she was wrong? Sure, maybe Eli was as afraid as she was. Maybe that was half of why he'd pushed her away. Maybe.

She jerked the backseat door open and pulled out the pet carrier, depositing it on the porch, checking to make sure Toby's food, water and litter weren't disturbed.

Then she looked out into the forest.

The place she'd always gone to escape, before she'd run for real.

She took a deep breath of the pine and salt air. And then she ran.

THE WAY ELI saw it, he had two options. The Connor option—really, the Garrett option—that meant drinking until you couldn't remember why you were sad.

Or the handle-your-shit option, which was a lot harder.

He stared at the bottle of Jack on the counter and placed his palms flat on the marble surface, looking at the bottle. As if it might tell him what to do.

"Drink it and it might," he said.

Then he shoved off from the counter and started pacing the room. What was he doing? He felt like hell. Or something worse than hell, whatever that was.

But he had order. He didn't have a blonde whirlwind with a strange emotional connection to a cat. He didn't have distractions. He had what he'd spent a lifetime cultivating.

"Loneliness," he said to the empty room. "You have loneliness. Give the man a prize."

And it was all he ever had to look forward to. An orderly life and an empty bed. All because he was too afraid to let someone in.

All because it was so much easier to keep everyone out and to never lose anyone or anything again. All because it was easier to blame himself so he could pretend he had some control in the universe when the simple fact was he didn't have control over any of it.

Mothers left. People died. Barns burned. And no amount of diligence on his part would ever stop it.

He slammed his fist down onto the counter and swore as pain shot up his arm, straight through to his heart.

What a terrible realization. And too late. Dammit, if he was going to have to deal with the fact that he had no control over his life, over anything, the least he could have done was grasped the concept before he'd lost her.

Sadie...

He looked at the spotless counter, where she'd once put her damned tennis shoes. Who did shit like that?

And even though the shoes were gone, and there was not a speck of dust from the tread left behind, the memory lingered so strongly there might as well have been a muddy footprint there.

It would have been easier to erase.

He turned away from the counter and looked out the front window, and his heart about burst. Her azalea. Her apology azalea with its pink flowers. Another Sadie invasion that had been obnoxious at first, but that he couldn't imagine life without now.

She was everywhere in his house. At the counter, drinking a beer. In his bed. His shower. His yard. His heart.

Dammit, she was in his heart.

He loved her.

The realization sent warmth blooming through him. Like a burst blood vessel around his heart, flooding his chest and making him feel weak.

He *loved her.*

He hadn't loved anyone but Kate and Connor in… ever. Hadn't wanted to because he'd been so busy trying to hold the world together. Trying to make sense of things that just didn't make sense.

Trying to keep his family from falling apart, so that no one else would leave. So that he would matter.

But Sadie had always acted like he mattered, even when he was screwing things up. Sadie had held him, stripped him of his inhibitions in a way nothing and no one else ever had, accepted him when he confessed his shortcomings. Sadie, who had shared herself with him when she hadn't shared with anyone else.

An offering of herself, but also a demonstration of the trust she put in him.

And he had turned her away to keep wandering

through life, holding on with an iron fist, trying desperately to earn the trust of strangers. To be seen as good enough.

When she'd already seen him that way.

"Probably not now, asshole," he said into the empty room.

No, probably not now.

And he couldn't blame her.

But he had to ask. He had to try. He had to beg forgiveness.

He had to tell her he loved her.

And damn the consequences.

Order meant nothing without her, control meant nothing without her. And the only acceptance that mattered was hers.

He shoved the Jack Daniel's bottle back into its place in the cupboard and walked out of his house. He strode toward the B and B, his heart in his throat, his hands honest-to-God shaking. Everything in him was shaking.

He'd never loved anyone. And he'd never asked anyone to love him back.

He'd tried to earn it, every day. But he'd never asked.

Today he had to ask.

He walked across the driveway and into the clearing in front of her house, and saw her car, the back door open, suitcases inside.

"What the hell?"

Just then, Sadie came down the stairs, a couple of pine needles stuck in her hair, tears on her cheeks, her face pale. Her eyes widened and she froze, staring at him like he was some kind of ghost. He walked toward her.

She was packed. She was leaving.

She was leaving him.

Hell no.

He reached out and wrapped his arm around her waist, tugging her to him, his lips crashing down on hers. He tried to make her feel what he did. To understand what he'd just started to understand. That he loved her. That she'd changed him.

She clung to him, grabbing his T-shirt and holding it tight, holding him tight.

When they parted, they were both breathing hard, and her cheeks were wet, tears tracking down her pale skin.

"Don't leave me," he said, his tone a command. "Don't go."

"Eli…"

"I am an idiot. You *are* distracting. And you did change things. But dammit, Sadie, I want to be distracted by you. I want to be changed by you. Hell, baby, I need it. And I was just about to drink a whole bottle of liquor to try to forget how much of an ass I am. But then I saw my counter."

"Your counter?"

"It's clean. Your shoes aren't sitting on it. Everything's in order. Everything. You're not there saying some…sexual innuendo I barely understand, and you know what? I hate it. I hate the order if it means I can't have you. I love you, Sadie."

"I'm not leaving," she said, her voice trembling.

"Then why are you packed?"

"Because. Because I was going to leave but I went and did some thinking. And now I'm not," she said.

"Why?" he asked.

"You know…it's hard to say. Because leaving is what I do. And even when I knew I would miss you like hell it seemed easier than this. Easier than standing in front of you and telling you I want more. But I'm going to do it anyway. I went back to my clearing. It was where I used to go when things got to be too much. When I needed to escape. But I didn't find oblivion there. I found you instead. And whatever power there was in escape, whatever I used to enjoy about it...it was gone. I don't want to run anymore. I want to stand and fight. I want to stay. I want more. Because I want you. I want everything. Good and bad and stick up your ass. I love you and I want to fight for that love like I've never fought for anything."

He felt like he'd been punched in the chest. It was one thing to confess his love to her, but he didn't think for a damn minute he deserved to have it returned. Not after the things he'd said to her.

"How can you love *me*?" he asked. "I failed you."

"That's the thing, though, Eli, you didn't. I wished that someone would have stepped in and saved me. Of course I did. And I think...it was easy to wish it had been you. But what I really needed was to save myself."

"You did, Sadie," he said, his chest tightening. "You left."

She shook her head. "No. That's not when I saved myself. That's when I learned to run. Which is the first step sometimes. But I realized something today, when I was ready to leave this place, to leave you. I realized it's not enough to have a life. You have to have all of life. And I haven't let myself do that."

"Sadie..." His throat closed up. "I haven't, either. I wanted to believe that I could control things. That somehow I could stop bad things from happening. But the problem with that is that... I can't. I thought if I could, if I got things in order... But it's not in my power. And admitting that is one of the scariest damn things I can think of because control is everything to me. Being the one taking care of things is everything to me. So that…" He felt like an ass even thinking this, much less admitting it. But it was time to say it. And it was time to let it go. "People leave me, Sadie. I thought someday I'd make myself so important it wouldn't happen again."

"Well—" Sadie wiped the tears from her cheeks and smiled "—Eli Garrett, future sheriff of Copper Ridge, you have made yourself so important to me that this woman, who always has her running shoes on hand, can't leave you."

SADIE LOOKED UP at Eli, at the deep concern in his dark eyes, at the sincerity. And the insecurity. And any remaining walls around her heart crumbled completely.

She threw her arms around his neck and held him close, stroking her fingers through his hair. "You're the best reason in the world to stop running. And you don't have to work to get me to stay. I'm offering to. Because you're the best man there is. And anyone who made you feel like less deserves to be dragged behind a horse."

"I love you, Sadie. More than a clean house, more than stability. If you kept running, I'd run after you. Even if I had to leave all this behind. Because it doesn't mean a thing without you. And I'm sorry. Sorry for all the crap I said to you. Everything I put us through. I couldn't run, so I guess the best I could do was try to make you run. Because you scare the hell out of me, woman. But I'm even more scared of living without you."

A tear rolled down Sadie's cheek, emotion filling her, so full she thought she might break with it. "Then it's a good thing I'm staying."

"Oh, hell, does this mean I'm part of the bed-and-breakfast?"

"Only if you spend the night."

"Yeah," he said, "about that... Do you think you could run it if you mainly slept at my place?"

"Mainly?"

"Always."

"I have a cat," she reminded him. "And he sleeps indoors. He basically lives indoors."

"I will give him his own bedroom."

"Holy crap, you do love me!" she said, laughing, another tear sliding down her cheek.

"I really do," he said, leaning in to kiss her. "I really, really do."

Sadie kissed him back, the feeling of completion when their lips touched unlike anything she'd ever experienced.

Whoever said you couldn't go home again had never been to Copper Ridge. The place hadn't changed at all.

But Sadie had. And for the first time, she was home, and she was ready to stay.

* * * * *

ACKNOWLEDGMENTS

THEY SAY IT takes a village to raise a child. Sometimes I feel like it takes a village to create a book. A huge thank-you to Margo Lipschultz, who encouraged me to send this series to HQN and who has put in so many tireless hours to make it the best it can be. Kate Dresser, my fantastic editor on this book, I only wish we could have done more together. You're amazing. I always owe thanks to my wonderful agent, Helen Breitwieser, who has believed in me from the beginning. To Jackie Ashenden for reading every word I write and serving up hard truths wrapped in encouragement. Many thanks to Nicole Helm for her insider knowledge on police uniforms and how they are removed, velcro belts, clip-on ties and all. And I owe the biggest thank-you of all to Victoria Austin for the snowballs joke that Eli tells in the book. You are a goddess of the corny joke, and for that I am grateful.

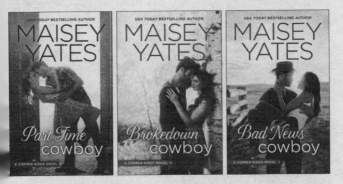

Fall in love with the cowboys in
The Montana Creeds series by
#1 *New York Times* bestselling author
LINDA LAEL MILLER

Available now wherever books are sold!

"Miller tugs at the heartstrings as few authors can."
—*Publishers Weekly*

Turn your love of reading into rewards you'll love with
Harlequin My Rewards

**Join for FREE today at
www.HarlequinMyRewards.com**

Earn **FREE BOOKS** of your choice.

Experience **EXCLUSIVE OFFERS** and contests.

Enjoy **BOOK RECOMMENDATIONS**
selected just for you.

PLUS! Sign up now
and get **500** points
right away!

Earn
FREE
REWARDS
HarlequinMyRewards.com
Join
Today!

MYR16R

LINDA LAEL MILLER

78906	BIG SKY COUNTRY	___$7.99 U.S.	___$8.99 CAN.
78897	MONTANA CREEDS: TYLER	___$7.99 U.S.	___$9.99 CAN.
78895	MONTANA CREEDS: DYLAN	___$7.99 U.S.	___$9.99 CAN.
78845	MONTANA CREEDS: LOGAN	___$7.99 U.S.	___$8.99 CAN.
77996	McKETTRICKS OF TEXAS: AUSTIN	___$7.99 U.S.	___$8.99 CAN.
77953	McKETTRICKS OF TEXAS: GARRETT	___$7.99 U.S.	___$8.99 CAN.
77870	THE MARRIAGE PACT	___$7.99 U.S.	___$8.99 CAN.
77866	THE BRIDEGROOM	___$7.99 U.S.	___$8.99 CAN.
77831	BIG SKY SECRETS	___$7.99 U.S.	___$8.99 CAN.
77681	McKETTRICK'S HEART	___$7.99 U.S.	___$9.99 CAN.
77677	McKETTRICK'S PRIDE	___$7.99 U.S.	___$9.99 CAN.
77642	McKETTRICK'S LUCK	___$7.99 U.S.	___$9.99 CAN.
77600	THE CREED LEGACY	___$7.99 U.S.	___$9.99 CAN.

(limited quantities available)

TOTAL AMOUNT	$_____
POSTAGE & HANDLING	$_____
($1.00 FOR 1 BOOK, 50¢ for each additional)	
APPLICABLE TAXES*	$_____
TOTAL PAYABLE	$_____

(check or money order—please do not send cash)

To order, complete this form and send it, along with a check or money order for the total above, payable to HQN Books, to: **In the U.S.:** 3010 Walden Avenue, P.O. Box 9077, Buffalo, NY 14269-9077; **In Canada:** P.O. Box 636, Fort Erie, Ontario, L2A 5X3.

Name: _____

Address: _____ City: _____

State/Prov.: _____ Zip/Postal Code: _____

Account Number (if applicable): _____

075 CSAS

*New York residents remit applicable sales taxes.
*Canadian residents remit applicable GST and provincial taxes.

HQN™

www.HQNBooks.com

PHLLM0216E